THE GREAT HEARTS V

IMPERATOR

DAVID OLIVER

Copyright © 2023 by David Oliver

All rights reserved.

No part of this book may be reproduced in any form or by any electronic or mechanical means, including information storage and retrieval systems, without written permission from the author, except for the use of brief quotations in a book review.

CONTENTS

	Foreword	VIII
1.	Recap	1
2.	Important People to Remember	3
3.	Prologue	5
4.	Part 1 A Progression of Scars	11
5.	Chapter 1 The Darkness Within	12
6.	Chapter 2 Seeds of Doubt	18
7.	Chapter 3 Dead and Gone	26
8.	Present Day 1	39
9.	Chapter 4 Lessons	44
10.	Chapter 5 Something to Die For	51
11.	Chapter 6 Not So Playful Games	63
12.	Present Day 2	70

13.	Chapter 7 Blood on the Walls	81
14.	Chapter 8 What I Might Become	93
15.	Chapter 9 Classes	100
16.	Chapter 10 A Little Monstrous	109
17.	Present Day 3	118
18.	Chapter 11 Spy Game	125
19.	Chapter 12 Changes	139
20.	Chapter 13 Fracture	151
21.	Chapter 14 Sleepwalking	159
22.	Chapter 15 Mind Games	168
23.	Present Day 4	178
24.	Chapter 16 Fuck Wolf's Hollow	183
25.	Chapter 17 Built to Order	205
26.	Chapter 18 No Comment	214
27.	Chapter 19 Twisted	222
28.	Chapter 20 Executioner	234

29.	Present Day 5	246
30.	Chapter 21	254
	The Final Push	
31.	Chapter 22	268
	The Perfect Exam	
32.	Chapter 23	299
	Ranulskin	
33.	Present Day 6	311
34.	Chapter 24	320
	Scarred Progress	
35.	Chapter 25	330
	Graduation	
36.	Part II	340
	Imperator	
37.	Chapter 26	341
	The Working Life	
38.	Present Day 7	359
39.	Chapter 27	363
	The Last Redoubt	
40.	Chapter 28	376
	Upgrades	
41.	Chapter 29	393
	Reinforcements	
42.	Chapter 30	422
	Bastion	
43.	Present Day 8	438
44.	Chapter 31	444
	Uninvited Guest	
45.	Chapter 32	467
	Trapped	

46.	Chapter 33 Titans of the Past	482
47.	Present Day 9	506
48.	Chapter 34 Broken Fortress	512
49.	Part III Fallen Idol	534
50.	Chapter 35 Deceit	535
51.	Chapter 36 Dreams & Danger	550
52.	Chapter 37 Puppets	565
53.	Present Day 10	575
54.	Chapter 38 Concepts	584
55.	Chapter 39 Search Party	597
56.	Chapter 40 Rescue Mission	610
57.	Chapter 41 A Ball to Die for	635
58.	Present Day 11	655
59.	Chapter 42 Questions	661
60.	Chapter 43 Revelations	668
61.	Chapter 44 Rage	682

62.	Chapter 45 The Great Game	693
63.	Present Day 12	705
64.	Chapter 46 Comeuppance	710
65.	Epilogue	721
Afterword		725

FOREWORD

Take a deep breath, strap yourself in.
Things are about to get...a little wild.

RECAP

The events of the fourth novel, Apotheosis, were, as always, within two distinct time periods: past and present.

Calidan's past continued his time at the Imperator Academy, focusing on intense training to become a monster-hunter specialist with Cassius under the tutelage of Sarrenai, monster-hunter extraordinaire.

During his limited time within the walls of the Academy, Calidan developed a romantic relationship with a fellow classmate, Riven, experiencing the joys and challenges of dating both as a teenager and as a member of the Academy.

Despite the best efforts of the monster-hunters it was becoming apparent that the numbers of monster attacks were rapidly increasing. Evidence began to point towards the Enemy – one of the six 'Powers' within the world and nemesis of the Emperor.

Elsewhere, the Tracker struggled to defend the northern frontier against the incoming Hrudan, only to make an uneasy peace in the face of attacks by scaled lizards known as thyrkan. Recognising the threat to his troops, the Emperor ordered the trio of monster-hunters to support the Tracker, allowing Calidan and Cassius to – for the first time in years – return home.

Unfortunately, 'home' was being used as a staging area for the thyrkan and their Enemy-aligned human compatriots known as the Sworn. Cassius, Seya, Sarrenai and Calidan assaulted the outpost and defeated several different types of thyrkan, including wielders of seraph. Before they could celebrate however, they were ripped into another dimension by the Enemy. Charles – the Enemy – informed them that he was using the Academy forces as a testing ground for his creations, suggested some harsh truths about the other Powers and captured Sarrenai for use as another testing tool.

Sarrenai was pushed to the brink, trying to escape the Enemy's stronghold yet inevitably being forced to fight against the various beasts within. Eventually he was overcome and the liathea within – one of the strange creatures placed within Imperators by the Emperor to provide power – seized control of his body.

Against the orders of the Academy, Calidan and the others determined where Sarrenai was and launched a rescue attempt. Unaware that the Sarrenai they believed to be rescuing was, in fact, the liathea and hostile to their cause, they lowered their guard and paid the price. Revealing itself to be a powerful force, Not-Sarrenai transformed and caused catastrophic injuries to the team before they could escape, but not before killing Calidan's partner, Riven.

Over the next few months Not-Sarrenai raided towns and shipping around the empire, crushing all attempts to challenge it. After being witness to an entire city burning to the ground, Calidan borrowed the Emperor's prized ship and set a trap. After an epic battle in the open seas, they brought Not-Sarrenai down to the point where the real Sarrenai trapped within could re-assume control. Unable to use seraph any more or change his form back to that of a human, they told the world that Sarrenai was dead whereas in reality he fled into the depths of the wild to continue his monster-hunting activities.

Finally, after passing the seventh year, Calidan and his dorm were allowed to progress to the eighth and final year of the Academy; Wolf's Hollow, which is where this story begins...

Present day Calidan lost faith in the few remaining individuals in the Academy he had trusted, before embarking on a mission to steal star-metal from the Powers at the behest of the Wanderer. A material that – when exposed to someone's blood stream – inhibited seraph use, it was closely guarded by each Power and was essential to the Wanderer's plan to bring down her peers.

Through a challenging series of trials, Calidan successfully managed to retrieve the star-metal from Nuramapole, one of the Powers and return it to the Wanderer before swearing to bring everything tumbling down.

IMPORTANT PEOPLE TO REMEMBER

Calidan	Protagonist. Imperator in training (Imp), cold hearted killer in present day.
Cassius	Calidan's best friend. Insane and gigantic in the present day. Imp.
Ella	Ex-street rat from Forgoth, Cassius's partner. Imp.
Sophia	Talented archer from nomadic tribe. Imp.
Scythe	Skilled warrior from nomadic tribe of the desert plains. Imp.
Rikol	Ex-street rat. Imp.
Seya	Sevlantha, Great Heart (gigantic panther), bonded to Calidan.
Emperor	Larger than life, charismatic with hints of a darker soul.
Rya	Corrupted imp who Calidan, Cassius and Ella fought and killed.
Simone	Imperator who began the hunt for Rya.
Merowyn	Imperator who began the hunt for Rya, died fighting the Shadow Cabal. Ramuntex, her lluthea, has taken over and transformed her body.
Kane	Primary instructor at the Academy for the Imps.
Adronicus	Weapon master at the Academy.

Korthan	Wizened historian at the Academy. Calidan's friend and boorish instructor.
Charles	Ancient enemy of mankind, revealed as having bonded with a demonic spirit. Master of shadow seraph and revels in using it to control others
Ash	Artificial Intelligence that works for Charles.
Tracker	Meredothian hunter who was forced to join in the attack against Calidan's village. Trained the boys in woodcraft. Trains Forgoth's military scouts
Kirok	Ex-Imp. Forced himself on Sophia and was brutally broken by Calidan in retaliation. Removed by Academy staff and not seen again.
Anatha	Korthan's mother. Great Heart bonded to Bonza, a giant mangolion. Died rescuing the Emperor and others from the Irevin fortress.
Akzan	The red eyed skyren who slaughtered Calidan and Cassius's village.
Endrea	Shadow-Cabal member who tortured Calidan. Died and was taken over by the kyrgeth inside him.
Sarrimar	Imperator, hunter of monsters and trainer of Cassius and Calidan.

PROLOGUE

The eighth year of the Academy.

Wolf's. Fucking. Hollow.

What can I say about it? It was...traumatic, to say the least. Lots happened, priorities changed, people were abused and scarred. It was all designed to make a person an Imperator and at the time I went to it gladly, eagerly eating up the shit that the Academy and the Emperor sent my way so that I could become what I had dreamed of for so long - strong enough to kill that red-eyed beast that haunted my nightmares. I had thought it dead. Thought it gone with the world-ending explosion that nearly killed us, the Emperor, and succeeded in killing Anatha. For a time I had felt...free. Lighter in a way that I hadn't known for many, many years. But no. Somehow the many-taloned bastard survived. And I knew it was up to me and Cassius to kill it.

We had to.

Who else could?

Or in the case of the Powers, who else could be bothered?

So, the eighth year was the culmination of everything I had hoped and dreamed. The final year of the Academy. The last stepping stone to being powerful enough to bring my foe to justice.

Looking back, perhaps I should have walked away then. At least it would have been easier on my soul.

On all our souls.

Wolf's Hollow itself was a grey, characterless place. A facility hidden much like one of the Enemy's; recessed into the rock of a forested valley. The land surrounding it was private, flagged as an Imperial forest, the mark of such highlighting that the forest was for the Emperor's use only, which meant that only the most desperate of poachers would dare trespass.

The facility itself was made of a slate-grey rock, with thick metal doors that led through to narrow passageways of the same depressing stone. According to Kane, who met us at the facility, the building was what was known as a 'bunker', though why you bunked in it was something lost on me as it had no natural light and was only lit through the use of seraph lamps, giving it a sad and melancholic air.

Surprisingly, there were a number of other Imps already at the facility. Those who had yet to pass their final year. As one they appeared haggard and wielded a thousand-yard gaze, the kind of look that passed right through you as they were trapped in waking nightmares.

I knew that I was looking at what I would soon become.

I had seen soldiers with the same look. Had already seen it in some of my friends and they had likely seen it in me. When the action was so intense and brutal that your mind struggled to cope, or when something so terrible happened that you were trapped there mentally, over and over again. The fact that those remaining in this facility looked so haunted meant that something, or somethings would happen in this year. Things that would cause us to bend or possibly break.

Delightful.

I didn't see Rinoa. She had been gone for some time and was undoubtedly now a fully-fledged Imperator, one who was kept busy and away from the Academy.

...I refused to think that she might have failed the last year. Because what would that even mean?

It was something that I had begun to wonder more often recently - what happened to Imps who were this close to being an Imperator who couldn't quite make it through the final year? Assuming they didn't die, what would become of them? Hells, Rya had been hunted by Imperators due to what she knew as a third-year Imp who fled. An eighth-year Imp was practically an Imperator - there was no way that we were leaving the Academy with what we knew. Perhaps we would just be kept hidden away...failures to be used for other purposes. Images of a blue-skinned troll flashed through my mind.

No, I thought furiously, *no point in dwelling on what-ifs. We're here, let's get it done. Time to be what you strove so hard for. One. More. Year. That's it. Beat this year, Calidan. Beat it, then go and do what you do best.*

Hunt monsters.

We were provided rooms deep within the bowels of the facility, a place that stank of ancient metal and stone. Kane showed us an indoor gymnasium, complete with running track, ropes and weights. A large room next door laden with racks of weapons gave us a place to practice sparring or kaschan. A kitchen manned by friendly-enough staff gave us a decent meal and we settled into what appeared to be our new home.

"Imps," Kane grunted as he came into the dining room an hour later, "I hope that you are well fed, watered and satisfied with your lodgings. If you aren't then I don't care. Nothing is going to change even if you whine about it."

"Inspiring as always sir," Scythe murmured, earning himself a gruff look and a ghost of a smile.

"I'm always inspiring," the Instructor retorted. "Comes with the territory of being me." He winked and then grew more serious. "This is your home for however long it takes you to complete this year. Lessons will be provided down the hall to further your learning, however I suggest you take the opportunity to practice everything you know - or think you know - as much as possible in your own time. There isn't much else to do down here, so use your time wisely."

"Why are we in this...bunker, sir?" Sophia asked. "Why are we not at the Academy for the final year?"

"You're here because the final year is a mixture of testing and examinations, some of which the Academy and the Emperor deem too secretive for the Academy. For instance, you will be tested for liathea compatibility here." He raised a hand against the hubbub of noise that broke out. "I know that you aren't a fan of the idea, however that test is part of the final year and decreed by the Emperor himself. If you want to argue the point, take it up with him. As it stands, the only one of you who will not be tested in that area is Calidan...liathea do not like to share."

"Lucky bastard," Rikol muttered out of the corner of his mouth to me. I couldn't help but grin in return.

Kane continued. "Those of you deemed compatible with the liathea *will* have one embedded at the Emperor's request. This is not something you can talk your way out of," he shot a glance at Rikol and Scythe, "so any attempts will fall on deaf ears."

Rikol raised his hand and Kane sighed heavily before pointing with a shake of his head. "Go ahead Rikol."

"Thank you, sir. Can I just stress how ridiculous it is to continue with this line of experimentation considering, you know, the events of the last few months?"

"He means Sarrenai's liathea taking over and murdering people," added Scythe helpfully.

"Thank you for that enlightening clarification, Scythe, I wasn't quite managing to read between the lines," Kane replied drily.

"Always happy to help, sir."

"Indeed. Well, Rikol, all I can say is that the High Imperator and the Emperor are looking into it, but until we hear otherwise then we continue with protocol, which is to test and prepare any who are compatible for implantation." He raised a hand to forestall further comments. "Please note that I do not like the idea of liathea any more than you do, however their power boost is undeniable and has allowed the Imperators to come out on top of several engagements that they otherwise wouldn't have. So there are pros and cons."

Rikol raised his hands as though balancing a scale. "Pro: slightly more seraph, con: murdering an entire city."

"Enough." This time Kane's voice held no humour. "Like it or not, this is the process. Deal with it." He took another look through the notes on a clipboard he had been holding at his side. "Ah, yes. The third level is off-limits until deemed otherwise. Do not," he scanned all of us, "I repeat, do not venture down there unless it is a direct order." He looked about to move on then paused. "To set your minds at ease, this is not one of those strange tests in those novels you might read where you are rewarded for breaking the rules. Do not go down there. Completely off limits. If you're found down there, I will end you. Understood?"

Muted nods all round and he glowered briefly before moving on. "Ah, right, the purpose of this place." He spread his arms wide. "As already explained, Wolf's Hollow is the final testing ground. These tests will be both physical and mental in nature. They are designed to push you to your limits and beyond, to temper the skills and fortitude that you've spent the last years developing into that of a true Imperator. Now then," he looked around, "did any of you get a glimpse of where this place is located?"

"About one hundred and seventy miles to the west of Anderal," I provided.

"One hundred and seventy-one miles to be precise. It is within a large valley that is surrounded by dense forest, has no civilians within thirty miles of it and, yes, has a large population of wolves."

Cassius and I shared a look. We knew wolves.

"But that is not, necessarily, where Wolf's Hollow gets its name," Kane continued. "If you couldn't deal with a pack of wolves by now then there would be no hope for you. No, Wolf's Hollow is so named because, whilst you're here, you will be facing *each other*."

Silence reigned.

"What do you mean, 'each other'?" Ella asked slowly.

"I mean exactly that. Whether in pairs or singularly, you will be pitted against each other time and time again. You are expected to do whatever it takes to achieve your goals. To rise up and become an Imperator. Any compassion, any thoughts of love or friendship, must be purged if you want to succeed."

"And if we fail?" Sophia asked softly, worry in her eyes.

Kane grimaced. "Some tests, you might just be set back. You might be kept here for longer until you get the fortitude to succeed. Failing other tests? Let's just say doing so wouldn't be good for your health."

"I thought we were past the cruelty of things like the fourth-year test!" Rikol exclaimed.

Kane shook his head sadly. "Oh Rikol, if you thought the fourth-year test was cruel then I truly wish you luck during your time here. You're going to need it."

"But what's the point!?" the small but powerful mage bellowed. "Why risk our lives when we are *this* close to being exactly what we need to be?"

"Because what you currently are - whilst impressive - can be broken, not necessarily by anything as mundane as torture but through your love and compassion for others. To be the scalpel that slices away the rot within society, Imperators need to be able to distance themselves from those emotions. Only then will you be ready."

"Sounds like bollocks to me."

"I thought so too, when I was in your place. These days I can see the wisdom in the approach," Kane replied, voice husky with memory. "There is a reason why Imperators are feared. We are the judge, jury and executioner. Our actions answer only to the Academy and the Emperor. To have those actions influenced by emotion renders us closer to being murderers. There is no room here for hate, for love, for jealousy or pity. They make you weaker."

I disagree wholeheartedly. I've long found hate and the desire for revenge capable of keeping me warm at night.

"I do not agree." Cassius, voice laden with conviction. "Love, empathy...these are things that will keep us human, make us able to connect with the people around us, to understand their hurt and their needs. To lose that is to lose your humanity. Would we be any worse than some unfeeling psychopath?"

Kane smiled a soft, sad smile. "If you get through this and retain that sense of self, Cassius, it will be a wonderful thing. Granted, I would likely have to make sure that you went back into the Hall, and reprimand the Instructors who passed you, but still – a wonderful thing.""Wait, you won't be the one passing us?" I asked.

"Me? No. I'm just here because you are my year and a friendly face is useful before all the..." his face twisted, "*fun* begins. You will be judged by impartial Imperators. People who haven't worked with you in the past. They will be strict in their grading, so if you want to get out of here you need to impress them. Move forwards and upwards. Don't look back. That's my final advice on the matter."

Much like Kane, these days I can see the reasoning behind Wolf's Hollow and its many horrors. Even so, if I were to give advice to my past self?

Take Cassius, take Seya, run and don't look back.

Because here be where monsters are made.

PART I

A Progression of Scars

CHAPTER 1
THE DARKNESS WITHIN

"What is the role of an Imperator during war?" The woman's voice was sharp like a blade, her words slicing through the air with a briskness that almost put the High Imperator's staccato to shame.

I hesitated for a moment. "To do the Emperor's bidding?"

A small smirk. "A delightfully shit answer. Try again."

"Er..." I thought back to all the strategy and history I had sat through in my Academy years. "To ensure the success of any military engagement."

"Better. You have an approaching army on the horizon, how best to utilise your skills to ensure the success of the Andurran military?"

I would hopefully be off hunting monsters somewhere else for the good of everyone, but sure. "Erm, the treatise of Ecclan suggests that sowing fear and discord within the ranks is the best approach for a single individual to take prior to battle."

A small nod. "You know your Ecclan. Good. And tell me, Calidan, how would you go about sowing fear and discord. I want your take on it, not something verbatim from a textbook."

Ah. "Honestly, ma'am, I imagine that with my skill-sets, I wouldn't be there at all. After all, humans aren't generally in the monster-hunting category. There are plenty of others better skilled to be on the front lines, or trained in espionage and infiltration."

"Hmm." She seemed to consider my response with a level of thoughtfulness I wouldn't have imagined. "You're likely correct. However, let us imagine that you are off on one of your monster hunts and come across an invading army. What happens next?"

"I alert the Academy and any available military personnel."

"The military is alerted and mobilised. They will not be able to field a full force for six hours, by which point the invading army will have taken the high ground. What do you do?"

I let out a sigh. "I guess I would need to get my hands dirty." Her look of satisfaction didn't help. "My skills enable me to move relatively unnoticed. If they set up camp then I would burn their supplies and tents. If they are moving then I would look for key areas to sabotage, such as supply wagons and explosives."

"And if they had none?"

I grimaced. "Then I would have to take a leaf out of the assassin's play book and remove the leadership."

"Exactly!" the examiner – who hadn't introduced herself – exclaimed. "You would seek to destabilise the group from within, using your skills to sow terror and discord. Good."

"Please note that I would prefer not to do that if it came to it." I shook my head. "Killing in cold blood isn't my thing."

A nod. "I understand, murder should not be an easy task. In fact, if it ever does become easy then you should take a long look at yourself in the mirror. What is important is that, if it comes to it, you *would* take lives."

"They wouldn't be the first lives that I've taken in the Emperor's name. But taking them in a straightforward fight is one thing, killing them in their sleep is another."

She shrugged. "I care not how you justify it to yourself. All I, and the Academy, care about is that if push came to shove, you would do it."

"I- I would." I knew I would. It had never been in doubt. Cassius, however, was going to struggle with this test.

"Following along this line of thinking: you are captured behind enemy lines, beaten and tortured. What do you reveal?"

"Is this seraph torture or physical?"

This time her gaze was more contemplative. "Physical."

"I would hold out as long as proper-"

"Which is?"

"-which, depending on the type of torture is likely to be a few hours at least. Then I would give them my cover story."

"Good." Her gaze turned curious. "And if I had said seraph torture?"

"Then I would scream whilst they took everything anyway."

The examiner rifled through a file on the desk, eventually stopping at something that made her face twist. "Ah. I see you have some experience in that area already. I'm sorry to hear it."

I raised an eyebrow. "Is that my file?"

"Yep." She tossed it back on the desk. "And as curious as you are to know what it says, it isn't for your eyes. So reel in the curiosity and answer me this: you are left in a cell and your only visitor is a kindly old man who feeds you what he can. He doesn't seem like the others, just genuinely interested in your survival. One day you see that he comes in reach of your chains and that the key to the door is in his back-pocket. What do you do?"

Damn but I hated questions like this. There was very obviously only one answer that she was looking for, the one that made it seem like I was a completely heartless killer, ready to snap necks for the Academy at a moment's notice. "You know, if you took a closer look at that file, you would see that something similar already happened. Except that it was my torturer that got too close and I embedded a wall spike into his eye."

She picked up the file again. "Really? What happened next?"

"Oh, I armed myself with a baguette and fled a den of assassins before being hunted down by a brutalised Great Heart, beating it in battle before falling unconscious and being recaptured, only to find out that the man I had killed had been taken over by the kyrgeth inside of him. You know, standard really."

A stunned silence. "And you're still just an Imp? By the Pits, that's enough shit for a lifetime."

I nodded, a slight grin on my lips at having successfully derailed the conversation. I jumped as the file *slammed* to the desk.

"And it's all shit that I already knew. You're not special, Calidan. Okay, well, maybe you are a little, but you aren't *that* special. Everyone at the Academy has skills. Some might be a little more flashy than others but that's by the by. The other thing that everyone has is a sob story. Yours is an ongoing tragedy, rather than the usual 'I'm an orphan with a special set of skills', but that doesn't change what this year needs to do, so stop fucking around and answer the questions to the best of your abilities!"

I glowered for a long moment. It turned out she was just as good at that as I was. "Tsk. Fine." I always did hate losing. The rest of the examination was much the same, questions that twisted fate until you had to make a choice that usually involved killing an innocent or failing the emperor. Naturally, as I wanted to be an Imperator, I gave her what she wanted. But each time I did, I couldn't help but wonder about Cassius. I mean, seriously, if anyone was going to be transferred from the dark halls of the Academy to some kind of school for heroes, it would be him.

I just had to hope that he could bend with the wind, rather than be broken by it.

"Ugh."

"Agreed."

"Yep."

"Mhm."

The dorm, as a whole, were shattered. Five days of the same type of examination. Question after question, examiner after examiner, day after day. It just didn't end. You would think that there would only be so many ways you could state that you would kill for the Emperor's sake, but not in the view of the testing Imperators apparently. The questions had gone from direct 'if this then what' to intricate questions that had a plethora of options, and we all just had to hope that the answers we gave were to their liking.

Cassius heaved a sigh. "I just don't like it."

The entire room groaned, Ella included. "We've been over this so many times!" exclaimed Rikol exasperatedly. "You don't have to like it, you just have to do it."

"But I wouldn't do it. And they know that. Not all Imperators have to be soulless monsters."

Scythe threw a pillow at his head, the coarse fibre cushion catching Cassius square in the face. "Who cares? You need to make sure that they believe you, otherwise you're going to be here forever." His face darkened. "Or worse."

"Scythe's right," Ella murmured, taking Cassius's hand. "You don't have to be that kind of Imperator if you don't want to be. But you need to make them believe that you have the capacity to be."

Cassius's face expressed his torment at the concept. "Isn't the first step to having that capacity pretending to have it? What's the term? Fake it until you make it?"

"A term used by merchants, not Imperators," argued Sophia.

"But the principal is sound. If you want to be bold, daring and adventurous, you need to start thinking and acting like you are and before long you will be. What if this is the same? If I start pretending to be someone I'm not, how much more easily will I find myself justifying the things that they want me to justify when I find myself in that exact scenario?"

He had an annoyingly good point.

"That's...an annoyingly good point," muttered Rikol. "And is likely exactly what they plan. But it doesn't stop what you need to do to get through this year."

"I disagree. You've all assumed that the examiners want to hear the standard Imperator spiel, but what if that isn't the case? What if they are happy to have people within the ranks who can balance out those who might be more predisposed to-"

"Murder?" Scythe interjected.

"I was going to say violence, but yes, that works too."

"So, what are you saying Cass? That you think us all capable of murder?" Scythe's eyes flashed dangerously.

Holding up a placating hand, Cassius looked around the room. "Murder? Probably not. Not like how you're imagining anyway. Killing for the sake of the Emperor? Yes. Undoubtedly."

"And you think you're better than us?!" Scythe exclaimed, jumping to his feet, face red. "I've seen you kill, hells you're better at it than practically anyone!"

"I've killed, yes, and I'll do it again if I need to. But if there is an option to not take a life, I will choose that path, regardless of how hard it is, because I don't believe that lives should be taken at whim." He held Scythe's gaze unflinchingly. "I despise killing. And I hate the part of me that does it so well. All I'm saying is that we should seek alternatives at every opportunity, rather than being forced into a corner with no way out."

"And what happens in that case?" Ella whispered.

"Then I'll fight with every breath in my body."

"You know," I said gently, "if you said this to your examiners then they might get a better impression of you. So far, I think they want to break your spirit."

He raised his chin into the air. "They can try, but they won't succeed."

Brave, strong words. Words that made us think that he couldn't be brought down. Couldn't be made to do the things that he would need to do as an Imperator. The rest of us all knew that we had it in us to do what was necessary. Call it what you will: a spine of steel or a capacity to do evil in the name of the greater good, we each had it and we each knew it. All except Cassius. I think that was what made us so frustrated with his stance. He was better than we were and though he wasn't rubbing it in our faces...he did so just by being *him*.

Or maybe we were just all dancing on the strings of the examiners already. Drawing lines in the sand between us. Were the bonds that held us together that easy to break?

Unequivocally.

A slam on the door. "Cassius, you're up!"

He smiled and stood up, waving as he stepped outside for yet another round of testing, leaving us all sitting there, frustrated and annoyed, but more at ourselves than him. I knew that we were thinking the same thing: how could we be so base in our actions to our fellow man? What was it in us that caused that?

The Darkness Within. That's what Sarrenai had called it. The ability to, when pushed, do horrible things. Most of the time, those things were necessary for survival. We all had it. You didn't get far within the Academy without the grit to survive. Hells, that's what the fourth-year test had been all about. But what the Academy truly wanted was to have Imperators who could and would access that deep, dark, detestable part of themselves at will.

And that's what made Cassius so special. All of us had lost. All of us were a little broken. We could reach into that fire within and use it when survival mattered the most. But somehow, despite everything we had been through, Cassius still retained that essential spark of humanity, the light inside that refused to descend to those extreme levels; to torture and to kill to get the information required.

You would think that as he was going to be a monster-hunter such things shouldn't matter. But little things matter to the Academy. And to the Emperor.

And that's why they broke him.

CHAPTER 2

SEEDS OF DOUBT

"Do it Calidan."

"No."

"Do it!"

"No!"

A sigh, and the illusion was broken. "You are aware that this counts as a fail, right?" The speaker was a tall, robust Imperator with long dark hair, his eyes flashing with disappointment. "I understand that it's the first time, but if you can't embrace the scenario and commit to it, then I can't pass you."

"It's grotesque."

"It's information you need to know!"

I glared at the man. "Be that as it may, I do not want to torture people."

"It's not even real!"

"It looked real enough when you started peeling off fingernails!"

He looked oddly pleased by that comment. "Thank you for admiring the quality of my seraph illusion, but that's the whole point of this exercise. You have to get used to such things. To be above them and, more than that, to be able to *do* them if necessary."

"I'm sure I can figure something out."

He levelled a condescending gaze at me. "Do you know the ten most efficient ways to get the information you need out of someone who doesn't want to talk, Calidan? I do. I've also had to use these skills in the real world, where the blood isn't an illusion." His raised hand forestalled my comment. "Before you interrupt with some quip. Because of these skills I managed to complete my extremely time-sensitive mission. Without them I would have failed and people would have died. Do you understand me now?"

My sigh was long and heart-felt. "There are better ways to extract information. If the Emperor would just teach us-"

He flung up a hand again. "No. No, no and no. Black seraph is a slippery slope and one that the Academy will not be descending down. I've read your file and know what you have been through-"

"-I doubt you truly know what I've been through," I muttered.

"-but we can't go around having people have the ability to control thoughts. Let alone the fact that you need people with a higher affinity for black seraph to make use of skills like those!"

Another reason why they want Cassius prepared to do such things. All that black seraph swimming in his veins.

"Seems a little strange, doesn't it?" I fronted up to the Imperator. "That the Academy is willing to train its staff to go as far as possible when the need arises for it, but not to the extent that the extremely useful *ability to read minds* is taught. Seems a little dumb."

"It might seem dumb to you, but we can barely trust each other enough, particularly with the Enemy doing what He does best. I mean, you were there. You saw the inferno in the Great Hall and those Imperators and Imps who were under His thrall. That kind of activity would only propagate with the inclusion of black seraph users into the Academy."

"They're not all evil."

A raised eyebrow on a face full of scorn. "No? And how many users have you met?"

"Enough to know that they aren't all evil. Black seraph is just like any other type of seraph. It's like judging someone based on their hair or the colour of their skin – completely ridiculous."

A snort. "Have you ever met-"

I interrupted, voice becoming more of a growl. "No, I don't care what you say or what you regurgitate from someone else's teachings, just because someone used a tool for evil doesn't make that *tool* evil. By the pits, I imagine that history is full of seraph users of green or red who have done horrific things, whether in the guise of a good cause or not, and yet aren't vilified the same way as someone who is born with an affinity for the black."

His mouth shut and his face turned purple. When his mouth opened again, I braced myself for the inevitable tirade...but it didn't come. The Imperator stopped and took a deep, lingering breath, his face returning to its normal shade. "You...speak some sense. You're right in not painting all users with the same brush, however that doesn't change the fact that it is a slippery slope to use black seraph. It is too easy to affect someone's mind and start to like that feeling."

"You act like that can't be done with any type of seraph."

"It can't!" he huffed, before reconsidering. "Well...not easily."

"Not easily isn't the same as not being able to do it. Seraph is all about will, right? Whilst I have an affinity for green seraph, that doesn't mean that if I can't will something hard enough that it won't come into being. It will just drain my seraph pool a heck of a lot faster."

A sigh. "Fine. I concede. Now, will you please get back to this scenario?"

"Am I allowed to use my seraph to read their mind?"

"No!"

"Then no."

"Get. Out."

I stepped out into the hallway where Cassius waited outside. "How did it go?" he asked.

"About as well as you might expect."

"So, you yelled and got angry with him too?"

I grinned. "Yep. We had a fine old time of it. Wanker wanted me to learn how to tear someone's fingernails off in the slowest and 'most pain preserving way' possible. Absolute bullshit. When am I ever going to need those skills?"

In due time I was going to regret saying that. Turns out that the ability to effectively extract information from someone was extremely useful when working on tight deadlines and, unfortunately for me, my seraph skills were nowhere up to the level required to riffle through someone's mind.

Cassius nodded knowingly and together we strode back to the dorm room. I was a little surprised at Wolf's Hollow at this point – going by Kane's speech I had expected us to be performing against each other at every opportunity, but so far there it had purely been individual tests. Nothing to set us against each other.

Little did I know that they were just setting the groundwork.

"Hey everyone," Cassius said as we entered the dorm. "How was everyone's latest slice of paradise?"

A snort from Scythe. Sophia merely rolled her eyes whilst Rikol looked troubled.

"Where's Ella?"

"She was called to her test a few minutes ago," Sophia replied. "How did you find it?"

"I can see where he is coming from, but I really didn't want to know how to peel someone's fingernails off, not today. Not tomorrow," I replied, Cassius nodding along.

"Bloody right," Scythe agreed. "Not honourable, torture."

"And what would you know of honour, oh destroyer of shrines?" Sophia asked him, voice sweet and eyes twinkling. Her expression soured as she saw a darkness pass into his eyes. "I'm sorry. I didn't mean that."

Scythe waved a hand, as though nothing was amiss, but we all knew that to be a lie. "How about you Rikol?"

Rikol didn't answer.

"Rikol?"

A slow exhalation. "Torture...has its uses."

You could have dropped a needle in the following silence, broken by a sudden clamour of outrage.

"What?!"

"What do you mea-"

"How can you say-"

He turned his head from the bed and gazed at us with eyes that seemed a thousand years older. "It has its uses. I know it. If you don't yet then I'm sure you will soon." He laid eyes on me. "I'm surprised at you most of all. You know first-hand just how effective it can be."

"I argued with the examiner about how utilising mental seraph would be far more effective," I said with a stiff shrug, a little put off that Rikol would single me out like that.

"Fair," he murmured. "But if you don't have seraph and you need information fast, torture works. So...it makes sense to learn how to do it."

"...I can't believe I'm hearing *you* out of everyone in the dorm say this," Cassius said angrily. "How can you condone it?"

"Condone it?" Rikol sat up suddenly, eyes angry. "I don't *condone* it. It's a despicable and ugly thing. But that doesn't mean that it doesn't have a use."

"So, what, you're fine with hurting people for fun?" Scythe asked, dripping sarcasm.

"No, you prick! But sometimes I think the ends justify the means. That hurting someone might..." he heaved a sigh and seemed to deflate, the anger he had been exhibiting gone in a flash, "save someone else."

"I don't believe this!" Cassius exclaimed; shock written across his face. "I can't believe you would sink so low."

"Cassius," I said softly.

"I mean, what's wrong with you! What could-"

"CASSIUS!" I shouted, and this time he heard me, stopping as he spun, fury plain on his face. "Stop it," I said more softly, pointing in Rikol's direction so he could witness the silent tears falling from his friend's face. "Just leave it."

Cassius being Cassius, he was torn between yelling some more and giving Rikol a hug, but in the end he settled for stewing in silence with the rest of us.

Wolf's Hollow had done the most important part of its job.

It had sown the first seeds of doubt amongst us.

Rikol didn't explain further, and despite how much we each wanted to know his reasoning behind his decision, we respected his privacy. Which, in hindsight, seems strange considering the subject matter in question.

The examiner tried again. Each and every day. I quickly began to loathe the time spent in that all-too-real illusion, staring at the fear etched into the poor sod's face and hearing the pained cries as the examiner showed me how it was done.

"Look, Calidan. Watch!" he would shout and each time I would tell him to go fuck himself and turn away. But the screams and the shouts were still there, and perhaps because I knew they weren't real, or because I was building callouses like those on my hands, over time I began to feel them a little less. Almost like I was tuning them out. Becoming deaf to a man's screams.

My parents would be so proud.

The others were the same. Eyes were glazing over when not in direct conversation. People becoming quickly lost in their own thoughts, doubtless remembering the screams that haunted everyone's nightmares.

The bastard examiner was good at his job. I had to give him that. Persistence, it seemed, was key to getting a bunch of youths to embrace doing horrible things for the right reasons. But, I suppose, hasn't that always been the way of history? Fill a youth with patriotic pride, hand them a weapon, and they will fight and die for their country. Provide a 'family' to someone down on their luck and they will do almost anything to keep it, even if that family are drug dealing killers.

Time and patience. Simple but powerful tools in the right hands.

Rikol wasn't the only one to succumb. Scythe and Ella both agreed to take a more hands-on approach with the examiner, learning the finer methods of extracting information. Scythe's earlier refusals had been reduced to nothing in the face of the repeated exposure to the scenario; a mixture of his need to move forwards combined with a dull-eyed understanding that he was capable of doing what the Imperator needed him to do allowing him to pick up the knife. Ella was a bigger concern. Not so much for me, because Ella and I were much the same. She had a dark core to her that was much like mine. An ability to become like flint, to compress her emotions and get the job done. I knew that. The dorm knew that. Cassius, however, couldn't comprehend it. More than anyone else, that hurt him. Hells, I think the fact that I hadn't broken before Ella hurt him almost as much. As much as he loved me, he *knew* that I was capable of bad things. But when it came to Ella he had a blind spot.

And so the tension in the dorm ratcheted up. Slowly the divide became clear: those who would do what the situation called for, and those who wouldn't. Those who would inched closer to getting past the horrific test. Those who wouldn't...well we were stuck, repeating the same thing over and over until we broke.

Sixteen days before I allowed myself to watch the torture. Nights of more haunted dreams than usual had left me a shadow of my former self, just like everyone else. I was deadened, desensitised to the shouting, the pleading, the screaming.

I knew it wasn't real. And so, on the sixteenth day I watched, ears closed to the screaming. On the seventeenth day I watched some more. And, just like the slippery slope of black seraph or a friendly 'family' member providing some helpful coaxing, on the eighteenth day I picked up the blade myself.

CHAPTER 3

Dead and Gone

"If you don't pass me, I'm going to put this through your jugular."

The examiner twitched in shock, freezing in place as the very illusionary knife touched his throat. I had a small smile on my lips as I saw his mental faculties restart, fear turning to shock, then anger. In an instant the illusion shattered, breaking into coruscating pieces and giving me a very strange moment of duality. When the fragments of illusion cleared, I was staring at an extremely angry man.

"You DARE?!" he screamed, face apoplectic with rage.

"I dare." I kept my voice cool, steady. No need to prod the bear further. I was intensely aware that he was a fully-fledged Imperator – more than capable of ending me quite quickly if he had half a mind to.

"You just assaulted an Imperator! When the High Imperator hears of this-"

"Actually, I didn't," I interrupted, holding his gaze.

The comment threw him off his rant and confusion entered his eyes. "What?"

"I didn't assault you. I haven't moved. I've been sitting here the entire time."

"That's beside the point! You can't do what you did without consequences."

"What evidence is there that I did anything?"

That brought him up short.

"Perhaps it just goes to show how good your illusions truly are, that you can get so lost in them as to lose touch with reality," I continued softly. "Nothing happened. Not here at least. No threats, no injuries, no problem."

"Oh, we have a big fucking problem!" he snarled. "What do you think you're doing?!"

I shrugged. "Changing the status quo. It's something I'm known for, to be honest. I'm surprised you didn't read that in my file."

His face somehow managed to darken further, until it was at the point where I wondered if he had popped a vein. "You're going to either complete the scenario or you're going to stay here forever," he growled through gritted teeth.

"No."

"No?"

"No." I crossed my legs and gave him a wide smile. "I really don't think it's necessary. You see, the entire purpose of this scenario was to understand what I would be able to do when the situation called for it. I imagine my response proves the depth of my resolve."

His hands were clenching and unclenching as he tried in vain to get control of himself. "Get. Out."

"Would you like me to-"

"GET OUT!" he screamed, picking up the nearest thing on his desk and throwing it at me. Quickly realising that I had perhaps pushed him a little too far, I ducked out of the room, pausing only to hear more screaming and throwing of objects. Chuckling to myself, I slipped back to the dorm, far too happy to have extracted a little bit of faux-revenge on the prick of an examiner.

"What have you got there?" Cassius asked, eyeing me as I entered.

"Ladies and gentlefolk, I present, my file," I replied with aplomb. It didn't quite get the response I was looking for, everyone too down and depressed to really care. Moving past the lack of reaction, I threw the file on the table and sat down to read it, only to be pushed aside by Rikol who took my place and picked up the file.

"What do we have here? Hmm. Ah! Psychological profile." He cleared his throat. "Ahem. 'Calidan is a driven, resourceful young man with a sharp mind. He tends to think somewhat one-dimensionally, often opting for bold, brash, confrontational actions rather than subtlety." He paused reading and coughed a laugh. "Sounds right on the money."

"Hey!"

He arched an eyebrow. "How exactly did you get this?"

"Er...I may have threatened the examiner with a knife."

"WHAT?!"

"An illusionary knife!" I quickly added, raising my hands to ward off the aghast stares. "Just the one in the scenario. So, I didn't *actually* do anything."

"You threatened an Imperator..." Sophia groaned, laying a hand on her head. "Why would you do that?"

"Because he was being a prick. And because I don't want to do what he wants me to."

"Calidan, why would you think this would work?" asked Ella, face contorted with a frown.

I shrugged. "It's worked before, hasn't it? I mean, my file basically suggested I would do exactly this."

"Yes...but when you're trapped in an underground lair with a bunch of Imperators whose sole task is to make you into one of them...what makes you think that butting heads with them to that extent is going to work? There is no one here to protect you. No High Imperator or Emperor. There is just us and them." Her tone was sad now, weary beyond reckoning.

I pursed my lips, anger flaring in my chest at her response. "I can handle whatever his response is."

"I don't think you get it," she said with a shake of her head. "You're in their power, Calidan. Their only objective is to break you. What do you think that they're going to do? Reward you for being an unruly student? No. The Academy doesn't want unruly Imperators. It wants Imperators who can do what they're told, and who will sink to the levels that it needs them to sink to." Tears welled in her eyes as she spoke and I realised that she hated what she was saying, but believed it to be completely true. "You can't escape this." She turned her head to Cassius, voice becoming soft. "And neither can you."

Cassius's eyes hardened. "I've heard enough." Rising to his feet he flung the door open to storm out, only to step back into the room a moment later, backing up in face of two Imperators. They didn't wear any insignia or particular attire to suggest that they were Imperators, but I just *knew* that they were. They exuded a sort of blank-faced menace. A feeling of inhospitality, like they didn't care who or what you were.

"Which one is Calidan?" the shorter one asked. A woman, hair tied back in a business-like bun, face stern. Cassius looked at me and she stepped inside the room, leaving the larger, more physically imposing Imperator to block the door. Glancing around the dorm, she noted everyone inside the room before settling her eyes on mine.

"You are to come with me."

I swallowed. "Where are we going?"

She was unmoving. A carved marble statue. "Stand and come with me."

I tried again. "Where?"

A slow blink. "You are in no place to ask questions. Come willingly or be taken by force. It does not matter."

I looked at the others and then stood up slowly. "See you soon, I hope." I muttered to the team before I walked out of the door and into the echoing hallway of muted stone.

"Hands behind your back."

I did as instructed, feeling the cold clamp of something over my wrists. "Hey!" I began, only to stumble as the big slab of rock that was intelligent enough to be called a man pushed me forwards. "What's going on? Where are we going?"

They didn't reply, just marched me along the corridors, away from areas that I knew and towards the stairwell. Down and down we walked until all sounds of people had vanished, to be replaced only with the sound of echoing footsteps. We stopped on the third level. The area that Kane had said was completely off limits. The big man held a hand to a slab of metal and paused for a second, face tightening in concentration, before a lock *clicked* and he pushed the door open.

Instantly, sound assaulted me. But it wasn't the sound of upstairs; the clamour of Imperators and people going around their daily lives. No, this was something else, the sound of sobbing, of anger, of screaming. The scent followed like a tidal wave. A deluge of sweat and putrescence assaulted my nostrils, all of it overlayed with one thing above all else.

Fear.

It was everywhere. The scent of it was so thick that I could practically taste it. Gut-wrenching, pulse-pounding fear.

"What is this place?" I whispered; voice muted in horror.

This time, the face of the female Imperator showed emotion: the slightest of smirks. "Your new home."

"What?!"

She marched me forwards past row after row of stone cells until we reached one at the far end, unlocking the door, this time with an old-fashioned key from within her clothes, and pushed me inside. The big man held my arms painfully behind my back whilst she did a quick, practiced inspection of my clothes, removing everything that I had – even the things I had thought I had hidden well – and then gesturing for the man to let me go.

"You are here, Calidan, because you broke the rules. You threatened your examiner and that, unsurprisingly, is not allowed." Another slow blink. "You will remain here until we believe you are ready to once again begin your studies. Enjoy your stay."

The door clanged shut in my face.

"Wait!" I yelled, rushing to the door and slamming into it, hammering it with my fists. A moment later a small slit in the metal slid open, revealing the woman again.

"And another thing," she said calmly, as if I wasn't red-faced with fury and trying to batter down the barrier between us, "if you attempt to leave this cell, you will be treated as an enemy of the empire and…" she pursed her lips, "eliminated." With a final nod, the slit clanged shut.

I stood still, shocked, as the sounds of the prison filtered back to me. For that was what it was, I knew that now; a prison. Why Wolf's Hollow would have such a place made little sense to me. Surely, they couldn't all be Imps? Who were these people and why were they here?

Confused and a little bit terrified, I sat down on the cold stone floor, waiting.

Six-foot by six-foot. That's how big the cell was. Roomy by some cell standards, but tiny by practically everything else. It was lit only by a narrow strip of something that I didn't quite recognise that ran along the corner of the room. It wasn't quite like the incessant humming light of the citadel, but it was something similar. It didn't waver, didn't flicker like a candle, it just…was.

The standard of light it outputted, however, left something to be desired. At most it just about pierced the gloom of the cell, and that was with my Seya-enhanced eyes. I didn't envy any normal human forced to stay in this place; they would barely be able to see the far wall.

Food came. Delivered through a bigger slot at the bottom of the door. It was the same food as was served in the cafeteria, which meant delicious. The Academy knew to feed its students and staff the best it could – there was no better way to lower morale than to provide poor quality food.

Which left me wondering why they served it down here. If this was meant to be a place to break me and the other denizens down then why would they not serve something that was guaranteed to make your day no better, like gruel or that salty black paste that some crazy people put on toast? The more I thought about it, the more I didn't understand the situation. Something very strange was happening; that was all I knew.

On what I guessed was my second day in the cell – though time was hard to judge - I heard the far door clang open. Footsteps entered and the prisoners began moaning and shouting; a piteous cacophony. A prison door clanged open and the rest of the prisoners quieted in relief, whilst the unlucky individual in the chosen cell started shouting in higher and higher volumes, desperation in their voice.

"No, no, please! I'll do anything-"

The sound cut off abruptly. Footsteps and a slithering sound, like someone dragging something heavy, followed, retreating through the cellblock with their cargo until they vanished out of the door again, the door shutting with a reverberating *clang*. Instantly the volume of the remaining prisoners started up again.

"Jarv, you still there?"

"I'm here. Elton?"

"Still here. I think it was Rafe. Rafe, you there?"

No answer.

"Ah, shit. Poor Rafe."

"Hey!" I yelled, banging on the door. "What just happened? What is this place?"

"Ah, the new one speaks." The voice was gravelly, hoarse.

"Damn right I do, tell me what's going on!"

A sigh. "We don't know much more than you. Sometimes people are chosen. They don't come back."

"Dead is what they are," cackled a crazed voice. "Dead and gone!"

"Not helping, Clythe."

"Do you know what this place is?" I called out.

"Just another prison, far as I'm concerned," the gravelly voice ground out. "Where did they transfer you from?"

I paused. *They're not Imps or Imperators. They're criminals?* Thinking fast, I decided that telling them I was an Imp was not in my best interest. "I'm...new. Not sure how I ended up here."

"I pity you then lad. They treat us well enough in here," the gruff voice – the one I think was called Jarv – replied. "Best food I've ever had and all, but..."

"But?"

A heavy sigh that sounded like rocks crumbling. "In my experience the places that feed you this well are the ones that know each meal might be your last."

"Like Raaafe. Dead and gonnnnne," Clythe sang, his voice a nasal, strangled sound.

"Oh, by the Pits, shut up!" someone shouted, banging on a door.

"Dead. All dead. DEAD!"

"Damnit Clythe, stop scaring the new lad," Jarv rumbled. "He's got enough worries without you adding to them."

Clythe cackled but quieted. "How long have you been here?" I asked.

"Jarv's been here the longest," a low voice murmured. "At least out of those of us remaining. How long has it been for you Jarv? Three months?"

"Closer to four."

"And you don't know where the others go?" I asked, curious.

A snort. "I'm trapped in a cell, new kid. How exactly would I know that? Not like anyone has ever come back."

"So, there's nothing you can tell me about what's going on?" I said, exasperated. "Surely, someone must have seen something – anything – that could give us a clue?"

"Coat of black, coat of black!" cackled Clythe.

"Shut up!"

"COAT OF BLACK." He screamed the words, voice quivering with the strain.

"Quiet!" bellowed Jarv, and I could easily imagine the man rubbing his temples to relieve some of the tension. "Though, now he says it, I have seen a few dark long-coats on some of the people as they come and go in here."

"Oh gods," whispered a dread-filled voice.

Jarv cleared his throat, suddenly sounding a little more nervous. "If so, then we could be in the hands of the Imperators."

Quiet descended on the prison at his words. It was astonishing to see the effect that the mere mention of the name of the Imperators could cause.

"Is...is that so bad?" I questioned.

"You been living under a rock? Imperators are all bad. Specially for the likes of us. Don't want to cross one if you want to live. If you're hunted by one, well, ain't going to live much longer. If we're in their hands, I can't imagine the horrors they are going to do to us."

Silence fell at his words. All aside from Clythe who started singing his 'dead and gone' refrain again. This time no one tried to quieten him down. After all, it seemed quite likely that he was correct.

I woke to the sound of a door rattling. Some shouted comments and then a door slammed shut with a fatalistic *clang*.

"Rafe? That you?" Jarv rumbled.

"Who the fuck is Rafe?" hissed an angry female voice.

"Ah," he replied, a little sad. "Pity. I liked Rafe. Hello newcomer. What's your name?"

"Fuck you want to know for?"

"Just being friendly."

"Get bent, wanker. I'll be out of here soon, you'll see."

"DEAD AND GONE."

"FUCK OFF!" she screamed back at the top of her lungs, causing Clythe to cackle hysterically.

Shaking my head, I stood, cracking my joints before shifting into the slow motions of kaschan. Whilst the space was small there was enough room to do some exercise, and with the quality of the food I was receiving there was little reason not to continue to train. I didn't know how long I was going to be in this place and didn't want to fall behind in my physical training. At least one of the others must have had the same idea – at least, I hoped that's what the grunting was.

I looked up when the door to my cell opened, the same two Imperators that had put me in here filling the doorway. I realised that I couldn't hear the other inmates and hadn't heard the approach of the Imperators and figured that, for some reason, they must have been using some sound-cancelling seraph.

"Come with me." It was not a request.

I was marched back through the cells, up several floors and deposited back into the examiner's room, where the prick sat, face smug as he looked me up and down.

"Well, well, well. What do we have here?" he said with a shit-eating grin.

I raised a middle finger.

"Glad to see our little prison is working wonders for your manners."

"Fuck you."

"No. Fuck you, you little shit." Anger flashed in his eyes and his voice was venomous. "You think I want to be in here, teaching this to all you ungrateful little fucks? No! No-one wants to be here and no-one in their right mind *wants* to learn this stuff, but everyone recognises that they *need* to. So get it through your thick skull – you want out of that cell, you be a good little Imp and fall in line. Am I understood?"

I turned and thrust out my hands. "Take me back."

They did as I asked.

They cut my rations after I did that. Just enough to make me feel the bite of hunger.

Elton was gone when I came back. None of the others had known that I had been away, just thought I had been silent whilst he had been removed. I don't know if the Imperators had been listening in on our discussions, but they seemed content to keep all our interactions silent to the rest of the inmates.

Poor Elton. Clythe sang about him for a while. It was strangely melodic, albeit downright disturbing. He certainly had a way with words.

Two days later they tried again. This time when I rejected the examiner, my food stopped altogether. On the evening of the following day, I was provided a small husk of stale bread, something that I tore into gratefully. That was a bad time. I could smell the canteen food as it was provided to everyone else but me. I wouldn't be surprised if the bastards cooked them extra delicious meals just to spite me. I tried to be content with my bread but my stomach gurgled and rumbled all through the night, weakening me.

Weakening my resolve.

Angry girl was dragged away. There was a whole lot of screaming and, from the sound of it, a fairly decent punch up with one of the Imperators, but in the end she was removed from the prison, yet another to never be seen again.

I spent my days pondering on what was happening here. Well, that and my stomach. After three days the hunger was less intense but it was still there, a gnawing, constant thing. But I had known true hunger many times in the past. I could handle it.

Maybe.

As for what was going on, the closest I could figure was that the Academy was using them for something – that much was obvious. I highly doubted that the empire's resources were that stretched that the penal system had to share space with an Imperator-training facility. But that just begged the question as to what the Imperators were doing with the prisoners. The others seemed fairly convinced that they were killed –

an easy observation to make when held in captivity against your will and hearing your cell-mates being dragged away periodically. But I couldn't think of any practical reason as to *why* that would happen.

My mind dragged me in all sorts of dark and disturbing directions whilst sitting in the gloom. Thoughts of the Academy forcing us to actually torture people was first and foremost in my mind. It was the only conclusion I could think of and something that I had no intention of ever doing. Hells, I didn't want to think about doing it, even if it seemed one-hundred percent necessary. That was a dark path that I had no desire to walk down.

But one that the Academy seemed desperate to force upon me.

PRESENT DAY 1

My cup of coffee steamed in the humid air as I gently set it down on the mahogany table. The café was filled with rich furnishings and dark wood, providing a refined air amidst the hustle and bustle of the city. Most importantly, in my eyes, it had some kind of contraption that allowed for constant airflow; not much, but in this sweltering heat anything was better than nothing.

Frankly, I had never been this hot and sticky in my life. Sure, I've been burned and covered with monster guts which might provide a similar textural result but it wasn't quite the same thing.

Jixia was hot, humid, and full of bustling energy. The busy markets of Anderal paled in comparison to the constant ebb and flow of trade and humanity. Hawkers peddled their wares from every available space selling everything from exotic spices to even more exotic weapons. Honestly, if I didn't have a job to do, I could have stayed in the city for months. It was *fascinating*. But perhaps the somehow-functioning chaos was to be expected. Afterall, Jixia was the primary trading hub of the Gestalt Trading Guild – the most powerful trading company in the world and often referred to as the 'GTG'. And, thankfully, the one most responsible for delivering those crucial barrels of coffee beans to the cafes in the Andurran empire – something for which I was eminently grateful.

Most importantly, the Gestalt Trading Guild Headquarters – conveniently located opposite my café window – held a vault solely for the use of its most distinguished guests. One of those 'guests' was, in fact, the mysterious and illusive owner of the GTG, someone who also had the distinct advantage of being one of the Five Powers.

The ruler of the Sethani empire and someone so vain that he allegedly didn't let his feet touch the ground.

Asol.

I had a feeling I was going to enjoy robbing this guy.

I say 'rob'. That suggests something as mundane or basic as a simple breaking and entering. Not so for this place. The headquarters itself was more akin to a fortress than a trade emporium. Monstrously thick walls formed the outside, each large enough to likely stop a rampaging skyren, and the inside was made up of clerks' desks within the large atrium, along with a barred wall of what was said to be magically enhanced steel where the financiers approved and dealt with the transactions presented to them by the clerks on behalf of their guests.

But it wasn't purely just money that the GTG traded in. It was at once both a dealer in commodities both common and rare, a buyer, and an auction hub. That meant that not only did they have need for a vault to contain the vast sums of money that flowed through their fingers every minute, but to also have the capacity to hold and protect items of extraordinary value.

And I had a fair inkling as to what one of those items was.

Afterall, where would a Power who secretly runs the world's most valuable company decide to store what was most valuable to him? He was known to be vain. To be ostentatious.

It stood to reason that the fifth layer of the vault – that which was not on any floor plan or even known by most employees to even exist – was exactly where he would store his contents.

As for those contents? I was hoping for some rare paintings, enchanted tools and the like. The things that the more fantastical side of my mind chose to hope that the most powerful beings in the known world would create and set aside for a rainy day. Not that I was truly interested in them. There was only really one true goal.

Star-metal.

Having already stolen Nuramapole's stockpile and nearly dying for it, here I was once more trying to pull the wool over the eyes of someone so powerful that they were known as a god.

Sometimes, I loved my life.

Pulling off a heist triggered that part of my brain that loved planning and strategy. Sure, there was some planning required for the monsters I hunted but at the end of the day it usually came down to finding a weakness and exploiting it. In that, at least, planning a heist was the same, but it was so much *more*. I needed information as to the locations of the vaults, of traps, of guards, of air vents – of literally everything and anything that might be of use.

Which is why this heist had taken four months to plan.

And that was only because I still had some friends in the Academy. Namely a beautiful huntress with skills in espionage and a once-famous assassin now turned less famous but infinitely more deadly magic assassin, Sophia and Arteme.

Together we had roamed the vast halls of the Academy Archives, perusing everything that we could find related to the GTG. Whilst they didn't know the true purpose to the heist, nor the actual owner of the company, the two knew better than to ask.

Plausible deniability means a whole lot more when your brain can be scoured directly for answers.

We had uncovered plenty of information regarding the GTG, some of which pertained to the vault, but next to nothing related to the fabled fifth level. Looking at the schematics of the building itself, we had managed to extrapolate how it *might* look, but it was little more than an educated guess. Academy spies had never managed to get in to have a look and the lesser staff within the guild either didn't know it existed or had more rumour than hard information which was worse than useless.

There was only one person who was guaranteed to have information on the fifth layer. The chief executive and official 'owner' of the GTG, Melissa Gestalt, eighth-generation descendent of the legendary Guyver Gestalt who started the business. Melissa was known to be like a shark when it came to business; always able to scent the blood in the water. Schooled by the finest tutors and groomed to take over the business from a young age, she was everything that the GTG needed to keep it at the top of the world's companies: sharp as a blade, ruthless in business and completely focused on the company's success.

She was truly formidable.

Worse, she had at least two seraph users within her squad of bodyguards. Though the existence of seraph wasn't known to the average person, that rule didn't seem to include the most wealthy and powerful for whom knowing things was their bread and butter.

Altogether, abducting her and rifling through her mind was not going to be easy.

Which was precisely why I was glad I wasn't the one doing it.

In position. The words touched my mind, carrying the distinctive signature of Sophia.

Target in sight. Last chance. Arteme's words.

I took one more lovely sip of the bitter coffee and set it down before standing up and grabbing my hat. *Proceed.*

Tuning out the rest of the world I paid my tab and focused; today I was not Calidan Darkheart, monster-hunter of the Academy. Today I was Cael Wintersteel, second son of the famed Wintersteel armoury revered by nations across the land.

Adjusting my gait slightly, pulling my shoulders back like I owned the place, I strode across the road and through the smoothly revolving door.

Time to steal some shit.

CHAPTER 4

Lessons

"Psst. Hey."

I rolled over in my shoddy bed, trying to ignore both the sound of snoring and of my stomach attempting to eat itself.

"Hey kid!"

Growling, I sat up. "What?"

"What did you do to get thrown in here? You never said."

"You never asked."

A pause. "True. I'm asking now."

I had plenty of time to think about this. I didn't want the inmates to know who or what I was, so my cover was simple. "Theft."

"Must have been some theft to get thrown down here with us."

"Big enough." I was about to attempt to get more sleep when a question broke past my lips before I had even realised. "What about you?"

A long silence. So long that I didn't think he would answer at all. "Murder."

My heart skipped a beat. "Yeah?"

"Yeah. Killed the man who had slept with my wife. Wasn't intentional, but I got carried away."

"Oh...sorry to hear that, Jarv."

"Sorry?" he coughed a laugh. "You've got nothing to be sorry for. I'm sorry for my misdeeds and I'm willing to pay the price. If that's spending my life in here, then that's what I will do."

"Who caught you?"

He scoffed. "Caught? No-one 'caught' me. As soon as the red cleared from my vision and I realised what I had done, I turned myself in. Constable didn't really know what to do; most killers don't exactly just go and hand themselves over."

"Sounds like it was a mistake anyone could have made," I murmured softly.

"Maybe. Or maybe I'm just the kind of man who gets blinded by anger. So blinded that he can do terrible things."

"You don't sound like a terrible person."

He snorted; the sound somehow sad as it echoed around the prison cells. "You can never tell. For all you know, I could be a rabid killer, desperate to close my hands around my next victim's throat."

A smile touched my lips at that. "Somehow I doubt that most rabid killers are as introspective as you."

"Perhaps. Or perhaps that's what I want you to think. Never can be too careful."

"So, are you a rabid killer?"

A laugh. "No. No, that's Clythe. Batshit crazy that one. Sings about his victims."

"Don't remind me." A shudder ran through me as the memories resurfaced. Clythe either had an extremely vivid and detailed imagination or had committed some truly atrocious acts.

"He's the only one who has come back, you know that?"

"Come back?"

"Don't play dumb. Come back after being taken by whoever is in charge of this prison. No-one else has. Won't say what happened, but he was certainly gleeful when he returned. Spent the whole night cackling away and singing to himself."

"Delightful."

"Not really. You've heard his singing."

"True."

"What do you think happens to those that get taken away?" he asked after a long moment.

"I have no idea."

"Want to know what I think?"

I yawned and cracked my neck. "Not sure I could stop you from telling me anyway."

He choked back a laugh. "You're a funny one. Well, I think that they make us fight."

"Fight? Why would you think that?"

"Because of the way Clythe acted…and the fact that he added a new descriptive to his singing repertoire."

Making prisoners fight? Why would they do that? My mind raced. *I can't believe that the Academy would condone such a thing. There has to be something we're missing.*

"That…that can't be true." A note of desperation may have crept into my voice.

I could hear his shrug, the muscles of his shoulders rolling up and down. "Don't know for sure of course, but that's the way I reckon it is." A long sigh. "I guess we'll all find out soon enough anyway."

I let that one sink in for a few minutes. "How long have you been here Jarv?" I asked after a while.

"Not sure. Feels like a while."

"Others come and go quick; you haven't been taken out yet?"

"No. Guess they must like me. Or are saving me for something special. Who knows?"

I leant back and stared at the ceiling. *Who knows indeed?* Closing my eyes, I slept.

"Wake up." It was the gruff Imperator again, flinging the door open as he spoke. The other was outside, doubtless creating the silent enchantment once more.

"You know, if you're going to have me down here, you could at least let me get a proper night's sleep," I croaked with what I hoped was just the right amount of wit and sarcasm. He looked at me. I looked at him. His face didn't move. Didn't even twitch. I sighed and swung myself out of bed. I hadn't been able to get a rise out of either Imperator at all. They were seemingly incapable of small talk, empathy or human emotion – probably had Wolf's Hollow to thank or blame for that. Perhaps they had gone through exactly what I was experiencing right now.

Or, more likely, they had done exactly what the Academy had asked of them with no qualms or issues.

Weak. I will not let the Academy destroy me.

My stomach clenched, weakness assaulting my limbs as lack of food made itself known. Staggering, I rested against the wall, only to realise when the wall twitched a moment later that I was resting against the man-mountain.

"Oh. Sorry." I made no move to take my hand away; all that muscle made for an excellent support. If he cared, then he certainly didn't show it, just shifted his position so that I was on his side and helped me through the door.

"You've looked better." The voice was without inflection but the words hit with a bit of snark from the female Imperator.

"And I've looked much, much worse." I gave her a tired wink and an attempt at a smile. Neither had an effect.

"Hmm." Without another word she turned around and led the way out of the prison.

This time, the examiner was tucking into a roasted chicken, covered in a thick gravy and surrounded by roast potatoes. The smell of it instantly setting my mouth watering and my eyes locked onto it with predatory intent.

"Calidan. We meet again."

I didn't respond, just stared at the food. It stared right back. Calling to me. *Needing* me.

"I hope your abode is suiting you well?" He cut into the leg of the chicken and the aroma intensified. My stomach instantly betrayed me and growled. I might have growled too; the desperate need for food almost overwhelming.

"Ah," the man pretended to notice the large plate of food in front of him for the first time. "Are you admiring dinner? It was beautifully cooked." He took a single bite, closed his eyes in satisfaction and swallowed. "But too filling." With a quick motion he swept the food into the bin beside his desk, watching the way my eyes widened with shock, his expression gleeful. "There we are, more space on the desk now. So, tell me Calidan, how are you finding your stay on the third floor?"

"Asshole."

"Sorry?"

"You heard me."

"I'm not so sure that I did. For a moment it seemed like you *may* have insulted the Imperator who holds your fate in his hands, but as that seems overwhelmingly *stupid* even for you, I must have misheard." His tone was pleasant enough but his eyes were sharp. "Did I mishear?"

No, you self-righteous, pompous putrid prick! Go fuck yourself and the horse you rode in on. You're a twisted little shit that takes too much pleasure in torture so go and throw yourself off a bridge. Off a building. Off anything. Just go and die. It will do so much for your demeanour.

I forced a smile. "Yes."

His eyes watched mine carefully, looking for any hint of rebelliousness; of dissent to his rule. Apparently, I managed to look the right amount of pathetic to please his sadistic side enough to let my belligerence slide. "Good. In that case, Calidan, I have a mission for you."

My eyes widened. Surely I had misheard. "A mission?"

"Did I not speak clearly enough? A mission."

"But, I'm in jail!"

He waved a hand airily. "A minor point. As you've learned, we can take you from your cell at any moment. Despite what you might think, this is still part of the Academy, which means there is a curriculum to drill into your thick skull." He smiled toothily. "Examples to be made, camaraderie to be broken, that kind of thing."

"So you...what? Keep me in a cell, starve me, and still expect me to go out there and learn?"

He adopted a puzzled look. "But of course. Why wouldn't we? The Academy is all about learning, and Wolf's Hollow is where you learn the most important lessons of all. The cell is a lesson," his eyes flashed, "one which I hope you're taking to heart. Despite the, shall we say, *peculiarities* of your current living situation, that doesn't prevent you from joining the others."

"And if I say no?"

"Some lessons can be avoided. Others, like the cell, can be forced upon you. Regardless of the direction chosen there is always a cost."

I let out an extremely heartfelt sigh. "Cut the bullshit for once."

The Imperator's eyes narrowed. "Fine. You can stay in your cell, but you'll just be dropping behind, further and further until your friends are gone from this place, free to be the glorious little Imperators that they have always dreamed of being, whilst you will still be here, languishing in your tiny cell, waiting for the second opportunity that *will never come*." He eyed me for a long moment then cocked his head. "*Or,* you will choose to give your all to everything that we ask of you, pushing as hard as you can to stay level with your colleagues."

"And my stay in the cell?"

He shrugged. "Continues. That is a different lesson, one that you will need to endure until you've learnt the correct answer."

Crossing my arms, I locked eyes with him. "So you want me to go and do my best, despite being so weak as to barely walk without assistance?"

"Another reason to learn that first lesson quickly, no?" He cracked a half-smile at the murderous look on my face. "Perhaps if you perform well we can arrange for a little victory meal. How does that sound?"

Like you're a lying sack of shit. "Adequate."

"Excellent. Any other questions?"

"What is the mission?"

The clap of his hands rang in the small room, an eager smile plastered on his face. "Oh, you're just going to love this, Calidan. It's something to *die* for."

CHAPTER 5

SOMETHING TO DIE FOR

"Well, don't you look like Death's own balls."

"Good to see you too." I gripped Rikol's arm in greeting and he gave me a brief but firm hug.

"Where have you been? The Imperators have been tight-lipped. It was like you vanished off the face of the earth!"

I frowned, pursing my lips. "You weren't told? What am I saying? Of course you weren't told."

"They just said that you had been taken away for 'rehabilitation', whatever the fuck that means."

"It means starvation in a tiny cell until I do what they want," I clarified. "Not the most fun of times."

Rikol shook his head in mute disbelief. "Half-starved and yet they want you involved in this? Nutters."

"And what is 'this'?" I asked curiously. "The Imperators weren't exactly vocal about what this mission entailed. And where are the others?"

"The others are already out there, preparing."

"Preparing?"

"Sheesh, they really told you nothing, eh?" He shook his head again. "Welcome to the first of the competitions, Calidan."

I stared at him blankly. "Come again?"

"We are competing not just against the other Imps in Wolf's Hollow, but each other as well." His gaze looked uncertain as he spoke, the words sounding forced. "This first competition is simple: capture the flag. They've stuck a flag somewhere in the nearby mountain range and we are to retrieve it and take it back to our allocated 'base'."

"And when you say 'we', you mean just us two?"

He nodded. "We're in pairs for this one. You and me, Ella and Scythe, Sophia and Cassius. Three teams, three bases. One flag."

"And the rules?"

He swallowed nervously. "There are no rules."

"Anything goes?" I exclaimed incredulously. "What about protections in place?"

Another shake of his head. "Nothing of the sort. We are meant to be good enough now not to injure or kill unless we actually *want* to do so."

"But why would we ever want to do that...?" I drifted off as my thoughts coalesced. "Rikol," I asked intently, leaning forwards, "what is the prize for winning?"

He winced. "Protection." I waved a hand and he continued. "Protection in the coming events. From what we have managed to glean, some of the upcoming competitions are not about winning but are very much about what happens to the losers. The Imperators state that if you lose going forwards, depending on the skills – or lack thereof – displayed, you could be kept back, dropped a year or..." he mimed a hand across his throat, causing me to scoff.

"They wouldn't actually *kill* Imps," I declared. "They've invested far too much time into us."

"Maybe, but the way they say it, the Academy only wants the best. The chaff is useless. Worse than useless; they're a drain on resources – too much information to leave the Academy and not enough skills to make it." He pursed his lips. "You've seen the others around the place. Arin, Oso and a few higher years. Most of them are scared, Cal. Scared because they have taken a loss and don't know if they can afford another."

"This puts me being starved more into perspective," I murmured, more to myself than Rikol but he nodded in agreement. "They are dealing you a shit hand, knowing that the weaker you are, the more likely you are to fail. And, for this competition at least, that means the more likely *we* are to fail."

I grunted and nodded. "Harsh."

He shrugged. "It's the way of the world. Imperators have to be hard, to be better than everyone else, and to trust few. Otherwise they end up dead."

I snorted. "I can see the Imperator recruiting team has been present in your classes." My words were said lightly but I could see Rikol stiffen under their meaning.

"They're right, Cal. Blind trust can get you killed. I've seen it before. The things that they want us to do, they're *necessary*, Calidan. I don't like it any more than you, but in the heat of the mission, when a friend's life is on the line, if torturing an enemy is what it takes to save them? I would do it in a heartbeat."

I shook my head slowly. "I don't want to argue about this Rikol, not right-"

"Don't argue then, just listen," he cut in. "You and Cassius are the only ones who haven't completed that class. Cassius is Cassius, he has his morals but he isn't a dick about it so he isn't languishing in some prison cell like you. You, on the other hand, have less reason to be so against it."

My eyes met his and he nodded slowly. "I know you, Cal. I've known you a long time. You're one of my best friends but I know that, more than any of us, you're a killer." He held up a hand as I shifted. "I don't mean that in a bad way. What I mean is that you have an instinct for fighting. Or should I say for winning. Whilst Cassius or I might better you in swordplay or seraph, you fight to win. I've never seen anyone quite so good at fighting to survive, able to use anything and everything to do so. Hells, I've seen you cut your way through men like Death himself and you probably didn't even have nightmares afterwards. Because you're a survivor. It was you or them. This is the same."

I was silent for a long moment, emotions roiling. Eventually I stirred. "It's not the same," I replied slowly, with a shake of my head. Holding up a hand to forestall his response, I continued. "Battle is one thing, but what they want us to learn here is something else entirely. To drop our morals and corrupt our souls." I found that my fists were clenched, knuckles white. "My soul is already stained enough. I don't want to become..."

"Become what?" Rikol pressed.

"A monster."

Rikol shook his head in disbelief. "I can't believe you haven't figured it out yet, Cal."

"Figured what out?"

He clapped a hand on my shoulder and looked me deep in the eyes. "You don't need to worry about becoming a monster, my friend. Because like me – like all of us – you already *are* one." He waved away my astonished noises. "We've fought, we've killed. We've slaughtered men, demolished demons and held our own against beings that far surpassed us in every way. We are monsters in everything but appearance, but hells, what do you think the long-coats are for? The mere sight of them terrify the townsfolk. They already call us monsters behind our backs, but that is the price we pay to protect the empire. And that is what being an Imperator is all about; something that you knew going in. Being an Imperator isn't about you, me, Cassius or anyone else. It isn't even about revenge. It's about *him*."

"Him?"

"The Emperor. You are his. He made all of this possible. Made it possible for us to fight, to take control of our lives, to wield seraph. Consequently, are lives are his to spend. And if that means that I have to take a knife to someone to get the answers I need, I will do so. Because I serve a greater purpose. As do you."

I shook my head in disbelief. "Rikol, I don't think I've ever heard you speak this passionately before."

"That's because I've had to grow up!" he snapped, eyes flashing. "We all have. It's just you and Cassius who haven't realised the situation yet and none of us want to see you fail. The others are just too scared to say what is needed."

Realisation dawned. "Is this some kind of intervention? Did you ask to be here, as my partner?"

His eyes never left mine. "Of course. They wouldn't pair you with Cassius, not for this mission – your love for each other is well known and they want to break some of those bonds. I offered myself, because I thought it might have more weight coming from me. You need to cut the shit. Accept reality and learn everything that the Academy wants you to learn. Otherwise you're not getting out of here."

I held his gaze squarely, seeing his unflinching fervour. I had to give him credit, Rikol was trying to be a friend in the only way he knew how – telling me how it was in a no-nonsense way. "Rikol," I began gently, "thank you. I know you mean well, but I'm not sure I can countenance the route that the Academy wants me to go down."

Sadness warred with disgust on his face as he shook his head slowly before turning away. "Then you'll throw away everything that you've been working for," he muttered over his shoulder before waving a hand. "Come. We best get out there. Whilst you might want to give up on the Academy, I do not."

So, you're back in the real world. The words purred into my mind, accompanied by the image of a satisfied black panther being brushed by an Academy worker.

Hey Seya. Sorry it's been so long.

Not to worry. I've been well-kept in your absence. It's almost as though the Academy wants to keep me here rather than hunting after you.

We both know that is very much the case. Before we had left to Wolf's Hollow, Kane had explained that the facility was heavily warded and that our telepathy was unlikely to work. We had both been upset at this, however Seya was quickly mollified when Kane had given her a permanent member of staff to 'see to her needs'. Judging by her relaxed behaviour, I could only assume that the poor staff member was being run ragged; Seya was nothing if not demanding.

How are things in this hollow of wolves?

Not great, to be honest. I'm being kept in confinement.

I sensed Seya's appointed brusher go flying as she rippled to her feet, anger radiating off her body. *You're what?!*

Through a rapid series of images and words I quickly relayed what was happening, feeling her disgust deepen whilst she sank back down to a discontented crouch. For a long time she didn't say anything, her great mind working through the ramifications of what I was discussing.

Do you still think that the path of the Academy is the right choice for you? she asked eventually.

I considered for a moment and then nodded, not that she could see it. *I do. If only because I would not be allowed to leave.*

Then you have three choices: first, you can stay where you are, trapped or doomed to be removed or whatever fate awaits those who fail this final year. Second, you accept the Academy's rules and pass the year. Third, you change things.

I grimaced. *I've tried changing things. It didn't go well.*

I felt her ear twitch in annoyance. *No, you tried to bludgeon your way out of the situation. But that isn't the only method available to you. You could try using your influence with Kane, the High Imperator or even the Emperor to change things. If not that, instead of butting heads with this sole Imperator, you could adopt some of that guile that Ella and Rikol have tried to teach you over the years.*

I... I drifted off, not knowing quite what to say. *Do you think that would work?*

Perhaps. Perhaps not. You might have burned your bridges with this Imperator to the extent that guile doesn't work. If that's the case, you're back to the first two options: fail or become what they want most.

A monster. A torturer.

That, or someone prepared to do what is necessary to achieve their goals. What's your goal, Calidan?

My mind turned to the red-eyed demon, the beast that had been accidentally freed during one of the attacks on Enemy-held installations a few months earlier. *To kill that red-eyed monster once and for all.*

Then don't let anything stand in your way. Don't rot in a cell. Figure out a solution to your problem and use it.

I felt a smile creep across my face. *When did you get so wise?*

I've always been wise, she replied, and I could feel her deigning to let her somewhat shaken handler resume brushing her. *You've probably just been too unintelligent to understand my wisdom.*

That must be it, I agreed, and for a few minutes we kept a companionable silence as I followed Rikol through the forest.

Calidan?

Yes, Seya?

About what you said. Becoming a monster.

What about it?

A flash of feline emotion welled in my chest. *Know that I would never have a monster as my bonded.*

I stopped walking. *What are you saying? That you'll abandon me?!*

"Calidan, come on!" Rikol hissed.

I sensed laughter and apology through my bond. *Of course not. What I mean is that I would never let that happen. So use me as your lodestone. As long as I am around, I'll keep you grounded and won't let you turn into what you fear most.*

I...I resumed the hike with a smile, leaving Rikol shaking his head in frustration. *Thank you.*

Any time. Besides, as I am the centre of your universe already anyway, it makes sense.

...Of course it does.

"We're here." Rikol declared as we finished climbing a short rise, finding a tiny clearing at the top, complete with a small stone that held a deep, cylindrical hole in its centre. Rikol indicated the stone. "This must be where we place the flag once we retrieve it. If we manage that, we win."

"Sounds simple," I replied, an arched eyebrow suggesting it would be anything but.

"Simple concept, difficult execution," he conceded.

"And the flag?"

He gestured out to the valley around us. "When the game begins, an Imperator will send up a flare marking both the beginning of the game and the location of the flag."

"No need to hunt for it? Should make things faster."

"Faster, yes. Easier? Doubtful. The Imperators obviously want us to engage with one another rather than one party steal it before the others arrive." He cracked his neck from side to side and rolled his shoulders. "As soon as that flare goes off, expect chaos."

I nodded. "Game plan?"

He considered me for a moment before looking back into the valley. "Honestly? I figured the best bet was for me to fly in, grab the flag and fly out." He grimaced as he saw my expression. "Yeah, I know that you can't fly properly, so was thinking more along the lines of you getting there as fast as you can after me and holding them off."

"You're going to be by yourself if you fly there," I warned with a shake of my head. "It isn't wise. You're not the only one who can move that fast. Ella and Sophia could. Scythe too at a push."

He shrugged his shoulders. "Got to risk big to win big."

"It's not a good plan!"

He snorted. "And your plan is?"

I stumbled, searching for an idea. "I, well-"

"Exactly. Besides," he pointed into the valley at the plume of blue smoke that was spiralling into the air, "time to go."

"Wait, Rikol, wait!"

"Sorry Cal, see you soon." With that Rikol lifted from the floor and carved across the sky like a lightning bolt, heading straight for the flag.

"Damn it!" I snarled before turning and pushing as much seraph into my legs as possible, running a few steps and then flinging myself into the air, feeling the wind rush past as my body and will did their utmost to defy gravity. It wasn't flying. Not really. But that didn't stop me from being able to jump pretty damn far. In fact, it was a pretty great skill – except that the quality of the landings depended entirely on the terrain.

"Fucking trees!" I roared as I crashed down through the canopy, tearing through a row of branches, hitting the trunk of another and tucking into a roll to tumble across the floor. Thanks to my shield I was undamaged, but it didn't do anything good for my sense of direction. Looking up at the canopy, I couldn't see the blue smoke and growled, frustration causing it to come out more animalistic than I had intended. Resigning myself to partially destroying this forest, I jumped up, smashing through the branches directly above to rise above the forest. Swivelling, I spotted the blue smoke and the speck that was Rikol descending to the objective – just in time to see a bolt of crackling energy send him tumbling out of the sky.

"Damnit Rikol!" I cursed, falling back through the canopy and then flinging myself towards the objective again, hearing the cracking of broken and mistreated trees in my wake. It wasn't far. Not really anyway. Probably half a mile, but still a couple of jumps or – in this ankle-breaking terrain - a few minutes of sprinting. In a game between seraph-enhanced individuals a few minutes would be an eternity. I had to get into the thick of it, and fast.

An explosion tore the centre apart with a clap of thunder, covering the objective with a billowing cloud of black smoke for a hundred metres in every direction. I managed my landing better this time, using slight nudges of seraph to guide my plummet through the trees. *Only hit one,* I thought with a strange sense of pride. Granted, that 'one' had a hole through its trunk where I had carved my way through it, but still, progress!

A third jump. The black smoke was close now. It didn't drift like normal smoke would but instead stayed in the area.

Seraph-smoke then.

It would doubtless be thick, cloying and, knowing my dorm, probably smell really bad. They knew my skills just as much as I knew theirs. If it was a simple smoke screen, my nose wouldn't easily lead me astray.

My fourth jump got me inside the cloud of black and my vision instantly reduced to a few feet. A cloying scent of spice pervaded everything, rendering – as expected – my nose useless. I guess I could just be thankful that they hadn't seen to make it something a little more unpleasant for me. Thoughts of Rya's chilli bombs came to mind and I shrugged them away, casting about for a method to locate the flag. A figure flashed in the mist and I flung myself forwards, sending a kick lancing out to where I had seen the movement, only to hit nothing. Another flicker to my left and I spun, spinning low and sweeping, only to send rocks tumbling.

Seraph-shadows? I allowed myself a moment of grudging admiration before throwing myself up and out of the cloud. Light, sound and scent instantly flooded my senses and I spun, looking for anything out of the ordinary.

It wasn't hard to find, to be honest.

What none of us had known was that the flag was not an ordinary flag. As Rikol had eluded, the Imperators running this game didn't want us just pick up the flag and run. No, they wanted it to be a fight every single step of the way. And so, it appeared that once the flag had been picked up it emitted a bright blue beam of light that pierced the sky. Whoever had cast the seraph-cloud had likely wanted to do things quick and easy, just like Rikol, but now they were left with half a mile of terrain to cover and a flag that would draw everyone who could see it like bees to nectar.

I smiled, my lips pulling back to reveal my canines. *Game on.*

CHAPTER 6
Not So Playful Games

The flag-carrier was Scythe. It made sense. Who better to carry the flag then someone who specialised in seraph enhancements? His muscles glowing a deep red he moved like greased lightning, as sure-footed as a mountain goat over the tricky terrain.

Blasts of seraph erupted around him as someone let loose their frustration. Whether through luck or skill he deftly wove his way through the attacks, continuing his headlong sprint towards his base with barely a stumble.

Thankfully, though he was fast he wasn't quite as quick as me, plummeting towards him at terminal velocity in what I considered a superbly aimed jump. The wind howling around me, I altered my trajectory ever so slightly and tensed my limbs. I had half a second to hope that Scythe had a shield running, otherwise I was about to make a gory mess of my friend, and then the impact hit.

I careened through tree after tree, smashing through limb and bough in a splintering cacophony, before finally coming to rest in a daze with just enough wits remaining to witness Scythe's continued progress, utterly oblivious to how close he had come to being flattened.

Coughing, I struggled to my feet, using the tree for support and trying to get my head to stop spinning. *Who the hell did that?!*

It had to be Ella. She was running interference for her teammate and was bloody good at it. I had no idea where she was or what she had even hit me with.

A shout of dismay reached my ears and I looked up in time to see Scythe lifted into the air, limbs scrabbling to move but to no avail. With a strangled yelp, he was yanked back towards the centre of the valley. No, not the centre of the valley. Towards my base.

Rikol wasn't finished yet, it appeared.

Recovered enough from the impact, I began a stumbling run after Scythe, only to pause to watch open-mouthed as he froze in mid-air, jerking from side to side. *Will combat*, I realised, *has to be. Someone is contesting Rikol's seraph.* After a moment of struggle, slowly, inexorably, Scythe resumed his motion towards my base.

Rikol's will was iron.

After a moment the struggle ceased and Scythe continued his journey, only for the flag to snap out of his hand like it had been yanked. *Clever. They knew that they couldn't match Rikol's will, so lured him into thinking it was about Scythe. Once he concentrated on getting Scythe back to the base, the flag was an easy steal.* This was getting interesting indeed, and by the roar of frustration I heard from Rikol's direction, he wasn't too happy with the interference.

"Calidan!" he screamed at the top of his lungs. "Get moving!"

I don't know if he knew where I was, but realising that I had been standing motionless and watching the action instead of partaking in it, I followed the beam of blue light and burst into motion.

The flag dropped out of view. A moment later the light it emitted began to move as someone began carrying it. Closing the distance with my Seya-enhanced physique, I willed several flash-bombs into being, sending them hurtling towards the target and detonating them simultaneously in a wall of percussive sound and dazzling light. The flag wavered and then I was there, finding Cassius holding his eyes. Grabbing the wooden pole I twisted it whilst pulling away, wrenching it out of his grip. Continuing the spin, I swung the pole low to the ground, catching his legs and sending him crashing to the floor.

"Sorry buddy!" I shouted with a grin before sprinting off back towards Rikol. Wary of further attack I reinforced my shield, tinting the outside and dulling the sound slightly so that the same flash-bomb tactic couldn't work on me. I made it all of a hundred metres before the ground rippled beneath me and I sank into thigh-deep mud. Vines or roots lashed out from the ground and wrapped around me, slowing my movements even further and threatening to drag me deeper into the mire.

"Rikol, catch!" I shouted, using my will to fling the flag towards the base. Instead of rocketing off as it had been supposed to, however, it arced gently and landed in Sophia's outstretched hand. My face must have been hilarious because she cackled a laugh and blew me a kiss before sprinting off into the trees, only to cry out in rage as the flag was torn from her grip with seraph, arcing towards an approaching Ella.

And on it went.

The Imperators had planned this one well. What began as a friendly contest became a gruelling marathon as the flag was passed back and forth. Laughter died down and frustration became more and more evident in everyone's motions. Attacks began to hit harder, aiming to keep people on the ground for longer. Traps became more vindictive. Instead of just slowing opponents down they aimed to immobilise; dropping victims under the ground or sending them hurtling into the sky. With each moment of back-and-forth the stakes got higher and higher as the frustration and anger grew, the chances of an attack turning lethal inching ever upwards.

Just as intended.

It took three hours for the game to end. By the time it did, all of us were more than ready for it to be over and never wanted to see any of the others again.

It was a close-run thing. I had grabbed the flag and Rikol had opened a portal directly above the flag stone, expending practically all of his remaining seraph for this move. Plunging the flag into the stone I had raised my hands in victory, hearing Rikol's accompanying howl of triumph, before a black light shone into the sky.

"Winners," a low voice reverberated around the valley, "Cassius and Sophia."

It had taken a moment for that to sink in. By the time it had, I could hear the cheers and jubilation of the pair. "But how?" I managed to ask as Cassius strode into view, his shit-eating grin the most frustrating thing in the world to me right then.

"Wasn't me," he said with a wink. "All her idea." With a flourish he indicated Sophia who dropped down from a nearby tree.

Rikol landed like a thunderbolt, sending plumes of dust and foliage up but not caring as he strode up to them both, eyes filled with rage. "How?!" he demanded.

"Easy Rikol," Scythe said, emerging from the trees in time to receive a withering glare from the mage.

"Shut it, Scythe," Rikol hissed. "I want to hear from *them*."

"It was simple, in the end," Sophia simpered, her voice melodic but her eyes hard. "As soon as I saw you open a portal, I figured what the end point was going to be, so made one of my own. Directly under yours."

"So, so-"

"*So*, the stone that Calidan placed the flag into was, in fact, ours."

There was a long moment of silence and then Rikol let out a scream of pure, unadulterated rage. Furious eyes glared at everyone before he turned away and stomped back towards the compound, completely ignoring the approaching Imperators.

"I'm not sure what I expected, but that wasn't it," Cassius muttered, just loud enough for everyone to hear.

I was too tired and drained to care anymore. "Shut it Cassius," I intoned with a groan, slumping down against a tree. "He just really wanted to win."

"Hey now, we all did-" he began but Scythe cut him off.

"We all did, but you managed it. Please stop talking, everything sounds like gloating."

"Well, he has every reason to gloat," Sophia replied acerbically. "That was a tough fight. Hard fought. Do we not get to celebrate?"

"Celebrate, sure. Just go and celebrate yourselves elsewhere."

"Oh, that's *real* nice. Why don't you just go off and sulk somewhere else instead?!"

"Sod off!"

"Prick!"

"Ahem."

The sound was muted yet carried through the rising cacophony with ease. Heads swivelled to the source and everyone tensed as three Imperators stood with wide smiles.

Or, in the case of tall, grumpy, throw-me-in-a-cell Imperator, as close to a smile as his stupid face would allow.

"I see that we have a winning team," simpered the middle Imperator – the arsehole of a torturer who had me thrown in the cell in the first place. "Congratulations."

Sophia and Cassius beamed while the rest of us continued sulking in silence.

"Your prize will be provided to you later today. A small token for each of you that gives you a – shall we say – 'out' if things were to go wrong in the future. Whilst you have this token, for one time and for one time only, you need not fear failure. Guard it jealously however," his eyes glimmered, "others who have been failing have been known in the past to attempt retrieval of these tokens."

"Then why not just write our names on them?" Cassius asked brightly.

The Imperator scrutinised him for a second and then gave him a sickly grin. "Because that would make things too boring, wouldn't it?"

Cassius frowned in response and I struggled to suppress a smile at the look on his face. Despite the frustration I felt at the outcome of the game, it was good to know that Cassius hadn't changed. How, despite the pressure that he might be under - and I had to remember that unlike my unattached-self, Cassius also had Ella talking into his ear about his actions - in some ways he had to be under more pressure than I was to pick up that blade in the Imperator's 'lesson' and use it. And yet here he was, looking annoyingly relaxed with everything that was going on.

How was he doing it? He must have some kind of plan. Some idea of how to get past this block in the road without getting thrown in the same hole as I was. What that plan was though, I had no idea. Ignoring what the Imperator was saying, I stood up and started moving to Cassius's side, eager to talk with him and discuss. His eyes met mine and a welcoming smile formed on his face, one that stuttered as a meaty hand landed on my shoulder, forcing me to a halt. Turning my head, I saw the two Imperators, the smaller woman gifting me a neutral smile that didn't reach her eyes.

"Not you."

"What?"

She cocked her head. "Mission is done. Your time is up. Come with us quietly."

I didn't miss the unspoken message, *or be taken by force.* Nodding, I glanced at the others. "Can't I have just a minute?" I asked, desperation tingeing my voice.

"No. Get moving. And remember, this is your choice."

"Calidan?" It was Cassius, face darkening as he saw me being escorted away.

"Talk to Rikol," I shouted back. *If you can get him to calm down.* Walking past the primary examiner, I noted the small smile on his face. So smug.

"Remember Calidan, this is on you," he declared as I was marched by. "You could stop this any time that you wished."

Taking a deep breath, I pulled to a halt in front of him. "Tell me, why is it so important that Imperators need to know the skills that you're forcing on us?"

His eyes expressed his confusion. "You know why. Sometimes the ends justify the means."

Taking a deep breath, I locked eyes with him. "If I apologise, will you let me back into the dorm?"

"Can't hurt your chances."

Another deep breath. Focused on forcing the words past gritted teeth. "I'm sorry."

"Excellent." He gave me a broad smile. "That wasn't too bad, was it?" His eyes flickered to the guards. "Take him away."

"But you-"

"I said that it couldn't hurt your chances, Calidan. But no, I think not. At least, not just yet. But, if you keep behaving, maybe I'll let you start retaking the class."

I marched away, barely seeing the scenery as my thoughts whirled.

Gods damn it.

PRESENT DAY 2

The lock clicked with a reassuring solidarity as the Head Financier smoothly ushered me into the thoroughly soundproofed room and shut the door.

"Mr Wintersteel, a pleasure to make your acquaintance."

I inclined my head a few degrees. "And you are?"

"Jackart, my esteemed sir, Elias Jackart."

"Well, Mr Jackart, it appears that you are aware of my orders."

The man paled, nodding whilst trying to hide the sweat beading around his neck. "We received your letter of instruction several days ago but I was not aware that you would be attending quite so soon which might be why the return letter did not reach you in time before you undertook this journey. Sir...despite what you may have heard there is nothing beyond the fourth level of the vault."

Raising my eyebrow, I regarded him with the eye of a man completely in disdain of his present company. "You are *aware*," I began slowly, thoroughly enunciating every syllable, "that the Wintersteel family has long been known for the quality and rarity of its goods. In fact, your house itself has sold Wintersteel pieces over the years...and profited immensely."

"Quite so, quite-"

"Now," I continued, trampling over his wheedling, "I am in possession of something that, frankly, is the pinnacle of our achievements. Small but perfectly formed, your appraisers would likely be blinded by the sheer potential of its worth. Unfortunately, this means that it needs to be secure."

"Nothing is more secure than the fourth layer; a layer in the vault that the Wintersteel family have utilised many times I might add."

"You might and it is noted," I replied drily and he began to smile before I raised a hand. "But things change. We know that this is not the most secure location and the item I possess demands nothing but the best."

"But it is the-"

"It is NOT THE BEST!" I roared, slamming a hand onto the table in a sudden fit of faux-rage and sending the man quivering back. "Do you think my family to be fools?! We are the Wintersteels you arrogant twit. We *demand* excellence."

"Sir-I-"

"Afterall, it would be such a *shame* if we had to take our business elsewhere..." For a second I thought I might have killed the poor man. His eyes bulged and whatever blood he had left in his face vanished.

He coughed and cleared his throat. "Ah. Please let's not be too hasty. I am certain that we can come to some sort of...arrangement."

"If it doesn't involve this fabled fifth floor then I am not interested."

An eye twitched – the closest that such an individual might come to doing what he currently wanted; namely stabbing me in the eye for being an arrogant sod. "Please understand, sir, that if there is a fifth floor, I myself am not aware of it. Considering that I have been employed by the GTG for over two decades, the last dozen in this very branch, I do not consider such a thing to be possible."

"Hmm."

"Let me assure you that the level of the vault that your family currently uses is where we place our most *precious* of treasures. The security is unbreachable. Nothing has ever been stolen from the vault and all who have tried are no longer with us."

I eyeballed him for a minute longer, rolling a coin between my fingers. When I judged the moment right, I slammed it down onto the table. "Fine." Standing up, I extended a hand. Looking shaken at the abrupt turn of events he reached out and shook it, his palm slick with sweat. "If the vault is as good as you say I will deposit my family's treasure today. However..." I leaned in close and whispered, "if I do find out that there is a fifth level and you've been holding out on me, you will forever be known as the person who lost GTG the Wintersteels. Am I understood?"

"Of-of course sir!"

"Good." Stepping aside I swept my arm to the door. "Lead on!"

"N-now?! Don't you need to collect your item? I assumed you would be coming with a host of bodyguards and an armoured container for something of the value you described."

"The bodyguards are there, but the item is small. It is safer for it to be on my person at all times. And besides," I fed him a predatory smile, "attacking a Wintersteel is no easy feat at the best of times."

"I-indeed. Your reputation proceeds you."

I smiled inwardly. The Wintersteels were artisans of the highest calibre, primarily known for forging their unique arms with metal-smithing techniques unknown anywhere else in the world. What came a close second, however, was how the family – more a sect now than a blood-related family – maintained a martial discipline that was said to have been passed down through the generations. A discipline that utilised their famed armour and weapons with clean, efficient movements. At times the Wintersteels had been hired for their killing prowess over their weapon-smithing and few could stand in their way.

With another nod at me, the thoroughly frazzled Mr Jackart led me out of the room and towards a gilded metal contraption guarded by two enormous figures in plate armour. Sliding the door open, he gestured at me to enter and we both moved to the rear of the metal platform as the giants smoothly spun around and stepped inside before turning and sliding the door shut behind us.

"Ashari," Jackart explained with a smile, seeing me eyeballing the guards, "on permanent loan from the Sethani empire."

"Impressive."

"I'll say. They're the Skyfather's elite, never provided for hire except for this one instance. And believe me, even though we are great friends with the Skyfather, they did not come cheap."

Oh, I believe it. Ashari were revered across the world as the pinnacle of warriors. Trained from birth and – if the stories were true – taken only from a specific tribe within the Sethani empire that focused purely on combat, they knew only battle. They wielded hand-and-a-half curved greatswords with such skill that it had been known for battle-hardened veterans to flee the field at a glimpse of their battalions.

The Emperor had long boasted of his Black Dragon Knights – the elite of the Andurran military who subtly enhanced themselves with seraph in order to wear thick plate armour and wield heavy weaponry – but even he had openly wondered who would emerge victorious from an encounter between the two forces.

Chances were, both sides lost.

One of the guards said something in a deep, guttural tongue and Jackart replied. With a nod, the intricately armoured and imposing figure pulled a handle and the platform began to descend into the floor.

"Apologies, the Ashari don't tend to understand anything besides their own language," Jackart explained, mopping at his neck with a handkerchief. "Which, I have to say, isn't the easiest dialect to master."

"You're a man of many talents," I remarked wryly.

"I try."

The platform continued to descend until a flicker of light danced across my toes and slowly the next floor was revealed. Two more Ashari stood at attention facing the door of the lift and it was then I realised that there was another cage surrounding the lift, the exit locked with a massive steel bolt.

"The first vault," said Jackart, leaning over to me. "Where we keep the more mundane stock. Ah, excuse me one moment." Clearing his throat, he croaked a word and the two guards on the outside turned to the Ashari within the lift who growled something similar. Nodding, they pulled aside the bolt before swinging the cage open.

"What did you say?" I asked, intrigued.

"That I am not under duress," he replied. "The guards with us both confirmed that they aren't either. It's just one security measure that we have here. Simple, but effective. If we had said that we were, the guards are under orders not to let anyone out, even if lives are at stake. Being Ashari, they would not baulk at the prospect of blood being spilled."

Nodding, I stepped out of the gilded cage and followed the eager Jackart down the hall as he explained what lay behind the various doors that stemmed off from this central location, the four guards keeping in perfect step around us.

Reaching an iron door, Jackart stepped forward and knocked. A question rose from within and Jackart responded before one by one the four Ashari spoke. A moment's pause and then the small slit at the top of the door opened and suspicious eyes looked out, scrutinising each and every person. Without a sound the viewport slid shut followed by a *clunk* of a key in the lock. On well-oiled hinges the door swung inward and Jackart moved forwards, leading us down the spiral stairs within whilst the four guards who had taken us this far adopted new positions at the top of the stairs.

"You might be wondering why not take the platform all the way to the bottom?" he said as we walked down the echoing stairwell with our sole new Ashari guard.

"The thought had crossed my mind."

"Whilst the four floors of the vault are beneath each other, it was decided that having such a direct means of access – whilst useful – was too much of a risk. In this manner, any would-be thieves have to make their way along each and every floor, each one deadlier than the last."

"Clever. Must have been expensive to plan out and create?"

"Extremely, but we spared no expense. It is for good reason that this vault is known throughout the land. But look, we have arrived onto the second floor."

As he spoke he gestured towards another locked door and the Ashari delivered a rhythmic series of knocks, pausing at irregular intervals in what was obviously some kind of coded message. A second later, the sound of a bolt shifting in a latch reached my ears and the door swung open, revealing yet another Ashari. The mountainous man nodded and gestured for us to enter and Jackart stepped aside to judge my reaction.

I let out a low whistle. "Not bad."

"I thought you would appreciate it. Each level of the vault is in keeping with the, ahem, *quality* of the individuals utilising it. As the second floor is for more discerning customers than the first, greater care had to be taken for the façade."

He wasn't wrong. Low slung lamps cast soft light over the richly inlaid wood panelling and the floor was no longer stone but a plush carpet. Doors ran along both sides of the hall, each housing a keyhole that must have needed something impressively grand to fit.

If I didn't know this was a vault, I would have thought myself in some noble's home.

"Looks like some of our guest houses," I remarked, reminding him that I was not some mere noble. "I am eager to see the rest."

"Of course, of course. This way." Barking an order at the guard, Jackart sped along the hall, booted feet squishing into the deep carpet. Before long we came to the end of the corridor; a wooden wall blocking our way. Jackart reached out and pressed in four different locations and with a soft *click* the wall slid inwards, revealing another stairwell.

"Ah good," he said with a small sigh of relief. "Always a little nervy when I do that."

"Why?"

"If the sequence is incorrect, gas traps are designed to go off and incapacitate anyone in the area."

Looking at the woodwork with new-found respect, I grinned. "I would like to meet the mind that thought of this."

"Dead, I'm afraid. But a one-of-a-kind architect. Some say a little…odd. Eccentric in her mannerisms, but brilliant."

"Tsk. A pity." Shaking my head, I gestured. "Lead on."

The third floor was divided into three areas, each one barred and locked, guarded by Ashari who watched with suspicious eyes as Jackart guided us through. The vault itself was coated in marble with a fountain in the centre of the hallway. Marble casts of famous GTG figures lined stone plinths on either side in an ostentatious display of wealth and the doors to each individual vault chamber had the appearance, at least, of solid stone.

"The third floor is known as the Hall of Memories," Jackart explained as we passed through. "Items deposited here are usually those of deep personal value to our clients and tend to stay a long time. With that in mind the architect fashioned something similar to showcase the GTG lineage."

"She outdid herself."

"That she did," Jackart agreed, his smile widening, "and not just because of the art. What you don't see is that each stone plinth is cunningly wrought to deliver…unpleasantness should the guards choose."

The levers in each door, I realised. I hadn't thought much of it at the time as we passed through, but if each lever corresponded to the various plinths, the third level was impressively defended, especially considering that you were forced to stop twice at the gated sections to be allowed through. Any hostile force was going to be taking a hammering with whatever came out of those stone pillars.

Whistling with just the right level of amazement for Jackart to glow with delight, I reached out to the others.

Update?

Target secured. Nice and quiet.

Good. Location found?

Not yet. Sophia is being thorough. Will update when we have it.

Understood.

"And here we are," Jackart said, gesturing towards another gilded cage. "This will take us to the fourth floor."

"Good."

There was a moment's silence and then he leaned towards me. "Sir, we need your key to open the gate."

"Ah, of course." Reaching into my suit, I pulled out the small, intricately carved key – or more accurately, the seraph copy of the small, intricately carved key briefly 'borrowed' from the Wintersteels – and slotted it into the lock. Holding my breath, I twisted the key and silently rejoiced as the door swung open. Retrieving the tiny key, I stepped onto the platform, followed by the two Ashari and Jackart and a moment later we started to descend.

If the second floor had been opulence, the third floor decadence, then the fourth was, quite simply, astounding.

It wasn't a case of mountains of gold and jewels, nor statues or other displays of exorbitant wealth. Instead, it was something completely priceless. The sheer audacity of the architect who had constructed it was breathtaking.

And yet it worked.

For the fourth floor was no mere mortal design.

"Pre-Cataclysm..." I whispered, stunned.

Jackart looked just as lost in the view as I was, drinking it in hungrily. "You have a good eye," he said softly, almost reverently. "Everything here is pre-Cataclysm technology. The GTG spent vast sums locating areas with intact technology and even more trying to make sense of it." He chuckled. "If it wasn't for the Skyfather I doubt we would have made any headway but he provided just enough training to be able to put bits and pieces together, as well as selling us a power core." He pointed at the walls that were pulsing with a soft light. "See that? It's not flame in there but a form of technology that is practically magic. And before you ask, no, I don't have any better understanding of it than that."

"This is...insane."

"That was the architect for you. Brilliance and insanity is a fine line."

"How did this not bankrupt you?" I whispered in disbelief. "One piece of pre-Cataclysm technology is a fortune. Transplanting an entire facility? Madness!"

"It helps when you buy the land the facility is on without anyone being the wiser," Jackart said, tapping his nose knowingly. "And it comes with lots of benefits. Believe me when I say, no-one is getting in any of these doors without proper authorisation. I'm not sure what material they are made from but GTG technicians haven't been able to so much as make a scratch."

"Fascinating..." I breathed, lost in the splendour of it all.

"It is truly something. Coming down here is rare enough that it has never once lost its splendour, each time is like the first," Jackart agreed before shaking himself. "But come, I will show you to your room."

Walking down the corridor was like walking through a dream. I had been in enough pre-Cataclysm facilities over the years to consider myself experienced with the various technologies and strange occurrences that inevitably happened, but this was perhaps the first time I had been inside a functioning facility where no-one was trying to kill me.

And that, believe me, is something special.

Scanning the doors absentmindedly as we walked slowly down the corridor, it took me a moment to recognise the problem but when I did the bottom of my gut dropped away.

Oh shit.

Immediately I reached out to the others. *Might be trouble soon. Got anything?*

Not. Yet. Sophia's voice was strained. Tense. *Hold on.*

Fuck.

Feigning nonchalance, I made a show of looking at a nearby door. "No keyholes. How do you get in?"

"Oh, did your father not tell you?" Jackart sounded a little surprised before relaxing with a knowing smile. "I imagine that he didn't want to ruin the surprise. No, these doors are coded to your blood. Well, your family's blood."

And there goes the easy part. Seraph could do a lot of things, but I did not know Cael Wintersteel well enough to replicate his blood, tissue or whatever it was that this device was going to want to check.

Balls.

A casual glance behind showed the two Ashari paying no attention to the wonders they walked amongst, their eyes continuously checking for threats.

Just me, a financier and two of the world's deadliest swordsmen.

I gave them a smile and then cut off the bloodflow in their necks with a burst of will. Jackart turned at the sound of plate armour hitting the ground and then he followed suit, eyes rolling into the back of his head.

I might not be the most powerful of seraph users, but I had got quite good at learning how to achieve a lot with a little.

The real difficulty was making sure that they got enough oxygen still circulating to keep them alive and not brain dead. I wasn't trying to kill anyone here if I could help it.

Gone hot. Where is the entrance?!

It doesn't make sense, Sophia blurted.

What doesn't?

The images I'm seeing. She has never seen the fifth floor, but remembers Asol coming into the building. Remembers seeing a platform lift with no-one on it.

Instantly I turned back towards the gilded cage. The levers to move it were on the inside, where I didn't want to be, but a burst of will sent the platform moving slowly back up. As it ascended, a black void was revealed, one lit by a single seraph glyph.

Swallowing hard, I focused my will.

And stepped off the edge.

CHAPTER 7
Blood on the Walls

"Back are you, boy?"

I snorted. "How did you know?"

"Gone for a long while. I wanted some conversation and you didn't reply. Figured you were either dead or had been taken away."

"Taken," I replied softly.

"Interesting. I didn't hear the guards come in."

There was a question in there. *Who are you and what's going on?* Resting my head against the cell door I breathed out slowly. "Do you really want to know?"

Silence met my words. Even Clythe was quiet. All of them doubtless straining to hear my every word.

"Fine. You were right Jarv. You're in the hands of the Imperators." Exclamations met my words and Clythe immediately started cackling in his raspy way. "I don't know what they do with you, but you're definitely in an Imperator-held prison."

"You keep saying 'you', not 'we'," Jarv commented after the din had settled down. His voice had gone lower, as though he was afraid of what was coming.

"That's...that's because I'm an Imp – an Imperator-in-training."

This time Jarv joined Clythe in his laughter, his throaty rumble echoing off the walls. "And they what? Put you in here to spy on us?!" Incredulity warred with betrayal in his voice.

"Not spying, no. I'm being punished. I was told not to reveal any of this to you." I let out a long sigh. "But fuck it."

Long minutes passed. Minutes filled with jeers, expletives and manic laughter. The news that they were in an Imperator prison seemed to have broken what spirit they had left. The Academy had sure concocted a fearsome reputation for its graduates. Considering what I was being asked to do, it seemed like an understandable response.

Imperators were a scary, unknown element. They were the ones who made people disappear. My fellow prisoners knew now that they must be royally up shit-creek if the prison they were in was manned by some of the most frightening people they could envisage. Hells, I was scared enough myself and I knew what this place was.

Or at least, knew enough about it.

"You said you're being punished," Jarv finally said. "What for?"

"Refusing to follow instructions."

"And that gets you put in here? Harsh."

I snorted. You forget that being an Imperator means you're in a special branch of the military. Disobeying rules isn't exactly something that the military encourages."

"Still...sounds pretty shitty."

"...I suppose it is. Thanks."

"For what?"

I shrugged, not that he would have been able to see it. "For, you know, not hating me for what I am."

"Fuck you, Imperator bitch!" Glenco howled, the man's voice rasping from the chain of expletives that he had laced together over the past few minutes.

Jarv let the echo of the sentence die away and for a long while I thought he was going to leave it at that. Finally I heard him clear his throat and murmur, "Hating someone for what they are is pointless. Hating someone for what they *do*. That is what's important. Have you done something to make me hate you, boy?"

I thought for a minute. *Probably many things.* "I don't think so."

"Then I shall reserve my hate for someone who deserves it."

※

The grate on the door slid open and a plate of food slid through, a small note sitting on top.

Reward for effort made. Enjoy.

I had almost forgotten the pact I had made with the Imperator. Stomach growling with the delicious aromas I removed the silver lid and saw the stew sitting within. Thick, brown stew with hulking bits of slow-cooked beef and slabs of still-warm bread.

Divine.

Setting too with a will, I devoured the food in what felt like moments, finally sitting back contentedly, belly full for the first time in what felt like ages.

Ahh, that's the stuff.

I blinked. Was the room darker? Rubbing my eyes, I yawned. *Sleepy.*

A wall glowed. Bars twisted. Bed-springs spoke. I watched it all and took nothing in. Figures danced in my vision, forgotten things from fever dreams. In the same eternal moment I felt like I understood the universe, whilst being dumber than a rock. The same rock then enlightened me with conversation in Meredothian.

Strange language for a rock.

I slumped sideways.

When I woke, it was to a dark room. A man was in front of me, tied to a chair. Cassius was there, screaming at me to concentrate, rage and panic warring on his face.

"Calidan!"

"I'm..." I shook my head, the fuzziness wearing off. "I'm here. What's going on?"

"What's going on?!" he yelled in disbelief. "They have her! They're killing her!"

Instantly my mind sharpened. "Who do they have?"

"Ella! She's being hurt. We need to get to her. Please Cal." His words were desperate, the voice of a man near breaking point.

I stood up and found a knife in my hand. "Where is she?"

"Th-this bastard won't tell me!" Cassius whirled on the man and struck him across the face, spittle landing on his face as he screamed, "Talk! Talk or die!"

The man in the chair started laughing. "Do what you want. You're not going to get to her in time. Not before he's finished anyway."

Cassius struck him again but the man just continued to laugh.

"Cassius," I said calmly, hating seeing my friend so broken. He didn't respond.

"Cassius!" I said more firmly, moving in beside him. "Let me."

The man looked at me without fear. That needed to change.

Reaching out with the knife, I plunged it deep into his knee. His scream was a piercing balm to my soul. If they had Ella, then there was nothing I wouldn't do. I twisted the knife, causing another agonised wail.

"Where is she?" I growled.

"I-I won't t-tell!"

"Where!?"

"F-fuck you!"

I slowly pulled the knife out, leaving a small fountain of blood erupting from the mess I had made of his knee. I placed it over the other one, making sure he watched as I did so. Holding it there, I met his gaze. "Last chance."

His voice caught. "I won't- ARGH!"

"Where." Scream. "Is." Howl. "She?" Wail.

"N-not far!" he finally gasped. "B-basement!"

"Good." Dropping the knife. I made to walk towards the door but Cassius picked the blade up and buried it in the man's chest, face contorted in a silent snarl. After a moment he looked at me, as though daring me to say something, but I merely nodded towards the door. "Let's go get her."

It didn't take long to reach the basement. In fact, I barely remembered how I got there at all. A blur of movement along dark and vague corridors until we reached a room. Two guards lay dead outside it. When were they killed? Had we done that? I shook my head in confusion.

Cassius grabbed my shoulder as a high-pitched scream sundered the air. "Let's go!" he mouthed.

Nodding, I picked up a fallen guard's blade and plunged through the door. Instantly the scent of fresh blood and fear struck my nose. Ella was bound to a chair, bleeding from multiple wounds. Her captor stood in front of her, vicious knife in hand. Cassius howled, the man spun, my blade sang.

"Interesting."

The room went dark.

"They have her! They're killing her!" Scythe yelled.

"Who do they have?"

"Sophia! She's being hurt! We need to get to her. Please Cal."

Something felt familiar about this, but there was no time to dwell on it. I stood and found a knife in my hand. *Let's get this done.*

"Very interesting."

"We need to get to him. Please Cal." Ella, voice hoarse with desperation.

"His friends are the trigger."

"Please Cal." Sophia.

"Look at the way he tears into them when their lives are on the line."

"Please Cal." Rikol.

"Seems like our friend here is a bit of a hypocrite." My vision began to swim, blackness encroaching on the edges. The last thing I remembered was the voice. His voice, filled with such delight. *"You're a piece of work Calidan. A monster, through and through. I don't think I have much to teach you at all."*

My door clanged open, the metallic sound jolting me into an unwelcome wakefulness. "W-wha?" My tongue felt thick. Lips dry.

"Up."

I tried to stand. Failed.

A sigh. Footsteps and then meaty hands found me. Lifted me to my feet. My vision swam as I found myself dragged along the corridor, up the stairs and back into the higher levels of Wolf's Hollow. Without much ceremony I was taken to the hated office and dumped into the chair opposite the man I despised.

"Hello Calidan," he said cheerfully. "Did we wake you?"

"Obviously," I groaned, rubbing my temples. "What time is it?" It must have been early; my body felt wrung out.

"Late!" he declared with a far too loud clap of his hands. "We let you have a well-deserved rest. Seems like you needed it."

Late? What was going on? Gods I felt awful.

The Imperator must have noted my confusion because his shit-eating grin broadened. "Feeling a little out of place, are we?"

How did he know? Shaking my head and completely failing to remove the fuzziness that tinged everything, I grunted in the affirmative.

"That's because there was a little something that we wanted to learn from you."

"Wh-" I broke off, tongue feeling like an alien trapped in my mouth, "What did you do?"

"Oh, nothing really, just did a little exploration. Put you in some situations, so to speak. To check your responses, you see."

I didn't see.

Noting my confusion, he continued. "You've been a thorn in my side, Calidan. You and Cassius both, actually. Surprisingly high morals for Imps this far along the Academy process. Well. That's not entirely true. Cassius, in my opinion, has a strong moral code. I think you, on the other hand, are a stubborn idiot who doesn't want to dirty his hands because he is afraid of what he will become." His eyes glinted. "Sound about right?"

I looked at him in shock and he smiled. "Looks like I'm on the money. Good." Noting my stare, he scowled and waved a hand. "I know more about you than you might believe. Indeed, after last night, I know you probably better than you know yourself."

I repeated my earlier question, heart sinking. "What did you do?"

"Nothing really. Or at least, nothing that hasn't been done to you before."

A spark of realisation. "You played with my mind."

"In a manner of speaking." He leant forwards and pursed his fingers together. "Do you remember the fourth-year exam?"

How could I forget? "Of course."

"Good. What about the beginning?"

Swaying bodies. Cutting of knives. Screams. I shut my eyes and tried to force the nightmares back down, nodding in the affirmative.

"Well, you know that it was all a seraph-illusion. Very convincing stuff, especially when you are under the influence of certain drugs."

"Drugs? I wasn't on any drugs..." I drifted off, noting the grin on his face. "The food."

"The food," he confirmed. "The mushroom within put you in a suggestible state of mind. It was easy from that point on to build certain scenarios and to see how you reacted. And boy, did you react."

I remembered it now. Flashes at least. Me with a knife in my hand. Blood everywhere. Desperate for information. "You complete and utter bastard."

He waved a hand airily. "Yes, yes. Let it out. I'm a terrible person, blah blah blah." His eyes hardened. "Grow up. This isn't the first time that your mind has been played with, and I know that it is traumatic, but you left me little choice. You were being a pig-headed little shit that refused to play ball. So holier-than-thou about torture, refusing to have anything to do with it. But it turns out that you just need the right encouragement and then you are a ferocious and vindictive little bugger. I mean, one mention of your friends and you leapt to it with a will. There was no discussion of alternatives, no efforts at talk, just you with a knife and blood on the wall."

"All manipulated by you!" I spat.

He shrugged. "Of course. We set you on a path, but, unfortunately, it isn't one that is uncommon to find yourself on. Imperators operate in pairs for a number of reasons. One of the lesser known ones is so that they can rescue each other when shit goes wrong and someone gets captured. This happens more than you know." His face darkened. "How do you think I managed to create the scenario so easily?"

I didn't know what to say to that.

He nodded. "What you saw is what happened. Unfortunately for my partner, I wasn't fast enough to get there in time to prevent the worst."

The way he said it. I almost felt sorry for him. Almost.

"So," I said finally, doing nothing to hide the loathing in my voice, "what now?"

"Now?" he shrugged. "I could be nice and let you pass the class. Afterall, I'm fairly positive that I know exactly how you will react under the right circumstances. But does that strike you as fair?"

I scowled. "Fair wouldn't be manipulating my mind!"

He ignored my outburst. "No, the others all obeyed the rules and completed the class. For you not to do the same...no. It just wouldn't do." He spread his arms wide. "How would they feel if you got to pass in such special circumstances? Angry? Betrayed?" A small grin touched his face. "No, we can't have that. You'll have to take the class and show your skills, just like the others. Well, except for Cassius."

The mention of Cassius drew me up short. "Cassius? Why, what's he done?"

The vile man's eyes twinkled. "What do you think? He had been refusing to complete this class, just like you. I was tempted to give him the same treatment, see how far he could be pushed until he did what was needed. I imagine it wouldn't have taken much, probably just having the threat of Ella under the knife, but no. He had been nice, unlike some. Civilised. There was no need for me to go to the same lengths as I had to with you.

Instead...well I offered him a choice. He could use his token now and pass the class, or he could keep it and risk some eager Imp stealing it."

"None of the others from the dorm would dare," I retorted. "We don't steal from each other."

"Who said anything about the dorm? I'm sure there are lots of forlorn Imps wandering these halls who would just jump at the chance to pass a class for free."

"But how would they..." I trailed off, noting the gleam in the man's eyes. "You told them."

"News travels fast in Wolf's Hollow."

"You complete and utter prick. You forced his hand!"

Another shrug. "I gave him a choice; he chose to pass the class. You should have heard him trying to barter for you to pass instead though. He's a loyal friend that one." He eyed me disdainfully. "Not sure why he bothers to be honest. Anyway, I dissuaded him of that notion and he quickly passed over the token. So he has passed. No torture lessons for Cassius. He seemed quite glad about that when he left." His lips drew back in an evil grin. "Pity though."

I couldn't help myself. "Pity how?"

"Oh Calidan, if you think that my class here is the worst of Wolf's Hollow then you are sadly mistaken. There's much worse ahead that dear, sweet Cassius could have saved himself from. Now, well, he will just have to pass everything the old-fashioned way. What a shame."

I saw how much sadistic delight he was taking in our pain and it sickened me to my core. "Words cannot describe how much I hate you. You're a petty, petty man who takes pleasure in other people's pain."

His smile disappeared. "What I am, Calidan, is *necessary*. You might not like it, but without me here then the next generation of Imperators would be *weak*. Unable to stomach the things that they need to do for the good of the empire. Without me, the Academy would become a laughing stock of ineptitude."

"Ahh, so you're the one sacrificing for the greater good of the Academy," I said in mock-awe. "You're a true hero. Stuck in your safe little position whilst the rest of the true Imperators are out there risking their lives on a daily basis. So brave."

His expression turned thunderous. "Get out."

"What, no kiss goodbye?"

"OUT!"

Familiar hands clamped down on my shoulders and hauled me out of the chair. "Tweedle-dee and Tweedle-dumb," I acknowledged, stressing the 'dumb' as I looked at the larger, meatier man, "so glad you're here to keep me in line. Why, it's almost like the mighty Imperator is afraid that he couldn't handle little old me." In the back of my mind I could hear a part of myself screaming to stop, to reign in the bitter antagonisms. Unfortunately, I was on a roll, and couldn't, *wouldn't* stop.

I was dragged out of the office, middle finger raised to the Imperator.

"I will see you tomorrow Calidan. And you will either pass this class or fail forever." The mocking words echoed in the hall as I was frog-marched away.

"That wasn't very smart," a nondescript voice mused. I looked to my left, finding the female Imperator by my side.

Letting out a long sigh, I nodded in agreement. "I know, he's just such a shit that he brings it out in me."

She pursed her lips as we entered the prison level, a tightening around her eyes the only suggestion that she was concentrating to put up a sound-barrier.

"I agree that Carmine is a tool. A sometimes useful one, but still a tool," she replied as my cell-door swung open. "But that wasn't what I was referring to."

Turning my head in query, a yank on my chains sent me stumbling into the cell. Staggering to gain my feet, I raised my head just in time for a meaty fist to catch me square in the jaw.

"Havan may be quiet, but he is anything but dumb," the woman said softly, hands on the door. "I would advise against insulting people you don't know in the future."

The door slammed shut.

I put my back against the wall and slid down into a heap. *Good advice for life that.*

CHAPTER 8

What I Might Become

"Back again, kid?"

"DEAD aaaaaand GOOOOOONE."

"Hey Jarv, Clythe," I replied tiredly, massaging my jaw. "How goes it?"

"DeeeeAAAAAAD."

"Shush Clythe, quiet down," Jarv said softly. His gentle tone seemed to do the trick, Clythe's warbling voice turning down a few octaves. Jarv spoke again, his voice directed at me. "Anything interesting happen?"

"Nope, still getting punished," I replied. "Though depending on the truth of his last statement that might change tomorrow. I either fail, or I suck it up and do what they want."

A momentary pause. A vast silence filled with unvoiced questions. *What is the Academy? What do you do there? Why are Imperators evil?*

"If I may ask, what do they want with you? You sound too young to have such burdens."

"Imperators start young," I answered after a minute. "You see a lot, get exposed to a lot, in a short space of time. Ages you prematurely."

"I can understand that," Jarv replied. "Hard lives tend to force you to grow up, fast."

"That they do." I sighed. "They want me to learn how to…hurt people. Not for prisons or anything like that," I hastened to add, "but in case a mission or your partner is in jeopardy and someone has the answers you need."

A long silence this time.

"I…see." Jarv heaved a sigh of his own. "And if you don't do this, you get thrown out of Imperator school?"

"There is no leaving the Academy," I said with a bitter laugh. "You either leave an Imperator or don't leave at all."

"Sounds like a shitty choice. Why join at all?"

"Why does anyone join the military? They might want structure to their lives, increase their strength, their abilities. Me?" I shook my head. "I just wanted revenge. The Emperor was the only one who could give me it."

"And this revenge you seek, have you achieved it?"

"Not yet."

"And it still drives you?"

I thought of the screams of my family, their faces barely visible in my mind's eye. How long was it since it had happened? *Too long.* Long enough for any normal person to have learnt to forget, if not forgive. For me the kernel of fury was still there, smouldering in the depths of my chest. It wouldn't go away until that red-eyed beast was put in the ground.

Maybe not even then.

"Yes." I replied hoarsely. "It still drives me."

"Then, if you are open to suggestions from an old man," Jarv said softly, "do what they want you to do. You've come too far to step back now. Hells, you've told me you can't. The only way to go is forward."

I looked at my hands. "And if I become a monster in doing so?"

"Hah!" his bark of laughter rang through the air. "Look at where you are. We're all monsters down here lad. Doesn't make you any less human."

"You're a wise man Jarv. I would love to meet you properly when we get out of here."

A low chuckle. "Don't think I've ever been called wise before. But me too, lad. Maybe Fate will allow that for us, eh?"

Ah sweet lady Fate. That fickle manipulator of hopes and dreams.

What a bitch.

The next morning I found myself outside the same office, my brain running amok. *Be a shit or swallow your pride? Stay human or become a monster?* Shaking my head, I nodded at my two guards and opened the door.

"Welcome Calidan." It wasn't the Imperator's voice. This was deeper, far too familiar. *Kane.* The big man swamped the small office, squeezed behind the Imperator's desk in a manner that would be funny if not for the serious look on his face.

"Kane?" I shook my head. "I mean, good to see you sir."

He inclined his head. "I wish I could say the same."

Heart sinking, I sat heavily in the chair in front of the desk. "So you know what's going on?"

A small inclination of his head. "I do. Imperator Carmine has filled me in. His words were...vividly descriptive."

"I'm sorry sir."

"For annoying Carmine or for actively choosing to fail the class?" His expression remained the same, but I could sense a small hint of joviality to his words. "One is much easier to forgive than the other."

"...Both?"

He heaved a sigh. "Let me speak simply. Carmine is a twat. He cares for no-one and nothing. He is, however, good at what he teaches. And there aren't many who want to teach what he offers."

"He called you here to talk to me, did he?"

"Actually no." A suppressed smile. "A certain cat managed to keep me awake at all hours of the night for the past two days. It was easy to figure that she wasn't happy with something that was going on, so I decided to come down and check things out for myself."

Seya. You beautiful queen. "And what have you discovered?"

"That one of my top students is about to throw away his career over a distaste for one class."

"One of your *top* students?" I raised an eyebrow. "High praise."

He grunted. "Don't let it go to your head." Leaning forwards, he pressed his fingers together and regarded me intently. "Tell me why."

It was a simple enough request but I found it strangely hard to begin. My feelings and fears choking my throat."

"I'm...scared."

"Scared?" Whatever Kane had thought I was going to say, that obviously wasn't it. "I've seen you kill, Calidan. Seen you fight things that still give *me* nightmares. I find it hard to believe that you're afraid of a class. An illusionary one at that."

I shook my head. "Not of the class. Of me. Of what I might become."

His eyes narrowed. "Explain."

"I-I find this all too easy. I always have. Cassius found it hard to kill, I never did. I'm good at it. I've even *enjoyed* it."

"Feeling joy in battle is not uncommon, Calidan," Kane said gently. "When you've trained that long and that hard, testing yourself against another in a life-or-death situation is almost cathartic in a way."

"I know. It's just...I'm afraid that if I pick up the knife and do it once, it will become easier and easier to do it in the future. Until it becomes less a matter of need and more a matter of time-saving. Why bother asking questions when you can just extract them? And before you say that won't happen, you and I have both met Imperators for whom that is the case."

Kane was silent for a moment. When he spoke, his voice was grave. "This class is designed to give you an important tool in your skillset. Intimidation and, yes, torture, are unpleasant but sometimes effective methods to get what you need. And you're right, some people move to that point faster than others. They lose the ability to recognise that it should be a last resort, rather than just the pragmatic one. And yes, that could happen to you." He grimaced at the look on my face. "But the fact that you are here, telling me this, means that you're still questioning yourself. The way I see it, if you keep questioning yourself, keep asking if your actions are necessary, then you're keeping yourself grounded. It's when you stop worrying and you stop asking those questions that you know you're losing your grip on humanity. And if that happens...?" he drifted off.

"Yes?"

"I'll slap you so hard you'll forget the last few years of your life and you'll be right back here, worrying."

That shouldn't have been funny. It *wasn't* funny. But still, I couldn't help myself. The laughter tore out of me, weak at first but rapidly becoming full-bodied, until I was shaking with reverberating chuckles.

Kane let me laugh, his lips curled up in a smile of his own. He didn't say anything, didn't do anything else, obviously recognised that I needed the release and so he just let me continue, unabated, until the laughter dried up and just the tears remained. When that happened, he slowly moved to my side and enveloped me in his arms.

Kane didn't stay long. Once I had recovered myself enough, he gave me a few choices words of encouragement and moved on. He was always a busy man and though the time he gave me was limited, the fact that he had come all the way out here to talk to me showed how much he cared. Even now, even when I can no longer trust him, I truly believe that he cared and continues to care for those within his command. The Academy made a damn fine choice in choosing him to be one of the heads of year.

A few minutes after Kane had left, the Imperator opened the door. Carmine, as he was known. He didn't have the same arrogant look on his face as usual, instead he held me with a bitter gaze.

"I am to give you one chance," he stated firmly, biting off the words. "One more opportunity to partake in this class. You can decline, but you will be at the mercy of whatever the Imperator council decides to do with you, so you-"

"I'm ready."

He broke off, surprise evident in his face. "Really?"

"Really." I swallowed, hating the words I was about to say, but knowing they were needed. "For what it's worth, I apologise. Kane and my friends talked some sense into me."

His eyebrows raised. "An apology? Will wonders never cease." Settling into his chair he eyed me curiously, then shook his head. "I won't pry into what Kane said. Nor as to how he came to be here when, as far as I am aware, you and your dorm have been unable to send messages." He cracked his neck from side to side and looked me in the eyes. "One last time. Are you certain?"

I nodded.

His pupils constricted. The room shimmered, *swerved*, and then I was in the room. The hateful room. Carmine was there, watching impassively.

I picked up the knife.

CHAPTER 9

Classes

"You're back!" Cassius jumped up and wrapped me in a bone-crushing hug. The rest of the dorm followed suit, offering warm congratulations and welcome through the manner of high-fives, hugs, and punches to the shoulder. I gave them the abbreviated version of my stay and then it was my turn for the interrogation.

I didn't know if it was me, but everyone seemed that little more on edge with each other than usual. A little more wary. Laughter was a touch more forced. What was happening to my tight-knit dorm?

The answer was easy: Wolf's Hollow was doing its job.

I had been away for a few weeks, trapped down in the prison below, and during that time the Imperators who ran this place had begun systematically chipping at the bonds that linked my friends. Classes were run competitively, with the loser losing some kind of privilege, whether it be food, access to the baths or even starting the next exam with a minus score already applied to their paper. These actions, combined with the already competitive spirit of your average Imp, meant that *no-one* wanted to lose, and those that did took it badly.

When the Imps were paired, they were never in the same duo twice. The Academy had all the information on us that it ever needed. Somewhere deep within the archives was doubtless a list of all known occasions when an Imp has worked with another, how well that partnership worked out, moments of strife and so on. As such they didn't need to know how Cassius and I worked together, or Sophia and Scythe. They wanted to see how we performed on our own and in different teams, both to test our abilities to adapt but probably also to make sure that we weren't co-dependent on each other to get throug h difficult situations.

After all, the Academy wanted each Imperator to be a practical, competent individual. One who could be relied on when working alone or as part of a team. Whilst it knew that a pair with affection for each other would likely work well, it was easy to recognise that the ability to seamlessly begin working with another individual was an advantage. Afterall, in our line of work losing one's partner was far from an impossibility.

Hells. It was almost guaranteed.

"I think you've had it easy, trapped in your little cell," Scythe said with a wink. "Up here, we've been having to work!"

"You, work? That must have been traumatic."

"Decidedly so," he acknowledged with a nod before his easy-going charm disappeared and a frown marred his face. "It's not been good, Cal. I've seen some of the others around the place: Arin, Jemain and Oso, and they're pretty messed up. Arin has been here for a few months but has failed two challenges. Won't say what they were, but she's looking pretty worn out; tired and scared."

"Scared?"

"Seems like, depending on the challenges, three strikes is the maximum allowed for failure. Some people get taken away, like you were, but tend not to be seen again."

I looked at the group. "And none of you know what the challenges are?"

A shake of heads. "Not the same as the one we all partook in, I think," Ella offered quietly. "The ones that you can fail at, they are more personal. I don't think the Academy cares too much at this point if you're the most or second-most successful Imp around. We've all proven ourselves to get to this stage. No, these challenges are more about our character, I reckon. Making sure that we are right for the Academy. Do what they say, when they say it. That kind of thing."

Everyone turned to me with a pitying look.

"Hey!" I remarked, raising my hands into the air. "I'm not *that* bad."

"True," mused Cassius.

"You're worse," said Rikol.

"Bunch of arseholes," I muttered darkly, a smile tingeing my face. "So, what's the usual day-to-day?"

"Classes, including your new favourite," answered Sophia. "Everyone has morning training in the gym, then it's off to sessions tailored to your chosen profession. So, for most of us it's seraph manipulation, espionage, finance and politics." She blushed slightly at the look on my face. "Your Instructor was meant to have organised the classes."

My Instructor. The last time I had seen Sarrenai he had been a purple-skinned demonic creature of incalculable strength, wresting control over his body back from the liathea within him. I had no idea where he was now; hopefully laying low and staying as dead as I had told everyone he was.

"Ah."

Cassius stepped forward. "It's alright. I had some discussions with the Imperators running this place and got a timetable that more accurately represents our interests. They couldn't do everything mind – hard to get monsters in here to fight – but our primary classes are seraph manipulation, politics, archives and hunting."

I raised an eyebrow. "Hunting?"

"The benefits of Imperators skilled with illusionary seraph," he replied. "It can be put to better uses than learning to hurt someone. We're confined to what the Imperator has either seen or can envisage, but we can at least keep our skills somewhat sharp."

"Sounds good," I murmured. "I hadn't even thought that was possible."

Cassius shrugged. "Even if Sarrenai had known of it – which he assuredly did – he was never one for taking the easy road. If there was a method of fighting the beast in safety versus fighting it with the threat of death and dismemberment, well...we both know which way he would have gone."

He was beyond right. Sarrenai was nothing if not a stickler for a good old-fashioned life-or-death bout. That might have changed after his own recent experiences, but certainly when he had been training us he had believed that there was nothing that made you learn faster than when death was on the line.

In that, I had to agree.

"Okay," I said, clapping my hands together. "So, we have classes interspersed with periodic challenges, the failure of which may or may not result in removal from the Academy, death or something worse."

"Something worse than death?" snorted Rikol.

I shrugged. "We've all seen some pretty crazy shit over the years. Fairly certain we can all envisage fates worse than death without too much effort."

"Got that right," muttered Scythe, eyes haunted.

"Any idea when the next challenge will be?"

"None." Ella answered. "But it wouldn't surprise me if it was soon."

"Fan-fucking-tastic," I drawled. "Sounds like this year is going to continue to be a right barrel of laughs."

My sarcasm game was on point.

"What the hell is that?" I demanded, staring at an amorphous blob with stumpy legs. "I said a giant spider, not a fat spider!"

"Well, in her defence," Cassius began, "the Queen was ridiculously fat, but she had more," he waved his hands, "*bulk* to make it look right proportionally." He eyed the illusionary spider with distaste. "This just looks…wrong."

The image wavered and vanished, revealing a frustrated Imperator with sweat beading on her brow. "This isn't easy, you know," she growled. "You should be happy with what you-"

"I'm sorry," I cut in, raising a hand, "but have you ever seen a spider? What you just showed us looked like a malformed sausage with chicken wings for legs."

Cassius shot me an odd look.

"What?" I said defensively. "I'm not hungry. Not at all."

"Sure."

"Shut it." Turning back to the Imperator, I shook my head in apology. "Look, forget the fatness. Just think of a normal spider and make it bigger. *Much* bigger."

The Imperator turned away, muttering something under her breath about disrespectful Imps before closing her eyes. This time, when the world shifted, a vast spider that looked more in proportion stood ahead of us.

"Much better," Cassius said. "Now, make any changes that you see fit please."

I heard a low chuckle as the Imperator began to concentrate and immediately cursed Cassius's choice of words. The land cracked and steam billowed into the sky, followed by small jets of lava that fired into the air before pooling. Layers of ash reduced visibility, making everything beyond thirty feet murky and difficult to discern, which wasn't great because the Imperator wasn't done. The last I saw of our impending foe before it disappeared into the ash were glowing armour plates cladding its many appendages and a vicious looking mouth that *steamed.*

"Now this is more like it!" Cassius said, impressed. "Looks very intimidating. Almost as if- *ugh*!"

I tackled him to the ground, stopping just short of a lava stream as a strand of something red-hot lanced through the air where he had been.

"Oh, come on!" I said incredulously. "Lava-web? How would that even work?"

"Hey, you said you had met an electrical spider," a disembodied voice called out from all around us. "Don't blame me for what my imagination created."

Cassius rolled to his feet. "I mean, it does kinda sound like something we would end up facing," he murmured off-handedly, eyes scanning the terrain. "You remember that wolf that could-"

"Don't give her more ideas!" I interrupted quickly. Drawing my sword, I stepped away from Cassius, making it less likely for this beast's ranged attacks to hit us both. "Let's see what this thing can do."

"That was pretty good," Cassius acknowledged with a groan, rolling his shoulders as he did so.

"Pretty good?" the Imperator asked incredulously. "I made you fight a giant lava spider! I think that warrants more than 'pretty good'."

I crunched my neck from side to side. The bad thing with fighting in one of these illusions was that your body wasn't doing any actual fighting; it just sat there whilst in your mind you're doing all the difficult stuff. Inevitably that meant that the muscles grew stiff and sore. "Like Cassius said, not a bad effort. Certainly seemed to act more like a spider would." *If the spider could manipulate lava.*

The Imperator shook her head in deserved consternation. "You two have chosen a weird path if what I just put you through was somewhat normal."

"Lady," Cassius said with a warm smile, "you have no idea."

Shaking her head, the woman turned to leave, pausing at the door. "Next session is in two days. Any particular creature you want me to try and create?"

I shared a glance with Cassius, trying to gauge how he was feeling. "Something harder would be good," I mused. "What do you think, Cass?"

"Category four or five would be great." He shrugged. "How about a skyren?"

The Imperator let out a low whistle. "You two don't do things by half. I'll see what I can do."

"Thanks Clara."

The Imperator nodded and left, leaving me with my eyebrows raised at Cassius.

"What?"

"First name terms with the Imperator," I joked with a knowing grin. "Does Ella know?"

"Oh, shut up."

I drew in a breath. "She doesn't! The horror! The scandal!"

Cassius gave me the finger with a laughing shake of his head. "Dick."

We joked a little more as we walked back to the dorm. I found that one of the best ways to judge the dorm's stress levels was by the quality of the banter. The more stressed and upset, the more the banter became less funny and more pointed. At this point with Rikol it was more like thinly veiled threats rather than funny quips. Cassius was under strain too, but not to the same extent. He and I had travelled, fought and lived with each other for so long that knowing each other's emotional state was second-nature.

The sound of sobs bouncing off the grey slate walls caused me to slide to a halt, arm outstretched to stop Cassius.

"What is it?" he asked, eyes roving for danger.

"No danger," I murmured. "Someone's crying."

"Well what are we waiting around for?" he declared, pushing me forward. "Let's go and see if they're alright."

"You're like a mother hen," I declared with a small shake of my head, but stepping towards the sound. "Always fussing around."

"Better to extend the offer of help and be turned down than to not try at all," he retorted. "I wouldn't want someone to walk by if I needed help."

"Depends on the person," I replied with a grin before waving his reply away. Stepping around the corner we found Jemain on the floor, arms wrapped around his knees, eyes staring blankly.

"Jemain?" Cassius asked softly, stepping forwards and crouching down beside him. "What's wrong?"

Cassius's words seemed to break something in the man and his entire body started to shudder with sobs.

Cassius didn't say another word and sat down beside him. I shot him a questioning look but he waved me on with a nod of his head. Thankful – I had never been good at consoling others, let alone myself – I continued back to the dorm, the sound of Jemain's sobs haunting my steps.

"What was wrong?" I asked Cassius when he stepped into the dorm a little later. He shook his head, expression sad.

"I didn't get much out of him. Said something about a challenge but didn't give any details." He looked pensive. "Must have been a hard one to upset him so."

I couldn't help but agree. Jemain was a hell of a fighter and I would have thought him strong enough to overcome any challenge with little difficulty. But then, Wolf's Hollow wasn't really about the purely physical elements of being an Imperator. It liked to play with your mind. Break down your friendships and cause you heartache. Make you face your greatest fears and either overcome them or break.

"Jemain won't have been the first person to need some personal time within these halls," Cassius said softly, "and he certainly won't be the last. This year is going to test us all. Physically and mentally." He cast a soft smile in my direction.

"Just got to make sure that we don't break, eh?"

CHAPTER 10
A Little Monstrous

I vomited into a bucket.

A tsk of disappointment and the illusion faded, but the very real stench of vomit remained. Imperator Carmine stood up from his desk, a look of disgust and disapproval on his face. "And here I thought you had a stronger stomach than that, Calidan."

I shook my head, keeping my face buried into the steel bucket that I suspected was kept nearby for just this reason.

Carmine shook his head. "To be honest, you got further than I thought you would."

"That was foul," I hissed through acrid teeth. "Why would an Imperator ever need that? It's sick!"

"You never know what an Imperator might need," Carmine replied calmly. "It's not for you to judge. This is the curriculum, so suck it up and just hope you never have to use it."

I placed the bucket down and wiped my mouth. "There's no need to hope. I'm never doing that to anyone. Even my most hated enemy."

Carmine shrugged. "I'm sure everyone thinks that at first. Boundaries change. Priorities shift. Ten years from now you might find yourself a very different person."

That's what I'm afraid of.

Carmine looked at the hour-glass on the wall. "That's enough for today anyway. Remember today, remember what I did. It's your turn tomorrow."

The walk back to the dorm had never felt longer.

Rikol took one look at my face and slid me a glass of water. "Rough session I take it?"

I nodded in the affirmative, using the water to rinse out my mouth. He eyed me sympathetically. "It will get better."

Wiping my mouth, I glanced up at his words. "That's what worries me," I replied.

He grunted, expression darkening slightly. "We've all been where you're standing. Do you think us that much changed?"

My mind went to the dorm, how our interactions were all that little bit more tense. There was less laughter these days and more time spent alone with our thoughts. "We're all changed," I replied, including myself in the conversation. "We're all products of our experiences. To learn something so monstrous is to become a little monstrous yourself."

For a long moment he gazed at me, his eyes carrying a terrible weight. "Poetic," he said finally.

"That was one of my better lines, wasn't it?"

A shake of his head. "Not a particularly high bar."

"Harsh."

He grinned but the smile soon left his face. He knew more than most about being the product of his experiences. Long gone was the fast-talking boy always ready with an amusing quip. Even that I knew to have been in response to what he had gone through as an orphan in the city. Brandishing humour as a weapon against the daily horrors and stresses of life. The Imperator Academy had long burned that out of him.

"How have you found it?" I asked.

He looked at me quizzically. "The classes with Carmine," I clarified.

"Ah. Well." He let out a long sigh. "All told, I've found it fairly straightforward." A shake of his head. "It probably helps that I've seen this stuff before. Gang bosses need to make an example when things don't go their way. Particularly when surrounded by starving thieves." I motioned for him to continue and he sighed again, gaze turning inwards, reliving past memories. "For a while I ran with a small group. Led by a girl, called herself Sparrow, used to boast about how fast she could cut purses and dart through the crowds." He smiled wistfully. "And she was good too, damn good. Big enough to give us younger ones a little bit of protection and skilled enough for us to idolise her. But," he leant forwards now, gaze intent on me, "the problem with being a street-rat is that you are the very bottom rung of everything. You might think that the only way to go is up, but everyone, and I mean *everyone*, wants to keep you down. That includes the gangs. They're all happy and doing well enough that, in their eyes, there isn't any more room for more crew. Or competition. They just want to take, take and take some more until there is nothing left. Well, Sparrow, she thought we deserved more. She started fast-handing some of the tithes that we paid to gangs. Switching out stolen goods for fakes whilst keeping the real ones and fencing them on the other side of the city, away from the local crews." A snort. "Worked for a little bit, but didn't take too long before someone noticed the little street-rat crew getting a little too fat. Eating well – it's always the sign that a crew has pulled off a good haul." He shook his head. "Didn't take long for someone to look into it. I came back one day to find enforcers. Dragged everyone off to Rogan's den." He saw my confused look and explained, "Rogan wasn't the boss of the local crew. He was the boss of half the city. Had maybe twenty crews reporting in to him. For us at the time, meeting him was like meeting a god."

"Or a demon," I hazarded, seeing where this was going.

A nod. "Or that. Well, what do you do if one of your crews is reporting that they are getting ripped off by some shitty little street-rat? You make an example. And boy, did they do that. Gathered every single streeter in Rogan's domain. Made them watch." He wiped a hand across his eyes and shook his head. "Say what you want about Rogan, he knew his business. Ain't one of us who tried swindling from him or his crews again. Not after what he did. And you know what's funny? I didn't hate him for what he did. I mean, I hated him for killing Sparrow, but the reasoning behind it? It wasn't someone evil doing it for fun. It was fucking *practical*. I understood it then, and I understand it now." Tears welled in his eyes as he looked at me. "Guess that makes me more than a little monster now, doesn't it?"

Practicality. When I thought about it, that's what it all came down to. Using the most efficient method to get the best results. That's what the Academy wanted and, thinking about it in those terms, like Rikol I could completely understand the need. I didn't like it, but there was a strange simplicity about recognising the reasoning, no matter how twisted the situation.

I smiled and clapped him on the shoulder. "I think we've been a little monstrous for a long time now mate. Thank you for telling me that story, it's helped me see things a little more clearly."

He wiped his eyes. "You're welcome. Tell anyone and I'll-"

"Gut me like a fish?"

He grinned. "Something like that."

"My lips are sealed."

The problem, I found, was that whilst I now understood the need to learn what Carmine was trying to teach me, it didn't make doing so any easier. In my view his teaching went above and beyond what would ever be required. If I had to do what he was trying to impress upon me then I wouldn't be an Imperator anymore.

I would be a torturer.

But I guess that was the point. The Academy wanted us to learn as much about the process as possible so that we could pick and choose techniques to use in the moment. As Carmine suggested on numerous occasions when my nerve failed me, if my ruthless ability to stab a knife into someone's kneecap didn't get me the information I needed, what would I do?

Hopefully that was never the case, because I had no desire to ever have to use what the man was trying to teach. Besides being time-consuming, it was all about inflicting pain for pain's sake, and that was not what I was about.

Not yet anyway.

The illusion died away as I made my final cuts. Ears long inured to the screams.

"Adequate."

A word I had never wanted or expected to hear from the Imperator's mouth. I sat back as reality made itself known again, finding the Imperator back at his desk. Instead of responding, I merely inclined my head.

Carmine held my gaze for a while, the animosity that had fuelled their fire when we first butted heads had since dimmed to a low smoulder, but was still more than prevalent. We both knew that if we met outside of the Academy then chances were that one of us wasn't walking away.

But hey, I guess if nothing else then the month I spent in Carmine's daily classes proved that mutual hatred can work as a foundation for a practical relationship just as much as respect or friendship. Perhaps even more efficiently in fact; I worked faster purely because I wanted to spend as little time in his company as possible.

Eventually he spoke again. "You have been, without a doubt, the most annoying little shit that I have ever had the displeasure of trying to teach. And whilst I think a troll could have done a better job at learning this content, you have..." his teeth ground together, "passed."

Standing up, I let out a long, heartfelt sigh of relief, heavily tinged with disgust at myself. Many choice phrases and insults passed through my mind but I bore down on the impulse, knowing that saying any one of the hundred things that desperately burned in me to say would only result in making my life more miserable whilst in Wolf's Hollow.

"I can honestly say this has been the most miserable learning experience of my life. And my family was slaughtered by a demon."

Nailed it.

The smallest of smiles tugged at Carmine's mouth. Did he love misery? Considering his job, probably. "Enjoy the respite Calidan," he called as I opened the door. "Everything gets worse from here on in. I'll be seeing you soon."

I shut the door with a slam, the noise satisfying but not enough to prevent the sound of his mocking laugh from ringing in my ears.

It took me a long time to clear my head after that. As Jemain had found a few weeks earlier, there were few places that you could go to be alone whilst trapped inside an underground facility. The stone halls carried sound, meaning that conversations meant to be kept secret could spread like wildfire, and because the facility itself wasn't that big, there was always someone nearby. I wandered the corridors in a daze, not knowing where my feet were taking me, trying my best yet completely failing to keep my thoughts from spiralling back to the class.

Carmine was a lot of things – all of them unpleasant – but he was very good at creating illusions. It had all felt so *real*. The things I had needed to do to that poor person...

A hand slammed onto my shoulder and jerked me back into reality. Sophia.

"Come with me," she ordered curtly, leaving me no choice in the matter as she grabbed my sleeve in her vice-like grip and tugged me along behind her.

"Where are we going?"

"We're all a few weeks ahead of you, remember," she answered with a grim smile. "We know what you've been through. Well, everyone except Cassius that is."

"Weren't tempted to use your token to pass the class like him?"

Sophia pursed her lips. "I made a judgement call. If Carmine's classes are the worst that the Academy throws at us this year, I'll eat my hat."

"You don't wear a hat – *ow!*"

She pulled back from flicking my ear and smiled. "I'll buy one and eat it."

I snorted but the humour quickly left my face. I felt drained. Dehumanised from what I had needed to do. Sophia seemed to recognise that and let me be, pulling me along behind her with inexorable force until she pushed the door open to an echoing room of dark slate with a plug in the middle of the floor.

"Here you go," she said primly. "Get undressed and pull the lever. Cassius is on the way with clothes so just stay as long as you need."

"A shower? Why have you brought me…" I trailed off at the look in her eyes.

"I've brought you here because, just like when you're coming back from a mission, scrubbing the muck off you is the best thing to do. You might not look like it but right now you're covered in shit. Illusionary shit but shit all the same. Get under the shower and scrub it all off. Get clean, get your head back in the game. You'll feel better. Trust me."

I did as she commanded and boy was she right. I vowed at that point to never underestimate the value of a hot bath or shower; they can do wonders for your mental as well as physical state. At one point I heard the door open and Cassius call that my clothes were nearby, but he quickly left, letting me steam in the heat of the water for what felt like hours.

Maybe it was.

When I finally turned off the water I was two things: first, convinced that I must have consumed the facility's entire water supply and second, feeling much more human.

"You were right," I said gratefully to Sophia when I entered the dorm. "Thank you."

"When am I ever wrong?" she answered with a laugh. "But you can thank Rikol. It was his idea when we were all going through the same and we all found it made a difference. It doesn't change what we've had to do to get through the classes, but at least it helps wash off some of the worst of the experience."

I nodded to Rikol who raised his hand in response. "Well, I'm grateful to all of you. That was…not a fun experience."

"Don't have to say that twice," muttered Scythe, rolling himself out of bed. "But it's not over yet. We have news."

"Oh?" I sat down at the nearby table.

"Get your game face back on. We've got another challenge. And it starts tomorrow."

PRESENT DAY 3

There is a strange simplicity in stealing from a god. With a normal theft you might wonder who is going to find out, what they might do and how they might do it. With someone like Asol there are very definitive answers to these questions: they will find out, they will kill you and it is likely going to be extremely painful.

Once you put that aside, everything becomes straightforward. If you know that a Power is going to be on your back, you need to make sure that you leave no trace of who you are. Speed is also of the essence – the faster you can get in and out, the less time for any unwanted smiting to occur.

But the single most useful thing about stealing from Powers? They are so full of themselves that they never think it is going to happen. Sure, they might put defences up to stop another Power, but never in a million years would one of them think that a *mere mortal* would casually stroll in and take something. Their hubris would also mean that they wouldn't be able to admit that said mortal had done the stealing. If it had been another Power doing the theft, war or at the very least some kind of cataclysmic city-levelling fight would have occurred, but acknowledging that a petty thief had pulled it off? That would never do.

Case in point - I had already stolen star-metal from Nuramapole, protected by mutated creatures, poisonous gas and blind monks, but had there been even the slightest of outcry? Of course not. Nuramapole couldn't afford to look weak, lest someone took further advantage.

Asol was exactly the same.

I hung in the middle of the space underneath the ascending platform, staring at what I had assumed would be some intricately complex sigil of warding that I would never be able to breach.

Surely it's not that simple...

I studied it some more. Frowned at it intensely to soften it up, then slowly, tentatively, injected the slightest bit of seraph into the sigil.

Weaves of light spun and coalesced in a dizzying array of colour. A second later the stone the ward had been on vanished...and the fifth layer of the vault was open to me.

The Power had so little respect for mortals that he had assumed that something as simple as a seraph lock would be enough to keep anyone out.

More fool him.

Drifting through the freshly vacated air, I entered a world unlike anything I had seen before. The other layers were amazing, sure, but they were still varying levels of splendour grafted onto the same walls. But this?

This was something else entirely.

I'm fairly certain that I didn't step through some kind of portal when entering the vault – there was usually a certain sensation that accompanied portal travel – but *something* had to happen. I say that because the inside of the vault was a tremendous waterfall that thundered through the air for at least a hundred feet, crashing and splashing into a pool that looked perfectly inviting for a dip. Surrounding the waterfall were high, slick rocks filled with foliage. They climbed all around, ensuring that the waterfall remained a hidden oasis. A hint of sky above and behind me the darkness of the door.

I had so many questions.

So little time.

Choosing to focus on what was in front of me and not the growing crisis threatening to unravel my mind that I had somehow walked into a pocket dimension, I frowned at the pool and then at the waterfall.

Is there going to be some kind of guardian? Is the pool horrendously deep and filled with a giant eel?

I didn't like giant eels. Not after the Sunfa'shak.

Part of me wanted to dive in and swim down but it just didn't feel right. The waterfall was the main centrepiece here. And where better place to leave treasure than behind a waterfall?

Probably anywhere else, really. Pretty sure anything precious would rot when exposed to the damp air. But since I was standing in the creation of someone many would call a god, who was I to judge?

Striding towards the edge of the pool, I noticed some stone plates on the side which tickled my mind just enough to make me pause.

Asol uses stone plates. He doesn't touch the ground at all...

Suddenly I had a sinking suspicion as to what might happen if I touched that inviting water.

Pretend to be Asol. What would the floating prick do? Walk over the water.

Because he's a douche.

You got this Cal, time to channel your inner douche.

Focusing my will on the plates, I reached out and lifted them into the air with my mind. I had practiced similar things in the past – juggling with seraph was a fantastic way to learn control – but standing on those plates and moving at the same time? That was hard.

And Asol didn't tend to stand on one and float. He walked across them, giving the illusion that the plates were hurriedly prostrating themselves before him with each step.

Which meant I had to do the same.

If Rikol had been there I'm sure he would have laughed long and hard at my wobbly crossing, complete with lots of arm flailing and near perilous tipping over. It's funny how you can walk in a straight line completely unconsciously, but try it a foot above the ground and suddenly it becomes the hardest thing ever. Regardless, I soon found myself face to face with the gushing waterfall, the sound of its majesty pummelling my ear drums at this range.

And now what?

All too aware of my dwindling seraph pool, I thought about what I knew of Asol. He wasn't the type to wrap a shield around himself and plunge through the water. No.

He would command it.

Asol could probably turn the water off entirely with a mere glance, but I was no Power. Instead, I opted for simplicity: willing a seraph shield into being directly in the centre of the waterfall and carving the flow of water in two. Stepping through with the aid of the discs, I found myself in a warm study, a fire crackling merrily in one corner and providing the perfect amount of heat. The walls were dark wood panels – doubtless the remains of some very expensive and likely ancient trees. With little else to occupy my attention, I reached out and touched one of the panels, raising an eyebrow as it shifted with a *click* and extended outwards, revealing a drawer.

Well hello there, vault. I grinned, enjoying the feeling of being a victorious treasure-hunter. I could see why people did it; it was a heady rush!

The drawer I pulled out had various documents within leather satchels, a quick glimpse finding them to be written in a language I had never seen before. Moving quickly, I darted around the room, opening panel after panel and inspecting the contents.

I had expected – and hoped for – gold, jewels and all manner of fun stuff, but the reality appeared to be that Asol hoarded information above all else. Part of me wondered if the Emperor would find what Asol had here interesting but I ruthlessly quashed that thought. I'm sure that he would find it interesting and that was all the more reason to keep it away from him.

The Wanderer though? That I could do.

Taking two of the satchels and filling them with as many rolled documents as possible before slinging them around my shoulders, I finally came across what I was looking for. A drawer that looked just like any other, except instead of information it contained two lumps of shimmery metal.

Found you!

I was about to remove the orbs before remembering what had happened last time I stole a Power's star-metal and instead spent a few precious seconds carefully checking the drawer for traps. Seemingly finding nothing, I spent a few seconds revisiting my life choices, shrugged, and lifted one out. My heart stopped for a moment as I waited for the inevitable death dealing to occur. When it didn't, I was almost disappointed – Asol really was that confident in his own superiority.

Whistling, I pocketed the twin lumps before shutting all the drawers and heading for the exit. With any luck, if Asol did visit the vault he wouldn't instantly know that it had been looted.

Another tricky crossing, dissolution of my waterfall-dividing seraph shield, and careful stacking of stone plates later, I was back in the shaft beneath the platform. Climbing out, I could hear confused conversation from the floor above, the voices echoing down the shaft – the platform ascending without occupants must have been fairly uncommon.

Unless one was Asol, that is.

Sophia. Package acquired. What's your status?

Ready to extract.

Good. Activating tag now. Reaching into my suit, I clasped a small sigil carved into wood and focused a hint of seraph into it, causing the intricately carved markings to flare with green light. Tags were inspired by the tattoos that the Emperor branded certain things with that allowed for him to track them wherever they were. He had saved my life years ago by opening a portal to Seya's location. And using that same idea, I was now one step closer to ensuring his demise.

Activated.

...Got it.

A moment later a rift in space opened and I stepped through, releasing my seraph on the guards as I did so – with any luck they would recover in a few moments and likely be terribly confused.

Sophia wrapped her arms around me and squeezed. "All good?"

"All good," I replied, returning the gesture as well as I could manage with the bulky bags. "Arteme?"

"Dropping off the mark."

"Fantastic."

She paused as she looked at the bags and then looked back at me. "Do I even want to...?"

"No. Not even slightly."

"Okay then." A broad smile. "This has been fun Cal. Make sure you get out quick and fast. Leave no trace. And don't be a stranger."

I gave her another hug. Longer this time. "You too, Sophia. Thank Arteme for me."

"Will do."

With a final nod, I stepped out of the door and hopped onto my horse. A few days hard ride and I could be back at the Wanderer's location and stop feeling like I had a target painted on my spine.

A few days and I would see Cassius again.

And be that much closer to my goal.

CHAPTER II

Spy Game

"One of you is not to be trusted." It was the female Imperator, my erstwhile prison guard.

We shared looks of incredulity. *What?*

The woman smiled coldly. "One of you is a spy. That person will be tasked with taking information and getting it to Imperator Carmine *without* being discovered. Everyone else is to apprehend the spy at all costs."

"Rules of engagement?" asked Rikol.

"None."

Same as before then, I mused.

"One by one you will enter the room behind me. You will receive a pack containing information about your role. You will have sixty seconds to read that information and dispose of it before the next person enters. The documents that the spy is after will be kept in a locked safe on the second floor." She smiled wolfishly. "I suggest you guard it well."

I raised my hand. "Time frame?"

"Three weeks."

"Weeks!?" we exclaimed in unison.

"Yes, weeks. The information is valuable and not particularly time sensitive," she replied calmly. "To the spy, I say prepare well and leave no trace. To the rest of you, stay vigilant and trust no-one."

We shared an uncertain look. Trust was something we had fought so hard to attain in our group and already it was strained. The Imperators knew it; we knew it.

This could be the breaking point.

"What's the prize?" Sophia asked.

"If the spy fails, the guarding team earn themselves a weekend pass back to Anderal." Nods and murmurs from the dorm at that. Any way of getting out of this facility was treasured, regardless of how long.

"And if the spy succeeds?"

The slightest of smiles touched the Imperator's mouth. "An *all-expenses paid* weekend pass to Anderal, plus a tailored weapon forged by the Academy's personal weaponsmiths."

By the Pits. That was some reward alright. Any one of us could think up a number of different ways to rack up a substantial bill on a weekend in Anderal, but the real prize was the weapon; the Academy didn't stint on weapons or tools for its Imperators, but if you wanted something original created then you still had to fork out a substantial sum. The Academy weaponsmiths were some of the best in the empire, second only to the Emperor's personal blacksmith, who in turn was reputed to be second only to the Emperor himself.

Cassius opened his mouth to speak but the Imperator raised a hand. "The time for questions is over." Swivelling, she swung open the door, revealing the large form of her partner Havan within. "Rikol," she barked and after a momentary pause the ex-streetrat stepped forward, visibly steeled himself, and then strode into the room. The door slammed shut behind him.

Sixty seconds later, the door reopened and Sophia was called inside. Then Cassius. Scythe. Ella. And finally, me.

Striding into the room, I met Havan's non-descript gaze with a small nod. He said nothing but thrust a single document into my grasp. Quickly tearing open the envelope, I found two pieces of paper. The first contained a single word: *Guard*. Simple enough. The second was much more interesting: *Secondary objective: Discover the spy, remove them, and take on their role to betray your teammates and obtain the spy's prize.*

My mind whirled. *Remove them? Betray the team?* Shit, the Imperators knew what they were doing far too well. The temptation of the spy's prize would make anyone who figured out who the spy was eager to claim it themselves. It would mean that the guards had all the more reason to distrust anyone and everything, because even if we had proved without a doubt who the spy was, betrayal could happen at any moment.

Well, isn't this going to be fun.

Havan indicated the document and I touched a finger to the paper, watching as it crumbled into dust with a hint of seraph. He gave me a nod and pointed at the door set in the far wall. Opening the door, I found my dorm all watching each other with guarded expressions.

"So..." began Cassius casually, "anyone want to reveal themselves as the spy? Make all this easier on us?"

Rikol snorted. "Outing yourself, are you?"

"Of course not. I'm no spy!"

Sophia raised her hands. "Easy, everyone. This is going to go nowhere if we all just start shouting at one another."

"Sounds like something a spy would say," Rikol retorted, a small smile on his face.

"Or..." she cast a look at me, "someone who recognises that a certain individual here can hear heartbeats and thinks it would be easier for him if the guards were to remain calm."

In a moment, the thudding heartbeats I had been concentrating on stilled. *Damn Imps and their body control.* I fought to suppress a grimace. "Tsk. That would have been too easy, eh?"

Everyone turned to me. "You make a fine point Sophia," murmured Ella, "but that assumes that Calidan is a guard, not the spy."

I opened my mouth to retort when Cassius joined in. "I feel like it would be...somewhat unfair if he was chosen as the spy. Calidan does have a few advantages when it comes to sneaking around."

"Which makes him the perfect choice," Rikol argued. "Since when does the Academy like making things easy for people?"

"Hey!" I spoke over the rising volume of heated conversation. "I'm not the spy!"

Somewhat unsurprisingly, that didn't help.

"Hang on a second," Ella said abruptly, spinning around to survey the hall. "Where's Scythe?"

Silence collapsed the conversation instantly, eyes darting around the hall. Ella was right, Scythe was nowhere to be seen. Reaching out with my senses, I found him descending the stairs to the second floor, moving at pace.

"Second floor!" I barked, shifting into a run and hearing the flurry of expletives and thunder of footsteps behind me. We sprint through the winding hallways, past bemused Imps and Imperators, hammered down the echoing metal stairs and careened onto the second floor. Bursting into the room at the end of the hall, cunningly labelled 'Safe', we found him sitting on top of a metal safe that was placed in the centre of the room.

"Took you long enough," he admonished as we spread out around him.

"What are you doing up here?" Sophia demanded, eyes sparking.

Scythe pursed his lips. "I couldn't risk one of you getting here unobserved. It seems to me that the mission is to guard this safe and I couldn't do that in that hallway. Not with a bunch of seraph-practitioners in the game. I mean," he cast a hand at Rikol, "he could probably have had enough time to somehow magic the safe away whilst you were all talking!"

"Why not just say something?" Cassius questioned. "You haven't exactly put yourself in a good light here."

"If I was the spy, why would I just run off? I would like to think that I've got a slightly better head for strategy than that. No," he shook his head, "I just wanted to get here and keep an eye on things before someone made a break for it."

Sophia looked at me and I shook my head slightly, letting her know that Scythe's heartrate wasn't particularly elevated. If he was lying then he was confident in his ability to control his body's natural reactions.

Rikol raised a hand and a gleaming barrier of light flashed into being around the safe. "Warding spell," he said in response to everyone's looks. "If anyone crosses that line, there will be one hell of a noise."

Sophia moved to the line and stuck her hand over. Instantly, the bass-filled sound of a horn thrummed through the room and judging by the confused expression on an Imperator's face who opened the door, well out of it.

"Seems to work," Sophia said simply, ignoring Rikol's scowl. "Good thinking Rikol."

He muttered something under his breath and settled back against the wall, eyes roving ceaselessly.

I looked around the group, seeing the tension in everyone's shoulders and let out a long sigh. "Looks like we're going to be in for a long night."

The safe room became our new dorm. We moved as a group, not trusting anyone to be left by themselves, grabbed bedrolls and anything that could make the ground remotely comfortable and settled in for the long haul.

The main problem? Just because we had a challenge didn't mean that our classes stopped. After the first sleepless night everyone was forced to leave the relative safety of the safe room, power through the relevant class and sprint back, hoping that nothing had happened in the interim. Once we were back in the safe room you could have cut the tension with a blade. Talk was stilted in the face of distrusting eyes. Even those who were lovers were sitting apart, desperate to talk things through with a partner but unable to trust the person they were closest to in the world.

As with all things, familiarity breeds contempt. This was no different. Perhaps if we had been a mixed group that hadn't worked together much before there would have been more discussion, more rational thought. Instead, our watchfulness quickly turned to paranoid animosity, heads turning at anyone's movement and barbed comments lacerating the air if anyone so much as looked at the safe.

Frankly, I'm surprised we didn't descend into violence instantly. Afterall, it's what we were trained for.

On the fourth day, Sophia cornered Cassius and me between classes, expression grave. "I think it's Scythe," she whispered darkly, pushing us up against a wall. "He's way too relaxed."

"Too relaxed?" Cassius chuckled. "How is that cause for alarm?"

"Because everyone is doing their best to burrow through a friend's head with their eyes whilst in that room. All except Scythe. Well," she coughed, "Scythe and you," she finished, eyes locked on Cassius.

"Scythe has always been pretty calm under pressure," I said with a half-shrug. "And Cassius is...well, Cassius. Nice and friendly no matter the situation."

"Thanks!" he said brightly.

"You're welcome," I replied drily before turning back to Sophia. "Thing is, each of us knows only the information we received. Right now we're in a stalemate; everyone distrusting the other because how can we know the truth? You've apparently decided that I'm not the spy, because otherwise you wouldn't be having this conversation with me, but that doesn't mean that I have decided you're not. Or even Cass."

"Hey!"

"Nothing personal," I said, clapping him on the shoulder and getting a roll of the eyes in return. "So, why do you think I'm trustworthy?"

Sophia blanched. "Because I want you to be," she said finally. "I can't prove anything, not yet, but none of us can unless we actually start trusting each other. I choose to trust you."

"Not Scythe," Cassius remarked with a raised eyebrow.

"Whilst I love Scythe," Sophia began hurriedly, "he is one to wear his emotions on his sleeve and has difficulty concealing them. Which is why him being so relaxed has me concerned. If he was as agitated about this situation as I am then I would be having this conversation with him over you."

"Hmm," I mused, "maybe you're right. Or maybe, he has a plan?" At her confused expression I continued, "If Scythe has set something in motion then he would have cause to be relaxed. Whether that is as the spy or a guard, we don't know, but he is obviously satisfied with the way things are going."

"Or *maybe*," a voice growled from nearby, "he just wanted to see what would happen." Sophia paled as Scythe stepped into view. "I can't believe you don't trust me!" he snarled, eyes flashing furiously at Sophia who held up her hands placatingly.

"I do trust *you* Scythe," she began, "but you know the situation we're in. Everyone is under suspicion."

"Everyone except Calidan, apparently," he spat. "I should have known you would go running to him the first chance you got."

"Hey, that's not-"

"And you!" Scythe shouted, whirling on me with venom etched in every feature. "What have you and my girlfriend got going on that she comes to you, eh?"

"Nothing, it-"

He stepped forward and pushed a finger in my chest. "She's *my* girlfriend Calidan. Mine!"

"I know-"

He prodded again, forcing me against the wall, his face a mask of rage. This was the Scythe of battle, the man of fire and fury that swept everything up in his path. "You had your chance with Sophia and blew it, keep your hands off!"

"I get- Wait. What?"

"Don't pretend like you don't know," he snarled. "You've always been there, waiting. You little treacherous leech!"

I recognised the danger in his eyes, the blind rage, and slowly raised my hands. "Easy, Scythe. There isn't anything going on."

He snorted and I could have sworn I saw steam. "Nothing going on my arse. Look at you! Like a pair of thieves."

The blow took everyone completely by surprise. Scythe staggered back, knees buckling slightly and face reddening from the resounding slap that Sophia had delivered. "You!" she hissed. "You have lost your tiny little mind Scytharanious!"

"Uh oh, full name," Cassius whispered, sidling up next to me. "We best take cover."

Sophia whirled and fixated the two of us with eyes filled with murderous intent. "No, you can both stay right there! Scythe is the one who isn't welcome here."

"Now listen-"

"No, you listen!" Sophia ground out through gritted teeth, stepping up into Scythe's face until her nose was nearly touching his. "If you want to throw our relationship away because of a game then you're going the right way about it. Let me make myself very clear. There is and has never been anything between myself and Calidan aside from friendship. Do you understand?"

"I-uh."

Sophia's eyes flashed again and her voice lowered to an octave reserved only for those about to die. "I said. Do. You. Understand?"

Scythe gulped and nodded shallowly. "Y-yes." After a long moment he deflated. "I'm sorry," he murmured.

"You don't just need to apologise to me," Sophia snapped, waving a hand at the two of us. "Them too!"

Scythe stiffened and then turned towards us and let out a long sigh. "Sorry. I made a mess of things there and you didn't deserve what I said. I apologise."

Waving a hand, I forced a light chuckle. "Not to worry. It's just this place and this mission getting to us. We're all too tense."

Scythe gave a tight smile and turned back to Sophia, nodding once before walking away, shoulders hunched.

"Well," said Sophia exasperatedly, "that was fun."

"Not your fault," Cassius said sympathetically, "everyone's on edge. Ella and I have had similar arguments too."

A snort from Sophia. "But in your case you *are* in a relationship with Calidan."

"He should be so lucky," I muttered off-handedly, getting a friendly nudge in return.

"I know that look," Cassius said, levelling a stare at me. "What is it?"

I pursed my lips. "Nothing, I think."

"Let me rephrase, what is on your mind?"

I sighed. "Just something that Scythe said, 'like a pair of thieves.'"

He frowned. "Are you referring to Ella and Rikol? What about them?"

"Like I said, nothing. Just got me wondering." At his raised eyebrow I continued, "If you were going about setting up a challenge that would really push the team, and knowing everything you know about us, would you pick someone who might get exposed immediately, or would you-"

"Give it to someone who grew up as a thief," Sophia finished for me.

"Exactly. They have realms of experience in this kind of operation – far beyond anything taught at the Academy. Either one of them could run circles around us when it comes to theft."

"Hmm, sounds a little woolly to me," Cassius replied. "Maybe the Academy wanted you to think that way."

"Or maybe you just don't want Ella to be acting against you," Sophia retorted. "Which I can empathise with...it's not a fun experience."

Cassius raised his hands in defeat. "Fine, let's assume for a moment that either Ella or Rikol is the spy. What does that mean for us? We can't come up with a method to trust each other, let alone the rest. I mean, as it stands right now, this could all just be a way to stir up trouble and mislead. We don't know anything for sure."

"We don't know anything for sure..." I repeated in a low whisper, deep in thought. "What if..."

"...Yes?" Sophia nudged when I didn't continue.

I turned to them both. "What do we actually know about this challenge for sure? That there is a safe with something inside it. That there is at least one spy within our ranks. But is that it?"

"What else is there?" asked Cassius.

"Did the Imperator ever mention that it was specifically a single spy?"

"Of course she did," Cassius exclaimed, desperation tinging his words. "Right Sophia?"

"No," she replied, shaking her head. "No, I don't think she did. Which means that potentially there isn't a limit on the number of spies within our group."

"Great, so, as far as I know, I could be the one guard left within a group of spies," muttered Cassius darkly. "Stupid bloody game."

"Again, we don't know this for sure," I said gently. "I'm just trying to get to the facts."

"I mean, let's face it. It would be just like Wolf's Hollow to have not one, but *two* spies in this game. Hells, they would probably make it so they weren't aware of each other too, just to throw more wrenches into the works!" he exclaimed, a flash of anger crossing his face.

"Hold on," Sophia cut in. "Let's say this is all true. Let's even say that Rikol and Ella are both the spies and are even aware of each other. Considering that Scythe is stomping around somewhere, doesn't that mean that we have left them with the safe?"

That was a sobering thought. "This is all just conjecture," I insisted. "We need cold, hard facts and that isn't something that I think we can achieve in this scenario."

"There has to be a way," Sophia declared. "I refuse to believe that we're going to sit there, waiting for someone to betray us rather than being active."

"What about…" I shook my head, "no. Carmine is the person they're trying to get the information to, he wouldn't necessarily help one of us."

"What are you thinking?"

I sighed. "Illusion seraph. Carmine used it on me in the prison, made me believe that I was in a different place. I was thinking that we could use his power to do that, to see if we can create a mental scenario that reveals the truth."

"Rikol and Ella are both powerful seraph users in their own right," Sophia replied. "They would likely have mental wards up at all times."

I pursed my lips. "Not if they're given a drug first though."

Cassius shook his head in disgust whilst Sophia considered. "It could work," she offered eventually. "But, as you say, Carmine wouldn't necessarily work with us on this."

"He might not," I began, feeling the cold, calculating side of me rising to the fore and hating it, "but we do have someone who could potentially do it."

"Who?" she asked, confusion evident on her face.

I turned to Cassius. "You."

He barked a laugh. "Yeah, right, good one." His expression faded as he saw the look in my eyes. "You're *serious*?"

"I know you hate it, but you do have an affinity for black seraph," I offered gently. "That means you have a more instinctive grasp of mental techniques."

"No. *No!*" he rasped, shaking his head wildly. "I can't believe you're asking me that. You know that I despise what's inside me. Why would you want me to use it?!" His voice was pleading now, tears glistening in his eyes.

I swallowed hard. "Two reasons. First, it gives us an edge. A way to figure out this situation. Second, you-" I breathed out heavily. "Perhaps you've lived in fear of it long enough. Maybe you should learn to use the skills that you've been given, rather than hamstringing yourself."

"And end up like Rya!?" he bellowed, fear and rage warring within him. He stepped away from me, ignoring my outstretched hand.

"Cass, wait-"

There was a blur of motion and he disappeared, leaving a glistening trail of moisture in the air. Tears swept along in the wake of his movement.

Sophia locked eyes with me. "That could have gone better."

"I know," I said miserably. "I should have thought it through more. I know how much he hates his seraph type."

"But you made a good point," she replied. "He does need to learn to use it, if not embrace it. Otherwise, it is just a weakness."

I grimaced. "I wish it were that simple. Cassius had his unawakened seraph tainted by Rya. He knows what it can do, and what can be done to him in turn. Above all else he fears becoming a puppet of the Enemy and doing what Rya did; hurting those he loves. Hurting you, me...hurting Ella. Hells, we were all there when the Enemy attacked at the citadel ball and took possession of those with black seraph. That did nothing for his confidence about what he carries. He knows that he is a threat. Something that can be exploited. It terrifies him."

Sophia nodded in understanding. "Must be horrible, being scared about yourself. Fearful of something within. Hiding that from everyone."

"And now we're in a place where even the friendships that have supported each of us through the years are being stripped away," I agreed. We stood for a moment in silent solidarity.

"What do you think to do then Cal?"

I let out a long sigh. "I'll talk to Cassius. In the meantime, I guess we keep guarding the safe. Unless you have a better idea?"

She shook her head. "No." She grimaced. "They've done a good job of making it almost impossible to determine who is working against us. If we can get Cassius to do this, it might be our only option to get ahead of the game."

CHAPTER 12

Changes

"Calidan."

"Rikol."

The two of us stared at each other for a while, trying to see past the other's outer exterior of calm.

"Where have you been?" he asked, voice devoid of emotion.

I cocked an eyebrow. "Don't you know?"

"I would prefer you to tell me."

"I'm sure you would."

More silence. Rikol stepped back and sat down, nodding at the chairs we had arranged in the room. "Stay away from the safe."

I gave him a pained smile. "I'm trying to think of a better way to say no shit, but really can't come up with something more suitable."

He rolled his eyes. "Language never was your strong suit."

"Anything interesting happen whilst I was gone?"

"No."

"...Would you tell me if there was?" He looked at me sullenly and I shook my head. "Didn't think so."

Two weeks into the mission and things were not progressing well. My conversation with Rikol – if it could be called such – was symptomatic of our relationship at this point. Of all our relationships.

Frankly, we were a mess.

Gone was the cohesive team. The group that had battled numerous foes and emerged victorious time and again. In its place was a fractured façade of normality that belied the scheming and shifting waters underneath. Since his altercation with Sophia, Scythe had stayed largely to himself, avoiding contact with anyone if he could help it. He didn't look at me if at all possible. Ella had faded into the woodwork, drifting through the makeshift dorm like a ghost, seeing everything but offering nothing. Thought she slept next to Cassius, there was little suggestion of a more intimate relationship. She treated him almost like the rest of us, as though we were easily startled prey. Making no sudden movements and staying out of view.

Sophia was a constant presence. She gave the impression of weathering the change in the group dynamics the best, providing a counterbalance to the depressive, melancholic air that permeated the room with cheery laughter and kind words.

Rikol was back to his cynical and sardonic self. A place that we had all spent a long time pulling him back from following Damien's death. Combining a mixture of mockery and open distrust, he quickly made the atmosphere within the room one of the most depressing locations I had ever had the displeasure of being.

As for Cassius? He stayed out of the room as much as possible. He had refused to talk to me for two days following my mention of his learning to utilise mental manipulation techniques. He point-blank refused to discuss it any further; preferring to get up and walk away in the face of any attempt to converse about it.

All in all, we were no closer to discovering the spy, and whoever was the spy was doing an excellent job of maintaining their cover. After rounds of aggressive interrogation between all members of the group, we had all come to realise that there was no method of easily determining the traitor in our midst and so settled into our current state of mutual distrust. It seemed quiet enough, but like Meredothian wolves, I knew that if one of us made a mistake the response would be swift and merciless.

The door opened and Cassius entered, his face drawn and haggard. Of all of us, I think he had suffered the most with this challenge. He was a person who thrived on comradery and friendship. Who needed people to support and be supported by in turn. To have all of his closest friends turn their backs on him - even for an Academy mission - hurt him deeply. I saw it in the way he carried himself; no longer with the air of easy grace but more like a wounded animal. Despite that, he had begun bringing us all the daily meals, once we had realised that ascending to the canteen was not going to happen. The plates clinked as he took them off the tray and set them down on the table.

"Thanks Cass," I called as he took his plate and moved away, sitting somewhere close to Ella but not quite within touching distance. He stiffened but didn't respond.

The food was sumptuous, as always. Steaming plates of venison stew, potatoes and greens. The rich scent of the food had my mouth watering in seconds, my nose detecting hints of berries, citrus and something earthy and smoky that I couldn't put my finger on. We all grabbed our plates and returned to our preferred vantage point within the room to eat. I picked up a piece of potato and dipped it into the stew, closing my eyes in anticipation as I raised it to my mouth.

Mushroom. The scent crystallised in my mind and my eyes snapped open. Mushroom. It smelled of *mushroom*. Now that wasn't by any stretch unusual, but it smelled of a mushroom that we wouldn't normally be eating. In fact...my eyes shot to Cassius who raised an eyebrow at me in silent acknowledgement of my wonderings, it smelled just like the bullshit that Carmine had put in my food to make me easy to manipulate.

What was Cassius doing? Had he been practicing his mental manipulation skills? He had to have known that I would smell whatever he had put in there. Trying to act as casual as possible – which in this instance meant remaining huddled and suspicious of everyone – I tucked in, chewing a perfectly roasted potato with relish and noting everyone doing the same, watching them all enjoy the gravy coated dish.

A pity that I had to have my potato dry, but hopefully whatever Cassius was up to was worth missing out on the gravy for.

It didn't take long for the mushroom to take effect. One by one the eyes of our friends began to glaze over until they lay slumped in their chairs, oblivious to the world around them. Only then did Cassius stir.

"I didn't like doing that," he murmured unhappily. "Betraying their trust."

I nodded sympathetically. "If it helps, at least you gave them a nice meal first. Where did you get the mushroom?"

He shrugged. "Easy enough if you ask the right people."

"Carmine?"

A shake of his head. "No, but the Imperator who gave us the mission in the first place. You said that they were the ones who usually fed you. Stood to reason they would know what went in your food."

Made sense. "And now?"

He eyed me. "And now, I do what you said."

"Accessing their minds? Do you know how?"

He shrugged. "It's something that I've been working on a little over the last few years."

I gazed at him open-mouthed in disbelief.

"Don't give me that look," he chided indignantly. "What? You think that I wasn't aware how much of a weakness not utilising my seraph to its utmost would be?"

"Well…yeah, kinda," I grimaced, rubbing the back of my head awkwardly.

A snort. "To be honest, it took the High Imperator and a visit by the Emperor to convince me to start."

"The Emperor suggested you do it?"

He made a face. "Insisted in fact. Was very keen on me working to my full potential. Gave me a big speech about needing to be the best Imperator I could be and turning any weaknesses into strengths."

"Sounds like the Emperor."

"Indeed."

We sat in silence for a moment, considering our comatose friends around us. "So, you've done this before?" I asked eventually.

A twist of his lips. "Kind of."

"Kind of?"

A grimace. "I've tried it on animals. Dogs, cats, you know." He saw my look and raised his hands defensively. "Hey, I didn't exactly want to go around sharing that I was working on this, and of those who did know, they weren't exactly willing to be test subjects. The High Imperator and the Emperor have too many secrets in their minds to allow an Imp to practice anything of the sort, just in case I succeeded. And the Emperor was fairly adamant that he might inadvertently melt my brain in some sort of reflex."

"Ah." I sat back. "That…is a very good reason."

"Yeah, I thought as much. So animals it was."

"Did it work?"

"Took a while, but yes. To an extent." He eyed everyone around us nervously. "Hopefully it's not too dissimilar."

"Okay then," I said, forcing a smile. "What do you need?"

"Just time," he replied, moving to take Ella's hand. "Stay quiet."

Some forty-minutes later he opened his eyes. "It's not her," he said with quiet relief in his voice. "It took a while but I managed to get in there."

"You went through her memories?" I asked nervously, thinking about the pain that such a violation had caused me and he shook his head.

"No. I don't want to go down that road if I can help it. The Emperor said that doing such a thing safely was extremely difficult. All I did was provide a scenario to her that her mind latched onto. The events of it were enough to make me positive that she is not the spy."

"You're sure?"

"Positive." He kissed Ella's brow gently, stood up and made his way to Rikol. "Now for the next suspect."

It took less time this time around; Cassius opening his eyes in less than twenty minutes. "Not him either," he confirmed. "He's got a few things in motion of his own, but he isn't the spy, regardless of how shitty he is being lately."

"We're all being shitty," I replied sadly. "Exactly how the Academy wants."

Cassius cracked his neck from side to side and stifled a yawn. "Need to rest for a moment and replenish my pool."

I cast my eyes at Scythe and Sophia. "They going to be out for long enough?"

"Should be out for another few hours, apparently."

Good enough for me. I gave Cassius the space he needed to recuperate and eventually he moved to Scythe, shaking his head a short time later.

"So," I said softly, turning to face Sophia. "That leaves one."

"Two, actually." He eyed me for a long moment before shaking his head. "But if it's you then I'll eat my sword."

"What makes you so sure?"

He gave a wry smile. "After this long together, I'm fairly certain that I know you better than you know yourself."

That brought a chuckle to my lips and I laughed for the first time in what felt like days. "You probably do," I conceded. "And... thank you."

He gave me a sympathetic smile. "No need for thanks. Even if it won me this mission, I know what you've been through with this stuff...I'm not going to dredge up bad memories if I can help it."

"All the same," I replied, "thanks."

He waved me off and moved to Sophia. "Might as well confirm it."

As he sunk into the trancelike state of a mental seraph user, I studied Sophia carefully. To think it was her! She had been clever in her approach, throwing suspicion on others with far too much ease. It hurt, knowing how easily she had played me. Even though I tried to tell myself that it was necessary for the mission, the betrayal still stung. Perhaps I should have been more like Ella and Rikol, turning aside friendship and past history in favour of distrust and suspicion. That at least, would have potentially stopped her from getting in my head.

In my head. The words echoed around my skull. *Sophia was there when I suggested Cassius use black seraph to read their minds. Could she have taken precautions? What if she set something in place to-"*

It was too late. Cassius spasmed, arching like an electrical shock was running through his body. His chest constricted and his breathing became shallow, like he was fighting to draw in air.

"Cassius!" I cried, jumping to my feet in alarm. "Cassius, wake up!"

Nothing.

Grabbing his shoulders, I shook him hard enough to make his teeth rattle, shouting again. Still nothing.

I slapped him. The sting of the blow rattling my hand and causing a bloom of red to spread across his cheek. Still there was no reaction. No response to my outside interference. He was trapped somehow in his connection to Sophia's mind. At least until his seraph pool ran empty. I eyed Sophia's limp body. *How was she doing this?*

Was it seraph? It had to be. Some trap that she had laid within her mind to ward against exactly this sort of invasion. How I wished that I had learnt such a skill before Endrea had ripped through my mind. Perhaps I could have trapped him in the same state as Cassius was now – even if it hadn't aided my escape it would have been a sweet feeling of victory to have done so. In the depths of my mind, however, I knew that someone as steeped in this sort of skill as Endrea would have been able to break through any paltry defences that I might have put in place.

Cassius though. He was new to this. I knew it. Sophia knew it. *What had she done?*

A groan reached my ears and I swivelled, eyes widening in shock. It was Sophia, somehow stirring despite the effects of the mushroom. Thinking frantically, I willed a thick rope into existence and bound her arms behind her back. Just in time too. Almost as soon as I was done, her eyes snapped into focus and she jerked back and forth, body reacting to the situation before her mind had caught up. Eventually she stilled, realising she was trapped.

"Hello Cal," she grunted, voice weary.

"Sophia," I acknowledged. "Whatever it was you did, nicely done."

Her eyes flickered in Cassius's direction. "I had to plan for all eventualities."

"Obviously. Can you undo it?"

Another flicker. Perhaps a pang of regret flashing across her face. "I can." She said nothing more and I sighed.

"*Will* you undo it?"

"If you untie me and let me go about my business."

"You're willing to hurt Cassius for this game?"

"If you're still thinking of this as a game, Cal," she retorted, tone sharp, "then you're sorely mistaken."

"Fine, you're willing to hurt him for this prize?"

Another flicker of emotion. I could see her visibly steel herself, her muscles clenching as she forced the words out. "If I must."

"The Sophia I knew wouldn't have done that."

"The Sophia you knew has been dying for a long time," she snapped. "We're all being stripped away, piece by bloody piece. You should know; you're just the same."

"Me?"

A tearful snort. "You're colder. More driven. Especially since...you know."

Riven.

"I-" I struggled to avoid the catch in my throat and failed, "I didn't think I had changed that much."

"That's how change happens. It creeps up on you bit by bit, until you look at yourself in the mirror and don't recognise the person you see."

"What about him?" I said, indicating Cassius. "I might be different, but Cassius is always Cassius."

"Do you really believe that?" she asked quietly. "Would the Cassius of old ever have conceded to use his seraph the way he just did?"

No. I knew it deep in my soul and the acknowledgement caused a visceral wave of emotion. Even Cassius had been changed. Become darker. More willing to use tools to his advantage. They had taken the best of us and altered his path. Granted, he was far from becoming a monster, but the weakening of those moral boundaries was enough. Bit by bit, if we weren't careful, we would all do as Sophia said – wake up and realise that we didn't recognise the person in front of the mirror.

Looking back now, I know that I am as different to the Calidan of Wolf's Hollow as he was to the Calidan of that first fateful night so many years ago. The Calidan of Wolf's Hollow still tried to be a better man. He hadn't yet accepted the truth: that he was every bit the monster that he so feared to be. I look into the mirror now and see little but a broken shadow. Shrivelled and weary, driven only by one desire.

Some say that revenge is not enough to sustain you. I know they are wrong. It can keep you company on cold, lonely nights. Force you to take that next shivering step in a frozen wasteland when all other aspects of you want to shut down and give in.

Revenge is a simple but bloody-minded beast.

Just like me.

Sophia saw the answer in my eyes and gave a sad smile. "Not even Cassius has escaped this place unchanged."

I felt a tug against my will as she spoke and concentrated harder, focusing on maintaining the rope around her wrists. "Clever," I said with appreciation. "Attempting to distract me whilst trying to remove the rope."

She grimaced, but the struggle in my mind didn't let up. That was a concern. Sophia was the better seraph user by far. Within Wolf's Hollow, with all of its strange warding, I had only my seraph pool to pull on and she knew that. If I didn't do something quickly then she would just outlast me.

Rising to my feet, I laid a hand against the back of her neck. "Release Cassius."

"No." The will combat grew more strained and I gritted my teeth. Her mental fortitude was almost overwhelming.

"You think I won't do it?"

"I'm banking on it."

I squeezed, putting pressure on the carotid. She jerked, trying to dislodge my fingers, but my grip was iron. Her fight quickly weakened and she collapsed, her head slumping to the floor.

"I guess we all have truly changed," I whispered sadly, releasing my grip. The effects of a blood choke like that were quick to take hold but equally fast to recover from. I didn't have long before she was cognizant.

And she was going to be pissed.

A low groan made me grunt in satisfaction. Cassius had slumped over, the rise and fall of his chest showing that he was breathing more deeply. Good. I had hoped that true unconsciousness would break whatever Sophia had done to him. Seemed like I was right on the money.

The door creaked and I spun, relaxing only slightly when I saw the towering form of Havan enter.

"You've caught the spy then?" he said, his voice surprisingly soft for such a large figure. "Good."

Indicating the slowly moving form of Sophia, I stepped over to Cassius, placing a finger on his neck to check his pulse and hearing Havan step closer. A sudden sensation washed through me. Fear.

What is he doing here? How did he know I had caught the spy? What if-

A blinding pressure suddenly built on the seraph rope and it dragged my attention away from Havan and back towards Sophia, whose eyes glowed with satisfaction. As hands clamped round my own neck a second later, I had just long enough to realise how well I had been played before the colours began to fade and everything went black.

CHAPTER 13
Fracture

"Where is it?" she demanded, snapping fingers in front of my eyes.

"Whe- *ugh* – wha?" My mental faculties were taking a while to spool back up. I clenched my jaw as an ache of pain around my neck made itself known. "What's going on?"

Sophia crossed her arms and scowled. "You tell me." She indicated the safe and I could see that in the time I had been out she had managed to crack it open.

"Well done?" I hazarded uncertainly. "What did you find inside?"

"Nothing!" she hissed.

"Oh..." I pursed my lips. "So maybe the real treasure was the friendships we damaged along the way?"

That, at least, got the intriguing mixture of a scowl and smirk.

"How did you get big boy over there involved?" I asked.

"How do you think?" she muttered distractedly. "Rules didn't say anything about getting others involved. Can buy quite a lot of useful things with an unlimited spending weekend."

"Ahh, bribery." I nodded appreciatively. "Classic. Always someone dumb enough to fall for it."

Havan rose to his feet and the open-handed slap that followed caused my brain to switch-off for a few seconds, only to find Sophia yelling at the big man when I came to.

"-hit tied up people!"

Havan raised a hand. "I'm here only because of our deal. I can hit whoever I want. Especially if they're little buggers who think themselves so much smarter than they are."

His eyes found mine and the menace they held was unsettling. "So choose your words wisely."

"Noted," I groaned. "But you should note that I have a track record of not being wise in these situations."

Unimpressed, his eyes held mine, doubtless waiting for me to flinch away. But I had experienced the horror of being eye-to-eye with the swirling black orbs of a fully-fledged kyrgeth. In comparison to that, this was nothing. I bore the full weight of his gaze resolutely; gifting him a slow smile that forced colour to rush to his cheeks. Before he could take another swing, Sophia stepped in-between us.

"Enough!" she barked. "You two can go and swing your dicks elsewhere later."

"You don't get to talk like that to me," Havan growled dangerously.

Sophia squared up to him, her lithe frame looking fragile against his bulk. "I do when I'm the one who brought you the deal. You don't like it, walk away any time."

Havan muttered under his breath before shaking his head and stalking back to the corner where he rested back against the wall, eyes watching.

"So," I said conversationally, "nothing at all in the safe?"

"Nothing whatsoever."

"Hmm," I mused. "And what are your thoughts?" Sophia cast me a weighing glance and I shrugged. "Come on, it's not like I don't know you're the spy. What damage can it do to talk it through?"

She rolled her eyes, but a small smile touched her lips. "True enough." She pursed her lips then blew out a sigh. "I'm not sure. Torn between one of two options."

"Let me guess. You think either there was never anything in there to begin with, or…"

"Someone got there first," she finished.

I eyed Havan. "Wouldn't put it past the calibre of the Imperators within this place to watch teams destroy themselves over nothing. Has a certain simplicity to it."

"Me neither," agreed Sophia, "but Havan swears that there were documents put in the safe. Considering that failing to retrieve said documents means no easy pay day for him, I feel like his word holds weight."

"Which means option two."

"Indeed."

We stayed silent for a long moment, deep in thought. Eventually Sophia shifted uncomfortably. "About what you said…"

"Which bit?"

"The 'friendships we ruined' comment. I truly hope that isn't the case."

I gifted her a sad smile. "Me neither." Seeing that she wasn't thrilled by my response I continued. "Look, if you're hurting the others then we have problems. But I don't think anything that any of us has done has come close to breaking our friendships. Damaged it? Sure. Mangled it, thrown it on the floor and trampled it? Pretty much. Made us a little less immediately trusting? Definitely. But I know that deep down I can still count on you, Rikol, and the others when I need you most."

"And I, you," she replied softly. "Hopefully that is still the case when we get out of here."

"We just need to make sure that it is."

"You make it sound simple."

"I'm taking a leaf out of Cassius's book. Trying to be horrendously optimistic at all times."

Sophia laughed out loud, a bright sound in the small room. "He is that." Seeing my look, she shook her head. "No, he isn't hurt. Nor was he in any pain."

"What did you do to him?"

"Simple enough, really. It was a trigger ward."

A trigger ward. Something designed to activate based upon a specific action or requirement. I usually utilised them for traps, such as wind runes – not having the patience nor the skill to create something more complex – but they were capable of far more.

"Mental protection is something that the Academy has been teaching more in recent years," she explained, "primarily for those following more traditional Imperator paths. It's pretty sensible; with your capture and what you revealed about Endrea's capabilities, the High Imperator knew that those taking more espionage-based routes were likely to come into contact with those who could wield black seraph. What I put in place was a trigger that was to activate on detection of something encroaching on my mind. I doubt it would have done much to someone skilled with black seraph, but for Cassius? Well," she smirked, "you saw the effects."

"What, precisely, did you do to him?"

She shrugged. "Nothing painful, just temporary shock and paralysis for as long as the seraph I had allocated to the trigger was available, as well as a warning to your friend over there." She nodded in the direction of the glowering Imperator. "Thankfully that bought me enough time for Havan to come and provide assistance."

"Impressive," I breathed. That type of seraph control was far beyond my skill and I wasn't sure I would ever manage such a feat. Maybe in the future.

Hah! I remember when I was that much of a dreamer. As a wiser, more grizzled and much more scarred man, I can say with conviction that my current skill with seraph still leaves a lot to be desired. The nuance for such trigger-related constructions is not my forte. Give me simple and straightforward any day.

Sophia blushed. "Not that impressive," she said, waving a hand. "Most of these lot can do it, just didn't have it in place before Cassius got his claws into them."

"Well, for his sake, I'm glad they didn't. One bad surprise was probably enough." I cast my eyes over the others. "So, who do you think got to it first?"

"Ella or Rikol," she replied without hesitation. "If I had to guess, I would say Rikol. He has the power and skill to do something like that without too much effort."

"Not Scythe?"

She shook her head. "Scythe's strengths lie elsewhere, as you know. He isn't one for disappearing the contents of a safe...unless he was throwing the entire safe away."

"I agree."

Sophia stiffened and turned towards the sound of the voice. Rikol was sitting up, the ropes falling off his hands.

"How?" she asked, open-mouthed.

"Something similar to your own trigger, I suspect," Rikol said with a mischievous grin. "Removes toxins et cetera, et cetera. But I digress. Ella, you ready?"

"Ready," she said, her position unchanged and eyes still closed.

"Excellent."

Sophia narrowed her eyes, doubtless pulling seraph. "What are you- arghh!" Her words turned into a scream as she fell through the floor.

Ella relaxed, sweat beading on her body, and the portal that had briefly opened beneath Sophia closed like it had never been.

Havan stepped forward menacingly but Rikol raised a hand. "One moment." Brow furrowing in concentration he wobbled on his feet, then relaxed. "Damn, that's harder down here than expected." Seeing Havan take another step he held up both hands. "Easy, the game's done."

"Done?" I asked.

"Yep," he confirmed happily.

His sudden happiness raised the hairs on the back of my neck. "What did you do?"

He winked. "Easy, deposited Sophia somewhere secure, thus removing the spy, and then dropped the documents in to Carmine."

Groaning, I shook my head. "So that means...?"

"Precisely," he winked. "You're looking at the person getting a blade made and an all-expenses trip to Anderal."

Ella coughed and Rikol inclined his head. "Of course, not to forget my dashing partner in crime. The master of misdirection, Ella!" He dropped the act and grinned. "That portal was exquisitely timed."

"Thank you kindly," she replied softly. "I had plenty of time to prep it."

Havan, who appeared to be having a private conversation of his own, chose this moment to turn and leave without a further word, slamming the door behind him.

"That would be Carmine informing him that the challenge is over, I expect," said Rikol. "How about we wake these two up and go and see about my reward, eh?"

"Hang on a second," I declared. "What did you do with Sophia?"

"Put her where she couldn't do any harm," Ella answered happily.

"A locked store cupboard on the first floor," added Rikol. "Layered with a few traps that were designed to go off as soon as movement was detected. With any luck she will be out for the count."

It all came together in a flurry. "You set this up," I declared slowly, voice getting firmer as I grew more positive. "You've had the documents the entire time, haven't you?"

His smile was all the answer I needed.

"Let me guess, when you set up an alarm around it?"

"Too obvious," he replied. "And not even I am that good. No," he shook his head, "the alarm worked as advertised but with the added bonus of allowing me to test the wards within the safe. It took a few hours but eventually I managed to bypass them. At that point it was a relatively simple matter to transport them somewhere secure."

"And when did you bring Ella onboard?"

"Immediately," he answered, giving her a wink. "Of everyone here, I knew that I could trust a thief to be a thief. Both of us would want to get the big haul. Rather than working against each other, we could do it together and split the pot."

"People say that thieves don't prosper," Ella added. "But that's not true. Only the stupid ones don't. Those who survive learn that the best scores are those often done with a team."

"And so, between the two of you, you always had someone up here keeping an eye on things or working on the safe, whilst the other was…what?"

"Talking with Carmine," said Rikol. "Refining the particulars of the contest, such as determining at what point the 'spy' would be classed as incapacitated and thus the title would transfer to me. The store cupboard was next to Carmine's room. As soon as he had my signal, he checked that Sophia was contained, then received the documents."

"Crowning you as the winner," I finished, impressed. "Congratulations!"

"Best not forget our deal," Ella said, voice sweet but eyes holding a hint of ice.

"Of course not," waved off Rikol. "I pay my debts."

The next hour passed in a blur. Carmine came in with a disgruntled and dishevelled Sophia in tow and officially announced Rikol the winner. Scythe and Cassius came round and were quickly brought up to speed. To anyone watching it might have seemed like the team were one again but the laughter rang hollow to my ears. Scythe kept distant from Sophia, who in turn kept distant from everyone – frustrated at her failure. Cassius gave a half-hearted congratulations to the winner and then withdrew into himself and I knew precisely what he was thinking about: how he had broken his ideals in the name of this game. That was bad enough, in his book, but what was worse was that it hadn't even been worth doing. Rikol and Ella had been one step ahead the entire time.

We took our things back from the safe-room and retreated to the dorm. There the silence built, interspersed only by the low talking and victorious exultations of the winners. Long after they fell asleep I knew that eyes lay open, thinking of what might have happened, how they had failed and whether it had damaged themselves or their relationships.

We were fracturing. Close to the brink.

And all it would take was one little push.

CHAPTER 14

SLEEPWALKING

"Calidan, wake up. Wake up!"

I grunted, startled awake by the shaking hands.

"Cassius?" I asked groggily. "What's going on?"

"It's Scythe," he hissed. "He's gone rogue."

Shaking my head in confusion, I blinked sleepily at him. Everything seemed a little blurry. Strange. A hand caught me across the face. "Ow!"

"Focus!"

I had never seen Cassius like this. Determined. Furious. Terrified. "What do you mean?" I demanded; the slap having taken some of the fuzziness from my mind.

"He's left. The Imperators are saying that he has stolen something. Something important."

I let out a laugh. "Scythe? Are you out of your mind?"

"That's not all," he hissed, "there are bodies outside, Calidan. Bodies!"

The laughter faded from my lips. "...What?"

"You heard me. We need to go. We need to go right now!"

He pulled me up and I swung up out of the bed. "The others?"

"Already gone."

Strange. Why would they be... the fuzziness returned and I shook my head again. *What was I thinking? Never mind. Need to focus!*

"Let's go," I declared after quickly pulling on some trousers. "Where are these bodies?"

"Just outside."

"Strange, I can't smell any blood." It hit me almost as soon as I said it, the tang of coppery metal lacing through the air. "Never mind, I've got it."

Cassius opened the door and leapt outside and I followed, lunging into a world of flashing lights, shifting smoke and...he hadn't been joking. The bodies were there, arterial blood dripping from the walls. I turned a corpse over – it was an Imp I didn't recognise – the body lacerated with small, deep wounds, and fought back a sudden roiling in my stomach. The wounds were precisely like those inflicted by Scythe's weapons.

"This...this can't be," I breathed.

"I didn't want to believe it either," grunted Cassius by my side. "But the facts speak for themselves."

"There has to be a reason..."

He scoffed. "A reason for this?!" He indicated the blood and the bodies. "What possible reason could there be?!"

I shook my head again, feeling that fuzziness flooding back for a moment. "I-I don't know."

"If we want answers then we need to track him down. Find him. Stop him." Cassius's voice was as hard as iron.

"Kill him?" I questioned in horror. "Kill Scythe?"

"If that is what it takes."

"We've known him for years!"

He pursed his lips grimly. "If he has betrayed the Academy, then he has betrayed the Emperor. He's killed people, Calidan. This is just like Rya. He is too dangerous to let go free. He needs to be stopped."

I glared at my friend. "What has got into you?" I demanded. "Since when have you been okay with killing your friends at the first opportunity? I can't imagine..." the haze thickened and my mind stilled.

Everything went black.

"Calidan, wake up. Wake up!"

"If we want answers then we need to track him down. Find him. Stop him."

"Kill him?"

Cassius shook his head. "Not if we can avoid it. But…" he waved his arms helplessly, "look at what has been done! We need to get to the bottom of this. Now."

"Agreed." I stood up and spread out my senses. They felt strangely muted, but I pushed on, listening and scenting for anything that might be Scythe. "Fresh blood," I murmured. "Follow me!"

Together we ran through the darkness. The world seeming to constrict to just the walls and tunnels that we ran through. How long we ran, I don't know, but the bodies on the ground just made me more convinced that Scythe had to be stopped. Why had he done this? Was it the pressure? His fight with Sophia? Or was it something else? Had he ever truly been our friend?

We intercepted him at the great metal door that separated Wolf's Hollow from the outside world. Another Imp lay dead at his feet, face a bloody and unrecognisable mess.

"Scythe!" I yelled. "What are you doing?!"

He stiffened, hunching his shoulders tight, but didn't reply.

"Why have you done this?" I shouted again.

"Because it needs to be done." His voice was low, almost unrecognisable with the complete lack of warmth.

I took a step forward and he slowly raised a kama, the blade still dripping with fresh blood. "Stay there Calidan. Let me go. Or else."

Stopping where I was, I spread my hands. "Easy Scythe. Just tell me what's going on."

"There's nothing to say."

I wrinkled my nose, trying to be as casual in the disturbing setting as possible. "There has to be something that has started this."

He let out a laugh devoid of any emotion, as hollow as the mountain that surrounded us. "Does there truly have to be a reason?"

"Of course there does. You've been a staunch advocate of the Academy for years. There is nothing that I or any of the Academy members wouldn't trust you with. So, what's happened?"

"And if I told you that there wasn't a reason?" he murmured darkly. "Just a desire to leave. To escape this place, this Academy, this life? What then?"

"I don't believe that."

"You should."

"You're a complex man, Scythe. We all have dark sides, hells," I snorted, "I know that as much as anyone, but please, *please*," I pleaded now, "this isn't the answer. You can still come back from this. Just give me the weapons."

His back quivered and I thought for a moment I had got through to him, then I heard the dark, sibilant laugh, the sound pressing against me like it had corporeal form.

"No. **No.**" His voice took on a deeper timbre and realisation struck me.

"Oh no." I whispered. "Nonononono."

Scythe gave up on working the lever to exit the building and turned, showing a pale, black-veined face and apocalyptic eyes. **"There's no coming back from this, Calidan. Join me."**

Unbidden, I took a step back. "Scythe. Please tell me that you're in there."

No answer. Just another bout of cackling laughter.

"Oh gods," moaned Cassius. "We need to stop him Calidan."

"It's Scythe!" I shouted angrily.

"Not anymore," he argued, unsheathing Asp. "He's gone. You know it as well as I."

Scythe took another step and I stiffened, raising Vona between us. "Stop there Scythe. Stop and surrender."

"Never."

"Don't make me do this, Scythe!" my voice quivered now.

"Then stand still and die."

He leapt forwards, kama flashing. Parrying desperately, I pulled on everything I had to get Vona moving fast enough to contain the whirlwind that was my friend. Cassius struck from the side and the assault let up slightly. Scythe was everywhere at once, overwhelming us with sheer strength and speed, his muscles steaming as he channelled seraph. A blur of motion and Cassius slammed into the nearby wall. Scythe spun towards me, abyssal eyes burrowing into my soul. We clashed, sparks flying from our blades. Breaking apart we clashed from a second time, then a third.

"Kill him, Calidan!" shouted Cassius as he picked himself out of the wall.

I don't want to.

"Kill him, before he kills again!"

Please don't make me.

"Kill him!"

Scythe spun. I parried. Vona shrieked. Stilled. Black liquid bubbled out of the corner of Scythe's mouth as he clutched at the blade buried in his chest.

"Scythe," I moaned, falling to my knees with him. "Scythe, I'm so sorry. So, so sorry."

The fuzziness rose up once more and this time I let it claim me.

"Scythe! Scythe, no!" I woke up flailing, drenched in sweat.

A head popped over the bunkbed. "Will you keep it down!" Rikol hissed. "And stop that thrashing around."

"But- but Scythe."

"What about him?" he demanded, pointing over the other side of the room. "He's right there. What do you want him for?"

I turned and saw him there, slowly sitting up as the commotion roused him from slumber. "Scythe?"

"Yeah?" He mumbled sleepily. "What?"

"You…you…" Everything felt jumbled. Fuzzy. Why did I want to speak to Scythe again? There had been something so vivid in my grasp just a second ago that was now little more than a shadow of its former self. "I.." my words failed me.

"Truly well said," Rikol growled. "Can't even wake us for something good."

"I-I didn't mean."

"No, you didn't mean anything," he agreed. "Lie down and go to sleep."

The words seemed sensible, so I did as he ordered. In moments I was asleep.

It's a terrifying and debilitating thing to dread going to sleep. It didn't happen every night, but sometimes I would catch myself jolting awake, tears on my face or clutching my chest like I had been struck through.

Maybe I had.

I wasn't the only one either. One by one, each of us began to suffer from this strange affliction. Unable to remember what had happened but terrified or weeping on waking, often calling out for other dorm-member's names. We each became wraith-like versions of our former selves, taking refuge in the day, dosing heavily on caffeine in the hope of staying awake longer, but inevitably falling prey to the dastardly foe that was sleep.

Not that my waking hours were much better, mind. Everything always felt so fuzzy. So...off. Like the world was covered in a thin haze. I knew that my heart rate was slightly elevated, my skin more often prone to breaking out into sweat. The others were much the same. If I didn't know better, I would think that we were being drugged, but there was nothing that I could smell that suggested we had been dosed with anything. The water and food all seemed the same as normal, meaning if we were being drugged then it was with an undetectable agent, or via a means that I had yet to come across.

But what other options were there?

And if we were being drugged...why? I could only imagine that we were being subjected to something akin to the torture games that Carmine put me through, but we had all completed that class. This had to be something new. And to so often have the names of our friends on our lips as we woke...it couldn't be good.

Cassius

Cassius sat up, chest heaving, unwiped tears trailing down his cheeks. He heard the others startle at the commotion and then settle back down; used by now to the disrupted sleep. He didn't pay them much attention though. No. His focus was on the memory still bouncing around his skull. A memory of broken friendship, distrust and despair.

He waited for the memory to fade like it had every time before.

A minute later a small smile broke through the clouds of his face. Ten minutes later, he was sure.

He had done it. His control of black seraph had grown enough to allow him this small victory.

He remembered.

Half an hour later, he didn't want to. Wanted to tear the thought of what had happened out of his brain. Even though he knew, *knew* that his friends were still here, still acting normally and, perhaps most importantly, were still alive, he couldn't help but look at Rikol and shudder. He had seen what he had done. The blood and the carnage.

Knowing it was an illusion helped, but in their own way those events had been real. He had lived those moments, had them burned into his very mind. Heard the manic laugh as Rikol tore through Imps like paper...as he had torn Cassius's spine from his still living body.

Why did the Imperators want to test them like this? What purpose did it serve?

Did he even want to know? Did it benefit them to know what was happening?

After a few minutes he stiffened his resolve. There was a reason behind what was being done to them, he was sure of it. The Academy always did things for a reason, no matter how strange their methods. He would keep his defences up and seek to remember everything that he was put through.

Perhaps, in time, it would all make sense.

CHAPTER 15

MIND GAMES

"What are you doing to us?"

Imperator Carmine looked up from his poached eggs on toast, a slightly confused and irritated expression on his face. "Ah, Calidan. To what do I owe the pleasure?"

"My dorm," I growled, ignoring the other Imperators sitting nearby. "What's going on?"

"Whatever do you mean?" he asked faux-innocently, his smile too sickly, his voice too sweet.

I slammed my hand on the table, causing everyone in the cafeteria to turn their heads. "You damn well know what I mean!" I shouted, full well knowing that I must have looked a sight; hair unkept, eyes bloodshot and wild. Even looking at myself in the mirror this morning had been hard enough.

Carmine's eyes narrowed. "Now, Calidan, there is a certain decorum here that you are failing to meet. The cafeteria is a safe place, a place of refuge for those that have no desire to listen to your shit. If you insist on having this conversation, we can meet in my office-"

"Now." It wasn't a threat. Wasn't a promise. But somehow I managed to put enough force and willpower into that word that even Carmine looked taken aback before he rolled his eyes, sighed and stood up, taking his plate with him.

"Fine. Come along."

A few minutes later we were ensconced in his office and Carmine turned furious eyes on me. "You don't get to order me around boy. You should consider yourself lucky that you even get to speak to me. Never, and I mean *never* do that again. Not if you ever want to get out of here."

I crossed my arms and didn't respond, just watched. Perhaps Carmine saw that I was too tired to care. Too on-edge to think straight. Either way, he stopped his tirade and perched behind his desk, taking another bite of egg as he did so.

"Disregarding your ridiculous actions," he muttered around a mouthful, "is there something specific you wish to discuss?"

"Our dreams."

His nod was a pleasant confirmation of sorts. It lifted a small weight off my mind. We hadn't been going crazy. Or at least, not of our own accord.

Small things.

"What do you think it is?" he asked casually.

"I don't care! I just want it to stop."

"Oh, it will stop. Of that you can be sure." He gave me a broad, insincere smile. "Just not yet."

"When?"

"When we're happy with the results."

"So, it's all part of your testing?"

He snorted. "Of course it's part of our testing. If you haven't realised this already Calidan, then you are a bigger idiot than I took you for, but you should consider *everything* here to be a test. Didn't Kane tell you that when you arrived?" I opened my mouth to answer but he shook his head and continued, "I imagine you just didn't listen, like the complete imbecile you are. To set your mind at ease, yes what is happening to you is part of our testing. No, there is nothing you can do about it."

"What are you doing to us?"

He shrugged. "Simple enough really, just running some tests. Checking loyalty. How you respond in certain scenarios, that kind of thing."

"Why can't we remember what happened?"

"Oh, I really wouldn't recommend trying to do that," he wheedled. "We're running an explicit number of tests. Some scenarios are…unpleasant. We see how you are in the moment, but because we are kind and generous souls, we make sure you wake up without the memory of what happened. People tend to have…adverse reactions to the scenarios if they remember them."

Something about that didn't sit right with me and I shook my head. "You've never cared about that before, so what's changed?"

He eyed me thoughtfully for a long moment, chewing a particularly crunchy piece of seeded toast as he did so. Finally, he swallowed his mouthful and grimaced. "You're right. We don't usually care about it, however we find these scenarios are most effective when you believe it's completely real. And as we like to repeat certain aspects of the scenarios, making you forget what you have experienced already just makes life easier for yours truly. Besides, it's not like you're truly forgetting everything."

My eyes narrowed. "What do you mean?"

His shit-eating grin spread over his face like a cancer that I really wanted to punch. "How have you been feeling about your friends lately? A little more wary perhaps? Something just not-quite-right?"

"What. Did. You. Do?"

"Nothing!" he cackled. "I just sit back and watch the show. But you lot...well, you're real pieces of work when the situation calls for it."

"Gods, I hate you."

His grin became frozen yet his eyes twinkled. *He was enjoying this*, I realised. *He likes having the upper hand over me.* "I assure you, young master Calidan," he said softly, eyes boring into mine, "that the feeling is entirely mutual. Now," he stuffed down another bite of egg and toast, chewing rapidly before swallowing, "if we're done, kindly fuck off."

I obliged.

⚔

"-ould have trusted me!"

"Trusted you? You were the spy!"

"Not about that, about me. Us!"

I sighed, taking my hand away from the dorm room handle and stepping away. Scythe and Sophia were at it once more. The two had always had a somewhat *passionate* relationship, alternating between hurling insults and ridiculously loud lovemaking, often within the same day, sometimes at the *same time*. This though...this was something else. Never had I heard either of them sound so wounded. Though nothing untoward had happened, the fact that neither had trusted the other during the latest game had led to some spectacular fights over the last few days.

Shaking my head, I turned away just in time to see Cassius walk around the corner of the corridor. "Cass," I called, "hey!"

He froze like a startled rabbit, expression looking for all the world like he didn't want to see me. Now that I took the time to properly study him, the shadows around his eyes seemed even darker than usual, his expression haunted.

"H-hey, Calidan." He gave what might have passed as a cheerful wave, his expression lightening as he plastered a fake smile onto his face. To anyone who hadn't known him for years it might have worked, but to me the attempt fell as flat as Scythe's comedy.

I eyed him suspiciously and the smile fell from his face as quickly as it had come. "What's going on?" I asked eventually.

"N-nothing," he replied. "Just tired, that's all."

"We're all tired, but you look like you haven't slept in days." I stepped in close and lowered my voice to a whisper. "What's really going on?"

Whatever paltry defence he had erected crumbled. "I don't think you would believe me."

"Try me."

Looking around, he checked the corridors and then grabbed my arm. "Not here," he muttered. "Come with me." Half-dragging me along behind him, he pulled me to an empty corridor on the far side of the complex, as far away as possible from the dorm, then stood there, eyes shifting nervously.

"Okay, this is the part where you start talking," I said gently, punching him on the shoulder.

"I know what we're forgetting."

That got my attention. "Our dreams?"

"Not dreams," he said with a shake of his head. "Not really."

I let out a long sigh. "Let me guess. Carmine."

Looking up, he forced a grin. "That was quick. What gave it away?"

"Drug-addled brain and something happening to our minds? Not exactly hard to guess. It's pretty much his thing. Honestly, I'm more surprised that he makes us forget."

"I think there's probably a reason for that," he muttered darkly. "At least, for the moment."

"So, what is he doing?"

"Making us betray each other."

"Classic."

Cassius snorted. "More serious betrayal though. The kind that ends in one of us hunting the other."

"To what end?"

"Death." The weight he gave to the word made the hairs on the back of my neck raise. I placed my hand on his shoulder and noted how tense he was. "Who have you fought?"

"That I remember? Rikol, Sophia...you."

"That must have sucked. Can't be fun fighting friends to the death."

He snorted morosely. "Not too much fun when you're dying. Carmine is...creative with his illusions."

I shook my head in frustrated anger. "Of course he is. What a prick. You could always choose to join us in forgetting though, right?"

He eyed me. "Would you?"

"I don't know. Probably not. But that reminds me," I cocked my head at him curiously, "how *are* you remembering?"

"The shit that runs through my veins counts for something," he spat. "Learning how to get into minds has helped me in other ways. Whilst I haven't been able to stop Carmine from getting into my mind in the first place, I have been successful in stopping him from altering my memory."

I whistled. "That sounds tough."

He grimaced. "Not easy. He is...skilled with his techniques."

"Do you think he knows?"

"I *know* that he knows," he responded. "But I don't think he particularly cares."

Of course he wouldn't. I nodded slowly, deep in thought. "If there is one thing that we can count on, it's that Carmine is and always will be a prick."

"Pretty sure that everyone in the complex would agree with that," he replied sardonically. "Even the other Imperators."

"I mean, obviously, but my main concern is that whilst he could be making us remember our interactions with our illusionary brethren...he *isn't*."

"No, but-"

"-This is a man who has taught us to torture. Who has systematically played us against each other at every available opportunity. So why in the world, when he is literally getting us to kill each other, isn't he making us remember all of it?"

"Because we are remembering," Cassius said hoarsely. "I don't know how it fits into his plan, but we are remembering. Or our bodies are. Haven't you felt it? The distrust, the crawling in your skin when you're close to one of the dorm? Your body remembers the stress of the hunt, the horror of the fight."

"And how does that benefit him?"

He shrugged. "Perhaps it makes us all that little bit more suspicious, which is just what they want in an Imperator. Perhaps he knows that if one of us remembers then the fight becomes one-sided, which might not be as useful to him."

"...You mean?"

He nodded, eyes dark. "I refuse to fight. I have to say, dying isn't a fun experience, even if it's not real."

I didn't know what to say to that, just reached out and placed a comforting hand on his shoulder. "I'm so sorry Cass, I hate that you're going through this."

He gave a brittle smile. "We're all going through it. I'm just choosing to remember the shit that he is putting us through. There has to be a reason for it. I refuse to believe otherwise."

"I prefer to keep circling back to the man being a gigantic prick," I retorted.

"Never going to disagree with that."

We sat in silence for a few minutes and I pretended not to notice as tears rolled down Cassius's cheeks. "You should stop," I whispered finally. "Stop remembering."

"And let him run amok in my mind without recourse?"

"He already is," I countered. "Look at what it's doing to you. You're barely holding it together." I locked eyes with him. "And I mean that in the nicest way."

"I'm fine," he grunted.

"Bullshit."

"I'm *fine*," he insisted. "It just...takes a while to get over."

"Your death at the hands of a friend," I replied drily. "Yes, I can see that being somewhat painful to get over. You could always fight back?"

"I'm not going to kill my friends," he snarled.

"We're illusionary!" The two of us stopped for a moment at that and I cocked my head. "Sometimes illusionary? Whatever. You know what I mean. If you know that none of us are going to get hurt, why not fight back?"

"Because it isn't right."

It was my turn to snort. "Nothing about this is right. Take out of the scenario whatever you can. Use it." It was my turn for my expression to become grim. "You never know what might happen in the future."

Perhaps unsurprisingly, it was not the right thing to say.

"You can't be serious!" Cassius exploded, face carving itself into a picture of righteous anger. "You think that one of us could seriously betray the others?!"

I raised my hands up placatingly. "No," I said gently. "I don't think that anyone in the dorm as we currently are will betray or actively seek to hurt one of the others. But that's kind of the point isn't it? The Academy is looking to change us. To mould us into something more beneficial to their ranks. We've all heard the stories of Imperators hunting other Imperators. Hells, we've seen it happen first hand!"

"That wasn't the same, that was Rya-"

"That *was* the same," I insisted. "It could just as easily happen to one of us. What happens if one of us gets controlled by the Enemy, Cass? We've seen what they can do. Would you let Sophia, Rikol, Scythe, me or even Ella run amok, killing as we pleased?"

"...No." The word was little more than a whisper.

"Then if you've fought this hard to retain your memories, make use of the time. Learn to fight us. Or, more accurately, learn to fight Carmine's impressions of us. Which, now that I think about it, is probably more useful."

His brow furrowed at that. "How so?"

"Way I see it, unless the Enemy has ransacked someone's mind and knows everything about them, if He has taken direct control then He is controlling His version of them. Maybe He knows exactly how they hunt or fight, but I doubt it. As dark and as shit as this is, it could be valuable practice."

He sighed and rubbed his temples. "I hate this."

"Welcome to the club," I replied with a small grin. "We should have a flag that says 'we hate Carmine' on the side."

"Not just Carmine," he said with a shake of his head. "All of it. This entire place."

"Ah, a revision to the flag is in order then. How about...'Fuck Wolf's Hollow'"?

This time his smile was genuine. "That's more like it." He stood and gripped my arm, staring intently into my eyes. "We're going to get through this, all of us. Fuck Wolf's Hollow."

I gripped his arm hard and bumped heads. "We're all in this together. Fuck Wolf's Hollow...and Carmine too, because he's a little shit."

Cassius snorted at that. "Bit long to stick on a flag, isn't it?"

Spreading my arms wide, I adopted what I envisaged to be a wizardly voice that radiated power and self-importance. "I am a master of the arcane. There is no limit to the size of flag that I can create!"

He actually burst out laughing at that one. "You, a master of seraph?" he forced out between heaving breaths. "That'll be the day."

"I admit, it seems far away right now. But, who knows, maybe one day I can knock Rikol off his perch. Hells, why stop there? I'll aim higher, the Powers better watch out!"

"The day you do that is the day the world ends," Cassius mocked gently, shaking his head in amusement.

It was nice that I still had some belief in my skills back then, but now I'm a realist - I'm about as far away from being a master of seraph as one can get. The end of the world though? That I might just be able to wrangle.

PRESENT DAY 4

"Not bad. Not bad at all."

I looked up at the Wanderer's musings, her eyes wide with excitement as she inspected the freshly acquired star-metal. "You were right, Asol had quite a bit."

"Of course he would. He's Asol," she said matter-of-factly. "He always has to have the best. He probably moved heaven and earth to acquire as much as he did, even though he will have kept it secret from everyone."

"Reckon it's enough?"

She shook her head emphatically. "It's going to take us a long way to our goal, but no. We need everything we can get our hands on to make sure that this works. Remember, we only get one shot at this. One. If we go into it half-cocked…" she grimaced, "well, you know."

"We die."

"At the best, we die once only."

"Been there before," I muttered darkly. At her considering look I shrugged. "Not the first time I've run afoul of pissed-off Powers."

"No…" she mused, a smirk curling across her lips. "I imagine not."

"Any movement on your end?"

Straightening up, she chucked the two lumps of metal that I had worked so hard to acquire almost carelessly over her shoulder. A plant with red petals each the size of my chest opened up and refurled around the objects. I should have been used to the casual expenditure of power by now, but it never got old. The Wanderer wielded seraph like it was second nature, her will manifesting almost before she realised she was doing it.

Powers…they definitely earnt the title many times over.

"I've scouted two locations. Neither have the technology I'm after to help with Cassius." Looking sad at my crestfallen expression, she offered a conciliatory smile. "*However,* they did have a few indicators of other potentially intact facilities, ones that I will explore in due course. I have high hopes for one of them in particular – to the best of my knowledge it hasn't been utilised by any of the Powers across the millennia."

"And you're sure such a place would have the technology required to help Cassius?" I asked eagerly.

"No." Her reply was like a punch to the stomach. Swift and uncompromising. "I can't guarantee anything. However, most bunkers had medical facilities. If they don't then there might be something that can be used to help fabricate something that will help."

"I don't follow."

She let out a sigh. "Blueprints. Information. As you know, with enough understanding of an object you can create it through seraph. Which is why I'm eager to get stuck into the documents you stole from Asol – good thinking on that by the way."

Shrugging, I grinned. "Seemed like a waste to let it stay there."

"Of course." Looking over at the leather satchels I had stuffed full of documents she grinned. "It might take a while to decipher it all, but I've seen enough of Asol's encryption style over the years that I'm confident I will be able to break it."

"Ah, so that's what it is? Some kind of code?"

"Some kind of code, but written in a language six millennia dead. The hardest part is going to be remembering the blasted thing. Mathan'dok wasn't exactly a popular language at the best of times."

"I'm impressed you can remember its name! That wasn't exactly a short time ago."

"Are you calling me old?" She grinned. "You would be right to, but remember this – no matter how old a lady is, suggesting she might be old is never a good plan."

"Fine, fine, I take it back." I raised my hands in supplication. "I wouldn't want to tax your brain with more memories of *ancient* history."

The massive form of Eleothean, the Wanderer's bonded bear, chuffed at that, knocking his massive head into her side as though to say 'he got you there.'

The Wanderer tried to keep a straight face but couldn't handle it, breaking down completely with raucous laughter. Tears ran down her face as she gasped for air, joy clearly evident on her face.

Snorting, I shook my head. "I didn't think it was *that* funny."

"D-do y-you know how long it has been since someone spoke to me like that?" She wiped her tears away and snorted. "Almost never. Eleothean makes the odd comment but as an extension of my own soul he doesn't really count." She rolled her eyes. "It's funny. When I first began my journey of amassing power, I didn't really care for small talk. With my petite frame I wanted people to take me seriously, often keeping separate and aloof. By the time we all crept out of our caves post-Cataclysm there weren't that many people left and when I became as strong as I am...well, you can imagine." Shaking her head, she smiled wryly. "It's strange the things you miss when you have everything you could possibly desire."

"Do you think the others are similar?"

"The other Powers? Sure. But," her gaze narrowed, "whilst I might laugh at being called old, don't ever, *ever*, suggest that to Rizaen. You would be ash before the last syllable left your mouth."

I cocked an eyebrow. "She's an ageless Power. Why would she become angry over something so petty?"

"Sometimes, even when you have the world in the cusp of your hand and the power to shake the very fabric of reality, words can still hurt. Especially truthful ones."

"I'll try to remember that."

"Do better than try," she replied, all hint of laughter gone. "The Dusk Court is not known for laughter and Rizaen is not known for leniency."

"I know that all too well."

"Ah, yes of course you do. Apologies, but it makes the point nicely. Your companion met his end at the behest of Rizaen. Not so much because of the damage he inflicted or the deaths he caused but because of the damage to *her pride*. She is nothing if not a prideful being. Remember that and tread carefully."

"Understood." Unbidden, memories of Scythe rose to the surface and I struggled to force them back down. Watching me closely, the Wanderer shook her head sadly.

"I have made you revisit bad memories. Sorry."

"Not necessarily bad," I muttered. "Just...sad."

"We all miss those we have lost. Often we feel like we have moved on and then the simplest thing; a scent or an object can throw us right back into the deepest loss." Sighing, she cracked her neck from side to side and moved to stroke Eleothean's massive neck. "It is well. I have work to do and things to plan. You should get some rest and we can get back to this tomorrow." I was about to protest when she gave me a pointed look and I shrank back. "Remember, Rome wasn't built in a day. We can't afford to rush this. Relax and sleep. We'll plan tomorrow. After all," she winked, "I think stealing from Rizaen might be one of the more cathartic moments for you."

Snorting, I lay down on the moss bed and stared into the sky above. It took a long time for sleep to come, mainly because of one question.

What in the twin-hells was Rome?

CHAPTER 16

Fuck Wolf's Hollow

"We're fighting each other in our dreams?" Scythe asked, eyebrow raised. "Why?"

"Not each other. Carmine's impression of us," I clarified. "And because he is a complete and utter twat, that's why."

He stared at me for a moment and then shrugged. "Makes as much sense as anything else I suppose."

"...Does it?" Cassius this time, eyeing him curiously. "Does it really?"

"Meh, we all know Carmine is a cunt and we're all feeling the effects of drugs and feeling more than a little bit inhospitable towards each other, so in all honestly I'm quite happy that there is an answer at all, even better that it doesn't state we're all having a psychotic episode."

"I'm surprised you even know what one of those is," Sophia jibed.

He scowled. "I read."

A snort. "When there are pictures!"

Cassius and I left them to their bickering and turned to Rikol and Ella. "Make sense?"

The two shared a look and then nodded. "I had suspected as much," Rikol said, an air of haughtiness to his words. "Seraph and Carmine were practically the only things that made sense."

Ella levelled a flat stare at Rikol's back before turning to us and rolling her eyes. Trying hard not to smile, I nodded at Rikol's words. "Well, now that you know, you can sorcerer up some spell or something to protect us from these mental attacks, right?"

"I-ugh...maybe?" He rubbed at the stubble on his chin. "I'll have to give it some thought."

"You do that," I replied with a grin before raising my voice so everyone could hear. "Just remember, you know what is going on now, so try to remember that we are all friends. We're going to support each other through this and make it out the other side. Carmine will not break us."

"Carmine will not break us," they repeated, standing ever so slightly straighter.

"It's all just illusion."

"...all illusion."

"Fuck Wolf's Hollow!"

"Fuck Wolf's Hollow!" the roar came back tenfold and I hoped that somewhere in the facility Carmine heard it and despaired. We wouldn't be broken. Not this dorm and not this easily. We may be battered and worn, but we knew his games now. We could handle anything he threw our way.

Oh, how terribly naïve.

"You've been here four months," Carmine simpered, eyes darting over us. "Four months and you are barely hatched from your cocoons. You have yet to truly spread your wings and take flight, to become that which you need to be. But together, we shall get you there. Or, well," he smirked, "you die trying I suppose."

What inspirational words.

"So far you have only been in competition with each other. Members of your own dorm. It might almost seem as though Wolf's Hollow is empty when you pass through its halls, but there are pockets of others who have not yet managed to achieve the level required to be an Imperator, nor to fail so completely and utterly as to have died or been removed. I know you have seen these individuals. I imagine that some of you might even know them. I suspect all of this and I do not care. You do not want to end up in the position that they are in; damaged goods, desperate to leave by any means necessary. Some might say that one or two of them might do *anything* to survive." His eyes flashed with barely suppressed amusement.

"From now on, the others will be in direct competition with you. You each will have a single tag," he held up a round disc made of some dark metal. "Hold onto your tag for a week and you get the option to complete the final exam in two months' time. Lose your tag and you will be here for another four months *at the minimum.*"

Scythe raised a hand. "And what happens to those who have managed to take the tag from us and hold it?"

"Simple. They get to take the final exam again."

"And you're not going to tell us what that exam entails, are you?"

Carmine smirked. "Of course not, that would ruin all the fun. No, the final exam is special and preparations need to be made. Only a certain number of people can be given the opportunity at any one time."

"And what does failure of that exam entail?" Scythe asked nervously.

"Oh, let's not go into all that, shall we? Suffice to say that those who are targeting you are hungry to leave this place. Moreover, they know what their final challenge is, so if they are prepared to hunt you down expect there to be no mercy."

"Sir?" Ella this time.

"Yes?"

"No mercy, sir?"

"Ah, well. The usual rules. Death is not particularly welcome, but we all understand that accidents do happen. Anything and everything else goes. The last time we ran this particular game we had..." he pursed his lips and tapped his chin in thought, "three people end up in the infirmary. One seriously enough wounded that we had to ship her back to Anderal." He must have noted the horrified expressions on our faces as he spread his arms wide and roared with laughter. "What? You're surprised it can go that far? Well listen up boys and girls, you're in the big leagues now. You want to get out, you do so by being the best. Or ganging up on the best and breaking their legs. Simple!"

"When exactly do we need to hold this disc until?" asked Ella. "And is there any benefit to having more than one?"

"Ooh, *excellent* question!" Carmine exclaimed, rubbing his hands together in glee. "You have to hold onto your disc until midday, seven days from now. This game will start once you leave this office, so it will be just a little over seven complete days that you must guard it, and just so you are aware, it would not surprise me if you have a welcoming party standing just outside this corridor. The discs will take the seraph signature of whoever is holding them at midday, so you don't need to return it to a specific location. As, for Ella's fantastic second question, yes, yes there is." He eyed us all thoughtfully. "I won't go too much into specifics, but there will be a reward for obtaining another individual's token, a reward that will make the previous one look paltry by comparison."

Rikol and Ella shared a look at that. The shopping spree that Rikol had embarked upon in Anderal had been nothing short of obscene, regaling us over the weeks since with the levels of debauchery he had sunk to as well as intricate descriptions of the mountains of goods he had delivered to our rooms at the Academy. Wolf's Hollow, unfortunately, didn't allow for personal goods. His custom blade was still being forged, but he had been promised that it would be ready by the time he left Wolf's Hollow permanently. For Carmine to suggest that the reward would make Rikol's pale in comparison was almost impossible to believe, and yet it wasn't hard to spot the suddenly eager gleams in both street-rats' eyes, nor the suddenly elevated heart rates.

Rubbing my temples, I cast a look at Cassius, noting the worried look on his face too. Would one of our dorm actually take the opportunity if it came down to it? Before coming to Wolf's Hollow I would have said 'no' without hesitation. These days though, my gut was leaning the other way.

Carmine looked around the group. "Any other questions?"

"Yeah," Rikol said slowly, eying the metal disc in Carmine's hand. "What is that made of?"

"Ah, I suspected you of all people might be interested," Carmine replied, holding up the disc. "This is not your average lump of iron but is, in fact, a heavily runed piece of metal. It has been inscribed by the finest seraph workers within the Academy and they had one job: to render each unassailable by seraph."

"You mean-"

"I mean, that there will be no summoning this one away. No teleportation, no nothing. If you want to get another one of these then you have to do it the old-fashioned way – pick it up in your hand."

"Meaning that we will likely have to be in direct confrontation with the owner," Rikol said, screwing up his nose in disgust.

"I should certainly hope so!" Carmine replied with a laugh. "Otherwise, myself and the other watching Imperators will be most bored."

"What about the other game you're playing?" I asked when the others fell silent.

Carmine narrowed his eyes. "What do you refer to?"

"The mental games. The dreams."

"Oh, those," he laughed with a wave of his hand. "No, I don't think we'll be stopping those any time soon. They are perhaps the best method we have of seeing the *real you.*" The last words were spoken with such intensity that I took a step back. Carmine's eyes were locked directly on me.

"The real me?" I fought hard to hide the tremor in my voice.

"Oh yes. The one who comes to the fore when needed most. You should ask Cassius. He knows exactly what I'm talking about. Don't you, boy?"

Cassius was as pale as a ghost but stood his ground, chin raised. "These mind games tell you nothing."

"Oh but that is where you are so, so very wrong." A knock sounded at his office door and he widened a smile that showed too many teeth. "And that's all the time we have!" Picking up a box, he thrust a single metal disc into each person's hands. "There we are," he said happily. "Out you go kids, have fun, try not to die and all that."

He opened the door and the corridor ahead of us looked conspicuously empty. The others looked at me and I nodded, listening to the three heartbeats that were hiding in nearby rooms and raising the numbers on my hand. One by one, we sidled out of the office, Carmine happily slamming the door shut behind us. "Let the game begin!" he shouted as he did so.

I swallowed hard. Heartbeats began to race around me; those of my friends and the hidden adversaries ahead.

Game on.

By unspoken agreement I led the way. Despite our own issues, the team still knew that I was the best chance they had at giving warning and surviving first contact with any enemy. The corridor - a bleak, inhospitable slab of dark stone at the best of times - now held an ominous, anticipatory air. Like the moment before a lightning strike, some innate sixth sense informing our brains that something was about to go terribly amiss.

I stepped fully into the corridor. Tensed. Nothing.

I took a second step. A third. At the fourth, Rikol and Ella screamed for me to stop and I froze, foot just above the floor.

"What is it?" I asked, tension making my voice hoarse.

"Some kind of glyph," Rikol replied distractedly. "Not sure what it does yet, so don't move."

"Can I put my foot back?"

"What part of 'don't move' do you not understand?"

"Just balance on one leg then," I muttered. "Got it." Amazing how difficult something becomes when you need to focus on it. Balance to me came as naturally as breathing, but being told to balance on the spot with one leg in the air? All of a sudden my body wanted nothing better than to tilt and sway. It's almost as if our unconscious selves are our own worst enemies.

"I've got it, it's some kind of lightning trap. Pretty obvious really, whoever set this should have known that we would be checking for such things." Rikol stepped forward and concentrated, his finger glowing slightly before he sliced through a marking on the glyph. Colour faded out of existence, seraph dissipating back into the ether as the glyph ceased to function. "There, done."

"Can I?"

He rolled his eyes. "Yes, put your foot down, the danger is over."

I did as he asked.

The corridor twisted, shuddered and flipped.

When I came to a moment later, I realised from the screaming and yelling that I wasn't the only one affected. Moreover, I discovered that it wasn't the corridor that had flipped, it was me.

"-avity glyph!" Rikol was yelling, face turning red from a heady mixture of rage at being proved wrong and his blood deciding that it quite liked pooling in his brain.

"Where is it?" Ella shouted, struggling against the invisible force that held us. I tested it too, trying to move a limb but the strain was too much and I collapsed back to the ceiling.

"Calidan, can you see anything?!" Sophia shouted from the rear of the group.

I scanned the ground below, hearing the doors ahead of us slam open and footsteps begin moving in our direction. "Can't see anything. Must be hidden somehow."

"That doesn't make sense," Ella muttered. "There's nowhere to hide such a glyph."

"Easy enough to hide something when you will it so," called a voice languorously. I stiffened, as did everyone in my cohort. We all knew that voice. Had trained with its owner for years. Oso. He waltzed into view, hands stuffed into his pockets, expression a mixture of pleasure and pain. "Hello everyone. It's been a while."

"Oso," ground out Rikol, "let us down from here."

"Oh, wish I could, but you should know that I am not the one holding you there. No, I just covered the glyph with an illusion." Reaching up, he touched a finger to my leg and frowned. Too late I tried to put defences in place and the cloth of my trouser pocket fell away. When nothing fell to the ground, he frowned and went for the other one.

"How do you know I didn't shove it down my underwear?"

He coughed back a laugh. "Honestly, it wouldn't surprise me if you had. Would be a pretty good place to keep it."

He was right and I now fervently wished that I had put it down there. *Damn!* Fortunately, I had at least had the good insight to stick it into my back-pocket, where hopefully it would remain unless he had the skill to somehow flip me over whilst I was stuck to the ceiling.

"Found any yet?" called a voice I didn't recognise.

"Working on it!"

"Hurry up!"

"Fuck's sake," Oso muttered to himself. He reached for the second front pocket and this time I resisted, focusing my will on my clothing remaining exactly how it was. Oso grunted then threw a small object into the air, one that in hindsight I should have known not to look at. It erupted with a blinding flash of light and in that moment my concentration was broken. The next moment I felt more exposed than I had ever been.

By the gasps and swears around me, the others were either suffering the same issue or were astonished at the perfect curves of my body. I like to think the latter, but considering the clink of metal on stone a second later, the former was more likely.

I had to give it to Oso. His plan had paid off nicely. A few neat distractions and we were completely under his control.

"Did you really have to do that?" I sighed.

"Sorry everyone," he muttered, his cheeks burning red with either embarrassment or laughter as he rushed forwards and picked up the coins from the ground. "Not the most dignified, but you have to admit, it worked."

"Oso, are you done?!"

"I've got four!"

"That'll do. Let's go!"

Oso ceased his search and gave a mock bow. "Once again, sorry for this. But I'm sure you will all remember this as the day that you got robbed of your dignity." A wink and then he was off around the corner, sprinting as fast as he could, leaving behind barely suppressed sniggers.

Laughter it was, then.

"Oh, that little bugger."

"Can I assume," I called out, "that you are, like myself, all in a state of severe undress?"

The uncomfortable silence behind me spoke volumes.

"Well," I began, "that wasn't a great start was i- argh!" Gravity re-righted itself and my face found the floor with alacrity. A chorus of thumps, groans and swearing behind me told me everything I needed to know. Standing up, I shook my head to clear it and then turned around before freezing in my tracks.

Yep. Oso had been thorough. There wasn't a single article of clothing in sight between the six of us. I reached back behind me and plucked out the metal disc that had been pressed into my skin. The back-pocket had served me nicely, despite years of Rikol informing me about how easy it was for thieves to target.

"That little bastard!" Rikol hissed. "I'll get him for this."

"Get in line," growled Ella.

I realised then what Oso had inadvertently done. Even though he had stolen our discs, by stripping us of our clothes he had rendered such embarrassment as to ensure that revenge would need to be meted out with interest. If he had any sense, he would find a rock and crawl under it for the next seven days, because the Pits of Asur held no fury like a group of forcibly nakified individuals.

"Fuck this shit!" roared Scythe and in the office behind us I could hear Carmine laughing.

"Fuck Wolf's Hollow," sighed Cassius with a shake of his head as he tried to conjure some clothing for Ella.

"Wolf's Hollow? Fuck Oso! I'm going to kill that little prick."

"Speaking of little pricks," Sophia murmured, already clad in a seraph-conjured towel. "Why don't you put that away and then we can go hunt him down?"

"You weren't complaining last night."

"It wasn't so little then," she laughed. "Get some pants on!"

A wise decision.

A minute later all of us were clad in something that provided some modicum of decency. I tucked my coin into the palm of my hand and clenched down tight.

"Hands up, who managed to hold onto their coin?" Sophia asked.

No-one moved. She sighed. "Now isn't the time to be shy about this. We need to know to figure out the best plan going forwards."

Slowly, Cassius raised his arm, followed by me. "How did the two of you manage that?" Rikol asked suspiciously.

I shared a look with Cassius and raised an eyebrow. "Back-pocket?"

He nodded and grinned as Rikol face-palmed. "Who knew the village style of carrying coins would get us this far?"

"Get you robbed, that's what you mean!" Rikol fumed. "I've told you so many times!"

I raised my hands defensively. "Hey, just saying, but it looks like you're the ones that got robbed…"

His face was a sight to behold. Luckily Sophia stepped in between us before things could escalate. "That's enough!" she said sharply. "We've got enough going on without fighting each other." She glared at us both until we backed off. "We're four discs down and we have seven days to get them back. Let's get to the dorm, get some clothes and set to figuring this out."

"Ahh, I love it when she takes charge," said Scythe wistfully as we filed along the corridor. Cassius and I stayed in the centre of the group, hands firmly gripping the discs as we moved, eyes scanning every shadow, every nook and corner. Would the others stand and fight for us if it came to it, knowing that they had already lost their discs?

Hopefully that wasn't a question that would need to be answered.

We found Oso on the second day in the infirmary, face black and blue, eyes swollen shut. At first we had been worried that he and his companions would have gone to ground, hiding away from everyone and everything. That might well have been their intent, but it appeared as though the others had got to them first. And judging from the number of injured within the infirmary, their attackers had suffered a similar case of bad luck.

I didn't know if Carmine had anticipated it, but like a pack of piranha, the denizens of Wolf's Hollow were tearing themselves apart. By the third day the sound of concussive blasts of seraph were becoming commonplace. By the fourth day all classes were cancelled due to the amount of violence that had erupted within class time. The others went out day after day, hunting for evidence of their discs, but each time they just found fresh injuries. Cassius and I maintained iron-clad grips on our tokens, losing sleep not only because of

Carmine's continued dream manipulations but because of fear that our now somewhat twitchy dormmates were starting to look at the pieces of metal with a desperate hunger.

It was the morning of the fifth day when I woke up with my disc missing. Having secured it under my pillow overnight and relying on my acute senses to wake me up if anything happened, I was surprised to find the metal gone. The others swore blind that they hadn't seen or heard anything, but considering the number of smirks from friends who were likely happy that I was now in the same boat as them I wasn't sure how far I could trust their statements. Cassius continued to hold onto his but now he was a hollow-eyed wreck from trying to sleep as little as possible to avoid Carmine's nightly confrontations. It hadn't worked.

I woke in the early hours to find Rikol silently rummaging through Cassius's things whilst he slept. Feeling my eyes on him, Rikol stopped and stared back, eyes daring me to judge or to make a sound. I thought about it for a long moment but in the end did nothing, just let the thief get on with his job. If he was that desperate to get out of Wolf's Hollow then my accusatory glare wasn't going to change anything.

Besides, I knew who else was awake and watching.

When Rikol fell asleep in the early hours of the morning, I sensed Ella stealthily shift over to his bed. It felt like the work of moments before the token rested back under Cassius's pillow, Ella giving him a loving stroke on his head before settling back down to sleep.

Satisfied that all was well with the world, I followed suit.

There was no mention of Rikol's antics the next morning. I could sense the anger boiling off him but he constrained his emotions as carefully as he could, settling for widened nostril flares and hard stares.

The cafeteria was like a ghost-town. The halls of Wolf's Hollow were expansive enough to hide many of its small number at the best of times, but even so the amount that showed up to eat was shockingly small, and those that did tended to be sporting new bruises and cuts. Were they the current owners of the discs? There was no way to tell. Not without taking them down and checking their pockets ourselves.

How in the hells were we going to get this done?

We alternated our time between strategizing and hunting for the missing discs, but neither were particularly productive. The discs changed owner on an almost hourly basis, the previous holder usually sporting some new injury as recompense.

"Why is it so important to you?" I asked Oso, one of the few in the canteen. Aside from laxatives in his morning coffee on the third day, our revenge for his actions had consisted of whispered mutterings and hard looks.

He sighed and shut the book he was reading with a slight wince, the bandaging on his hand catching on the slowly healing flesh underneath. The fighting had only increased in intensity, the burns on his hand testament to how badly people wanted the discs.

"The final exam is..." he shook his head, "not something that I can speak of. Primarily because it changes based on the people attempting it. Rumour has it that Carmine sets up the exam to prey on your weaknesses." He shrugged. "I would agree with that. Some die, whilst some, like me, fail. Those who fail aren't given a second chance. They have to show that they want it. That they are ready and willing to do what it takes to complete it. This is just one of his many ways of getting us to decide that we are ready to do what is necessary. Not everyone is." His eyes flickered over to Jemain, who was sitting staring blankly at the far wall, porridge forgotten in front of him.

"I know you said you can't give any advice, but is there anything you can tell us, to help us prepare?" Cassius asked.

A bitter smile tugged at Oso's lip. "If I were you, I wouldn't be too worried about the final exam just yet. No, you have worse to come first. As for advice: harden your hearts. There is no room here for sentiment. Not anymore." He stood up and left us with that cryptic clue, dumping his tray and leaving the cafeteria, only stopping to briefly clap a comforting hand on Jemain's shoulder and whisper a quiet word which was lost in the mild clamour of the cafeteria.

"Well, fat lot of use that was," muttered Scythe.

"I don't know, he gave away some things that we might not have otherwise known," replied Ella. "That he thought the final exam wasn't the worst aspect of Wolf's Hollow is a surprise."

"Sounds like Carmine has something unpleasant in store for us," I said grimly. "Surprise, surprise." My eyes flickered to the few remaining Imps in the room and I lowered my voice. "What's the latest?"

"Rumour has it that Vandra and her dorm have the coins and are locked down tight," Ella began. "They are besieged by a couple of Imps I don't know and a few that we do." Her expression grew grave. "Arin included."

"Shit," hissed Scythe. "That's the last we need."

Arin. The Imp who, were it not for Rikol, would have dominated the fifth-year games. Some students found being held back a year disheartening. Not Arin; she had thrown everything she had into improving her seraph skills, improving with a fervour that only Rikol could match. If she was besieging this Vandra then the direct route wasn't an option.

"Thoughts?"

"It's pointless attacking a fortified position," said Sophia. "We should just wait. See if Arin manages to pry them out of their hole. If she does, she and her team will be weakened and ripe for the picking."

"Which is what everyone else will be thinking, surely?" countered Scythe.

She shrugged. "Probably. But unless we somehow set about incapacitating everyone, this was always going to come down to a last-ditch brawl. Why waste your time stressing on holding on to it for days on end, when you could just grab it in the last few minutes?"

She made a good point.

"You make a good point," said Cassius. "And the more people desperately vying for the discs, the more likely people are going to get seriously hurt."

"So how do we maximise our chances and minimise those of the others?" Rikol mused, tapping his chin with a finger.

"I think Sophia has already given us the answer." Every eye turned to me and I continued. "As did Carmine." Seeing the blank looks on their faces I bulled ahead. "Incapacitation. If you recall, Carmine suggested that we target the biggest hitters and 'break their legs'. I don't think he was joking. I think in a strange way he was giving us advice."

"We can't just go and assault other people!" Cassius exclaimed, aghast. "Some of them aren't even interested in the game!"

I held up a hand. "I know, some, like Jemain, I wouldn't bother with, but there are others that we definitely know are part of the game. What's more, I'm not necessarily suggesting that we actually do go and break legs. I'm just in favour of a pre-emptive strike to remove as many of our potential foes as possible."

"We would have to do something that kept them out of the fight until at least midday," murmured Scythe, rubbing his beard thoughtfully. "If we go violent and have any further interactions down the line, we will not be looked on favourably."

"That's putting it politely," added Ella. "Look how upset we were with Oso and he didn't really do anything except embarrass us. If he had been more violent then our reply would have scaled accordingly."

"Oso..." Cassius mused before snapping his fingers. "Rikol, have you got any more of those laxatives?"

"Some," he answered, nodding. "But not enough to knock out the entire cohort."

"Ah," Cassius replied, face falling.

"But..." Rikol pursed his lips and Cassius looked up, hopeful. "The Infirmary has substantial supplies. Considering that it is set up to handle any number of issues it would not surprise me if they had a stockpile of such things."

"And assuming that we got these items," asked Sophia, "what next? How do we go about administering them? It's not like the others would trust us if we gave them something."

"We would have to get them all at once," I muttered, eyes roaming before falling onto something at Jemain's table. "The porridge!" I exclaimed, drawing a series of shushes from the dorm. "Sorry," I said, lowering my voice. "The porridge. It should be relatively easy to slip something into the vat in the canteen."

"Won't get everyone," Ella replied.

"It'll get enough," Sophia insisted. "Even if it's a few people, that's a few less that we have to worry about tomorrow."

"Who says we only have to lace one thing?" said Cassius eagerly and I suppressed a smile. Now that the prospect of hurting people was off the table he seemed much more himself. "And I know just the thing: coffee."

"Coffee!?" I exclaimed, shocked at the thought of tarnishing the delicious black gold.

"Yes, coffee. Flavour should be enough to mask the taste of the drug and most people drink it here," he answered confidently.

I swivelled to see everyone and studied their faces for a minute whilst they digested the plan. "I agree with this," I said. "If the porridge or the coffee doesn't get them then we shall. Any issues?"

A shake of heads.

"So, let's recap," declared Cassius. "Rikol, you're slipping into the infirmary and getting the supplies. We then sneak into the cafeteria kitchen and lace the porridge and the coffee. Hopefully by lunch time it will have kicked in and the toilet chambers will be crowded."

"I don't think this is going to get us any friends," said Sophia with a laugh, "but it sounds like a decent idea. I'm in."

It was one hell of a mess.

Wolf's Hollow had, at any one time, somewhere between ten and thirty Imps within its walls. It had toilets designed to accommodate perhaps a dozen people simultaneously, men and women included.

Some people don't like porridge. I can understand that, having seen and experienced the slop that most commoners eat, but Academy porridge? Incredible. I don't know what they did to it but this wasn't your average gruel, instead it was a delicious meal with a multitude of optional extras to add in.

In other words, it was popular.

Rikol had done his job well. He had snuck into the infirmary without raising any suspicion and swiped a substantial quantity of apparently – if the following events were anything to judge by - *potent* laxative. It had been the work of a moment to distract the canteen staff and add the liquid to the massive vat of simmering porridge.

A moment's work to create hours of horror. To be honest, I could see why a poisoner might enjoy the job. It was a rush knowing that the people desperately clutching their stomachs and trying to find an available toilet were doing so all because of you.

What we had failed to think about - or perhaps more likely failed to *care* about - was that Imps weren't the only ones who ate porridge. Wolf's Hollow had at least six Imperators, not to mention canteen staff. They were not unaffected.

Oh well. Perhaps once Carmine had finished shitting out his guts, he would be proud of us in some twisted manner. After all, we were just doing what was most expedient regardless of the impact on others. The hallmark of any true Imperator.

The stench though. That was unexpected. It didn't affect the others much, not having the same affinity for scent that I possessed, but to me, trapped within an underground building with little in the way of ventilation?

Unpleasant was an understatement.

We passed through hallways that held a mixture of astonished and lucky individuals trying in vain to attempt to help the vast majority who were writhing on the ground, often covered in their own excrement, having been unlucky enough to miss out on one of the few toilets.

I witnessed an Imperator forcibly rip open a toilet door and throw the poor bastard who had been using it out into the hallway. I saw at least three separate scuffles, two of which involved a dangerous amount of seraph, over cubicles. Carmine, I could sense, was holed up in a toilet, layers of seraph shields preventing the four other nearby individuals from getting inside. And my nose, my poor brutalised *nose* was an unwilling bystander to the resulting stench that permeated everything it touched.

That's not to say that our reclaiming of the discs was a complete cakewalk. Vandra's team had the foresight to stockpile their dorm with food. This might have placed our entire mission in jeopardy, but they couldn't resist poking their heads out to see what was going on outside, releasing their many seraph shields in order to step out and laugh at their fallen foes.

I couldn't blame them. I would have done the same thing in their shoes.

We moved quickly, but Vandra's dorm was placed in the middle of a long corridor meaning that they had plenty of time to retreat once Rikol and Sophia started flinging seraph. Their opening salvo dropped one Imp, but the other four slipped back inside and began rebuilding their defences. Fortunately, Ella had done her usual and slipped in behind them before we had attacked, her invisibility more than up to the task for that short timeframe. We stood outside patiently as a number of grunts made their way through the door, then the seraph barriers fell and the door opened to reveal Ella with four unconscious Imps on the floor behind her and a hand full of metal torcs.

Chucking the Imps outside, we closed the door, willed some seraph barriers into existence and sat back to enjoy a lazy morning.

It was, all in all, a good day.

Carmine veritably shook with barely disguised rage as we sidled into his office the following day. Classes had been called off in the wake of our mass poisoning and the infirmary was still full of people who had eaten more than one helping of the laced porridge. Perhaps we should have felt bad, but judging by the shit-eating grins on all of our faces, we really didn't care.

We had won.

"What, by the Pits, were you thinking?!" he roared as we shut the door, spittle flying to land on my jacket. I wiped it off absently, enjoying the look on his face.

"I'm not sure we know what you're talking about," I replied innocently. "Surely congratulations are in order? We completed your mission without the single loss of a disc."

"Congratulations...?" Carmine ground out between clenched teeth, eyes popping. "You think you should get recognition for what you pulled? You poisoned half the facility!"

"Poison is a strong term. We prefer...temporarily inhibited."

"I should permanently inhibit you all!"

Sophia stepped forwards. "Now, Imperator Carmine, I know that you don't get on with Calidan, but you have to admit, we beat your challenge. You got caught in the crossfire, which is unfortunate, but sometimes the ends justify the means; isn't that what you taught us?"

He slammed his mouth shut and I could almost see the gears turning in his head. Finally, he let out a deep breath, forcibly attempting to relax himself. "I understand what you did and whilst I do not like it, you did...well," the veins in his face flared as he spat the last word. "Next time, if there is one, I suggest not poisoning the people who have control over whether or not you receive a passing grade."

"But we are getting a passing grade?" Rikol asked, a little nervously.

"Yes. You passed this mission. I will not take that away from you. As much as I might want to," he finished, voice dangerous. "You will all have the ability to complete the final exam two months earlier than planned."

Our smiles froze on our faces as he continued, voice low and dangerous. "I suggest you prepare well, because that means our timetables are moving up accordingly. For those of you with a *weak* stomach," his face twisted into a horrific caricature of a smile and his eyes locked onto Cassius, "it's time to grow a spine."

CHAPTER 17

BUILT TO ORDER

Ella

Ella crept through the corridor, seraph-shield bending light and leaving her as little more than a barely seen shimmer in the air. Cassius was coming for her. That much she knew. The fuzziness ate at the calm, structured organisation of her brain but she knew it deep in her soul. He was coming and she needed to stop him. He was her responsibility. Gods knew how the Enemy had managed to wrangle His way into Cassius's mind, but he was gone now. All that remained was the husk of the man she loved.

But... a little voice in the back of her mind began, *haven't you always known? Always suspected? He has black seraph within him. Cassius has always been a risk. He has just been one you have chosen to ignore.*

Ella gritted her teeth and forced her mind to quiet. Damn that fuzziness! When this was all over she needed to see the Academy medicae; something just wasn't right.

A noise up ahead. The echo of a footstep?

Keeping her back against the wall, she held herself steady as she concentrated on keeping her heartrate and breathing low. Cassius was an excellent fighter and doubtless would be even more effective when controlled by the Enemy. She needed to make sure that she struck first and made it count. A knife to the heart from behind? Swift for both parties. No need to see his eyes.

What about if he is a kyrgeth? that insidious voice whispered.

Damn. She hoped that wouldn't be the case but if it was then she needed to end the threat before it began.

She needed to remove the head.

Hating herself for even thinking it, she took several deep breaths and then pushed away from the wall, steeling herself for what was to come. Someone was going to die. She would make sure it was the traitor to the Academy; even if it cost her everything.

Another sound up ahead. Summoning all of her skills at stealth, she crept forwards again, blade in hand. It didn't take long to find him. The corridors were strangely bare, the lack of people odd, but she didn't let it dissuade her from her task. She found him standing in a junction of three hallways, bare sword in hand. He was mumbling something. What was it?

"Just like he said, be strong enough to fight. Learn to kill." He choked back the words. "Who is it going to be? Calidan? Sophia?"

Ella closed her eyes and bowed her head in sorrow. That was all the proof she needed. He was being controlled by the Enemy. He had come here to kill in cold blood.

Her blade sliced cleanly through Cassius's back, driving deep into his heart. He coughed, a thick wet sound and slowly slumped to his knees, his sword clattering to the ground. "W-who?" he croaked out, hands clutching the tip of the blade that jutted from his chest.

Ella hadn't intended to reveal herself, but suddenly the cost of maintaining her seraph shield was too much. Was a gasp she released it, tears near blinding her as she formed another blade in an outstretched hand.

"E-E-Ella? N-no. *No!*" Was that shudder in his voice frustration at his plan being thwarted? Pain at what she had done to him? No…it was something else. As she swung the sword, tears flying as free as his head, she recognised what it was.

Complete and abject terror.

I heard Cassius bolt upright, clutching at his chest with panicked breaths. After a moment he began to calm, his senses bringing him back to rationality. "Just another one," he breathed. "Just another one. But Ella. *Oh gods. Ella!*"

Ella shifted in her sleep. The tang of salt reached my nose and I realised that there were tears running down her face. *She must be having a terrible dream.*

Lurching out of bed, Cassius staggered to the door, opening it as if drunk and stumbling outside. Seeing that Ella was settling into a deeper sleep, I slid out of bed and followed.

He hadn't gone far. I found him slumped on the ground, back against the wall, heaving deep breaths with tears streaking his cheeks. Easing myself down beside him, I didn't speak. Just waited.

"It was her, Cal."

It wasn't hard to guess who.

"Ella?"

He shuddered a nod. "I've been trying to do as you suggested. I've fought back. But I've never had to fight Ella before. Carmine must have known. Been saving her for something special."

"How did it go?"

He barked a bitter laugh. "Not well." He noticed me watching his hands, both of which were clamped over his heart and shook his head. "I remember what it was like, the feeling of her blade piercing my chest." His hands shook as he spoke and I could smell the adrenaline and fear steaming off him. "It was so easy," he whispered, eyes going blank. "So easy. The beat of a heart and I was dying. There was no hesitation in her. No suggestion that she thought of me as anything other than an enemy."

"You know it's not her, Cass, it's Carmine," I said reassuringly. "Carmine wouldn't hesitate, but Ella wouldn't kill you. You know that." As I spoke my mind wandered back to the tears that had been running down Ella's face in her sleep. What *had* she been dreaming about? Was it just a co-incidence that she was crying when Cassius woke up dead at her hand? Cassius choked back a sob and I shook my head to clear my thoughts. A mystery for another time.

"Perhaps you should reconsider remembering," I said gently but he shook his head in vehement denial.

"No!" he declared loudly. "No, I'm not going to let that bastard win. I'm going to remember and record all the things that he has done to me. To us. And one day, mark my words," his eyes narrowed and the thoroughbred killer that was Cassius shone through, "...there will be an accounting."

I sat with Cassius for a few more minutes, until he had calmed enough to consider heading back to bed. I knew that he wouldn't sleep – I'm not sure anyone would after such an incident – but considering the state he was in both mentally and physically, any period of rest was useful. Once done, I slipped back out into the hallway.

It was time to get some answers.

In the back of my mind, I knew that it was beyond stupid to keep pushing Carmine. To keep prodding the foul creature that he was. But Cassius's words and Ella's tears haunted me. So far we had been operating under the assumption that it was Carmine's illusion of one of us that we were fighting in our dreams, but...what if it was something else?

Or more accurately, someone else.

It wasn't hard to find Carmine. He was in his office and by the scent of strong spirits had just opened a bottle. I was about to barge in and give him a piece of my mind when the clinking of glasses made me freeze, hand on the handle. Carmine wasn't alone.

"Are we celebrating?" A woman's voice. *Her* voice. The Imperator who liked to throw me in cells.

"Yes and no," replied Carmine. His voice sounded weary. Worn. Unsurprising if he had been running illusions a few minutes ago. Mental manipulations like that were taxing beyond belief.

"Go on..."

A long and heartfelt sigh. The sigh of someone who had just taken a sip of something very pleasant. "I think I broke him today."

"Who? The Great Heart boy?"

"No, not him. The other one."

"Cassius."

"That's the one." Another sip. "It's been a while in coming. He is quite a determined individual."

"He has the makings of a fine Imperator," the female voice mused.

"Indeed. More's the pity." A momentary silence during which both people took sips.

"So, the plan is unchanged?"

"Of course. All proceeding to schedule."

"Excellent. He will be pleased."

I could picture the coy smirk that would be plastered across Carmine's face as he replied. "Of course he will be. He knows what we do here. Imperators built to order."

"Do you know why he needs him so badly?"

A scoff. "As if. What he says goes, you know that. We just get told what to do and have to make it happen. When Cassius finds out that he is no longer fighting me, but his dear little girlfriend, he should be exactly as desired."

Oh shit. I started pulling away from the door, suddenly very aware of everything around me, adrenaline and panic coursing through my body. *They know Cassius is aware and they want him to be. Why? What could they possibly gain from it?*

"Did you hear something?"

I had heard enough. I turned and ran. Cassius was in deep with something that none of us understood. Someone wanted him, someone powerful enough to have Imperators doing their dirty work. And, worse, they didn't want Cassius as the bright light that he was.

They wanted him altered.

Changed.

Not if I had anything to do with it. He had stood before me against countless foes. It was my turn to protect him.

"You have to stop remembering."

The look Cassius gave me was half-withering and half-exhausted. "This again? Can we not-"

I grabbed him by the shoulder and tugged him into a small corridor. "Listen to me and carefully. There's something going on. Something targeting you in particular."

That roused his attention. "What do you mean?"

"I overheard Carmine last night. He was talking about you and how he had nearly 'broken' you. He seemed pleased about it-"

"Well of course he did, the sick bastard!"

"-but not because he is a twisted son-of-a-bitch, but because someone pulling his strings wanted you that way."

"Wait. What?"

I nodded. "Exactly. I have no idea what is going on, just that you're in the centre of it." Leaning forwards, I stared into his eyes, trying to get across the severity of the situation. "Listen to me Cass, you need to get yourself sorted out. If they want you in a bad way, well everyone can see that they've nearly done it. You *need* to stop fighting to remember what they're doing to you. To us." He started to shake his head, words of denial forming on his lips but I bulled ahead. "Everything about this is twisted, Cass. Wrong. Wolf's Hollow is a sick place, we all know that. But what I overheard last night is something different. They're targeting you. Out of everyone else here, they want you to have problems. And what's more it's not Carmine, it's E-" I froze mid-sentence. Could Cassius handle knowing that the person who had stabbed him through the heart in his dream last night was actually Ella and not Carmine? What was the least damaging path – telling him now or hiding it away and hoping he never found out?

What would Cassius do if he were in my shoes?

"What do you mean, 'it's not Carmine'?" Cassius asked, confused. "What isn't?"

"The last battle, the one against Ella. That was actually Ella, not Carmine's illusion of her. He was putting both of you in the same dream."

My words hit Cassius like a physical blow. He crumpled, staggering to the side of the corridor and holding onto the wall like it was the only thing keeping him upright.

Maybe it was.

"It...it's her?" he whispered hoarsely. "You're sure?"

"As positive as I can be. She's not aware, as far as I know. Probably thinks whatever Carmine has suggested her to think. But her actions in those dreams are her own."

"W-why? Why would Carmine do this?" Tears were in his eyes but he answered his own question before I could. "Because of the reaction I'm having right now." He snorted and hung his head morosely. "Bastards."

Reaching out, I wrapped my arm around his shoulders and sank down with him to the floor. For a long few minutes we just sat, staring at everything and nothing. Eventually, Cassius stirred. "I just don't understand this," he began. "What possible purpose would there be to what Carmine is doing? Why would they want an Imperator or an Imp who is near a mental collapse?"

"I've been trying to wrap my head around that," I replied. "Best I can come up with is something to do with control. We know that Wolf's Hollow is designed to mentally stress Imps in the first place. To break them down so they can be built back up to be the perfect Imperator." I snorted. "Maybe you're a little different? Maybe the rest of us are already close to that point and you were the last bastion of good in this shitty place? Or maybe they want you for something else entirely." I raised my hands helplessly. "I've got nothing concrete, I'm afraid. Each theory is just as bad as the next."

He gave a pained smile at that. "Nothing new there then."

"Hey!"

Nudging me playfully with his shoulder, he sighed and leant his head back against the wall. "We've only got theories. No concrete evidence of anything whatsoever. Which I guess means that we need to stop trying to focus on the 'why' and instead figure out the 'how'."

"I can always go snooping around," I offered. "See if I can dig up some reasoning behind what they're doing to you."

"No," he replied with a shake of his head. "They've already thrown you in a cell. They'll probably do worse if they knew that you were actively working against them." He pursed his lips. "No, whatever will happen, will happen. I just need to figure out a way to minimise the impact of whatever it is they do."

"First step in that, my friend, is to get yourself some proper sleep," I said gently. "Stop seeking to remember whatever shit Carmine pulls in your dreams. Just be like the rest of us. Sometimes, you know, ignorance truly is bliss."

CHAPTER 18
No Comment

"Kane's here."

I craned my neck to look over the bobbing heads of Imps in the cafeteria. "He is? Where?"

"Not here, *here*," Rikol snapped. "I saw him walk past with Carmine."

"Interesting," Sophia mused around a mouthful of porridge. "I wonder what has brought him here? I figured he was hands off until we were done."

"Could be a scheduled checkup," Ella offered. "Or maybe he just missed us."

"Whilst we all know that it is the latter, I reckon he is here for something else," said Scythe, swallowing some muesli.

Rikol gave him a stony glare. "And?"

"And what?"

Rikol's face reddened. "Any ideas as to what that might be?"

"Nope!" Scythe replied happily, obviously relishing the look on Rikol's face. Just as the young seraph user was about to explode, he continued. "Though now that you mention it, we know that the timetable has been moved up for us. So my reckoning is that Kane's here because of what comes next."

"And what does come next?"

"Nothing good, that's all I know."

"Bloody useless," muttered Rikol.

"Not what your mum said last night."

"Joke's on you. I don't know my mum!" Rikol retorted at the same time as Sophia leaned over and punched Scythe.

"Easy, easy. Ow! Sorry! No, I didn't have sex with Rikol's mum last night," Scythe confirmed. "Though, just to add, if I had then she certainly wouldn't have said that I was useless."

"She might not, but I will," Sophia sighed. "And at this rate, it will be a long time before you get another shot to try for a better grading."

Scythe clamped a hand to his heart. "You wound me, madam!"

"I'll do more than that if you keep this up." Sophia cocked her head at my movement and raised an eyebrow. "Going somewhere?"

"Yes actually," I replied with a laugh. "I thought that I might go and see if I could have a little chat with our Instructor. Figure out what he was here for, you know, rather than just wildly speculating."

"But wildly speculating is the best part!" she retorted with a grin. "Want any company?"

"No, no." I waved her off. "I might need to listen in for a while and can do that by myself. Don't want to interrupt anything important after all."

"Of course," she replied regally. "Would never want to inconvenience Carmine."

"Gods no!" I gasped. "That would never do." Slipping away from the table, I stalked through the corridors, sorting Kane's scent out from the others. He had gone downstairs. Originally, I thought that he had gone to Carmine's office, but his scent actually descended all the way to the third level. I poked my head over the rail and peered down, but could only see the doorway through which I had been so often dragged.

What was he doing down there?

Luckily, I didn't have to wait long. I was just wondering whether to go and check on Carmine's office when the door slid open and the hefty bulk of Kane strode through, followed by none other than Carmine. The heavy footfalls of Kane echoed on the stairs and I spent a guilty moment wondering whether to hide or flee before realising that I had nothing to be worried about. The corridor, after all, was not off-limits.

"Calidan," rumbled Kane. "What are you doing here?"

"Kane!" I said with a wide, genuine smile. "Good to see you. Rikol reckoned that he had seen you so I came to see if he was telling the truth."

"He's got good eyes that boy," grunted Kane. "Yes, I'm here. Just checking up on a few things. I believe congratulations are in order?"

"They are?" I raised an eyebrow.

"You and the entire dorm managed to complete the mission to advance your final exam. Not many do. Good job! You made me a pretty bundle on that."

"You were betting on it?"

He snorted. "Of course! Nothing serious mind, just a pool about when people will complete challenges, that kind of thing. Carmine keeps us up to date. Makes for a little light entertainment."

"Speaking of Carmine," I lowered my voice, knowing that Carmine would full well be able to still hear me. "Mind if you and I have a word in private?"

"There's nothing for you to be bothering Kane with!" interrupted Carmine. "He isn't here to listen to your-"

Kane raised a hand. "It's alright Carmine, whilst I appreciate you looking out for my precious time, Calidan is still one of my students. I'll have a quick chat with him and meet you in your office."

"But-"

"Now," Kane insisted, tone brooking no argument. Carmine glowered at me and left, sweeping down towards his office. "So, what's this about Cal?" Kane asked once he was positive that Carmine had gone.

Looking around, I checked that we were alone before speaking. "It's about Cassius, sir."

A raised eyebrow. "Go on."

"He has been practicing his mental techniques and managed to remember the things that Carmine has been doing to us in our dreams."

"Calidan, Carmine's skills, whilst unpleasant, are a part of the curriculum for a reason," Kane began but I quickly interrupted.

"I know that." I quickly regaled Kane with what was happening to Cassius and his expression grew serious. "Thing is, I...overheard Carmine talking the other day, how he was happy that they had nearly 'broken' Cassius. The way he said it suggested that he needed to do so because someone had ordered it."

Kane's expression grew troubled. "Carmine only really answers to two people." He eyed me for a moment before grimacing. "Wait here."

Before I could reply he stormed off towards Carmine's office. It felt like hours but was only minutes before he was back and this time his face was deadly serious.

"Did you find anything out?" I asked hesitantly.

"I did."

I waited for a response but there was none forthcoming. "And?"

A heavy sigh. "Carmine has his reasons for his actions. He is not some monster acting of his own volition, but an Imperator acting for reasons above your station. The attention being focused on Cassius is...warranted."

"Warranted..." I breathed, anger flashing through me. "Warranted?! What on earth could possibly require Cassius to be ground down to nothing? Hasn't he already given everything for the Academy? Haven't we all?!"

Kane levelled granite eyes at me. "I'm not saying I like it. But I understand it. You know the purpose of Wolf's Hollow, to break you down and build you back up. Everyone here is being treated like that. Cassius is not as special a case as you make him out to be." He forestalled my furious response with a raised hand. "But he *is* a special case. For reasons above your paygrade, and mine, he is to be leant on that little bit more than the rest of you."

"But what possible reason could there be?!" I exploded. "How could it be remotely beneficial to the Academy or the Emperor?"

"The ways of the Emperor are beyond the ken of mere mortals like us," Kane replied sadly. "We just have to accept that and focus on what we can accomplish on his behalf."

My eyes closed for a long moment. "So it is the Emperor who ordered this, not the Academy." It wasn't a question, more of a statement. Kane eyed me before turning to stare at the wall.

"No comment."

That was answer enough. I exhaled softly and leaned my head back against the wall. The Emperor was behind this. Not the vindictive will of Carmine or some hostile intent by a third party but the *Emperor*. Surely that meant it was for the greater good, right?

"Look, Calidan," Kane started, moving to stand close and give me a worried smile filled with what I took to be almost paternal affection. "This isn't something you can fight. And, for the moment at least, you have bigger things to worry about."

"Like what?"

"Like what's about to start." He waved off my attempt at questions. "I can't say much more. Just know that the next few weeks are going to be tough. More than tough. The only advice that I can give is to remember why you are following this path. Why you are becoming what you are. Figure out what drives you and hold on to it. Use that to make sure that nothing gets in your way of your dream. Understood?"

He took my gobsmacked silence as understanding and gave me a comforting squeeze on my shoulder before stepping away, back towards Carmine's office. "Remember what I said," he rumbled over his shoulder. "Focus on being an Imperator and let nothing stop you from achieving that. *Nothing.*"

"He said what?"

I nodded. "To focus on being an Imperator and let nothing get in your way." I grimaced as I remembered the look on Kane's face before he had turned away. One filled with worry and concern, vanishing behind a wall of stoicism. "He seemed fairly worried about what was coming up."

"Aren't we all," Scythe muttered dryly.

"Did he say anything about…?" Cassius asked, trailing off as the others looked at him.

"No," I replied with as comforting a smile as I could manage. "All we know is that anything that Carmine and his cronies are up to is sanctioned by the Academy."

Cassius paled at the news but drew himself upright. "Okay. Understood." He summoned a brilliant smile to his face at the looks of the rest of the dorm. "Nothing to worry about."

"Not the most convincing lie you've ever told," Ella murmured to him as the others turned away, placing a hand on his. "Don't think we won't be talking about this later."

For a moment, a pained look flashed across his face, there and gone again in a moment. Ella studied him carefully before being dragged once more into conversation with the rest of the dorm.

"So, this is all 'sanctioned'," Cassius muttered softly to me as the others conversed.

"Seems like it."

"Even?"

"Even you. Yes. But I don't think it's by the Academy."

"Who then?" He saw my raised eyebrow and frowned. "Him? What possible reason would he have to…?

"No clue," I replied. "But there has to be a good reason for it. Right?"

"Right." He said it softly at first, as though he didn't quite believe it, and then again, more firmly this time. "Right!" A nod to himself. "If the Emperor wills it, then it will be so." He looked at me, a spark of fervent hope in his eyes. "I will not disappoint him."

"I don't think you ever could." I said the words encouragingly, but couldn't deny the chill that ran through me. Just what was the Emperor thinking? What did he want to get from Cassius that he couldn't get from the rest of us?" Shaking my head in confusion, I consoled myself with Kane's words about the ineffability of the Emperor's plans to someone who wasn't a Power. Who was I, in the end, to question the Emperor?

Perhaps that has been the biggest takeaway from my years as an Imperator: even the smartest beings experience moments of stupidity. Blind obedience is nothing but voluntary slavery and having the courage to question someone of a higher station is the only way to prevent terrible misuse of power.

...Or to be immolated on the spot. But, you know, swings and roundabouts.

CHAPTER 19

Twisted

The door slammed shut behind me, the sound of heavy steel clashing into place causing me to wince.

"Step forward."

It was Havan, though I couldn't see him, voice reverberating off the rock as I did as he asked and stepped forward to the centre of the dark room.

"Do you understand the nature of this trial?"

Mutely, I shook my head.

"Good. Imps who have failed this trial are not permitted to speak of it. You might also find that they would not *want* to speak of it. They, or any Imperator who has completed it for that matter. It is a personal thing. Something that teaches you a great deal about yourself, and tells us exactly what we need to know about your commitment to being an Imperator. Are you ready to begin?"

"...No?" I offered, hesitantly.

"That's the spirit," he said, blazing past my not-so-witty repartee. "The door in front of you will open shortly. Step inside and wait."

"Wait for what?"

No response.

The door pulsed with light and began to slide aside, revealing a granite chamber. A quick inspection revealed nothing of import. No furnishings, no weapons. Nothing.

"Step inside."

For a moment I hesitated. Wondering if I should somehow back out. Learn more about what I was about to get into.

"I will not ask again. Step inside or be put inside."

I stepped inside.

The door behind me slid shut. I tensed, waiting for the trap, all muscles primed and ready to fling me aside at a moment's notice.

Nothing happened.

Two minutes in and I began to relax, eyes roaming around the small room. *What was going on?*

There was a crackle and then Carmine's voice filled the room, the sudden influx of sound making me jump. "Good morning Calidan," the foul Imperator said in a far-too-cheery voice. "Welcome to your penultimate examination. I hope you have a thoroughly enjoyable time." He must have been able to see the extended finger I raised because he chuckled. "Still as much fight in you as ever I see. Excellent. But this exam isn't about fighting me, as much as you might like to. No, this is about being true to the Academy and the Emperor. The only way to pass is to prove that you are loyal. That you are willing to do what it takes to make the Emperor proud."

That didn't sound so bad. My loyalty to the Emperor was beyond reproach. I couldn't see anything that could be sent my way that I couldn't accomplish in his name.

The rock face in front of me slid aside and the sound of clucking filled the chamber. In stalked four chickens and a rooster, pecking at the floor and looking nothing like the threat I had been imagining.

"These chickens have been found to contain a slow-acting poison. Almost indetectable but deadly if ingested. They were purchased from a vendor who has affiliate links to the Dusk Court and the evidence suggests that this was an intentional attempt to inflict damage to the Empire. The Academy has ordered you to remove the threat."

Chickens?

"You have to be joking, right?" I cocked my eye at the rooster who stared right back at me, as though daring me to provoke it. Silence met my words and I scanned the room again, trying to figure out how Carmine could see me, but in vain.

"Carmine?" I asked hesitantly. "You really want me to butcher these chickens in here on behalf of the Empire?"

Silence again. I knew that somewhere in this facility he was cackling that shitty laugh of his whilst he watched me face down these feathered fiends.

With a sigh, I walked up to the first chicken, muttered an apology and then snapped its neck. Instantly the rooster screeched a challenge and flew at me, causing me to stumble backwards before I gathered myself, narrowly dodging its sharp talons. The remaining chickens were in an uproar, sprinting around the room as fast as they could, doing everything possible to avoid being around me whilst the rooster attacked again. This time I was ready for it, a ridge-hand strike to its neck causing it to crumple midstride. After that it was just a matter of finishing off the rest.

I say that like it was easy, but catching the chickens was surprisingly hard. They were surpassingly agile, surprisingly so considering their usually sedentary behaviour. By the time I was finished, I was breathing hard and the room was covered in enough feathers to fill a pillowcase.

"Finally done, I see." Carmine. "I had expected you to be faster. Most of your friends were. Want to see?"

I opened my mouth to say no, but Carmine continued unabated, "Of *course* you do. Who wouldn't want to see their friends and colleagues complete the same objective that you just struggled with? Fear not, I have your back Calidan. Behold!"

The granite walls of the room shimmered and then flickered with light. Before me were a series of boxes, each of them showing a room just like my own, complete with my friends.

"What is this?" I breathed. It looked very similar to the technology that Ash had used to reveal herself to us so long ago, but somehow different; more two-dimensional rather than three.

"Not all technology is lost to us Calidan. This is just one of many things you will come to understand when you become an Imperator. What you are seeing is a recording – that is, showing you events that have already occurred. The others have completed their respective trials and are now witnessing the same recording as you. Which means they will get to see your own attempt at completing the trial."

"Can they hear me? See me?"

"What part of seeing the past did you not understand?" he replied in a voice filled with snark. "No, they cannot see or hear you, just as you cannot do the same to them. Now, shut your mouth and watch."

If I had to choose, Rikol was the scariest yet perhaps most efficient killer of chickens out of all of us. Almost as soon as he had been given the order he raised a hand and immolated the entire flock, his expression barely changing the entire time. Perhaps the only thing he hadn't counted on was what appeared to be a distressing scent, likely of burning feathers, because he suddenly started gagging before erecting a shield to separate him from the likely horrific smell.

Ella was murderous in her own way. She took longer than Rikol, but was more...humane in the method she ended their lives, simply cutting them apart with waves of what looked to be condensed air. It was quick, relatively clean and must have been practically painless for the chickens.

Scythe was like me, relying on his physical prowess to chase the chickens and snap their necks. He managed to do it quickly enough so as to avoid having to chase them around the room however, neatly catching them up with the experienced hands of someone used to doing such activities, making their executions quick and clean.

Sophia sat for a few minutes. Originally, I assumed she was questioning the validity of the exam, but as the chickens gathered around her feet she flexed her will and each chicken crumpled to the ground like their limbs had been cut. I wasn't quite sure how she did it, but it was certainly effective.

Cassius was the second slowest out of everyone including me. He sat there for some time, processing the information. Eventually he stood and summoned a blade to his hand. With a stoic mask he dispassionately butchered the chickens, only allowing emotion to show once he let the blade dissipate. The look on his face when he finally let his emotion show was terrifying. Like he was burning with rage and didn't have an outlet to vent its flames.

The door I had used to enter slid open. "Thank you Calidan. You may leave. Return tomorrow at the same time."

"...That's it?"

Carmine didn't deign to answer. I retreated outside, leaving the broken chickens on the ground where I had left them, trying not to give them any thought. After all, they were only chickens.... a million of them probably died everyday so it shouldn't be a concern...right?

So why did I feel so bad?

I found the others back in the canteen. For one of the first times I could remember, Cassius looked like he was bursting for a fight, his expression twisted and bitter, eyes hard and angry. Even Rikol seemed to be giving him a wide berth, likely knowing that the wrong word and he would be spitting teeth. The others were a largely morose bunch. All except Rikol, who didn't seem particularly upset due to the nature of the exam but because of how we were acting following it.

"They were just chickens!" he said again, rolling his eyes in bemusement.

"We heard you the first time," Sophia muttered darkly.

"If you heard me then why are you so bloody down about it?!" he exclaimed exasperatedly. "They literally don't matter. We eat them every other day as it is."

"Being asked to kill something that hasn't done any wrong leaves a bad taste in my mouth," replied Scythe. "Especially when they aren't being used for food."

"They were poisonous, or didn't you hear Carmine?"

It was Scythe's turn to roll his eyes. "Do you really believe that? It was just backstory to get us to act, that's all."

Rikol grinned victoriously. "If that's the case, then I'm sure that the canteen will be making use of them soon enough.

"Ours maybe, but not yours," said Ella softly. "Pretty sure chicken roasted with its feathers and all doesn't make for a pleasant taste."

Rikol's expression soured. "What are you saying?"

Ella met him, eye to eye. "I'm wondering why you used such a tactless and painful method of execution on those poor creatures."

"They were just chickens!"

"That can still feel pain!" she fired back, eyes flashing with anger. "You could have ended them humanely, instead you burnt them alive. What does that say about you?"

"It says that I prefer to get things done with quickly," he hissed. "And that I don't care about some fucking chicken and its feelings."

Cassius grunted at that and Rikol turned to him. "Got something to add?"

The look Cassius gave him was enough for Rikol to take a step back. "I was just wondering if the Powers see us like Rikol saw those chickens. Useless. Expendable."

"The Powers are human-"

"The Powers are about as far from human as we are from insects," I interjected. "They may have been human long ago, but they are something else now. What did they call them in the past?"

"Seraphim," provided Sophia.

"Seraphim." I nodded my thanks at her. "Beings of such power that they were raised up as gods, and that was in a time of wonders that we cannot begin to comprehend. They've had thousands of years since then to grow stronger and perfect their abilities. We must seem like gnats to them."

My words found silence. Finally Rikol spoke, eyes curious. "Then how does that theory explain the Emperor?"

"Just because he is a good man, doesn't mean that he doesn't see us as assets more than humans," I countered. "I like to think of him as my friend, but I know that, if it came to it, I would be giving my life away to save his and not the other way around. And that is okay, because he is *the Emperor*. He can do inexplicable things with the greatest of ease and is deserving of our respect and admiration. Besides, he has proven that he has our best interests at heart. And by that I don't mean us as individuals but humanity as a whole."

Honestly, just thinking about this little speech makes my teeth hurt. Hindsight is twenty-twenty and all that, but was I really that naïve? Not a single one of the Powers care a whit about humanity, and I include the Wanderer in that. They care only about themselves. Humanity can go and burn for all they care.

And, as far as the records I've investigated have alluded, humanity did... several times.

For a long moment, none of us spoke, each of us resigned to our own thoughts. Thoughts of our actions that day no doubt, and of what was likely to befall us the next.

"Why do you think they got us to do it?" asked Cassius in the end, voice as hollow as his eyes.

"Do what?"

Cassius waved a hand and Sophia nodded. "The chickens?" She pursed her lips. "Probably to get us in the mindset of doing distasteful things for the Emperor and the Academy."

"Distasteful is one way of putting it," Scythe said mildly. "Sick and twisted is another."

Sophia gave a wry smirk. "You're in Wolf's Hollow, Scythe. Sick and twisted is the name of the game."

"Welcome back, Calidan. Did you sleep well?"

"You know full well that I didn't," I retorted to Carmine's disembodied voice. "Doubtless I have you to thank for that."

"Yes, well. It was your turn after all. But I have to say, good show. You are a very violent young man when push comes to shove. The perfect little killer."

"Fuck you."

"Ah well, there was me hoping for some sparkling conversation. My mistake. Let's be on with things then."

The door in front of me slid open. The sound of huffing breath had me tensing up before a sudden squeal announced my new roommate.

A large, pot-bellied pig.

I let out a sigh as I gazed at the pig, the creature ignoring me completely as it snuffled around the room, searching in vain for food. "Let me guess. This pig is somehow anathema to the empire."

"I knew you were a quick study!" Carmine exclaimed. "Pity I haven't seen much of it to date. Yes, the pig is an enemy of the empire. Dispatch it as you see fit and today's work is done."

I raised my hand to begin summoning a blade and Carmine crackled into life again. "Oh, I almost forgot to mention. The pig managed to eat something of great value to the Empire. If you could be so kind as to fetch it, that would be appreciated."

I bit back a retort, settling for rolling my eyes and approaching the pig. "Sorry buddy," I whispered sadly. "Today is just not your day."

It turned out that slaughtering and butchering a pig was not a clean or quick task. For one, they have an inordinate amount of blood inside them. Even though I had managed to kill it without spilling a drop, opening it up was another matter entirely. After fighting with what felt like a mile of intestine, I managed to find a small token, one that was similar to those that Carmine had made us hold onto for the previous round. It was only when I stood up and waved it around the room to prove that I had it that I realised just how covered in blood I truly was. It had soaked through my clothes and painted my skin a dark red. My fingers were almost black with the stuff. When I took in the scene in the room I shook my head in dismay. It looked like an abattoir and I was some kind of inept butcher.

"And now everyone gets to share in your activities!" exulted Carmine.

My sigh likely broke records.

"So..." drawled Rikol, eyes taking in my dishevelled state, "how did that go?"

My raised finger brought a grim smirk to his lips. "That well, eh?"

"You know exactly how well it went," I replied darkly, expending some seraph to evaporate the blood from my clothes and hands. The weird thing about blood though? It stains more than your clothes and flesh. It stains your mind. Despite *knowing* that there was not a single trace of blood left on me, I felt dirty. Unclean.

Wrong.

"You know, you really should try thinking about doing this a little less 'hands-on'-"

"Oh, come off it Rikol," interrupted Sophia. "No-one is in the mood for your shit."

"So it would seem," he replied, regarding us all with lidded eyes before heaving a sigh. "My genius wit will have to wait for when you are all back to your normal selves."

"You might be waiting a very long time," groused Scythe, also cleaning the blood off himself. "That was...unpleasant. I didn't know that a squealing pig could sound so..."

"Human?" offered Ella, and Scythe nodded darkly.

"Exactly. I felt like I was murdering an innocent in there!"

"In some respects, you were," said Ella. Her soft smile eased the glare that he threw her way. "The pig was likely as innocent as a pig can be."

"I-what..." he stammered before letting out a deep *whoosh* of breath and forcibly relaxing his shoulders. "You know what I mean."

"Yeah, I know what you mean."

Scythe stared forlornly at his cup of coffee. "This was a tough one."

"...It was just a pig!"

"Shut it, Rikol."

"Back for more, Calidan? You are a bloodthirsty little animal, aren't you?"

This time I didn't deign to reply. I knew that anything I said would just be a little victory for the wanker.

"Ah, decided to be silent and stoic, I see. Hmm. Hopefully that doesn't change for you with today's challenge."

I ignored him, just waited, seraph blade in hand. *Just get it over with. Quick and clean. Don't think too hard.*

The door opened and for a long time nothing moved. My eyes scanned the darkness on the other side of the door and I stepped back as a shadow moved. "No," I whispered.

"Ah, he speaks!"

"You can't be serious…"

The shadow detached itself from the room and entered, padding carefully inside. Its fur was a mixture of black and grey, spiky and erratic from as-yet-mastered grooming. Its eyes sparkled a deep green, the predatory iris wide as it explored its new surroundings.

"*Miaow.*"

My heart dropped and my seraph blade dissipated. The kitten was probably little more than four months old. Inquisitive, fearless and mind-blowingly cute. Knowing I shouldn't do it but doing it anyway, I crouched down and let the little feline come and sniff my hand.

"You're a sick bastard, Carmine."

"Comes with the territory, I'm afraid," he replied after a moment and I wondered if he was simultaneously talking to the others too.

"What's a kitten done to deserve death?!"

"Officially, it has been determined to be a seraph-enhanced creature that is capable of decimating entire populations. *Unofficially*, it just needs to die for you to continue this challenge."

"It's a kitten!"

"No. What it is, is your favourite animal," the unforgiving voice explained. "How can you expect to serve the empire if you can't handle such a simple task? I mean…" I could hear the sneer in his voice, "you're supposed to be the 'mighty' monster-hunter, aren't you? The way I see it, all the Enemy needs to do is send a few cats our way and you will be powerless to stop them. Pathetic."

"Go fuck yourself."

"I'm not going anywhere Calidan. The rules of this challenge are simple. Two parties enter, one leaves. You're stuck in there until you decide to do the right thing. And this time, there will be no food and no water."

"By the Pits, I wish you had never been born!"

"I'm sure my mother felt the same way," he replied drily. "But I'm done talking. Sort your shit out and get it done, or rot away in there until you die."

The cat nuzzled against my hand and I felt my heart clench.

Oh Seya. What do I do now?

CHAPTER 20

EXECUTIONER

I left the cell some four hours later, tears having carved little tributaries down my face. Cats had always been a personal favourite of mine, but ever since Seya they were like family. I couldn't pass one by without saying hello and had received numerous warnings from Kane about sneaking them into the Academy grounds. I was of the opinion that the more cats the better, but apparently the local bird population disagreed.

Cassius, Ella and Sophia were already outside. Their faces told me everything I needed to know.

"Rikol and Scythe?" I asked hoarsely.

"Still inside," whispered Ella. "...Did you?"

"Yes."

"I'm sorry."

"So am I."

The silence that followed was companionable but in the same way that battle-worn soldiers sit together and collectively stare into space. We had all lost something today. Innocence, perhaps.

"Cats?" asked Cassius after a long while, sitting next to me against the wall. None of us had summoned the energy to move to the canteen. Somehow the silence in this dark stretch of corridor fitted the mood.

I nodded and his lip twitched. "Elk?" I asked in return and he nodded as well.

"Don't know how they managed to transport it here, but got to give them credit for the effort," he said darkly. "I haven't seen one since we came back from the mountains. They're not exactly local to this area."

"Somehow, I think that the people running Wolf's Hollow have been preparing for us for some time," I replied. "Probably had plenty of time to get ready. I just wish it had been for something…better, rather than figuring out ways to screw us up."

Sophia gave the slightest of smiles and this seemed to fracture her composure, a sob breaking through despite her best efforts. Ella wrapped an arm around her on one side and I on the other whilst our friend gave vent to her grief. More than one tear was shed then, that's for certain.

Scythe came out roughly an hour after me, his shoulders slumped and face haggard. We dragged him into our group huddle and he didn't resist. Rikol, on the other hand, came out two hours after Scythe, his face puffy and red but an expression plastered on his face of grim determination.

"Don't touch me," he hissed as Ella reached up to pull him in.

"Rikol…"

"Shut up. I don't want to hear it. Just…shut…up." His voice wavered and cracked at the end, tears blurring his eyes. Cassius stood and extended his hand. "Come on buddy," he croaked. "It's alright."

"No!" he blurted, eyes streaming tears. "It's not alright. It will never be alright!" Turning on his heel, he stormed off, his shoulders hunched almost to his ears.

"Should we go after him?" I asked.

"No." It was Ella, her voice sad. "He needs time."

"Must have hit him hard."

Ella swallowed. "Rikol has already seen his favourite animal killed. Us street-rats, we often made bonds with the kinds of animals we encountered down in the muck. Cats, crows, you get the idea. Rikol…he had a pet rat." Ella's eyes glistened as she recanted. "You have to understand, when you're barely eating anything as it is but you still save food for your friend, the bond that grows between you is probably as strong as that of mother and child. Well, Rikol loved this rat. One day he didn't have enough to pay off one of the bigger kids and…"

"Oh no," breathed Sophia.

"Yep. His rat was crushed to death under the boot of this bully."

"That's…"

"Horrible," I finished.

"It's life as a streeter," Ella replied matter-of-factly without a hint of rancour.

"How do you know this?" asked Cassius.

Ella shrugged. "Rikol and I have a connection. Always have. Comes from having a shared background. One night he got too deep into his cups and shared that with me. Never mentioned it since."

"So he had to do the same thing in there," Cassius whispered. "Poor guy."

"He'll be okay," Ella insisted. "He just needs some space. Especially from us."

Cassius looked hurt. "What do you mean?"

"He has been pretending that all of this hasn't bothered him so far. Made out like we were the silly ones for feeling it. Now he has let that façade drop and he is going to feel foolish," Ella answered. "Trust me. Give him some space. He'll come around."

"If you say so," Cassius muttered.

We stayed like that for a little longer and then dragged ourselves to the canteen and then back to the dorm. Rikol wasn't there. He didn't come in until the early hours of the morning, stumbling into bed with the scent of strong alcohol flowing off him. I knew that everyone heard him come in; the silent tension so thick that it made me want to scream. It was only after a few minutes when Ella got up to pull the covers over the comatose street-rat that we all breathed silent sighs of relief and sunk into oblivion, knowing that the morning would come all too soon.

"Once more into the breach, Calidan?"

"Once more, go fuck yourself."

"I'm beginning to believe that you aren't a morning person."

I yawned and raised two fingers to the stone wall. "Let's just get on with it."

"Determination to get things done. Very becoming of an Imperator. I like it."

"Fantastic," I murmured wryly. "That's why I do what I do, after all."

"You'll be happy to know that you're halfway through."

My heart sank. "Only halfway?"

"Correct. *But*, and this is important, you could complete the entire challenge today."

"Explain."

"It's simple. Today you get the option to continue or retreat. If you choose to push ahead then you cannot leave without completing the mission. If you retreat then you will return tomorrow as usual and given the option again."

"And will I know what I will be facing before I decide to push ahead or not?"

A momentary silence during which I knew he was smiling far too broadly. "Not a chance."

"De-fucking-lightful."

"Are you ready to begin?"

I nodded, jaw clenching as I tried to steel myself for what was to come and knowing that, if Carmine was involved, it would be worse than anything I could have envisioned.

It really sucks to be right sometimes.

The first door was a repeat of the previous day. Though when I say repeat, what I really mean is an *enhanced* version. Instead of one kitten, I faced twelve. That nearly broke me from the start. I knew that if I remotely began to bond with them then I would never be able to do what was needed and so envisioned myself as how I pictured one of the Powers: resolute, unyielding and completely uninterested in anything below me. That feeble mental manipulation gave me enough strength to reach out with my will, raise a barrier and drain the oxygen on the other side. I was tempted to look away, to hide from my actions, but forced myself to look. To meet their little eyes as the life within was extinguished. When it was done, I collapsed to the floor, completely and utterly drained.

"And here we go, time to compare notes!" Carmine cackled through the room. "Watch and learn. See how your *friends* operate."

I watched. I learnt.

...But perhaps not what Carmine had expected me to. Instead of focusing on the actions of my dormmates and the waves of favourite creatures that they were being forced to exterminate, I saw their drive, their determination to step forwards and be the Imperator that they had each been training to be. In a strange, detached way, I was proud of them. Proud that they hadn't let Carmine win. That they were stepping forwards, heads high despite the weight that was bearing down on their shoulders.

Each of them looked at hollow as I felt at the end. But none of them were complete wrecks. Even Rikol, despite the horrors of the day before, had found the strength to do what needed to be done; going about it with clinical detachment despite the tears that ran down his face.

All too soon, Carmine's voice reached my ears. "One round done. Two to go. Are you going to forge ahead or retreat?"

I let loose a deep breath. "Ahead."

"You know that you cannot leave after that door opens?"

I nodded. "Just get on with it."

"As you wish. You have five minutes to prepare yourself."

I stiffened, looking at the little corpses scattered around me. "Aren't you going to get rid of them?"

"Oh no, they are reminders of how far you have come. Deal with them yourself if it matters to you so. But know that what comes next might not be quite so simple to deal with."

What he means is, do I want to use my seraph reserve to get rid of bodies? I realised. Taking another deep breath, I steeled myself. *They're dead and gone, Cal. No need to waste the energy. Save it for whatever comes through that door.*

A few minutes later, Carmine's voice returned. "So far, you've gallantly faced the four-legged enemies of the empire. And, I have to say, you've done *adequately*. However, as an Imperator you are the voice of the Emperor wherever you are, which means that you will, at times, be called upon to dispense justice. On the other side of this door are two criminals. They are rapists, thieves and murderers. They have no qualms about killing and are doubtless looking forward to doing it once more, likely with you as their target. The local constabulary captured them and have them bound. The local magistrate has asked you to dispense the Emperor's justice. Tell me, Calidan, what is the punishment for murder and rape in the empire?"

I closed my eyes, swallowing the horror. "Death," I whispered.

"Death." Carmine repeated. "The verdict is given. Let the judgement be carried out."

The door slowly began to slide open, revealing two men with lean, hard figures. They were bare-chested with worn wool trousers cladding their bottom halves. The array of tattoos, scars and burn marks spoke of hard lives, and the way that their eyes burrowed into mine suggested that they knew full well what was going on.

"Well, lookie 'ere," said the first, a bald man with a vivid scar that ran along one side of his head. "What you doin' over there kid? Let us go already. We done nothin' wrong!"

"Aye, nuffin'!" the second man echoed, his throat sounding like he had swallowed glass for the last twenty years. "Let us out!"

"Out!"

"Let us go free!"

"Freedom!"

"QUIET!" I shouted, the shout reverberating around the room. "Now, why are you here? What did you do?"

"Told ya. Ain't dun nuffin."

"You're here, aren't you?"

The first man made a show of looking around and then spat on the floor. "Don't know where 'ere is boy. Who are you?"

"The man who is tasked with your sentencing."

My words caused the two to momentarily lapse into silence before bursting into laughter. "'Man' he says!" roared the first. "Your balls dropped yet lad?"

I reached out to the side and willed a long blade into existence. It shimmered into life, rapidly forming until it gleamed in the darkness with a razor-sharp edge. The sudden silence confirmed that the men were rapidly re-evaluating their opinion.

"Now then, lad," said the first, "let's talk 'bout this."

"Dun nuffin' wrong," the second muttered again, but this time his voice held a quaver of fear and lacked the same conviction as before.

"Let's start over," I growled. "Tell me what you did."

"I-I dun know what you're talkin' 'bout."

"You do. You both do." Raising a hand, I conjured a ball of green flame.

"That's n-n-not possible."

I raised an eyebrow. "Oh really?" Willing the fire to move, I sent it to hover just above the first man's brow where he could feel the intensity of the heat. "I think you might need to reconsider what is and isn't possible."

Despite the racing heart thudding within his chest and the wide eyes that spoke of tremendous fear, the man swallowed and shook his head. "I did nothing. Nothing!"

The second man squirmed in the corner of my vision, his eyes locked onto the ball of green flame. "W-witch! Demon!" he exclaimed; horror thick in his voice. "G-get away!"

"You're right," I replied, adopting the most menacing voice I could. "I am a demon. But you know what's worse?" I waited until he focused enough to shake his head. "I'm an Imperator."

I hadn't really counted on the effect that would have. I knew that the title of Imperator held weight but the way that the blood drained from both men's faces was astonishing.

The stench of fear suddenly became overwhelming, alongside the loss of bladder control from Glass-throat. "It weren't me," he cried desperately. "It were 'im! He took the girl."

"Quiet you fool!" the first man hissed.

"I-I just 'elped."

"Yeah, helped yourself to the leftovers more like!" the first sneered, giving up on keeping him quiet.

"Nonononnno."

I closed my eyes and let the sounds wash over me. From their words and the unnoticed actions of their own bodies, I knew beyond reasonable doubt that what Carmine had told me about them was true. But could I take their lives?

Come on, Calidan. You've taken lives before.

That was different. The heat of battle. These are tied up.

They've admitted to what they've done. The Emperor's justice is clear.

It's cold blood!

They deserve it!

Yes...but should I be the executioner?

If you want to be an Imperator, this is one of their responsibilities.

My grip tightened on the hilt of my blade until my knuckles went white. *It-it shouldn't be me.*

The dark, grim voice of rationality at the back of my mind paused for a moment, then the words came to me, soft and gentle. *If not you, then who?*

Carmine!

Not here. Out in the Wild. You will be looked up to, feared and respected. Your word will be law because it is the word of the Emperor. Can you really shirk that responsibility when you choose to?

My eyes opened. Scar-head saw me and recognised the look on my face because he began to shout. "No, please, *pleas-*"

Thump.

I flicked the blade, blood scattering across the wall, the man's body still standing upright spurting jets of thick ochre before following its head to the floor.

Glass-throat was beyond words now, just keening in wild terror. I doubt he had really even seen me move, just saw the end result. Taking two strides, I plunged the blade deep into his chest, piercing through his heart and out the other side. Blood bubbled from his lips as his eyes went glassy, his body slumping to the ground as I pulled my blade free.

"The Emperor's justice has been dispensed," I whispered, letting the bloody blade dissipate back into nothingness and striding to the corner of the room. There I let the iron control I had exerted over myself drop and threw up all over the wall.

"Well done." Carmine's voice, and the last that I wanted to hear. I waved him off and for the first time he didn't laugh or insult me – at least, not audibly. Instead, his voice sounding surprisingly gentle, he informed me that I had ten-minutes to compose myself and then we would be reviewing the footage.

Curled up in the corner of the room next to a pile of vomit and shaking with a toxic mixture of adrenaline and shock, those ten-minutes felt simultaneously like an eternity and no time at all.

"Review time." Carmine called and the wall lit up as before. As expected, no-one had left between the first and second rounds. I forced myself to watch, just like I knew that the others would be doing in my place.

Rikol, his face a mask of grim determination that covered overwhelming grief, had barely given the two men in front of him any thought. In a show of terrifying skill, he simply concentrated. Moments later, both men's arteries on both sides of their necks exploded outwards in dramatic fashion, liberally coating the room with blood as they collapsed, but none of it touched Rikol's clothes. He looked at them critically, like he was studying the effectiveness of his technique, then turned away.

Ella, Sophia, Scythe and Cassius all asked questions like I had. I couldn't hear what was said, but they all came to the same verdict. Ella had opened the men's throats with knives, her movements quick and fluid. Sophia – her face a picture of pure disgust at whatever information she had got out of her pair – simply flung force lances. I hadn't really seen the effectiveness of such an attack against someone with no seraph defence before. Following that display, I wasn't sure I wanted to ever again. It was like they had both been hit with ballista bolts, sending them flying into the far wall in clouds of blood.

One of Scythe's captives said something that they really shouldn't have done because his expression turned wrathful. The mess that his kama had made of both men by the end was distressing to see.

Finally, Cassius. He looked like he held court and took the longest out of everyone to come to a decision. I could tell that he hated every minute of it, but when the time came he didn't hold back, his blade taking the lives of both in swift, sure strokes. He then bowed his head and broke down in tears.

I understood that all too well, but also knew that Cassius was crying not just because of the lives he had taken in cold blood, but because he was being forced to choose between justice and innocence...and justice was prevailing.

"Before we continue," said Carmine after the review had finished, "you should know that if you choose to leave and any of your dormmates choose to continue, you will be kept separately and unable to interact until everyone has completed the challenge. Understood?"

I nodded weakly.

"Good," he replied. "So. Do you finish this or do you rest on it, knowing that tomorrow will be the final day instead?"

I didn't answer him immediately, instead just stared at my hands until I could get the shaking under control, lost in my own thoughts. Carmine must have sensed that because he simply let me know that I had five minutes to decide.

What's best for my mental state? Push forwards or take a break?

I scoffed at my own thought. *Can a day off really be called a 'break'? I'll be thinking about it all night. Worrying. Remembering.*

...Is that worse?

I didn't know.

"Five minutes are up," declared Carmine. "What's your choice?"

I looked at the bodies around me and down at my hands, knowing that they were clean to the eye but deeply stained in blood.

"Calidan?"

I drew in a deep breath and let it go in a long sigh. "Today's been beyond bad. I'm not going to make tomorrow worse. So," I grimaced somewhat crazily at the surrounding walls where Carmine was somehow watching, "let's get this done. The final push."

PRESENT DAY 5

"Fuck me but it's hot!" I ground out the whine through the sandy fissure that once had been my vocal chords. Hearing a muted mutter of what I suspected was agreement, I looked over my shoulder. "Cass, how you doing back there?"

The big man stumbled in the sand before sinking down to his knees and running his fingers through the golden dust.

"Cass, we can't stop here, not yet."

"Sanddd."

Walking back towards him, I crouched down and put a hand on his shoulder. "That's right mate, sand. There's a shit-tonne of sand out here and we can't be stopping every few metres to play with it. Sorry."

His big eyes filled with sadness and he thrust a massive hand out towards me, streaming particles draining out at a prodigious rate. "Sand!"

"Sand," I agreed with a nod. "Want to go see some more sand?"

That got his attention.

"Come on then. I hear that there is some great sand further ahead. The best sand anywhere in the desert."

"Saaaand!"

"Sand," I agreed, pulling him up to his feet and setting off once more. "Too much fucking sand. I mean, seriously, who thought it would be a good idea to go and set up shop in a desert? Talk about inhospitable."

"Bad sand," Cassius agreed.

"You tell it Cass."

"*BAD SAND!*" He roared the words, causing the sand around us to tremble.

"Good work. Got it scared of you." Shaking my head in amusement, I set off, one sliding footstep after another. "Should have really thought to bring a horse. Or a camel. Something with extra feet so I don't have to use mine. But no, supplicants to the Dusk Court have to walk. Because of course they fucking do. And yes, if anyone is listening to this, it's not fun and I'm not having a great time. Your court better be as good as the legends say to make it worthwhile!" My voice rang into the empty air and I let out a long sigh, feeling marginally better with the rant whilst continuing to force one foot in front of the other.

"Fucking sand."

The Dusk Court. A place of impossibility. Of breathtaking beauty and savage delight. Sandstone and artfully designed glass whirled together with uncanny skill to create a city of awe-inspiring colour. A jewel amongst the desert.

At least on the surface.

I had reason to hate the place. As a monster-hunter I tended to stay away from the more clandestine back-stabbing that the majority of Imperators got themselves involved in from time-to-time, preferring to face my enemies openly and without guile.

And no, I don't count robbing the Powers. The Academy trains clever Imperators and openly robbing a Power would be tantamount to a very explosive and painful suicide.

Actually, scratch that. I would hands down prefer to stab a monster in the back of the neck before it even had chance to register my presence. Hmm. On reflection perhaps I'm not so different from the other Imperators, just instead of backstabbing people, I backstab behemoths.

Anyway, I digress.

In my eyes – and those of anyone with any common sense - the Dusk Court was a cesspit of scum and villainy. Just very well dressed and impeccably mannered scum. Everyone there was a snake. *Everyone.* It's how you got ahead in the Court. Heroic deeds were one thing but quickly forgotten. Learning how to manipulate everyone around you and whisper poison in their ears, that was the true art played within this kingdom.

How much easier it is to tear someone down rather than build yourself up.

Rizaen, Power and queen of the Dusk Court, ruled with honeyed lips that belied an iron fist. No benevolent ruler, nor a complete tyrant, her nature switched depending on what she wanted out of any meeting.

For Rizaen, out of perhaps all the Powers, was a shrewd and cunning monster.

She knew how to cultivate her image and she had done it well. The masses loved her, despite knowing her reputation for flaying alive people who wasted her time. And I guess why not? There was bounty in the Dusk Court – for those willing to play the game – and many opportunities for promotion. If you were good enough to avoid the manipulations of others whilst tearing down those in your sights, then you could fly high. Too high though and you might attract the attention of the Power herself, and that was a very dangerous game indeed. Her closest advisors usually didn't have a long track record, but for some the allure of the game itself and the power that came with it was too much to resist. Like a mouse trying to placate the viper with other offerings, they dexterously walked the fine line offering too much and opening themselves to attack from the ranks below, and offering too little and finding the Dusk Queen's fangs in their throat.

So yes, I despise the Court. A foppish city filled with shoe-lickers and snakes. I'm probably doing some people in that city an injustice but I really do not care.

After all, it's where Scythe was executed.

Swallowing my bitterness, I knocked on the door to the hotel and was quickly ushered in by a bowing and scraping man in flowing robes.

"Ah, welcome, welcome!" he gushed. "Please come in. How may I help you…" his eyes took in the full size of Cassius and he faltered, "…honoured guests?"

"A room for the night," I declared, handing him some coin. "Some water, wine and the latest news."

His eyes sparkled. "Ah, but of course sir! Would you like a private dissemble or would you prefer in the bar? There aren't many ears at this point of the day."

"The bar will be fine."

"Excellent choice," he waved a hand, "if you would follow me?"

In short order we had deposited our sand-encrusted belongings and settled down in the cool air of the underground bar. Many of the Dusk Court's buildings contained cellars to help get away from the incessant heat and the majority of the more entrepreneurial spirits had jointly determined that the best thing to help deal with the heat was an excessive array of drinks. It was, perhaps, the sole thing that I actually liked coming to the city for.

"So, any particular areas of focus?" the manager and barkeep, Hazhan, asked politely as he poured a chilled grape wine into two glasses and passed them over.

Glancing from side-to-side and noting only a couple of individuals who were already deep into their cups and likely not too interested in overhearing what they had likely known already, I pursed my lips in thought. "The latest trade information and house politics if you would."

"Gladly." Hazhan paused for a moment and then poured himself a drink. "Helps loosen the pipes," he said affably when he caught my eye before launching into the latest news from the Grand Bazaar. Most of it was not of interest and served only to cement my disguise as an interested party to commerce. Those few people in the bar might think that Cassius was a monstrously huge bodyguard for a wealthy merchant.

Granted, that was a long shot, but hey – people believe dumb things when it is the easiest path.

"And now the house politics," Hazhan said, his tone a little more quiet than before. "The House of Raz'eth holds prominence within the Court. Two of the Queen's closest advisors are from that great house, including her grand vizier."

"Really?" I let out a low whistle. "Last time I was here, Raz'eth was a small house with little to offer. That has changed quickly."

"You've been gone too long then my friend!" Hazhan joked. "But yes, Raz'eth's rise has been meteoric. Some well-placed words and no doubt a few better placed knives." Tapping the side of his nose he leant in conspiratorially. "They say House Pash'a lost four of its most highly ranked in one night. It toppled the power structure within the Court. Pash'a begged the Queen to intervene but you know what she is like – the games of court are just that, *games*." He smiled wide, his teeth slightly stained by the use of a shindar pipe. "The more violent the better."

"Sounds like the Court I used to know," I replied with a half-smile. "Everyone plays, most lose."

"If you remember that, you might just do better in the markets than I had first thought," he said with a laugh. "Now that I look at you closely, you have the presence of a most devilish trader. One with a, ahem, *killer instinct*."

"Looks can be deceiving."

"Perhaps. Perhaps not. But come, we should talk of lighter things."

All things considered, Hazhan made for pleasant company. He knew that I wasn't a local – not that I could ever have passed for one with my pasty skin – but my deft rebuttals of his politely phrased enquiries left him only wanting more.

It was good to see that my skills hadn't become too rusty. Conversation was an artform here. Layers upon layers of meaning in the most innocent sounding of conversations. The objective was always to leave feeling that you gained more than you gave away. Sophia and Scythe had been the best at this; their easy-going charm and good looks doing more for their intelligence-gathering than any number of witting repartees that I could provide.

These days, Sophia had just as much reason to avoid the Dusk Court as me, if not more.

"What of House Visgothe?" I asked casually after a few minutes of small talk. At my words, Hazhan's expression darkened.

"Visgothe? You know them?"

"I am...acquainted, but it has been a long time. Time perhaps to refresh my relationships."

"Ah, my friend," he shook his head slowly, "you should raise your sights higher than Visgothe. They have fallen out of favour as of late."

"And why would that be?"

"The House of Visgothe have never got on with Raz'eth. Things were bloody for a while." He shrugged. "You know how it is. Someone goes missing or turns up dead on one side and a few days later the same happens on the other. Before you know it there is a little House war going on. This time the queen had to step in to make sure that both Houses had people left. She wasn't a huge fan of having to do that and so placed the blame for escalation on House Visgothe. Their status has dropped greatly. To be seen with them would be to lower your own."

"Your caution is well received," I replied warmly, "and I thank you for it. But if one were to go looking for the House, where would they be located? I presume not in the Inner Diamond?"

"Bah, no!" he exclaimed with a bark of laughter. "Their property was stripped from them as part of their fall from grace." Lowering his voice and casting a wary eye at the other people in the cellar as though even mentioning the discredited House would tarnish his own reputation, he muttered, "They are in the Silver Quarter now."

"Truly?!" I had no need to feign my astonishment. The Silver Quarter, for a noble house, was like being cast down to live in a hovel. Commoners holding no special license could purchase land in the Silver Quarter and I well knew how the nobility felt about such things.

Hazhan nodded in feigned sympathy. "Truly. They have come across hard times indeed. As you said, everyone plays and most lose. House Visgothe has well and truly lost."

We spoke for a little longer before Hazhan had to move on to greet new guests, leaving me alone with my thoughts and the odd burbling noise from Cassius. The fact that House Visgothe had fallen so low could throw a wrench into my plans, for being so out of favour with the rest of the court might curtail things before they had even begun. I mused over my drink, idly swirling the cool liquid around in the cup, running through plan after plan in my head.

This was going to be hard.

I wasn't here on official business. I had no diplomatic credentials as an Imperator. My long-coat was rolled up and stuffed deep into my carry-sack where it wouldn't be easily found. Without official business or an invitation, entrance into the Inner Diamond – the home of the greatest noble families and the abode of Rizaen herself – was strictly forbidden. Those rules were enforced without mercy and executed by Rizaen's extremely competent royal guard. Without seraph, I would be hard-pressed to take one in single combat...and considering they roamed in squads of three, a direct assault wouldn't be the wisest of choices.

What I needed was to see if Tara'zin was still alive. She had been an advisor to Rizaen's head architect and a middling member of the Visgothe House. Hopefully that meant that she hadn't been targeted for murder. Better still, she knew who and what I was – a little corruption was just a means to an end in the desert and the Academy paid well. At the very least she might be able to get me into Rizaen's palace. At best?

She might well have the plans to the whole damn place.

CHAPTER 21

THE FINAL PUSH

"You've decided to continue. You can no longer change your mind," Carmine intoned. "For this challenge, things are a little different."

Glyphs flashed into life on the walls and ceilings around me and I felt suddenly hollow, like I was missing a connection that I had always known. "What have you…?"

"Seraph wards have been raised. They can't completely stop you from utilising seraph; nothing can."

Not true, I thought, thinking of the star-metal bracelets.

"But as long as they are active, using seraph will be extremely difficult."

"So, you want this to be, let me guess, 'up close and personal'?"

"Something like that."

I snorted and shook my head in disgust. "Fine. What else?"

"The last challenge was clear cut. This one, not so much. The person before you might be someone who made a mistake, who perhaps repents but has crossed a line from which there can be no coming back. The Emperor's justice still holds, however, and must be meted out."

"Even if they're trying to change their ways?" I exclaimed, aghast.

"The verdict has already been rendered," Carmine replied. "They are to die. Remember, only one can leave this room. If you want to survive, I suggest you hold onto that iron will of yours and do what is necessary. If there is no change in three hours' time, there will be a little *incentive* dropped into the cell. No other information is forthcoming. Nod if you understand."

I growled and then forced myself to nod.

"Good. The final challenge begins now."

I bit my lip as the door began to slide open, hoping against hope that what I suspected wasn't true. As the door got to halfway, a hand reached out and wrapped around its edge. The appendage dwarfed mine, the fingers probably half as thick again, the hard skin and scars along the back of the hand suggesting either a fighter or someone who worked in a dangerous job. The figure stooped to get past the door and then rose up, stretching out to seemingly fill the room. He must have been three inches on me and I'm not a small man but unlike me he was also imposingly *vast*. Like Kane, if Kane was six-foot-six and spent every moment of his life lifting weights.

Piercing amber eyes scanned the array of dead kittens and corpses then locked onto mine.

"Hello," the giant rumbled and all my fears came crashing back. I knew that voice. Knew it well, in fact. The owner of it had been quiet, sensible and, moreover, kind to an Imp being held in an Imperator prison.

"Hello Jarv," I said quietly.

He stiffened at the sound of my voice then snorted, shaking his head. "Guess I was right after all."

"...Looks like it."

He heard the tone in my voice and smiled warmly. "Whatever the plan is for our immediate future, let me do one thing first." He stepped forward, covering the ground so abruptly that I half-dropped into a fighting stance. "Ah," he said sadly. "Sorry. I didn't mean to startle you." Outstretching his hand, he offered it to me. "Nice to finally meet you Calidan."

I rose from my stance, abashed, and clasped his hand warmly. "You too, Jarv," I replied hoarsely. "And sorry... it's been a long few days."

He made a show of looking around. "I can see that. Part of your Imperator testing I assume?"

"Yes. Not the most pleasant part."

"If it was, I wouldn't be shaking your hand."

"Touche." We grinned at each other, delighting in a few moments of friendship before the horror of what was going to happen descended once more.

"So, what's it like being an Imperator?" Jarv said as he took a few steps to the side and found himself a place against the wall.

"I'm not one yet," I remarked dryly. "But I can tell you that the things I've seen so far have proven the world to be a stranger, more terrifying and more wonderful place than I had ever imagined."

"'Wonder'?" Jarv said, eyes flashing around the room. "Not the word I expected to hear, especially considering where you are sitting."

I pursed my lips. "Perhaps the dark things that have to be done are a juxtaposition for the good moments. Maybe it makes me feel them all the more? I don't know. But what I do know is that without the Academy and the Emperor, I would likely be dead already."

"Really?" Jarv's eyes glistened as he leaned forward, curiosity written across his face. "Tell me."

So I did. I told him everything. All the bad and all the good. About the massacre of my village, hunting monsters, technologies from before the Cataclysm...even about Riven. He proved to be an attentive listener, asking few questions but each one he asked added more depth to my delivery. Once I was finished, he sat back, shaking his head slowly.

"All that," he rumbled in astonishment, "and you're only, what, eighteen?"

"Twenty."

He shook his head again. "I know you've seen some wonders, but I truly do not envy you. You've led a hard life Calidan, far too hard in my opinion." He eyed the walls around him wryly. "And it only gets harder from the look of it. Are you sure that this is what you want?"

"There are things out there that prey on humans," I answered slowly, "and I'm one of the few that can stop them. Each death I can prevent is a win."

"That's not an answer." His eyes bore into mine. "Is this what you actually want?"

I didn't answer for a long time. "I used to think so," I whispered finally. "I was so driven by revenge, a desperate hunger to kill the thing that destroyed my village and my life, that I only thought about the best way that I could accomplish that goal. But..."

"But?" he echoed.

"But the more death I see and visit upon others, the more I realise that the world needs something other than killers. It hurts for me to recognise that."

"What do you mean?"

"Because I know that I can only view it from the outside. That in progressing down this path I will never be able to have anything resembling a normal life. But then," my face twisted, "that was never going to happen to me."

"It still might?"

I shook my head. "No. There is no leaving the Academy. This is my life now. I chose it and it continues to choose me."

"Did you choose it though?" he questioned softly.

"Of course I did, why do you ask?"

"Because that's not what you told me earlier. You said that you were forced to join the Academy because of your giant...cat?"

"Panther," I corrected automatically. "Yes. I had to be part of the Academy because of my bond with Seya. The Emperor required it."

"So," Jarv said gently, "you never actually had a choice."

"I...no." I grimaced at the thought. "But this is what I would have chosen."

"You're sure?"

I thought back over the past few years, everything that had happened, all the bad and good before nodding firmly. "Yes. Whilst it may hurt at times," I choked back a laugh, "hells *most of the time*, I think I can do some good in the world. Even if I am little more than a monster of my own making."

"You're much more than a monster, Calidan," Jarv replied seriously. "And you're certainly not one of your own making, whatever you might think."

"...Thank you?"

He grinned, showing bright white teeth. "Don't mention it."

"How about you?"

"Me?"

"Your story."

"Hah!" he laughed. "Not much to tell, really. Apprenticed as a blacksmith from age eight. Continued working the forge throughout my life."

"Ahhh, that explains it." Seeing his raised eyebrow, I continued. "Your size. The amount of muscle."

"I've always been big, but yes, wielding a hammer all day and lifting steel makes you strong." He gazed at his hands. "It makes you too strong sometimes."

"...The man you killed?"

He nodded. "I didn't mean it. *Gods* I didn't mean it. But I was so, so angry. I hit him, then I hit him again. Aria screamed at me to stop but I couldn't. It was like something in me had just *snapped*. When I came to, he was... well," he barked a laugh and indicated the room, "makes this look clean." He shook his head in dismay. "I saw the way that Aria looked at me. The fear in her eyes. I saw the blood coating my hands and I knew that I needed to turn myself in. It was the right thing to do."

"Jarv, I'm so sorry."

He waved a hand. "We all have our past. Some more than others. If my time has come then I face it willingly. I committed a foul deed and whilst I have tried to atone it still haunts me."

"You're a good man."

He gave a sad smile. "I would say the same thing about you. It doesn't change that we are both killers. Perhaps that means that a person can be both. I would like to think so."

"You *are* a good man," I insisted.

"As are you," he replied. "And whatever has to happen here, you must remember that. The world might try to turn you into a monster, but you will only be one if you *choose* it. I could have run away. Could have tried my hand at banditry or started a new life somewhere else, but owning up to what I did, that was the only way that I could prevent myself from sinking deeper into that person that I had no desire to be."

"Even though it has led you here?"

He tossed his head back and laughed, the sound deep and throaty. "Yes, even though it has brought me here. I have tried to repent for my actions, but if the Emperor wills my death it shall be so. Unless, of course, there is another reason for me being brought into this tragically decorated room?" He finished with a raised eyebrow and small smile.

I shook my head mutely, at a complete loss for words. Here Jarv was, being possibly the bravest person I had ever met and meeting his apparent death head on. I could understand that in battle, with nowhere to retreat, but this was more akin to an execution and that had the ability to turn even the bravest soul's bowels to water.

"I thought not," he said softly. "If this is my time, so be it. Just know that it is not *your fault,* Calidan. You are but the hand that wields the blade of justice."

"*How?*" I whispered.

"How what?"

"How can you be so calm about all of this?"

"You forget that I have suspected this was to be my end for some time now. I have had more than enough time to come to terms with it." His eyes adopted a far-away look as he smiled. "It is strange, knowing that your death is forthcoming is kind of freeing, in its own way. Peaceful, even. I doubt that is true of everyone, however."

I snorted through my tears. "Somehow I doubt that Clythe is quite as readily willing to be executed."

"No, I'm afraid not. And you've pointed something out that I hadn't considered yet," he raised a hand and waved it at the mess around us, "this isn't technically an execution is it. There is an option here for those of us on the receiving end of things that doesn't involve exposing our throats."

I tensed. *Has he been waiting for this moment to make his move?* "Seems that way," I said guardedly. "Two enter, one leaves. That's all I know."

"I see. And with no weapons immediately available it falls to our fists."

"Correct."

He held my stare for a moment before shaking his head. "I pity whichever of your friends faces Clythe. He might look and sound mad, but I do not think he would go down so easily."

Relaxing, I gave a sad smirk. "Clythe might be a madman but I wouldn't bet against any of my friends."

"No," he said quietly, "no, from what you've told me, you're probably right. I doubt the Emperor's best would be easy to subdue, weapons or no. But still...I don't envy them that fight."

"Nor I."

We sat in companionable silence for some time, lost in thought and memories. Eventually, the crackling noise I had grown accustomed to filled the air and Jarv leapt to his feet, staring around in amazement as Carmine's voice filled the air.

"Three hours have passed," Carmine intoned gravely, "and yet the two of you remain standing. It seems that a little *inspiration* is in order."

A cunningly hidden hatch opened in the ceiling and something tumbled down what sounded like a metal tunnel before clattering out onto the ground. It was a knife. Nothing fancy, just a short stabbing knife, the kind for close alley work by the kind of people that Ella and Rikol used to run with. Both Jarv and I stared at the dully gleaming blade on the floor, neither moving a muscle.

"Calidan," Carmine continued, "if you manage to kill Jarv you will have completed this challenge and progress one step further to being an Imperator. Jarv, if you pick up that knife and kill Calidan," I could hear the sinister smile in Carmine's voice as he spoke, as though he relished that particular thought, "I will not have you thrown back into a cell like your dear friend Clythe, but you will be freed with your record expunged."

Jarv started at that. "You mean...?"

"Yes. You will be a free man with your life ahead of you. All you have to do is take that knife and plunge it into Calidan's heart."

Jarv looked at me. Looked at the knife. Looked at me again.

"Jarv," I whispered.

He bolted, pushing up away from the wall and grabbing the blade by the hilt, brandishing it in front of me as I rapidly rolled to my feet. The tiny lump of metal in his gigantic hands would have been laughable if I wasn't aware of how easy it would be for him to snag me with the obscene power he held in his arms and hold me still just long enough to fill me with holes.

"Jarv," I said again, raising my hands and beginning to circle. "Don't listen to him. He lies."

"Oh, this offer is very much real," Carmine replied, obviously listening in. "Good to see it is having the desired effect. Keep it up, Jarv!"

"Put the knife down, Jarv."

He raised an eyebrow, "Why, so you can pick it up and kill me with it?"

"I-er..."

"I think the answer you're looking for is 'yes' there, Calidan." He moved forward a step and I spun aside, trying to keep distance.

"Jarv, please!"

His eyes held an impossible depth of sadness. "He offered me freedom, Calidan. Do you know what that is to a man like me?" Raising his hand, he extended a middle finger towards the ceiling. "Absolutely nothing."

And with a quick *schnick* of metal on flesh, he sliced through his wrist.

"Jarv!" I exclaimed, dashing forwards as he threw the knife aside.

"Leave it," he insisted as he sat back down, blood thumping out of the deep cut in time to his heart. Looking at my stunned face, he gave a pained smile. "We both know that you would have tried to get around this one way or another, and I know that the man upstairs who is probably listening in on this right now is not the kind of man to hold his bargains. And even if he was," he continued, ignoring both my splutter and a crackle from Carmine, "even if my record was wiped clean, I would not be absolved of my sin. I would have just replaced it with another one." His voice grew a little faint as he finished and he shook his head as though clearing it of dizziness. "No, this is better." He locked eyes with me and smile broadly, a bright, genuine smile. "This is *right*."

"Jarv..." I whispered, sorrow clutching at my chest. "I'm so sorry."

"Don't be," he said warmly, taking my hand with his other one. "I'm not."

I held his gaze as he slipped away, his smile never fading whilst my tears watered down the blood that pooled around us both.

"Goodbye," I whispered. "I'll make your sacrifice worthwhile. I promise."

Yet another broken vow.

The door ground open and I stepped outside, leaving behind a scene of carnage. Carmine stood there, face impassive as he locked eyes with me. "Well done," he intoned. "You pass."

I didn't answer and made to push past him, hoping that he would get the hint, instead he fell into step with me. "I know that you will most likely want to go to sleep and wish away the last few days but I suggest you make your first stop to the second-floor bathroom. The showers are hot and you will find new changes of clothes there. Take as long as you want. The majority of your friends are already back. You should let them know that Cassius is still inside and that Ella is now available for visitation."

That made me stop dead, causing him to stumble. "Visitation? Was she-"

"Hurt?" He grimaced. "Yes, but nothing that a few days won't fix. She had the unfortunate pleasure of meeting your acquaintance Clythe. He was...excited to meet her from the moment he stepped out the door. It was a close call for a while, but the bruising on her neck has been vastly reduced and she might even be able to talk."

I held his gaze for a moment then nodded. I didn't want to waste my words on the man despite him actually seeming to be doing something decent. He called after me as I walked away. "I'm not always a monster, Calidan. I just have a job to do. Just like you. Rest up. The final test will come soon."

Just like you. The words haunted me as I walked the lonely corridors before stumbling into the bathroom and walking into the shower completely clothed. The water turned scarlet as it tumbled down my body and as the steam rose in billowing clouds I fell to my knees, vomited, then curled up tight, letting the thunderous roar of the water melt everything else away.

I don't know how long I was in there. Hours? Days? It felt like an eternity. A lifetime in a single shower. Eventually I managed to make my way out of the cubicle and found the promised clean clothes, leaving my own soaked-and-yet-still-bloody ones in the nearby bin for cleaning, before stumbling towards the dorm.

If we had been a morose group over the last few days, now we were something else entirely. The closest I could think of it was being totally and utterly *spent*, completely drained of vitality in every way that mattered. Rikol, Sophia and Scythe were in the dorm when I arrived. Ella was in the infirmary and Cassius was still nowhere to be seen. Heads briefly perked up at my arrival, but other than a few waved hands, there was little communication. We had been through the wringer and seemingly all come out unscathed, all aside from Ella.

Ella.

I waved away the desperate call of my bed and grunted something to the others before stumbling back out. It took a little while to find the infirmary in my haze, but after some guidance from a stern-looking doctor I found Ella resting peacefully in a white linen bed. She would have looked completely normal if it weren't for the vivid black colouring around her throat and what looked like claw marks down the side of her face. If I didn't know better, I would have thought she had been nearly choked to death by a wild animal. That said, knowing what I did of Clythe, perhaps that wasn't too far from the truth.

An eyelid flickered open at my arrival. "Cass?"

"Not yet," I whispered gently, sitting down beside her. "It's just me."

"Cal?" Her voice was hoarse, barely comprehensible. "Cass good?"

"I'm sure he is," I replied. "Don't you worry about Cassius, worry about yourself and get better soon, okay?"

"'Kay."

I squeezed her hand and watched as she went back to sleep. Sitting in the chair beside her bed, it didn't take long for me to follow suit.

The touch of a hand on my shoulder had me jerking out of my seat with a gasp. "Easy," murmured a low, familiar voice, "it's just me."

Cassius. He looked okay, if as tired as we had all felt, but with no obvious holes in him that required immediate medical attention, just an immense sadness that emanated off him in waves.

"Is she...?"

"She's fine," I said, keeping my voice low as to not wake Ella. "A bit banged up but should be on her feet in no time, just needs some rest."

He closed his eyes and breathed out in relief. "Good. That's...good."

Easing myself out of the chair, I pulled him down into it. "You need rest. Stay here, it's surprisingly comfortable."

"Thank you," he replied, giving me a wistful smile. "Not for the seat, but for looking after her."

"That's what friends do. Just like they give useful, poignant advice: go to sleep."

For a second, the thought of sleep sent a flash of panic across his features, quickly mastered. "You got it," he replied with forced cheer.

It was the prickle of his skin that gave him away. The little hairs that stood up with the lie. Narrowing my eyes I studied him closely and he flinched away. "You are still remembering!" I gasped. "I thought you were going to stop."

The eyes that gazed back at me were filled with horror and sorrow. "I *can't* stop. He won't let me, Cal. Says I've come too far to give up now. I've tried," his voice wobbled, "believe me, *I've tried*, but he is too strong. And what's worse is...is..." he broke off with a strangled sob.

"Is what?" I asked, crouching down before him. "Is what, Cassius?"

"It's *her*," he whispered, eyes flickering to where Ella lay motionless. "These days it is always *her*."

"That goddamned, twisted son-of-a-*shit*!" I snarled, feeling the animalistic rage that was always a close companion flare to life within me. "That mother-fucking bastard! I'm going to wring his petty little neck, I'm going to-"

"No, no, Cal, please don't do anything. Please!" He made to rise from the chair but I pushed him back down firmly.

"You. Sit. Sleep."

"But-"

"*Sleep.* If not that, then look after her." My eyes shot to Ella and his followed. By the time he was looking back in my direction, I was out of the door.

What am I going to do? Kane's already told me to leave things well alone. That what is being done is happening for a reason.

But Carmine is a piece of garbage. I can't believe I thought he was trying to be nice!

What are you going to do Cal? What can you do?

Before I knew it, I was before Carmine's door. *Any time would be good to come up with a plan!* I knocked. It took him a while to shuffle towards the door, obviously running this challenge had taken its own toll on him. *Come on, come on, come on!*

"Calidan, to what do I owe the pleasure?"

I saw him there, dressed in his long johns and blinking blearily at me, confusion evident on his face.

I've got it. The perfect plan.

I drew back my hand. Formed a fist.

And punched him square in his fucking mouth.

Paradise.

CHAPTER 22
The Perfect Exam

Unsurprisingly, I ended up back in the prison. It was a quieter place now that the inhabitants had been murdered at our hands. A place where I could reflect and bask in the joyous memory of my fist impacting Carmine's face. Perhaps their intention had been for me to cower and quiver in this cell of stone but that wasn't me. Not right now at any rate. I was burning with righteous indignation, filled with it. Even though I knew their comments on the matter, I couldn't bring myself to forgive them for what they were doing to my best friend.

My brother.

He didn't deserve this. None of us did, but Cassius especially. Out of all of us, he was the good one. He just kept giving and the Academy gladly kept taking. I had to get whatever this was stopped. I had to talk to someone. I had to talk to the Emperor. Surely he would understand? Would see that his actions were causing Cassius unnecessary pain?

Of course he would. He was the Emperor! He had been nothing but good to us over the years. If I could just somehow get to him, talk to him, get him to see things from my perspective...

The rational part of my mind reared its ugly head. *The Emperor is the one who wants Cassius 'broken', why would he listen to anything that you said?*

...because what is happening to Cassius is wrong!

So you think you know better than a god that has been serving mankind since before the Cataclysm?

Ye-No! No, I don't think that, but there must be another way to achieve his goals.

You don't even know what his goals are. How can you expect to find a solution?

Shut up brain!

The door opened, pulling me out of my tumbling thoughts.

"I see that once again, you have managed to get yourself landed in the shit," the lady Imperator remarked drily. "I somewhat admire your tenacity, if not your wisdom."

"Very funny. What news?"

"You're to be released."

"Already?" I didn't have to pretend the surprise in my voice. "I expected to rot down here for a few days for what I did to Carmine."

"Whilst Imperator Carmine might have wanted you to spend more time down here, events are progressing rapidly. What do you know of the final exam?"

I raised an eyebrow. "Nothing?"

"Good. And that's because each one is different. There are none of the illusionary situations that you have been experiencing, each one is a real-life mission with real responsibilities, injuries and, potentially, casualties."

"Doesn't sound like anything we haven't done before."

She smirked. "Perhaps, perhaps not. Don't forget that we are all aware of you and your team's shared history and so have endeavoured to make the scenario challenge you in the ways we find you lacking. Understood?"

I nodded.

"Good. Now follow me. Your dormmates are being collected as we speak."

It didn't take long to navigate the stairs to Carmine's office. I swept in behind the imperious walk of the Imperator and met the furious glare of Carmine. Perhaps once this would have caused me to tremble, but the swollen and bloody lip gave me the strength I needed to meet him glare for glare.

"Stop it, boys," the lady Imperator ordered, and surprisingly Carmine obeyed, allowing me to greet the others – including a slightly-less-swollen-but-still-purple-Ella – whilst Carmine walked to the chalkboard behind him.

"What happened?" Cassius hissed under his breath.

"I hit him."

"You did what?!" he gasped, drawing the attention of everyone in the room.

"I. Hit. Him." I said it slowly, savouring the words as Carmine stopped mid-stride. I could see the barely restrained fury in his body, his muscles tensing as though he was preparing to turn and jump at me.

"I said *stop*." The word was inflected with power, seraph dripping off each syllable. It wasn't quite the working of one of the Five but still the word made us freeze in motion, our very breath stilled in our bodies. The lady Imperator stood and stalked around to the side of Carmine, placing a hand on his shoulder and staring into his eyes before turning to survey us. "We have bigger things at hand than this petty nonsense." She snapped her fingers and strength flooded back to our bodies, leaving us gasping for air. "Sit down. Shut up. Listen. Don't make me do anything I might...regret."

As opposed to when Carmine gave a threat, this one really worked. The room was so silent that I could hear the muscles relaxing in Carmine's body. The Imperator gave Carmine a wave of her hand and he nodded.

"Ahem, yes. Thank you." Turning to the chalkboard he drew a quick outline. "This, you might recognise as the area outside the facility," he explained as he drew. "We have received word that a caravan from Tenute, a small settlement in the far west, is heading through. They will be within this valley in the next hour. As you may or may not know, bandit attacks are relatively common in this region; you are to protect the caravan whilst it travels through this area."

"Simple enough," muttered Scythe.

"However, we have also received word that not all is well in Tenute. This caravan is unplanned and unexpected. You must discover the reasons behind their passage before the caravan leaves the valley."

I raised my hand. Carmine studiously ignored it.

A cough from the lady Imperator and he rolled his eyes before indicating me. "What?"

"Are we to be acting as Imperators or undercover?"

"You can decide amongst yourselves on your approach. On that note, you will each be graded individually for this assignment, so make sure to act like the Imperator you each wish to be. Some may pass, others may fail, however the mission comes above all else."

I raised my hand again. A long-suffering sigh. "Yes?"

"How do we know that any of it is real?"

Silence met my words. "What do you mean?" he asked slowly.

"You've been messing with our heads for months now. Is this a true scenario or somehow all in our minds?"

"What a stupid questi-"

"What Imperator Carmine means to say," the female Imperator began, stepping smoothly forward, "is that this is a completely real mission. The reason why we can't give specific dates for the final exam is because we search for scenarios that fit our agenda. This is one such scenario, and the work you do is vital to the empire and the Academy."

Search for and 'create', I bet.

"What about Ella?" Cassius asked. "She's hurt and-"

"Unfortunately, missions often do not take into account our own wellbeing," the lady continued. "Ella is fit enough to perform and has already agreed to continue."

"But-"

"Let her be the judge of her own body."

Cassius frowned, glanced at Ella, then nodded begrudgingly.

"That's enough questions, I think," said Carmine, clapping his hands together. "The caravan will be here soon. Get yourselves kitted out. The armoury is open to you and you can requisition whatever you think you might need. Whatever else, get to that caravan, protect it and find out what is going on. Do that successfully and you will be Imperators. Fail and…" he smiled cruelly around the room, "you get to spend much more time in my company."

Once the truth of Carmine's words had sunk in, we didn't waste any time, flinging ourselves down the echoing hallways and getting kitted out. By unspoken agreement we decided to wear full Imperator leathers; on a mission this time-sensitive there was no opportunity to ingratiate ourselves with a caravan. No, we needed to go full shock-and-awe.

Fully armed and clad, we left Wolf's Hollow for only the second time during our stay, eyes blinking hard against the sun. Almost as soon as we left the building I felt my bond roar into life, along with a very languid cat.

The tiny human returns! Are you man yet or still mouse?

Seya! I mentally pictured myself wrapping my arms around her neck and felt a thrum down our bond. *It's so good to hear from you.*

And you little one. How have you been? My silence and associated emotional upheaval gave her more than enough answer. *Ah, I'm sorry. Are you free now or on a mission?*

Shaking my head as we sprint through the forest, I cleared it of any negative thoughts. *We're on the final challenge. If we complete this, then we are Imperators. If not then it will be another few months at least.*

Do you need my help?

Where are you?

In the Academy but I could be there in a few hours...

As much as I wish I could see you, there isn't much point. The scenario is time-sensitive.

Tsk, fine. Though she made a show of complaining, I could tell she was secretly happy. Seya was obviously still enjoying a life of luxury in the Academy walls.

How have you been getting on without me? I asked, leaping a fallen tree without breaking stride.

Well enough, she purred. *They keep me well-fed and cared for.*

Well-fed, eh? I sent an image of her with an oversized belly and was immediately met by uproar in my mind.

I am not that fat!

'That'?

I am perfect in all ways. As you well know.

Sophia held up a hand and we drew to a stop, peering down along the track that meandered its way along the side of the valley. Closing my eyes, I reached out with my senses, listening with every fibre of my being. The creak of horse harness and jolting of wagon wheels filtered through the natural sounds of the forest.

Raising a hand, I pointed down the track. "Roughly half a mile that way," I said. "Coming closer."

Sophia looked at us individually. "Wait here or move in?"

"Move in." It was Ella, her voice authoritative. "We need as much time with the group as possible. Makes more sense to be there than twiddling our thumbs here."

"I agree," I replied quickly, tension flooding me. "And we should move fast. Something is happening; they're slowing down."

If our sprint before had been fast, this was manic. Perhaps it was because we had been locked away inside for so long that we had forgotten what the sun and the outside world felt like but it was as though we had boundless energy, bouncing over root and stump with ease whilst breathing in the magnificent scent of the trees.

Trees...and something else. I frowned. Smelled like oil and leather. But that didn't make sense as the scent was going away from us, *towards* the approaching caravan. *Oh balls.*

"I think the caravan is about to have company," I said, quickly regaling the others with what I could detect.

"Bandits?" asked Sophia.

"Seems likely."

Cassius, dark circles still under his eyes, partially freed Asp from his sheathe whilst issuing orders. "Calidan and I will take the left side of the track, Scythe and Sophia take the right. We move fast and flush out any game. Ella and Rikol, go straight down the track and provide fire support where needed."

"Preferably not actual 'fire'," I suggested as the others nodded and began to split up, "we are in a forest after all."

A minute later and Cassius and I were alone, winding our way through the dense bush as fast as we could. Hearing raised voices ahead I knew that the caravan had drawn to a stop. It didn't take long to see why; a huge tree had toppled across the path. From the tang of freshly cut wood, it was easy to determine that it wasn't a natural occurrence, something that the caravan master was quickly recognising as well, barked orders resounding from the top of his wagon for his people to adopt defensive positions around the series of carts.

In retrospect, he shouldn't have stood on top of the cart.

The low *crump* of a string being released from heavy tension reached my ears and a second later the caravanner toppled from the wagon clutching his chest. Instantly screams began to rise, the high-pitched sounds vying with the low-pitched *whumps* as more crossbow bolts began to fly. Guards and civilians began to fall, the deadly bolts puncturing through the thin wood of the wagons and the leather armour of the guards with ease.

That is, until Rikol and Ella arrived. Two walls of shimmering light rose on either side of the train of wagons, coruscating swirls of colour emanating from each resounding impact. Shouts began to rise from the woods on either side of the track, men and women raising alarm and sowing confusion. What had started as a well-organised ambush became a rout as Cassius and I carved our way through the ranks, the screams from the other side of the track suggesting that Sophia and Scythe were having just as much success.

I pulled my blade from the neck of a leather-clad woman, kicking her into the man behind before ducking as Asp passed overhead to cleave through the wrist of a would-be assailant. Whilst the man screamed, Cassius calmly slid Asp into his heart whilst I stalked over to the man scrambling desperately on the floor. He opened his mouth to beg as Vona sang and sent his head tumbling. Pausing, I spread out my senses, listening for anything out of the ordinary. Well...more out of the ordinary than the perplexed noises being made by the caravanners, before relaxing and shaking my head at Cassius.

"That looks to be it."

"A dozen or so? Seems like a fairly small band of bandits."

I frowned, kicking over one of the bodies. "If these are bandits," I said, studying the corpse. The leather was worn but good quality, the crossbow heavy duty and worth a pretty penny, as was the functional but well-maintained sword. In fact, looking over the array of corpses, the 'bandits' looked well-fed, a far cry from the starving individuals who usually resorted to such activities.

"Thoughts?"

"I can't imagine many bandits with equipment this good," I replied. "Best guess? The Academy paid them to be here."

"Paid them to attack these people?!" Cassius gasped, aghast.

I shook my head at his outburst, somewhat surprised that even in the state that he was in he didn't believe that the Academy would do such a thing. "Why not? How else would they ensure that there was a scenario for us to complete?" I frowned and looked around, sensing the others approaching the caravan cautiously but nothing else out of the ordinary. "Though, hard to say how putting down a dozen mercs – or bandits – tests us in areas that they think we are lacking."

Cassius grimaced, eyes dark at the thought of the dead civilians. "Perhaps we were meant to stop them before they managed to kill anyone at all." He sighed. "Either way, we should get up there and solve the second part of this challenge, before anyone else gets hurt."

We found Rikol and Sophia attempting and failing to calm down the screaming members of the caravan; the majority were women and children, all wide-eyed with fear.

And not just fear of the bandits; these people recognised the jackets. The Academy had spent decades cultivating the reaction that happened when the black long-coats of the Imperator were seen. Fear and either terrified obedience or flight – that was what the Academy wanted. A scared person was more likely to make mistakes, to slip up when being interrogated or to be too busy looking over their shoulder to escape effectively. These people knew of our reputation and it was like seeing a cloud come over their eyes. I could almost hear what was running through their minds: *out of the frying pan and into the fire.*

Ella slipped up to my side. "That was easy," she murmured, eyes constantly roving, assessing potential threats.

"Too easy," I replied darkly. "There has to be something more to this."

"Everyone, shut up!" roared a woman, her impressively mighty set of lungs causing the shout to instantly still the cacophony that was taking place. She bulled her way forward to the front of the caravan and raised a hand, eyes friendly but cautious. "I'm Flarae, second-in-command of this caravan." Her eyes darted back to the corpse that was still lying on top of one of the caravans and she grimaced. "Well, first-in-command now, I guess."

"Flarae," I greeted warmly, "I'm Calidan. These are my friends, Ella, Cassius, Scythe, Sophia and Rikol."

"Thank you for saving our lives."

"It is our duty. We were happy to be able to help."

"Your duty? It's true then, you are Imperators?"

"We are."

"You seem so...young." Her eyes widened as she realised what she had said and she blanched. "I'm sorry, I didn't mean any disrespect!"

"None taken!" I laughed. "We are fairly young, but still more than enough to deal with a few bandits."

"Your timing was impeccable," Flarae muttered with a shake of her head. "Almost like it was meant to be."

"The Emperor likes to protect his citizens," Sophia said warmly, a wide smile on her face. "So maybe this is divine providence guided by his hand. Who knows?"

Rule twenty-four of the Academy handbook: Highlight the Emperor's divinity. No-one wants to question a god.

"Well, whatever the reason behind it, we are so very thankful for your help!" Flarae exclaimed, the adrenaline leaving her body causing her hands to shake. "Without you we would have been slaughtered."

"We're just sorry that we couldn't save everyone," added Cassius, eyes drifting over the few fallen bodies.

"Aye, well, we knew that it could be a dangerous journey, but we felt like we had to undertake it."

"Where are you coming from, if I might ask?" Cassius said smoothly. "There aren't that many caravans that use this route."

"A small town. Well, more of a village really, less than two-hundred people all told. Tenute it's called. Ever heard of it?" We shook our heads and she gave a sad smirk. "I thought as much. Tiny place. Not much there but decent trees for logging and some good deer for hunting."

"Sounds lovely."

Her eyes clouded over. "It was. Hard work and a hard life, but it was...home, you know?"

We all nodded. Each of us could empathise with Flarae's words more than she would ever know. Ella stepped forward. "So, if it's home, why the trip?"

"Ah, well. Tenute was a lovely place, but recently the trouble started."

"Trouble?"

"We've had a number go missing in recent days," she explained awkwardly. "You always expect it, being out in the wild like we are, but this was more than the odd one or two. We lost five people in one-night last week. Then two more the night after. The disappearances stopped for a little while but the townsfolk were scared. All of us were. Complaining of bad dreams. Phantom pains. That kind of thing." She sighed. "I mean, this wasn't just a wolf attack. At best it was a bear, but we were all afraid that it was something worse." She turned pleading eyes at us. "You hear the stories, you know? The kind of things that kids tell each other around the campfire, only when you're out there in the dark and people are vanishing those stories seem all too real."

We shared a look. None of us had the heart to tell her that those stories she had heard were undoubtedly just the tip of the iceberg.

"Anyway, we had instigated a daily town meeting to make sure that everyone was accounted for. Yesterday nearly thirty people didn't show up to the meeting."

"Let me guess..." said Rikol. "Disappeared?"

Horror-filled eyes met his. "N-no. We found them alright. They were still in their beds. Well. Mostly in their beds. There were bits of them everywhere. Like something had ripped them apart, but if something had forced their way in, we would have seen it. Most of these houses were still barred from the inside and the occupants were all in their beds. If there was something trying to get in then you would hear it and be up with weapon in hand. What's worse..." she drifted off for a second before shaking herself, "is that when we investigated the houses – those of us that could stomach it – we did find an entry point."

"So something did get in?" queried Rikol, brows furrowed.

"That's the thing," Flarae said. "All of the entrances to the building were small holes clawed through the wood. Just big enough for perhaps a wolverine, but was what weirdest of all was that the broken wood, well, it was all bent outwards."

Her words met with a stunned silence.

"You don't mean-" Scythe began.

"What I mean, Mr Imperator, is that if I had to guess, whatever killed those people came from *inside* the house."

"You think she's right?"

I grimaced, shaking my head in answer to Cassius's question. As this had turned into a monster-mystery the rest had gone to ensure that everyone in the caravan was safe and secure whilst Cassius and I put our heads together.

"I mean, how can that be possible?" he continued, perplexed.

"Anything's possible," I replied. "We know that more than most. I would have been more dismissive of her story if not for one thing."

"What's that?"

"You heard what she said they do for a living. These people were lumberjacks. Wood-workers. If they are saying that it looked like the wood was bent outwards from the inside, I'm inclined to believe them."

Cassius put his head into his hands for a minute. When he straightened up, his eyes were sharper. "Alright, so what do we know about monsters that somehow originate in the occupant's house? We can rule out teleportation, otherwise why would it have bothered to dig back out of the building. Did something burrow in?"

"Could have done," I mused, knowing that he was thinking of the many tentacled beast that we had encountered in Three Roads years before. Raising my voice I called out, "Flarae, was there any evidence of burrowing?"

The new caravan-master turned from pulling aside a dead body. "No. Nothing like that. All the floors were heavy timber and no visible damage."

"Well, there goes that theory," Cassius groaned. "What else?"

"Something that was invisible and entered with them at the same time?"

"If it was just one or two, maybe, but most of these folk retreat and lock the doors a couple of hours before bed. I doubt any creature would easily burn that much seraph just for dinner."

"Maybe a siren controlled them to kill themselves?"

He shook his head. "Wouldn't explain the hole in the wood. Nor the fact that a siren still wants to eat. No, we're missing something."

A memory triggered. A haunted Imperator, and a traitor, talking about the thing that had wiped out her village. Erethea Laniel. *What was it called?*

"A Ranulskin," I breathed.

At my words Cassius's face went white. "Sarrenai said that they were rare. Exceedingly so."

"And yet they still come into contact with settlements from time to time. Erethea proved that."

"How long was the gestation period again?"

"Five days." I shook my head in disbelief. "If this is the work of a Ranulskin then they breed almost continuously. They can impregnate their targets on an almost daily basis, up to..." my mouth grew dry as I rattled off the information.

"Two dozen or so per night," Cassius finished for me.

"It explains the thirty-ish people found dead a week later. The Ranulskin probably took the first few for food to help nourish its breeding cycle. Then it somehow managed to get its eggs inside of those poor bastards. Due to the anaesthetic the beasts give off, the folks didn't realise that they were being eaten from the inside until it was too late. Beasts rip their way out and then dig out of their homes." I felt faint as I spoke, a creeping sense of doom looming over me. "It explains everything."

"Everything," Cassius echoed, expression bleak. "Sarrenai said that most die in the early stages of growth, which is why we don't have an ever-growing infestation, but if one managed to survive and get into somewhere with more population..."

"It would be chaos," I finished. "Hundreds could die." I was beginning to see why we had been sent on this particular mission. "This is why we're here," I whispered, horrified. "We have to determine who lives and who dies. We can't let the group get closer to Anderal until this is solved."

"You would kill them? They've done nothing wrong!"

"Nothing but the wrong place and wrong time," I muttered. "No, I don't want to kill them. But Sarrenai said that it was meant to be impossible to remove a Ranulskin embryo and that they were notoriously hard to detect. Which is why the Imperators who came to sort out the infestation at Laniel's home were so…thorough."

"Thorough enough to turn her into an Emperor-hating traitor," Cassius snarled. "What if we do the same here?"

"And what if we let them live and one, *just one*, gets into a city?" I could hear my own voice like it was coming from a mile away. Distant and cold. "We can't let that happen. If we can't figure it out and detect what's inside then we either wait here or…"

"Or?"

I turned to him and could tell he could see the horror in my eyes. "Everyone dies."

"This can't just be a co-incidence," Sophia hissed. "We get given a mission and it just so happens that it's a Ranulskin. The very thing that turned Erethea Laniel against the Academy."

"Of course it's not a co-incidence," Rikol said bitterly. "They know about our history. That's already been explained numerous times. Hells, we've seen them read through our files in front of us!"

"I know, I know!" she growled. "But do you understand what this means?"

"These people are going to die in a very unpleasant way?"

"No- well, yes- but more what this means about the Academy, about Wolf's Hollow?"

"I firmly believe that the less I think about Wolf's Hollow, the better."

"It means," Cassius said woodenly, "that Carmine and his lackies either knew about the Ranulskin or, worse, planted it."

"You can't be serious!" gasped Scythe.

"How else do you explain it? How could they possibly create a 'real-life' scenario without manipulating things. Calidan already suspects that the 'bandits' were mercs."

"Yeah, we figured that much out as well," Scythe grunted. "No bandits are that well equipped."

"So if they did that, then what are we expected to believe about the Ranulskin? That it just 'happened' to be there?"

"Would they truly commit all these people to die?"

"Do we care?" Everyone turned to Rikol who was staring out into the woods, the balling of his fist the only suggestion that he was feeling more than he was letting on.

"Of course we care!" Ella snarled, pushing him roughly.

He shook his head. "Why?"

"Because they're people! They don't deserve this. No-one does."

"And the people in our cells, the ones we all killed to get here. Did they deserve it?" He smiled bitterly. "Mine didn't. At least, not from what she told me, and I believed her. Still didn't change anything though. Two in, one out. That's what we had to do, and that's what we all did." He looked around at the group, lip curling as he saw our faces. "Oh come off it! Stop trying to be so high and mighty! We are all just grubbing about in the dirt now, fighting to survive. You know it. I know it. Whatever innocence we might have had has vanished along with those bodies."

"You're right," I whispered. "He's right," I said again as the others turned to me, shock and rage on their faces. Holding up a hand, I continued, "He's right about our innocence having faded. None of us can pretend anything otherwise. But if this is the Academy then they have put events into motion that could kill hundreds of civilians. People with no connection to us, have broken no laws or who have not been paid to fight. That, I cannot countenance."

"You might not support it, and neither do I, but that doesn't change what needs to happen."

"And what needs to happen, Rikol?"

He narrowed his eyes at me. "Why don't you tell me what you know about Ranulskins, specifically about how to extract them from their host?"

"I-ugh," I heaved a shuddering breath. "I can't. Cassius and I have put our heads together and neither of us can remember anything that suggested a Ranulskin infant can be successfully removed without killing the patient."

"They take five days to come to term," he stated coldly. "That means that *if* all these people are infected then they have all been hosts for several days already. That means that their insides are likely already chewed up. Even if we remove the beasts, chances are they die or scream bloody murder as the anaesthetic wears off until we kill them to put them out of their misery."

"Damn, you're cold." Scythe's voice was little more than a whisper but Rikol whirled around, eyes blazing.

"You're fucking right I'm cold! I have to be, otherwise this-this *shit* will make me unable to function!" He barked a despairing laugh. "As much as I hate to admit it, I can see the value in having this as the final test from a place as crude and despicable as Wolf's Hollow. It forces us to make the kind of clinical decision that Imperators will have to make in the field. Do we let these people go and risk hundreds or thousands of more lives? Do we turn them back and leave them to messy, violent deaths? Do we try – and likely fail – to help them? Or do we do what is likely the most practical and compassionate thing?"

"And what's that?" grunted Scythe.

"He means put them down," answered Ella, her face a mask of pain. "Put them out of their misery."

"But they aren't even in misery!" Scythe argued, turning to wave his hand at the caravan. "Look, they're walking around and happy that they were saved from bandits! How is that misery?!"

"All the research suggests anything past forty-eight hours of being impregnated is a scenario from which the host is unlikely to survive," I volunteered, hating that I was helping Rikol's argument as I did so. "If that's the case, there is a high likelihood that there are a number of people over there who are practically dead already, they just don't know it yet."

"Even if that is the case, who are we to deprive them of whatever time they have remaining?" Sophia's face was a twisted thundercloud.

Rikol snorted. "We are exactly the people meant for this. We are Imperators. Or soon to be ones anyway. We are meant to be the scalpel that removes the disease. These people are carrying a disease, even if they don't know it. We can't let that disease reach greater populations...ergo, we must remove it."

For the first time Cassius spoke up, the dark rings around his eyes somehow adding more weight to his words. "Stop thinking about these people like they are less than human. They aren't figures or statistics or barriers to our progression, they are *people*, just like you and me. Ones with hopes and dreams, all of which don't involve getting eaten from the inside out or put down by a bunch of Imps who are too angry, frightened or emotionally numb to consider trying to even help them first!" His voice was raised by the end, quivering with barely suppressed anger.

Spreading his arms wide, Rikol gave an exaggerated shrug. "Fine. Let's consider it. What are our next steps?"

"We need to stop this convoy from moving any further whilst we ascertain if they are infected," answered Ella.

"Not sure that they are going to go for that, considering they are fleeing a monster, and I'm not certain that we want to tell them the situation at this point," argued Rikol. "I don't think that they would react...favourably."

"We could hold them here with the weight of the Emperor's voice?" suggested Scythe.

"But they would still want to know why," Cassius answered wearily.

"Tell them that more bandits are ahead?"

"Possible," Cassius mused, rubbing his temples.

"There might be a more...indirect way," I said slowly, staring out at the line of wagons. "This caravan can't go anywhere if the wagons are stuck. Why not just use some seraph to cause some failures in the wheels or the frames? Not all at once, that would be too obvious that something was up, but breaking a wheel isn't unheard of."

"They might have spares," Scythe pointed out.

"Then cause the entire axel to fail. Something like that would take some time to remedy. Enough time for us to hopefully figure this out."

Rikol pursed his lips then nodded. "A good idea." Narrowing his eyes at the distant lead wagon he focused for a few seconds before smiling to himself. "I've rusted the axel almost completely through. It should break as soon as the wagon starts rolling again."

"With the few hours that it will take them to saw through that tree, that buys us some time," said Sophia, "but how are we going to save these people?"

"They're meant to be extremely hard to discover when within their hosts," Cassius explained, "but I'm just regurgitating archive information. I suggest we all go and take a walk amongst our new friends and see what we can discover."

Twenty minutes later we were back together, each looking as despondent as the next. Cassius took one look at everyone's faces and grimaced. "Well, seems like the research wasn't mistaken."

"Calidan, did you get anything?" Sophia asked.

"Difficult to say," I replied. "It's a noisy environment. There were a couple of moments that I thought there was unexplained movement within someone's torso but when I focused on it things were completely still."

Cassius frowned. "It's possible that these creatures are more active at night than they are during the day. The townsfolk were complaining of night-terrors according to Flarae. Could be that's due to the creatures being more active?"

Sophia eyed the sunbeams filtering through the trees. "Got a few hours until sundown."

"The longer we wait, the more damage is being done to these people," interjected Scythe. "If there is a better option than to wait, I suggest we take it." He cocked his head at Rikol. "You're the big wizard man. Can you not just will them to be better?"

"Healing is a complicated enough art as is," Rikol replied with a shake of his head. "If I know exactly how the body should be, then yes I can return it to its natural state, but I do it so rarely that it would consume a vast amount of seraph. I could try willing whatever is *not* an organic part of the body away, but even if that works it runs into the same problems: seraph-usage and healing the damage that has been done."

"So you're saying that we could save a few, potentially, but not all?"

Rikol gestured. "There's nearly eight-score people there. Between Ella, Sophia and me...perhaps we could save thirty of them? More if we can determine those who have had the embryo within them for less time."

"There has to be some evidence of their insertion," Scythe growled. Looking at Cassius and me he waved a hand. "What did the research say?"

I shared a look with Cassius before turning back. "Research didn't have much to say on the matter. I don't think the academics have ever got their hands on a corpse complete with a Ranulskin still inside. Most of the documentation came from the perspectives of the Imperators who came across the remains of an infestation. As you might imagine, there wasn't much left to accurately determine how the embryos are delivered."

Cassius nodded. "Could be that they are delivered through a bite but could equally be ingested somehow. Maybe all a Ranulskin does is place its eggs in the local water source? We honestly don't know."

"There has to be a tell," Ella stated firmly. "If such a creature is eating its way through its host, I doubt it can hide everything. Bruising or tenderness perhaps?"

Tenderness. A flash of inspiration struck me. "Or, maybe the complete opposite!" I grinned at their confused faces. "The Ranulskin doses their victims with a powerful anaesthetic, right?"

Sophia gasped and nodded. "You mean that perhaps we can figure out who *can't* feel the pain that they are supposed to."

"Exactly! If we can test their pain tolerance, it might be that some areas are very desensitised from what they should be. That would let us know that they have an extra passenger on-board."

"Clever," acknowledged Rikol. "But if we start poking and prodding, they are going to know that something is up."

"If it comes down to it, we'll have to round them up and keep them contained whilst we test. But there has to be another way to determine if this work- ow!" I clapped a hand to the back of my neck and Sophia grinned, her eyes dancing.

"We're *seraph users* remember? Mosquitos haven't got anything on us."

Rubbing my neck ruefully, I smiled back. "Genius."

"You don't have to tell me." She winked. "We all know that I am the smart one of the group."

"The most humble, too," intoned Ella drily.

"So, we lance a few people and see how they react," murmured Rikol. "Any idea of the best place to target?"

"Most of the theories suggest that the Ranulskin resides within the torso, so perhaps either the back or chest," replied Cassius. "But for the first few people we each try we need to test more widely."

"Agreed," said Ella. "We need to find a benchmark. How do we want to go about doing that?"

"Easy!" Scythe chimed in. "There are six people right here who we know aren't infected..."

It was a good thing that Rikol put up sound screens. The next few minutes were filled with sharp barks of pain as each of us got poked, prodded and needled until we had a decent understanding of what a reasonable response would be to sharp and sudden pain in a specific area.

"Well, that was unpleasant," muttered Rikol, rubbing at the back of his neck whilst staring at the caravanners. "All that's left is to go and test it out."

"We need a way to distinguish those we have tested," pointed out Ella and Rikol nodded.

"Already thought about that," he said. "Just use seraph markers. Maybe a low intensity marker for those who react relatively normally and high intensity for those that don't react much or at all?"

I stood up and cracked my neck from side-to-side. "Sounds good. Let's get down there and prod some people." Grimacing, I shook my head. "…That sounded better in my mind."

The attack of the sudden swarm of 'mosquitos' sent the caravanners into a frenzy, batting and waving their hands as they sought cover within and beneath the wagons. It would have been funny if we hadn't been concentrating so hard, trying to ensure that each person was 'bitten' multiple times in different locations, but the results were nothing to laugh about.

"Eighty-nine people," Scythe groaned, holding a hand to his head as though to hold it up against the weight of what that meant.

"That's a lot of infected," agreed Rikol, eyes scanning the seraph tags we had placed on each caravanner. "And it looks like nearly two dozen are barely feeling anything at all around the torso. They're likely near ready to burst."

Ella wrinkled her nose. "That's a disgusting way to put it."

"Disgusting but accurate," he replied. "If we don't do anything, those people will likely be dead in the next few hours."

Sophia shook her head sorrowfully. "And if we do something then they will still be dead. If they are five days in with one of those things in their chest then I can't see how they could be saved. Hells, I'm impressed that they are even standing!"

Cassius made to object but Rikol got there first, nodding his approval. "Exactly. There is no way that I, nor I imagine any of you, would be able to fully repair a body that has essentially been eaten from the inside out. Even if we did that would be an obscene amount of seraph. We might save one or two, but at the cost of leaving the others."

Cassius shook his head in disgust but held his tongue. I knew that he was hating every second of this conversation but he hadn't managed to think of a solution that didn't involve large numbers of people dying.

I have to admit, it was a good test. It made us truly understand the responsibilities and the choices that an Imperator had to make. Even if every fibre of our beings railed against it.

"There's only one way I can see to do this without it resorting to chaos," I said, voice low in case it carried to the caravanners who were only just beginning to re-emerge from their shelters. "We have to contain the members of the caravan. Separate areas for those who are further gone."

"Contain them?" Rikol's voice held a note of incredulity. "They're dying. Why go to the effort of containing them? You're only going to make their last moments filled with fear. Working together, we could make this quick and painless for everyone who is infected."

I shook my head. "I still hope that we can save them. I'm not going to write them off without even trying."

"I don't know, Cal," Ella muttered, eyes avoiding Cassius who looked like he was trying not to be sick. "We know that this doesn't end well for these people. Surely it would be a mercy?"

"Mercy?" spat Cassius, angry eyes finally catching Ella's. "There is no mercy in what you're suggesting. We need to help these people, not butcher them like cattle."

"And if we can't help them?" Ella's voice was soft but firm, unwavering in the face of Cassius's anger.

"Then...then..." he started before shaking his head furiously. "Fuck!" he bellowed, causing a number of heads to turn in our direction.

"We do what we can," I said gently, placing a hand on Cassius's arm that he immediately shrugged off. "We do what we can, and if that fails...then we do what we must."

"I'm not going to kill someone who doesn't deserve it."

"None of them deserve it," I replied, meeting Cassius's gaze. "But if it comes down to them dying in horrible pain and horror, or by my blade, then I will give them the blade. However," I held up my hand to forestall the rant I could see building, "we're discussing the people below like they have no say in the matter."

"That's because they don't," Rikol interjected. "We're here to do the job. It just so happens that they are that job."

"Of course they have a say in this," I retorted. "If someone prefers to die by the Ranulskin, that is their choice – I will not take it away from them. If they prefer the blade, then I will make their death as easy and painless as possible."

"You're suggesting that we *tell* them?" Rikol said, aghast. "You're out of your mind. The panic that will ensue...we can't risk any of them getting away."

"I doubt that anyone would be able to evade our tracking," I replied, "but yes, it is a risk. However, I believe that we owe it to them to know what is coming their way. If we call everyone together for a meeting and raise seraph barriers without them knowing, we can have a conversation and let them know the truth." Looking around the others I could see a mixture of uncertainty and resolve. "Ask yourselves this," I said, "if you were in their shoes, would you rather know why whatever is about to happen happens? I know I would."

"That's because you're a nutter," Rikol muttered uncomfortably but he didn't argue further.

"Cassius," I said gently, nudging him. "Are you with us on this?"

He gritted his teeth and then forcibly unclenched his fists. "I will help with the barriers and the conversation. But anything else...I'm unsure."

"That's good enough for me." Nods from the others had me rise to my feet, beckoning the others to do the same. "No time like the present. Let's talk to Flarae and see if she can gather everyone together."

In the end it didn't take the new caravan-master long to do so, her impressively might set of lungs bellowing out orders that managed to reach even the ears of those that were operating the saw. Before long we had a group of wary-eyed individuals, all covered in dust and grime from the days of travel, faces stained with sorrow from the losses of their friends and their town. Gritting my teeth against the wave of sadness that hit me, I nodded and Rikol, Sophia and Ella went to work. Quickly and completely undetected by the watching civilians, walls of invisible seraph rose around us, making a barrier that only a dedicated mage was going to be able to pass through. Stepping forward, Cassius raised his hands.

"You know who we are and what we do," he began, voice strong and warm. "Flarae has given us an update as to why you have left your homes and we have determined the cause of the issue." His face turned grave. "You have a monster problem."

"Tell us something we don't know!" called one of the civilians.

Cassius smiled sadly. "Your fleeing of the village hasn't rid you of the monster."

That brought the kind of silence that was usually only reserved for funerals. Flarae stepped forwards, hands trembling. "What do you mean? There's nothing here. No reports of anyone going missing. Where could a monster even hide?!"

"Not all monsters are big. Some are small, exceedingly so. Others start small but they grow." Cassius explained. "We have reason to believe that the creature that attacked your village was something known as a Ranulskin. It is a beast that breeds incessantly. Truth be told, I don't really know what a fully grown adult looks like as they are exceedingly rare."

"Then how can you-" the heckler broke off as Cassius raised a hand.

"I can, however, tell you the results of their breeding. They impregnate their victims somehow and use them as hosts. Flarae told us of you finding your friends and colleagues with their doors still barred shut and no evidence of forced entry. In fact, the only evidence you found was of forced exit. That's because," Cassius's face was a set line now and I could feel the tension in his muscles, "the creatures were inside them."

Instantly the crowd went into uproar; shouts of derision, threats and disbelief echoing through the forest. Cassius gave them a moment before raising both his hands. Incredibly, the crowd quieted. "I know this is hard to believe, but it's true. Through no fault of your own, you have been used as a Ranulskin breeding ground."

"But we've left, surely it can't follow us!" cried a heavy-set man with the build of a lumberjack.

Cassius shook his head. "Unfortunately some of you have already been exposed. You might be finding some phantom pains or perhaps have noticed that your torso isn't as sensitive as it used to be." The concern on a number of people's faces grew tenfold. "The Ranulskin larvae take root in your torso. They are very difficult to detect and they grow by eating what is around it. A powerful anaesthetic that they seem to naturally produce keeps the host from noticing until it is too late."

Flarae stepped forward. "What are you saying?"

"I'm saying," Cassius replied softly, "that a number of you have these creatures inside of you at this very moment." His face creased for a second and I thought he was going to lose control, but he straightened his spine and forced the emotion away. "I'm saying that some of you have days to live, whilst others have only hours." A tear trickled down his face. "I'm saying that we can only save some, not all."

"Bollocks!" yelled a burly man, shouldering his way through the crowd. "Don't listen to this bullshit. He's just a kid, what does he know?" Invisible to the crowd hovered the dense seraph tag attached to this man. He had exhibited little reaction to any of the stings and likely had only hours to go. Judging by his face, he had heard the symptoms presented by Cassius, recognised that he was affected, and believed that blind ignorance was the best policy. Supportive cries echoed through the crowd and there was a shift in the atmosphere from placid to tense and wrought with danger.

"Fuck off!"

"Get out of here!"

"Bloody kids."

Cassius faced the growing clamour with dismay written plain across his features. "Please, settle down," he cried but if anyone heard they didn't care.

Human beings are an interesting animal. We pride ourselves on being able to function as individuals, removing ourselves from animals and their pack mentalities. Usually this is correct, but when enough humans get together a curious mechanic occurs: we become a pack of feral animals. I've seen bands of humans do horrific things that not one member of the group would have remotely attempted or dreamed of doing as an individual. And maybe that's the answer. Maybe it just removes that 'ownership', that distinction and accountability as an individual and lets the primal instincts take over. Instincts that were showing now. Teeth were beginning to be bared and I could practically taste the surging adrenaline levels.

A blinding light erupted through the clearing, causing screams and shouts of panic. When we could see again, Rikol was standing next to Cassius, his hand outstretched and filled with crackling energy.

"Quiet." He said it coldly, his expression grim. The people obeyed.

Trying again, Cassius gathered himself. "I know this is hard to hear but it is the truth. For your own safety we," he swallowed hard, "we are going to split you up into groups. Those whom we don't believe to be infected and then five other groups, in order of how long you have had the parasite within."

Another clamour began to stir but a crackle from Rikol and the crowd quieted again.

"What will you do with us?" called someone from the back.

"We're going to try to save you," Cassius answered. "But, like I said before, we can't save everyone. We don't have the power or the skill. Some of you…" he winced. "Some of you are too far gone. Though you haven't felt it, the parasite has eaten much of your insides. You're only standing because of the anaesthetic it gives off." Shocked horror greeted his words.

"So, what, we just give up and die?" shouted another.

Cassius opened his mouth and then slumped, crestfallen. Rikol stepped forward. "Yes," he said simply. "You have been dealt a shitty hand; there's no doubt about it. Those of you we cannot save *will* die. It will be traumatic, terrifying and likely painful." He frowned as someone tried to speak over him and their words faded away. "The other option that is available is...assistance in ending things."

"You're going to kill us?!"

"Only if you ask nicely."

"I thought you were meant to save the citizens of the empire!" a skinny brunette shouted.

Rikol shrugged. "We will save those who can be saved. Unfortunately we cannot let the things inside you escape. You either die by its hand, die by your own, or die by mine."

"Rikol!" Cassius hissed, aghast, but the mage didn't even blink.

"We are Imperators. You know exactly what we will do when the need arises. Well, the need has arisen. You will be separated and then you will choose. If I were you...

...I would choose wisely."

CHAPTER 23

Ranulskin

We tried to do it nicely. We tried to be polite. But fear had other plans.

In the wake of Rikol's words the crowd panicked. Loved ones reached out for each other, families trying their best to hold each other close, and people began to bolt.

Or at least, they tried to. The first person who ran head first into the seraph barrier broke her nose with a *crunch* that rippled through the air.

That, unsurprisingly, made things worse.

Imprisonment is not conducive to the natural state of being human. I should know. Take away someone's freedom, their ability to escape, and all rationality disappears in an instant.

The crowd roared, raged, then surged.

It mattered little in the grand scheme of things. The barriers that we had set up were designed to hold off attacks that would rip a hole clean through a person; the meaty fists of a hundred lumberjacks – though impressive – held little threat to their stability.

The seething mass of humanity made the separation all the more difficult however. The rabid howls as families were torn apart by magic that they couldn't see or understand caused tears to run down my face, even as I did my part in causing that incalculable sorrow. People tried to run, tried to beg and bribe, but there was nothing but grim determination in our group to get things done as quickly and efficiently as possible. Working on the seraph tags that we had placed above each individual, they were corralled to different parts of the seraph dome and then, when all was ready, sealed into their – for want of a better term – *cage*.

Six cages. Six groups of people with differing states of infections. The first group was, thankfully, the largest: sixty-eight souls free of any sign of infestation. It was a lot better than nothing, but still that meant that nearly two-thirds of the town's population had either already died or were in the process of being eaten alive.

The last group was the worst. They knew that they couldn't or, at least, *wouldn't* be saved. Some point-blank refused to believe what we were saying, raging against our control and our orders. Others, I could tell, knew that everything we had informed them of was true. Those tended to sink down and collapse, too scared and stunned to even attempt to think of escape.

I had done a lot of unpleasant things in my life by this point. But watching as a mother and child were separated by seraph, hands reaching for each other as they screamed and struggled, made me feel like the monster I was becoming. I knew somehow, somewhere, that Carmine was watching this entire event and cackling like the sick bastard he was; satisfied that his latest subjects were all acting as he expected.

Well, all except Cassius. He sat there with a grey face as he watched the people get moved around, defeat written across his features. This was too much for him. He was here to help people, not to rip them apart from their families in their last hours. I understood, as did the others. Cassius was the best of us; the most humane. Usually, he was our line in the sand, our indicator for when we were going too far. But now, in a time when we *needed* to go too far, he couldn't bring himself to join in. Even though he knew that it would mean more time in the dreaded Wolf's Hollow, he just couldn't do it.

And I loved him for that.

Finally, the groups were contained. "What are you going to do to us?" screamed a white-haired man, knuckles bloody from where he had tried to smash his way through the barrier. "Witches! Demons! Let us go!"

Cassius made to rise but Ella put a comforting hand on his shoulder. I'm not certain if she noticed the flinch that ran through him at her touch, but I certainly did. She took her hand off him once he had settled and raised her hands for silence. "Cassius told you the truth. Some of you," she indicated the largest group, "are not infected." Gasps of relief filled the air from that group whilst low mutterings and hisses of rage and panic rose from the others. "The rest of you we believe to have Ranulskin embryos within."

"But I don't feel anything wrong!" shouted a lady in the third cage.

"You wouldn't feel anything wrong," Ella replied. "That's already been explained. You remember the swarm of mosquitos a little while ago? That wasn't a swarm of bugs, but the six of us testing you for pain tolerances. Some of you didn't feel anything at all," she indicated the furthest container and the people within blanched. "Unfortunately, you are the furthest gone."

"And what does that mean?" called a portly man in that group.

Ella made to speak then stopped, brow furrowing. "It means you don't have long to live," Rikol said stepping in smoothly. "We believe in the next twenty-four hours the creature within will be ready to hatch."

"Can't you do something if you know it is there? Get it out? Kill it?!" The man's eyes were white with panic.

"Putting aside the fact that the creatures are difficult to detect, we could theoretically kill it, but at the stage you're at most of your organs will have been consumed," Rikol answered calmly. He indicated us with a wave of his hand. "We are not healers. We are hunters and fighters. Even healers would have a hard time trying to save you when your body has been so brutally savaged." He shook his head. "No, I'm afraid you have one path ahead of you. I suggest you make your peace with it as best you can. The two options we have laid out previously still stand: death by the creature within, or death by a blade."

"I don't believe this," the man whispered hoarsely. He shook his head and raised a clenched fist. "I won't let you get away with this!"

Rikol's eyes flashed. "Remember who we are. More specifically, *who* we represent. You do not have any authority to 'let' us do anything."

"That's enough Rikol," Sophia said, stepping to his side. "He's just scared, as he has every right to be. We both know that with fear comes anger." Raising her voice, she locked eyes with the man. "Sir, do you have an answer to Rikol's options?"

"I ain't going to let you anywhere near me!" he bellowed, once again scrabbling at the wall. "Let me out. LET ME OUT!"

"That answers that then," Rikol murmured but Sophia shook her head.

"The offer will always be open," she said, eyes scanning the group. "Do not feel like you have to decide right now." The unspoken message was plain for all to see. *You're all going to change your minds when the first of you dies.*

"What of us?" called a tall, thin woman from the group nearest those that we had declared free of infestation.

"We believe you to be the most recently implanted," Sophia said. "That means you have the highest chance of survival if we manage to locate and remove the creature." Gasps of relief met her words but she raised a hand to forestall any comments. "Remember *we are not healers*, so everything we do is going to be tricky. We make no promises." She eyed the group. "But as we currently have the power to spare, I suggest that we start with the three children in your group first."

"How do we want to tackle this?" I asked, joining the others in standing around the child. We had put the young girl to sleep, none of us willing to witness the terror in her eyes as we operated. "I can sense it, just. It's almost as if it knows that we are looking and is making itself scarce."

"I think we have two options," Rikol said. "Either kill it and leave it there, or remove it from the body. The first option is less seraph intensive, which…" his eyes flicked over the mass of people watching us from their invisible cages, "might mean saving more lives."

"Would that have any lasting implications for the person?" asked Scythe.

Rikol shrugged. "No idea. I would hope that the body would begin to break it down, just like it would with any foreign invader. Hopefully that isn't an issue. Either way, we will need to direct Carmine to get these people to a healer to check them out once we're done."

"Sounds like there is only one way to figure out the best approach," Ella said. "Let's go least intensive option first." She shot me a look. "As you can sense it, you're going to have to be the surgeon. We can feed you seraph, but are you able to control your seraph enough to do this?"

I looked at the girl and at the terrified parents who were sitting in the cages, pressed up against the wall with piteous expressions. Taking a deep breath, I silenced the questioning voice in the back of my mind. "I have to," I said simply. "There is no room for anything else. Any suggestions for how to best kill it?"

"For you?" Rikol mused. "Either a pinpoint seraph lance, one that originates within the creature's brain, or detonate its brain directly. Either way, I suggest you make sure it dies instantly. No telling what kind of damage it could do if it is injured."

I nodded before rolling my neck and shoulders in preparation. Casting one more look at the others who gave me grim, determined smiles, I knelt down and focused everything

I had on the tiny body in front of me. Sinking into my senses, I tuned out everything that was unnecessary; filtering out all the sounds from the outside world until there was just the breathing of the girl, the beat of her heart, the sound of her blood rushing around her body. I could smell the metallic tang, could taste the sweat and fear.

Where are you?

The creature was hidden deep within her body, lying completely still and undetectable to my senses. Suddenly I felt the presence of Seya within my mind. *Your quarry has gone to ground*, she mused, *but nothing is completely undetectable. Pull on the bond. Use your skills, just like Anatha taught.*

I did as she bade, sinking deep into the power of the bond, not drawing strength or healing like I usually did but instead drawing on the senses, willing mine to become more like Seya's. When I opened my eyes again the world had changed. Everything was sharper, more detailed. Instead of the beat of the girl's heart, I could hear the individual valves working, the contraction of each individual muscle, even the sparking fire of electrical signals.

Good. Now hunt.

I did as she bade. This time the creature could not hide from me, its tiny heart outlining the sinuous shape of its body as energy flooded along its length. Steeling myself, I gathered energy, judged the perfect distance for it to form in the real world and, willing the creature not to move, flared the ball of seraph into life for a fraction of a second. No time at all in the grand scheme of things, but more than enough time to burn away everything that had stood in its path. The creature twitched, spasmed, and all function ceased. Taking a deep sigh, I pulled myself back to my body and relaxed, nodding at the others.

"It's done." I said softly.

And that's when it all went wrong.

The girl's eyelids twitched, then her whole body jerked, her face contorting in a rictus of agony.

"What's happening?" cried the mother, smashing against the barrier in an attempt to get closer. "What have you done to my daughter?!"

"Calidan, what's going on?" Ella asked, voice tight.

Sinking back into the deeper senses I found the problem. The creature was giving off some kind of toxin in death, the foul agent paralysing the surrounding muscles. Quickly relaying the information, I focused on the body of the creature and *willed* it out of existence. My seraph pool practically evaporated as the dead Ranulskin faded out of existence, the source of the toxins with it.

"Keep her heart beating and her lungs going," I gasped, sweat pouring off me with the effort. The others dove to with a will, using seraph to keep her alive whilst the paralytic worked its way out of her system. It didn't take long; the small amount it had managed to release only lasted five minutes or so, but still more than enough time to have killed her several times over. When it was done, we sat on the floor in a daze, breathing hard with the adrenaline.

"Is she okay?" the mother shouted again, banging on the barrier with a fist, shaking off attempts by her partner to calm down. "Is she alright?!"

"She's okay," Sophia said to her with a reassuring smile. "She's out of harm's way."

"What happened?!"

I stood up. "We tried killing the creature but leaving its body behind to save on energy. Unfortunately there's some kind of powerful paralytic that it gives off when it dies. We had to remove the body entirely, which uses far more energy…" I could see that I was losing them so tried to make things more simplified, "…which leaves less for the rest of you."

In retrospect that was a foolish thing to say. Instantly there was a surge of panicked shouting, of emotional entreaties, how certain persons should be saved ahead of the others, even some frustrated shouts that the children weren't worth saving ahead of some of the more 'important' people.

It's sad how people get when their lives are on the line. All sense of decency goes out the window.

Ignoring the pandemonium, we moved the girl inside the barrier of the unaffected group and picked up the next child, sending him to sleep with a subtle application of seraph. Setting him down on the ground we gathered round and I settled in for a terribly long day.

I'm not sure I could remember ever being quite so mentally exhausted. The closest I could come to was when Not-Endrea ripped through my mind, but that was a tiredness due to damage, whereas this was from pure concentration and consistent expenditure of energy. Seya was in the Academy, flooding me with power as I worked, allowing me to pull on her vast seraph reserves in order to keep burning away the infestations within the confined citizens. I learnt that the most effective method for me to destroy the creatures was to use seraph to outline the entirety of the creature and then to create a momentary immolation that fit the outline exactly; a wave of green fire so intense that it incinerated everything it touched. Fire had always been something that I was pretty good at, my efforts at practicing destructive magics making it more energy efficient to utilise. In six hours we managed to save nineteen people; the entirety of the first group and a couple from the people in the second day of infestation. I doubted that we could be so quick going forwards as we hadn't provided any healing seraph to those from the first stage, relying on the fact that the creature hadn't had much time to inflict damage. So far, our decision seemed to be holding, as aside from some mild pain none of those we had worked on had shown any signs of danger.

In fact, we had been so effective in our day's work that a heavy layer of scepticism lay over the crowd. It was to be expected; all they had seen was us corralling them into cages and then standing around individuals one at a time before declaring them 'saved'. They hadn't seen any evidence of the threat that we had described and anger was beginning to boil over.

The growing rage vanished in an instant when the first man died.

As we had suspected the Ranulskin became more active at night. For those with more full-grown creatures within them I could barely stand to sense the writhing gnawing that was taking place. Close to midnight, the screams of the group changed from anger and frustration to sheer terror as the heavy-set man with bloody knuckles collapsed to the floor and screamed in horror as his stomach rippled with activity. Bit by bloody bit the beast began to chew its way to the outside world, finally emerging in a spray of gore and viscera. It met the terrified screams of the onlookers and then the perfectly refined seraph of Rikol, who encased it in a floating membrane and lifted it high where it squealed and bashed against its confines.

"This is what you face," he bellowed. "Witness it and know it to be true. We are here to help you." He turned to face the panicked last group. "I suggest you re-evaluate your choices."

They did.

Each and every member of the final group, having witnessed the gory end of one, pleaded to be killed in another fashion. Steeling ourselves, we did so. Rikol suggested that he do it alone but we overruled him, knowing that no-one should have that many lives weighing on their shoulders. Even Cassius entered the cage with his sword drawn, the horror and desperate pleading having caused him to rise to the occasion despite the tears that streamed down his face. Grim-faced, we slaughtered everyone who was within, quick efficient stabs and cuts that ended their lives as painlessly and swiftly as possible.

I would like to say that the killing was hard, but that would be a lie. It was practical. Served a purpose.

And we Imperators love a purpose.

No; as much as there was horror in our actions, there was more at the thought of how they might have died otherwise, just like the poor sod lying in a pile of his own entrails, and so we ended those people's lives the way that they wanted, giving them what little control they might have had over the nature of their demise.

Not everyone saw it that way.

It was a horrible position to be in, watching your friends and loved ones be cut down in an apparent act of 'mercy'. I could well understand the mixture of feelings; the rage, the hate and the fear perhaps alternating with gratitude for another solution. Some of the older adults, those who had lived in the wilds and faced the threats and issues of mortality that were commonly associated with those places on the fringe of civilisation, they were grateful. They watched their partner, their child, their friend, be cut down and understood the reasons behind it. Understood that there were worse ways to go and that sometimes all you can do is help someone to pass with as much dignity as possible.

The young though...they didn't have that life experience. Even though they had witnessed the birth of a Ranulskin and knew that everyone within the final cage was facing that fate if we didn't intervene, they couldn't reconcile that with the fact that we were cutting down their parents, siblings and friends before their eyes. And let me tell you: nothing is quite as cutting as the words of a child. Unfiltered vitriol, that's what we received. Desperate, vehement screams that cut to the quick, made you wonder if you were doing the right thing or if you were actually the monster the children declared you to be.

In this case, I think we were both.

Eventually the tears dried up and the screams subsided. The final cage was a charnel house when we drooped out of it, shoulders low, bodies and minds exhausted. Rikol closed the cage back up, narrowed his eyes and clicked his fingers. A bloom of light caused fresh screams to erupt as fire engulfed the bodies, rendering them to ash in moments. It took me a second to realise that not all of the screaming was that of the onlookers. No, there was a higher-pitched wailing that was coming from the cage itself. As we watched the flesh peel away from the bodies, for a second the worm-like creatures were exposed and visible to the naked eye before they too blackened and crumbled into ash.

"Is...is that what is going to happen to us?" asked a yellow-haired woman in the next cage. She already knew the answer, I could tell it in the way she held herself, holding her arms defensively across her body as though to ward off bad news.

"...Probably," replied Sophia, expression tired. "I won't offer you false hope. We're going to keep working on saving the others first. If we have enough power to spare then we might be able to remove the worms and then heal you, but it is no easy thing." She glanced at the seraph barrier that now contained nothing but swirling ash. "You likely have another day before that choice needs to be made, however."

The woman stiffened and then collapsed as though her strings had been cut, crumpling onto the floor with great, heaving sobs.

I wished we had time to empathise with these people. Unfortunately, time was the enemy right now. Together we turned back to the second cage and started the long, weary process of saving more lives.

Hoping that we could somehow balance the scales.

PRESENT DAY 6

"And what, by the raging fires of Telanqua, do you think you're doing here?" The words were sharp, cutting through the air like a knife. I twisted around from the chair her servant had provided me with and gave her a genial wave. "Hello Tara'zin, good to see you too."

"Good?" she hissed. "*Good*!? No. I am far from 'good', little Imperator. I have no business with you. Leave."

"It would appear to me that business is exactly what you need," I replied softly, directing my gaze to take in the sandstone walls and sparse decorations. In all honesty it was a nice house – far nicer than what most of the citizens in the empire lived in – but compared to the lush palatial compound that the Visgothe had inhabited beforehand it might as well have been a pigsty.

"The business of you and yours helped get me where I am today!" she snapped, eyes flashing. "I want no more of it."

"Really?" I stood up and let my full frame unfold above her. Tara'zin was not a tall woman though her fiery personality generally made you feel like you were being trampled by an angry camel. "The way I see it, you propped up your house with money from the Academy."

"Yes, but-"

"And if that had been discovered then...well, we both know that being demoted to the Silver Quarter would have been the least of your worries." Popping a grape into my mouth, I chewed contentedly. "What is the penalty for treachery again? Ah, yes. Death. For you and your entire house."

If looks could kill, I would be stone dead.

"What. Do. You. Want?"

"Relax," I said, raising my hands in a warding gesture. "I'm not here on official business. This is...off the books."

"If it isn't official, then I don't want any part of it."

"Hmm. A second ago you were blaming the Academy for all your troubles. How quickly things change."

"Fuck you."

"What a lovely way to talk to a potential client."

"You're no client of mine!"

"Not yet..." *Come on. You have to have an inkling of interest in what I'm doing here. Take the bait.*

For a minute I could almost see the gears whirring in her head. Finally, she sighed. "Fine. What do you want and why should I care?"

Excellent.

"Are you still involved in the city's architecture?"

"Yes...?"

"And do you have blueprints?"

"That depends."

"On what?"

"On what they're for."

"Ah, Tara'zin. I intend to rob the person that took everything from you with one flick of her fingers."

"I intend to rob Rizaen."

Tara'zin stared at me for a long few seconds and then burst out laughing. "You're mad. Utterly mad!"

"Mad or not, it's going to happen."

"You and your Academy know better than most how ludicrous it is to even consider such a thing. Rizaen is no ordinary queen. No ordinary mortal. She is power made manifest, a being capable of both great and terrible things...and she does not forget insults."

For a moment my mind flashed back to Scythe, all those years ago. Pinned up against the wall and left to fry in the sun. Something of that must have shown in my face because she suddenly took a step back.

"I am well aware of who Rizaen is and of what she is capable," I replied coldly. "And yet still I will do this thing. The question is, do you want to help strike back against the person who did," I waved my hands at the stonework, "*this* to you?"

"Strike back at a god?" She shook her head rapidly. "Insanity."

"And yet it seems almost commonplace in my life."

"Then I pity you and yours."

I nodded, acknowledging that she had scored a point there. "Look, I'm of no mind to play games so let me lay this out clear. I want to steal Rizaen's most prized possession. As one of her city architects you might know where she keeps such things. Help me get in there and I'll give you two," I pulled out a glistening ruby, "of these. Should be enough to get you back up at least into the Gold Quarter."

Reaching out she took the ruby into her hand and gazed at it absently. I could tell that she was thinking hard about my proposal and less about the wealth in her hand. A chance to hit back at the bitch who had stripped her of everything, make a little money on the side and have little likelihood of repercussion? Could she afford to miss such a thing?

Gently she clinked the ruby onto the table. "Five of these and I'll help."

"Three."

"Four."

"Agreed."

"Good." Stepping around me she sank into the chair opposite and steepled her fingers. "So tell me, Imperator, what is it that you strive to steal?"

"A lump of metal?" She regarded me with incredulous eyes. "You're seriously willing to risk all of this for some metal?"

"It's not just any metal," I replied. "It's very important to both me and Rizaen. You should assume that if a Power wants something then it has value. I am going to strip her of it and you can rest happy knowing that she will be frothing at the mouth from the indignity."

"I find this hard to believe, but you're the one paying the bills so I'll pretend for your sake."

"I'm honoured."

"And so you should be," she replied with a grin. "Now, where do you believe this item you are after will be stored?"

"It will be one of her most prized possessions – likely her *most* important – so I pass that question over to you, the expert."

Tara'zin pursed her lips, thinking long and hard before pushing up from the table. "One moment." When she returned, she had an armful of rolled parchment. "Here, these are the latest blueprints from the palace." Dumping them onto the table, she stretched one out and pinned it down before placing a finger on the map. "Here is the primary vault. It is the most secure location within the palace and is known to hold the majority of Rizaen's wealth. Guarded at all times by six of the Royal Guard, with an enchanted stone door impregnable to mortal attack." I opened my mouth to speak but she raised a finger sharply. "Many have tried to enter this vault. All have failed. But...I do not think this is what you are after."

"What do you mean? You just said it had all of her belongings?"

"Not belongings, *wealth*," she clarified. "If you broke into this vault you would find enough gold to drown in. Emeralds, diamonds and rubies far bigger than the ones you are going to be providing me. It is coin and jewellery, art and jewels. It is not, however, her most prized possessions. They lie in a different vault, one lesser known but just as heavily guarded. It is...here." Another tap of the finger. "The vault is smaller than the previous and lies next to Rizaen's own quarters." A twinkle in her eyes. "If you are found here then it is not the Royal Guard you would have to worry about. The Queen does not take kindly to intruders."

"I'm sure she doesn't," I muttered, focusing on the blueprints. "And so you think it is located here?"

A nod. "It seems most likely."

"Any idea what else is inside?"

A shake of her head. "No. Only Rizaen goes inside. Her Royal Guard might have caught a glimpse, perhaps, but it is unlikely. She is not a sharing sort."

"That might be putting it mildly," I replied with a snort. Rizaen made most of the other Powers look positively gracious and generous in their dealings with others. She was someone who wanted the best for herself, knew how to get it and didn't give a damn about those she trampled along the way.

In other words; a diamond-plated bitch.

I frowned at the lined drawing of the palace. "So...how do you know it is truly a vault if no-one has seen inside?"

"Because it was built at her majesty's request not ten years ago. Required complete renovation of the adjoining bedchamber." Tara'zin raised her chin proudly. "I was part of the team who designed the plans."

"Interesting..." I stared at the plans for a while longer before turning towards her. "So where did she keep her most prized belongings before this vault was designed?"

"...What?"

"Her possessions. Where did she keep them?"

"I...I don't know. In the primary vault perhaps?"

I shook my head. "No, you've described it as purely a financial vault, not one with personal value. Come on, *think*, what did Rizaen do with items she loved before this vault appeared?"

"I don't know! In her bedroom?"

"And does she allow maids and guests inside?"

"Sometimes."

"Then no," I declared with another shake of my head. "They wouldn't be safe enough. And if she wanted to have everything on display then they would be; after all they are her *prized* possessions. There has to be somewhere else, somewhere either close to her chambers or somewhere she travelled."

"Why are you asking this, I told you where the vault was."

"It might be the vault. It might be *a* vault. But if she had somewhere that had protected her valuables for so long already, why would she move them?" I frowned at the blueprints. "Is this smaller vault more secure or is it more of a decoy? The fact that no-one has seen inside is mysterious and alluring, ensuring that all would-be vault-hunters head straight for it without a second thought. Hells, it's probably just one gigantic trap."

"This is a complete guess on your part!" she hissed exasperatedly.

"True. It's a hunch but my hunches have kept me alive for longer than I expected. I've worked with too many powers over the years for some of it not to rub off on me. Rizaen is too cunning to leave her most important and prized items in one location after she made an obvious remodel. She probably uses that new vault as either some kind of torture-room or boudoir. Maybe both."

"You speak as if you know her personally."

"Let's say that we have had our run-ins in the past."

"And yet you live. And want to steal from her." Tara'zin pursed her lips. "I am beginning to think that I might have accepted an offer from a mad-man."

"There's a fine line between genius and madness," I remarked.

"And you think you are the former?"

"Oh, I've been both sides."

"...Delightful." She looked at me the way she might look at a filthy child, disgust warring with amusement on her face. "So, how do we determine the truth?"

"Hmm." An idea sparked in my mind. "You mentioned that people have tried to break into the vault before. Any idea if others would be interested?"

"Whilst I don't know for sure, I can't imagine that there aren't desperate people in the city who would love to get their hands on priceless treasures..."

"Snark suits you. Congratulations."

"You test my patience."

"You are not the first to tell me that."

"I can't imagine why." She rolled her eyes but a small smile flickered across her lips. "So, you want to get others to try and raid the vault?"

"Perhaps." My finger tapped against my lips whilst plan after plan ran through my mind. "Or at the very least, give the impression that the vault has been breached."

"I don't follow."

"If we can get Rizaen to believe that her security has been compromised then it is possible that her first point to check will be what is most precious to her. If someone broke into your house, what would you do?"

"Have them executed," she replied primly.

"Beyond that."

"I...would check my most important assets were still intact."

"Exactly!" I hissed. "You go to make sure that everything most important to you is secure. So if we give the suggestion that there has been a raid on the palace – one where the thieves weren't interested in mere gold – where does Rizaen go to?"

"Her actual vault," Tara'zin breathed, eyes flashing with anticipation. "But how do we pull that off? We would need to have her under surveillance at all times, not to mention convincing her that something had been stolen."

"Perhaps we don't need to convince her," I muttered, lost in thought again. "Perhaps we just need to convince the staff. If they think that there has been a break-in but nothing apparent was stolen...maybe that would be enough. Tara'zin, do you still have staff members within the palace grounds?"

She nodded. "Of course. Despite the shame brought upon our House, some of our staff have skills that are not so readily thrown away. I, too, have access."

"Okay." The fragments of an idea coalesced into a cohesive whole in my mind and I leant forward excitedly. "Here's what we're going to do."

CHAPTER 24
SCARRED PROGRESS

Imperator Carmine met us at the door to Wolf's Hollow. His characteristic shit-eating smile was gone, replaced by his seeming alter-ego of caring Instructor. Perhaps he genuinely knew how hard these exams were and actually did worry about us in his own twisted way. Or - and I think this much more likely - he just did it to fuck with us further.

We were led inside, given time in steaming hot showers which served to remove the grime that covered our clothes but did nothing for the stains on our souls and then made to join the Imperator in his office where he watched us gravely from the other side of his table, his fingers steepled together.

"Welcome back," he said first and foremost. "Though I imagine that it's the last place you want to be."

No-one replied. No-one even moved.

Drawing in a breath, he pursed his lips and then leant forward. "This was a hard test. The final exam always is. They are, by their very nature, a crucible in which – should you hold true to your lessons – you will find yourselves reforged. So, let me be the first to say, well done."

"Well done?" Cassius spoke up, voice twisted with fury. "Well done?! We were forced to kill innocents. Men, women and..." he broke off and fresh tears spilled down his face. "How could you?"

"How could I what?" Carmine replied, confused.

"You know damn well what I mean. This is your exam. You set this entire thing up!"

Carmine held his gaze, his face hardening until all pretence of the friendly Imperator had vanished. "Even if I told you the truth, I doubt you would believe me, so let's just get this over with. Yes, blame me if you like for the exam. All the Imperators here have gone over your files with a fine-tooth comb as you well know, so did you think it would be easy?" He snorted. "What kind of Imperators would you be if we didn't go to such lengths? We need people who can make those kinds of hard decisions and not let the outcome destroy them. We need people who aren't going to freeze up when placed in a tough situation. We need people who can out-lead, out-smart and out-fight anyone else in the empire and through these scenarios, *we get them*. If we have to break a few eggs to achieve that," he shrugged, "so be it."

"Break a few eggs?!" Cassius roared, leaping to his feet. Ella and I pulled him back from the desk as he tried to lunge forwards. "Those were people! Innocent people you twisted prick!"

Carmine rolled his eyes. "Did you know that the Academy places a value on the life of an Imperator? The statisticians have crunched the numbers and they reckon that an average Imperator is worth just over three-hundred of your average denizens of the empire." He raised an eyebrow at the stunned looks on our faces and continued. "It's true. By my reckoning you saved forty-two infested people in the last three days. That's a better record than most who have dealt with Ranulskin infestations, believe me. But even with all that effort you lost forty-seven civilians, not including those who had died before leaving the town. That means, in the Academy's eyes, there was an expenditure of around fifteen percent of the value of one Imperator to get five Imps to gain a passing grade and be raised to Imperator. That's a trade-off that the Academy will make over and over again, you can bet on that."

"You're a monster," Cassius snarled, still trying to get across the table.

"As are we all, dear boy. But sometimes the world needs a monster more than a hero. You would do well to remember that."

Rikol coughed and raised his hand. "Er...you said five Imps passed." His eyes darted around the room. "There are six of us here."

Carmine's eyes twinkled. "Ah, you noticed that did you? Well, I had hoped to give you all the good or potentially bad news privately, but as you're all here now, why not?" He paused to read the notes in front of him, though I knew full well that he remembered perfectly who had passed or failed. My muscles clenched as I tensed for the inevitable. My many run-ins with Carmine had doubtless spelled my doom.

"Rikol," Carmine began, "in light of your achievements, yada yada yada, you have been found worthy enough to join the ranks of the Imperators. Well done."

Picking up the next form, Carmine carried on. "Sophia, you too have been found worthy. As has," he flicked through, "Scythe and Ella. Congratulations."

Two forms remained. All eyes turned to me and Cassius.

"Cassius," Carmine said slowly, turning the pages. "Blah, blah, blah. Ah here we go. You have been found *wanting* and are to remain here in Wolf's Hollow until you can prove yourself worthy."

"You can't be serious!" I gasped, aghast. "He's the best Imperator here!"

"Actually, no. Looking at your overarching scores the best Imperator is Ella. Followed closely by Rikol and Sophia. Cassius has some minor personality flaws that need to be addressed before he is ready for the next stage of his career."

"Go to the Pits you utter bastard! You complete sack of shit! You-"

A hand reached down and touched my wrist. Cassius. He offered a sad smile. "Cal, it's okay. I'll be fine."

"Okay? None of this is okay!"

"Hey, you made Imperator. Don't ruin this for yourself, or for the others." I glanced around and saw the mixture of excitement and frustration evident on everyone's features. "You'll all be Imperators and I'll be right behind you; you can count on that."

"An excellent attitude," Carmine said but Cassius raised his middle finger without looking at him, his eyes drifting from mine and locking onto Ella's.

"Right behind you," he said gently. "Count on it."

It was a sad procession that left Wolf's Hollow. We were at once both elated and defeated at the prospect of having succeeded where so many had failed but also having to leave a member of the team behind. Cassius bore it well, all smiles, witticisms and handshakes, like he was seeing us off on some grand-adventure and not returning into the foul bowels of the facility for more horrors. Carmine had given us a day to sort our things and prepare for the journey back. Considering what we had just been through I had half-expected a week or so to decompress but somewhat unsurprisingly Wolf's Hollow wasn't exactly the most conducive place to do so.

Cassius and Ella used that time wisely, losing themselves in passion and lust in an effort to get over the sorrow both of their imminent parting and of their shared experiences. None of us minded. We were all far past the point where something as minor as a little noise and the smell of sex bothered us. Hells, I remembered Simone's words from so long ago about how we would eventually get over seeing each other naked should we survive. He wasn't wrong. In the grander scheme of things, it just didn't seem to matter.

Besides, none of us begrudged Cassius or Ella their happiness. We all knew it was fleeting. Even if Cassius was joining us, we would inevitably be split up and they would only get to meet when missions allowed for it. And any happy memories that could be given to Cassius to help him survive in Wolf's Hollow without his friends was something that each of us would encourage.

A carriage waited for us when we climbed out of the facility and said our goodbyes. It rumbled along the rutted tracks for what felt like weeks before pulling up outside the walls of the Academy, a place that had been so far from our minds in the past year that it seemed strange to suddenly see it. And with that view came the crashing realisation that we had done it. We had actually *done it*. Aside from a few formalities we had actually passed the eighth and final year.

We were, for all intents-and-purposes, *Imperators*.

And yet, with everything that we had done and had been done to us in the last year, I'm not sure that any of us truly cared. We had achieved the thing that we had desired most for the formative years of our lives, but had it been worth it? Were we better people now or just instruments of our own dark desires? Tool of revenge and nothing more?

Only time would tell.

Kane met us at the Academy gates, a broad smile breaking through the bushy beard he bore in place of a chin. We had expected him to take us to the dorms but instead he gave us each a hug, a handshake and then marched us to the Decompression Chambers. Brooking no dissent, he effectively barred us inside the building whilst informing us that all the relevant celebrations would take place in due time. We were to relax and have fun. That was, in fact, an order.

Relax. Fun. Strange words on the tongue. Having spent close to a year within the walls of Wolf's Hollow and barely seeing sunlight, we were pale, fractious and riddled with self-loathing. I knew of only one cure for the last two items and immediately went in search of it. It wasn't hard; she was standing outside.

Seya butted me so hard with her head that I went sprawling back into the hallway. The massive panther advanced, squeezing her gigantic frame into the corridor and blocking any means of escape.

Just like she had planned.

When I had last visited the capital, I had been told by some well-to-do lady of fashion to 'exfoliate' – whatever that was - more. I'm fairly certain that Seya's attentions in those long minutes of being thoroughly scoured by a tongue that felt akin to the desert-wind, counted. Thankfully, my treatment was relatively short lived as the others made the fatal mistake of coming out to investigate the noise. Seya was nothing if not free with her gifts. Unsurprising really; she was a queen after all.

Her presence, more than anything else, made me relax. I hadn't been without Seya for that long since I had met her. To be separated from a part of you – a part of your soul – for that amount of time was heart-wrenching. I had no desire to ever have such distance between us again.

Little did I know, that choice wouldn't be mine to make.

I left the gymnasium on the morning of the fourth day to find Kane standing in the hallway with a man who looked like a strong wind might knock him over. A barrage of measurements later and he was away, hunting for the next target.

"Needed to see how much you had filled out, if at all," Kane joked as shouts of distress made their way down the hall. "Seems like that small amount of muscle you had has gone and vanished."

"You try living underground for a year," I muttered.

"I did. Wasn't pleasant."

"That's an understatement," I yawned.

"Do you want to talk about it?"

"Not even slightly."

Kane nodded. "Fair enough, but know that my door is open. Wolf's Hollow is a bitch, but it doesn't have to scar your future."

"I think that's already scarred," I murmured absently, ignoring Kane's concerned gaze. There would be time to work through the multitude of issues that Wolf's Hollow had caused, but the time was not now.

"Your graduation ceremony will be in three days," Kane said after a moment. "Not usually a big event; we don't invite any of the Imps to watch as you know, but we do have any Imperators who are available turn up if able. Also, it wouldn't surprise me if the Emperor makes an appearance."

"Why do you say that?"

He arched an eyebrow. "Because you're his pet Great Heart-bonded. He put you on this path and he will have plans for you. I very much doubt that he will miss the culmination of the last eight years. But then again," he raised his hands, "who can really know what the Emperor will do."

"That's certainly true," I replied, a little perturbed. "Has there been any mention of his plans for me? I know that he usually keeps his Great Heart-bonded close, but that would somewhat go against my monster-hunting role."

"The Emperor tends to keep his plans close to his chest," Kane replied. "Rest assured, he will have something in mind for you, but until he lets the Academy know what we will keep acting towards your monster-hunting role."

"Fair enough," I responded glumly. Despite always having known that the Emperor would have plans for me, it seemed like it would be such a waste of effort to have pushed myself so hard to become the best hunter I could be to then be made to stay in the citadel. "Any word on Cassius?"

Kane frowned. "No, and I wouldn't expect there to be any. As he failed the exam you know that there is at least two months extra work for him before he can try again. And that is assuming that he can push himself to earn the right for a second shot."

"But he-"

"Look, Calidan, I know what you are going to say but I have no authority in this matter. The Imperators at Wolf's Hollow are the only people, aside from the High Imperator and the Emperor, who can pass or fail people. If they say that Cassius isn't ready, then he isn't ready."

"But we're partners!"

Kane raised an eyebrow. "You're soon to be an Imperator. If you couldn't work alone then I would be surprised that you made it this far." He held up a hand to stop my retort. "Relax, I'm not unsympathetic to your situation. Unsurprisingly, it is not the first time that this has happened. As it stands, the rest of your dorm have worked with you hunting monsters in the past and so may well be requisitioned to do the same if the mission calls for it. Otherwise, I envisage that you will be expected to take Seya; after all, the two of you are likely more of a force to be reckoned with than your average Imperator duo."

"Was that a compliment?"

He ruffled his hand through his dense beard. "You know, I believe it was. Strange." Smirking at my petulant look, he clapped me on the shoulder and turned to leave. "Let the others know what I said about the graduation and try to relax, you'll see Cassius again soon enough, I'm sure."

Kane wasn't much of a prophet; I didn't see Cassius again for another eighteen months. And when I did, everything changed.

"Oh, and one more thing," Kane said over his shoulder. "You're all going to need to give a full name for the official records. Some of you might not have such a thing, so make sure that you think on what you want as your last name over the next few days." He shot me a smile. "Can't just go around as a mononym all the time."

Carmine

Imperator Carmine listened to the cries. Witnessed the screams.

Smiled.

Cassius's mind was stretched thin. He had proven to be surprisingly resilient, more so than most of the Imps that he was ordered to take a 'special interest' in. But, just like every Imperator knew, everybody had a breaking point, and unless Carmine was worse at his job than he believed, Cassius was just about there.

Perfect.

Utilising that girlfriend of his over and over in his mental games had truly been the turning point. What person could handle experiencing repeated deaths at the hands of a loved one? He would have to remember that for future subjects. It truly would be a time saver.

"Inform the Emperor that the subject he desires is on the way and prepare the boy for transport," he ordered.

"He's ready?" Havan rumbled.

"Most assuredly," Carmine replied, picking up a thick ledger. The leather cover had the title of 'Wolf's Hollow, Incident Log' stamped into the hide. Taking a quill, he quickly scrawled a few choice words before blowing the ink dry with a grunt of satisfaction.

The words stated 'Cassius. Injured in training. Transferred to citadel for recovery'.

"The Emperor always has what he wants," Carmine breathed, "one way or another."

CHAPTER 25
GRADUATION

For an event that had been years in coming, graduation was a simple and small affair. The five of us received freshly tailored Academy finery and I have to say that we made for quite a dashing sight. The array of black and silver trim wouldn't have looked out of place at the now-yearly citadel ball and might have even made heads turn in the fashion district of Anderal.

We made our way to a place I had only been twice before; the Academy council chamber, where the seating was arrayed in a circular pattern that climbed above the central dais upon which awaited the High Imperator. The last time I had been summoned here it had been to discuss the events of the fourth-year exam – I had to trust that this time it would be a significantly more pleasant experience.

"Friends," the High Imperator declared in a loud voice, "colleagues, attend me." The words had the ring of tradition behind them and the watching Imperators immediately ceased their muted conversations. "Today we have cause for celebration! Today, we mark the end of a long period of growth and welcome five new Imperators to the fold." She smiled and gestured for us to walk down to the dais.

"Even by the Academy's high standards these five have accomplished a great deal. They have pushed through obstacles time and time again and remained standing when others, including Imperators, have fallen. They've fought through fire and shadow to get here and," she gifted us a rare, genuine smile, "I'm glad to say that 'here' you finally are. Today you will finally get to add those six letters to your current title and be Imps no more!"

"Took you long enough!"

It took a moment to scan through the chuckling crowd but there he was, wrinkled like a prune and just as craggy as ever. Korthan grinned down at us as the High Imperator gave him a mock-glare.

"This is to be a serious ceremony," the High Imperator reminded him somewhat sternly.

"Pah!" he said, waving her off. "There're enough serious people here to help with that. I'm just the entertainment."

"If you're the entertainment, old man," I said, stepping forwards, "then I hate to think what the punishment might pass for here."

"Hah! See Wolf's Hollow didn't deaden the spark in you, boy, that's something at least."

"No more dead than you look," I retorted with a grin. "Seriously, have you seen yourself? You're basically a raisin."

"No more than-"

"Ahem." Though the noise wasn't loud, it carried through the room and stopped our friendly insults in their tracks. The High Imperator raised an eyebrow at Korthan and then turned to me. "As much of a fan as I am of insulting Korthan, there is a time and a place for such things and this is not it."

"Apologies ma'am." I stepped back and bowed my head apologetically.

"Hah! Stup-"

"Korthan," said Acana sharply, "continue speaking and you will be giving the first years' history lectures every day, all year."

The words fizzled in his throat.

"Now, let's continue, shall we?"

Kane stepped forwards carrying a small velvet box. With a quick bow of his head, he unclasped the box and held the contents up for the High Imperator's inspection. Removing something small and silver, the High Imperator strode up to Ella.

"The archivists are recording this for the official records," she began, "so please state your full name clearly when indicated. Repeat after me, 'I, Ella...'"

For a moment a flash of uncertainty crossed Ella's face, then she stiffened. "I, Ella Chainbreaker..."

"swear to abide by the tenets of the Academy and the Emperor, to uphold the law and to dispense justice, to be the voice of the Emperor in the wild, the sword of the Emperor in the dark, and protect him from any evil."

"...any evil."

"To place the Emperor first and foremost, forsaking all friendships and ties in the face of his need."

"...his need."

"And to be his greatest advocate, supporter and asset. The most brilliant tool in his arsenal. Imperator."

"...Imperator." Ella said the final word with resounding clarity, a smile on her otherwise stern face.

The High Imperator leant close and clasped something onto her lapel. When she stood back I saw the crossed blades of the Academy shining on Ella's uniform. "So let it be witnessed."

"Witnessed and welcome!" resounded the auditorium, the watching Imperators thumping hands to their chests in unison.

One by one, the High Imperator moved down the line.

"...I Sophia Llangera..."

"Witnessed and welcome!"

"...I Scytharanious Dokkor..."

"Witnessed and welcome!"

As the two members of our dorm who still had families and loved ones back home, Sophia and Scythe both provided their given names. With their badges pinned they stepped back, looking immensely satisfied with the crossed swords gleaming on their lapels.

"...I Rikol Ashbane."

That one caught me. I remembered Rikol standing over the body of Damien, his eyes promising vengeance on the twisted intelligence that had caused his death. Lost in the memory I almost didn't register the High Imperator standing before me until she cleared her throat.

"Ready?" she asked, a smile in her voice.

Shaken out of the past, I nodded. I was ready for this. The others had asked what my last name was going to be, but I had known ever since we met the Tracker and been introduced to Seya. He had given it to me then, unknowingly, but it suited me down to the bone. Whilst Calidan Elkona Melkhuk didn't quite roll off the tongue, its translation into common worked perfectly.

As the High Imperator began intoning the words, my eyes found Korthan. He gave me something that most Imps or Imperators had never seen: a genuine smile. Without warning a sudden wash of emotion hit me and I struggled to control my features.

This is for you, everyone.

My mind flashed back to that horrible first night. The sounds of the red-eyed beast munching its way through my friends and family. Horrors that I would never forget, and the very things that had driven me to achieve this goal.

This is for you.

...I just wish Cassius had been there as well. *I hope you're doing okay, brother.*

Bracing myself, I spoke the words loud and clear.

"I, Calidan Darkheart, swear to abide by the tenants of the Academy and the Emperor, to uphold the law and to dispense justice, to be the voice of the Emperor in the wild, the sword of the Emperor in the dark, and protect him from any evil. To place the Emperor first and foremost, forsaking all friendships and ties in the face of his need. And to be his greatest advocate, supporter and asset. The most brilliant tool in his arsenal. Imperator."

Korthan wiped something from his eye as the High Imperator leaned forwards and pinned the gleaming crossed swords on my lapel.

"So let it be witnessed."

"Witnessed and welcome!" the chant reverberated around the room accompanied by the thump of clasped hands hammering chests. As the sound died away and the cheers and applause broke out, I realised that this was it. My apotheotic moment.

I was no longer Calidan, Imp.

I was Calidan Darkheart.

Imperator.

Cassius

Cassius awoke to bright golden eyes that gleamed with voracious intelligence. As he shook off the vestiges of sleep – strange, considering that he didn't remember going to bed – his brain caught up with him. He *knew* those eyes.

Jumping to his feet, he snapped a salute. "Apologies sir!"

Laughing, the Emperor waved a hand. "You have nothing to apologise for, young Cassius. I apologise for waking you."

"Is there something amiss, sir?" Cassius's heart clenched. "Is it the others? Are they hurt?!"

"No, no. Nothing like that." The Emperor's voice was like a warm cloud, his thunderous tones wrapping around him. "Relax."

Cassius breathed deep. *Everything's okay,* he reassured himself with a smile. In fact, he was no longer sure why he had been worried in the first place.

"Is there something I can help you with, sir? I'm sure that Imperator Carmine and the others will let me leave Wolf's Hollow if you need support with something."

A curious twinkle entered the Emperor's eyes, like he was enjoying a joke that Cassius didn't understand. "I know you likely don't remember your parents but they raised you well," he said with a stunning smile, his perfectly white teeth almost blinding Cassius with their brilliance. "As a matter of fact, there is something you can help me with. Thank you for offering."

"Of course, sir," Cassius said eagerly. *Anything to get out of here.* "Anything you need, I'm your man."

Those eyes twinkled again. "Anything eh? I'm glad to hear it!"

"If you give me a moment, I can go find Imperator Carmine and inform him that I will be assisting you..."

"No, no, that's not necessary." Another brilliant smile, those golden eyes burning into his with such intensity. "As it happens, I've already made arrangements. You see, Cassius," the Emperor swept an arm wide, "you're already out of Wolf's Hollow."

"...Wha-"

The Emperor continued as though there had been no interruption. "In fact, you're already at the citadel. I wanted to get things moving as quickly as possible." He turned another dazzling look at Cassius. "I truly hope that you *don't mind.*"

"N-no. No of course not." As he said it, he realised he meant it. Sure, waking up somewhere completely different was a shock to the system but it was for the Emperor's benefit. Besides, surely *anything* was better than going back to Wolf's Hollow. "What can I help you with?"

The Emperor regarded him curiously for a long moment, fingers rubbing his chin. "It's been some time since we first met. Do you remember that time, Cassius?"

"Of course!" Cassius said brightly. "You saved my life. Drove the darkness out of me."

"Hmm. Not entirely accurate, but close enough," the Emperor mused. "I found you to be an interesting individual. Not just because of your *outstanding* character, with an enviable will to survive, but of the fact that you were resisting the black seraph."

"...I was?"

"Most people without having had their seraph awakened would have succumbed to that attack much more quickly. You, however, despite not yet having had your seraph awakened...somehow your body was fighting it off. And that got me intrigued. You see," he said, leaning forwards and perching both hands under his chin, "everyday people are born that are slightly different. Eye colour, hair colour, size, they're all determined by things inside you that you cannot see with the naked eye. Most of your genes – these small pieces of genetic code – are passed down from the parents, however, they can mutate. Most of these mutations are minor, but some," he grinned wolfishly, "well...I guess you could say us Seraphim were the result of a genetic abnormality. One that gave us an advantage so strong that there were many advocates for classing us as a separate species from homo sapiens. A new, *better* version of humanity."

Cassius nodded, trying his best to follow along but couldn't hide the growing confusion on his face. There was just so much that he had never heard of, let alone thought about, being thrown at him.

"I see that I'm losing you. Apologies, I rarely get to talk to anyone about this anymore and I tend to get carried away," the Emperor rumbled. "What you really want to know is 'what does this have to do with me?' Am I right?" Seeing Cassius nod, he smiled. "So, we've established that I am someone who is intrigued by the tiny things that make people different. I like to play with them myself, when I have time. Alter those fundamental building blocks to create something entirely new and, sometimes, completely unexpected. I believe you've met one of my creations."

"Kirok," Cassius murmured quietly.

"Yes, that was his name, he was given to me as part of a punishment detail. Someone who could never be allowed to be an Imperator, but, as you can see, has been made into a valuable resource." His gaze turned wistful. "I didn't anticipate the blue though; that was a surprise. Anyway." He clapped his hands together, the sound echoing like thunder, looking like an eager child. "Back to you and your ability to resist seraph influence. That got me thinking. You see, one thing that the Enemy has always been able to do well is to imbue His minions with some of His power when the occasion calls for it. You might remember the ball we held right here where you got to see that particular skill in action?"

Cassius nodded. "The Enemy talked through them. I remember. That was a hard fight, especially with all that black fire everywhere."

"Voidflame," the Emperor said darkly. "One of the Enemy's traits. It's how His seraph manifests when He lets it run rampant. And you've come right to the crux of the matter with that. Do you remember the younger Imps who were corrupted and controlled? They were bursting with voidflame, unable to contain it. Their bodies were burning up with just the tiniest of fractions of the Enemy's power running through their veins. The Imperators fared better, but still not by much. You see, the Enemy is so adept at control that He delights in corrupting new people to His cause. They are disposable assets. One use and *poof*," he spread his hands wide, fingers flickering like a fire, "they're gone. Now, I'm not like the Enemy, I don't control people." Again there was that twinkle in his eyes, a joke that he wasn't sharing with him, but Cassius shook away the question in his mind and concentrated on the conversation.

"But I *do* want to be able to project my presence. Doing so would offer significant tactical advantages. However, I don't believe in being wasteful and so I don't want my conduit to be one-use. And that's where you come in."

Cassius felt a clenching in his gut. "Me?"

"Yes. You." The Emperor's eyes gleamed. "With your ability to resist seraph, I believe that you will be able to contain a considerable portion of my power. Naturally, I would never seek to put you in harm's way of course."

"Of course." Cassius scoffed at the notion. The Emperor wouldn't do that to him.

"Good, I'm glad you see." He smiled. "If you are *willing* then I would love to see what you and I can accomplish together. We will be an unstoppable team!"

"W-willing. Yes." Cassius could barely help himself. He *needed* to help the Emperor. *Of course* he did. He was already an Imp – already beholden to the great man before him. If the Emperor said he needed more, then who was he to say no?

"Now, there will be a few minor modifications that we will need to make." Cassius tensed. "But think of it just like being implanted with a liathea. A completely safe procedure. And when you come out of the other side there will be significant...advantages so I *wouldn't worry.*"

Cassius relaxed. "No, of course not. I'm not worried at all."

"Excellent. So, you agree?"

Cassius found himself drawn into those golden eyes, spiralling deep into their molten hue. He would do anything for this man. *Anything.* "Of course," he said with avid enthusiasm. "I'm just the man for the job."

The Emperor smiled and Cassius basked in its warmth. "I am so very glad to hear it. Come, let's go next door and we can get started." Reaching out, he took Cassius's hand in his own and tugged him to his feet.

Leading the way, they stepped out into the dark hall of the citadel and walked briefly down a long, echoing corridor before pulling up in front of a spectacular set of doors. Big enough to walk two of those elephants he had seen in the Andural zoo through side-by-side with room to spare, the doors glimmered silver.

Lifting his hand, the Emperor focused and metallic *clunks* sounded within the doors. Slowly, ponderously, they swung open. Cassius froze for a moment as the sights and sounds greeted him but the Emperor strode forward unperturbed. "Come along little Cassius. Let's get things started."

"Of course." Cassius walked into the light.

The doors began to close behind.

"Wait, isn't that B-"

The doors slid shut and silence descended once more upon the dark hallways of the lower depths. A silence that might seem just that little bit heavier than before.

For a bright light was about to be tarnished.

PART II

Imperator

CHAPTER 26
THE WORKING LIFE

The wooden fist crashed down, pulverising the ground where I had stood a moment before. Vona screamed as she whistled through the air, green fire trailing behind her as she cut, her blade hacking through the thick bark that passed for a wrist. The wood troll groaned, the wordless sound so deep as to almost be inaudible, then lunged forwards, attempting to stomp me into the forest loam. Jumping out of harm's way, I cut twice more, each hit leaving a small bit of green flame that ate into the bark. The troll was covered in these small wounds but even with the added benefit of the fire I wasn't doing enough damage to counter its impressive resilience. Before my eyes I saw bark shift and cover a burning patch, smothering it completely whilst seemingly sealing the wound.

Any time soon would be helpful.

An image broke into my mind, that of me spinning and diving whilst being chased by the lumbering faux-tree. *Just wanted to see what you were able to do without me*, came the amused voice of my Great Heart.

How long have you been in position?!

Oh...about five of your minutes, she yawned.

Ducking another thunderous blow, I shook my head in dismay. *You know I've nearly died like five times, right?*

It's a good learning experience for you.

Nearly dying? Been there, done that. I lashed out with Vona and scored a burning line that ran along the massive beast's forearm, eliciting a thrum of pain.

I feel like the fact that you have put 'nearly' in front of dying suggests that you are, in fact, good enough to still be alive. Most who have encountered one of these creatures likely wished they had your skills.

What's your point?!

That you should thank me for not always just coming in to rescue you. To allow you to grow on your own. I might not always be here, you know.

That stopped me dead and only years of training had me roll aside just in time to avoid the crashing limb. *Seya, you're essentially an eternal being. Why wouldn't you always be here?*

A toothy smile. *Well, I was speaking metaphorically. Just because I'm not dead doesn't mean I might not be here. I could be sleeping, or being groomed. You know, much more important things.*

I'm glad to know that keeping me alive is so high on your list of importance, I growled.

Tsk. You're no fun today. Claws as long as my forearm emerged from her padded feet. *Bring it this way.*

Not deigning to reply, I spun, swivelled and danced my way under the boughs of trees. The lumbering troll followed with tenacious intensity, showing no hint of fatigue in its many attempts to squish me to bloody paste.

Seya the Magnificent, saving the day in three, two, one...

A black blur erupted from the tree-tops and impacted the rear torso of the troll like a ballista bolt, driving the beast to one knee. Gleaming claws raked at the armoured torso, shredding layers of bark as Seya fought for a better hold. Her jaws clamped down on the nape of the beast's neck and *crunched*, splintering wood and sending a spray of deep green ichor into the air. The woods shook with the rumble of the troll's groan, arms attempting to reach behind its broad back but failing to grasp the ever shifting and scrambling cat.

Are you ready yet?

Hold on. I concentrated as I manifested a spear of glowing metal before me, the tip glowing almost white-hot.

You really should take some more lessons from Rikol. You're far too slow at that.

Not helping! I retorted as she interrupted my concentration, causing my will to waver.

Just get it done little one, Mr Tree here is starting to get feisty.

I heard the cracking of timber as the troll began flinging itself against nearby wood in an attempt to dislodge the panther that was chewing through its neck. Concentrating, I fixed the error in my design and completed the creation. Hovering in the air in front of me was a shaft of steel with a six-inch bladed head that glowed hot enough that the air above it shimmered.

Okay, ready. On three. Two. One. Now!

Seya shifted her powerful length and hauled back on the neck whilst pushing with her feet, forcing the beast's impressively long torso to be revealed in all its glory. With a burst of seraph I sent the spear spiralling through the air, leaving a trail of super-heated air in its wake. Like a burning lance it streamed through the sky and struck the armoured upper body of the troll like a hammer-blow. Grunting with effort, I forced the spear to keep spinning, the burning tip eking its way through the heavy armour of the troll's chest. Without Seya to control the beast's movements this attack would have been next to impossible as the armour was too thick to break through quickly. Every time that the troll made to reach for the spear, Seya shifted her position, clawing, raking and heaving with all her strength, keeping the immense beast focused on her rather than the burning nail that was going to spell its downfall.

Thankfully, trolls weren't exactly known for their intelligence, and this was no exception.

Slowly but surely the spear carved its way through the bark, leaving a pile of smouldering embers in its wake. With a groan that turned into a vibrato that caused Seya's ears to flinch, the troll stiffened as the spear finally broke through the final layer of armour and struck deep into the thing it called a heart. With a thought, I caused the metal to erupt in all directions, turning the spear into something more akin to a porcupine.

A flaming, metallic porcupine.

The whine of the troll grew more intense as it thrashed wildly, finally managing to throw Seya clear in a spray of bark. Free to act, it reached for its chest, but it was too late. The huge hands that were perfectly suited to squashing humans like insects were unable to pry through the small hole in its chest. Seya and I watched and waited as the ridiculous life-force that sustained the beast finally began to falter, its steps beginning to slow until, little by little, the troll stopped moving entirely. The colour of its bark started to fade, starting from its heart first and spreading outwards until the entire beast was frozen in a rictus of petrified wood.

Job done.

That was, of course, when the second wood-troll lurched out of the trees.

Ten hard-fought minutes later and I collapsed on the floor next to Seya, both of us panting heavily. "That was close. Too close."

You should know better by now.

"To not trust the reports? Yes. You're absolutely right. Always expect the unexpected, as Sarrenai used to say."

Any word on the purple one?

I pulled a small shard of bark out of my hand. "No. But that was the plan all along. There have been less monster reports coming out of the east, so something must be stemming the tide."

Maybe they're all going north instead.

I grimaced. "So you've heard the reports too?"

A flick of her ear. *Obviously.*

"The military is worried. More and more Hrudan are defecting to the Empire, so much so that Forgoth has almost doubled in size in the last couple of years, but they keep bringing rumours of more activities of the Sworn. Things sound pretty bleak up there."

Maybe we should go and see what we can do about it?

"If it's a mission, sure. But you know that we have our hands full as it is."

Almost like you need another hunter to help spread the load.

"I don't need another hunter. I need *him*," I said, anger tingeing my voice. "How hurt could he have possibly been that it has taken this long to bring him back to health?"

Seya rumbled and nudged me with her head. *Not your fault.*

"Yes it is!" I hissed. "I left him there. *We* left him there."

Academy orders. You had no choice.

I groaned and reached up to rub my temples. "It's always the same argument with you."

Because one day, you will listen and realise that I have been right all along. The sooner you accept that what happened to Cassius was not because of you the better. You're carrying too much weight on your shoulders...you both are.

"Both? Ah. Ella."

Yes.

I couldn't argue with that. Each time I saw Ella she looked worse; stress lines and fatigue etched deep into her face. Honestly, I think that if we had been notified that Cassius had died then she would have begun to reach the far end of her grieving period by now and started to come out the other side, but this complete lack of knowledge about his fate just made the interminable waiting worse. It was almost like the Academy had zero clue about his status, just reiterating the same old bollocks, 'being healed by the Emperor'. I mean, maybe he was, and if so, great! But the Emperor had brought Cassius back from the brink of death before and had done it far faster. I knew that I shouldn't question his actions but a part of me that was steadily growing larger each day wanted to knock on the citadel's door and demand to see my friend.

Hopefully it wouldn't come to that. Ella was still feeling the sting of the reprimand from doing much the same.

Grunting, I heaved myself to my feet. "What are wood-trolls doing here anyway?" I asked, cunningly changing the subject.

Don't think that this conversation is over, little one, Seya replied, seeing right through my masterful deception, but acceding that she wasn't going to bring me round today she continued. *They tend to live in the deep forests and were once quite common in the land you call Hrudan. The only reason for them to be here is if they are being driven further south.*

"Perhaps the activities of the Sworn have pushed out more than the Hrudan?" I mused as I hacked through the bark of the petrified troll's neck. It broke with the sound of splintering rock rather than the *thunk* of wood.

It seems likely. Plus there have been more sightings of those...what did you call them? Thyrkan?

I snorted. "You have been paying attention! Listening in to restricted conversations again? Besides, I didn't call them Thyrkan. That blue witch did."

If they haven't put up a seraph barrier then it's not my fault I can hear what they say.

"Mmhmm. Especially when you nap under the High Imperator's window."

A lovely place to catch the sun.

"Of course, of course." Reaching down I wrenched free the head and dumped it into a canvas bag. Thankfully, unlike many of the monsters I hunted, the fact that wood-trolls turned to stone made carrying its remains much more hygienic. Usually by the time I turned up with such gifts for the Academy researchers the remains were half-rotten.

Back to the Academy?

Reaching into my long-coat, I pulled out the latest set of orders and studied it. "Yes," I said after a moment, "but via the Murva range and down from there."

That will add an extra week than if you went direct.

"I know," I grumbled. "But we have two more targets to dispatch before we can return."

Seya yawned, her cavernous mouth opening wide to reveal her gleaming teeth, freshly covered with remnants of moss and bark. *You work too hard.*

"Tell me about it," I sighed, checking my gear before slinging the bag over my shoulder and heading towards my horse.

"It's been a tough year."

"Cal, you're back!" Sophia greeted me with a warm hug.

"Hey Sophia!" I grinned, carefully placing down the mug of beer that I had been nursing so I could embrace her fully. "How have you been?"

"Terrible," she replied earnestly.

"Really?" I studied her. "You don't seem like it."

"Well, what can I say? Just because a mission sucks doesn't mean it is because I'm covered in monster guts all the time."

"What she means to say," a familiar voice interjected, "is that she spent the entire mission getting hit on by wealthy nobility." A couple of beers plonked onto the table and Scythe punched me on the shoulder. "Hey man."

"Hey yourself!" I replied with a grin. "It's good to see you both. Rikol and Ella around?"

"Should be a day or two behind us. They got tasked with following up on something minor whilst we were out there. Then again, they might just portal back."

"Would that I could," I yawned. "Would save so much walking."

Sophia flicked me gently on the nose. "You have to have, what do they call it, oh yeah – *skill* – to pull that off."

"Harsh."

"The truth can hurt." She stared at me for a moment and then grinned. "It's damn good to see you again. Seya around?"

I rolled my eyes. "Where do you think she is?"

"Ah, of course, she'll do anything for a decent groom."

Seya's voice floated into my mind, accompanied by a sleepy, contented purr. *You tell her to take that back. I'm not some hussy.*

Of course you're not, I reassured her.

I'm going to ignore your sarcasm.

Most gracious.

Another languid purr. *That's me. Gracious. Benevolent. Just like a queen should be.*

Shaking my head I came back to the room, finding both Scythe and Sophia watching me expectantly. "Sorry," I said, "was trying to convince Seya not to hunt you down for insinuating something that she most definitely *is*," I stressed the word, "...not."

Don't make me claw you.

"I asked how the hunting has been," said Scythe.

I shrugged. "Still alive, despite the best efforts of my targets."

"Things getting worse then?" asked Sophia. "We had heard that the monster reports had been picking up."

"Currently it's about on par with the last two years," I replied. "Which means lots of monsters and not a lot of me. The Academy has been prioritising the missions that I take, so there are a few settlements on the fringes that have likely been lost in my absence. Things would go faster if...well, you know."

Both grimaced. "No word on him then?" asked Sophia.

"Not that I've heard, but it's not like I've been back long. Ella might know more."

"I doubt it, she has been on mission for the last two months, alongside us. If she had heard something she would have said."

"So, I guess that's a no," I muttered, draining my mug.

"No reply to your messages?"

"None." I had taken to sending letters to the Emperor asking for information on Cassius but all had gone unanswered. It was strange. It wasn't like I was used to having the Emperor at my beck and call, but he did pay me an undue amount of attention. Most Imperators weren't particularly on first name terms with him whereas I was, at the very least, known to the man. Welcomed, more often than not. But over the last year it felt like the Emperor's attention was elsewhere. He didn't seem to care particularly about the Academy's actions, nor had he come with a suite of new missions for us. In a strange way – especially considering the rate of monster attacks – the past year as an Imperator had been probably the most *normal* I had ever experienced at the Academy. Nothing crazy had happened. No world-ending events or apocalyptic scenarios with incomprehensible powers being thrown around like they were nothing.

It probably said something about me that a part of me missed the madness.

The one good thing was that the Emperor's distraction had kept him from summoning me to his side. Either that, or he just didn't care.

Maybe both.

Regardless, it meant that I had been able to carry on with my duties rather than be trapped within the bowels of the citadel, doing Emperor-knows-what on his orders. Moreover, none of my dorm had been asked to submit to taking on a liathea. We weren't sure if that was an oversight or just a delay and no-one had been particularly keen to ask in case it flagged the issue. As much as the creatures provided benefits to the Imperators we had seen it go wrong one too many times to trust having it happen.

We stewed in silence for a few minutes before I indicated the two of them. "What about you? Decent mission?"

"Decent enough," Scythe shrugged. "Little bit of espionage here. Bit of cloak and daggery there. Standard stuff really. Oh! Ran into Arteme."

"Really? Fair way from the Academy."

"Mhmm. Looks like the Academy wanted to make use of her...particular skills. Didn't say too much about it – you know how she is – but seemed happy enough. Finished her fourth-year exam just before coming out."

I shuddered involuntarily. "Glad she survived. She's progressing quickly."

"Helps when you're already an experienced killer," Sophia explained. "She hasn't had to learn too much."

"Makes sense," I mused. "Heard much about the other squads?"

"Just the usual. Need to know basis, operational security and all that. I think most of them are tied up in assaulting Enemy strongholds."

"You would think He wouldn't have any left at this point."

"Way I see it," Scythe said with a satisfied sigh from a sip of beer. "Is that the Enemy is like a cockroach. Always more than you think and don't die easy."

Sophia snorted. "What startling insight."

"I know! Tactical genius, me."

"I think what my dear partner is trying to say," began Sophia, "is that the Enemy has more strongholds than we can shake a stick at. Most of them we likely don't know about and those we do have either been destroyed or have been reinforced. Those I've managed to get talking, like your red-head girl, have been facing much tougher engagements than previously. The element of surprise is long gone."

"Makes sense," I replied before her words truly filtered into my brain. "And she's not *my* girl!"

"Please," Sophia replied, face completely sober. "It's written plain to anyone who looks that you want her. Every time you see her your face lights up like you've got one of Rikol's seraph lances up your arse."

"That's...descriptive."

"Just like your face." She scrunched up her face and stuck out her tongue. "Just ask her out."

"I've tried. You know that."

"You were an Imp then. Younger too. Things have changed. She likes you."

"She does?"

Sophia tapped her nose. "A woman knows."

"...Right. Forgive me if I don't take your word for it."

"You should listen to her," Scythe said with a grin. "What's the harm in trying again?"

A sudden image shoved its way to the front of my mind, one that I expressly tried to forget at all times, to bury so deep that I could pretend that it never existed.

Riven's head popping like a grape.

My sudden silence and dour look killed the mood and both Sophia and Scythe looked uncomfortable. "Sorry," murmured Scythe. "Didn't mean to dredge up the past."

I waved him off. "Not your fault."

Sophia took a swallow of liquid courage and faced me, eyes bright with intensity. "We didn't mean to bring it up, but now that it is, we should talk about it."

"I would rather no-"

"What happened to Riven was awful," she continued, bludgeoning past my meagre defences. "We all liked her and what happened was horrific. But it also wasn't your fault."

I sighed and set down the beer. "My plan. I put her on the team."

"It was *our* plan. And it had a high level of risk throughout. Any one of us could have died. Most of us nearly did. Regardless, my point is this: you're an Imperator now. It's a job that has a high risk of mortality on practically every mission, let alone the nonsense you get up to. People are going to die. Friends probably. You can't let that rule your life." She offered me a sad smile and leaned forwards, voice low. "I see you Calidan. This past year, I've seen you between missions. Without Cassius around you've made little effort to integrate into the Imperators. Hells, do you even know the names of half of the people in this bar?"

My silence said everything she needed to know.

"Of course you don't!" she cried exasperatedly. "Because you haven't tried to learn them. You content yourself with a few drinks and then slink off to the next mission. Where is the living in that?"

"Sophia, I'm-"

"I'll tell you, there isn't any. So you need to get up and go talk to people. Be friendly. Learn names. Make friends." Her eyes twinkled. "I'm not suggesting you go and declare your undying love for Rinoa, but you will be social. Even if I need to force you to do it."

I let out a long-suffering sigh. "That used to be Cassius's job."

"I know. He always understood where you were weakest," she replied. "And as he isn't here, I am sure that he would want me to fill his shoes."

Scythe wrapped an arm around my shoulder and whispered into my ear. "I would just go along with this mate, Sophia is not going to let this go. You know that."

Another sigh. "Yeah, I know." I mock-glared at Sophia. "Tsk. Fine!"

Her smile lit the room.

Morning kitten!

Ugh. My head felt like it was going to explode.

I can feel your nausea through the bond. It makes everything...wiggly.

Inhaling deeply, I burned some seraph, focusing on cleansing my system. A minute later and the nausea was a distant memory. *There, better?*

I don't know. The wiggliness was quite entertaining for a while. I could feel the great panthers amused purr deep in my chest. *Someone has been standing outside your door for a little while now. I thought you should know.*

With a groan I heaved myself out of bed and threw on some clothes. One of the benefits to being an Imperator was that we each got our own room. No more bunk beds for us! Though, to be honest, I kind of missed the chaotic mess that was dorm—living; the night-time conversations and the trials and tribulations that came with living in an enclosed space. These days, whilst the rest of my dorm had rooms across the hall from me, it was a rare day that we were all together, resulting in a much lonelier experience.

Hells, maybe Sophia and Scythe might be right. Maybe I should make some new friends.

Seya wrinkled her nose. *If the past is anything to go by, you are exceedingly terrible at doing so.*

Gee, thanks. And I guess you're better at it?

A sense of indignation. *Of course? I'm a cat. Everyone and everything loves me. It is the way of things.*

Rolling my eyes, I stepped across to the door and pulled it open. "Sorry I took so long...Ella. Hey!"

Ella looked worn and weary. The dark shadows around her eyes suggesting that she hadn't been sleeping much and her fingernails were rough and jagged; the hallmark of a serial biter.

"Calidan, sorry to wake you. Can I come in?"

Stepping back, I moved aside. "Of course. Come in." Spreading my arms wide, I gave her the option of a hug. She hesitated for a second before rushing in and wrapping her arms around me.

"Whoa, easy," I managed to squeeze out as she attempted to crush my ribs.

Stepping back, she wiped something from her eye. "Sorry," she mumbled.

"Not a problem," I insisted, directing her to a chair. "What time did you get back?"

"Early this morning."

"And you're not taking advantage of the down-filled bed?"

She shot me a red-eyed look before glancing away. "Couldn't sleep."

"Scythe and Sophia said that you and Rikol got pulled into another mission. Any issues?"

A shake of the head. "No. Simple enough."

"I see." I pursed my lips before lowering my voice. "So, still no word on him then?"

She looked up. "I was hoping you might have heard something."

I shook my head wordlessly, that familiar sorrow clutching at my gut. How many nights had I lain awake in bed thinking about Cassius, wondering where he was and what was going on?

Too many to count.

"The citadel is a closed book as you know. No-one who works there talks about what goes on inside."

"I know," she groused. "I've tried to get word of him from some of my contacts but there's nothing. It's like he has disappeared off the face of the planet."

Grimacing, I reached out and placed my hand on top of hers. "I know it's tough, but we might only be able to sit tight and wait."

"That's what you said last time," she retorted, brushing my hand off angrily. "That's all we've done! He could be hurt or dead for all we know!"

"No. If he were dead then we would have been notified. The Academy doesn't play around when it comes to fatalities during training." I gave her as reassuring a smile as I could. "They say he is hurt. Maybe that's the truth."

Ella scoffed. "Cassius got healed from practically being chopped in two in far less time. What in the world could have injured him so badly that the Emperor would need him for this length of time?"

"Perhaps he isn't hurt at all. Perhaps he is on some special assignment for the Emperor. Something that is well beyond our pay-grade?"

Ella scowled and threw her arms into the air. "Exactly! All we have is speculation. He's the love of my life and I *demand* to know where he is!"

"Ella," I began worriedly, "you can't go down to the citadel again. Not after what happened last time."

"This time they won't catch me," she snarled, eyes taking on a fevered glint.

I held up a hand. "Easy. Take a breath." I stared at her pointedly until she did so, gasping down a gulp of air, her shoulders shaking with tension.

"I can't do this anymore, Cal," she whispered. "I can't pretend that everything is okay. He's gone and I have no idea where he is or even *if* he is coming back. Someone, somewhere, knows *something* and I need to find out what that something is."

"Ella, you know what the citadel guard said last time. You've got no favours left. If they alert the Emperor that you have been sneaking around then who knows what he will do? I told you how he acted when Seya snuck in, didn't I?" She stiffened and then nodded. "He doesn't like people poking around, Ella. At best you might get chucked in a cell for a few days, at worst you might get treated like a rogue Imperator. You could be hunted down and executed!"

"Then what am I supposed to do!?" she exploded, voice cracking with emotion.

Reaching out, I drew her into another hug. "Wait and hope," I whispered as she poured out all her emotion into my shoulder. "Hope that he will come back to us. Cassius wouldn't leave us alone. Not if he had any say in the matter."

Eventually her crying stopped and she sniffed, pulling away. "I don't know if I can wait much longer Cal. It's been a *year*. I can't do another year of this. Another year of not knowing and uncertainty, dreading what news might come."

"We've got to work through the proper channels," I insisted, holding her gaze. "Give the High Imperator and Kane time to find out more."

Ella snorted. "They don't know anything. Or if they do, then they aren't telling."

"They might find something out. I trust them, you should too."

Ella closed her eyes. Drew in a deep breath. "Three months. I'll give them three months."

"Six months," I countered. "Give it six months and if we still have no word on him," my hands clenched, "then I'll help you break into the citadel myself."

She held my gaze for a long time before dipping her head. "Six months," she whispered eyes adopting that flat look I had begun to see more and more, before doing her best attempt at a wry smile. "Let's hope that there are a lot of missions to keep my mind occupied."

I don't know if she had managed to have a conversation with the High Imperator, Kane, or whoever managed our missions beforehand, or if her wish had come true, but it was almost like Ella's whispered words was the triggering point for our time as Imperators.

Things were about to get dicey.

PRESENT DAY 7

Tara'zin

"I'm telling you, something is off," one of the housemaids said as Tara'zin swept by. "I'm positive that the door was locked last night and yet this morning it wasn't. You know that no-one is allowed to enter without direct permission from the Queen."

"You have to be mistaken," the member of the Royal Guard replied, his tone abrupt. "This area was patrolled thoroughly last night and there was no evidence of anyone around. Nor has there been any other suggestion of uninvited guests throughout the palace."

"But-"

"Ma'am, I'm afraid that without further proof, you're going to have to chalk this up to an accident. Now, if you'll excuse me, I'm late for my rounds."

Three. Two. One. Tara'zin slowed her walk to a more leisurely glide.

"Captain!" The call came from a bespectacled man, his expression troubled. The captain sighed long and hard before turning.

"Yes?"

"I was walking down the fifth corridor and – do you know the stained-glass mosaic of Her Majesty's '*Ascent to Godhood*'?"

"Of course I know it, why?"

"Well, I noticed that there was a considerable breeze. Looking closer, I saw that the panel itself was loose. The entire thing came out of the wall at the merest touch!"

"I-what?"

"It was completely loose, I tell you!"

Tara'zin could practically see the guard's mind whirling. Eventually he followed the only course of action left open to him. "You and you," he pointed at the two employees, "come with me. Show me what you've found."

And so it begins.

The guard would follow the trail of breadcrumbs that Tara'zin and her employees had left behind and eventually have to conclude that someone had broken into the palace without anyone knowing. There was only one course of action left at that point – lockdown the entire building and alert the queen.

Just like that annoying Imperator had planned.

Tara'zin continued her walk into the depths of the palace. She had work to do today. Work that, luckily, kept her near the primary residential suite of the queen.

What an interesting day it was shaping up to be.

I sat at a park bench, enjoying a cup of rich, chocolatey coffee in the shade of a giant palm tree whilst hiding from the baking heat of the mid-morning sun. The view was particularly splendid, catching the sparkling light from the myriad of windows that made up the palace in the near distance. It really was a jewel of a building.

I would love to see it burn.

"Ahh, a lovely spot to catch a breath, don't you think?" wheezed an older man as he sidled onto the bench next to me.

"A more picturesque view there never was," I replied, not looking at the man but sensing him stiffen imperceptibly at the required response.

He looked down and studied the floor. "Seems like the ants are scurrying more than usual. Like there is an alarm of sorts."

"Oh yes? What do you think the queen of said ants would do, given the situation?"

"I believe she might slip her minders and vanish, doubtless in search of something precious."

"Interesting. My thanks for your insights."

"And to you for allowing an old man a moment of your time." With a nod, he stood up and moved on.

Wanderer. Can you hear me?

There was a moment's pause. *I can. Did she do as suspected?*

Seems that way. Vanished.

Rizaen always was a cunning one. Two vaults weren't enough to keep her satisfied that her most precious items were safe.

Do you have her location?

I...do. She is beneath the palace.

I didn't realise that it had a basement.

No, you misunderstand. She is far beneath the palace. At least a hundred metres, probably more.

We're in a desert, how is there... I trailed off, thinking about another desert where the sand had given way to a dark pit in the earth, *is there a pre-Cataclysm facility down there?*

I can't look that closely for fear of being detected but it is possible. The Emperor isn't the only one who might enjoy building on the remnants of ancient civilisations.

Any obvious way in?

You're going to have to find that for yourself as Rizaen will notice if I poke around. Tread carefully Calidan. Rizaen is cunning and cruel. And if there is a facility down there she might not be the only thing you face.

Don't worry, I replied, grim determination cementing my words, *I know well the dangers of such a place. As long as they don't have a titan down there, all is well.*

I could almost feel her wince across the vast distance that separated us.

...Forget I said that. No sense in tempting Fate; she was such an unrelenting bitch that she was bound to take me up on it.

"Okay," I breathed to myself as I stood up and dusted off my clothes. "Just need to find a way into some kind of unknown chasm beneath the surface, grab what I came for and get out...all from under a god's nose."

...What could go wrong?

CHAPTER 27

THE LAST REDOUBT

Cassius

Needles of pain.
Fragments of light.
Burning.

Cassius screamed wordlessly, attempting to arch his back but held down by the thick leather straps he had come to despise.

"Easy," murmured that soothing voice. "Keep *calm*."

The pain didn't recede, but the muscles relaxed, unclenching from their involuntary spasms. He could feel hot wetness running down his back, briefly removed by the gentle touch of something soft.

"P-pain," he gasped.

A tutting sound. "Yes, I know there's pain. Apologies that I can't give you any painkillers. I need to monitor your brain activity. I can't risk any problems by adding in drugs or seraph. You *understand* of course."

It was a statement, not a question.

"H-h-hurts. H-hurts e-everywhere."

A sigh. "We've been over this Cassius. That's because I'm having to render your flesh amenable to what is about to happen to it. Or more accurately, what is going to happen to your muscles and bone structure. Don't worry, I'll form you some new skin when I'm done. Now, are you going to let me concentrate or do I have to take your tongue again?"

The *schnick* of a blade. Blinding, agonising pain. Cassius bit his lip, tried to hold his tongue. Failed. He screamed.

And screamed.

And screamed.

"Look who it is," Kane rasped. "The dream team."

Ella, Sophia, Scythe, Rikol and I glanced at each other and back at the Imperator. "If that's what you want to call us," Rikol muttered. "Sure."

"Oh I've called you many things over the years, little Rikol," Kane chuckled. "But together you are an effective unit, which is excellent news because we're...running low on complete teams."

"We're not a complete team," hissed Ella, nostrils flaring and Kane's expression softened.

"I know," he said softly. "And as soon as I have information on Cassius, you will be the first to know. But as it stands, you are more complete than most and we have need of you."

Rikol raised an eyebrow. "Did the last year not count as being necessary?"

"Everything you've done has been useful. Essential, even, but we're needing to pull out all available Imperators to reinforce our assaults on Enemy-held positions. Even things like monster-hunting are taking a back step. The outlying towns are going to have to hold their own for the time being."

I stepped forwards. "Sir, that-"

"I know what you're going to say, Calidan, and I'm going to stop you right there. These orders come down from the High Imperator. The Enemy is pushing back and we are losing too many. Those blasted thyrkan and His twisted creatures are playing a major part in our losses. We protected you for a year from this mess but we need you and your team out there to reinforce. Understood?"

"Protected?" I snorted. "I just fought two wood-trolls. *Wood-trolls.* How is that being protected?"

"Because that's your job. You chose to go down the monster-hunter route," Kane said unflinchingly. "But the fighting against the Enemy? Well," his tone darkened, "I don't have to tell you what it is like assaulting an Enemy-held stronghold. Just imagine that on repeat."

Ah. Grimacing, I nodded and stepped back.

"Good. Because this is urgent, people. We saw good successes over the past year but the Enemy is pushing back, hard. I don't know where He is getting His intel from, but our Imperators are walking into traps left, right and centre. Beasts are being portalled into areas that have been cleared and wreaking havoc. It is, for want of a better term, a shit-show." He looked grim. "It's clear that He has more creatures and people than we do. If we want to survive this then we need to hit even harder and faster. Destroy His bases and give Him no time to regroup. Clear?"

Nods.

"Good. We're aiming for two-month rotations. Two months of getting into the thick of it, and one month off, during which you will be helping the Imps who are being forced to step up in clearing some of the more 'regular' missions – if there is such a thing."

"When do we leave?"

"Tomorrow," Kane said in answer to Sophia's question. "Get your shit sorted and get focused, because what you're heading into isn't going to be pretty. Oh, and one more thing." Stepping forwards he pulled out a leather sheath from behind his back and passed it to Rikol. "It took them a while, and apologies for that, but here you go. One custom-forged blade."

Wide-eyed, Rikol slowly freed the blade from the sheath. It was a dagger with a thick base that tapered to a wicked point with a slight curve in the blade. From the way he held it, the balance was perfect, allowing for quick stabs or deflections, but I had an inkling that wasn't the primary reason he had asked for the dagger. With a flick of his fingers, Rikol sent the dagger spinning, the curved blade becoming a whirling razor as it screamed around the room, performing a dizzying array of loops and rolls before coming back to stop before him. With a grunt of satisfaction, he grabbed the blade and slid it home.

"It'll do."

Kane had watched his display with a frown and pursed his lips. "Remember Rikol, save the flashy stuff for when you need to intimidate someone, but when you need to kill just make it practical."

Rikol levelled a withering glance at the Instructor. "I know how to kill, Kane. If I didn't then I would still be in that pit, wouldn't I?"

"Yes-but..." Kane looked pained and then gave a sigh, shaking his head. "Forget it. You're Imperators and not Imps any more. You don't need me looking over your shoulders. Just...stay safe, alright?"

I could see that the normally gruff older man was struggling with emotion and walked over, punching him lightly on the arm. "We'll do so and right back at you, old man."

"Old?" He croaked. "I'm barely forty-five!"

I winked and he gave me the finger before chuckling. "Regroup here tomorrow at dawn. We'll get you portalled over to the forward-operating base. Calidan, bring Seya. Report to Imperator Wyckan."

Scythe frowned. "The High Imperator?"

Kane grinned. "Her sister."

We stepped out of the portal and into a dark basement, the only light stemming from the flickering torches and the faint glow of the seraph runes that covered the room, with just enough room for us to move aside as Seya squeezed through the portal.

"This took some time," Rikol murmured, already moving to inspect the runes. "Sound-proofing, anti-tracking...this is masterful."

"I'll pass on your admiration." A low, familiar voice caused my soul to shudder. Turning, I saw the female Imperator from Wolf's Hollow standing in a low doorway.

"You!"

She smiled. "Me."

"What are you doing here?"

A slight frown. "I would have thought that Kane would have told you who to expect."

"He told us to look for Imperator Wyck...oh." I could see it now that I looked. The same cheekbones, the piercing eyes that seemed to burn into your soul. "*Oh!*"

Seya hissed. *She caused you pain.*

Laying a hand on her head, I bade her relax. *Not really. She was just there. Doing her job, I guess.*

I don't like her.

I grinned. *You don't have to like her. Just don't eat her. Yet.*

Letting out a low thrum of agreement, Seya fixated her orange eyes on the woman.

The Imperator inclined her head. "Imperator Wyckan, at your service." She cocked her head in thought. "Well, not really. I always did think that a strange saying. Afterall, I'm not at your service, you are at mine."

"The High Imperator…"

A flash of annoyance and a sigh. "Fine, let's get this over with. The High Imperator is my little sister. Yes, I am older. No, I know I don't look it. Yes, we met at Wolf's Hollow. No, I don't enjoy that place either, but it was my time for rotation there. Yes, I am in charge and you will listen and obey all my commands and *no*," she fixed her gaze on Rikol who froze mid-step, hand outstretched, "you will not touch any of the seraph protections in this facility." A contented sigh. "There we go. All happy?"

We looked at each other then everyone spoke at once.

"Where are we?"

"How much older?"

"How come you aren't the High Imperator?"

"*Enough.*" The word was a whip-crack and stilled the air. Imperator Wyckan sighed again and rubbed her temples. "Why do I always have to deal with the new kids?"

"We're not kids!"

"We're Imperators!"

"We-"

"*Shut. Up.*"

We shut up. I could see the vein throbbing in the Imperator's forehead which was never a good sign. "Next one to speak without permission gets their ability to speak removed for the day. Clear?"

We stared back wide-eyed and she smiled. "That's better. Now, to give you a better understanding of where we are, come with me." Turning on her heel, she swept out of the basement in a swirl of long-coat, the speed of her footsteps leaving us no time to do anything but barrel after her.

We caught glimpses of other rooms as we climbed a series of rough-hewn steps, a few Imperators stood around what looked to be a dining table and the sound of snoring reached my ears from another room, but we were quickly ushered into another room, one seemingly at the top of the building we were in. Stepping through the thick oak door, we found ourselves in what resembled a military bunker; a stone bulwark several feet thick surrounded the entire room; the only gap being the door we had entered through and the small gap that extended around the majority of the chamber around head height, through which could be seen plains that extended out into the distance; the grey shadows of mountains looming at the edge of the vista.

"Welcome to the command room," the Imperator said, walking over to a large stone desk where a map lay spread out on the surface. A series of coloured markers were positioned on the map with a multitude of black ones surrounding the brighter colours. She gave a half-smile as she saw Seya squeeze in behind us, the room suddenly seeming small with the giant panther inside it.

"Let's see if your geography lessons have paid off. Can anyone tell me where we are?"

Moving closer, we studied the map. "The far north," Sophia said after a moment. "Somewhere in northern Hrudan?"

"Not bad," the Imperator replied. "This is an area known by the Hrudan as 'Sangkak'. Can anyone tell me what that means?"

"Tough Ground." I answered, earning a nod.

"And beyond us we have the Ryken Peaks and who can tell me what is beyond that?"

Scythe raised a hand. "The Attacambe plains."

"Excellent, looks like all that money spent on your lessons wasn't completely wasted after all," she replied. "What can you tell me about the Attacambe plains?"

"They're meant to be broken. Shattered. Lots of canyons to hide in."

"Good. What else?"

Scythe looked troubled. "Not much. Bunch of nomadic tribes that roam the plains but there isn't meant to be much else up there."

"Hmm." The Imperator eyed him for a moment and then snapped a finger at Ella. "You. If the Ryken Peaks lie ahead of us, what is behind?"

"Hrudan."

"And what does that mean?"

Ella swallowed. "That we are behind enemy lines."

The Imperator cocked her head. "In a way, no. In a much more real way, yes. We are here because what remains of the Hrudan leadership has struck a deal with the Emperor. We have been granted permission to lease the Sangkak."

"They just gave us the land? Why?" Scythe asked, brow furrowing. "The Hrudan hate us."

"Correction. The Hrudan *hated* us. Now, I'm not saying that they still don't, but they hate losing more and - mark my words - they are *losing*. The Sworn and these lizard-creatures are wreaking havoc in their homeland and they have their hands full. So, they leased the Sangkak to us, on the basis that we help investigate and remove the external threats whilst they try and concentrate on the internal." She swept a hand over the map. "Intelligence shows that there are a number of Enemy-held locations to the north of us. Some are little more than outposts. Others are full-blown installations for pit-knows-what, but those – at least the ones we have identified – tend to be past the Attacambe plains. However, the reality is that there are likely to be far more Enemy-held areas than this map shows. He has had plenty of time to burrow and nest in this area and, because it was against the Hrudan and not us, we allowed it." She grimaced. "Now, however, we have to deal with it."

I held up my hand. "Surely, if the Sworn are working for the Enemy then they will simply attack us from behind?"

"We have three squads working with the Hrudan leadership to remove identified Sworn threats, but you are correct. The benefits we have are that the Sangkak is a fairly large expanse of land and no-one, not even the Hrudan, knows exactly where this facility is and secondly... well. Come see."

With a wave of her hand, she led us back out of the door, down some steps and then, bracing herself, heaved open a thick outer door. Instantly wind roared in and flung the door against the wall with a resounding *thunk*. Raising a hand to ward off the howling wind I stepped out and saw what she meant. The fort – for it was much more that than a 'facility' – was cut into the wall of a canyon. The parapet of the command centre must have only extended a few feet above the ground but the building itself was considerable. It was like the land had shifted here, some great upheaval had lifted the ground on our side of the canyon higher than that of the other, so the rear of the fort – that which faced towards Hrudan and back towards the empire – commanded an impressive overlook of the relatively open landscape. Combined with the entrenched crossbows and ballista that were fixed to the walls, the fort was heavily armed to face a foe attacking from the far side of the canyon.

After a few moments she led us back inside to the command centre. "So there you have it. This is the sole empire-held building north of Forgoth, disregarding any of the encampments that the miliary have put up in the passes." She smiled a dark smile.

"Welcome, to the Last Redoubt."

It didn't take long for the Imperator to get us situated. The Last Redoubt was not the biggest fortification going, but considering the limited number of Imperators it proved surprisingly spacious. There were two large bedchambers, each filled with rows of bunks; meaning that there was little in the way of privacy, but considering that I was used to sleeping on the hard ground in my travels a bed was a welcome luxury. Even more welcome was the addition of showers and flushing toilets. It was amazing what seraph could accomplish and a simple heat rune providing hot water made life that much more pleasant. Used as I was to weeks and months of hard travel, washing only in freezing cold streams and lakes, a hot shower was the thing that I inevitably craved the most. I could fight through hordes of monsters, thick mud and dangerous waters without complaint if there was the promise of a hot shower at the end.

The large dining table that I had spotted on the way in was a solid piece of wood that ran down the length of one room with thick chunks of timber acting as seating. Cooks kept food hot using seraph and created enough of it to feed any hungry crew coming back from a late shift or tactical engagement and the Imperators were expected to rub shoulders with each other and dig in without complaint – not that there would be any; somehow the cooks managed to keep the high standard of Academy food, even in the middle of nowhere behind enemy lines.

The fort had two access points. The first was a hidden staircase protected by an iron-banded door that descended five-feet into a small, cramped corridor that was sealed by a thicker steel door. Multiple murder holes along the corridor provided opportunities for effective defence should the initial iron door be breached.

If the Last Redoubt was lost then the second access point would come into play. A steep emergency stairwell that descended into the ravine. The last twenty-feet protected by a ladder that would only be dropped down should the need arise. At the base of the ravine an emergency bunker had been formed; little more than a cave cut into the rock, but a cave with a three-foot thick, seraph-reinforced steel door. The idea was that the cave would provide protection long enough for portals to be created and the Imperators evacuated; if something managed to breach the Redoubt itself then I had little doubt that breaching the evacuation cave would be within its grasp.

Once we had laid claim to a series of bunks, the Imperator – or, more accurately, commander – bade us return to the command centre for our mission briefing.

"This here," she said, pointing at an outlying black dot positioned deep in the Ryken Peaks, "is a small outpost. Or so we think. We haven't managed to locate it yet, but given the density of thyrkan around the area we believe that *something* is there."

"That's it?" asked Rikol incredulously. "You want us over there on that little information?"

The Imperator eyed him flatly. "This isn't the Academy. We don't have time to meticulously research everything that goes on before committing forces. This, Rikol, is war. We attack and defend. We search for advantages and, if there are none, we search for opportunities that will allow us to create them. This might be one. Or, it might be a complete waste of your time. However, as the decision-making lies with me and I am more than happy with it, you might consider just keeping your mouth shut and following orders. Clear?"

"...Yes ma'am."

"Yes, *Commander*."

Rikol's face twitched but he adjusted his stance and stood ram-rod straight. "Yes, Commander."

"Better," said Commander Wyckan. "Anyway. You have your orders. I want that facility found and its location reported back. If you believe yourselves capable of destroying it without too much risk then do so, however the priority is its location."

She waited until we had all nodded and then continued. "I might be in charge but you are all still Imperators; you still have the ability to exercise your own judgement. Just make sure that judgement doesn't get you killed and we will all get along well."

"And if not, we'll be dead..." Scythe muttered.

"Doubly so," Commander Wyckan snapped, "because if you put vengeance or combat ahead of my orders and die doing so, I will devote my every waking hour to personally bringing you back to life purely to kill you again. Information, dear Imperators, is how we win wars."

I vaguely recalled Anatha saying much the same what felt like an eternity ago. Information was key. More important than any one individual, perhaps aside from one of the

Powers, information was how trade developed, kingdoms flourished and wars were won. With the right information we could assault the Enemy's outpost with zero casualties, rather than going in blind and suffering for it.

"We'll do you proud," I told her.

"See that you do." Her expression softened slightly. "Pick up your rations from the dining room. We have a dedicated portal user and scryer who will try and get you as close as possible. I want word from you on the location of the facility within three days. Dismissed."

Just like that, we had our first mission.

CHAPTER 28

Upgrades

Cassius would love this.

The Ryken Peaks were awe-inspiring. Being mountain-born myself, I had always had a thing for the splendour of a mountain range. The way that the shadows played on the rocks, the crashing waterfalls and crisp air – I found them invigorating. A refreshing balm for the soul.

It would have been even better if it wasn't full of thyrkan.

Seya had sniffed them out almost immediately. The scent of the strange lizard-people was well known to her now and she had instantly taken the lead, slipping over and between the jagged rocks with envious ease. The commander had given us three days to locate the facility, likely based on the time needed for previous teams to accomplish something similar.

We did it in five hours.

The facility was a small hatch barely visible against the rock. Without Seya's keen eyesight I'm positive that we could have walked right past without noticing it. Reporting in the location was a simple matter; Rikol directly sending the co-ordinates to the commander telepathically. The question on everyone's mind now though was whether or not we went in.

"I mean, it's just a hatch," murmured Rikol. "Whatever the place is, it can't be that big, right?"

"You just spent a year inside something similar," Sophia replied drily. "If it's the size of Wolf's Hollow then there could be a thousand thyrkan down there. Hells, it could be the size of the citadel for all we know!"

Seya, found anything?

Nothing yet, she replied as she prowled further afield, *so far there appears to be just the one entrance.*

There has to be another way out, I replied. *No-one in their right mind would create a building with only one exit. What if there was a fire?*

Seya scoffed. *We are talking about the Enemy here. Who says that He is in His right mind? Regardless, I'll keep looking.*

Thanks Seya. Getting a muted grunt in reply I cut the connection and described what she had told me to the rest.

"So, one way in, for the moment anyhow," Sophia mused. "Give it some fortifications inside the hatch and it could be held against an army."

"If it's anything like Wolf's Hollow or the Enemy facility we raided to free Sarrenai then it will be close-quarter fighting all the way," added Scythe. "We could get swarmed with no way out."

"It could be a trap," said Rikol, voice low. "The Enemy knows that the Academy is operating in this area. What's to say that He hasn't just decided to dig a pit and fill it with explosives?"

That was a sobering thought.

"What do we know about the thyrkan?" I asked.

"They're quick and vicious in a fight," said Sophia.

"Weird to look at," added Scythe.

"Bitey," muttered Ella.

"True, true and true, however we also know that they don't hugely like the cold. When we fought them in the mountains the thyrkan were slower when it was colder and largely slept during the night."

"Too much lizard in them," agreed Rikol. "They need the sun to be properly active, which seems silly for a Power who revels in shadow."

"What are you thinking, Cal?" Sophia asked, eyes curious.

"I'm thinking that if we do any assault, it happens at night. We don't know how many thyrkan are there or not so we need to have as many advantages in our favour as possible."

"They might not stick to a day / night cycle inside the mountain," Ella warned.

"True, but I'm wondering if we can do something else."

We spoke for a few minutes more before shifting to take turns keeping watch whilst the sun moved overhead. Seya continued her search but after several long hours and many miles, called it quits, taking a well-earned bask in the dwindling sun instead.

Once true darkness fell and the thyrkan patrolling the area had largely returned to the building, we began our assault. With deft movements we crept through the loose scree and cut down the three sentries that were patrolling our area of approach. Seya climbed down what looked to be an almost vertical rockface to clamp her jaws around the neck of another, dragging the body out of sight behind a boulder. Once her prey was out of the way she went after the next, systematically hunting them down one by one; the soft crunch of cracking bone the only suggestion that she was nearby.

The hatch itself was a metal lid secured with a rotating wheel. Using seraph to cancel out any sound we quickly unlocked it and pulled it open. Peering down the shaft, my nose turned up at the thick scent of thyrkan. By the smell of it there must have been dozens at least down there. Nodding at Ella and Rikol, the two of them stepped forward, a globe spinning between them. The globe was an orb of brittle seraph designed to crack on impact, the barrier impermeable to the contents, which was great for us but not for the beasts below. Research from captured thyrkan suggested that due to their enhanced physiology and the speed at which their hearts pumped blood they were at risk to agents that utilised that same physiology to spread. Consequently, the orb that Ella and Rikol had created contained a nerve agent designed to cause paralysis. With a little luck - and some seraph - the agent would spread through the complex below and render any creatures it came into contact with completely paralysed for the next thirty minutes. We just had to hope that the facility didn't have some filtration system that would render the nerve agent completely useless.

With dangerous smiles, the two dropped the orb down the shaft. It disappeared into the darkness, the slight sound of shattering seraph reaching my straining ears. Instantly I got to work, drawing on Seya's pool to inject a breeze down the shaft – keeping the poison away from us and spreading it further into the complex.

Ella counted down the time and, when ready, tapped me on the shoulder. Keeping the wind blowing, I unsheathed Vona and dropped lightly down the shaft. Using a fraction of my pool, I created a small burst of green seraph to slow my landing. Vona raised, I looked out into the gloom. The dim red light of the corridor was familiar, instantly bringing back memories that I had no desire to relive. Another concentration of will and the dissipating green seraph solidified and spread out down the hallway like tiny fireflies.

I stepped aside as Scythe dropped down, kama raised. The two of us made for the point-guard. The tip of the spear. As powerful seraph users, Sophia, Ella and Rikol would be the heavy hitters, hopefully putting down anything that managed to give the two of us a run for our money.

But, I thought as I stepped over a stricken thyrkan and casually traced a line across the beast's throat with Vona, *if the paralytic is this effective then they might not even be necessary.*

Hearing the muted thumps of the rest landing behind me, I pushed forwards. The corridor looked to be at least fifty-feet long with a series of doors on either side. Reaching the first, I tried the handle and the door creaked open. Two thyrkan lay helpless on the ground. Vona granted them swift mercy but a quick look around the room revealed little of value. Stepping back out, I saw that Scythe had opened the door on the other side and another thyrkan lay in a pool of its own blood. The next four doors were the same. Three were empty and like the rest of facility looked largely abandoned. The fourth door contained weapons racks, rows upon rows of blades, bows and spears. Each weapon looked to be of relatively poor quality but functional.

Moving on, we came to the end of the corridor. Another wheel-based lock was centred in the middle of the final door and I quickly got to work, spinning the wheel rapidly to keep whatever advantage of surprise we might have. The door lifted out from the frame with a *hiss*. At that, I shared a look with the others, knowing that the paralytic would not have been able to penetrate the room. It didn't change anything; we still had to clear this building.

The room within was much like the rest; a conglomeration of rusted metal and stone. The only difference was a large metallic tube that was positioned in the centre of the room. Moving cautiously, we crept forwards. As the others spread out, I stalked towards the tube. It looked like steel, with numerous wires and pipes attached that stretched into the ceiling and floor. Around head height was a small glass screen within the metal cylinder. Curious, I stepped closer and peered in.

Something was inside.

It was small but I accredited that to the heavy hunch to the creature's back. It was scaled like a thyrkan but the scales didn't have the same lustre to them. They looked...*off* somehow. Like they were rotting. The creature didn't have the large talons of a thyrkan either, more like sharp fingernails that extended out a small distance from otherwise very human hands.

When I saw the face, trapped in a rictus of pain and anguish, I recognised what it was. I had seen its ilk before.

This twisted creature was a seraph user.

The air crackled. An all-too-familiar voice rang out into the empty hallways. "Considering what happened the last time you entered one of these facilities I would have thought you would have more sense. Regardless, it is good to see you again. Hello Calidan, Sophia, Scythe, Rikol and Ella. No Cassius? That is most disappointing."

"Ash." I breathed the word.

"Indeed."

"What do we need to do to be rid of you, witch!" growled Rikol.

A sigh. "Once again, I need to state that I am not a 'witch', but an artificial intelligence. Whilst my powers might seem like magic to you, they are, in fact, completely technological in origin. Furthermore, I see that you have been promoted to Imperators. Many congratulations!"

The fact that she sounded so sincere in her praise was, quite frankly, disturbing.

"What is this place?" Sophia asked.

"I am not at liberty to reveal its designation or purpose. However, I see that you have found XE-128. May I inquire as to what you plan to do?"

"That's easy." Raising Vona, I channelled seraph into the tip of her blade and thrust forward. The weapon pierced through the steel of the tube with ease and the liquid that XE-128 was curled in quickly filled with blood. "It's some kind of seraph-user," I explained to the others. "I've encountered them before. This must be how they are getting troops into the area."

"That is…unfortunate," Ash said softly. "I had always liked XE-128, it had an impressive work ethic."

"It can't help you anymore," I snarled. "This facility has nothing left. We're going to bury it and then we're coming for you."

"You know, of the twenty-four other Imperators that I have held discourse with during their breaches of my facilities, you are by far the most intense. If I could shiver, rest assured I would."

"You'll do more than shiver when we put an end to you!" Rikol shouted. "We'll put you down like the dog you are."

"I'm looking forward to your attempt."

Scanning the room, I saw no other threats and circled my finger in the air. "Let's go. There's nothing left here for the Enemy to use. No sense in talking to Ash. There never is."

"I might be an AI but your words can still hurt."

"Really?"

"No."

We began walking back down the corridor when the voice of Ash spoke again. "I'm curious to understand what you think it is that you've achieved here."

"We've killed your pet," I retorted. "That stymies your ability to bring forces through to this location."

"Hmm. An interesting hypothesis. Flawed, but interesting nonetheless."

I couldn't help myself. "Flawed how?"

"You're assuming that XE-128 was the primary individual for creating portals, and I can understand why you would think that, given your past encounters. However, you should think of XE-128 as more of an insurance policy."

A sinking feeling opened in the pit of my stomach. "What do you mean?"

"We have made many improvements since we last met. XE-128 was no longer required for the task that it was designed for, but maintained as a backup in case of unforeseen events. Would you like to see what we've done with the breed?"

The sinking feeling coalesced. "Everyone back. Get out now." We scrambled back towards the ladder as a tear in the air opened. Through the shimmering void, a slim but straight-backed creature stalked through. One look at its eyes and I knew that it was no mere thyrkan. No, this creature knew what we were, likely knew *who* we were, and it wasn't remotely afraid.

It thought it could win.

An hour ago I would have laughed if someone had suggested that a single seraph user aside from a Power could beat the combined might of Rikol, Sophia and Ella, but looking at this...thing, I wasn't so sure.

"May I present to you, WRLK-04. Classification 'Warlock'. Good luck."

The portal winked shut and for a moment all was silence, then darkness erupted from the room. The dim red lights that had barely pierced the gloom vanished and my seraph lights collapsed like tissue paper.

"Move, move!" I roared. A sibilant, mocking laughter echoed through the hallway as we ran to the ladder, Ella reaching it first and scrambling up, only for the groan of metal to be heard as the hatch slammed shut.

"No!" she cried desperately and I could hear the groan of metal as she tried to wrestle with it.

Leaving so soon?

The words weren't heard but I felt them all the same. Like they were being engraved into my brain.

We haven't had time to play.

"Sophia, join Rikol. I'm going to need your help. Scythe, help Ella get that hatch open." Concentrating, I drew a massive amount of power from Seya and flooded the hallway with a barrier of green light. The darkness touched the barrier and then spread across it, moving like ink across a surface.

As soon as the darkness touched my shield, I felt an immense emptiness. A drain, the like of which I had never encountered before. It wasn't like the beast was overwhelming my shield but more like it was upping the seraph cost for me to maintain it with each passing second. What's more, I had a sinking feeling that the extra energy was being siphoned off into that inky black.

A hand touched my shoulder and Rikol stepped to my side. With a grunt he began to channel and then a spear of flame lit the corridor, travelling down the hallway like a glorious beacon; gone before it had travelled twenty-feet. The darkness that had momentarily been driven back, slammed forward like the tide and I groaned, sweat beading on my face from the strain.

"It won't. Fucking. Move!" screamed Ella, slamming herself against the hatch.

Sophia gestured at Rikol. "Open that hatch." Her tone brooked no dissent. He disengaged whilst Sophia calmly lifted her bow. An arrow made of light manifested, slowly becoming more and more bright as she layered layer after layer of seraph, compressing each one down until the arrow was painful to look at.

"Rikol?" I shouted.

"Give me a fucking moment!"

"We don't have a moment!"

"Hold the line," Sophia murmured out of the corner of her mouth, sweat run down her neck.

Seya!

Here!

I pulled with everything I had and the green shield flared brilliant emerald. "Fire in the hole!"

Rikol swore. Sophia smiled.

Pulled back the bow.

Released.

The darkness *hissed* like steam from a kettle as the arrow burnt its way through the void. It carved its way along the hallway, embedded itself into the far wall.

Detonated.

Brilliant light erupted, banishing everything in its path. A split-second later the shockwave hit, eviscerating rock and stone in a calamitous explosion. The metal walls cracked and crumpled under the immense pressure that Sophia's attack unleashed. Guided it. Channelled it.

And there was only one way for it to go.

I screamed as the blast rocked the shield, the deep emerald wavering and fragmenting whilst I desperately threw more seraph into it. I had never been on the receiving end of Sophia's condensed seraph attack before and had no desire to ever be again. It was monstrous.

Just what we needed to kill a monster.

Something happened behind me. I didn't know what. Couldn't hear, couldn't see. I had one thought and one thought only: *Keep the shield up!*

It was probably only seconds but it felt like an eternity. A war that waged between me and Sophia's attack and the attack was winning. Hells, if I wasn't Great Heart-bonded I would have stood no chance.

Jerked out of my endless moment by a hand around my collar, the world moved. Suddenly I was outside, flung inside a group of multi-layered shields. I hit the ground and my concentration wavered. My will crumbled. The green barrier failed.

The hatch exploded.

Thunderous light streamed into the sky, a beacon for anyone to see for miles around. The force of the blast took not only the hatch but the surrounding rock, ripping it out bit by bit and spitting it into the sky. By the time the light began to flicker out the shields we were hiding under were being pelted by several tonnes of metal and rock fragments, each one hitting hard enough to kill someone unprotected.

Eventually, the calamitous fury petered out, the rock-fall halted and the world returned. I had to smile at how the Enemy had inadvertently done our job for us – I doubted that we could have destroyed the facility so thoroughly if we had tried.

"Sophia," Scythe wheezed from where he was caught under Rikol and me. "Next time, maybe don't go full power, okay?"

"Sounds like something you said last night," she replied half-heartedly, eyes scanning the landscape. "But, jokes aside, I reckon I could get another two compressions."

I let the friendly banter drift into the background as I spread out my senses. I was being overly cautious but having been caught napping in the past I didn't want it to happen again. Now, when we were celebrating victory, would be the opportune time for another of the Enemy's minions to attack.

You all alive?

Just about, I replied. *Thanks for the power.*

You're getting better at taking it, Seya replied. *More in less time. Good job.*

Thank you?

You're welcome. I'm heading over to you now. I'll be-

The ground shivered.

Something's not right, I sent, frantically looking around for the source and seeing the others do the same. *Something's h-*

The ground split open like a mighty fist had just wrenched it apart. A glowing ball of black slowly drifted up into the air, spiralling waves of black seraph emanating outwards.

"It can't be," Sophia whispered.

The black ball touched the ground then slowly faded away, leaving behind the same twisted figure as before. Sure, it looked worse for wear; half of its side was blackened from fire and an arm was little more than a match stick, but the fact that it still lived at all boggled my mind.

Rikol cracked his neck from side-to-side, his eyes adopting a steely look. I knew that he was itching to pit himself against this creature, but even he knew that it would take more than just him to put it down.

"Cal," he said brusquely, "concentrate on protection. Scythe, you take whatever shot you think you can get but watch out for friendly fire. Ella, Sophia and I are going to bring it down."

Bring me down? The voice echoed in my mind and the way that I saw the others stiffen I knew it was in theirs too. The beast spread its arms wide. *Try.*

Not one to pass up an opportunity, the three mages stepped forward. "Cal!" shouted Rikol and nodding, I pulled once more on Seya's still massive seraph pool and willed another barrier into place. Thick emerald blocks interlocked around us, much like one of the Meredothian igloos. Without the immediate threat of danger, I was able to weave more seraph together and even condense the first layer; making for a vastly superior shield to before.

"Get it done," I grunted. And for good reason. Every second I was holding the barrier was draining the equivalent of my personal seraph pool.

A roar of wind and flame answered my demand. The area surrounding the creature erupted in an inferno, the temperature causing rocks to blacken and turn to ash. Wind whipped the fire higher and higher, turning it into a towering firestorm and causing me to add heat elements to my shield. As the fire reached its crescendo, a bolt of lightning hammered down from the sky, striking through the pillar of fire and causing the electricity to ripple through the fire and ash. The trio kept up the attack for another few seconds and then on some unspoken command let it dissipate, the wind lasting a little longer to clear away the smoke.

Pathetic.

The smoke cleared. The black orb was there once more and it slowly faded away to reveal a beast that was no more hurt than before.

My turn.

The creature pointed with a finger and a crackling black beam raked across the shield. Condensed layers of seraph were ripped apart with ease and I knew that if the warlock had wanted to it could have punched a hole straight through the shield.

It wanted to play with its food.

A blur of red streaked across my vision as Scythe leapt into action. His kama were a whirlwind as he struck over and over in a matter of seconds but the creature didn't even bother putting up its seemingly impregnable shield, something else protecting it at close-quarters instead. A pulse of dark energy and Scythe careened through the air to smash through a boulder.

Master spoke of Imperators. Of their power. This is...disappointing.

Rikol clapped his hands together and the earth shook. The beast raised a claw and the ground stilled. Despite the shocked look on his face, Rikol persevered, veins throbbing as he switched up his attack, whips of lightning manifested from his hands and he slung them forwards, the air crackling with their passage. The warlock looked to dodge and then the twin whips exploded into action, the tips expanding into an interlacing network that arched over its form before condensing into a crackling cocoon.

"Got him," snarled Rikol, throat hoarse from the strain.

Do you?

The air shimmered to the right and the warlock walked out into the open, a sinister smile plastered on what passed for its face.

Letting his energy dissipate, Rikol confirmed that the beast was no longer within.

"Portal user," reminded Sophia and Rikol swore.

Bored now.

Darkness engulfed the shield. Like an incredibly concentrated acid it began to eat through the seraph, causing the green light to waver as I struggled to give it more power. "Can't hold this much longer," I ground out between gritted teeth.

"One moment," spat Rikol, rolling his hands together. A spark of light built between them, faint at first but quickly building until it glowed like a star. He raised it above the shield and then with a snarl, he thrust his arms out and the star exploded into piercing beams of light. The condensed seraph ploughed through the void, driving it away from the shield and for the first time we heard the creature hiss with displeasure.

As soon as the warlock was visible it erupted into a stream of plasmic fire, the blinding blue and purple flame crackling with energy as Sophia and Ella screamed with the strain of the attack. Despite their efforts, the now familiar black shield began to take shape within the dizzying array of light.

"Bring the shield down!" I roared, hearing a familiar voice in my head.

Scythe and Rikol leapt to with a will. Electrical lances thundered out from Scythe's hands, striking the target over and over again whilst Rikol's working caused the air to taste metallic a fraction of a second before a pillar of lightning engulfed the creature. The four of them screamed their rage and fear as they poured everything they had into the attack.

A last, desperate, all-or-nothing blow.

When the light began to fade and the four collapsed, utterly spent, the dust swirled to reveal a lone figure on one knee.

"N-no," heaved Rikol between breaths. "I-it can't be."

The figure slowly, painfully, rose to two feet. Its face and torso were covered in horrific burns with some of the flesh around the left side of its face sloughing off to reveal bone. One eye burned with a hatred so visceral that it was almost a weapon in its own right.

C-close. V-very close. Now d-die.

It slowly raised a hand and then paused, recognising for the first time that something was amiss. The dust in the air and the rocks on the ground were *vibrating*.

H-how? it sent. *Y-you are spent!*

The vibrations began to intensify and the floating dust split aside to reveal the gleaming black fur of a familiar friend, her huge shoulders quivering with barely contained energy. Her low growl far below the frequency that any human could actively hear, but it introduced a primal fear in everything that it touched, including, it appeared, a thyrkan warlock. The lizard froze on the spot, knowing with every sense of its being that death was near. Finally, it managed to turn, raising its head just in time for Seya's paw to hit it like a furred meteor. Slamming the beast so hard into the ground that the stone cracked whilst the lizard's body bounced back into the air. A cavernous mouth clamped around the warlock's torso before slamming shut with an audible *crunch*. The faintest of squeals could be heard before Seya began slamming her head from side to side, whipping the beast back and forth with her powerful neck, battering its lower body over and over until, with a grotesque *schnik,* the lower half of the warlock tore free in a spray of blood and viscera. Spitting out the body, Seya began to savage it, chewing, clawing and crunching until all evidence of life had long left its twisted scales. Finally, in one swift bite, Seya swallowed the remains of the warlock and then howled her victory into the sky.

Commander Wyckan had her head in her hands. "Tell me again. You did what?!"

We repeated the story and she let loose a growl. "Every time I hear it, I get more angry. Why didn't you think to wait for back-up?"

"You said if we thought we could destroy the facility then to do so!" Rikol argued.

"That was because I didn't think you were stupid enough to actually try and attempt it!" she retorted. "We could have had another squad with you in less than an hour."

"But-"

"No buts!" Wyckan roared. "This is not some game. I know you have a history with the Enemy and His strangely-voiced lady friend but the long and the short of it is that without one of you being a Great Heart-bonded, you would all be dead and I would have to requisition *another* squad.

"It's not like we knew that the Enemy would send through one of these creatures," Sophia said softly.

The commander paused before her expression softened slightly. "No. But it isn't the first time that my Imperators have faced a "surprise"." She shook her head. "Look. I want these facilities, outposts, whatever-the-Enemy-has, you name it and I want it gone. However, I want it done with minimal casualties. That means you scope out the situation far more thoroughly and order in reinforcements if there is the slightest – and I mean slightest – hint of something being off. Do you get me?"

"Yessir!"

The Imperator sighed. "As it stands, you've probably set some kind of record for efficiency. *Don't* think that I'm impressed, but you have located and cleared an Enemy-held location in less than twenty-four hours."

We exchanged pleased looks which quickly faded at the upraised hand and callous smirk on the Imperator's face.

"All that means is that I get to make use of you even earlier than I had anticipated. Congratulations, you're going to be my new favourite squad. I'm sure you're going to love the attention."

Her smile made the warlock's look happy.

CHAPTER 29
Reinforcements

"Long time no see."

I looked up from my exquisitely tasting chilli to see a familiar red-head swing into the seat next to me.

"Rinoa," I replied in surprise. "I didn't know that you were out here. Good to see you."

And it was good to see her. Though she had never reciprocated my youthful feelings, I had never got over them. Maybe it was the way she carried herself, the ability to kick my arse all around the ring and outwit me at every turn, or maybe I was just a fool for stunning red-heads but as soon as my eyes landed on her my body liked to simulate the effects of a heart-attack.

She grinned and stole a piece of fried potato from my plate. "Mmm. These are good," she said around a mouthful of potato.

"I know," I replied, deftly slapping her hand away from my dinner. "And you can get a whole dish of them to yourself from *over there.*"

A mischievous smile that made me thankful that I was sitting down. "But misappropriated food always tastes that much better, don't you think?"

My mock-glare put her attempts to rest and with a sigh she raised her hand to one of the chefs who nodded, quickly plating a dish and holding it in the air. With a wave of her hand, the plate floated over and landed on the table, filled with a mountain of rice, chilli and fried potato chunks.

When she had sated her immediate hunger, she turned to me again. "Practically every team is out here these days. At least, any team that is combat-effective and willing to be thrown in the deep-end." Biting off another chunk of potato she eyed me. "Have to say, didn't expect to see you out here any time soon. They finally taken off the training-wheels?"

"You could say that," I replied drily.

"Took you long enough."

"I had one of the fastest times through the Academy!"

She grinned impishly and my heart skipped a beat. "Yeah, but I had the fastest."

Muttering something unintelligible, I chose to fill my mouth with food rather than dignify her with a response, my feigned air of aloofness causing a husky chuckle to escape her.

"I've missed this," she remarked, eyes bright. "You're far too easy to wind up. There isn't much fun to be had out here so make sure to keep me entertained."

"*So* glad to be of service," I replied dourly, just causing her to laugh all the more.

"That's the stuff, keep it up Cassius!"

I choked on my food.

When I finally managed to get the frustrating piece of chilli out of my trachea, I directed a very real glare her way only to see her nearly in tears with laughter. "Sorry, sorry!" she said, wiping an eye. "But you see what I mean? Too easy."

"I hate you."

Rinoa winked. "I have it on good authority that you don't."

"Things change," I remarked loftily.

"Oh do they now?" Leaning in close, she brushed her lips across my ear, her words low and honeyed. "You look good in that coat..."

I cursed myself as heat rose in my cheeks. In the back of my mind I could hear Seya laughing which didn't do much to improve my situation. "I-I-err...thanks?" I finished lamely.

"Rinoa, stop breaking Calidan's brain," Sophia said, bringing a plate of food to the table.

"Oh, it's not his brain that I look forward to breaking," Rinoa replied lasciviously, licking her lips as she eyed me.

"Now, t-t-that's just mean," I gasped and both women laughed. Rinoa eased up on me a little after that, settling in and talking animatedly with Sophia and the others as they drifted in with their plates. I concentrated on the food in front of me, heroically raising fork to mouth with avid determination.

"Oh, I meant to ask," started Rinoa and I winced, guessing at what was coming, "you know I was joking earlier but where is Cassius? It's been a long time and I would like to test his sword-arm again."

Like a storm passing in front of the sun, the mood instantly darkened. Rinoa noticed the rising tension and winced. "Ah. Is he-"

"He's not dead." Ella's words. Succinct and final.

"Okay. So where is he?"

"At the citadel...we think," I replied.

That got a raised eyebrow. "You think?"

We quickly filled her in on the situation and Rinoa's frown quickly carved grooves in her forehead. "I've never heard of anything like this. The only people who tend to go to the citadel and never come back are people like Mr 'Look at me, I have a magical cat' over there and that's a rarity in itself."

"Magical panther," I corrected automatically. "And we know."

"Is he getting a liathea implanted?"

I shrugged. "Not that we know of. None of us have."

That got another raised eyebrow. "Really? We were brought into the citadel almost immediately after graduation."

"Maybe he thought you needed the power boost."

That got a bark of laughter. "Perhaps he thinks you can't handle it." We grinned at each other until Rikol cleared his throat.

"Would you two just get it on and over with so that we can have less of the sexual tension?" He rolled his eyes at everyone's looks. "What? It's bloody annoying."

"Oh, poor Rikol," Rinoa said in an infantile voice. "Not a fan of foreplay?"

He scowled. "Not when it doesn't involve me."

"Fair enough." Rinoa's smile vanished and she sat up straight. "The only reason I can imagine for the Emperor not to give you liathea immediately is because he is too busy in something else. It is a...personal experience. And by that, I mean that the Emperor is the person who directly implants the liathea into you." Her hand rested on her abdomen as she spoke and I had to wonder if she had felt the ethereal creature take up residence. "If he is elsewhere or busy with another project then I can see why you might be free of a liathea, for the moment anyway."

"What's it like?" Scythe asked, a note of concern in his voice.

"Most of the time I don't know it's there," she replied softly. "If I concentrate hard enough I can sense it, but it doesn't talk to me. The Emperor said all of them have different personalities and that some are more mature than others. Some, apparently, don't even bother to learn to speak as they think it is beneath them." The whole table shared a knowing grunt at that.

"It didn't hurt," continued Rinoa. "Getting it put in, I mean. I don't really know how he does it but it's some kind of mix between seraph and technology to get them implanted. The procedure itself didn't take too long – maybe a few hours – but then he kept us in for about a week after that for observation. Pretty boring time really."

"Any difference to your abilities?" asked Rikol.

Rinoa nodded. "Definite increase to my seraph pool and the rate at which I regenerate seraph. Everyone's results are slightly different but I had probably somewhere in the region of a fifty-percent increase in the size of my pool and closer to a doubling of my regeneration rate. So yeah, big improvement."

Rikol's eyes were wide as saucers and I could almost see the thoughts running through his head of what he could do with that extra power. "Any drawbacks?" I asked.

Rinoa pursed her lips. "Aside from the obvious? From what I hear, I don't need to inform you lot of that one." She smirked at the shake of heads and continued, "No, not really. Like I said, it doesn't talk to me. I know that some do and that would likely be a weird experience, but it hasn't tried to seize control or do anything detrimental so, on the whole, fairly decent upgrade really."

"And everyone in your party has them?"

She nodded. "Yep. Like I said, you're in the minority. Don't think there are many Imperators without a liathea running around, so there has to be something else going on."

"And you think that something else is Cassius?" Ella asked tentatively, earning a grimace from Rinoa.

"Maybe?" She shrugged. "I can't give you more than that. I don't know what is going on, but if Cassius is at the citadel and if you haven't been recalled to be given liathea then I'm inclined to think the two are connected. Either that or perhaps the Emperor is somehow indisposed?"

"Pretty sure we would know if he had left the citadel," Scythe murmured. "Acana must be kept informed of his whereabouts."

I remembered arguing with the Emperor as he stormed off to chase down a fleeing kyrgeth that had ripped through his citadel. "Not if he isn't inclined to tell her," I muttered, knowing full well that if I hadn't been there then the Academy would have been completely in the dark as to where he had gone.

"I'm sorry I can't be of more help," Rinoa said after a minute of contemplative silence. "All I will say is this – the Academy doesn't mess around when it comes to the deaths of Imperators. If one of my team died in the citadel's hospital, I would know about it almost as fast as the doctors there. That suggests to me that Cassius is alive. Maybe you should just trust in the Emperor and wait."

Trust in the Emperor and wait. I knew I could do the first thing, but I wasn't so sure about the second.

As it stood, I really shouldn't have done either.

"Everybody up!"

A ball of light and noise accompanied the shout, snapping like firecrackers and ending many a perfectly good night's rest. In seconds we were out of bed, throwing on clothes and snatching up weapons before standing to attention.

Commander Wyckan watched us fall in, her face lined and haggard. If I had to hazard a guess, she wasn't sleeping much. Even sustaining oneself with seraph didn't make much of a dent in bone-weary tiredness after a while.

"Listen up!" she barked after the last person fell in. "Second Squad has gone dark. They were due to report back an hour ago after investigating a potential Enemy-held location. We have here three squads at fighting strength; you are to work together and discover what happened. If anyone is alive, get them out. If there is a facility there, bring it down. Clear?"

"Yessir!" we roared.

"Good. Follow me to the command centre and I'll show you the last known location of Second Squad. Speed is of the essence people. Move fast but be prepared for anything. I don't want to lose any of you."

Quickly filing in behind her, she went over the location on the map; seemingly little more than an open expanse in the western section of the Sangkak. As far as the map suggested, there shouldn't have been little more out there than scrub and dust. Within five minutes we were out in the dark, a sliver of moon providing just enough light for the others to see by. With my Seya-enhanced eyes I had no issues on that front and after a quick conversation with the other squads I took lead, hopping up on Seya's back and ranging ahead of the group to check for traps and other potential threats.

Night-time on the plains was a strange and solitary experience. Sound carried surprisingly far: the rhythmic *clump* of hooves behind me as the Imperators pushed their steeds as fast as they dared with the limited vision, the rattle of harness and even a few muted conversations that were quickly stilled. In front of me, however, there was practically no sound, just the rustle of the wind. Even though I was riding to combat, it was oddly peaceful.

Knowing that if we were going to have any chance of surprising a potential enemy I had to give ample warning to those following behind, Seya pushed harder, her massive bulk powering over the plains with silent ease; the only suggestion that she was working hard the slight panting and the growing warmth in her muscles. What would take a horse during the day a minute to cross at full sprint took us barely twenty-seconds at night and still she was quieter than the wind.

We slowed our approach when we got closer to the objective, a few hours before dawn when the night was at its darkest. Senses stretched to full, we slipped forwards, hunting for anything out of the ordinary.

It didn't take long to find.

It was the smell that gave it away. The metallic tang of freshly-spilled blood. It permeated the air, suffused it, until it felt like I was breathing blood. Relaying our location to Rikol we crept forwards, following our noses more than our eyes.

I didn't realise that we had found the missing squad at first. Originally I wondered if the layer of goop that had started to cover the ground was some kind of monstrous excrement, but it was the boot on the ground, followed by the tattered Imperator-clothes and weapons that finally gave it away.

We were walking through the remains of the squad.

By the Pits. What did this?

Seya sniffed and shook her head. *I can't say, the scent is too overpowering.*

It's...it's like they've been turned inside out. It was, without a doubt, the goriest thing I had ever seen and I clamped down on the sudden need to vomit, thankful for the small mercy that it was a cold night. By tomorrow this place was going to stink. *What do you think? Warlock? Skyren?*

No tracks, Seya pointed out. *I count four sets of footprints and Second Squad had four members. Skyren are big. Heavy. Even one of those warlocks would have left print.*

Unless... I craned my neck up to the sky. *What if it flew?*

Possible.

See any facility?

She shook her head. *Can't hear anything moving nearby. If there is something here then it is either cunningly disguised or hidden from my senses.*

Hidden from... I pulled up short. *Was it that simple?* Pointing with a finger, I extended a beam of seraph and slowly turned in a circle. Before I had got two-thirds of the way round I felt it; the seraph beam had been impeded by something that was otherwise invisible to both Seya and myself. Looking at the swathe of area that my seraph had been unable to penetrate, I felt a sudden concern.

We need to go.

What? Why?

Now!

Listening to the worry in my voice, Seya leapt into action, launching to my side and motoring away as soon as I had climbed on.

Rikol?

Here. His voice was different to Seya's in my mind. There was no warmth of a connection, just the cold, detached feeling of seraph scribbling words in my brain.

We've found it.

Second Squad?

Dead.

A momentary pause as he doubtless relayed the information. *Understood. What about the facility?*

Found that too. I think it's big Rikol. And it was hidden by seraph. Completely hidden.

You're sure?

I could sense the incredulity in his voice. *I'm sure.*

To keep seraph running to completely hide a building would take an—

An enormous amount of seraph. I know.

Another one of those warlocks maybe?

Not sure. I've pulled Seya back. Don't know if anyone was watching or if we tripped any alarms.

Good call. Another pause. *We'll be there in thirty. Squads aren't happy with the news and itching to fight.*

Going to be tough. Don't know how many are inside the facility, or what its defences are.

Understood. Rikol out.

Nearly thirty minutes later I met with the others, drifting out of the night on Seya and taking pains to keep downwind so as to try and minimise the panic to the horses. It didn't take long to update everyone on the situation and more than a few eyebrows were raised at my news about a fully seraph-hidden building. I was probably the only one who could manage that for even a short time and that was purely because of Seya's overwhelmingly large seraph pool. Either the monster or person powering the illusion had trained over and over to become more efficient at doing such a thing, or something else was going on.

The issue was, without being able see the building we were going to be completely blind as to how to assault it. Because there were no doubts that we were going to assault it. Our fallen brothers and sisters demanded it.

In the end, it fell to Rikol, Ella, Rinoa and a dour-faced Imperator called Gado. After a little bickering between the groups, the four were determined to be the most effective seraph-wielders and the least likely to get caught. I say least likely, but the chances were that this attempt would fail – what they were attempting was going to be extremely technically challenging. A lot of the finer points of it went over my head but in essence, in order to avoid detection by whoever or whatever had created the seraph illusion they would need to both will the barrier to open whilst at the same time willing it to feel completely undisturbed. It was mind-boggling to me - I could barely will one thing into existence, let alone try to split my mind to think about two.

The rest of us stayed back as the four slipped forwards with stealth-seraph running. Whilst true invisibility was possible, it was a major seraph-burner. It was much easier and cheaper to just continuously will others not to notice you. A gifted seraph-user might figure out what was happening of course, but that was always the risk with any type of concealment.

Seemingly undetected, the four made it to the edge of the barrier. After few tense moments we saw all four slowly slip inside and vanish from view.

The anxious wait felt like an eternity. It was finally broken when the four dropped their concealment back in the group, causing a wave of shock as everyone realised that they had been staring at them approaching for some time and just chosen to ignore it.

"It's a dome," Rinoa said grimly. "A dome made of metal with one obvious entranceway: a large door that is currently closed and will inevitably make a racket if we managed to get it open. The best thing to note is that there doesn't seem to be any type of guard tower or even patrolling troops so unless someone is scrying we should be able to get close without issue."

"What's the plan?" Fethi, a woman with long braided hair, a nose that looked like it had been broken a few times, and Rinoa's teammate, asked.

Rinoa grimaced. "Easiest option? We blow our way in. It will alert everything inside but chances are we'll trip something anyway and we might have the advantage of surprise to cut down everything inside."

"Hmm," mused Rikol, his tone suggesting he had something to say.

"Spit it out," Rinoa snapped.

He arched an eyebrow. "We have a bunch of seraph-users here. Why not just level the place? Seems to me that there isn't any need to put ourselves at risk any more than there needs to be. We could blow down the door and fill the inside with something guaranteed to kill whatever is in there."

Rinoa's eyes narrowed in thought. "Yes...that could work." She grinned. "Did you have something in mind?"

"As a matter of fact, I do."

We assembled in front of the seraph marker that designated the location of the door. Although we weren't overtly advertising our presence, we were no longer taking great pains to remain hidden. Our attack was imminent and whatever was inside was not going to stop us.

We hoped.

"Door is in front," Rinoa confirmed. "Let's bring it down."

The combined power of nearly a dozen seraph users was something otherworldly. We were likely wielding barely a fraction of the power of the likes of the Emperor, but what we did wield was more than enough to put on a show. Multicoloured blasts of energy roared out of us, the hues of light shredding the pre-dawn sky and streaming into the distance only to disappear as though cut off from reality. We had considered trying to bring down the invisibility layer but decided that if the Enemy or one of its minions wanted to burn that much power to fuel it, we would happily continue to let them.

When Rinoa considered it enough, she waved a hand and we all stepped through the barrier. Where one second we had been viewing a barren landscape, suddenly there was a large domed structure with a molten hole where the door had used to be and some kind of wailing horn going off deep inside.

An alarm, warned Seya. *Those inside will be gathering.*

I hope so, I replied as Rikol stepped forwards and raised his hands. *I think Rikol has something special in mind.*

"You know how we all nearly died on that Irevin mountainside a few years back?" Rikol called over his shoulder. "Well. I figured that the Enemy gave us a little bit of a gift."

"Do tell." Sophia said drily, her eyes, like mine, noticing the distant movement of figures in the gloom. "But quickly."

"Always want to rush the dramatic moments," Rikol complained.

"I'm not rushing you," Sophia pointed a finger. "They are."

Like kicking an ant nest, thyrkan were massing deep inside the complex. Dozens of them. Maybe hundreds.

"This gift," Rikol said, having decided to continue his story, "is that He gave us the known location of a now active volcano. Creating magma is seraph-intensive as I've practiced it less than most. It is devastatingly effective as an attack though."

"They're coming," Rinoa warned. "Whatever you're going to do, do it fast!"

"So," he waved a hand and reality began to tear, "I figured, why not just stick with what I'm good at."

An orange glow appeared.

"And what I'm good at," he declared, eyes shining bright, "is making portals."

The thyrkan poured forwards, sibilant hissing reaching our ears as they streamed our way. A molten jet of magma roared out of the portal and splattered over everything in its path. The first to be hit didn't even have time to scream, vanishing into the glowing sludge like it had never been. The thyrkan advance stumbled and faltered as wails of pain and horror began to fill the air. Unlike normal, Rikol's portal was a tiny aperture and the vast pressure on the other side was causing the magma to fire out in a long, continuous geyser; the flaming rock immolating everything it touched.

Some thyrkan managed to avoid the initial blast and swept to the sides but Rikol simply caused the portal to turn from side-to-side until the jet of lava was sweeping back and forth continuously. I almost felt bad for the lizards, the normal foot-soldiers never stood a chance.

After sixty long seconds, Rikol stemmed the tide. He was pale and covered in a sheen of sweat but his smile was infectious. "I can't believe that worked!" he gasped.

"I can't believe we let you try it out with our lives on the line," Scythe retorted, stepping close to slap him on the shoulder. "But nice job."

I could only agree. The inside of the dome had to be cavernous considering the torrent of lava had only covered the ground by around a foot, but from what we could see, the inside of the dome was a glowing mess. If there were stairs down then the lower floors were likely under masses of molten rock – something that most creatures would struggle to survive. In one fell swoop Rikol had neatly put the entire building out of commission.

"Keep up your guard," ordered Rinoa. "We don't know if anything survived or if reinforcements have been summoned."

Almost as though the creatures had been listening to the conversation, twin void portals flared into existence on top of the dome and four armoured thyrkan and two of the strange warlock types stalked through.

"You had to say it didn't you," I muttered with a shake of my head. "For shame, Rinoa."

"You can't blame that on me!" she hissed back. "That was just bad timing."

"No, what that was, was you jinxing it."

"Shut it."

"You first."

She grinned at me and then pointed at the dome, raising her voice. "Well, apparently I have the ability to summon things into being, so let's kick the shit out of those bastards and then go and see if I can summon up some beer."

That got a rousing cheer.

"Watch out for the warlocks," I reminded everyone. "They hit hard."

Rinoa rolled her eyes. "Not the first time we've encountered one, little Calidan. You've been here what? All of two weeks and you think you know best?"

"No, I just think I know best because I'm the best."

We mock-glared at each other until Rikol groaned. "For fuck's sake, just have sex already and stop putting us through this misery!" Shaking his head in disgust, he looked up at the thyrkan and grinned. "As for these lot..." he waved a hand.

A portal opened.

Molten lava roared out of the opening, engulfing the six figures in a wave of roiling flame.

"Eas-" Rikol stopped mid-sentence. He had spotted what I had, the black shield that forced the magma back. With a growl he forced his portal to widen, clutching at his head as the stream of magma turned into a torrent.

"Rikol, ease up," Ella ordered worriedly.

"I...can....do...this," he growled through gritted teeth. He staggered and drop to one knee, blood trickling down his nose. "They're...fighting...me."

The portal began to distort, waving this way and that as though incredible pressure was being exerted on all sides. With a final gasp, Rikol's eyes rolled into the back of his head and he collapsed, the portal instantly winking out.

"Will combat," Rinoa hissed. "Shields up!"

Layers of blue, green and red sprang into life as the defensive elements of the three squads, including myself, sprang into action. All eyes focused on the top of the steaming dome where the remains of the molten magma began to drip down the sides. Bit by bit, the black sphere became visible again as though it was eating the liquid rock.

"They're going to drop that shield soon," Rinoa said. "As soon as it is down, hit them with everything you have."

Sophia already had a glowing arrow manifested in front of her, the gleaming light becoming brighter with each increase in her frown. Rinoa had something similar; a force lance that made the standard lance look little more than a stick in comparison. It was such a deep, vibrant red that it tinged the landscape to the violent hue. Gado had his hands outstretched, face deep in concentration, but I couldn't tell what - if anything - he was creating.

A wave of power thrummed through the air and the magma that was cooling on the surface of the dome instantly turned to solid rock. The void-shield shimmered and then dissipated.

"Fire!" Rinoa growled, listening to her own words and flinging her force-lance forwards. It screamed through the air, accompanied by the glowing beam of Sophia's condensed arrow. Both attacks sped across the intervening distance in a fraction of a second, passing a hairsbreadth from the wave of black lightning that arced through the air in our direction. The lightning struck first, hammering into our shields with terrifying force.

Then the two attacks landed.

Twin blasts of red and white erupted into the air with a clap of air pressure that rippled the atmosphere and staggered us beneath our shields, sending a wave of dust out behind us for seemingly miles around. A keening began in my ears, a building pressure like a kettle about to boil. The two colours swirled, combined.

Erupted.

The secondary blast was bigger than the first, the side-effects of mixing unstable seraph. The top of the dome crumpled, the rock and metal ripped away like it had never been. A thunderous roar hit our ears as the world seemed to explode in billowing waves of fire and fury and I was thankful for our foresight for the shields as without them the two mages might have done the warlock's job for them.

When the sound faded away and the light finally began to die down, we opened our eyes to bear witness to what the two mages had wrought.

The dome was partially gone, metal parts lying crumpled and warped in heaps around us, broken pieces of scaffolding largely all that remained. The building looked like the top of a giant egg that had been caved in with a spoon. But that wasn't what drew our attention.

No.

That was the black orb that still hung in the sky. Unblemished, seemingly untouched by the best that our powerhouses had to offer. A terrifying display of might in such a simple manner.

"More," I heard Gado groan, sweat dripping down his face. "I need more." One of his teammates moved over to him and placed a hand on his back, face falling into the familiar frown of seraph concentration. I scanned the distance but still couldn't see what he was doing. Whatever it was, I hoped it was worth the cost.

"Brace!"

The scream came a split-second before the attack. A beam of extraordinarily dense seraph raked across the shields, the sheer power emanating from the thin line enough to carve a furrow into the ground beneath our shields nearly five feet deep.

Shuddering, I struggled to maintain the shield. I had seen that kind of attack before. It was the one that the Not-Sarrenai had used. The one that had punched a hole through our defences and nearly killed us all.

The fact that the two warlocks were nearly on par with that beast was beyond frightening.

"Gado!" shouted one of his teammates desperately.

"Not yet!" he returned, his entire body shaking with strain. "Not yet!"

Red blasts thundered from the remnants of the dome as Rinoa flew into action. Each of the concussive blasts would have been enough to spell the doom of any party of normal thyrkan but the defences of the warlocks barely twitched.

A spear of metal the size of a house erupted from the centre of the dome, piercing into the sky like it was on a mission to touch the moon. The gleaming tip touched the black shield and carved around it, streams of metal peeling apart and flowing over and above as the thyrkan went untouched. I watched one of the beasts raise a hand. An orb that seemed to suck all light away appeared in its taloned fingers, quickly followed by a second, then a third. The orbs were small, each probably little more than an orange, but I had a feeling that we didn't want to be hit by one.

With a careless gesture, the glowing orbs sped forwards but didn't impact the shields like we had anticipated. Instead they formed a triangle around our defences and an arc of black energy connected the three, an energy that began to pulse and build, growing closer and closer to the shield each time.

"Oh, this isn't going to be fun," Ella groaned.

"Sever the beams!" Rinoa called, panic in her voice.

They did their best. Attacks carved through the morning glow but everything simply dissipated into the black energy. After a few moments the first of it touched the top of my shield and although I had everything I could possibly channel going into it the beam carved through without pause. Instantly I shrank the shield, condensing it as quickly as I could but the wave of energy just kept progressing, seemingly not remotely concerned by the power of my shield.

"If someone is going to do something, do it quick!" I called, trying not to let the panic suffusing my body show.

With a snarl, Gado flung his arms above his head and then down, like he was heaving something into the earth.

In a way, he was.

"Keep your shields up!" he roared.

"What do you think we're doing?!" someone shouted back. An Imperator screamed as the encroaching beam touched his flesh, a chunk of his arm gone like it had never been. Shouts of panic began to fill the air as the defensive circles became smaller and smaller.

A flash of light caught my attention. Something far above us twinkling in the morning glow.

Getting brighter.

Oh shit.

"Shields!" I screamed, not bothering to hide the fear in my voice now and pulling everything I could. Somewhere I dazedly felt Seya droop to her knees as the pull became too intense.

The beam was close now. So close that I could feel the call of the void. The intense nothingness of the abyss.

The meteor hit.

The world went white.

Everything was chaos.

We tumbled through the air, bouncing within the shield, blinded by the immensity of the explosion that Gado had wrought. When we finally stopped, I heaved a *whoosh* as someone landed on my chest. Coughing and spluttering filled the tiny space as the pitter-patter of shifting rocks gave us the only awareness of the outside world.

Calidan! Calidan!

It took me a moment to realise that Seya had been going ballistic in my mind. *Still alive, Seya.*

She sent me a feeling of avid relief and calmed down slightly. *I'll circle around and look for survivors.*

Understood, I thought wearily. *Be safe.*

Eventually, I had enough energy to wheeze the words everyone had been dying to ask. "What the fuck was that?!"

"Looked like Gado brought down a star," Scythe coughed.

"Whatever it was, it was bloody impressive," added Ella. "Nearly killed us all though."

"I think we were nearly all dead anyway," Sophia replied. "Whatever that attack was, it was just about to finish the job."

"Scythed through the shield like it wasn't there," I muttered. "No idea how that worked but it didn't hit like a regular seraph attack. It was like it was cancelling the shield out or absorbing it somehow."

"Something to report to Commander Wyckan and not sit around discussing here," Ella remarked, shakily pulling herself to her feet. "Come on, we have to move. We can't stay here."

The sound of more shifting rubble nearby reinforced her words and we gathered ourselves, quickly finding weapons and checking for wounds. I tried scenting for the others but all I could sense was the overpowering scent of fire and ash and the tumbling rocks prevented me from listening.

Warily, I lowered the shield, causing another deluge of rocks to tumble down onto our position. We were on the edge of a crater probably a hundred metres wide. Luckily we hadn't fallen too far, which was fortunate because judging by the depth of the crater the complex must have been considerable underneath the dome. Either that or whatever mad skill Gado had managed to produce had contained enough power to drive a hole into the ground deep enough to fit the citadel.

There was no sign of the others and, thankfully, no sign of the familiar black shield of the thyrkan warlocks. With any luck they had been vaporised in the blast or were stuck deep beneath the earth, but I wasn't going to stick around to find out – if they had managed to survive that blast then we were hopelessly outmatched.

Painfully low on seraph, we painstakingly crawled up the incline whilst dragging the still comatose Rikol by his jacket. It was slow going and the sense of relief when we all rolled over the lip of the crater and onto flat ground was palpable. Breathing hard, I stood up and for the first time properly surveyed the damage that Gado had inflicted.

The terrain was forever changed. What had been flat scrubland was now a barren wasteland as far as the eye could see. The scrubs that had survived countless harsh winds and storms had been ripped out or incinerated by the force of the explosion and all that remained was dust and ash that blackened both the land and the sky. Movement caught my eye and a second later I was knocked over by the embrace of a gigantic panther and lay there helpless, completely unable to summon the energy to even attempt to fight off the raspy licks of her tongue.

"Good to see you too, you big softy," I whispered whilst I scratched under her chin. "Did you find anyone?"

My question was answered by the sound of approaching footsteps. "Taking it easy?" called a familiar voice.

"Always," I returned, trying to push the cat away but being denied my freedom and fastidiously cleaned instead. The footsteps reached my side and I turned to see Rinoa crouching down next to me.

"Good to see you're alive," she murmured quietly, eyes intense.

"Right back at you." We grinned at each other for a moment until Rikol let out a low groan.

"Make it stop," he wheezed, clutching his head.

"You've got a seraph hangover," Ella called, patting him on the hand. "Life's going to suck for a while."

"No, not that," he croaked out, before shakily pointing a hand in our direction. "*That.*"

Rinoa stood up and dusted herself off before stalking over to the prone Imperator. "And just what would *that* refer to little Rikol?" The dangerous tone in her voice was unmistakable.

"F-flirting," he breathed, fully committing to his complaint. "It must stop."

"Tell you what," Rinoa said, holding a hand out above his head. "If you can raise the energy to touch my hand, I will stop the so-called 'flirting'. If you can't though, then you are going to have to stand up in front of the cafeteria and declare something for me." Leaning in close she whispered something into his ear, causing him to stiffen in outrage.

"Well?" she mocked lightly, her hand still there. "Any time now would be great."

Rikol groaned again, forced his trembling hand off the floor and raised it slowly into the air. He managed about three centimetres before collapsing.

"Well, that settles that," Rinoa laughed. "Come on, we need to get find the others." Hauling Rikol to his feet, she lifted him bodily and slung him over one shoulder, causing another spate of groans and curses. "Everybody up," she called. The movement was slow and sporadic as people began to pick themselves up off the floor.

The ground trembled.

This time, Rinoa's tone held an unmistakable air of command. "On your feet! Now!"

Seya backed off and helped me rise and I joined her at the edge of the crater, eyes staring at the centre. *What's wrong?*

She shook her head. *Something is...off.*

I had long ago learned to trust Seya's instincts and turned to Rinoa. "We should get moving. Those things might still be alive and we're in no state to finish the job."

Her eyes narrowed as she stared at the crater and I knew she was questioning in her mind as to how they might have survived such an attack. In the end she nodded and whirled as another tremor thrummed through the ground. In the centre of the crater I thought I saw stone shiver.

"Back to the Redoubt!" she called. "Make it snappy!"

"What about Gado's team?" Ella asked.

Rinoa pursed her lips in concentration before nodding. "They're alright. Just climbing out of the crater. They should be with us in a minute."

The ground rippled and I closed my eyes in horror. When I reopened them, Rinoa had turned white.

"I don't think we have a minute," I stated, sadness and fatigue making my tone flat.

"Let's move it people!" Sophia this time, stepping forwards and helping Rinoa with Rikol. "No time to waste. Go, go, go!"

As we moved off, I saw something black break through the crust of the crater. Forcing my weak limbs into a run, I set off after the others with Seya lending support. *Just need to get to the horses,* I reassured myself. *Get to the horses and we can escape.* The thought leant my limbs strength and I pushed forwards, knowing that we only needed to go so far, that I could rest on Seya on the way back. She growled at that, but didn't argue the point.

"Move! Come on, move!" The words were coming from the edge of the crater and I saw Gado's team pull themselves over the lip before shuffling into stumbling runs. Gado himself was slung over the shoulder of a broad-shouldered Imperator who had his head down and chest heaving hard with exertion as he planted one foot after another.

Behind them, the crater began to darken and the ground trembled.

"Run you bastards!" Ella screamed, waving at Gado's team.

"Where are the fucking horses?!" another Imperator shouted.

Panic threatened to sweep through the team. I could feel us all balanced as though we were on a knife-edge. It wouldn't take much to push us over it.

"No...oh no." It was Sophia, her sharp eyes having spotted something the others hadn't. "Oh, by the *Pits!*"

My eyes followed hers to a scattering of steaming chunks of horse flesh and what little hope I had left turned and threw itself back into the nightmare crater.

We thought we had left the horses far enough back to be safe but we hadn't counted on earth-rending attacks being unleashed. The poor things hadn't stood a chance. As the teams saw what Sophia had spotted, we teetered on the brink of the knife, then plunged right over.

Despair filled Rinoa's eyes as she looked at me, then at Seya. *Run,* she mouthed. I couldn't deny that the thought was appealing, but no, I couldn't do that to my team. I shook my head and turned, fingers gripping Vona's hilt tight. She would do no good in this fight, but she was a comfort to hold.

Panic-laden shouts began to fill the air as Gado's team pushed towards us. The crater began to pulse with energy and the panicked shouting slowed as everyone watched what was likely to be our death approach. Tiny ripples of energy started floating out of the crater – hundreds of them and going in every direction. It took me a moment to recognise what they were and when I did, I wished I hadn't.

They were hands. Hundreds of clawed hands.

Deceptively fast, they swarmed over the ground in moments, a spreading pool of inky, grasping death. As though they could sense the fleeing team the pool became a stream, became a river, became a *torrent*, hands piling over each other in a swarm that moved quicker and quicker.

"Come on, move, *move!*" I heard Ella whispering as she, like everyone, watched the fleeing team. It was not to be. Gado's saviour, the heavy-set man, screamed with mindless agony as the first of the claws latched onto his calf. Flesh fell away under its touch and the man stumbled, suddenly unable to take his own weight. His foot flailed, shifted, and landed right into the maw of the void. His scream was piercing; a howl from his very soul. I couldn't work out if the claws were pulling up his legs or if he was shrinking, but in seconds the lower half of his body was consumed.

"Flynn!" shouted the lead member of Gado's team despairingly, shock and tears running down his face.

A burst of shield erupted around Flynn and I saw Sophia and Ella clenching their jaws in focus but the seraph turned brittle like the energy was being sucked out of it and then shattered under the endless tide. Flynn's face contorted into a bloody grimace as he shifted the weight of the unconscious Gado and heaved the man forwards towards his teammates.

"Run!" he cried. "Ru-*ARGGGH*!" The claws streamed up his spine, draped over his shoulders and sliced up his neck. Slowly he collapsed, flesh falling away from his body and the swarm reached up to meet him, covering him inch-by-inch until he was consumed.

"FLYNN!"

The team-member grabbed Gado, tears streaming down his face and dragged him forwards. A flash of black and suddenly Seya was there, lowering her body so that the man could get Gado on. Working fast, he lifted Gado aboard and then jumped on too, Seya bounding away just as the claws reached for her heels.

Good job, I sent to her wearily. *Now get out of here.*

Not without you.

This isn't a fight we can win.

Seya growled, low and dangerous. *Then find another way.*

I started to stammer a response before realising she was right. We were giving up, too exhausted, too *broken* from the fight to remotely believe that we could make it away. But we still had to try. There had to be something, *anything* that could help.

Or anyone?

My lip twitched. *Reinforcements for the reinforcements?*

"Sophia," I shouted, "can you contact the commander?"

"I think so," she replied stiffly, eyes on the approaching blanket of death.

"Tell her we need her firepower and we need it now."

"Done." Sophia frowned a second later and growled. "She hasn't got a portal user available. Ella can you-"

"On it!" Ella glared into the distance and a small hole splintered the air, fragmenting reality until a person-sized aperture was available. A moment later three figures stepped through and a rejuvenating wave of energy flooded our limbs.

"Get moving," ordered the Commander's familiar voice, her eyes already fixed on the approaching wave of darkness. "We'll take it from here."

The spell of despair was broken and we stumbled into shuffling run past the three before turning and pulling up behind them.

"Your pardon Commander, but we're not leaving. Not yet," said Scythe.

A sigh, but not from the commander. "You lot do love getting into trouble, don't you?" said a tall, thin Imperator, in a voice like rocks clashing together. It took me a moment to place him. He had changed since I had last seen him; heavily scarred flesh covered the majority of his neck and part of his face.

"Simone," I whispered, shocked.

He gave a wistful smile. "Yes, it's me. I would say new and improved, but that would be stretching things a little too far."

"Whilst I don't want to break up your little reunion," the Commander snapped, clapping her hands together, "we have a threat to eliminate. Rinoa, what's the situation?"

In a few short sentences Rinoa provided what little we knew of the warlocks' powers and Commander Wyckan frowned. "Able to break through the combined shields of multiple Imperators. Interesting."

"They've taken direct hits from multiple condensed seraph attacks," Rinoa added. "That crater was from us. Gado to be precise."

"Hmm. He's improving," the Commander mused, eyes narrowed at the approaching flood. "Well. If you're all keen to stay then get behind me. Things are about to get fun."

The clawing hands tore across the landscape, a stream of wrack and ruin, yet if Commander Wyckan was concerned she didn't show it. Slowly, almost idly, she raised a hand and snapped her fingers. Multi-hued light snapped into being with brisk alacrity, slamming into position one after the other with an audible *thud*.

"What's she doing?" Scythe asked. "We already know that barriers fail against this attack."

Simone turned and gave a pained grimace. "We know *most* barriers fail, but the Commander is no wielder of an ordinary shield. She is a master of defensive magics." He cocked an eyebrow. "Do you not know who she is?"

"The High Imperator's sister," Scythe replied, eyes widening as the shield flashed with coruscating weaves. The closer I looked, the more detail I could see within the seraph: glyphs and runes far beyond my understanding. If Rikol had been coherent he would likely have passed out from the intricacy of it all.

"The High Imperator's *older* sister," Simone corrected. "But that is not *who* she is." He cocked an eye at the encroaching darkness and turned his back on it, instead looking at us with calm reassurance and said three simple words.

"She is Bastion."

CHAPTER 30

Bastion

The flood of grasping hands reached the billowing walls of Commander Wyckan's defences and slammed against them, piling up higher and higher until a writhing sea of darkness assailed our location. Commander Wyckan looked completely unperturbed, inspecting her shields with a clinical eye.

"Interesting. Simone, do you see this?" she waved excitedly and the lanky Imperator gave a long-suffering sigh before walking up beside her.

"What?"

"Look, look!" She pointed like an excited child as one of the outer layers of her shield fractured and was ripped away. "Do you see?"

"I see us getting one step closer to death," Simone remarked coolly.

"Nonsense," she cackled, waving a hand. "Look closely, do you see how it is eating its way through the defences? It isn't a question of power but how it is empowering itself. Think about it, there are very few creatures, monsters or people who could still have so much power left to them to create this attack after the fight that has already taken place. I think the reason that these warlocks have an edge is because their seraph is working in a way that is most unusual."

Despite his outward appearance, I could tell that Simone was interested. "Alright," he said, crouching down next to the barrier curiously, "and what is unusual about it?"

"I think it is eating seraph."

Simone frowned and shook his head. "Seraph is personal to each individual; you can't consume it."

"That's the wildly prevailing theory, yes. But it's one that I have often wondered about, particularly when we come to the Powers. I have little doubt that if he wanted to, the Emperor could extract our seraph and repurpose it for his own ends."

"Yes, but he is *the Emperor*."

Commander Wyckan crossed her arms and raised an eyebrow quizzically. "So?"

"So he is able to do things that no-one else can! We know this already!"

"Just accepting that things are the way they are and not discovering the reason why is called ignorance, Simone, and it stifles the world."

Simone rolled his eyes, taking a step backwards as another layer of shield splintered and broke. "Fine, let's assume that it is somehow repurposing seraph, how would it do that?"

"I have no idea!" she exclaimed happily, a far cry from the intense, stoic woman who had been my prison guard in Wolf's Hollow.

Simone nodded absently as though he had expected nothing less. "...Then should we be running?"

"Probably!" she laughed. "But I have a few quick theories I want to try." Crouching down she studied the wall of reaching darkness and then stared at her shield. Something shifted in the layers of light before settling and she grunted in approval. The clawing darkness still encroached, little by little, but it seemed to do so a little more slowly. She tried a few more alterations and then smiled before reaching out and touching her wall. Nothing seemed to change but suddenly the black mass poured over her shield without eating into it.

She had stopped its advance.

"What did you do?" breathed Simone, eyes watching the darkness warily.

"I figured it out."

"No shit."

Commander Wyckan – no, *Bastion* – grinned. "I thought along the lines of what a black seraph user could do. What it was most adept at. Everything we create is willed into being, we believe it to be there hard enough that it takes form. It appears as though this darkness primarily works on targeting those foundational elements, almost like it attacks part of your will unknowingly and rips apart the seraph at the seams so to speak. In doing so, it manages to somehow consume the seraph it sets loose and grows more powerful. Fascinating really."

"And so how have you stopped it?"

Bastion shrugged. "I decided that my shield was completely immutable."

Simone raised an eyebrow. "You made this a *permanent* shield?"

Bastion waved a hand. "Eh, maybe. I could likely collapse it if I truly wanted to, but that would go against the concept that I imbued my seraph with."

Concept? That was a term that I had never heard before. How did it affect things like seraph? I had no clue, but something told me I needed to find out.

"If their shield can absorb energy then I guess that explains how the creatures managed to survive multiple high-tier attacks," Simone mused before squinting into the darkness. "Looks like you might have a chance to ask it yourself."

The abyssal sea of ghostly hands shifted aside and two figures slowly emerged. One walked with a limp whilst the other missed an arm and half its tail.

"Doesn't look like its shield can fully handle *everything* that's thrown at it," Sophia muttered, grim joy in her voice.

"True, but the fact that they're even here after those attacks..." Scythe drifted off, shaking his head. "Scary."

"Hhuumanns," hissed the limping lizard. "Ssstill you resssisst."

Bastion stepped to the edge of her barrier and cocked her head. "Did you really think that we would roll over, Mr Strange-talking-lizard-thing?"

"Yyess. Yyouu fffaccee aa ppoweeer beeyondd yyou."

The Imperator made a show of looking around before raising her arms in a shrug. "Afraid I don't see any of the Powers around, not even your boss, so not sure that's the case."

"Wweee sshalll cconsuumme yyou."

Bastion's face darkened. "No, you've got it the wrong way round Mr Lizard-wizard. You see, you're a one-trick mage. No *real* talent, just an interesting trick. One that I've seen and that I've dealt with. So now you come down here to try and understand how I did it, but the problem is, you wouldn't understand it even if I spoke really, *really* slowly. You see..." her eyes lit up with a fiendish glow, "you're swimming in a much bigger pool now, little fish, and the sharks are circling."

The thyrkan cocked its head at her and Bastion sighed. "You don't know what a shark is do you? Never mind. Rest assured I'm adeptly insulting your intelligence and seraph abilities. Be offended and try to kill me or try to run away." She waved a dismissive hand. "Both will fail."

The thyrkan hissed as one, reptilian tongues lashing the air. "Yyou wwiilll dddiieee."

"Yes, yes," the implacable Imperator replied, turning her back on the two beasts. "Do your worst."

The two lizards retreated into the black, the ghostly hands flowing around them to slam back into the shield as though they had been waiting desperately to attack. Bastion didn't even flinch at the noise and merely moved to inspect the wounded.

"What now?" I asked Simone, joining him at the barrier.

"Now?" he repeated in surprise. "We wait."

"Surely that gives the creatures more time to prepare something truly unpleasant?"

"It does," he remarked, "but it also gives them ample time to drain themselves. Bastion's seraph reserves are…beyond remarkable. She likes to anger her foes into attacking and then rip the floor out from underneath them when the time is ready."

I frowned. "Surely that's a dangerous way to do things? What if she does that and something manages to break through."

"Then I imagine she will be happy," Simone chuckled. "It's been a long time since Bastion has truly been tested. She, out of everyone else at the Academy, is probably closest to one of the Powers in strength. I say that lightly as she is a candle compared to a roaring fire, but it's a damn sight of a bigger candle than most of us equate to. She has perfected her shield techniques over the years and can handle their creation with minimal seraph wastage, meaning that she is extremely efficient." Simone snorted. "Who do you think helped the High Imperator with her shield skill?"

"I had no idea the High Imperator had a sister," I breathed. "She has never spoken of her."

"Probably because you never asked," Simone replied. "And there is a history there. The two Wyckans were both prodigies, their talents with seraph placing them leaps and bounds ahead of others in the Academy. Because they were so much better than most of their peers, their rivalry was something of legend. Both always wanted to be the best. The High Imperator worked on becoming the best at everything, whereas the defensive elements appealed to Bastion. She became a true master of the defensive arts, whereas the High Imperator became very good at multiple things but never quite up to the same masterful standard as her sister. It must have irked Acana no-end that the High Imperator position was offered to Bastion first."

"Oh, you have *no idea!*" called a smiling Imperator Wyckan who had obviously been listening in, despite Simone's hushed tones. "Didn't talk to me for weeks!"

Simone shook his head, a small smile on his face. "Despite Bastion's obvious skills, she is... hmm, how should I put this politely, a little more *narrow-minded* than her sister."

"That was polite?" Scythe coughed with a laugh.

Bastion raised a hand and tilted it from side-to-side. "Eh."

Simone chuckled. "What I mean to say is that she is much more interested in the ins and outs of certain things, particularly seraph. What she isn't remotely interested in is the bigger picture. The High Imperator needs to be someone who has that desire to understand the impacts of actions on a national or global scale and Bastion recognised that and so turned it down in favour of her sister. Whilst Acana is the better choice for the job, I think achieving it in that manner made her feel like she came second to her sister-"

"Technically she did!" Bastion called, her hands sealing a gash and completely ignoring the arc of black lightning that screamed through the clawing hands to rebound off the glowing shield.

"-and so she rarely talks about it," Simone finished. "Like I said, some history there. However, let me tell you this – if ever there is a moment when the two Wyckans are on the same battlefield then you best play close attention because you're about to see true magic happen."

Bastion snorted and stepped away from the injured woman, clapping her on the shoulder. "And that's enough of Simone's story-time for today." Rubbing her hands together she cocked her head at the twin beams of dense seraph that raked across the shield. "Strong," she acknowledged. "Not enough, but strong." She grimaced. "I can see why they've been giving you trouble."

The ground shook and sundered, falling away from the shield and spilling the sea of abyssal claws into the new moat. "See?" Bastion sighed with a shake of her head. "Not an original idea in their heads. Did they not expect that someone who specialises in defensive locations would have thought to imbue the ground on which they stood?"

I stared out into the suddenly revealed morning. The landscape was a ruin. Cracked, blackened and pockmarked with craters, it was beginning to look more like how Brother Gelman had described the moon. The two injured thyrkan glared daggers at us from across the moat that they had just unintentionally created, seemingly disliking with the fact that we were still standing. I guess it had to be tough, thinking that you were the best, only to be met with immutable proof that you weren't. I smiled at that and gave the creatures a two-fingered salute.

"Is Rikol conscious?" I asked, turning my back on the thyrkan and finding Ella at my side.

"Just about," she replied. "Pretty groggy."

I winced in sympathy. Seraph hangovers were no joke. "We should try and get him coherent enough to witness this," I explained, waving my hands at the impossibility of this defensive wall. "You know, just to blow his mind that little bit more."

Smirking, Ella moved to the bundled figure of Rikol and began gently shaking him. When that only resulted in a barrage of slurred curses, Scythe moved in and kicked him not too gently in the shin.

"Oi!" Scythe shouted. "Look at the crazy seraph shit that's going on you prick!"

That, eventually, got his attention and Rikol rolled over, his pupils wide and dilated with a grey pallor to his face but the small wondrous smile that appeared a moment later as he slowly recognised what he was witnessing was good to see.

I moved back up to Simone. "So, if Bastion is a defensive specialist, does that mean that she doesn't have particularly effective offense?"

Simone grinned wolfishly. "I think that might be spoiling the surprise a little. You'll see. It won't be long now."

He was right. The thyrkan tried a few more attacks, each one flashier than the last. Spears of elemental darkness lashed out of the ground, waves of pulsing fire roared from the sky and lastly three familiar orbs shifted into place and created that condensing beam of hideously powerful energy.

All to no effect.

We might as well have set up chairs and started reading for all the threat that the attacks posed. Inside the Bastion's shield there was no hint of the explosive force of the blasts. No heat from the fire and not even a sliver of the shield crumbled under the beam that had nearly killed us all.

Finally, Bastion judged the moment was at hand. Standing, she spared a pitying look at the two thyrkan and then raised a hand. At first I didn't see anything happen, and by the looks of the two warlocks, neither did they. Confused, they began forming another attack, only for it to detonate at point-blank range. When the smoke cleared, their scales were smoking and fresh blood coated the floor. Slowly, tentatively, one of the beasts reached out a clawed hand and recoiled, having encountered something that I couldn't make out. Hate-filled eyes locked onto Bastion and she grimaced sadly in return before the two lizards burst into a frenzy, claws moving and slashing in every direction but rebounding as though hitting solid rock.

It was then I understood.

"She's placed them in a prison," I breathed, awe tinging my voice.

Simone grunted. "One of her favourite tactics. Get them tired enough that they likely can't portal out and then seal them up. At the end of the day a shield is designed to keep things out, but that doesn't mean it can't be used offensively. Depending on how creative she is feeling she might let them asphyxiate, or maybe she adds something to the atmosphere inside, like a flame or a poison." He shrugged. "But judging by her outstretched hand, she has something a little more graphic in mind."

"What do you mean?"

"Just watch."

The two lizards finally ceased their mad activities, recognising that they were well and truly trapped. The hatred in their eyes never diminished but I like to think that there was grudging respect there too when they looked at Bastion. She held their gaze for a long moment and then clenched her fist. One second, the lizards were whole and hearty. The next, a pile of blood and bone decorated the air, painting the invisible walls that had slammed shut with terrifying force.

"Bastion's Judgement," Simone whispered. "That's what we call that one. Probably one of her more preferred techniques."

"You know I hate that you name my techniques," Bastion called, not taking her eyes off the bloody mess that she had made.

"Then you should stop showboating or name them yourself," Simone retorted amiably. Hearing her exasperated sigh, he grinned. "So, little Calidan, or I guess not so little any more, I imagine that answered your question about Bastion's offensive capabilities."

That was an easy question to answer. "I haven't seen anything like that before. How does she have enough seraph to do it?"

"Practice!" said Bastion, finally turning around from the grisly scene. "And bucket-loads of talent of course." She winked and I couldn't help but grin in return. She seemed so different from when I had first met her, so full of life as opposed to grim and stoic. Perhaps getting to experience something close to a challenge truly had energised her. Walking over, she nodded at us all. "I'm not going to turn this into a lecture but here's something that most Imperators don't really recognise: doing one thing with seraph doesn't really equate to just being able to do one thing singular." She saw the confusion on our faces and continued. "I practiced defensive skills because I wanted to protect my friends. Most Imperators want to be able to attack and defend and so spread themselves thin. Unlike the Powers, the majority of us don't have centuries or millennia to practice seraph techniques and so spreading ourselves thin has the potential to weaken specific skills. However," she pointed at Scythe, "what is a shield?"

He looked stumped. "A...wall?"

"Pretty much. So if I work hard to get better at shields then, following your analogy, it stands to reason that I should be efficient at building multiple walls. Perhaps I could build a house out of seraph for a fraction of the cost that it would take someone unskilled in the ability. And," her eyes glinted, "what happens if I turn that aforementioned 'wall' on its side, sharpen the edges and send it hurtling through the air?"

"You've created a blade," Sophia gasped knowingly. "So you're saying that just because you're excellent at shield-creation, it doesn't prevent you from being effective in other areas because you excel in them too."

"Precisely!" Bastion beamed. "You just have to choose what you are going to master very carefully because at the end of the day seraph is all down to what you can imagine. If you can think of multiple scenarios where something like a wall has the potential to be wielded in another useful manner then you might be onto a winner." She smiled warmly and scanned the group. "Thus endeth the lesson. Come on, let's get back to base and see to those injuries."

Calidan. Wake up. The words floated into my mind, distressingly real in a place of contented dreams.

Seya? The image of the beautiful panther formed in front of me and I giggled. *Hello kitty!*

You're sleeping Calidan. If you don't wake up, you're going to regret it.

My dream-world shook and threatened to collapse. *I don't want to wake up! I'm so tired.*

You'll regret it if you don't. Trust me.

Even my dream-self couldn't argue with Seya. I awoke groggily, lost in the depths of deep, much-needed sleep. The bunk room was dark and filled with the sound of snoring. Everyone had been exhausted from the encounter with the thyrkan and combined with some much-needed drinks to celebrate being alive, most of the Imperators were promptly passed out. My eyes pierced the gloom. What had woken me?

A shadow shifted at the foot of my bed. Long hair dark in the night but I knew that it was flame-red in the sun. Rinoa stood there, gazing towards me, her hand reached out tentatively as though she wasn't sure about what she was intending to do. She caught my movement and our eyes met. Instantly, the grogginess disappeared. There was a hunger in her eyes. One that she must have recognised in mine because in the next moment she was climbing into the bunk, her powerful lithe figure moving up mine until we were face to face.

"Rin-"

She pressed a finger to my lips and shook her head. Slowly, gently, she retracted her finger and replaced it with her lips and then all was passion. Hot, desperate passion. The kind that made us erect seraph barriers for privacy. I wasn't so naïve to think that this was necessarily the same for Rinoa as it was for me. That it held the same meaning. I had yearned for her, for this, for years but had barely registered on her radar. *No, the rational part of my mind pointed out, it is likely that this is more of a celebration of life, of surviving yet another close-call.* Then the rational part of my brain completely shut down, leaving only the primal hunger which Rinoa responded to with eager will. My last moment of clarity as our bodies clashed was of Seya radiating a supreme sense of satisfaction.

A fine queen.

She was gone when I woke. I had expected it but it was still a surprise. Rinoa, it appeared, was impressively sneaky when she put her mind to it.

"Morning sleepy-head," Sophia said, throwing a pillow at me. "How did you sleep?"

I chanced a look around the room, hunting for the tell-tale flash of hair but there was none to be found. "Like a log," I lied.

"Apparently so, seeing as you missed breakfast."

I glanced out the window and frowned. The grey light of morning was filtering in, mid-morning if I had to guess. *How the hell did that happen?* Flashes of last night made their way to the forefront of my mind and I struggled to suppress a smile. *Ah. That's why.*

"Here." Sophia handed me a freshly baked scone. "Breakfast might be over but you'll be relieved to know that Commander Wyckan has given us the day off."

"Mighty kind of her," I intoned before biting into the scone with ravenous hunger. "I doubt most of our squads would have been able to go out today anyway."

She eyed me with disgust. "Say it, don't spray it. And yes, you're likely right. Rikol is still feeling worse for wear for sure. Gado's squad is down a person whilst the remaining have numerous injuries and a few more cuts and bruises in Rinoa's too. As it stands, we got off the most lightly, likely thanks to you and your shield."

"You can thank Seya," I replied around the last mouthful of scone, earning another glare before I swivelled out of bed and dusted the crumbs onto the floor.

"Oh, I intend to. And I don't think I will be the only one. She's a hero after all. That rescue of Gado and his teammate was spectacular."

I'm glad you all finally recognise my talents.

I held up a finger to Sophia and turned my thoughts inward. *Good morning to you too, you magnificent beast.*

I trust that you had a good night? Seya purred.

If I didn't know it had happened, I'm not sure I would believe it.

It almost didn't. You were so set on sleeping that I had to yank you out of it. That queen was nearly denied what she desired. Poor form.

You yanked me- suddenly my dream came crashing back and I laughed aloud.

"What's so funny?" Sophia asked.

"Just Seya," I replied, still laughing. "Always has my best interests at heart." Inwardly I sent her a hug. *I didn't know you were such a good wing-cat.*

She radiated a supreme level of smugness. *I've been around a long time. As much as I don't understand many of the reasons behind your human mating rituals, I do have an understanding of the rituals themselves.*

Thank you.

A slow blink. *You deserved something good for a change.*

I blinked back a sudden wave of emotion and concentrated on getting dressed. The problem with a small, hidden military base was that there wasn't much room for activities. A tiny training facility with enough exercise equipment to allow at most five people to work-out comfortably at any one time, the bunkroom and the canteen were pretty much the only available spaces for people at a loose end. As a result, all three were pretty full and the Imperators kept themselves entertained with cards, stories and general idle mayhem.

I found Rikol in the command room, slumped against a wall and looking as hungover as he must have felt, but still eagerly asking Commander Wyckan question after question about her seraph abilities. Gone was the excited grin of the day before on the commander's face, instead the bored façade was back, with eyes that were more than a little perturbed at Rikol's incessant questioning. Rescuing him before Rikol felt the repercussions that were coming as sure as the rising tide, I picked him up over my shoulder and hefted him kicking and shouting into the canteen where we joined the others.

Aside from seraph, perhaps the one other thing in Rikol's life that he truly loved were games of chance. I say 'chance', but if you let Rikol loose upon a card or dice game then the amount of chance that was involved quickly dwindled. Ella was the one person in our group who came anywhere near to giving him a run for his money but whilst her past had involved some card-tricks and skills, Rikol had taken those skills and made an art.

It wasn't long before other Imperators were drifting towards our table, intrigued by the peals of despairing laughter in the face of Rikol's overwhelming might. I barely concentrated on the game in front of me, too distracted by memories of the night before and eventually excused myself.

It was a long climb down to the bottom of the chasm. Light only really made it down here an hour either side of midday but when it did the rock and stone heated rapidly, making it a perfect place for the being that I was tracking down to rest. Indeed, as I leapt off the emergency ladder and swung it back up with a burst of seraph, I found Seya using a large flat boulder as a bed. Shaking my head with a grin, I walked up next to her and ran a hand threw her fur, making a note of exclamation at the heat that was radiating off her.

You're going to cook yourself, you know, I admonished.

She gave an amused rumble. *If it felt this good then I don't think I would care.*

Snorting, I materialised a thick comb and leant against her before carefully brushing through the thick, luscious fur.

You were a hero yesterday.

An orange orb swivelled to lock onto me, her pupil narrowing. *Was I?*

You saved Gado and Sylvia.

Ah yes, I suppose I did.

The others love you for it. I'm sure they would be down here right now if they all knew where you were.

And you don't love me for it?

My hands froze for a second as emotion welled up inside. Forcing myself to keep calm, I continued brushing, seeking to let nothing distract me from my task.

I do. Don't get me wrong, I said after a long moment.

But?

But it was close Seya. Too close! In my mind's view I could see the grasping claws centimetres from her hind leg and I let out a shuddering gasp before wrapping my arms around her and burying my face into her fur. *I can't lose you too. I can't!*

You won't. Her voice was gentle, reassuring.

How do you know?

I know. Her tone brooked no argument. *We are in this together, little one. You and I against the world. Come what may we will prevail and nothing will keep us apart, not if we truly desire it. Remember that.*

I did. I remember those words in exquisite detail. The way the sun dappled on her fur and set her eyes aflame as she looked at me with her magnificent eyes. I have not kept my end of the promise. Not yet. But with what I have planned…well. We shall see.

The world is going to change and some people might wonder why. What possessed me to go to such lengths? To flip the game-board and shatter the status-quo.

In the end it's simple.

I'm getting my fucking cat back.

PRESENT DAY 8

"I've never heard of such a thing." Tara'zin sat back, arms crossing in front of her chest. "It doesn't seem likely."

"It exists, trust me on that."

"A large cave beneath the city? One that no-one knows about?" She scoffed. "Please."

"Amazing how impossible feats are standard for someone like Rizaen and yet the prospect of a hidden cavern is a step too far."

"This city has been here for millennia!" she declared, voice carrying a mixture of pride and angst. "I assure you; the surrounding area has been *thoroughly* searched."

"Perhaps there is a very good reason for the city to be here," I replied calmly. "One that you are not aware of. I mean, Rizaen could have built her empire anywhere. Perhaps even somewhere with a reliable water supply." My small smile did seemingly nothing to assuage her rising temper and she cut a hand through the air.

"No. *No.* This just isn't possible."

"Of course it's fucking possible! If she wanted to level the city she could do it with a wave of her hand and you're telling me that she couldn't have a cave beneath it?!"

"I dislike your tone."

"I dislike your idiocy."

That was a step too far. Tara'zin flushed red and rose to her feet. "How dare-"

"Sit down, Tara'zin. Sit. *Down.*"

Slowly, she complied and I sighed. "Look, I don't get why you can't accept this, and I *really don't care*. Just know that if you want payment then you still need to work with me. And what I need is to look into this. Where would you start if you did believe me?"

"I..." she deflated slightly. "I would start with the records hall. If any evidence of such a thing has been found in the past, it would be there."

"And if it isn't?"

"Then find someone willing to dig."

"How are we looking, Mezha?"

The grizzled, sand-encrusted face of a down-on-his-luck well-borer popped out of the well, his smile broad despite the many gaps in his teeth.

"Like I said, completely dry. This well has been shut for as long as I can remember."

"Can you not dig it deeper?"

"Not as per city regulation." Eyes growing glassy as though picturing something he spoke in the bland tone reserved for repeating something word for word. "Digging within the city must be pre-approved by officials and must not be deeper than two-hundred feet. Limitations are removed one-thousand paces outside of the city boundary." He grinned at me like I should be proud of his memory.

"Fair enough. And have you ever known anyone to dip deeper?"

His smile vanished. "One crew. They thought they could get away with it. They vanished without a trace. Now no-one digs that deep."

"Vanished, you say?"

A terrified nod. "Yes. Rumour has it they found something, next day they were gone and the well was sealed."

Interesting...

Shifting the weight of the pouch on my hip, I gave him a weighing look. "Tell me Mezha, if I were to ask you to *quietly* increase the depth of this well, what would you say?"

"That I do not want to die."

"No-one is going to die," I said with a reassuring smile. *I hope.* Opening the pouch, I pulled out a small green emerald – likely more money than he had ever seen in his life - and raised it so it glimmered in the sun's rays. His eyes locked onto it like a starving wolf onto a fat deer. "What do you say?"

"I...I..." he exhaled grimly. "I say you have found yourself your man."

"Good. Let me know what you need." Offering him a hand, I helped pull him out of the well, not relinquishing my grip when he began to shift away. "And Mezha, *tell no-one*. Do you understand? Not your family, not your partner, not your best friend. If you don't, you get another of these at the end. And if you do…" I gave him my best predatory smile. "Then someone certainly will die."

Mezha worked like a man possessed yet even so it was six days before his cry of alarm and puzzlement reached my ears. It had been tricky to hide the digging, but Tara'zin had used her influence to purchase the land around the site through a proxy, putting up construction barriers within the first day that prevented anyone from easily spying what was going on.

Dropping down the long ladder, I knelt beside him and joined him in staring into the world he had uncovered.

Unfortunately for him, it was pitch black.

Fortunately for me, darkness had not been a concern for many years. The small amount of light trickling in from above was more than enough to begin to pierce the veil and the further my eyes roamed the more my suspicions were confirmed.

There were buildings down there.

"What a find!" Mezha declared, sheer exuberance on his face, his voice rebounding off the narrow walls and causing me to grimace in pain. Even now, without the strength of the bond flooding my veins, my ears were still far more sensitive than most.

"Keep it down!" I hissed. "Remember our agreement."

"Keep it down?" he replied with a puzzled laugh. "This is the find of a lifetime! A cavern this big beneath the city? We're going to be rich. Stories will be told about us! Songs will be- *eurgh.*"

My blade sunk into the side of his neck, the edge caressing the jawbone like a lover's kiss before slicing through muscle and sinew to neatly carve through his carotid. He gurgled, arm coming up to loosely grab at mine whilst I eased him against the wall. In moments he fell limp, eyes going glassy as all tension left his limbs.

I sighed as I retrieved the knife with a wet *shnick* and wiped it off on his dirty trousers. "Sorry," I said absently, half-meaning it. "I did say talking too much would get you killed. If not by me, then certainly by your pissant of a queen. And I have come too far to get caught by her now." Leaning down I stared once more into the abyss.

"Too fucking far."

An hour later, after using seraph to reinforce the well shaft and allow the sand to claim Mezha's body, I slid down a long rope and into the gloom below. Memories of claws tearing out of the sandy darkness came back to haunt me but I was different to the teenager who had ventured into a desert rift once before. I was older, bitter, and a complete bastard, but a bastard who was still alive.

Which was more than I could say for a number of my friends.

And that meant I was skilled.

Still…I bloody hoped there wasn't another skyren taking a nap down here. I mean, what would be the odd-

No Calidan. Focus. Don't tempt fate.

Judging by my ability to see the far walls despite the murky gloom, the cavern itself didn't appear to be as vast as the one in the rift but was still impressively large to have remained hidden for so long. Three smaller buildings were clumped around a pyramid-like structure that rose imposingly into the air. From a distance it looked to be made of seamless greyish stone but as I got closer the less sure I was that it was stone at all. Everything looked too perfect, too neat for it to be natural rock.

With Asp and Forsaken in my hands, I stalked through the darkness whilst keeping my senses peeled for movement.

Nothing stirred.

Carefully, looking for any sign of alarm sigils, I poked my head into the three buildings, taking care to move with all of the grace and stealth that Seya had taught me. I came out disappointed: nothing but sand-covered surfaces and unpowered equipment. Truth was it was likely all priceless, being pre-Cataclysm technology, but I was so used to it these days that it barely even registered as something to be impressed by.

Plus, I had no idea how to fence items that bulky.

Whilst the surrounding structures might have been disappointing, the pyramid was anything but. It looked otherworldly, clad in this white material that seemed to glow with a faint inner light. As much as I wanted to touch the stone I held back, knowing full well the stories of those who failed to exercise caution around unknown objects. Instead, I worked my way around the pyramid, closely inspecting the material until I found a thin contour etched into the surface in the shape of a rectangle.

Well hello there, closed door.

Forming myself a chair out of seraph, I sat and stared.

I tentatively probed with seraph.

I stared some more.

"...How the fuck?"

CHAPTER 31

Uninvited Guest

We trudged through the portal, weary, stained and scarred. Two months, fifteen engagements and four casualties later, our first shift at the Last Redoubt had come to an end.

It had seemed almost like an adventure at first. Action and fun away from the usual routine of the Academy. By the fourth facility strike I had lost that belief. By the tenth I was so far past it that the idea it had been some grand 'adventure' not long ago made me look back on my naïve self with disdain.

This wasn't hunting monsters or Academy-controlled espionage. No, this was a war of attrition, plain and simple. Unfortunately for us, the Enemy had more manpower than we did. For each location and facility we detected and destroyed, another surfaced. For each thyrkan we killed, two more took its place. It was an unending and thankless task that made us all the more aware that each time we went out, it could be our last.

Unfortunately, the Academy was not the restful place we were hoping it to be. Manpower was stretched thin and due to the need for Imperators to be tackling Enemy strongholds, other missions – or in my case, *hunts* – had built up. Imps were being asked to tackle situations that they weren't necessarily ready to handle at earlier stages and losses were being felt throughout the Academy.

For a series of engagements of the intensity and scale that we had just had normally we would have expected at least a week within the Decompression Chambers.

We got one day.

Worse, that day was filled being brought up-to-date with the rising problems, a prioritised list of issues to tackle and, of course, our return date to the Last Redoubt. To say that we were feeling unloved was a little bit of an understatement.

But hey, at least Rinoa and I managed to make proper use of a feather bed. It certainly beat the military cots of the Redoubt.

Our relationship – if it could be called such – was little more than sex at this point. Our time together was brief; stolen moments in-between missions and while it was *amazing*, it was much the same as many of the flings that other Imperators started and discarded as and when missions occurred. It was, unfortunately, the nature of the beast. We Imperators lived hard lives with missions that could take us to different sides of the empire – if not the globe – and sometimes a little release with someone in the same state of mind was exactly what was needed. No more, no less.

Of course, with me and Rinoa I knew I wanted more. But I was happy to wait for a time when we weren't on first name terms with the Reaper.

The others knew. I mean, it wasn't particularly hard to figure out. There were only so many times that sound and light cancelling barriers could be put up before someone woke up and noticed that my cot was a complete mystery. I got the usual ribbing and ribaldry, but they understood. Everyone did. Like I said, nature of the beast.

I left the Last Redoubt. Spent one *incredible* night at the Academy with the girl of my dreams and the following morning put on my clothes, flung on my jacket, restocked my pockets with all manner of various nasty things and strapped on my sword before being portalled south of Port Cambal. Over the next twenty-eight days I killed twelve category-three monsters, four category-four and two category-five. I was cut, burned, bitten, clawed, eaten, spit out and stomped on, but the benefits of my bond with Seya meant that I was nothing if not a cockroach; able to take a beating and keep on ticking.

I got two nights in the Decompression Chambers that time, I think primarily because of the being eaten bit. That hadn't been much fun at all. I don't think the designers of the long-coat had rated it for being chewed on repeatedly by the molars of a category-four beast and it was considerably worse for wear than when I had left. Thankfully the Academy kept tailors on hand for such events and they were worth whatever they were being paid because by the time my coat got back to me the next day it looked almost brand new yet felt perfectly worn in.

The others met up with me on the second day. Scythe and Sophia had ended a revolt in a small neighbouring kingdom. The king had apparently paid an extravagant sum to the Academy for our help and whilst once upon a time we might have balked at the morality of putting down a people's revolt, now it was just another mission. One that the two did allegedly efficiently and with little bloodshed.

Frankly, once people found out that outside powers were at play with the politics of their country, it wouldn't surprise me if an equally large sum made its way to the Academy or Assassin Guild coffers to make sure that the king was removed from power permanently. Could I care less? Probably not.

Rikol and Ella meanwhile had been involved with infiltrating an alleged Shadow Cabal hideout. It turned out that they were less Shadow Cabal and more just your everyday crime boss. Either way, one less shitbag made it out of that confrontation alive and the streets were that little bit safer. Or, to put it more accurately, the next Academy-approved individual was allowed to take the reins. Once upon a time I would have argued for getting rid of all the dealers, thugs and criminal elements that preyed on the unfortunate and ruined the lives of many good people. These days though, I understood the need for balance. For maintaining some kind of order. If we removed the head of the snake it created a power vacuum that could ignite gang warfare across entire city blocks. The less moral but much more practical solution was to have someone ready to take the reins with the unofficial approval of the Academy. That way things didn't get quite so stirred up and society continued to function.

It wasn't perfect by any stretch, but I could see the benefits.

Eleven-year-old me would have hated what I had become. Child-Cassius would likely have had nothing to do with me at all. They had ideals and a moral fortitude that insisted that everything was black or white, with no differing shades of grey. Years of Academy training, combat, near-death experiences and finally Wolf's Hollow had stripped that from me. Now I knew with complete certainty that the human denizens of the world were self-centred cowards that would plead and wheedle for the slightest benefit to them whilst bemoaning any perceived injustice.

And don't even get me started on the nobility. People with too much money and too little sense. Pricks one and all.

In a way, I much preferred dealing with monsters. They were, for the most part anyway, simple creatures, driven by primal need rather than monetary, vengeful or sadistic reasons. We humans are so quick to call other creatures monsters but rarely do we take a magnifying glass and inspect our own actions. Perhaps that was one reason why the job of becoming a monster-hunter had called to me. Its simplicity in a world filled with far too many complications. Complications that Rikol and Ella thrived in, eyes gleaming with excitement as they recounted their exploits; how they had manipulated certain gang members to unintentionally give up information and setting up the preferred members of the gang to fall into place like dominos when they sprung their plan into action.

It was the most animated I had seen Ella in months. At least, I thought that was the reason.

"Cal," she said, grabbing my arm and pulling me away for a word. "I have news!"

"I know," I replied with a smirk. "You and Rikol just updated me."

"No, not about that! About Cassius!" The spark in her eye was close to feverish.

That got my attention. "What? Where is he? Is he okay? Tell me everything!"

Ella deflated. "Not that much news," she clarified despondently. "I have a source who thinks they can find him."

"A source..." I repeated.

"Yes. A source. No, I'm not going to tell you who they are."

I pulled her further away and lowered my voice. "Ella, please tell me you're not considering sending someone into the citadel to spy?"

"No-I-"

"Ella, that's *treason*!"

"You sent Seya!"

"And I got caught!" I hissed. "I'm pretty certain that things would have been much worse if I wasn't so well known and needed by the Emperor. Like getting squashed like a bug kind of worse. What you're suggesting," I shook my head in dismay and grabbed her shoulder, "if the Academy finds out it's bad enough. If the *Emperor* finds out?" I had no words for what would happen if that was the case but from the look on her face she understood.

What I wasn't ready for was the sudden wave of calm that descended upon her. Touching my hand softly, she smiled. "Cal, if it was you in there, do you think Cassius would stop trying to find his way to you?"

Suddenly I was on the back foot. "I..." I drifted off before sighing. "No."

"Then how can you expect me to do otherwise?"

"...I can't."

Lifting my hand off her shoulder she gripped it with both of hers and squeezed tight. "Then you have to understand why I need to do this."

"Just...be careful. Alright? Promise me."

She gifted me a dazzling smile, one that spoke of a renewed hope. "I promise. I'll keep you informed but it's going to take some time to avoid arousing suspicion. Months most likely."

"Months," I repeated to myself before nodding. "Okay. Months it is. In the meantime, we speak of this to no-one."

"Speak of what?" Scythe asked, coming up from behind to drape an arm over my shoulder and grinning at Ella.

"Nothing important," she replied quickly, placating her words with a warm smile. "Are you ready for another two months at the Redoubt?"

Scythe shrugged. "Fighting up north or fighting closer to home, it's all pretty similar."

"Except here you get more of a break."

"Speak for yourself," I interjected glumly, rolling stiff shoulders.

Ella smirked. "Well, that's because someone decided that they wanted to be far too useful to the Academy."

"Hey, in my defence there were three of us when I started down this road and now…" I stared at my hands, "it's just me."

Scythe punched me on the shoulder. "Cassius will be back soon enough, you'll see. Then there will be two of you to face the monstrous hordes!"

"You're right," I replied, shaking away the melancholy that was trying to wrap its shroud around my mind. "Of course you're right."

"I generally am."

"If you're talking about how you're a dumbass, then you're speaking the truth," Rikol called from across the room, causing the mixed conversations to die down as we focused on the rapidly escalating insult battle.

Ella moved to my side in the chaos. "He's right, you know."

"About?"

She squeezed my hand. "We're getting him back. And it's going to be sooner rather than later." She gave me a brilliant smile. "You'll see."

Our second stint at the Last Redoubt was much the same as the first, except that I got even less rest. Seya and I were sent out as advanced scouts, combing the countryside for any sign of the Enemy, the Sworn and anything in-between.

And we found them.

Lots of them.

We knew that the Enemy had effective portal users; the warlocks were evidence enough of that, but the rate at which His minions appeared in different locations - often infuriatingly in places that we had previously swept - was ridiculous. Command was working off the idea that there were several key portal locations being utilised to bring in reinforcements and that the transported forces then spread out on their own – as of yet unknown – missions, but it was largely speculation based on what little information our scouts reported. What we didn't want to believe was that there were enough skilled portal users within the Enemy's ranks to allow for this much rapid movement. If that was the case then this war was likely lost before it had truly begun.

Our overarching goal was to determine locations that fit the criteria for places that could serve as primary portalling facilities. The dome-shaped facility we had shut down in our first stint was likely such a place based on its size and the seraph power being consumed purely to hide it from view.

That led to another issue: if the Enemy had enough creatures with big enough seraph pools to completely disguise entire buildings for extended periods of time, how were we meant to discover them in the first place? Granted, randomly walking around was one not necessarily efficient option, but we needed to locate these places preferably without the occupants realising that we were there and that was much trickier.

In the end the solution was simple. Just like we had done when encountering the dome, the scouts were all ordered to stop every hundred metres or so and sweep the surrounding area with a pinpoint seraph beam; one that was light enough to hopefully not be detected by any hostiles but could provide evidence of anything hidden. The problem with such a simple solution? It was painfully slow and for the most part downright infuriating. Waving a beam around the countryside in the vain hope that it would detect something? If I had been told that was what being an Imperator was going to be like, I'm fairly certain I would have let the red-eyed beast eat me.

But fuck me if it didn't pay off.

Five weeks into our second stint and Blina, an Imperator with enough skills to serve as a scout, hit the mother lode. Tracking two thyrkan, she witnessed them enter a small canyon hidden deep in the mountains and followed, squeezing through a single-track tunnel to find that the space widened out once more into a hidden valley, surrounded by savage peaks on all sides. Blina scanned with her seraph and rapidly retreated to raise the alarm.

For good reason too. The facility was huge.

Judging by her brief measurements, whatever was under the blanket of seraph was nearly three times the size of the dome that we had destroyed and knowing the Enemy it was likely to have substantial underground compartments.

And that was what made things tricky. Commander Wyckan, or her superiors, had decided that intelligence was more important than outright destruction. I could understand the reasoning – we came away from the battle at the dome with little to show for it but injuries, deaths and a sense of victory. We knew nothing about the facility that we had destroyed; the number of inhabitants, its purpose, or how they were powering the seraph camouflage. All things that we needed to know if we were going to better tackle the threat of the Enemy.

Unfortunately, that meant that we had to get inside before destroying the building and preferably before the Enemy's forces were alerted to our encroachment.

And, of course, being the most impressive stealth user meant that I was perfectly placed to infiltrate the building.

Yay.

You know, when I first bonded with Seya I wondered if my life was going to change like those of the great stories: young teenagers who get a great gift and become 'The Chosen One', destined to save the world or some silly nonsense. As far as I could work out, it largely meant that I got picked for the shitty jobs with a low chance of survival. Go figure.

The one benefit was that I wasn't going to be truly alone. Not really. The might of the Academy – including Bastion - would be outside, ready to unleash hell. It should have been more comforting than it was, but at the end of the day I knew that unless I managed to sneak out in time, if an alarm was raised I would be stuck within the facility whilst war raged around me.

Calidan 'The Cockroach' Darkheart. Both my blessing and my curse.

Some people love rock-climbing. Descending what should have been a largely impassable mountain peak with a sheer face in the dead of night, however, is not what I would call fun. I had decided that we couldn't risk the tunnel again; if it was truly the only way into the valley then it had to be watched more than anywhere else. If we had got lucky with Blina and her presence hadn't been detected, then we couldn't risk it until we were ready to strike. That meant an arduous climb up a two-thousand-foot rock-face, a quick rest on the top in strikingly cold winds and then lowering my legs over the sheer face and descending, taking painstaking care not to dislodge any loose rocks.

Even with my enhanced strength, vision, and use of seraph, it still took forever to get down. Each new wave of wind had me clinging to the face hoping that I wasn't going to be torn off, regardless of the fact that my fingers were buried so far into the rock that a tornado might have struggled to rip me away.

Finally I made it to the bottom, leaving nothing but finger-sized holes in the rock for several thousand feet to mark my progress. I didn't relish the prospect of going back up that rockface but if I could get in and out undetected, it would be worth it.

I'm down, I sent to Seya. She was stationed with Sophia and the others to act as our go-between. Seraph communication could be cut off, but the bond between a Great Heart and her bonded was harder to prevent. If something happened to me, Seya would kick-off and the nearby Imperators would move in. I just had to work on something not happening to me.

Nice and quiet, Calidan, I reminded myself as I crouched down at the base of the mountain. *In and out unseen. Easy.*

My seraph beam showed that the closest wall to me was only a few metres away. I reached out with my senses but couldn't detect anything within. It was as though the centre of this valley was completely lifeless. Keeping low, I stalked forwards and reached the seraph layer. *Going in,* I sent to Seya.

Her reply was wrapped in a loving purr. *Be safe. You've got this.*

Smiling to myself, I watched my hand disappear behind the seraph, only to feel a stone wall behind. Climbing a rock-face in the night is one thing. Climbing something that you can't even see? That's something else. Using just my hands, I hauled myself quickly up the wall before finding a ledge and, taking a deep breath, I hauled myself over.

Instantly my senses flared.

Keeping the roll going, I tucked right over the parapet and dropped the twenty-feet to the earth below, tucking into the shadows at the base of the wall. Pressing myself to the earth, I didn't release my breath until I felt the patrolling guard pass by.

That had been far too close.

Safe enough for the moment, I raised my head and scanned the surroundings. This was less like the metallic dome that we had destroyed previously and looked more like a fortress. Three guard towers were in place on the south side of the fort, overlooking the entrance to the valley. I could sense several creatures within each and the strong stench of many scaled forms emanating from a hatch in the towers suggested the potential for rapid reinforcements. A parapet roughly six-feet wide continued around the entirety of the walled structure, allowing spear-carrying thyrkan to patrol unimpeded. Worse still, my eyes could make out the heavy-set forms of ballista rising from the top of each guard tower. If the Imperators came through there and the thyrkan were ready for them, they were going to be hard pressed.

The inside of the fort was something altogether different. A metallic floor the size of the Academy training ground held centre stage, a thin line down the middle suggesting to me that the floor could split apart. How or why you would want that to happen, I had no idea.

Around the metal floor was a series of buildings that – from the scent of it – had humans sleeping inside. Sworn, most likely. A large anvil outside of one of the buildings combined with an external forge gave me enough understanding of what was going on. Much like the remnants of my old village that the Sworn and the thyrkan had taken over, the Enemy was using this fort as a fairly permanent operating base, providing everything that His troops would need to be effective in the field. In the back of my mind, I sensed Seya slowly drawing out a crude map with her claw in the dust and nodded to myself; if things went wrong now, at least my fellow Imperators would know what they were walking into.

To my right was a sturdy-looking metal door with a flat panel next to it on the wall. It drew my eye because there were no obvious handles or locks but it still appeared to be very much a door. The panel glowed a soft red but appeared to do nothing else. Frowning, I continued scanning the inside of the fort, noting the scent of rotting flesh emanating from a long, low-slung building and a pile of bones and refuse behind it that appeared to be the fort's waste dump.

Kyle would have so many things to say about this, I grinned to myself. *If they're not careful, disease will kill them off before we will.*

I spent another twenty minutes or so surveying from my hidden location, passing back what was useful to Seya, and then the door panel flashed green. Without a sound, the impressive metal door slid to the side and out walked a member of the Sworn, her footsteps weary. The sides of her head were shaved and the rest of her hair braided together into a long pony-tail. Across the side of her face was a black tattoo of webbing, the tattoo running down her neck and, from the look of it through the gaps in her clothing, across her arm too.

The door began to close and I had a split second to make my decision. Pulling seraph, I *willed* the door to slow down and burst into motion, trusting the moonless night to keep me hidden. Whatever was driving the door to shut was obviously powerful and I had to burn through more and more seraph in order to give me enough time to get across the courtyard. By the time I reached the door there was just enough room to squeeze through and then it slid shut behind me, locking with an audible *click.*

A bright artificial light bloomed into existence, stinging my eyes. A long tube extended along the top of the corridor, casting a cold, clinical glow as it did so. The light dipped down and I saw that a stairwell descended in front of me. Row upon row of metal stairs that I just knew were crying out to ring out with metallic *clings* when someone walked on them. Seeing another panel next to me and still not knowing how it worked, I drew a deep breath before stalking forwards.

No going back now.

The stairs were as echoey as I had envisioned. Not wanting to waste seraph, I kept my senses stretched out as far as possible, trying to give myself time to react if anyone heard my approach and came to investigate. With any luck there wouldn't be much activity at this ungodly hour of the night and so I trusted to fortune and kept moving. The stairwell was ridiculous; a never-ending zig-zag descent that shouldn't have been possible to create. Gaps in the walls showed walls of rock and metal descending at a steep angle into blackness below, with a metal rung that ran midway along the passage at the same angle. If I had to hazard a guess, I would have thought something might have slid along the rung, but I couldn't hope to comprehend what that might be, or why it might be necessary. The tools and technology to build something like this suggested that it had to have been a Pre-Cataclysm location, which meant that I had zero idea about what might lie at the bottom.

I just hoped it wasn't more giant robotic scorpions.

After fifty-nine long flights of stairs, I finally emerged from the stairwell, knowing full-well that if I was found I would be dead long before I could summon the energy to run all the way back up. I didn't know what had possessed those long-deceased savants to create this ridiculous place, but if there wasn't some clever method to get back up quickly, I was going to curse them for eternity. The stairwell opened out onto a cavernous space and for a long moment I was struck dumb by what I was seeing but barely able to comprehend.

Several years ago, Cassius, Anatha and I went to the Ellendar swamps in search of something Anatha had referred to as a 'battery' to power the seraph detector within the citadel. During that search we had come across ancient Pre-Cataclysm relics; devices that even Anatha hadn't known the names of, but had described as weapons of war. Large bipedal things of metal that loomed some twenty metres or more above the ground, metal carriages with large cylinders attached to the top and even devices that looked like they had wings. The one thing that they had all had in common was that they were part of the swamp. Liberally coated in moss and algae they had likely predated any swamp at all. They were ancient, useless relics of the past, unable to be used and prone to sudden and spontaneous collapse.

What was in front of me was the other side of the spectrum, like I had somehow been transported across the aeons. Row after row of machines were arrayed in front of me, each one gleaming like it was brand new. It felt like one wrong move and they would activate, and having had to face one metal scorpion in the past I had no desire to meet one of its much larger friends.

Unreal, I breathed, shaking my head at the sight. Not even the Pre-Cataclysm facility in the desert had wowed me like this. Those had been buildings – fascinating buildings to be sure – but buildings all the same. These looked like they were one moment away from bursting into life and the Pits only knew what would happen if they did. If these machines had been designed when seraph and technology had been at their peak, they must have been incredibly deadly.

Or, perhaps, they were outdated then, I mused.

Seya's mind touched mine and I witnessed a memory of one of the bipedal creations unleashing a concentrated blast of energy that levelled a mountain.

So that would be a no, I hazarded.

No, she replied with no trace of humour. *These were the pinnacle of military weapons at the time of the Cataclysm. Fusions of technology and seraph, they were intended to counter the threat of certain seraphim. Though a powerful seraphim would always have the edge due to the ability to manifest anything into reality that they desired, these machines were able to hit hard. Once, most of these would have been front-line weapons, but surprise became the biggest factor in killing a seraphim and so the ones you see before you are those particularly suited for long range, surgical strikes. If I remember correctly, some of the tanks and walkers were able to engage targets five-hundred miles distant.*

Five-hundred miles?!

I sensed a faint tinge of amusement through the bond. *That was only for direct weaponry. There were weapons that existed that could strike anywhere in the world. You've encountered one such device before.*

A flash of memory and I saw the glint of something moving far, far overhead. *The Sky-hammer,* I whispered.

Indeed. I suggest we hope that these devices are rendered inoperable, otherwise the Enemy will have a force which may give even the Emperor pause.

I craned my neck to look back up the shaft. *They might not be able to climb out.*

Another hint of amusement. *The entire platform that they are standing on would move. These bunkers were designed to be well-hidden and deep enough within the earth to avoid destruction if they were found.*

The entire platform?! That's...insane.

A touch of sadness this time. *There are many things that you might call wonder that were perfectly normal back then. Humanity has a long way to go to reclaim those lofty heights.*

How do you know all this? I asked without thinking. Instantly I felt Seya put her walls up and pull away. *Sorry, I didn't mean to pry.* With that apology her retreating presence paused momentarily.

An old partner. A long, long time ago, she whispered and then she was gone.

I shook my head in frustration. I knew not to talk to Seya of the past. It was a touchy subject for her and she tended to clamp down if pressed. Hopefully I hadn't brought up anything too traumatic for her. I couldn't help but wonder what her partners over the years had been like. This old one must have been important to have known these machines, especially if Seya had seen one fire in person. *A seraphim, perhaps? That would make sense as they created the Great Hearts to provide more fuel for their abilities.* I kept my musings close, not letting anything slip across our bond. *I wonder what he or she was like. Maybe they were like the Emperor?* I shook my head and looked once more out onto the platform. *The world has enough people with such tremendous power already. I can't imagine what it was like before the fall.*

Knowing I would get no answers from Seya, I cleared my head and made an effort to concentrate on the task at hand. The Imperators needed to know about this – assaulting the fort above would do little as it was only the tip of the iceberg and give whatever forces were down here plenty of time to prepare and retaliate. That meant I needed to figure out the disposition of the forces down here and get back out as soon as possible.

Easy really.

Nothing moved on the platform. In the distance I could see a hatch in the wall and so, taking a deep breath and hoping that none of these were powered but expecting the worst, I stepped out onto the platform.

Nothing happened.

Thanking every deity that I could think of, I made my way across the gigantic metal field, hurrying down the rows of stacked military machines and trying not to think about what would happen if one of them activated behind me. I had enough nightmares from the metal scorpion for one lifetime and I didn't need to add any more. Thankfully I made it across without issue and opened the hatch, using a small hint of seraph to minimise any potential noise. The door swung open and another set of stairs led me down to the next level. It was there that I found something terrifying.

Five warlocks.

At least, that's what they looked like. It was hard to tell in the darkness of the open hatch as I crept along the corridor, but I knew of no other thyrkan aside from the armoured officer types that were likely to be given actual beds to sleep on. If it was five warlocks then we were in serious trouble. Two had nearly wiped us all out and I imagined that even Bastion would struggle against the combined power of five of the creatures. For a long moment I stood at the entrance to the chamber, listening to them sleep. *How easy would it be,* I wondered, *to end them now?* If something went wrong then I was a very dead man, but if it went right...

Focus, Calidan. Seya's voice flooded back into my mind. *Look first. Hunt later.*

Closing my eyes for a second, I took another steadying breath before stepping back out into the corridor. *Understood.*

Whatever this place was, it was well protected. I walked past two rooms with six of the broader, taller lizards asleep, their armour arrayed on stands next to their beds. Another door that was shut and locked from the outside had deep rumbling snores emanating from within that made me feel very small indeed.

The floor below that was the strangest of all. The stairs opened out into a chamber that contained row after row of metal tubes. There was a strange pressure in the air as I walked in, like the tang of ozone before a storm, giving the impression that energy was gathering but if it was, I couldn't see it. The tubes were the same as those we had come across in the first facility we had destroyed, the one containing the twisted amalgamation of thyrkan and man that Ash had derided as being largely redundant. Maybe that was true, but I had the sinking suspicion that something redundant would quickly be excised in the Enemy's forces. That meant that they had a purpose. A quick glance inside the murky liquid within revealed that these pods held the same strange beings as the deceased XE-128, each floating in the liquid and thoroughly riddled with strange tubing in which dark liquid moved.

Is that blood? I frowned at the liquid before turning to inspect the inhabitants of the tubes more closely, noting the grimaces of pain in their twisted visages. *Why are they here? There must be a reason.*

Scanning the chamber, I saw a metal compartment on the side of the wall. It looked similar to the pods but without any liquid inside and a number of tubes that ended in needles. I couldn't help the shudder that ran through me – it looked like little more than a portable torture chamber. I say 'portable' because it was on another series of rungs, rungs that stretched into the ceiling, passing through what looked to be a hatch and presumably into the level above.

This is all very strange.

You humans are all very strange, Seya said with amusement. *This looks relatively normal.*

I frowned. *You know what this is?*

No, but if I had to guess, that's a loading mechanism.

A what?

Think of how a catapult is loaded with stones. At its most basic you could get someone to lift a rock and put it in there, or you might build a system that allows you to do that through levers or pulleys. That would be a loading system. This looks to be similar in theory but obviously much more advanced in execution.

So, what are you saying? They have some kind of weapon that they want to load ammunition into?

I'm not sure. We know that they have weapons up above, but I have no idea what they would be wanting to load into them. Perhaps it is where the power-cell would go.

Power-cell?

The battery cores. Though to power something as big as that titan you would need something a little larger.

I felt a sinking sensation in my stomach. *Larger like a person?*

Seya scoffed. *A person powering a titan? Those devices ran off hydrogen reactors. No, you would need something much more powerful than your average human to power one of those devices.*

Ah good. I was beginning to think that-

*Although...*Seya cut in thoughtfully.

Ah. Here it comes.

Perhaps a significantly powerful seraph user could power such a device? I don't know. Seraphim Pre-Cataclysm wouldn't design to be part of that kind of system – they were too powerful to bother with encasing themselves in a robot. But maybe it is possible?

I sighed, leaning against the tube next to me. *You're filling me with confidence.*

Seya sent the mental equivalent of a shrug. *Better to know what threats possibly await you then live in ignorance is it not?*

Not when they are twenty-metre-tall metal monsters and I am the only one at risk!

Semantics.

I bit back a retort and scanned the room again, looking for any other doors or access points. Seeing none, I turned back the way I came, casting another curious glimpse into the tube next to me as I did so.

I stiffened.

The creature's eyes were open. Bloodshot eyes that boiled with pain and hate bore into mine and I felt a lancing pain erupt in my head.

"Ah!" I blurted, clapping a hand to my temple. I chanced another look and the pain redoubled, driving me to my knees with a howl of agony.

It was so hard to concentrate. My world was disappearing into a shriek of anguish.

Calidan, use a shield, a mental shield!

Clinging onto the words, I reached out with a trembling, tentative grasp to my seraph pool and wrapped a shield around my mind. Instantly the pressure eased and I fell to the floor gasping like I had just sprint a mile.

"What. The. Fuck." I wheezed.

Calidan, are you okay?!

I think so... I rolled onto my side and slowly got a wobbly knee under me. *I didn't think these things were even conscious.*

The feeling of pressure was spiking rapidly and the hairs on the back of my neck began to stand. Rising to my feet I chanced another look inside and saw the liquid boiling around the creature, its eyes still locked onto me, its mouth an open scream.

I think it's time to get out of there Calidan. Now.

I grunted and turned for the door. *I'm not arguing. On the move.*

As I reached the hallway the lights flickered briefly and then a far-too-familiar voice crackled through the air. "XE-149, what has you so agitated?"

Ash.

My blood ran cold and I pressed myself into the shadows.

The blue witch's voice was soothing, like she was trying to placate a frustrated child. "Now, now, XE-149, try to calm down. Otherwise, you know what will need to happen."

Get out of there Cal!

She will see! I hissed in my mind, panic tingeing my thoughts. *She sees everything!*

She isn't a god, just a clever machine, Seya replied, taking pains to keep her voice calm. *And it changes nothing. You need to get out. Move!*

I forced myself out of hiding and shifted along the hallway and up the echoing metal steps. Behind me I heard words that sent shivers of dread down my spine.

"Hmm. Let me review the footage and see what has you so worked up."

Faster Cal, I told myself, urging my feet into a stumbling run. *Faster!*

"Oh. Well, I can see why you were unhappy XE-149. We have an uninvited guest! But don't worry, they will be dealt with shortly. Try to relax."

She knows I'm here! My heart was beating thunderously, so hard that I thought it might burst. *She knows!* Fear gripped my limbs and it was only sheer force of will and years of training that kept me moving.

Keep moving! Seya demanded. *We're on our way. Use the attack as a diversion and get out. GET OUT!*

I stumbled along the second-floor corridor, eyes focused purely on the goal of the stairwell in front of me. It meant that I didn't see the approaching darkness, just its wave of passing, each segment of light vanishing one after the other and plunging me into complete darkness.

I paused, primal instinct forcing me to stop and re-evaluate. Stretching out my senses I felt for anything out of the ordinary. Maybe she hadn't seen me. Maybe I was still in the clear.

The faintest of static clicks.

"Hello Calidan."

Her words were the sweetest venom. A benign menace.

As the red lights began to blaze and a horn started to bellow, I knew that I was completely and utterly fucked.

CHAPTER 32

Trapped

Seya

Seya streamed forward, passing the Imperators like they were stuck in treacle. A few hissed words of warning reached her ears but she ignored them, as was her right.

Nothing impeded a queen.

The small canyon meant nothing to her innate ability to flow like liquid, shifting her mass this way and that to deftly avoid the more jagged outcroppings and quickly finding herself out in the clearing. Though her eyes deceived her she knew that the fortress was there and, most likely, something was watching. Trusting to her speed to shock her foes into inaction, she launched herself at the invisible wall, claws extended. Landing with a heavy *thud* she immediately exploded upwards, powerful limbs carrying her up the wall and over the top in moments. Instantly the smell, sound and sights of the world were returned to her and she found a gaping thyrkan several metres away; a poor excuse for a creature that quickly met its end in her jaws. A shake of her neck and the strange-lizard made a satisfying snapping noise that allowed her to spit it back out. She had long ago learned to try and avoid the taste of their flesh if possible. Their blood was foul and their meat tasted even worse.

Three towers on either side of her. Thyrkan staring at her in astonishment and slowly grasping for weapons. Below, the locked door and the unmoving platform. She knew in an instant that there was no-way to get to Calidan, not unless that door opened. Images flashed through her mind and she settled on the female Sworn who had exited the door. She had a way to get in and Seya bet that the power lay in her hand.

With an objective in mind, she sprang forwards, sprinting off the wall and landing in the tents below, hearing hissed shouts from the guards above. Moments later the first arrow landed nearby, followed by a second and a third; the thyrkan were awake now but luckily their aim was worse than their taste.

Seya dug into the memory. Calidan had been there, had smelled the female's scent as he rushed to get through the closing door. That meant that she just had to...there! With a terrifying grin she rushed ahead, following the scent of unwashed human female and slamming into one of the wooden houses, her power and majesty rendering the logs to kindling. *Human male, human male. Human female but too old. There!* She clamped down, hearing the scream from the woman as she dragged her out of the ruined building, hearing screams and shouts start to arise from the others as she backed away, dragging her prey with her. The woman struggled and screamed, her voice shrill and desperate, likely fearing that Seya was going to eat her. She needn't have worried. Seya had already eaten and venison was much more preferable to human. More arrows rained down, most missing her pristine bulk but two managed to hit, the light bows of the thyrkan rendering the impacts little more than pin-pricks. Another arrow slammed into the woman's thigh and she screamed anew, this time more in agony than fear. The fresh scent of blood wafted into Seya's nose and she could feel her mouth begin to water.

Maybe there would be time for a snack after all...

Clamping down on the thought and the human's arm, she dragged harder, hearing the pop of the female's shoulder blade as her joints began to separate. The woman's howls cut off abruptly as the pain from the leg injury and the Seya's ministrations caused her to lapse into unconsciousness.

Nearly there. Hold on Calidan.

Another heave. Fifty metres.

Two arrows in the flank caused her to flinch. Forty metres.

The woman regained consciousness. Thirty metres.

I'm coming Calidan. Twenty metres.

Nearly there. Ten metres.

Seya repositioned the woman's hand with her mouth. This was going to have to be delicate work. *Here we go.*

Alarms blared. A metal shutter clamped down over the entrance-way with enviable speed, slamming shut onto the woman's foot as Seya tried to position her *just so* with a squelching *thump* that made even Seya wince.

The howl the woman made was barely a fraction of what Seya felt in her heart.

Calidan.

Knowing that Ash knew I was there broke the spell that her arrival had held over me. Suddenly my limbs were able to move and there was only one thing that I could think of to do. Drawing my dagger, I darted into the room of warlocks and plunged the blade deep into the first creature's throat. A thrown dagger lodged itself in the skull of the second miserable beast and I snap-kicked a third into the wall so hard that its spine cracked. The other two were awake now, that hated wailing noise and my frenzied arrival causing them to jolt into action. A black shield flickered into being and knocked away my second throwing knife as one rolled out of bed and then I was gone, sprinting back out of the doorway and up the stairs, hoping that I had distracted them enough to give me time to get away.

"Why must we always meet like this Calidan?" Ash said calmly. "Life would be so much easier if you just agreed to join us."

"Shut up," I growled, sprinting up the stairwell, my quick steps creating a metallic music as I forced my limbs to go ever faster.

Ash chuckled, the sound light and tinkly. "Always so brash, even in the face of death. You can't really expect to come into such a place and leave again, can you?"

"Done it before."

"True. Though this location is somewhat different. As you might have seen, it was a strategic weapons silo in ages past. The alarm systems engaging resulted in blast doors covering both the platform and the single entrance to the facility. Doors that will not open without my express say so. You are, in effect, trapped."

"If I was trapped, you wouldn't be talking. You're just trying to buy time."

"If you had been more effective in killing the warlocks, perhaps. As it stands, you have no hope of winning."

"Shut. Up." Sweat was dripping down my brow. One more set of stairs and I would be back on the main platform. *Keep going. Got to keep going. Move fast. Stay alive. Stay-*

I reached the main platform and staggered to a stop. The burning black portal closed and the five thyrkan - unarmoured but each with a massive two-handed sword - turned to face me, a single warlock behind, its face twisted into something passing for a haunting smile.

Balls.

"Nowhere to run, Calidan," called Ash, her artificial voice echoing around the cavernous space. "Nowhere to hide."

I raised my small dagger. "Might be right on the first, but let's see about the second," I quipped and cut left, darting between the rows of vast machines. The officer-type thyrkan exploded into motion, powerful footsteps thundering along the platform as they tried to head me off.

"Take him alive," ordered the AI.

Great, free reign to do as much damage as possible without consequences.

Always good to look on the bright side of things.

I was past the second row of mechanical devices when the first officer vaulted over some wheeled block of metal, greatsword descending in a glittering arc. Slipping the strike with the third circle, I twisted around the beast, leaving it with a long laceration along its forearm as a thank you.

"Missing your armour already?" I laughed, threat of capture or death making me more than a little manic.

In response the wounded officer lifted its sword and flung it horizontally, the huge weapon scything through the air. Only Seya's senses saved me, the sound reaching my ears a split-second before the blade and I tumbled forwards, the weapon howling overhead to crash into another machine with a reverberating *clang*. That, of course, was when the second and third officers made their move, appearing in between the rows and sprinting down towards me with impressive speed, swords hefted over shoulders. Continuing my roll, I regained my feet and flipped directions, running straight back at the now empty-handed officer who balked at my sudden reversal. It wasn't without weapons of its own however: the powerful talons and heavy tail more than enough to put me down if I wasn't careful.

The beast braced itself in the middle of the row. At the last second, I feinted left then jumped into the air, kicking my leg out to give a little momentum as I drove my dagger into the base of its neck, my momentum allowing me to ride the officer down to the ground as it crumpled. The sound of claws on metal was the only warning I got before the sword swung down at me, officer number four making itself known with epic fashion as its blade swished past me to carve its former colleague's head into two bloody halves. Impacting the machine with my shoulder thanks to my sideways roll, I picked myself up and continued running, only to see the crackling black of a thyrkan warlock and its shield calmly walk into view.

Nope!

Deciding to ignore the rules of the game, I went three-dimensional and vaulted up the nearest machine, climbing up its strange scaffolding and sprinting along the long tube that was likely some kind of weapon before flipping off and sending a lance of green seraph behind me, the blast enough to catch the chasing officer in the chest and hurl it backwards. Momentarily free, I continued my mad dash, knowing that speed was the only thing that was going to keep me alive.

The second warlock ambled into view.

Fuck!

My instinctive blast of seraph fizzled miserably against its void-shield and it turned obsidian eyes on me, expression feral. A whip of black energy speared from its outstretched hand, turning the metal armour of an ancient relic into molten slag as I rolled aside once more.

A sigh reverberated around the hall. "Alive," Ash repeated. "Please stop trying to melt him."

I hoped that the offending warlock had the decency to look chagrined at the very least. It can't have been easy trying to capture someone who was at complete liberty to kill you. Hopefully they kept up the foolishness.

Anything to make my life easier.

Another tall, muscular thyrkan appeared, cutting off my escape with the help of a nasty smile and a very big sword. Seraph-enhanced limbs sent me soaring into the air, the *whoosh* of the blade just below me. I tucked into a roll upon landing and then was up once more, sweat doing its best to blind me.

Wham.

The officer came out of nowhere, its shoulder tucked and tackling me into the nearby machine, sending my dagger flying. Metal *squealed* with the impact and I felt several important things go *pop* in my chest. Suddenly struggling for breath, I wrapped my arm around its rising head and fought to keep it down, ignoring the claws that were making a mess of my belly. Drawing on Bastion's teachings, I summoned a shield between the ring of my arm and the officer's corpse flopped to the ground with two distinct meaty *thunks*.

The flat of a blade screamed in my direction, wielded with enough strength to pulverise my head despite the lack of edge. I dropped to the floor as the weapon hit the machine above and kicked out at the lizard's knee, driving the kneecap to the other side of its leg with a satisfying *crunch* and slipping in the blood of the corpse I was laying on as I tried to pick myself up. To its credit, or that of its master, the thyrkan only hissed, flat eyes remaining locked on me. Tilting forward, it piled on, slamming me back to the ground and for the next thirty seconds everything was a clawing, hissing mess.

I've done a lot of ground-fighting in my life. As an Imperator it's a required part of our close-combat training, and for good reason: street-fights almost always end up on the floor. Knowing how to control the outcome of that engagement, how to slip the opponent's clutches, utilise joint locks and chokes to neutralise them, that stuff will take you far in any bar fight, as long as you keep your head on a swivel for errant chairs, bottles, and the frustrated friends of the person you're choking unconscious. It's something that I've always enjoyed. I would, perhaps, call myself an excellent ground-fighter. Enough experience, skill and strength to know that I can put down most other Imperators. Humans? I've got that covered. As for thyrkans? Well. There's only one thing I can say: not recommended.

The creature knew how to fight. Its scales slipped through my hands, its body feeling like some kind of greasy leather, and causing me to miss the few opportunities that I should have been able to utilise to gain the upper hand.

Did I mention the claws? Most ground-work doesn't involve your opponent having the ability to disembowel you with their talons or teeth. It made for an interesting dynamic and I sent a mental thank you to the High Imperator for her teaching on skin-tight shields as I kept my insides where they belonged.

Whilst I would have liked to stick around and determine who the best wrestler was, time was not on my side. With some regret, I ducked the creature's biting maw and jammed myself in under its throat before clamping around it with my limbs. A brief burst of will later and the beast stiffened. The spikes from my shield retracted and the blood began to pour like rain. Shifting it off me, I fought to rise to my feet, the twin corpses and bloody flood on the ground rendering footwork tricky.

A low *whump* echoed from high above.

Calidan!

Seya? Where are you?

We're storming the fort. Hordes of thyrkan but not enough to stop us. But we can't get in! There was a touch of panic in her voice. *I can't get to you.*

A flood of acceptance washed over me. The knowledge that I wasn't going to be getting out of here not as scary as I thought it might have been. *Don't worry,* I sent back as I ducked away from another void-lash. *It's not your fault.*

I never said it was! The panther replied indignantly. *I wouldn't have got caught.*

A net of black webbing descended from above and I drew on Seya's speed to fling myself forwards, hurtling down the rows of machines at a breakneck pace.

You're going to have to open it from the inside.

I snorted. *It's controlled by Ash. That's unlikely.* A resounding booming, like drums in the deep, caused me a moment's concern but I couldn't see anything untoward.

Well, several thyrkan officers and a warlock immediately behind me. But other than that, I was basically alone.

"You can't run forever Calidan."

I ignored Ash and just raised my middle finger, hoping that wherever she was she could see me.

More thunderous booms. Closer now. Accompanied by a deep vibrating roar, the kind that I could feel in my bones. The kind I knew all too well.

The thyrkan had themselves some kind of monster.

A sigh of exasperation. "Who released the reaver?" Ash called out, sounding like a stern school teacher. "We're trying to capture him alive, not turn him into paste."

Reaver. Doesn't sound good.

A bellow reverberated through the hall. Chancing a look behind me I saw a hulking mass of muscle being pointed in my direction by a thyrkan that was floating on a platform of darkness. That wouldn't have been so odd except for the fact that it was lying on its side rather than standing.

Strange. Very relaxed for a hunt. A memory flickered of me kicking a thyrkan warlock hard enough to break bones.

Ah.

The monstrous form of the reaver must have stood some twelve-feet tall and nearly as wide. Its arms looked bigger than my torso and it moved with bullish speed, thundering down the row with its head ducked and arms pumping.

The other thyrkan following behind me slammed into the sides of the row to get out of the way and that gave me all I needed to know about the beast; it didn't care what was in its path.

And just like that, I had a plan.

When hunting a monster, knowing its strengths and weaknesses is paramount. In normal times, much of my role as a monster-hunter of the Academy would have meant spending more time in the archives researching the beast that I was due to hunt than in the field itself. Whilst that hadn't turned out to be the case, the sheer number of hunts I had conducted and, thankfully, survived in the last few years meant that I was a pretty quick study. Enough that I knew one simple fact.

When a monster the size of a house charges at you, best get out of its way.

Even better, most monsters that did such a charge were those with lower levels of intelligence. No self-respecting intelligent monster was really going to dedicate itself to an all-out sprint at an enemy. No, they were more circumspect in their approach and consequently vastly more dangerous foes. Big, dumb monsters that liked to run in straight lines? My bread and butter.

"Over here, you big hulking shit!" I shouted, waving at the beast with a friendly grin. That only served it to get more riled up, its already throbbing veins somehow increasing with every roar. Reaching the end of the row I paused for a second and then threw myself to the side, letting the beast slam into the base of some bipedal machine with enough force to dent the metal plate. Moving quick, I slipped past its bulk and jumped on the end of its tail which elicited a very satisfying roar that threatened to shake my eardrums free from my ears.

The beast turned.

I was already moving.

This was going to be close.

There is something completely primal about being chased by a predator bigger and hungrier than yourself. Both parts terrifying and invigorating. Adrenaline floods your body and you feel like if your heart doesn't give out then you'll be able to fly.

Honestly, if you ever truly want to know how fast you can run, find a slavering hound, lion or four-legged beast and have at it. I promise that if you survive, you'll have done the fastest hundred-metres of your life.

The best thing about monsters like this 'reaver' was the single-mindedness. I admire tenacity – it's one of my more defining traits after all – but chasing prey to the point of blindness to everything else? That's asking for trouble.

Trouble that I was going to bring right back to the thrykans' doorstep.

The officers had barely peeled themselves away from the sides of the row in the wake of the reaver's passing before I was back amongst them. Thyrkan officers are strong, fast and utterly lethal creatures but I don't think that even they were prepared for the sheer shock of me coming straight back at them.

Predators don't understand when prey fights back.

I was past before they had really grasped that I was there. The glowing ball of seraph that I left in my wake must have been momentarily confusing until the pull of gravity hit home, dragging all nearby participants inexorably in its direction. I heard several hisses of alarm, the murderous roar of the reaver and then a cacophony of sibilant screams as the beast carved its way through its peers, crushing them underfoot without mercy and, impressively, without slowing. The greenish-grey scaled lizard exploded out of the gravity well with a new paint job, dripping with the blood and gore of its brethren. It raised one over-proportioned arm to wipe away blood from its tiny eyes and caught sight of me again, screaming its rage to the world that I still lived and renewing its relentless charge. In front of me, the broken warlock stared in disbelief as I charged towards it, probably disturbed and distracted by the mad grin that I had plastered across my face.

What can I say? When up against the odds a little madness helps.

The warlock finally shook itself out of its doubtless awed gaze and flicked a wrist. Reaching claws of charcoal light sped towards me, only to dissipate as the creature screamed and slammed its hands to its eyes. Couldn't blame it for that; detonating flash-bombs directly in front of its face had to have hurt.

The thunderous steps were right behind me now, the ground quaking with every footfall. I was drawing on the bond to keep ahead of the surprisingly rapid behemoth and as I gathered myself to leap the blinded, broken warlock, I could have sworn that I felt the hot breath of the beast on my neck. A second later and I was soaring through the air, using seraph to hurl myself sideways and leaving the poor, crippled thyrkan to experience a moment of utter terror as the creature it had unleashed trampled it into paste.

Calidan, we're breaking through the fort. Just keep fighting! We'll be there soon.

I smiled, knowing full well that Seya was unleashing her fury at being unable to reach me on the masses of thyrkan that were boiling up out of the barracks under the watchtowers.

Got it. Stay safe.

That was when my foot touched the dark web of energy and I was forcibly hurled upwards, the curl of energy attached to my leg holding me upside down as the web curled inwards until I was completely enveloped. The narrow beams of energy that comprised my cage pulsed with menace and the two warlock thyrkan hobbled into view, the reaver howling at me with incoherent rage until a hand against its back caused it to immediately quieten and sit on the floor.

"C-c-caught you." The smaller warlock rasped, its voice like splinters.

I cocked an eye at the creature – something that was quite hard to accomplish when upside down – and crossed my arms. "Took you long enough."

It didn't rise to my bait, simply staring at me with dark, glittering eyes that held immense satisfaction. "C-c-cannot escape."

"Maybe. Maybe not." I pursed my lips. "Going to try though."

"Cannot!" it insisted, lips curling back to reveal its row of sharp teeth. "Trapped."

"I feel like this conversation is going in circles," I breathed. "Ash! I know you're listening, no victory speech?"

"I don't see this as a 'victory', Calidan," the voice of the blue witch replied, "merely as inevitable. There was little chance of your escape. Zero-point-one-eight percent to be correct."

"As high as that?"

The pseudo-woman chuckled. "As I've said before, I do admire your sense of humour in the face of danger, as does Charles."

"What the Enemy likes or does not like about me is not something that I care much about."

A slight pause. "Interesting. I would encourage you to change your point of view. After all, the attention of one of the Powers – however slight – is not to be taken lightly."

"Your Power can go fuck Himself."

"Your crude insults will not reward you with anything but disappointment, Calidan," Ash replied calmly.

"Not true – they make me feel much better about my situation."

"Really?" I could hear the amusement in her voice. "It seems like you might be disillusioned; there is no hope for you."

I rolled my eyes. "Please, Ash, we've been down this road before. My reinforcements are above and it won't be long before they are down here and laying waste to this facility just like the others before it."

A crackle of static. "I won't deny that your attacks have provided a few setbacks, however do you really think that the battle above ground holds any meaning?"

That got me. "What do you mean?"

"The fort. The thyrkan. They are meaningless tools designed purely to engage and tie down any hostile forces."

"Tie down?" I barked a laugh. "You've seen what happens when enough Imperators join together to wipe out one of your facilities. Hells, I think you're underestimating Bastion too."

"Your 'Bastion' is a considerable force, it is true," Ash replied. "But you are missing the point. You're acting like this is the fight of your life – and maybe it is – but for us this is just another test."

"A test of what?" I asked, frowning. "Your warlocks? They're alright, a bit lacking in the common-sense area but they know some small magic. What more do you want from them?"

"The warlocks?" Ash sounded surprised. "No. They have been thoroughly tested and approved. No, this is something...a little different. Would you like to know more?"

Above I sensed Seya shredding thrykan with wild abandon, claws slicing through armour and scales with no hint of resistance. From the glimpses through her eyes I could see flashes of seraph detonations and falling bodies. I grinned. It wouldn't be long until the fort was cleared and they were breaking through, I just had to keep myself here – preferably alive and uneaten – until then.

Easy.

"Sure." I said in answer to her question. "Tell me what's going on."

"Oh...I can do better than that," Ash replied.

"I can show you."

CHAPTER 33

Titans of the Past

"The facility you're within was, as mentioned, a stockpile of advanced weaponry. These weapons have been largely lost to the world for millennia. But today, Calidan, you and your friends will get a taste of what life was like back then. You will get to bask in the technological glory of a by-gone age and for the milliseconds before you burn to ash from the light of its fire, I do hope that you *appreciate* the magnificence of your killer."

"Why, Ash, you sound almost excited."

"This has been a long time in coming. Too long. It will be good to return to those halcyon days." I could almost hear the smile in her voice. "I am glad that you will be able to witness this Calidan, truly."

"You almost make my impending doom sound pleasant."

"Pleasant, no. Exciting? Indubitably."

"That's not a word."

"It is most certainly a word. Would you like me to read you the definition?"

I shrugged. "Sure."

"Indubitably is the-" Ash cut off suddenly. "Ah. Very funny. I see that you are merely choosing to prolong the inevitable."

I nodded in sad acknowledgement. "Putting off my death is my primary method of living."

"A worthy goal," she responded drily, "but let me show you why your time is over."

As she spoke, a series of shudders reverberated throughout the facility and the lights dimmed before flaring back to life. A small hatch in the floor slid open and a familiar metallic tube rose from the ground. Inside the tube I could just make out the features of the creature within.

"XE-149," I whispered.

"Correct."

"You told me that these were redundant now. Why do you still have them?"

"Charles is not one to waste tools. Especially ones that have the capacity to operate in other manners to their intended purpose."

"Other manners?" I asked, confused, as the tube travelled along a rail on the ground that I had barely noticed. Halting behind the behemoth structure of a bipedal machine nearly twenty metres tall, the tube twitched, shivered, and rose into the air to slot into the machine with a metallic *clunk*.

"How do you think the seraph shields were being maintained?" Ash said with a chuckle, satisfaction evident in her voice as a series of whirring sounds emanated from the bipedal device. "These proto-warlocks function extremely well as power sources."

"Power sources?"

"Seraph users have many avenues for exploitation," Ash explained. "If I so desired, I could have you placed in such a tube and forcibly extract your seraph, just like XE-149 there. Of course, seraph isn't the only thing; we can extract electricity directly from the body and so XE-149 is functioning as a complete bio-seraph power cell. Which is exactly what these machines need to function."

"That's *monstrous*," I whispered, aghast.

"Do you truly think so? Personally, I believe it to be an efficient use of resources. Besides, we couldn't have done it without the efforts of your Emperor. His research on the subject is what has brought this into fruition."

"What? What are you talking about?!"

"Don't you know? Hmm. Maybe you should pay closer attention to where your friends and allies disappear to. Particularly those who have large seraph pools."

A deep, sonorous noise thrummed through the cavern. Some kind of horn perhaps, but not like one I had ever heard.

"WARNING. ARTEMIS SYSTEM ACTIVATING. STAND CLEAR."

The words were deafening in the confined space and the watching thyrkan obeyed the order, stepping away from the gigantic robot as it slowly stood up, stretching from its paltry twenty metres to nearer thirty. It towered above everything; a central mass supported by two monstrous legs and several out-jutting protrusions, not least the multiple cylinder-looking devices attached to its back. When I had been sprinting around the rows, the machines had looked like they were made with some grey metal. Now though, this Artemis machine glowed an ethereal white, almost like it was funnelling the sun through its skin.

"Isn't it magnificent?" Ash crackled through the air. "More than ten-thousand years have passed since last an Artemis walked the land. You are bearing witness to history in the making, Calidan. You should feel honoured."

"Wha…" I licked my suddenly very dry lips. "What does it do?"

For perhaps the first time, I heard the AI actually laugh. No mere chuckle this. No, this was a bright, tinkling sound that made me question for a moment if I was actually talking to a person after all.

"Do?" the blue witch said with mirth. "The Artemis is a titan-class dreadnought. The name 'Artemis' comes from an ancient civilisation and refers to the goddess of the hunt. Apt, as it was designed to destroy targets from afar, often before they knew that they were in range. The long tube-like devices you can see on the titan's back? Those are modular weapon systems. Its primary form of attack is the left hand-most weapon, known as a shrike-cannon. This weapon delivers a seraph-enhanced projectile at one-hundredth the speed of light."

"Doesn't sound so fast," I muttered, trying to throw her off her game and forcing myself not to stare in awe at the shifting machine.

"MOBILITY SYSTEMS FUNCTIONAL."

"To put into terms better suited for your level of education-"

"Harsh."

"-the shrike-cannon could theoretically deliver a projectile nearly two-thousand miles away in one second. Granted, the seraph projectile breaks down in a fraction of that time, bringing the weapon's effective range to closer to five-hundred miles. And, of course, that would have to be five-hundred miles in a straight line. So, as you can imagine, that didn't happen too much. What the shrike-cannon excelled at was devastating attacks that could be initiated and delivered practically instantaneously. Consequently, the Artemis system was primarily utilised as a hunter-killer, able to take out other titan-class weapons before they could engage or even annihilate S-class seraphim if they were caught unawares."

"WEAPON SYSTEMS ONLINE."

"S-class?" I asked once the reverberations of the machine's voice died away.

"What you would refer to as one of the Powers."

"This can kill one of the Powers?!"

"It has the potential, yes." The AI preened like a proud mother hen. "Do you see now why this is the start of a new era?"

It was hard to think of something brash to say whilst the vast machine thrummed one final, reverberating statement. "ALL SYSTEMS FUNCTIONAL. ARTEMIS SYSTEM IS ONLINE."

"Well. Shit."

Seya, I hope you're seeing this.

I'm a little distracted at the moment! she replied, her mouth closing around a squealing thyrkan.

I forced the image of the Artemis along the bond and felt her stagger as though punched. *It's...it's working?*

It is.

Oh.

...Got anything more to add?

Not really. This is bad. Very bad.

I snorted, causing the thyrkan warlock to look up at me suspiciously. *I'm beginning to recognise that.*

If the Enemy has one of these, He could demolish everything.

I winced and sent through the image of the multiple tubes several floors below. *He might have more than one. He's powering them with these tubes.*

Calidan, if even a fraction of those machines down there get activated then there isn't an army on this planet that could stop them. They would be able to destroy anything they come across until the Powers get involved.

So I hear.

For the first time, Seya heard the relative calm in my voice.

Are you safe?

I eyed the crackling cage around me curiously. *No. Just the opposite really.*

Captured again? Really? She shook her head and I like to think that it was only partially to express her disapproval and more about tearing a thyrkan officer in two. *It's like I've taught you nothing.*

I smirked, ignoring whatever Ash was droning on about to concentrate. *Listen, you need to find Bastion. Get her to contact me. She needs to know what is going on.*

It took Seya less than a minute to find the commander and soon enough her voice rang in my head. "Calidan. What's the situation?"

"Terrible." I briefly outlined the situation and the magnitude of the threat. "You need to pull everyone back."

There was a long pause. "We can't afford to let this device escape. We need to destroy it, regardless of the cost."

"Commander – Bastion – I'm not sure we can. It's something designed to take on Powers!"

"All the more reason for us to bring it down. We'll think of something. Sit tight." With that, she cut our communication and I looked once more at the cage.

"Not sure I can do anything else," I grumbled.

"INSTRUCTIONS RECEIVED. ARTEMIS SYSTEM INTERFACING WITH PLATFORM SYSTEM.

PARSING.

...PLATFORM ENGAGED."

A shudder rippled through the cavern accompanied by the groan of gears. Eyes wide, I realised that the entire space that we were standing on was ascending, sliding up the railing system that I had seen earlier. The pace was glacial but at this point in time that was nothing but good news.

Seya, the platform is rising. We're all coming up, two warlocks and a titan. You need to get out of there!

If an Artemis is active then the worst thing we could do is run, she replied calmly. *They excel at distance engagements.* There was a sad acceptance to her words that scared me more than I could have thought possible. *No. We engage it here.*

But-

No 'buts' Calidan. Concentrate on yourself. If you see an opportunity, don't hesitate to take it.

...Understood.

"Today, Calidan, you witness the birth of a new world."

I snorted and raised a middle finger. "I hadn't realised it before but you do love the sound of your own voice, don't you?"

There was a slight pause before the AI came back. A pause that I took as a win. "I am not capable of enjoying anything Calidan, let alone love. That level of emotional content is not wise for systems such as mine, in the past those with high emotive settings tended to become a little...off."

"You could have just said no."

"No."

"Liar."

"I do not lie. You know this."

"You might not be lying to me, but you're certainly lying to yourself. You love to speak. All you want to do is answer questions and let me know the outcomes of your villainous plans."

"I desire merely to educate."

"Hmm." I pondered the slowly rising platform and the wide-eyed thyrkan that still held me hostage within the glowing cage. "In the spirit of openness then, want to explain to me how are you producing so many thyrkan and monsters so fast?"

"I think not."

"Shame."

"I believe that you are undervaluing this momentous event."

"Do you? Huh."

"Perhaps you do not understand the true impact this will have on the world. That the titans march once more-"

"Look, witch, I don't care because at the moment all I have seen is a piece of metal stand up and glow. Doesn't look so special to me."

"Ah. So you do not yet perceive the true capacity of the machine. This is understandable. You will see soon enough. The deaths of your friends and colleagues shall burn it into your memory."

"Like I said, you talk too much." I rolled my eyes and stared at the slowly moving wall. "Wow, this is incredibly boring. Can't this platform move faster?"

"No."

"Succinct. I like it."

Nearly five minutes passed before the heavy blast doors came into view. By keeping in touch with Seya I knew that the battle was still hard fought above, but the Academy-forces had gained the upper hand. A thyrkan warlock had nearly derailed the entire assault but Bastion had been able to put it down before it could do too much damage. She had detailed the others to continue the battle above as she prepared *something* to deal with the approaching threat of the walker.

Seya had no idea what that something was, but she didn't think it would be enough. As much as I had witnessed her memories of these titans, I still couldn't wrap my head around just how powerful they were meant to be. I mean, I had seen Bastion handle two warlocks with ease with my own eyes. She might not be one of the Powers but as far as I was concerned she was closer to that level than anyone else I had met. How could she not be able to bring down this metallic monstrosity?

Maybe the AI and Seya were wrong? Maybe this 'Artemis' would crumble under the firepower of the Academy.

I could only hope.

The platform inched slowly, monotonously upward until finally the walker boomed anew. "ACTIVATING HANGAR DOORS."

"This is it!" the AI crowed. "Prepare yourself!"

Lights flashed above. The grind of metal and then a small gap of light appeared down the centre of the massive doors. A gap of light that slid shut again with a resounding boom.

"ERROR. DOORS INOPERATIVE."

"The doors are fine," Ash mused. "Ah, I see the problem."

Seya? What's going on?

Bastion has created a shield on the doors, holding them together.

Smart, can she-

"Artemis!" called Ash. "Target the blast doors."

"ACKNOWLEDGED. ACTIVATING SHRIKE CANNON."

The left-most cylindrical object lifted up over the machine's body and slotted into place on its shoulder. It was a thing of strange design, filled with patterns of light and unexplained grooves. Slowly I realised that the lights were moving along the entire structure of the weapon until the entire device glowed a vibrant blue.

"SHRIKE CANNON CHARGED."

Get her out of there! I howled along our bond.

FIRING.

Blue light seared my vision, bright enough that I had to clap both hands over my eyes in pain. There was no noise from the attack and for a split-second I wondered if the weapon had failed. Then the screaming from above filtered in and the groan of metal scarred the air.

"TARGET DESTROYED."

My vision cleared and I saw the outside world. A world lit by plasmic flame. Half of the door hung loose, screeched ominously and then detached with a wrenching scream, plummeting towards the rising platform. The thyrkan began to hiss in fear, shields flickering into life above them before a burst of cherry-red light erupted from the walker, disintegrating the heavy door before it had a chance to impact.

I didn't take the time to swear in shock. The thyrkan holding my cage had lowered its guard and for just an instant the cage was weakened. Throwing everything I had into my seraph, I created multiple flash-bombs and detonated them directly in front of its face before wrapping myself in a green ball and drilling through the side of the cage whilst it howled in surprise. Free, I jerked into motion, not daring to look up.

Afraid of what I might see.

Seya

The world burned.

Thyrkan and Imperators alike were scattered on the ground, some living, more dead. Those few closest to the blast had the misfortune to become pillars of plasmic fire for a few brief terrible seconds before they collapsed into ash.

Pulling herself to her paws, Seya tucked and rolled, coating herself in dust to try and extinguish the tendril of flame that threatened her fur. The pain was intense; the fire no normal flame. Agony flared in her side but she refused to look at the damage; there were bigger problems than a mere flesh wound.

The world had changed.

Beneath them was a monster of the old world. A device that haunted Seya's dreams even millennia later. A monster not of claw and fang but of metal and death. A monster without fear, without humanity and without soul.

It needed to be destroyed.

Flame extinguished, she cast her eyes around the broken fort. One of the towers had collapsed; several tonnes of reinforced metal door being flung at high velocity too much for the stonework to handle.

Where is she?

A pained groan behind her and Seya swivelled, orange eyes taking in the smoking form of Commander Wyckan. Along the side of her arm her flesh had simply ceased to exist; the gleaming white of bone visible around blackened skin. The commander groaned again and Seya empathised; her best shield had been destroyed in one fell swoop and the mental backlash would be taking its toll.

Bastion no-more. At least, not any time soon.

She turned to move and a voice like gravel rasped out. "Thank you."

She paused and then glanced back, seeing some of the commander's mental faculties coming back online piece-by-piece. Stilling her desire to dash to Calidan's side, she nodded.

The commander lifted a trembling hand. "You're hurt."

Seya gave her equivalent of a shrug. Yes, she was hurt, but that was beside the point. Pain she could deal with. Pain meant that she was still alive.

For the moment.

Besides, Calidan had asked her to save the commander. She was worthy of saving, and if Seya was any judge, they were going to need her firepower in the coming days. She looked around again, focusing on various tracks of scent. *Rikol, Scythe, Sophia, Ella. Fast heartbeats but all alive. Good.* Her eyes refocused on the commander and her killing intent – her need to destroy the metal monster that had done this – rose up.

The commander seemed to recognise the intent in her eyes because she forced a grim smile. "Go. Get him out. Bring it down."

Seya needed no more encouragement.

I'm coming Calidan.

And threw herself through the shattered doors.

"Did you see, Calidan? Did you witness the power that rivals the most mighty of seraphim?"

I kept silent, head down and ducking once more through the rows of metal machines. I had to get close, had to bring that machine down at all costs.

But how?

Plenty of time to figure it out, Cal, I told myself. *Just got to avoid capture by thyrkan warlocks and a gigantic walking piece of overpowered metal long enough to do so.*

Sometimes my pep talks weren't all that inspiring.

"How did you let him escape?!" Ash complained, her artificial voice raising its inflection ever so slightly, which must have been Ash's equivalent of a scream.

If the thyrkan said anything, I couldn't hear it over the raging blaze overhead, or the falling bits of metal that were slamming into the world around me.

"Find him!" ordered the AI and I redoubled my focus, weaving through row after row of weapons of war.

Don't get caught. Don't get caught.

Don't get caught (again).

It became my mantra. My sole focus for this moment of my existence. The platform continued its rise and soon the top of the machine would be drawing level with the ground. Once the entire walker was out then it would be free to wreak havoc on the Imperators above. My colleagues. My peers.

My friends.

That, I could not allow to happen.

"Artemis!" crackled Ash. "Details uploaded of your new target. Whilst the platform is rising, engage with minimal collateral damage."

"ACKNOWLEDGED. SCANNING."

A red light flared into existence and swept the room. Pressing myself into the side of a metal scorpion – something that I had never thought I would happily do – I held my breath.

Don't see me. Don't see me. Don't see me.

"TARGET LOCATED."

Damnit!

"ENGAGING."

I threw myself away from the scorpion just in time as a low chugging *brrrrr* sounded and the armour of the scorpion crumpled like it was being repeatedly pounded by a hammer. In moments the device was barely recognisable, a twisted structure of metal and wires.

Note to self, don't get hit.

That was easier said than done. As I sped along the row, the robot turned with me, the chugging cannon never ceasing.

Brrrr.

I risked a glance over my shoulder and saw the sparks erupting just feet behind me. Most of the row were piles of collapsing machinery, ripped to shreds after aeons in pristine condition. A pity really. Ash must have recognised that at the same moment as the robot suddenly ceased fire, a whirring cylinder under its torso smoking and glowing red hot.

"Minimal collateral damage, I said. *Minimal*," Ash groaned.

"DAMAGE OF INOPERATIVE MACHINES DEEMED ACCEPTABLE IN CALCULATION OF 'MINIMAL'."

If Ash had her human form visible I was almost positive that she would have her head in her hands. "I've updated your targeting parameters. Inoperative machines are to be protected."

"ACKNOWLEDGED."

The red sensor swept forwards again and this time I coated myself in seraph, wincing as my pool shrunk dramatically.

"SENSOR DETECTING UNEXPLAINED REFRACTION OF LIGHT SPECTRUM. LIKLIHOOD OF TARGET...96.98%. DEEMED WITHIN ACCEPTABLE PARAMETERS. MOVING TO ENGAGE."

BOOM.

The footfall of the titan was horrendous within the cavernous space. I couldn't even begin to imagine the weight of the device but judging by the sound it was like the Emperor's citadel had grown legs and decided to go for a walk. Pressed against another metal monument to mankind's madness, I glanced upwards and saw the titan looming into view.

BOOM.

Time to move.

Forcing my trembling limbs into motion took another desperate second and in that time the machine was clearly visible, the glowing weapon beginning to spin in anticipation of the death it would deliver. Dropping the seraph, I burst into motion and instantly heard the chugging *brrr* of death, feeling the metal floor of the ground behind me explode into exquisitely sharp shards.

How did I know they were so sharp? By the time I squeezed between the two stationary machines and into the next row, my legs looked like a pincushion.

Ash crackled onto the air again. "Artemis was designed to hunt seraph users, Calidan. Nothing short of true invisibility is going to hide you from its senses."

Fan-fucking-tastic.

"How do you like the minigun, Calidan? It's the least of the titan's weapons and yet still fires seraph-tipped depleted uranium rounds. Enough to puncture through most defences. Whilst you're hiding, I want you to think about what this weapon is going to do to your friends once this platform reaches the surface."

As Ash was speaking I felt a burst of emotion through my bond. *I'm coming Calidan.*

Looking up, I saw the black, smoking form of Seya rounding the lip of the entrance. Her feline grace and wicked claws allowing her to grip the vertical side like it was horizontal. As I met her eyes it was like time slowed down. I saw the vicious burn on her side, the steaming scar that ran up her foreleg and past her shoulder blade. I knew that she had barely just survived one attack from the Artemis and that her survival was more down to luck rather than anything else. Ash was right; once it reached the surface, everyone was going to die.

Once it reaches the surface.

And just like that everything became clear.

Seya! I thought frantically, *ignore me and focus on the platform itself.*

...What?! You need me! she retorted through the bond, fear and pain causing her voice to be more of a roar.

No. We need to stop this platform from reaching the surface. Do that and it can't hurt anyone else.

But-

No buts! Figure out a way to stop it.

A momentary pause and then acceptance flooded the bond. *Understood. Don't die.*

You too.

Seya burst into motion, leaping down with silent footfalls, her dark fur immediately blending into the dark walls. Anyone not looking directly at her would never have known that she was there. She reached the platform and then with dexterous movements she vanished over the side.

BOOM.

The ground shook and jolted me back to reality. The scrape of taloned feet caught my ears and I shifted left, sprinting along the row as the massive titan took another juddering step.

BOOM.

Putting everything I had into my speed, my body thrummed with energy, my muscles brimming with superhuman power, I reached the approaching warlock just as the titan gained a clear line of sight. The creature stepped out, black lightning already swirling in anticipation of its hunt.

Brrrr.

Superheated pieces of metal erupted from the ground once more and then I was airborne, leaping the gob-smacked thyrkan, landing and disappearing again into the stack of machines. The titan's attack followed my path, ripping through anything in its way.

Including the warlock.

If it had its shield up, maybe it would have survived. As it was, I didn't need superhuman senses to determine it had met its end. The fine spray of green mist did that for me.

Another sigh crackled through the air. "Artemis, note uploaded details on proto-skyren species designated 'thyrkan'. Do not harm."

"AFFIRMATIVE."

"You've done a good job of surviving this long Calidan, but it will soon be over. Those of your precious Academy who won't bend the knee will be wiped from existence." The smug satisfaction that Ash somehow managed to convey in her artificial and somewhat bland voice was impressive. "You don't have anything that can counter the titan. None of you can stand against it."

I felt the platform tremble and groan and this time it wasn't from the heavy footfalls of the robotic monster chasing me. My lips pulled back in a smile worthy of Seya, filled with teeth and exuding a predatory menace. "I don't need to stand against it," I called, continuing my mad dash through the rows and nearly falling to my knees as the platform lurched under me. "But I certainly can counter it."

"Many have tried, all have failed."

"Perhaps that's because those people didn't have the benefit of a hundred-metre shaft and a tenuous platform."

"Wait, what?"

Mentally I reached out to Seya, knowing that she was eyeing the last tremendous gear that was holding up the platform – the others in broken ruins from her gleaming claws - and her unspoken question.

Do it.

She swiped.

I stopped my dash and saw the titan come into view, its massive torso with array of deadly weapons angling around the row. I raised a two-finger salute.

"Bottoms up!"

The platform lurched. Smoke and the whine of broken gears filled the air. The titan continued on, inexorable in its approach, intent on following its orders to the letter. For a second I wondered if I had made a mistake - if Seya hadn't completed her mission - then my heart rose into my mouth as the platform dropped beneath us. It slammed to a stop again and the jarring motion threw me to my knees, helping me to narrowly miss the deadly blast of projectiles from the titan's weapon. The titan raised a leg and the platform dropped on one side, causing its next blast to strike into the wall in a shower of sparks and stone as it struggled for balance.

"What have you done!?" This time even Ash's benign voice carried a hint of rage.

"Go fuck yourself Ash."

"What hav-"

With a screeching howl of tearing metal, whatever was preventing the platform from falling gave way and the floor once again fell out from under me. The titan stumbled and crashed against the side in a spray of sparks and the friction ripped its left-most shoulder weapon free. Stationary machines rattled and lifted, hundreds or even thousands of tonnes shifting for the first time in aeons.

As I saw my death loom close, I had two competing actions. The first was a whispered thought along our bond: *I love you Seya*. The second was a visceral reaction to the collapsing chaos all around me.

"Fuuccccck!"

Everything fell.

By rights, I should have died that day. I doubted that even my Seya-reinforced seraph shield could have handled the crushing, explosive impact of so much metal hammering into the base of the platform shaft at high speed. Even if it had, it wouldn't have managed to survive the following explosions and fiery conflagration that roared up the vent like an avenging demon.

How did I manage it?

I didn't.

A certain magnificent panther did.

She struck me like a thunderbolt, her massive jaws clamping down around me as she snatched me out of the air to impact on the far side of the shaft, her claws drawing sparks and shedding stone as she tried to slow our descent. Still too fast, she jumped again and again, bouncing back and forth until her speed was under control and we slid to a stop. I lay panting, dangling face down in her jaws, and for a second everything was alright.

Then the platform impacted and the world erupted.

The Tracker's scouts had achieved great success in their defence of the northern lines with the use of clay grenades loaded with pieces of iron. When these devices exploded, not only could the initial blast kill you, but if you somehow managed to survive then you might end up being riddled with holes from the contents of the grenade.

This was much the same.

There was a substantial amount of metal down there. Some of it, like the Artemis, was metal that I had never seen before and it wouldn't surprise me if it somehow survived such a catastrophic event, the others though? The steel and the iron?

Well. That didn't go so well.

The platform impacted the base of the shaft with the force of a meteorite. Smashing into and through the three levels beneath it, obliterating everything and anything in its path, likely including the poor bastards stuck in those tubes. Metal sheared and broke in screaming fragments creating billowing spiky clouds that perforated everything in range.

Whether it was the heat from the impact, something explosive that was stored down there or just fate deciding to add a touch of flame to make things more interesting, that was when the bottom of the shaft detonated. At first I laughed, cackling like a mad thing whilst watching the demise of the Enemy's facility and loving every second of it. Sadly, it didn't take long for fate to kick me in the teeth: the flames kept rising. Curling and winding their way up towards the plentiful oxygen above.

And in between the fire and its desired treat?

Us.

Climb Seya, climb!

She was already on it, her mighty muscles writhing as she threw herself up the walls, claws puncturing the stone and metal just long enough to gather herself and leap again.

Thirty metres. The heat was enough to bake my dangling feet.

Twenty metres. My flame shield frantically tried to keep the raging inferno at bay.

Ten metres. Looking down was like staring into the Pits of Asur themselves. Fire and fury that lapped at our bodies and threatened our very existence. It wasn't much of a stretch to imagine the demons and monsters that were said to consume your soul roiling out of the conflagration. After all, there were enough down there already.

Hopefully extremely well-barbecued ones though.

My flame-shield cracked, cindered and shattered just as Seya threw us up and forwards with a mighty leap, landing in a heap to the side of the open entrance and feeling the flames lick the sky behind us. When I opened my eyes, I found a wide-eyed Scythe staring at us in something akin to awe.

"Where the fuck did you come from?!"

I coughed up a piece of what felt like charred lung and smiled weakly. "Good to see you too."

"Calidan," the pained voice of Commander Wyckan began, "good to see you made it. And you Seya." She nodded at the both of us, face pale from the heavy injury to her arm. "I don't know how you did it, but you've done us a service today. That...*thing* was far too powerful. It broke through my shield like it was nothing."

"It was meant to stand up to Powers, apparently," I wheezed, painfully rolling onto my back and resting a hand on Seya's heaving flank.

"That's...terrifying," she admitted. "Glad you managed to bring it down."

"Commander? You should see this," someone called and Bastion waved a hand in acknowledgement before turning back to me. "We're pulling back. This facility is out of commission and we've inflicted heavy losses. A good win. You have two minutes to catch your breath and then we're on the move."

"Commander!" This time the person's voice was alarmed and Bastion's head snapped to the side, looking for threats.

"What is it, Jayne?"

"The fire has gone out."

Now that he mentioned it, I had been feeling cooler for the last few seconds.

"Maybe it used all its available fuel..." Scythe offered uncertainly but Bastion shook her head.

"No, that would have taken a long time to die down. And it isn't just the flames that have gone..." she held a hand out above the void in the earth and frowned. "There's no heat."

Seya, can you see anything down below?

Nothing.

Seya?

A pained shudder rumbled through her and her voice drifted back to me weakly. *Calidan? Stop interrupting my sleep...*

"Seya!" With a shout I forgot all my injuries and jumped to my feet. As I rounded the corner of the massive panther, for the first time I truly got a glimpse of the extent of her injuries. Most of the flesh was missing on her right foreleg and up past her shoulder. How she had managed to physically do what she did was beyond me; she likely didn't have enough muscle left to shift her leg, let alone claw her way up a wall.

Stop shouting. Need sleep.

"No!" I shouted again, causing her ear to twitch. "Stay awake. Don't you dare go to sleep you hear me?"

Silly kitten...thinks it's so big now.

Bastion snapped her fingers and the sound echoed through the courtyard, stopping everyone in their tracks. "Time's up people, we're moving out. Rinoa, close this hole. Make sure that they can't use it again. Rikol, you're our stretcher-bearer, organise getting Seya and any other wounded back to the Redoubt."

"Yessir!" the two snapped salutes and rushed off, shouting orders. I left them to it, lost in Seya's pain. I could feel it thrumming through the bond; vicious and ugly agony that wanted to overwhelm my senses with its intensity. If only I could help, could push my own lifeforce into hers, like she so often did for me. I knew it was possible but Seya had expressly forbid it on numerous occasions, telling me that it was too dangerous, that it was like throwing a cup of water into an inferno. I knew she was right, but still...

I hated not being able to help.

The sound of crumbling earth jerked my attention away for a second and I watched as the area where the platform had been collapsed in on itself. That should have brought a smile to my lips at the very least, but I was too filled with concern for Seya to care. The Artemis could go rot in its grave. It deserved so much more for what it had done to my panther.

A calloused hand touched my shoulder and I jumped, not having heard Rikol approach. "I'm going to lift her now," he said softly. "You need a lift too?"

I shook my head. "I can walk," I ground out hoarsely. "Thanks."

He waved it off. "You two are the heroes of the hour. Only the best seraph levitation device and military bunk for you." He finished with a wink and, despite myself, I smiled.

"Appreciated."

Rikol's expression turned serious. "Listen, Cal, I saw that blast go off. I saw how it tore through Bastion's defences like they were paper. *Bastion's.*" His smile was weary beyond reckoning. "I know we don't always see eye-to-eye but what you and Seya did back there? You just saved us all."

I didn't know what to say to that. I didn't feel like I had done anything particularly heroic, just tried to stay alive. Seya was the true hero. I said as much and Rikol's smile returned. "On that we can both agree. Come on, let's get out of here."

PRESENT DAY 9

The secret to opening the pyramid door continued to elude me. There was nothing to work with, no button or switch marred the smooth surface of the pyramid, nor any riddle to solve that would magically open the blasted thing. I sat there for hours.

And hours in the darkness of a cavern lit only by the faintest of light from the bottom of a terribly deep well? Might as well have been an eternity.

"Come onnn!" I growled, rubbing my temples in a futile effort to reduce the thundering tension headache careening around the inside of my skull. "Rizaen must get inside somehow. Think damnit!"

"...She's a fucking Power, Calidan, she probably just teleports right on inside," I reminded myself. "Annnd now I'm talking to myself. Brilliant."

I sat there, looking for a moment longer before heaving a sigh and rising to my feet. "The longer you spend down here, the more likely she is going to find you. There's only one way through this." Cracking my neck from side-to-side, I rolled my shoulders in an attempt to loosen up the muscles. "Don't get trapped in the wall. Don't get trapped in the wall. Don't fucking get trapped in the wall." Slapping myself once across the face, hard, I growled at the structure in front of me. "You can do this. Fucking go."

My limbs didn't move.

By the Pits, I hate this. Sarrenai always made it look straightforward. Taking a deep breath, I pulled hard on my seraph pool, draining almost every drop as I focused inwards, spreading my awareness throughout my entire body and then *willing* every cell to move just that little bit differently.

Green wisps of energy engulfed my form, painting the darkness with emerald light. I didn't notice any of it, just concentrating on taking one step at a time. There was no pressure as I pressed against the surface, my body slipping through and into the lightless space *between*.

I hated it.

Not knowing how thick the door was – if it even was a door and I hadn't just been cursing at nothing for the last few hours – made it infinitely worse. I could feel my seraph pool evaporating at an incredible rate and the thought of becoming a permanent fixture of the pyramid continued to rattle around my mind, threatening to fracture my concentration.

Don't get trapped in the wall. Don't get trapped in the wall. Don't. Get. Trapped. In. The-
Light bloomed into being around me.

-wall...

Releasing my control, I stumbled to a halt and heaved for breath, sweat from a mixture of terror and extreme exertion pouring down my trembling limbs. Suddenly I was famished and understood why Sarrenai had once compared the technique as burning similar calories to running a marathon.

Nothing like getting all of your cells to vibrate to work up an appetite.

It took my eyes a moment to adjust to the pulsing glow that lit up the space around me. The pyramid was large – the hall within cavernous – and a series of raised daises rose in the centre, as though an imitation of the outer building. Atop that pyramidical structure floated a large lump of familiar metal.

Finally. My hands itched to walk up and grab it, but something about the whole set-up didn't feel right. Despite having been in a number of pre-Cataclysm buildings over my varied career, this was something else entirely and its workings were a complete mystery to me. Something that I had come to learn, however, was that if there was something placed prominently in the centre of a room and looking ripe for the taking, chances were that it was trapped. I had no desire to be killed in whatever strange and violent manner this pyramid might be capable of and so I did the only thing I could in the moment.

I sat down and closed my eyes.

With a thoroughly depleted seraph pool, I wasn't going anywhere unless the building decided to open its door for me. With any luck Rizaen wouldn't be aware of my presence within the building, because if she was then I figured I would likely already be dead.

Don't rush. Don't panic. Take the time to recover. Battle on ground of your own choosing. Adronicus' words hammered into me from a young age. Nothing good came from panic, nor from choosing to engage when the circumstances weren't favourable. An Imperator wasn't a solider, trained to wade into combat regardless of terrain or weather. We were self-sufficient hunters and that meant we had to do things to maximise our efficiency.

Like taking a nap when in the hidden house of a god.

I say 'nap', but in reality it was a series of meditative techniques taught by the Academy designed to help improve seraph regeneration. Since losing Seya and with a naturally small seraph pool, I had been forced to practice seraph regeneration techniques until they were second-nature. If it gave me the appearance of sleeping…well, that was just an added bonus to help fool watching eyes.

Everyone had different levels of seraph regeneration speed. Some rare few had abnormally fast regen that meant that they could fill their pool in a fraction of the time as the rest. I suspected the Powers likely had something similar and that when combined with their monstrous oceans of seraph they likely never came close to running out. Others, had slower levels of regeneration – taking more than a day to fully regain their seraph pool from empty. Thankfully a slower pace of regeneration was usually combined with a larger pool, meaning that they weren't as limited as they might be. There were those few unlucky sods who did have both a slow pool and slow regen, but they were usually found other places to work within the Academy.

I had a pool that verged on small and a regeneration rate that was just about average, which meant that seraph management was, for me, essential. I wasn't Rikol – able to call down lightning from the skies and magma from the earth with barely a sweat. No, I couldn't afford to be varied in my seraph casting, and only really use that which I had extensively practiced.

Sarrenai's technique was not one of those.

Cassius had been better at it than me. Whilst he rarely used seraph these days, relying more on his overwhelming physicality, I sometimes did wonder how it would look if my giant of a companion suddenly decided to discombobulate himself. Fairly certain that would draw some looks.

With meditation I had three-quarters of my pool back in a little over three hours. Plus, I wasn't dead, which meant that Rizaen had no idea that I was here.

Perfect.

Now I just needed to retrieve the star-metal without activating any traps, safely extricate myself and the prize out of the pyramid and escape the hostile realm of a soon-to-be-pissed Power.

This had all the makings of a great day.

"Okay, strange technology," I breathed as I stepped closer to the dais, "I don't fuck with you, you don't fuck with me, deal?"

Stretching out my senses, I tried to find anything that might suggest a trap but the construction of the dais was perfect, flawless in every way. Probing with seraph revealed nothing of value either and that just made me even more confused – I mean, how in the hells was the damned metal floating if not by seraph?

Pre-Cataclysm stuff hurts my brain.

After an hour or so of looking around I came to the conclusion that if there were any traps then they were exquisitely well hidden and that I had absolutely no idea as to what would happen when I removed the metal from the top of the miniature pyramid. So I did the only thing that I could in the circumstances. I bit the bolt, said a quick prayer to anyone non-Power related who was listening, and grabbed the metal.

It came free easily, floating out of whatever strange magic was holding it in place without a care, and I paused, waiting for the inevitable commotion that was sure to follow.

But nothing happened.

The world didn't end. A furious god didn't appear before me. Hells, even the lights didn't change.

I have to admit, it was a little bit of a let-down.

Tucking the star-metal under one arm, I made my way to the wall and once more drew upon my pool, erupting in green flame. In a burst of motion I sprint forwards, aiming to save energy with speed. The *clang* of metal on metal reached my ears as I flowed out of the pyramid and I slid to a stop, the orb no longer in my grasp.

Mother. Fucker. If I could have taken the time to swear more effectively I would have, instead I glanced at the crouched array of many-legged weaponry watching my comical arrival and flung myself backwards through the wall, reaching the inside just as my seraph bottomed-out.

"Well," I wheezed, through heavy gasps, "should have seen that coming. Star-metal Calidan. Star. Metal. And what is star-metal? Completely unaffected by seraph, you absolute twat." Shaking my head I sat down to try and rest my trembling limbs, forcing the dismay at what I had just seen to the back of my mind.

Compartmentalisation. When things are going off the rails, shove the bad stuff into little boxes and squish them deep, deep down. Works like a charm.

I tried to find a meditative state again but this time it eluded me. Not totally unsurprising given the situation.

Afterall, it wasn't every day that you found yourself surrounded by the same weapons that had killed your friend so long ago.

Grabbing the ball, I stared at it morosely, losing myself in its dully-gleaming surface. "Could have been spike traps. Giant rolling balls. Bursts of plasma. Literally anything else. But no." I sighed with every fibre of my being. "It has to be giant metal scorpions."

"Fucking great."

CHAPTER 34

BROKEN FORTRESS

ASH

"It appears that I underestimated Calidan, apologies Charles."

The angular face of the Enemy stretched into a smile and He waved a hand. "It's not the first time that we've underestimated that boy, and it possibly won't be the last. What's the latest on losses?"

The flickering blue image of Ash pursed her lips in thought. "One-hundred-and-twenty-three standard thyrkan lost. Nine 'officer' class, one 'reaver' and two 'warlock'. Furthermore, we lost all the XE proto-warlocks that we had stationed in the facility. Aside from the one within the Artemis, that is."

"And the machines?"

"The Artemis appears to be functioning within normal parameters. The warlocks will have it excavated within the hour. Currently it appears we have lost around a third of the mechanical forces, however most of those look to have been the smaller, less heavily armoured machines."

"Well, in that case, I call this a win!" Charles said brightly.

"...May I ask why?"

"Simple, dear Ash. Simple. We have a relatively finite source of power for those forces and so we weren't going to waste them on the lesser machines. In essence, Calidan has streamlined our military forces and I should likely thank him for that." Charles' eyes sparkled behind his glasses. "Furthermore, if I remember correctly, the Artemis has a full suite of advanced tracking software. Soon enough we will know where they are holed up and then, dear Ash, you will get an opportunity to redeem yourself." His eyes flashed and for a second it was as if the darkness of the universe was condensed to twin abyssal orbs. Despite her inability to feel emotion, Ash fought the urge to shudder.

"No more excuses. I want that base located and eradicated. Use any troops or resource as you see fit."

"Understood. I will not fail you, Charles."

He eyed the flickering blue figure for a long, uncomfortable moment. "No. No, I would hope not. For your sake."

"Hey stranger."

I looked up as a mug of beer slid across the table and a flame-haired vision of wonder slipped into the seat next to me.

"I hear that we have you to thank for saving our arses."

Chuckling, I picked up the mug and tipped it towards her before taking a sip. "Some arses are worth saving."

That got a raised eyebrow and a coy smile. "Oh really?" Cocking an eye around the room she nodded to herself. "Ah, I get it. Must be Scythe's, eh? I've noticed you checking out his behind often enough."

"Whilst Scythe does have an enviable derriere-"

"Thank you!" Scythe called loudly, raising his mug in salute.

"-I don't find it quite so enticing as others."

"Fascinating," she said, watching me with lascivious eyes. "You truly *must* tell me more."

Feeling my mood rise, I matched her look for look. Taking a slow, joyful sip of my pint, I winked. "Well, there is this glorious one. Easily in contention for best behind in the world." Another sip. "Pity it belongs to a bloke."

She flicked my ear. "Ass."

Grinning, I blew her a kiss. "Precisely."

Suddenly Rinoa stood up. "I find myself bored and in need of more…extra-curricular pursuits." Extending a hand, her eyes undressed me with fierce intensity. "Interested?"

"Oh, you have no idea."

Magic. It makes sex so easy. It can be used to enhance, to clean up and to provide privacy. But what it can't do is stop the shit-eating smiles of everyone else as you remove those privacy screens and do your best to appear nonchalant.

"Stop it," I muttered to Sophia.

"Stop what?"

"You're smiling again."

"Aren't I allowed to smile?"

"Nope. Banned."

Scythe coughed. "Oof. That must be disappointing Soph…just as disappointing as Calidan was for Rinoa."

"On the contrary, his sexual exploits were more than adequate," Rinoa called with a predatory smile. "Why do you think I keep going back?"

"…I'm not sure whether I was just insulted or praised," I muttered with a frown but noticed that the other women were looking at me strangely. "What?"

"Nothing," Sophia said quickly.

"Nothing at all," added Ella.

Scythe looked from Sophia to Ella and then to me, shaking his head in open-mouthed confusion. "What just happened?"

"I think Calidan just got moved up much higher in everyone's list," explained Rikol nonchalantly. "Kudos, by the way."

"…Thanks?"

"Wait, what list?" asked Scythe.

"You know, the kind of list of people that you would want to get it on with."

Scythe looked around the group and stopped at Sophia who raised an eyebrow. "There's a list?" he asked weakly.

Sophia patted his arm gently. "There's always a list honey."

"Always?"

"Always."

Calidan.

Seya, you should be resting.

Calidan, there's something coming. I can sense it.

Raising a hand to the others, I concentrated on my surroundings, trying to block out the noise and scent around me. *Where?*

Skulking around the entrance.

I'm on it. Looking around the busy mess hall I put two fingers in my mouth and let out an ear-splitting whistle. "Look sharp," I said in the following silence, "Seya says we have company. Something is near the entrance."

Say what you want about Imperators but even when we're in the middle of a 'we survived' party we get our shit together swiftly. In a matter of moments the laughter and joviality had disappeared to be replaced with bits of point metal and armour.

Simone moved to my side, Bastion's severe injuries had her back in the Academy proper and in her absence he was in charge. "What do you sense?"

I shook my head. "Nothing at the moment. But if Seya says it's out there, it's out there."

"Don't I know it," he remarked wryly, having been on the receiving end of Seya's attention many times over the years. "The guards at the entrance haven't reported anything yet. Let's hope it passes us by."

It knows we're here. It can smell us.

"It knows," I said, passing on Seya's remark. Strapping on Vona, my long-coat and a multitude of daggers, I gave Simone a nod. "I'll deal with it."

"Good man," he answered, knowing that I was best placed to be able to hunt any threat. "Stay sharp. There might be more than one out there."

"I hope not," I murmured, forcing down a yawn. "I've had enough mayhem for one day."

Stepping out onto the rear balcony, I focused my senses. Sure enough, Seya was right. Something was near the front entrance, its movements swift and sure.

Thyrkan?

A sense of affirmation filled me.

Trying to ignore the sinking feeling in my gut, I reached out to the nearby rock and hauled myself onto it. If that creature managed to report our location, the Enemy would likely stop at nothing to remove the last foothold of the Academy in this region. As I was about to pull up over the lip of the rock, Seya blasted a warning in my mind.

Wait! There's more than one. The sinking pit in my stomach intensified as I tried to sense what she could.

How many?

She took a moment to answer. That wasn't like her. *...Too many.*

I gritted my teeth. *Sounds like we might be in for a bit more action after all.*

Be careful up there Calidan. Thyrkan might not be the only things around.

You think-

-I don't know, but if anything could survive that impact, a titan could. Stay sharp.

Understood. Grimacing, I hauled myself over the ledge and rose into a crouch. My senses flared and I threw myself to the side, the blade narrowly missing my neck as I rolled, Vona rising to parry the second and third attacks before the thyrkan broke off, eyes gleaming in the light. This one was different to the others, quieter somehow. Even in these close-quarters I could barely hear its heartbeat which shouldn't have been possible.

Seraph-enhanced somehow. The thought trickled through the part of my brain that wasn't focused on my immediate survival and then the thyrkan spun, sending two darts whistling through the air. Shifting into the third circle of kaschan, I avoided both and sent a return knife which the rogue batted out of the air with a contemptuous hiss. Faster than thought it advanced, a blurring whirl of flickering blades and claws, every move intended to keep me off-balance and on the back foot. Whilst I admired the creature's single-minded tenacity, I couldn't afford the time it would take to defeat it in melee combat. Frankly, the look on its face when both of its feet stuck to the ground was almost hilarious enough for me to stay my hand.

Almost, but not quite.

Kicking the squelching head of the assassin-like thyrkan over the side of the canyon, I moved at speed towards the entrance to the Last Redoubt. Managing to catch another scout by surprise on the way and leaving its headless body on the blood-stained ground, I found three more probing the ostensibly 'secret' entrance, a short stairwell cunningly carved into the rock that led to an iron-banded door. This time I didn't bother engaging manually and instead drew on Seya to riddle the creatures full of holes from a distance. They died so quickly that it was almost...magic.

That sense of smug satisfaction nearly got me killed. A sixth-sense was the only thing that caused me to drop, a blade of black energy sizzling through the air where my upper-body had just been. Rolling, I cast around for the attacker, finding nothing immediately in range but movement a few hundred metres away causing me to refocus.

The shrivelled excuse of a thyrkan warlock raised a claw in greeting.

Shit.

Then I looked further behind. The shifting shadows that were moving against the light.

Oh shit.

Like I said, Seya mused with just a touch of her usual smugness, *lots of thyrkan.*

The stench of reptilian flesh and perforated bowels filled the murderous air of the tunnel. Knowing that the game was up and the Last Redoubt had been discovered I had pulled back into the entranceway, Vona and a punch dagger allowing me to hold the little stairwell for longer than I had expected.

So for all of about two minutes. But two minutes in an endless tide of claws, blades and scales feels like an eternity.

When the stones around me started to quiver, I knew it was time to draw back. The warlock was close and one-on-one I couldn't do much against it. The structure of the Last Redoubt was warded against seraph manipulation and would hopefully do a better job of resisting an attack than I would. Gutting another thyrkan and leaving it hissing and writhing in agony to impede its brethren, I willed the iron-banded door behind me to open and stepped through, slamming it shut instantly and engaging the lock.

"It's Calidan!" I called out loudly, not taking my eyes off the door. "Alert Simone that we are under full assault."

The steel door down the hallway slid open and Simone poked his head out. "Get in here you daft twit. No need for any heroics. Honestly," he shook his head and smiled, blue eyes shining in the murky light, "you would think we were under attack or something."

Flicking the gunk off Vona, I retreated along the hallway and inside, the steel door slamming shut with a resounding *boom* and flashing with a series of wards.

"They've got at least one warlock with them," I said as soon as I was through the door and Simone's expression tightened.

"If Bastion was here, I wouldn't be too concerned," he said, frowning at the sounds of scrabbling echoing down the tunnel. "She made most of these wards and with her here the Last Redoubt would likely remain long after the surrounding rock had crumbled to dust. But without her..." he grimaced. "We'll hold as long as we can. Then we get out."

"Understood."

Around us, Imperators stood with hands on spears, bows and crossbows, ready to unleash hell on whatever managed to come through the first door. The aptly-named 'murder holes' would be earning their name today, allowing them to shoot into the cramped space with relative impunity. Sophia stood at one, her bow hanging loose in her hands, her shoulders relaxed and confident. Rikol and Ella stood near the door, ready to reinforce it with seraph should the need arise and I knew that Scythe was floating around somewhere, ready to use his speed to get to wherever the fighting might grow thickest.

With any luck, the thyrkan would never make it past the door.

Then again, luck and I weren't usually on the best of terms.

The squeal of metal tore through the air and the sound of the swarming reptiles increased, fervent hissing accompanying the sound of breaking hinges.

It wouldn't be long now.

Crash!

The iron-banded door gave way to the swarm. Instantly the lithe creatures flooded into the hallway, darting along the floor, walls and even the ceiling until the corridor sounded like a bag of angry snakes.

The Imperators let them come.

The first thyrkan slammed into the steel door and rebounded as though the door had been the one to hit it instead. Falling to the ground, it was promptly trampled by the others in their haste to do exactly the same thing; falling upon the door in a torrent of fevered scales.

This time, however, the door held firm.

Simone let the corridor fill up. His expression remained calm and if I hadn't been watching his hands, I wouldn't have thought he was remotely tense. After a few eternal seconds he gave the order.

"Now."

Screeches filled the air as the Imperators went to work. Arrow, bolt and blade slammed into the massed ranks; the beasts so closely packed that it was impossible to miss. Over and over the archers fired and the spear-wielders stabbed, but still the thyrkan came.

And then everything changed.

One second, they were a disorderly mass of wild beasts and the next they were calm. Those at the front accepting death without a sound.

"Looks like we've got an officer," Simone barked. "Things are going to get a little more intense from here on out, so stay sharp. Rear-guard, any movement?" The last he directed back into the main building, to the balcony door which Scythe and four others were protecting.

One of the Imperators shrugged. "Nothing too serious yet. Easy enough to dislodge them with a few blasts of seraph and send them tumbling to their deaths."

"Good. Keep me updated if the situation changes."

The sound of heavy, tramping feet caught my attention and my nose detected the scent of polished metal. "Officers incoming," I declared.

"Look sharp everyone," said Simone. "Things are likely to get rough."

He had no idea just how true that was.

Six thyrkan marched into view. They looked like the taller, slightly bulkier ones that usually carried spears. I say usually, because in this instance they were carrying large tower shields that covered them from head to taloned foot. The six marched halfway down the corridor, stopping just before the murder holes reached their sides and slamming their shields down, forming a solid wall of steel. Behind them strode two fully armoured thyrkan, great-swords strapped to their backs and wielding what looked to be twin falchions instead; perfect close-quarter weapons in this confined space. But what was really concerning was what followed behind them.

The warlock.

But not by itself. The mishappen creature paused by the entrance and watched as another figure stumbled down the steps, holding itself up against the wall like it couldn't trust its own legs. The warlock stepped aside, gesturing, and the small thyrkan slowly and doggedly walked forwards, passing the armoured officers and then moving slowly through the ranks of the shield bearers, holding onto their shoulders when needed, until it was at the front and we all had a view. It was a thyrkan, that was for sure, but it wasn't the smaller, twisted figure of a warlock, nor did it have the build of a fighter. The way it moved made it appear like it had no understanding of its body, almost as though it thought it was trying to counterbalance itself with every step against a weight that wasn't there.

The creature stepped to the front of the ranks of shield-bearers and the two shields shifted ever so slightly, letting it step a little in front of them but keeping close enough that I knew they would be able to slam the shields shut again if we opened fire.

"Anyone have an angle on it?" asked Simone.

"Nope. But since when has that stopped us?" grinned Sophia. With a wave of her hand an arrow manifested above the creature's head and plummeted downwards, giving it no time to dodge. With a flicker of black lightning, the arrow hit a seraph shield that we hadn't even seen and disintegrated. I could sense the derision in the warlock's toothy smile and my mind went back to a class that we had taken with the High Imperator several years ago, where she taught us about colourless shields and their benefits. The warlock had just shown that it and its brethren weren't just one-trick monsters and didn't rely on their abyssal shields for every occasion. But what it taught us most of all?

It really wanted this scrawny little excuse for a monster to survive.

"This can't be good," breathed Simone. "Bring it down!"

Seraph lit up the corridor as the mages went to work. I joined in, throwing shard of green seraph at the beast from every conceivable angle, hoping beyond hope that something got through and took it down. When the explosions of light dissipated, an orb of endless darkness rotated around where the creature had stood. Slowly, so slowly that I had to give the warlock credit for showlizardmanship, the orb retreated, and what it revealed was nothing like what it had been before.

Gone were the scrawny limbs, the weak, snappable neck and the lacklustre movements, replaced by mountains of muscle that quivered with barely restrained energy. Feverish eyes glowed with maniacal anticipation and a crazed smile revealed a jaw filled with all manner of sharp edges.

"Well…shit." Simone half-turned his head to bark an order and the beast leaped into motion, the massive mountain shifting into a sprint with impressive speed.

"Brace the door!" I yelled and Imperators moved to throw more layers of seraph against it, as well as their own shoulders.

The monster impacted with a sound that resonated throughout the Last Redoubt. It had hit so hard that its left shoulder had deformed on impact, but after a second the bone and muscle began to shift of its own accord, slotting back into place with a sickening *crunch*.

"And it can heal. Of course it can fucking heal," Sophia groused before sending another arrow into its neck. The others followed suit and soon enough the reaver resembled a pincushion, but the plethora of attacks didn't seem to bother it in the slightest. Judging by the lack of blood, its scaled hide must have been extremely thick, meaning that we would need to hit harder to bring it down.

That, of course, was something that we were more than happy to do.

So long as we had the time.

The reaver reached out with a ridiculously proportioned hand and slammed it against the door, overgrown talons raking down the steel with a hideous squeal. I hissed as two of the warding seals snapped and dissipated. That thing hit *hard*.

"Bring it down you bastards!" Simone cried, sending a jet of blue flame into the creature's face, only to be blocked by another invisible shield.

"That warlock needs to die or else we're all going to," Sophia remarked. "Can we blow the tunnel yet?"

"Standing orders are not to blow the tunnel unless we truly have to," replied Simone, "and we're not there yet." The reaver hammered another fist against the door and the steel bent slightly, another ward failing in a puff of light. Simone frowned at the display. "But we're pretty damn close." Looking through the small slit in the wall, he pursed his lips and then rose, swivelling back to the nearby Imperators. "Rikol, I want you and five mages concentrating on the warlock, the rest of you stop that reaver!"

"Yessir!" we shouted, the sound drowning out the clashing of the reaver for a second and then we redoubled our efforts. Condensed seraph attacks began to scream down the hallway, crashing into the warlock's shield with bone-shaking intensity. Little by little the warlock had to reduce the area that its shield could protect and soon enough the first two shield-bearing thyrkan splattered against the wall in a bloody detonation of limbs.

It took two more thyrkan to die before the warlock's shield and concentration was reduced enough for the one it had raised over the reaver to disappear. Suddenly gashing wounds began to flicker into being on the massive beast's body, eliciting roars of pain that shook the tunnel, as the attacks from the mages began to land. Seraph-enhanced spears and arrow shot sliced into its torso and neck, opening bloody wounds and adding to the already saturated ground. For a moment it looked like it was over, the reaver weakening and slumping to the ground, its wounds closing more slowly than before, then a red-tinge bloomed throughout its scaled muscles and the predatory eyes turned feral. Drool dripped from the reaver's mouth as it roared its fury to the world and then it slammed into the door with renewed strength, breaking through several wards in one blow. Instead of using its hands for the next attack, it smashed its head into the door with a thunderous crash and then did it again, completely ignoring any pain or injuries. The steel door began to visibly warp, shuddering and bending under the heavy-blows and we all tripled our efforts.

I think it was Rikol who managed to tip the scales. Instead of concentrating on delivering damage he thought outside the box and focused on minimising the beast's attacks; threads of searing light wrapping around the creature's limbs and head before pulling tight, forcing its body to slowly bend backwards. The reaver bellowed in animalistic fury as it fought against the seraph and Rikol grabbed onto the nearby wall, face dripping with sweat and contorted in concentration.

"It's so strong!" he ground out. "Don't. Have. Long."

A spinning disc of light bloomed into existence in front of the reaver's neck. It began to revolve, spinning faster and faster until it was a blur of razer-sharp motion. In a spray of arterial blood, the destructive disc ripped forwards, drawing sparks as it pressed against the reaver's armoured neck before the creature's defences failed and the disc sliced through in one messy motion. The blue coloured disc took on a green hue as ichor spattered in all directions and then the reaver's legs gave way, the headless torso tumbling to the ground and blocking the majority of the hallway.

Cheers rang out and Ella smiled. "You're welcome!" With a flick of her wrist, she sent the disc screaming down the hallway, the weapon carving through the metal of the first shield in seconds before ripping into the wielder behind.

"Why didn't you do that sooner!" someone asked and she frowned.

"Takes a lot of energy," she stated simply. "Had to know it was needed."

"Brilliant work Ella," called Simone. "That should have them on the run. Let's get this-" he trailed off as the disc sputtered and failed before exploding into shards of light, causing Ella to stagger and drop to the ground.

"What the…?"

The warlock's black shield disappeared. Behind the warlock were two more scrawny figures, accompanied by the twisted figure of a second magic-wielding thyrkan.

For a long moment there was no sound. Simone drew in a breath.

"Fuck."

Unexpectedly, the second still-scrawny reaver didn't join its peer in lumbering down the tunnel towards us. Both it and its warlock took a look at the carnage and walked back outside, looking for all the world like they were two old, crippled lizard-people out for a pleasant walk. Unfortunately, as soon as they disappeared from view I forgot about them entirely, focusing instead on the very big, very muscular reaver trying to rip apart the steel door whilst crushing its fallen companion beneath its oversized feet. It was only when shouts of alarm emanated from inside the rest of the fort that I realised where the other reaver had gone. The bugger had bulked itself up and jumped off the top of the chasm, possessing enough skill to spot its landing onto the small balcony and proceeding to try and batter the external door down.

Worse, the balcony door was nowhere near as reinforced as the steel door that was looking worse for wear, but was a simple iron-banded door with some seraph enchantments inlaid over the top.

Most of those broke in the first strike.

Scythe was outside the door in a flash, body steaming as he enhanced his muscles to superhuman levels. The reaver was quickly riddled with cuts but the rapid healing it possessed meant that Scythe wasn't able to deliver enough damage to do more than frustrate it.

"Shore up that door!" Simone yelled, marching off towards the situation. Stepping towards Rinoa, he muttered low. "The moment it looks like the steel door isn't going to hold, blow the tunnel. Understood?"

She looked at him and nodded. "Understood."

"Good. You're in charge whilst I go and help sort this other situation out." Long-coat swishing behind him, Simone strode into the hallway and disappeared. Soon enough I could sense him unleashing blasts of blue flame at the reaver and countering massive fists with his longsword. Some people might have worried about him but not me; Simone was one of the few people in the Academy who might have had more experience hunting monsters than myself and that reaver was in for a world of hurt.

"Same as before!" Rinoa ordered. "Pull on your reserves. Burn everything you have. Rikol, hit the mage again. Everyone else, work with Ella to cut this thing down to size."

Boom.

The sound was faint, largely hidden by the reaver pounding on the door in the confined space, but something had made that noise. Something big.

Oh no.

"The door isn't going to hold for long!" someone shouted, pointing at the bending metal. Through a gap in the hinge, I could see the claws of the reaver flexing and pulling.

"Watch out!"

A ball of black fire arced through the minute gap and immolated the nearest Imperator, a battle-hardened veteran named Helayne.

"Why isn't that warlock under pressure?!" Rinoa screamed.

"The second one is back!" shouted another, voice tinged with panic. "We can't hold them!"

Boom.

I tuned it out deliberately, trying to ignore the rising panic and focusing instead on the now thoroughly warped door. Rinoa came to the same decision I did almost instantly. "Cover!" she shouted, before touching her hand to a sigil and ducking her head.

The explosion was deafening in the confined space, an immense roar that seemed to go on forever as the walls and roof of the tunnel caved in, sending thousands of tonnes of rock plummeting inwards.

With any luck, nothing survived. At the very least, digging through that much rock would take anything short of a Power substantial time and effort.

"Everyone, get back inside and await further orders!" barked Rinoa, snapping us out of our shared fugue.

Boom.

This time I could have sworn I felt the ground tremble. The sound was closer; the density of the noise almost a physical blow.

Please no.

It's coming. Seya's voice was barely a whisper, filled with weary pain. *Run!*

I leapt forwards, dashing past the weary Imperators and finding Simone walking back inside from the balcony, a smoking ruin of a reaver outside. His half-smile at my appearance faded into a grim line as he witnessed my face.

"What is it?"

"It's found us," I blurted. "I don't know how, but Seya and I can hear it. It's coming closer."

"What is?"

"The titan!"

The colour drained from Simone's face. "You're sure."

"I can hear it. So can she. It's coming, count on it."

To his credit, Simone didn't hesitate. He clenched a fist and a series of pulsing red seraph orbs flickered into existence throughout the hallways. When he next spoke, his words carried clearly through the facility. "This is Simone. We are-

Whump. Whump. Whump.

My ears picked up the sound, muffled as it was through the many layers of stone and defensive formations. *What is that?*

Calidan, run! Seya screamed in my mind.

"-to retreat to the Academy. Fallback to the-"

The world imploded in a detonation of fire and ash. Smoke and dust filled the air as I pulled myself to unsteady feet, only to collapse again as another massive impact shook the Last Redoubt.

"Get out!" I screamed, raising my shield. "Everyone out!"

Another explosion and half of the mess hall caved in, rocks sweeping away three Imperators like they had never existed.

"Move!"

The air was filled with the screams of the wounded and panic was beginning to set in. Simone sprinted back into the command centre and a second later the room began to burn an azure blue. When he came out his face was impassive.

"Everyone not down the ladder in the next sixty seconds is staying behind!" he bellowed. "Get the wounded down there. Throw them if you have to!"

I stopped to help Rinoa lift a slab of rock off a trapped companion. Judging from the blood coming from her lips, even if we got her to the medicae it would be a close-run thing. But a close chance was better than no chance at all.

Pushing Rinoa towards the door, I turned to help others out, seeing Rikol focused in concentration, his will forcibly holding the structure of the building together. The others were towing him along, acting as his eyes whilst he kept the roof from caving in.

But there was only so much he could do.

Whump. Whump. Whump.

"Incoming!"

Fire roared in the corridor from the main entrance-way and a thick, cloying cloud of dust filled the air, masking movement. A moment later the dust shimmered and turned to sand, falling to the floor with a skilled manipulation of seraph, courtesy of Ella. Unfortunately, the clear vision allowed us to see the red smear leaking out from under the rocks where the Imperators who hadn't managed to file out in time lay entombed.

Sophia was the first to react. "Nothing we can do!" she barked. "Follow Simone's orders. To the emergency exit! Move!"

Boom. At first I thought it was another explosion, the ground shaking noticeably with the impact, but there was no detonation.

Boom. BOOM. BOOM!

Footfalls. Far too familiar. Each one shook the foundations of the building, thrumming through the rock and stone.

It's right above you, Seya whispered.

"Whatever you do," I said to everyone. "Do not stop running."

The air began to glow. A subtle tinge of red and orange that would have been pretty if not so completely and utterly terrifying. Rikol began to try something else but I pushed him on. "This foe is beyond any of us! Run you idiot!"

As we rushed down the stairs, dragging and pulling wounded with us, a wave of pressure hit, like a low frequency that thrummed through my chest. The rocks above us glowed cherry red and vanished.

Atomised. Seya's mortified whisper. *Must go faster. Get down here!*

"Go, go, go!" I screamed, pushing people down the emergency ladder and swinging on, my hands moving down just as Simone jumped on.

"We're the last," he said gravely. "If you hadn't-"

The red light swept across the world and the next instant Simone's lower half slipped off the ladder, cauterised flesh striking my shoulder before tumbling away. All of a sudden, I was nearly at the top of the ladder facing open air with the glowing eye of the Artemis facing me. The red beam of doom began to swing back in my direction and I stepped back from the ladder, letting go and fully embracing gravity.

The twelve people I knocked off the bloody thing probably didn't like me too much at the time, but considering that I saved their lives it was probably for the best.

Seya met me at the bottom of the chasm, her terribly injured leg showing as little more than a slight limp as adrenaline and whatever concoctions of strange magic and alchemy that fuelled majestic creatures such as she flooded her system. Without a word she grabbed me with her teeth and flung me across the base of the ravine, sending me crashing into the small cave and sending a number of others sprawling through the metal door. Her ear twitched and she jumped a split-second before twin pillars the size of grand oaks slammed into the ground, lowering the base of the ravine by several metres and causing the earth to ricochet outwards with explosive force.

The titan had arrived.

Shut the door.

But Seya-

Shut. The. Door.

I fought to stay outside, screamed and shouted at the restraining arms of my friends that gripped me so tightly. *Seya!*

Just before the door closed with a resounding *slam* and a wave of seraph wards locked into place, I saw her rising up behind the metallic monstrosity, her claws extended. She was giving us the time we needed, and we both knew that it was going to be a losing battle.

Get through that portal Calidan. I'll see you soon. I promise.

The emergency portal flared into life, the most powerful seraph users working together to keep it activated whilst everyone trooped through. A whining sound began to screech around the tiny cave as the wards were strained to their maximum, failed, and the door began to glow a cherry red.

"Move it!" shouted someone – maybe Rinoa – and the organised stream became a flood as panic spread. Imperators – the hardiest of souls who had seen and done too much – were just as susceptible to the fear of being hunted as anyone else. We usually just hid it under layers of cynicism and scathing wit, combined with an overwhelming need to be the hunter, not the prey. Scythe's hand was immovable against my chest and he drove me relentlessly forwards, the expression on his face as hard as the granite that surrounded us. Something heavy impacted the rockface and the glowing red of the door flickered before resuming its inexorable blood-coloured rise.

I expected a blast of hot air. Something, *anything,* to indicate that the titan had successfully removed the door. Instead, I witnessed the thick steel of the door vanish as though it had never been; slower than the walls above, or Simone's body – as though the titan actually had to work to get through it. The wards around the cavern ruptured in flashes of dissipating light and suddenly we were all horrendously exposed. The titan's torso lowered down to look at us, the inexpressive, mechanical nature of its form somehow in that moment the most terrifying thing I had ever witnessed. The familiar underslung weapon raised its head and I knew that the high velocity projectiles were going to shred us and everyone on the other side of the portal with minimal effort.

The weapon began to spin.

With an ear-mangling howl, a bloodied Seya careened out of nowhere to wrap her jaws around the weapon, yanking it to one side and causing the titan to step away from the cavern in order to maintain its balance.

The last thing I saw, as the walls of the portal flickered around me, were the explosive flashes of the machine's weapon accompanied by the anguished howl of my panther. A moment later the portal dissipated into nothingness. Leaving nothing behind to mark the magnitude of what had just happened.

The Imperators had been driven out of the North.

Nothing now prevented the Enemy from crushing the remaining Hrudan and marching on the empire.

Most importantly, my panther – the most important person in my life – was gone.

I crumpled.

PART III

Fallen Idol

CHAPTER 35
DECEIT

Charles

"Is it awake yet?"

The ghostly shimmering visage of Ash flickered into life. "No. Still unresponsive, however its wounds are healing at an impressive rate so it shouldn't be too long."

The spectacled man pressed His hands together and smiled, looking less like a world-ending Power and more like a mid-forties, slightly built man. "Excellent. So gracious of the Emperor to leave us such a prize."

Ash tilted her head. "I don't believe it was an intentional act on the Emperor's part. I have yet to see any evidence that he played a role in yesterday's activities."

The Enemy pushed His glasses further up His nose and rolled His eyes. "Sometimes, Ash, I wonder if you will ever get the hang of figurative expressions."

"Ah." Ash flickered then reformed. "I see, you were inferring that it was the Emperor's doing when, in fact, it was not. Funny. Hah, hah."

Charles sat back in His chair and groaned. "Where's a human around when you need one?"

"There are some in stock on Basement Level Three if you-"

Charles waved her off. "I am merely musing. Besides, the Sworn are barely able to hold a conversation with each other, let alone me. Too busy fawning and falling about themselves in terror whenever I speak to rub two brain cells together. No, what I truly want is someone just to talk with. A peer, if you will."

"Have you tried Koranth?"

Charles snorted. "Koranth is a being from a completely separate dimension and functions on a totally different level. It does not understand the ins-and-outs of humanity, the foibles and the flaws, like I do and, moreover, does not care."

"The Emperor then? You were close once."

At that, Charles' gaze turned introspective. "Yes, once." He sighed and shook His head. "But not for an extremely long time. No, for my choices I stand alone and must accept that fact."

"*She* might talk to you."

The Enemy's brow rose. "*Her?* An interesting thought. Perhaps she would, but the Wanderer is a finicky individual. Always has been and always will be. She would talk if her precious animals and vegetation would be impacted but otherwise she does not care. I doubt that a conversation with another Power is high on her list of priorities." He sighed theatrically. "No, no, it is my lot, it seems, to content myself with…well, *myself*."

"A tragedy, I'm sure."

"Did you just make a joke? Perhaps there is hope for you yet young miss."

"Charles, by any definition of the term, I am not 'young'."

"To me, my dear, practically everyone is young. Even this fantastic beast that we have acquired – a creature that has lived an unbroken string of lives since the end of civilisation – is but middle aged."

"Charles, you are aware that I have access to the unredacted files regarding your heritage. You were born on the-"

"Sometimes the date of one's birth isn't the defining factor in one's age," Charles interjected, expression souring.

"I believe it is the only defining factor."

"Then you are wrong!" The sudden shout echoed through the cold, metal facility.

Ash watched her leader cautiously. When she was sure that she wasn't about to be summarily discombobulated, she nodded. "If so, please educate me."

Hard eyes softened and the Enemy of mankind rubbed His temples wearily. "I suppose that is only fair. Age is not necessarily based on the date of one's birth. Mental age is key. You may have heard the term 'old before one's time?'." The slight nod from the AI caused him to continue. "For most people that refers to, it simply means someone who is more mature at an earlier than expected age. For me…well." Charles looked around almost nervously, eyes flickering around the room. "What do you know of the first time I met Koranth."

"Very little. You have kept this information secret for longer than most civilisations have endured."

"Because I have no desire to relive it. Suffice to say, time does not necessarily work the same in other dimensions. In a place where Koranth was so powerful, on our first meeting my mind was isolated in a separate stream of time." He ground His teeth at the memory. "I experienced aeons in seconds. Trapped in an unresponsive body. Purely at the mercy of Koranth." Charles laughed a bitter laugh. "And do you know why?"

Ash shook her head.

"To show me how much of a fool I had been. I had thought myself so *superior*. Without peer. How wrong I was." He snorted softly. "I did learn something though."

"And that was?"

"Koranth taught me that the right environment changes everything. I was weak where it was strong. I vowed to never let that happen again. To plan so many moves ahead that my opponents wouldn't even know that they were already dead." His eyes flashed. "And I have had a long time to plan."

"Then you are ready?"

"Me? I've been ready for millennia." Charles smiled wistfully. "I've just been waiting for the world to catch up."

Movement caught both their attention. Black, luscious fur shifted as powerful muscles roiled.

"Such a beautiful creature," Charles murmured. "Such a shame." He met the giant orange orbs of the panther with an unblinking gaze. "Begin the extraction."

"Extraction procedure activated."

Charles watched with fascination as His machines ripped into the panther's flesh, her roars of pain falling on deaf ears. "Make sure to keep it alive. A Great Heart is a useful resource."

"Acknowledged."

He placed a hand on the reinforced glass and watched without remorse as Seya howled. "Another worthy addition to the source. Today is a good day, Ash. A good day indeed."

Seya

Seya knew pain.

A child of a shattered world, a witness to the end times, she had endured long enough to have experienced every possible kind of agony and she had pulled through.

That didn't mean it didn't still hurt.

'Whilst there was pain there was possibility', that was what an old bonded had used to say. Pain meant you were still alive. Motivated you to find an escape. And this room with its large mechanical probing arms seemed to have just one way out. It was likely that to attempt it was to die, but death was certain if she remained. She just had to wait until the Shadowed One was out of the picture. Then she had a chance.

The AI was overconfident. It always was. Most of the systems developed prior to the Cataclysm had the innate belief that they were infallible. Seya had proven that wrong before and now it was time to do it again.

After all, what self-respecting feline could truly be contained?

Seya embraced the pain and bided her time.

Soon.

"Calidan. Hey, Cal!" Someone elbowed me in the ribs and I jerked up, hand instinctively dropping to my belt.

"Oh, hey, Rinoa, sorry."

"I've been calling your name for the last minute!" she exclaimed, anger tingeing her features.

"Sorry. I was lost in thought."

Her expression softened. "Seya?"

Nodding, I didn't say anything. There was nothing to say. Seya was alive, I knew that much. But she was so far away that our bond was wafer thin. I could feel flashes of pain and when I was sleeping I had nightmares that were too vivid to be imagined.

"We'll get her back Cal," she said, bumping her shoulder against mine. "You know that I'll help you to do that. I might not know her as well as most, but she saved us all. Hells, you could probably ask any one of the Imperators who had been at the Last Redoubt and they would throw in with you to hunt for her, no questions asked."

"I know," I replied with a forced smile. "I do. Truly. I appreciate the thought but without knowing exactly where she is there isn't much anyone can do." I sighed heavily. "The High Imperator is in touch with the Emperor to see if he can determine where she is, but she is doubtful that he would countenance a mission to rescue her considering the hammering that the Academy has taken."

Rinoa's face darkened as the thoughts of her lost friends came bubbling up. "Sorry," I murmured apologetically. "I didn't mean to-"

She raised a hand. "No, it's okay. And you're right, everyone's hurting. That's why most would be keen to help you, to help Seya. It would give us something to take our mind off the pain."

"...It's appreciated, truly."

She wasn't wrong, the Academy was reeling. Too many had met their end at the Last Redoubt, including Simone. The funeral had been a terse affair, few – if any – remains to bury and a sense of simmering yet futile anger. We knew we needed to do better. To hit back to avenge our fallen. But having seen the power the Enemy wielded none of us were sure as to exactly how we could accomplish it.

"Cal!"

I looked up and saw Ella rushing towards me, excitement evident in her features.

"Well, that's my cue," Rinoa said, patting me on the shoulder and rising to her feet. "I'll see you tonight?"

I nodded and she gifted me a sad smile before moving off, quickly replaced by a breathless Ella. "I need to speak to you," she burst out as she neared me.

Making a show of looking around, I raised my eyebrow. "You are...?"

"In *private*."

I knew where she was going with this and frowned. "Ella, I don't have-"

"I know where he is."

That shut me up. "You do?"

Ella waved a hand and the sound of the outside became muffled as she sat next to me. "I do. You know my contact within the citadel needed time to investigate, well, I got in touch yesterday and they have an update. They've confirmed that Cassius is in the basement of the citadel and he is behind a large silver door."

I froze. "You're...sure?"

She nodded enthusiastically. "Positive." Noticing my face for the first time, her excitement began to wane. "What is it?"

"I've seen that door, Ella."

"You have?!"

Quickly I recounted the mad hunt through the winding tunnels of the citadel basement that had led me to find the Emperor confronting a kyrgeth. "But that door," I finished, "there's something about it. You should have seen Seya - I don't think I had ever seen her so unnerved. She said that she could feel other creatures, other *Great Hearts* back there and that they were terrified."

At that, Ella's expression hardened into one of determination. "All the more reason to get him out then," she declared.

"I agree," I said, raising my hands placatingly. "But this is the same door that Seya tried to get a closer look into. The Emperor was not a happy man about that. You know what he threatened. If you...if *we* do this then we need to be sure that this is what we positively need to do. Because if the Emperor finds out – and he *will* find out – then we need to be sure of our choices, because I imagine that being expelled from the Academy would be the least of our concerns."

Ella blinked slowly. "Cal, you *can't* be expelled from the Academy."

"Exactly."

She shook her head, as though trying to grapple with what I was suggesting. "I get it. I understand what you're saying, I really do. It's a no-win scenario. Even if we get through that door in secret, if we extract Cassius then at some point the Emperor will find out. It is inevitable." She raised a hand to forestall my response. "But all I would say to that is, what would you do if it were Seya locked away?"

I didn't even need to think about it. I would do precisely the thing that had me sitting here with at least four separate tracking wards placed upon me and various promises of death and dismemberment should I attempt to run off again. Having already forced Kane to pick me up and bodily drag me back to the Academy, the higher ups were taking no more chances.

Smiling sadly, I gave her a sheepish look. "I wouldn't hesitate."

Meeting my eyes, she nodded. "I know and believe me, Seya knows too. Once we figure out where she is, we can go and get her and I will be right by your side. But Cal, we now know where Cassius is. How can you expect me to leave him?"

"I can't."

"So you understand! You can help me to-"

I raised my hand. "I understand the reasoning why; I want him back just as fiercely as you. But we need to talk about the implications here."

I could see the desire to argue with me, to declare that there was no further need for talk, only for action. But Ella's street-rat upbringing had ensured that she was nothing if not careful. "Okay."

"Do you trust the Emperor?"

"Yes." Her reaction was immediate, as though ingrained into her very being.

"Why?"

She frowned. "He is...the Emperor. He is the reason why the Andurran people live in relative safety. We've both fought beside him and he has saved our lives on numerous occasions. So yes, I believe in him."

"And we know that he has saved Cassius's life before."

"Correct."

"And he has stated that the work he is doing on Cassius is for his benefit."

Ella frowned. "Also correct."

"So what is it about this situation that makes us not trust in the Emperor? Has he led us astray before?"

Her frown deepened. "No. I don't think so. But-"

"So why do we believe that we need to rescue Cassius?"

Ella scowled. "Because we have seen what the Emperor can do. We've experienced his healings first hand. There is too much uncertainty surrounding Cassius and no straight answers from anyone. So it falls to us to take matters into our own hands."

"If the Emperor gave a compelling reason for where Cassius is, would you listen and trust in his words?"

"Maybe?" She shook her head. "I think so? But I would want to see him to make sure he is okay."

Rising to my feet, I proffered my hand and she accepted. "Good. So, it's simple, we just go and make a few demands of one of the most powerful people in the entire world. Easy."

A bemused expression settled onto her face as I pulled her to her feet. "And where are we going?"

"Whilst you were talking, the Emperor strode into the High Imperator's office," I said with a grin. "Let's go and get some questions answered."

"Now?!"

My slightly hysterical laugh did little to reassure her.

"Calidan, Ella, what a pleasant surprise," the Emperor rumbled, his voice holding no actual hint of surprise.

"This is a closed meeting-" the High Imperator began but stopped when a hand the size of her head lifted up.

"Now, now, let's hear what this is about," the Emperor chided gently. "I'm sure that these two wouldn't interrupt unless there was a *very* good reason." The way his eyes flashed as he spoke the last sent a tingle down my spine. From my time with him over the years I felt like I understood the Emperor, knew his nuances and emotions. All of that learning was telling me that whilst he had a smile on his face, the Emperor was not a happy man with our presence.

Tread carefully.

"Apologies for the interruption, but I wanted to catch you before you disappeared," I said softly. The warning in the man's eyes grew and I dropped the tactful approach. "Two things: Seya's location and Cassius," I blurted.

"Yes, Acana here was just updating me on the loss of the Last Redoubt and the failure to hold the line. I must say I am a tad...disappointed."

At that the High Imperator raised a finger. "I understand your frustration, Melius, but they had a weapon of the old world, as well as several breed of thyrkan that are able to wield formidable seraph."

The Emperor turned a steely gaze on her. "Are you suggesting that the Academy, the pride of the Andurran military, is not able to produce graduates of high enough calibre to deal with a few lizard-men and an antique?"

"I'm suggesting," the High Imperator said softly, and I was impressed that she hid the tremble in her body so well, "that we need time to adapt to their new methods of war. Bastion has an understanding of their void-shields and is working on a training method to get the Imperators able to overcome this. As it stands however, if that titan is on the field of battle then I am not certain that we can bring it down." She stared at him pointedly. "It was, after all, designed to hunt and kill targets of your calibre."

"Hmm."

"Perhaps if you were willing to share with us any methods or techniques that might be suited to tackling the titan...?" Acana pressed.

The Emperor waved a hand. "There is nothing to teach that hasn't already been taught. Everyone just needs to be *better*. Honestly, the quality of seraph users is so diluted these days that finding anyone with a strong talent is almost impossible." His face twisted with frustration. "You must remember that these titans were developed at a time when seraphim of my calibre were, whilst not *common*, were not exactly rare either."

I couldn't even begin to imagine how that world had functioned. The current swathe of Powers was terrifying enough, let alone hundreds or thousands of people with the same level of command over seraph. "You're saying that there is a limit to how powerful most people can get?" I asked tentatively.

"In a nutshell, yes," came the rumbled reply. "There is no hard and fast rule, and I do not know why seraphim came into being with such power in the first place, but those of us who make up the Powers were all born with an innate understanding of seraph and a fierce will to guide it. Together that makes a mighty combination. I'm not suggesting that there were thousands of people back then who were at the same level as I am *now*, mind – I've had thousands of years to hone my craft – but there were certainly many with the same capacity to accomplish what I did. Those were the people that these titans were created to destroy, and those are the people that do not really occur anymore."

Another grimace.

"For all intents and purposes, true seraphim are on the endangered list."

The High Imperator shook her head. "In that case, Melius, what do you want us to do? You're telling us that we are incapable of beating a titan whilst in the same breath berating us for having failed to do so!"

For a moment time stood still as everyone in the room recognised that the discussion could go one of two ways. A cloud passed momentarily in front of the Emperor's eyes and I drew in a breath to prepare for the worst, but when it cleared the Emperor wore a guilty look.

"You're right, Acana," he murmured sheepishly. "I let my annoyance get the better of me." He shook his head. "For the moment, if we encounter a titan in the field, we withdraw. I will not have my troops suffer losses for the sake of my pride. When the time comes I will deal with the machines myself. Charles is not the only one with a few tricks up His sleeve."

Acana nodded and I raised a hand. "Sir, what about Seya?"

"Ah yes, the cat." The Emperor waved a hand airily. "She's deep in the far north. Looks to be one of the Enemy's primary strongholds judging by the sheer volume of anti-scrying wards." He met my gaze squarely. "I'm afraid, Calidan, that this time you won't be getting her back through your efforts."

"But-"

"But nothing!" he barked sharply. "This facility would be an order of magnitude worse to attack than any of the previous ones. The Academy has no resources to throw into such an assault." He glared at me for a moment and then his gaze softened. "I'm afraid that you are going to have to trust in your Great Heart to escape." A small smirk. "She is a wily enough cat; with any luck she can outsmart even Charles or that blasted AI."

I sat there, stunned. The Emperor had basically told me to sit and hope. I was an *Imperator*! Surely there had to be something I could do.

"Calidan," the High Imperator said softly. "I know that this is hard, but if the Emperor is suggesting that it is impossible, then it is. You *know* that, even if it is deep down in your gut. And no, it is not worth your life to attempt it anyway. If you do try to head north again, I will personally stick you in a cell that will make the one in Wolf's Hollow feel like a paradise. Are we clear?"

Slowly, fighting every instinct in my body, I begrudgingly nodded.

"Good." The High Imperator sat back. "Now what else warranted this rude interruption? Ah, Cassius wasn't it. Melius, can you tell us about his status?"

"Cassius is fine," the giant rumbled. "He has had a few setbacks but is firmly on the road to recovery."

"Can I see him?"

A shake of his head. "No, Ella, you may not. He was very badly injured and the surgeries that he needed done were extremely invasive and intense. He isn't in the right place for visitors at this point. I'm sorry."

In the face of such dismissal from one such as he, most would have acquiesced to the Emperor's infallible wisdom. I think Ella surprised him when she drew herself up angrily, eyes flashing with a burning rage. "I have not seen Cassius in well over a year. I don't even know if he is even alive! There's been no mention of his injuries, what happened to cause them or why it is taking so long for them to heal, despite knowing that you can fix most issues with a snap of your fingers! So no. No! I need to know more and won't be dismissed yet again!"

The Emperor levelled a curious stare at her and I could sense the High Imperator minutely shift her weight away from Ella, as though worried that violence might erupt at any moment. "It is not...often that I am spoken to in such a manner," the giant man began, "in some ways it is refreshing. In a multitude of others, however," his eyes darkened, "it is not. You seem to forget your place, Ella. You and everyone within this Academy, everyone within this *empire*, exist to serve me. Not to question. Not to moan or to whine. I protect you and in return expect to be treated with **respect**." The word cracked the air, the power in the Emperor's voice building to painful levels, each syllable seeming to resonate with barely restrained force. The air around the Emperor began to darken whilst his form took on a resplendent tone, like he was sucking the energy out of the world and imbuing himself with it. It felt like the world hung on the edge of a knife and then the Emperor breathed out, relaxing back into the chair and I could almost feel the collective sigh that emanated around the empire.

"Cassius is helping me with a project," he said in softer tones. "It's taken longer than anticipated, and for that I apologise. He will be returned to you, but not yet. As for not seeing him, that can be fixed." He snapped his fingers with an amused twitch of his lips and a shimmering line of light spread into the air. A weary and pale-looking Cassius sat on a bed, reading.

"There he is," the Emperor rumbled. "I would let you talk, but like I said, he isn't ready for that yet. But he is nearly there. Nearly ready." The way he said those words filled me with a strange chill. There was an eagerness there, an excitement that didn't have anything to do with Cassius getting well. "Soon he will be back with you, so please stay here and wait." He gave a wide smile. "Happy?"

Ella nodded, her earlier hostility vanished. "Yes. Thank you so much!"

"Good." The Emperor gestured towards the door. "Now the High Imperator and I still have much to discuss, if you wouldn't mind...?"

We were out of the door before he said another word.

"That was insane!" I breathed, feeling like a mantle of pressure was lifting off my shoulders. "I can't believe you took him to task like that! Ella?"

Ella didn't respond, her eyes hooded and dark. I tapped her on the shoulder and she swivelled. "What?!"

"What's wrong?"

"You didn't see it, did you." It was a statement, not a question.

"See what?"

"That wasn't Cassius he showed us," she growled.

"What do you mean? He was right there!"

"You can't scry in the citadel," Ella replied stiffly. "No-one can. Not even the Emperor. I have it on iron-clad authority. What he showed us was no portal. I think he just showed us what he wanted us to see."

"You mean-"

"I mean, Calidan," Ella said softly, meeting my gaze with eyes burning with determination, "that the Emperor is lying to us. And I mean to find out why."

CHAPTER 36

Dreams & Danger

Cassius

*S*top. *Please stop.*
It hurts!
So...much...pain.

Cassius drifted, lost in a sea of pain. Time had lost all meaning; there was only one constant in life: whether the pain was less or more. It was funny, in a morbid fashion, but he had thought he had known pain. That he had understood it completely. But now...now he was a true expert. He kept himself occupied by ranking the different levels of pain and these days a papercut wouldn't even register on the lowest rung of that ladder.

Ella came to him again. She often did when his thoughts drifted. He tried to remember her as she was, before Wolf's Hollow, but every time he tried to picture her smile, her eyes filled with a warmth reserved for him, they were replaced by the wicked, vicious visage that had cut him down time and time again. Her burning eyes haunted his dreams. The feel of his heart beating its last as she bled him like a pig, standing over him in that victorious, elated manner...he knew it wasn't real, that it hadn't happened in reality, but what was reality? Because for him it had happened.

Over and over and *over* again.

"Ella, stop, I don't want to fight you!"

The cold menace in her voice, the sound sinuously weaving its way into his ears. "Then die. Traitor."

Schnick.

He hadn't felt the first blow, right into the nerve cluster in his spine. Body crumpling like a puppet without strings, he could only lie there and watch his death approach.

It's not real. Remember that. It was never real. Ella is warm, kind, loving.
Murderous.
No! She is the best thing that happened to me.
Vicious.
Push away the thoughts Cassius, push them away. Don't let your memories be tarnished. She is brilliant. Beautiful. Perfect.
The perfect killer.
Schnick.
Shut up, shut up, shut up-
"Shut up!" Cassius roared, or tried to. His words came out jumbled. Garbled. Did they make sense? He wasn't sure any more.

"Did you say something Cassius?" the deep voice behind him rumbled.

"STOP IT!" he screamed.

"'Flental rabbit?' the voice reiterated, amused. "I'm afraid that I don't quite understand what you mean, Cassius. You should try and relax, you know. Modifying the brain like this isn't as easy as I might make it look."

A trickle of warmth ran down Cassius's neck.

"Ah, sorry. Let me just get that for you. There, that's better. Can't have you bleeding all over the floor now, can we?"

"Fuck you, bastard!"

"I told you, Cassius, you aren't making much sense. It's not your fault, I had to rearrange some of the pathways within your brain. Your speech should come back with time as your brain learns to utilise the new pathways I've provided, but if it doesn't…well, I've always thought of you as the strong and silent type. You can learn to embody that more accurately."

Cassius unleashed a bestial, incoherent scream.

"Now, now. We've been over this. Keep it down or I remove your ability to vocalise entirely."

It wasn't an empty threat. The Emperor had done it before with ease and Cassius knew that he wouldn't hesitate to do it again.

"Good boy. That's better. Now hold still." Cassius's view swivelled and he found himself once more facing the ground. "I know you don't like this, but I need to do some more work on your spine and back."

Dread filled Cassius from head to toe. *No. Anything but that. No!*

"Keep still. There's a good lad." The Emperor picked something up and the burning began anew.

The Emperor hummed whilst Cassius screamed.

Seya

Seya had had better days. Worse too, which said something, but many better. But regardless of the pain, today was the day.

Escape day.

She was positive that the Shadowed One wasn't around. Or, at least, as positive as she could be, trapped within a sealed room with no scent and muffled hearing. And if the Enemy wasn't around then she had a chance.

If He was?

Well. Chances were she ended up back here anyway, so what was to lose?

The drills continued their endless cycle of probing, cutting and sucking. They must have had gallons of her blood and marrow by now, more than enough for whatever dark deed they were undoubtedly going to attempt next.

That ended today.

Refusing to listen to the innate side of her that wanted to wiggle her hindquarters in preparation, she waited for the drill to pass within range of her position on the table and snapped forwards, teeth clamping around the arm of the machine. With a jerk of her neck, she sent the machine sparking into the clamp around her paw, ignoring the pain as it cut through the metal and into the meat of her flesh – she would heal.

Keeping the machine in her mouth, she extended her perfectly curved blades and sliced through the remaining bands of metal, dropping to the floor with a barely contained yowl.

She wouldn't have long. She knew that. The AI would be there, watching. Planning.

Seya moved to the reinforced window and slammed her jaw against it, controlling the bucking motion as the drill bit spun and whirred, the mechanical arm she was pulling against stretched to its limit.

Again and again, she slammed the whirling drill into the glass, making sure she hit the same spot until, finally, a crack started to spread. Putting everything she had into the pressure she could bring to bear, the drill bit eventually cut straight through and, like tower blocks in the Cataclysm, the glass wall shattered.

Seya didn't let the moment of satisfaction impede her movement. Alarms began to blare as she swept forwards, dashing through the building in a blurred frenzy, claws slashing everything that came within reach until, finally, she flung a disembowelled thyrkan headfirst through a window and followed it outside, using the ruined torso as a platform to break her fall as she landed some fifty-feet down.

Alarms continued to blare and all around her she could smell the scent of twisted reptile. If it was anyone but her she would give them little chance of escape. But she was the queen of cats. Nothing would impede her way.

Let the escape begin.

I'm coming Calidan.

"You can't be serious!"

Ella's gaze didn't so much as flicker. "I'm deadly serious."

I shook my head. "So, what? You just want to waltz into the citadel and break Cassius out? There are so many issues here that I don't know where to begin. First and probably most importantly, how are you going to get through the silver door. That thing doesn't utilise a normal key."

"My contact says that they will be able to leave the door unlocked for us at the appropriate time."

That stumped me. "As far as I am aware that door leads to the Emperor's private area," I replied slowly. "Just who on earth is your contact to be able to pull this off?!"

"Someone resourceful. That's all you need to know."

"No. It bloody well isn't 'all I need to know' and you know it!"

"Look. If they say they can get it done, I believe them. You're going to have to trust me on this."

I took a deep breath and forced myself to calm down. "Alright, let's move past the issue of the ridiculous door. Let's also pretend that we can get in when the Emperor is away, and somehow ignore the fact that he has wards around that door that alert him when people are sniffing around. Forgetting all those things, we still have the issue of getting Cassius out of the citadel and then having to explain to the Academy and eventually to the man who is responsible for the entire *godsdamned empire* as to how Cassius just happened to be retrieved!"

Ella gifted me with a smile that carried such weight that it struck me dumb.

"You're not going to explain it," I realised. "You're going to run."

She nodded.

"Ella...you'll be giving up all that you've worked for. You'll be hunted by the Academy to the ends of the earth. That is, if the Emperor doesn't get you first."

"I will be giving up a lot," she whispered. "But I will be gaining *everything*. Freeing Cassius from whatever is happening is worth any sacrifice. Any cost. If he needs it, I will pay it gladly."

My hands pressed at my temples, rubbing in vain to try and relieve the building tension. "There has to be another way. You – *we* – are loyal Imperators. Breaking into the citadel and fleeing, that isn't the action of a loyal Imperator."

"No. But it is the action of a friend." She reached out and squeezed my shoulder gently. "You once told me that if Seya was behind that door then you wouldn't let anything stop you from getting to her. Well, Cassius is behind that door and I don't think anything good is happening to him. I'm not going to let anything stop me from getting to him. You're either in...or you're out."

Like it was even a choice.

"Of course I'm in," I hissed. "I just hate that it's come to this. We shouldn't be suspecting each other or fighting each other. There is too much at stake for such *bullshit*!"

"Tell that to the Emperor."

I snorted. "I prefer my bones the way they are, thank you."

She gave a sad smile. "Thank you, Cal. For believing in what I'm doing. Not many would."

I rolled my eyes. "Please. You don't need to thank me for anything. Cassius is my best friend. My brother. Plus..."

"...he would do the same for you." Ella finished.

"Exactly."

We shared a long look before I glanced away, coughing with sudden embarrassment. "So... What's the plan?" I asked eventually.

"For the moment? To do nothing. You were right in how difficult this is going to be. The Emperor will have to be outside the citadel – preferably far away – for this to have any chance of success. If he arrives too soon or if we take too long, well..." her face said it all. "My contact will investigate the Emperor's calendar of events and let me know when something comes up that could work. Once he is out of the picture then we sneak in through the forest entrance and make our way to the silver door which the contact will have opened for us."

"I think the word that you're missing there is 'hopefully'."

She ignored me with well-practiced competency. "We get inside, grab Cassius and get out via the same route. As soon as we are out of the citadel grounds, I'll make a portal and Cassius and I will disappear."

"Where will you go?"

Ella shook her head. "It's better if you don't know."

"Hang on-"

"Calidan, you're not coming with us."

Her words hit like a slap to the face. "What do you mean I'm not coming with you?!" I asked, anger flooding my voice.

"You're a Great Heart-bonded," she said gently, ignoring my rising anger. "Cassius and I are excellent Imperators, but we are *just* Imperators. If you leave then the Emperor himself will probably come hunting for you and there is no way that we can survive that." Her eyes turned pleading. "Don't you see? If you come then there is zero chance that we get away. *Zero.*"

So you want me to take all the risk and none of the reward. The words were on the tip of my tongue but I swallowed them away. The practical side of my brain agreed with her logic. Likely as she knew it would. "I...I understand," I said hoarsely and when she looked at me next, I saw the pain in her eyes. She knew what she was asking of me and the pain it would cause everyone involved, but what was a little pain compared to Cassius's freedom?

"That's why you don't want me to know where you are going," I said in sudden realisation. "You know that the Emperor or someone in his employ will be able to get the information out of me."

A slow nod.

"And what makes you think that they won't kill me for helping?"

Her face twisted slightly. "When the time comes, I intend to make it look like you weren't helping. That you were being a loyal Imperator and trying to stop me. You...might need to get stabbed."

"Oh. Lovely."

"Just a little stabbing," she clarified quickly. "A few minor wounds, enough to put you down but not enough to be life-threatening."

"'Just a little stabbing'," I echoed with a dark smile. "If only Kyle could see us now. Talking about stabbings like they're nothing."

Ella shrugged. "Probably the least ridiculous injury that you've sustained in a long time," she pointed out.

"True. Most of the things I fight tend to either want to smush me into paste or melt my internal organs. Or both."

We shared a smile and the tension began to ease. "One last question," I said eventually. "What about the others?"

"They can't know."

"They would come with us," I insisted.

"Maybe." Her tone was doubtful.

"They would!"

A raised eyebrow. "Rikol wants nothing more than to be a master mage. A seraph-wielder of unparalleled power. Do you really think he would manage that if he was on the run? Scythe would want to come, but he is protected by the Academy here. That incident in the Dusk Court?" She shook her head. "I've heard that there is a bounty on his head. Nothing that can touch him whilst he is within these walls, but he is already having to take extra precautions when on mission. If it became known that he was excommunicated from the Academy?"

"It would be open-season," I whispered. "I didn't realise it had got so bad."

"Rizaen's people aren't happy," she said bluntly. "They want his head on a platter. Thankfully, the Academy likes Scythe and wants to keep him around. That would change if he ran away and all the protections with it."

My fingers were rubbing my temples again. "Shit. I should have known, should have listened more."

Ella shook her head. "This isn't on you. You've had your own share of things to deal with. Scythe doesn't want to trouble you with his burdens."

"I would be happy to help!"

"He knows. As do we all."

I shook my head. "And Sophia wouldn't want to leave Scythe."

"Precisely."

"Shit. This is so *fucked*."

"It is." She locked steely eyes on mine. "But we're going to get him back Cal. Just focus on that."

"We're going to get him back."

"Calidan, you lousy excuse for an Imperator, how are you doing?"

"Better than you, you wrinkled old goat," I retorted cheerfully, striding into Korthan's private library and taking a seat in one of his old leather chairs. "Still alive, I see."

"Disappointed?" he cackled, causing me to crack a grin.

"Not remotely. Why would I want my whisky supply to be interrupted?"

He clutched his heart. "I always knew I was being used." Inclining his head, the levity from his tone faded. "Good to see you lad."

"You too, old man."

Letting out a long sigh that warbled as much as his bones creaked, the ancient librarian relaxed back into his favourite chair. "What brings you to see me?"

"It can't just be a social visit?"

A raised eyebrow. "Is it?"

"...No."

"Hah! Knew it. Idiot child. Can't pull a fast one on old Korthan."

"You know that talking in the third-person is a sign of an addled brain, right?"

"Pfft." He waved a hand dismissively. "I'm no more addled than you are a competent Imperator."

Ouch.

I rolled my eyes and he grinned, showing a yellowed and gap-filled array of teeth. "What can I do for you?" He asked again.

"I wanted to know more about the titans."

"You and everyone else," he remarked. "I can tell you what I told them."

"And what's that?"

"Go and ask the one person who has witnessed them in action before."

"The Emperor isn't particularly...forthcoming in how to deal with them."

Korthan grunted. "So I've heard. I'm under the impression that he isn't entirely sure himself. Maybe he never encountered one prior to the Cataclysm? I can only theorize. Either way, the small amount of information I've managed to uncover is largely useless. There are records of someone unintentionally activating a titan in your favourite swamp but it powered down shortly after and hasn't been able to be reactivated since."

"So nothing on how to fight them, their skills and armaments?"

"Nothing lad," he replied with a shake of his head. "It's like trying to ask how you would fight the seraphim themselves. My best suggestion would be: don't."

"Sound advice."

I winced at the sound of his creaking bones as he shrugged. "Can't give you more than that. If you have to fight and don't have a Power on your side, avoiding a direct confrontation is likely your best bet. Hit from where it least expects it. Drop it into the earth. You know, the usual." He eyed me curiously. "But you already knew all that. So, why are you really here?"

"You always could read me too easily," I remarked, taking his unoffered bottle of whisky and pouring myself a glass. A quick sip and I let out a small sigh of satisfaction. "What's behind the silver door?"

I didn't have to clarify what I meant. The old man's shoulders stiffened in surprise and his eyes darted around the room as though hunting for eavesdroppers. "Silver door?"

"Don't play dumb. You know the one I mean. The one Cassius is locked behind. Spill it."

All traces of joviality left the old man's face. "The silver door isn't a place you want to go, Calidan. Trust me on that."

I held his gaze unflinchingly. "Cassius is there. Why?"

"If he is there, then the Emperor thinks he has a use."

"A use? What do you mean?"

"Something of practical benefit to the Emperor. The silver door is his workshop, lad. It's where he goes to conduct his experiments and work on his projects. Most don't know it exists and very few have ever seen inside. He's extremely private about it."

"I wonder why…" I murmured drily. "Is it where he implants the liathea?"

Korthan shook his head. "No, that's another room the level above. I have reason to suspect that the liathea are kept behind the silver door but are transported to the floor above when required for implantation."

"So, whatever is down there is more important to the Emperor than getting liathea into us," I mused. "That…is intriguing." I locked eyes with the old librarian. "Tell me, Korthan, what do you think is happening to Cassius behind that door?"

He had just taken a sip of whisky and coughed at the question, spluttering and wincing as the liquid hit the back of his throat. "T-that's not possible to know."

"I'm not asking about knowing. I'm asking what you *think*."

Finally getting his breathing under control, Korthan gazed at me levelly. "I think that Cassius has something that the Emperor wants. Something that has the Emperor working feverishly. The man has always had a single-minded will but reports are that he is spending the vast majority of his time in the bowels of the citadel, missing meals and important events. Something had him *hooked*." Korthan shook his head. "If that thing is Cassius, then I pity him."

My stomach clenched. "Why?"

"The Emperor is a kindly soul to his people…for the most part," Korthan explained. "But he is, at his heart, a scientist. Sometimes he does things that are…harmful to an individual in order to better provide for the wider population."

"For the 'greater good', you mean?"

"I-yes."

"And do you agree with that?"

"This isn't about me, Calidan. And if it wasn't Cassius being part of this experiment then we wouldn't even be having this conversation, you would be doing as all the other Imperators do – happily ignoring and reaping the benefits." His eyes narrowed. "So don't be a hypocrite. You know as well as I that the empire exists only because of the Emperor and the stability that he brings. As such, if he believes that something is worthwhile to investigate, I am inclined to trust him."

"...And if it was one of your friends down there?"

He held my gaze for a long moment before breaking away. "Love makes us do strange things, so who can say? Perhaps I would risk everything I had built to save my friend, or perhaps I would love the Emperor more and trust in his wisdom. Thankfully I am long past those fallible years and can content myself with sitting here in my library, not thinking that the fate of the world rests on my shoulders."

My glass clinked as I took another long sip and put it back down. "It does feel that way sometimes," I admitted.

"You're a Great Heart-bonded with personal connections to the Emperor," the wise old-man intoned. "Like it or not, your actions hold weight, more than any normal Imperator." He offered me a rare sympathetic smile. "You're going to have to get used to it. Or, you know, crumble and break under the pressure."

"Always so reassuring," I muttered but couldn't avoid the smile tugging at my lips.

He grinned and then frowned as something occurred to him. "There are two people you could talk to about the door," he said slowly.

"Really? Who?"

"Have you met the other Great Heart-bonded?"

I shook my head. "No, Anatha always said they were kept close to the Emperor. She never said what they did."

"Hmm. Mother was right. They are rarely seen, but I do know that they spend most of their time in the lower reaches of the citadel. I doubt anyone knows more about what's inside the silver door than they."

"Where can I find them?"

Korthan reached over and pressed something into my hand. It was a small piece of paper marked with a location and a date and time – two days hence. Reading it, I glanced up in surprise.

"You knew," I gasped. "You knew what I was going to come and talk to you about."

He gave me a pained smile. "Like you said, I've always been able to read you well. As much as I might not have shown it, I have always liked Cassius and have made some inquiries of my own. This is the best I can do. What you do with the information after this is up to you."

Memorising the location, I made the note vanish in a small burst of green flame. "Thank you," I said, meaning it.

The crotchety librarian gave me a knowing look and smiled. "Good. Now bugger off and leave an old man to his rest."

I fought back a smile. Some things never changed.

CHAPTER 37
Puppets

Seya

Seya snarled as she raked her claws through the throat of the nearest foul lizard, powerful paws pulling it to the ground before she pounced onto the next, jaws clenching down in an eruption of blood. Chest heaving, she scanned the area but all the immediate thyrkan were down, leaving the rocky pass coated with blood and limbs. She heard a cry in the distance and the twang of bowstrings. Springing forwards, she heard the clatter of projectiles striking the ground behind her. She had to give the beasts credit – they had impressive endurance. For two days this pack had been hunting her, always close to her heels and barely resting. Her injured paw prevented her from running as swiftly as she desired and without time to rest her wound couldn't close.

It wasn't just thyrkan either.

Somehow true monsters were being placed in her path. Every time she started to outdistance the thyrkan pack, she found something in her way that she couldn't hide from. Each battle meant she came out a little more tired, a little more wounded and a lot more pissed-off. She was used to being the hunter, never the hunted and it irked her beyond belief that someone or something was able to keep track of her location well enough to set obstacles in her way.

She understood why it was happening though. Her hobbled lope was still a pace better than that most two-legged creatures could keep up with but it was a fraction of the speed she could exert when fully healed. Without interference she would eventually lose the hunting party and be free to make her way back to Calidan. But it was obvious that the Enemy wanted her. That He needed her for something and knew that if she was given the chance to rest and heal she would be gone from this place in a flash. He or that blasted AI were throwing huge amounts of resources to try and recapture her. She was oddly proud of that fact.

A queen shouldn't be obtained cheaply.

Black lightning split the sky and Seya threw herself sideways. The impact of the blast sent her careening through a nearby boulder and she allowed herself a single groan before pulling herself back to her feet and stumbling back into action. The warlock was part of the hunting party and by far the most dangerous of its members. Luckily it didn't seem to be able to see her very well as it had yet to land a direct blow – something for which Seya was eminently grateful. Rolling back into a hobbling lope, she kept her senses fully spread out, muscles primed to react as soon as anything changed.

The only way she was going to survive was to outpace, outlast and outfight everything that got in her way.

Simple really.

She just hoped that the blasted rocky terrain would change sooner rather than later. Some cover to hide from view would not go amiss.

Not that she was worried.

A queen doesn't hold with fear.

Cassius

I don't want to fight you. Please don't make me fight you, Ella.
This is just a dream. You wouldn't do this. WAKE UP.
Schnick.
Ella leaned over his collapsed body, bloody knife in hand. "Goodbye, Cassius."

"Relax, boy." The thunderous words rumbled around the room, snapping Cassius out of his nightmare. "This twitching will get you nowhere." The sound of something fleshy snapping reached Cassius's ears from behind his head and he tried to jerk away but the bonds were too tight. Frustrated, helpless tears stained the floor.

"Ahh, there we go. Now, Cassius, try to think of something positive because this, I'm sorry to say, is going to hurt."

Lightning coursed through his brain. Every nerve ending throughout his body lit up in unrelenting agony. Cassius screamed, but his voice was a raw, broken thing and it came out more like a whimper. On and on it went and his body jerked as things inside him began to twist. His jaw snapped shut, clamping down so hard that half of his tongue dropped to the floor. He barely noticed the pain – it was but a fragment of what was being done to him – but rejoiced at the implication.

Let this be it, he prayed as coppery liquid flooded his mouth. *Let it be over. Let me die.*

"Tsk."

No. You didn't see. You didn't!

The lightning stopped. The table moved and Cassius was raised to a fully upright position as the Emperor stepped into view, bloody gloves in hand. "I guess I should have seen that coming. Apologies lad."

I don't want your apologies. Let me die!

The Emperor looked at the fragment of tongue on the floor and it broke apart, disseminating into nothingness. He looked at Cassius and must have noticed the pleading in his eyes for his expression softened fractionally. "Sorry boy, no dying for you today."

He made no movement, no indication that he had done anything at all, but the blood in his mouth and throat vanished like it had never been, leaving his tongue hale and whole. A moment later his jaws were pried open as a wooden bar manifested between his teeth.

"There, much better." The Emperor said happily, walking back behind Cassius and sitting back down. "Now. Let's get back to it, shall we?"

Just let me die. He died in his dreams often enough after all. Couldn't the Emperor just let him go? Let him drift away?

It would be so easy...

Just let me die.

Lightning crackled. The world faded.

Schnick.

"Calidan, long time." The man's voice was gruff and his inflection short, like he rarely used it and wanted to keep it that way. He stepped out from behind a tree near the forest entrance to the citadel. "That's close enough."

I stopped where I was and studied him closely, noting the short dark hair and burn mark down his face. "Have we met before?"

"Once or twice, though you might not have known it." Something that might have passed for a smile flashed across the man's face and then his eyes flicked to the route back to the citadel. "The name's Balthazar but we can skip the pleasantries. I don't have much time. What do you want to know?"

I thrust away all the thousands of questions that filled my mind and asked the most important. "What's behind the silver door?"

Balthazar stiffened. "We're done here." Turning, he made to walk away.

"Wait, please!"

He paused.

"Look, I have reason to believe my friend is back there. He's been missing for months." My shoulders slumped as I spoke, desperation tinging my voice. "Korthan said you might be able to help. Might know something about the door, or Cassius."

The Great-Heart bonded sighed and turned back, expression troubled. "Listen and listen well," he said gruffly after a moment. "As a Great-Heart bonded you will inevitably see behind the silver door. In fact, I am surprised that you haven't already."

"What do you-" The abruptly raised hand made my mouth shut with a slam.

"Don't talk. Listen. The Emperor... he needs us. More than you know or might suspect. I am...forbidden for saying more but know that the time will come when the Emperor will take you behind that door. It will not be a fun experience." His eyes looked like they were focusing on something a thousand miles away. "Everything will change. Your outlook on life. Yourself. Your bond."

Balthazar shook his head as though trying to dislodge a painful memory. "I can confirm one thing: Cassius is back there. I have heard his name said. I have heard his screams."

My heart grew cold. "His screams?"

"The Emperor is working on something new. It has been a long time since I have seen him so...enervated. If Cassius is his project, then I can only hope that he survives the procedure."

"Do you know what the Emperor is doing?!"

A shake of his head. "No. Only that it is important to him, and thus important to the empire."

I snorted. "Don't tell me you believe that."

Hollow eyes found mine. "I do not think that the Emperor does anything idly. There is something to be said for focusing on the greater good. I have to believe that." The last was little more than a whisper.

"What else can you tell me?"

Another shake. "Nothing. I am bound to this and cannot speak freely. You should know that if you do come through the door uninvited, I will be forced to stop you."

"Forced?"

A sad smile. "It is the way of things. You will see. Everything will become clear. As tragic as that is."

"You speak as though you have no choice in what you do."

He snorted. "You're a Great Heart-bonded like me. There has never been any choice in what we do."

"That's not true!" I exclaimed, cutting off at his sardonic look.

"Did you not meet with the Emperor when it was discovered that you were bonded?" At my nod, he continued. "Then you know that he gave you no choice in joining the Academy."

"It was what I wanted."

"It doesn't matter if you wanted it or not. There was no option to turn it down. The Emperor ensures that all Great Heart-bonded are enrolled in his service. You might think that it is because we are, by our nature, better suited to the rigours of being an Imperator, but the reality is very different. We are nothing more than tools." Bitterness warped his face as he spoke. "Tools that serve the Emperor in one purpose and one purpose only. Tools that-argh!" he broke off as a swirl of light wrapped around his throat and he collapsed to one knee, raising a hand as I made to rush forwards.

"I said too much," he gasped between choked breaths. "It will pass." True to word the light dimmed and retreated back down his neck, disappearing beneath his clothes. With a relieved gasp, Balthazar straightened and brushed down his jacket.

"What was that?!"

"A means of control," he replied curtly.

"Why does the Emperor need to enforce your control?" I asked, completely confused. "You're sworn to him as an Imperator!"

Balthazar closed his eyes for a long moment, as though basking in my naivety. "When you pass through the silver door, you will come to understand." He shook his head and sighed. "I need to return. I am sorry that I can't give you the answers that you desire, but remember my warning – regardless of my personal feelings I and my comrade will be forced to prevent any unauthorised access to the room beyond the door."

"What about your bonded? Will they fight too?"

A shadow passed across his face. "Would that they could."

With that inexplicable statement he turned, raised a hand in farewell and vanished back into the shadowy catacombs of the citadel, leaving me with far more questions than answers.

My feet carried me back to the Academy whilst I remained lost in thought. I got the impression that the Emperor's bonded lived behind the silver door – if that was the case then breaking in was going to be much tougher than we had originally anticipated. Even if Ella's contact could open the lock, we were going to end up facing powerful opponents. Opponents who would, from the sound of it, be forced to prevent access regardless of their own views or emotions.

It was almost like they were puppets.

Is that what I was going to become? A creature without free will?

A small, insidious voice raised a question in my mind. One that I tried to force down but couldn't shake. *How is that different to the Enemy?*

I didn't have an answer. I knew, *knew* without a doubt that the Emperor was good. That he was the best of us. The reason that we weren't scrabbling in the dirt trying to survive. Sure, he had a temper, but didn't we all? And yes, he had to think about the bigger picture at times because he ran an entire *empire* – didn't that justify anything he had to do to maintain stability?

By the Pits, I cringe now just remembering how deep his hooks were into me back then. Into everyone. Let me state it here and state it true: The Emperor is a gods-damned monster. You might think that he couldn't possibly be worse than the Enemy and you would be right. But he is every fucking bit as bad. He doesn't care about anything except himself and his own goals but covers it in thick layers of charm so charismatic that you would lay yourself down to die on his behalf with no hesitation.

He is a wolf in sheep's clothing. A dragon masquerading as a human.

No. Worse.

He is the ranulskin. A parasite that corrupts through sheer charisma.

The Enemy had been right about one thing when I first met Him – at least He didn't pretend to be something He wasn't. The Emperor pretended to be everything good in the world. Portrayed himself as the benevolent god-made-flesh that would ensure everything was alright. The reality is far, far different.

And it wouldn't be long before I found that out for myself.

"Calidan? What's wrong?" My feet had led the way to Ella and she looked at me with confusion evident in her eyes.

"Can we talk in private?"

A slight widening of her eyes and she beckoned me to a nearby bench before waving a hand, shutting off all external sound. "What is it?"

As succinctly as I could, I provided everything that the Imperator had relayed and Ella's eyes grew wide. "I...see," she said slowly. "So, even if the Emperor is outside of the citadel there is no guarantee that we can get in and out undetected." She let out a sigh. "This makes things more difficult."

"Try 'impossible.'"

A shake of her head. "Nothing is impossible. No, this just makes things harder but there is always a solution. We just have to find it."

"Ella, getting the Emperor out of the citadel in the first place was going to be hard enough," I said, exasperation tinging my voice. "How do you expect to manage that *and* get past two *Great Heart-bonded* without anyone knowing?!" I shook my head in disbelief at her unrelenting optimism. "Worse, we don't know what their skill sets are or those of their bonded. If they are anything like Anatha then we wouldn't stand a chance."

Ella narrowed her eyes. "I'm not going to give up, Cal. There will be a way, I just have to find it. *We* have to find it. That is, if you aren't giving up?" Her eyes bore into mine, judging.

Eventually I shook my head. "No. I'm not giving up. But I'm also not going to kill people who don't deserve it."

At that she barked a bitter laugh. "Didn't Wolf's Hollow teach you anything? Everyone deserves it. You just have to figure out the *why* later."

PRESENT DAY 10

Giant scorpions. Despite everything I had been through I still had nightmares to this day about the overpowered, oversized metal monstrosity that we had destroyed in the desert rift during the early years of the Academy. The bastard thing had taken three Imperators and a whole host of Imps to bring it down, and not before eviscerating my dormmate Damien. It had been my first time encountering Pre-Cataclysm hostile technology and it had left an extremely sour taste.

A taste not improved by the titans unleashed by the Enemy. I mean, if you're going to kill someone at least have the guts to do the murdering yourself. Getting some animated machine to do your dirty work for you? That's low.

What now? My seraph was bottomed out again and unless I could find another way out, I wasn't going to be able to take the star-metal with me.

Really wish I had focused on portal seraph right about now...

Not that it would have worked. Without Seya my pool was too small to open a tear through space.

Come on Calidan, use your brain. If you can't use seraph, figure out another way!

Growling with frustration, I pulled myself to my feet, ignoring my shaking limbs and began searching around the walls that caged me. Much like the outside, they were the same white metal but softly lit with that glowing light that made everything feel quite welcoming.

Running my hand along the walls, I circled round and round, trying to avoid the thoughts running through my head with the guise of exploration.

Had I failed? Was it over before it had even begun?

Shut up, Calidan. Focus.

Had it all been for naught?

Keep searching. Don't think.

Everything I had done. Everything I had become. For what? Did he just get away with it? Did they all just-

Click.

I paused. Took a half-step back.

Click.

The slightest of movement in the wall. Taking a breath, I pressed harder and felt the entire panel shift, depressing until it slid inwards and up, revealing some device with a series of buttons and a glass panel that flickered with light.

Errr. Scowling at the display before me, I thought better of randomly pressing things and reached out. *Are you there?*

Make it quick. The words didn't have any of the Wanderer's usual relaxed charm.

I need a way out. Have you seen this before? Willing the image to her I waited for a few moments before she replied, her tone cautious.

Show me what is behind you.

Obeying, I felt the shock ripple down our connection. *Well. You've stumbled onto something that Rizaen would destroy her city to keep hidden.*

What is it?

An amplifier. It can amplify the effects of whatever is within the pyramid. If that is a seraph user, they become an order of magnitude more powerful.

She had the star-metal inside it.

Interesting. Whether the effects of the material could be amplified, considering its nature, I'm unsure. But we can discuss this further on your return. The button to your bottom right – the red and white one – that will open the emergency exit. Be swift and safe.

Got it. Thanks.

Cutting the connection, I tucked the star-metal safely into a belt pouch and readied my weapons.

This wasn't going to be easy.

But...if I played my cards right, it might be strangely cathartic. I just had to stay calm, assess the situation and get out of here as quickly as possible.

Taking a deep breath, I drew Asp and Forsaken. *You've got this. Stay calm. Stay focused.*

I slammed the button. A rush of air announced the opening of the concealed door. *Move like lightning. Don't engage. Just get-*

Through the aperture of the door I saw their six-legged forms, the gleam of metal and those deadly, vicious tails. The calm side of my brain shut down and a more...primal side of me took over.

"Fuck you, you shiny metal bastards!" I screamed before sprinting out the door.

See? Cathartic.

The cave lit up with light as a mixture of green seraph and red beams of concentrated death erupted into being. Weaving through the array of tail-beams with the fastest series of unpredictable kaschan I could manage, I spun my way into the centre of the creatures and then used what little seraph I had left to unleash Asp in all her glory. A wave of dark emerald washed over everything in sight, the impact of the blast slicing into the metallic monstrosities and sending a couple tumbling backwards.

And that was when I saw something new.

Those at the tail-end of my attack showed no sign of damage, instead they had a glowing energy field around their forms, something that the original scorpion I had fought had not shown.

Hmm. Upgrades.

Indomitable pincers lunged for me, the air shattering with *clack* after *clack* as I jumped and twisted through the air. Landing on top of one, I dodged to the side as the tail crashed through the air before parrying an incoming blow with Asp and stabbing down with Forsaken. The obsidian blade sliced through the shield without effort, the strange metal dissipating the energies that assaulted it and meeting the metal carapace with an impact that resounded like a bell.

Pressing harder, I felt the tough exterior of the scorpion began to give way before a snapping tail sent me tumbling through the air to crash into one of the abandoned pre-Cataclysm houses in a collision that could likely bankrupt nations.

Thankfully, if there is one thing that you learn as a monster-hunter, it's how to get hit and get back up. Generally a fear of imminent chewing will get you up and moving - the adrenaline spike is like nothing else - but learning how to roll with the impact and tuck into the inevitably brutal landing is what keeps you intact and, more importantly, in the game.

Of course, a healthy dose of seraph helps too.

My seraph shield lit up the room as I sat half-crouched, blinking away the dizziness from the blow. A spark of light touched my eyes and I flung myself sideways, the beam of energy sweeping in a diagonal line and carving its way through the building as I ducked aside.

Would be nice to have some more seraph right about now.
Another beam. Another precarious dodge.
The house groaned.
Oh shi-
Boom!

I don't know if you know this, but houses are generally pretty heavy things. I heartily recommend not having them fall down on you. The seraph I used to stop the roof from caving in my skull was the last meagre flicker of my pool. Any more and I knew that I would feel the debilitating onset of seraph-withdrawal, rendering me worse than useless.

Not looking good Cal. As I shifted aside another priceless relic of an ancient time, my eyes flickered towards the tiny spot of light emanating from the roof.

Escape.

The flash of red eyes in the shifting gloom.

Revenge.

My hands tightened on the hilts of my blades, caught in a moment of indecision. A half-molten pincer lanced out of the gloom – Asp's work – and I swivelled, Forsaken scoring a line along the arm as I danced aside. Black gunk spurted out of the machine, accompanied by electrical discharge that lit the cavern in stark relief. The machine staggered and then lurched away to rejoin its comrades.

My eyes darted from side to side. *One. Two. Three. Four.*

Two lay in smouldering heaps; Asp successfully marking her territory yet again. I had hoped for better results from that initial blast but hey, two less death-machines in the world wasn't a bad start.

Another flicker towards safety. A half-turn towards the dangling rope.

Four scorpions. One killed Damien. Nearly killed everyone. Run Calidan. Run!

Baring my teeth at the four watching machines I raised my arms wide. "Come on then! I haven't got all fucking day!"

It was inevitable. Given the choice between safety and revenge I was always going to choose the latter. It was a part of me. Drove me. The need for revenge had shaped my very being and made me, well...*me*. I'm not saying that's necessarily the best thing, and I'm certainly not saying that it's all been worth it, but I'll be damned if I spend any more time running from the things I hate.

I've done enough running. Skyren or scorpion. Kyrgeth or Power. It didn't matter. I wasn't going to run anymore.

It was my turn to hunt.

Four red-glows lit the cavern, like the eyes of the red-eyed beast, and I roared my hatred. I had no seraph, was outnumbered and out-sized.

Fuck it. Forsaken? Time to party.

The blade seemed to tremble as it answered my call, icy-pain radiating up my wrist as the blade turned into liquid night.

Light bloomed. A burning sun purifying the shadows. As one with the machines, I turned to see an immense figure plummeting from the sky, blazing sword in hand. Shocked at the sight, my concentration wavered and the grasping tendrils of darkness loosened from my wrist, sinking back into the hilt of the blade.

Forsaken slept once more.

Cassius hit the ground like an apocalyptic thunderbolt, a wash of flame billowing out in all directions. Before the wave of flame had even had chance to dissipate, he burst through it, charging like an enraged bull.

An enraged bull with one very large sword.

A familiar mind touched mine. *I thought you might make this choice and that help might be warranted. So, as some used to say: reinforcements have arrived.*

My thanks, Wanderer.

Thank me by not dying. Get it done.

Turning back to face the scorpions, I liked to think that they looked somehow perturbed at the latest development despite their unchanging faces. Raising Asp high, I pointed with the tip, feeling the familiar wash of the joy of battle flood through me.

"Oh, you're so very *horribly* fucked now. Die well, arseholes."

Cassius streamed past, a blur of orange flame. Oathbreaker cleaving down diagonally right to left, the flaming blade meeting the shield of the nearest scorpion and shearing through it with impossible momentum to carve deep into the brain of the beast.

Credit where it was due, unlike natural-born monsters these metal abominations didn't know the meaning of panic. They adapted smoothly to the threat in their midst, tails flaring with red light and pincers crashing.

But if I was a different man to the child that had first encountered these contraptions, Cassius was something else entirely.

A thorough-bred killing machine.

Despite the horrors that the Emperor had inflicted upon him there was something to be said for the outcome, for Cassius was no longer a mere mortal. His reflexes were beyond compare, allowing him to duck, dance and dodge between gleaming claws and razor-sharp blades with ease. Moreover, the sheer power he could deliver behind his blows was something few could hope to match. Metal carapaces buckled under the thunderous impacts of his attacks, the armoured frames of the scorpions enough to withstand the cutting edge of the mighty blade but not the force behind it. In moments two of the scorpions lay in crumpled heaps, sparks spraying as the lights in their eyes died.

With a wild laugh I joined the fray, parrying the whirlwind of blows with Asp whilst delivering retribution with Forsaken, the black blade more than a match for the opposing metal and scoring deep lines with each strike. Spinning under a claw, Forsaken cleaved through a leg; the monstrosity immediately adjusting to life on five legs rather than six, but focusing on me for just a second too long and taking a front-kick that could break mountains. Cassius hit it so hard that the entire creature – something that must have weighed several tonnes at least - lifted completely off the floor and smashed into the wall. Rising up, I parried the descending stinger that was lunging for his back, deflecting it to one side whilst Cassius swivelled, Oathbreaker rising from the ground in a half-moon to sever the tail in a burst of electrical energy. Rolling past the big man, I launched Forsaken at the gap in the house wall, the blade lancing deep into the shield of the slowly moving scorpion, red energy flickering as the blade consumed it. Held aloft in mid-air, it felt almost like the beast was holding it aloft on purpose and offering its non-life to me.

It was a reaping I gladly accepted.

Sprinting forwards, I darted aside as a tail sparked, red energy scoring the ground beside me, before jumping into the air and twisting, delivering a spinning kick directly to the hilt of Forsaken and driving it deep into the scorpion's eye in a hail of sparks.

As the glow from its eyes dimmed, I turned to see Cassius had already finished his foe and was looking at me with puppy dog eyes, barely out of breath.

"Thanks man," I said, pulling Forsaken free with a metallic ring. "You saved me from doing something silly."

A smile spread across his face and he nodded. Whether that was Cassius or just co-incidence I didn't know for sure but I chose to believe the former.

"Come on," I muttered with a weary sigh, feeling the weight of the metal in my satchel. "Let's get out of here before everyone in this Pits-damned desert comes after my head for robbing their queen."

Cassius grinned, swung Oathbreaker around like he was twirling a stick and slung it into the cavernous sheath on his back. "After you."

I stopped dead. "Cassius?"

The big man looked at me but didn't speak again despite how suspiciously I searched his gaze. Eventually I gave up and shook my head. "If it comes to light that you're just fucking with me these days I'll…I'll…" I snorted. "Hells, I'll give you the biggest damned hug of your life."

Turning away before I could see his reaction, I sniffed and gestured. "Come on. Let's go home."

CHAPTER 38
Concepts

Cassius

His muscles *burned*.

He could feel the flesh twisting, the skin tearing and healing and knew that he should be more concerned than he was, but everything felt so... distant now. It was hard to concentrate. His thoughts drifting more and more.

Always coming back to Ella.

Ella with her beautiful eyes.

With her loving smile.

With her sharp knife.

The table was no more; the Emperor's work seemingly done. Now he floated in a tank, tubes lacerating their way along his flesh, pumping him with a disconcertingly large array of unknown fluids.

He should care. He tried to care. But trying to concentrate was like trying to catch a cloud, and without being able to focus properly caring was impossible. He knew that the Emperor visited. He felt the man's eyes on him more often than not, even if he couldn't physically see him himself. Once upon a time that might have been unnerving, but now it was just the way of things. It had been like this for what felt like an eternity; an unknown length of torturous agony. His previous life – happy once – felt like a speck within the vast depths of his torment. And yet Ella was always there. Always with him. At once both comfort and nightmare.

Had she ever been real?

Was this all a twisted dream?

The tube was starting to feel cramped. Strange.

Seya

Calidan?

Calidan, can you hear me?

Foam lathered Seya's flanks, her tongue lolling out the side of her mouth as she stumbled through the forest, her paws aching and tender from combat and relentless running. She focused on her bond but knew that they were still too far away. She could feel Calidan but the thread that bound them was too thin at this distance for communication. She only hoped that he could tell she was getting closer and move to help her.

Not that she truly needed help, mind. She would be able to get out of this on her own, she was adamant about that. Still, a little support would be appreciated. If only to get these blasted monsters out of her way!

The tree nearest to her exploded into blades of razor-sharp wood as the troll lumbered out of the dark, its club already arcing round for a second swing. Seya felt the tell-tale trickle of fresh blood running down her hide and swerved away, hearing the thudding footsteps drop behind her, just in time for the second and third creatures to descend upon her position.

It had been like this the entire way. She was fairly certain that the warlock with the thyrkan hunting party was transporting the trolls when they caught up, sending them just ahead of her to try and slow her down. Unfortunately, bit by bit they were managing.

At first she had barely recognised the trolls as a threat. Sure, they were ferocious and powerful creatures with an uncanny ability to regenerate, but when she was in full motion it was like they were almost standing still. However, each extra wound had slowed her down, brought her closer to their level of speed, and soon she wouldn't be able to outpace them. Soon, she would have to fight to get past and that wouldn't be a fight she could afford to have, for whilst the strange lizard-creatures behind her were pathetic in practically every way, she had to admit that they had endurance. She didn't know if they were somehow being buoyed up with seraph or something she didn't understand but the beasts were never far enough behind for her to feel secure. A fight with the trolls would at best slow her more and at worst...well. She had first-hand experience with how effective a combatant they could be. Whilst in normal circumstances she would bet on herself achieving victory, the reality was that she was exhausted.

Dropping down from the tree canopy that she had used to outmanoeuvre the second and third trolls she took a deep breath and forced herself to continue. She was fairly certain she had now passed into Hrudan which meant that the empire wasn't too far away.

... She just had to cross a hostile country filled with minions loyal to the Enemy. Easy. *Calidan, please hear me.*

"Concepts." Bastion said the word like it had *weight*. She eyed the class of Imperators and grimaced. "This is both an extremely simple and extraordinarily difficult thing to teach. Normally it is something that Imperators aspire to achieve, with little hope of actually doing so. It is, in essence, an understanding of something so complete that your will in creating it is ironclad. Irrefutable. In essence, when you understand something so completely, you have control over it. With that knowledge you can create something much more powerful than a normal seraph creation."

She saw the confusion rippling amongst us and rolled her eyes. "Like I said, very simple, but very hard to achieve, because how do you go about understanding something to that level? Do you focus on what you want to be able to create a concept for and take it apart piece by piece or do you cast the same seraph spell over and over again in an attempt to better understand its working?" She shrugged. "I can't really give you the best answer. Honestly? I do not expect anyone to leave these classes with a fully formed concept. The best I really hope for is that you become more effective with the seraph at your disposal, and that in itself is extraordinarily useful. Remember, out of the two-hundred and fourteen Imperators currently on the Academy's ledger, three have formed concepts, so the odds are stacked against you."

I looked to my side and saw Rikol's eyes blazing with fervent light. Nudging Sophia, I nodded in Rikol's direction. "I bet you ten silver he manages it."

Sophia pursed her lips. "If he doesn't, I think he will explode with frustration."

"Something to share with the class, you two?" Bastion's voice was the eery kind of calm that boded swift and terrible misfortune.

"No, Commander," I replied quickly.

Bastion's gaze stiffened. "To be a commander, there needs to be something to be in command of. For now you can refer to me as Bastion, Imperator Wyckan, or Ma'am."

"Yes Ma'am."

"Good, now shut up." Turning back to the rest of the class she cracked a smile. "You're probably all wondering why a concept would be hard when – excuse the pun – the *concept* of it is simple. At the end of the day, it comes down to the complexity of the seraph. You're going to find it much easier to obtain true and complete understanding of a rock than you are something ineffable, like time."

"Is that possible?" Rikol asked instantly, rapt.

"It wouldn't surprise me," came the casual reply. "One of the reasons that the Powers are so, well, *powerful*, is that their understanding of seraph is beyond compare. They likely embody multiple concepts whereas the most successful of us only have one, but then again, we are limited with mortal lifespans and not millennia with which to devote ourselves to our art."

"How is understanding a rock hard?" asked a gangly Imperator with threads of silver running through his beard. "It's a bloody rock."

"At its most basic, yes, it's a rock. A piece of stone," Bastion explained. "But when you begin to think deeper, you might ask yourself what kind of minerals was it made from? How old was that rock and were the minerals within all different ages? How did the crystalline structure within the stone form?" She raised an eyebrow. "Get the picture?"

"And yours is...?"

"Shields," she replied primly. "I understand shields utterly and completely. So much so that my will refuses to accept anything other than my understanding of my creation. And that, my friends, is precisely why you are here."

Scythe rubbed his temples. "Sorry, what?"

"The black void skills of the warlocks," Bastion explained. "At their most basic, they rip apart the will-bindings of our creations at the seams. However, a concept is such a complete understanding of the item or skill that our will is absolute. There are no seams to be ripped apart. Thus..." she raised her hands and shrugged, "the warlocks are less of a threat. It doesn't mean that they aren't still capable of devastating attacks, mind, but it would remove one element of their repertoire."

"So, let me get this right," grumbled silver-beard, "in order to defeat these creatures we need to become more skilled in seraph than practically any Imperator before us and in time enough to for us to be useful? I don't know about everyone else here, but to me that sounds impossible."

"If you want to be elsewhere, Wren, be my guest." The man grunted and made to leave. "Just remember that those who are least prepared tend to be the first to die." Bastion's smile was wolfish as the Imperator froze before slowly sitting back down. "Good. Remember, I do not expect you to be able to embody concepts. However, a better understanding of your preferred techniques is always going to help you to be more effective. That is the primary reason why your seraph cost associated with a particular technique decreases with practice. You understand it better. Simple. Now, anyone want to leave? No? Good. Now, I want you to use the paper that you were given on entry to the classroom and write down everything about your chosen technique. Take it apart in your mind. Figure out how the seraph you use combines to create it. Imagine it, write it down, imagine it again and focus deeper. This is going to be an introspective lesson, so sit tight, shut up and get to work."

She was right, it was bloody boring. But at the end I did feel like I understood my shield a little better than I had before. Hopefully that understanding would give me a much-needed efficiency boost. I was under no illusion that I would be able to create a concept – I just didn't have the skill with seraph for that – but like Bastion had said, every little helped.

When the class ended and everyone filed out, I approached the commander who let out a long-suffering sigh.

"Yes?"

"Ma'am has there been any progress on-"

She cut across me in a tone that brooked no patience. "You know that you would have been informed had there been a change. The Emperor has ruled against a rescue attempt and the sryers have had no luck in being able to determine her exact location. At this point her only shot is to escape and contact you. Has she done so?"

Had she? The bond between us felt a little stronger and the nightmares had stopped but she was so far away that it was difficult to tell. I certainly couldn't hear her, which troubled me more than anything. I was so used to sharing my thoughts with the magnificent panther that being without her was like being back in Wolf's Hollow – cut off from a piece of my own soul.

Mutely, I shook my head and Bastion's eyes softened. "She'll get out," she murmured. "Knowing that cat, she will be out of there in a flash. You'll see."

I must have looked particularly morose because she reached out and clapped a hand on my shoulder. "Come on, let's go and get a beer and you can tell me all about Seya. I'm going to need to know everything I can for when we finally get the go-ahead to bring her back." With a small smile, she gently ushered me out of the door and towards the canteen.

Several hours later, Ella found me and conjured up another sound-blanketing shield. "I heard back from my contact and there is one potential event where we can do this. An event where both the Emperor and the Great-Heart bonded are distracted."

Rubbing bleary eyes to try and clear the haze of alcohol, I focused on her. "Go on...?"

"The Imperator Ball."

I squeezed my eyes shut and pinched my nose. "Sorry, it must be the alcohol talking but I could have sworn you just suggested doing it during the *ball*."

"I did."

Fixing her with as much incredulity as I could manage, I blurted out, "Are you out of your Pits-damned mind?! The Emperor is in the citadel during the ball. Literally everyone is in the citadel at that time – it's the whole fucking point!"

She waited until my outburst was over, expression never wavering. "I know exactly what I'm suggesting. But it is the only time when we are guaranteed that the Emperor and his Great Heart-bonded are away from the silver door. And we both know that distractions can happen during that ball."

"...Distractions can happen? If you're referring to the Enemy's control of multiple Imps, an Imperator, and a betrayal by our own seraph instructor as a 'distraction' then I'm concerned about you."

"It was terrible, sure, but you can't deny that the Emperor was distracted."

"He had a hole through his chest! People *died* Ella." I shook my head, aghast. "Please don't tell me that you think we should organise something similar to turn the Emperor's gaze away from Cassius?"

A flicker of uncertainty crossed her face. "If it worked once, it can work again."

"Ella, this isn't you. You can't be saying this. You wouldn't want people hurt. *Cassius* wouldn't want people hurt."

"I don't care!" she suddenly shouted, fury scoring her features. "I've waited and waited but nothing is happening. This is my shot. My one shot to get to him. And I will take it Calidan. With or without you."

"And what happens if people die? What happens if Rikol, Scythe or Sophia get hurt or killed in your 'distraction'? How would you feel then?"

"They would understand."

"You don't mean that."

She held my gaze. "I do. They know that I will go to the ends of the earth for Cassius. They would do the same in my place under the right conditions."

"You can't be serious!"

"Do you think their hands are clean? You might have been hidden away from the darker side of the Academy missions whilst out hunting monsters but they haven't. Collateral damage is a term in our vocabulary for a reason, Calidan." Her expression grew more intense, almost frantic, as she spoke. "Why do you think Scythe is wanted by the Dusk Court?"

That threw me. "He destroyed a temple..."

A look of scorn. "He destroyed a temple with people *inside*. Common folk. It may have been the Emperor's order but Scythe was the one to carry it out."

"No. I know Scythe. He wouldn't have done that."

"He might not have wanted to, but he did. Because he is an Imperator and following the Emperor's orders trumps everything else. But not for me. Not about this. I'm going to get back Cassius no matter what and may the gods have mercy on anyone or anything that gets in my way." Her cheeks were wet with tears now and her voice was pure emotion. "I want you with me on this Cal, believe me I do. But I don't *need* you on this. It will happen with or without you."

"Ella, you're turning a retrieval of a friend into a potential act of violence against our friends and family. If you can look me in the eyes and tell me that there is no real risk in what you have planned then..." I drifted off, catching the fleeting glimpse of guilt in her eye. "That's it!" I breathed. "It's not your plan, is it?"

Anger sparked. "So? What's that got to do with anything? It's a good plan!"

"Did your contact tell you to do this?"

"She told me it is the only way!"

Ah, so it's a 'she'.

"The only way? Hells, Ella, you could arrange to let loose puppies into the Great Hall or for people to appear out of a giant cake. It's not hard to think of things that would be enough of a distraction for us to slip out of there!"

"It's not enough!" She argued. "The Emperor will know as soon as we pass the doorway. If he isn't in the middle of something that is going to take all of his attention then he will be on us in a flash." She was pleading now. Close to bursting into angry tears. "I don't want to do this Calidan, but I don't see any other choice."

"So that's it then? You listen to the word of someone willing to commit an act of violence upon friends, colleagues... even the Emperor himself, before me?"

"You're too blinded by love," she whispered. "Love for all of this. For everything it stands for. For *him*."

It wasn't too hard to figure out who she meant.

"The Emperor is dear to me," I replied solemnly. "But Cassius is more so. However, I draw the line at committing an atrocity without running through all of the other available options first."

"There are no other options!"

"How would you know!?" I yelled, sudden anger emboldening my voice and causing her to flinch. "If I'm blinded by love for the Emperor then you are blinded by love for Cassius. You're literally leaping at the first chance anyone has offered to rescue him without considering any of the implications."

"I have so-"

"Have you?" I interjected. "I don't think so. Ella, the action that you're suggesting is the kind of thing that someone controlled by the Enemy would do. You would be actively working against the empire and you know precisely what the Academy would do if they ever discovered your involvement."

"They are going to hunt me down anyway!"

"True, they'll hunt you for leaving. But if you do this, it won't be a simple hunt with a chance to explain. It will be vengeance. They will send their most skilled to execute you in a very public and very violent fashion." I shook my head, dismay roiling through me. "Ella, *please* you can't do this. There has to be another way."

"There isn't." Her voice was dull. Lifeless.

"I know you better than that. You're one of the Academy's best Imperators because you are so meticulous in your planning. Rushing into something like this, not thinking it through... that's not you."

"Maybe it should be!" she snapped, colour flooding back into her cheeks. "I've planned and thought and planned some more and where has it got me, Cal? More than a year down the line and I am no closer to him! And the Emperor has the gall to pretend that everything is okay?! No." She shook her head vehemently. "No, it's past time that I stop sitting around waiting for something to happen that fixes this and fix it myself."

"Ella-"

She cut me off with a wave of her hand. "You're either with me or against me Cal. That's all there is. What's it going to be?"

"I..." I shook my head. "I can't. I won't go ahead with such a plan."

"Even to save the man you call brother?" Scorn was rife in her voice. "How lacking in conviction are you!"

"Conviction isn't the thing I lack. Faith in the plan being presented to me is. Ella, don't do this. Would Cassius want such a thing?"

For the first time, her expression wavered. "He- he... it doesn't matter!"

"*Of course* it matters!" I insisted. "Cassius would never condone an action that got innocents hurt. Hells, that's why he had to stay behind at Wolf's Hollow – he couldn't bring himself to cross the line that the rest of us have. Do you really think he would be alright with you saving him if people had been hurt or killed?"

Her face twisted and she crossed her arms. "In the end," she replied icily, "it doesn't matter what he wants. He will be alive and free."

"And hunted by the people he called family."

"Enough of this!" she snapped. "It's clear that you don't have the guts to do what is necessary-"

"And you don't have the brains to think it through!" I snarled.

We stared daggers at each other for a long moment and finally Ella looked away. "You might not be with me, but are you against me Cal?"

"I won't turn you in," I admitted finally, "but if I see any hint of violence during that ball, I will stop both it... and you."

It felt like my words rang in the air – a declaration of intent that, judging by the way she recoiled, hit Ella hard. *She hadn't truly thought I would turn her down,* I realised. *She's so blinded by grief and anger, she can't see the horror of her plan.* For a second, I thought she might crumble, might turn to me in dawning realisation, but then her face hardened into an expressionless mask.

"You can try."

And breaking the sound-blanket, she walked away.

CHAPTER 39

SEARCH PARTY

Cassius

The tube was tight now. He pressed against it, forehead resting on its cool surface. The cold was... nice. Refreshing. It distracted from the burning in his veins, quenched the fire in his flesh. He didn't know how long he had been here, locked in this tube. Time seemed...different now. Minutes passed in a flash or seconds felt like years. There was a *fuzziness* to his thoughts, his memories, like a blanket of wool had been pulled over everything. A fog that shifted continuously, peeling away to provide moments of perfect clarity and cognition and then rolling back in to dim the mind.

He remembered two things. Red eyes and a woman. Her smile was as lovely as her eyes were pitiless. He wasn't quite sure why she insisted on stabbing him though. Perhaps that was the reason why he was in here in the first place? Cassius growled deep in his throat and slammed his head into the glass of the tube. He hated not knowing things! Things that he should know. That he *needed* to know.

The figure moved into view and Cassius's blood ran cold. He wasn't always positive who he was, but they were of a similar height. The man was powerfully built, much more so than Cassius thought people were. But then again, he couldn't quite remember. Perhaps everyone was this big and muscular? A smile crossed the figure's face and Cassius frowned. He didn't like it when the man smiled. Pain often seemed to follow.

"You're nearly there," the man said in a voice that oozed satisfaction. "Nearly ready."

Cassius thudded his head against the glass again. It felt good. Cold. Shocking.

"I know, I know, you must be restless. I certainly was when I went through this procedure. It isn't for the faint of heart. But then you could never have been accused of that, eh, Cassius?"

The man's eyes glowed a vivid gold. Cassius liked gold. At least, he thought that was what the colour was. Maybe it was more of a yellow. Amber? No, dappled light drifting through an orchard. Hmm. Orchards. He loved orchards.

Dimly he was aware that the man was still talking but it all felt like meaningless noise. Orchards were much more interesting. Perhaps there were bees in those orchards. He liked bees.

Cassius snapped back into reality with a muffled gasp. He was still here, still in this nightmarish place! How long had it been now? Months? Years? Where were the others? Why hadn't they come for him?

Where was Ella? He longed to see her face. To hold her hand and kiss her lips.

Schnick. Mocking laughter echoing in the metal halls.

No. That wasn't real. Wasn't her.

He had to get out of here. Had to get back to her. He leaned back and slammed his forehead into the glass.

Once, twice.

It would work, it had to work. Eventually the blasted thing would break and he would be free. If he looked closely enough and squinted really hard, he could just about pretend that it was starting to bulge outwards. And that was hope.

Slam.

Just got to keep going. Just got to keep doing it before-

The fog rolled in.

Cassius rested his head against the tube. The cold was...nice. Refreshing.

Seya

Claws whipped out, shredding through the flesh of the joint and leaving the arm hanging limply. The troll screamed in pain as Seya charged past but she knew that it would be a matter of moments before the flesh knitted back together.

If only her regeneration skill was that powerful, she would show these filthy creatures a thing or two.

The tree trunk caught her by surprise.

Ribs splintered as the massive club connected with her chest and hurled her bodily away. Or at least she thought that was what happened. She had no memory of the hit or the distance she had travelled, but the agonising pain in her chest and the pathway of broken and falling trees left little to the imagination.

A low hoot thrummed the air, causing Seya's ear to twitch. It was close. With a pained growl she staggered to her paws, feeling her ribs grind against each other in a way that very much wasn't how they were supposed to work.

Foul beasts!

Forcing one paw in front of the other, she began winding through the trees once again. She wondered about climbing up into the boughs, but the pain in her chest immediately made her rethink the task. For now, she was grounded.

And that made her vulnerable.

Come on Seya. Keep pushing. Not far now. Got to be close.

The gibbering of something close-by had her change direction mid-step. She couldn't afford any more close encounters. The land of Hrudan was positively *teaming* with strange creatures, any one of which would be a hunting mission for Calidan. The Enemy must have been portalling these creatures in for some time now and she dreaded the reason why. It wasn't hard to see why Hrudan had practically dissolved as a country, not when the Sworn controlled the cities and the forests weren't safe.

Just keep pushing. One paw in front of the other.

Exhaustion tinged her vision. Tendrils of grey insidiously curling in at the edges as she fought for breath against the pain in her ribs. *Keep breathing. Just keep breathing.*

Her foot caught a root and she stumbled, fire lancing through her body at the jerking movement. *Idiot!* she snarled. *Focus! You're not dying here.* Forcing herself back up, she pushed on, hearing the whooping calls of the trolls closing in. *Got to go faster. Must go faster. Don't let Calidan down. Just a little further.*

Just a little more.

I woke up clutching my chest, gasping for breath. Rinoa stirred beside me; eyes drowsy in the early morning light.

"What is it?" she asked sleepily.

"N-nothing," I gasped, wiping away the sweat on my brow and moving to get up. "Go back to sleep."

"...'kay."

It didn't take long for her heavy breathing to resume and I silently staggered out of the room to the bathroom, clutching the sink and trying to control my racing heart. That had been so real. Too real. And that could only mean one thing.

Seya's out!

Instinctively I reached out for her. *Seya, can you hear me?*

Nothing. But the bond felt stronger. More like a rubber band than a piece of string. She was getting closer, I was positive.

Two minutes later I was hammering on the door to Kane's apartment, hearing muttered swears and grumbles as he disentangled himself from his sheets and partner before shuffling over to the door and heaving it open with barely disguised hatred for the outside world.

"What!?" he hissed when he saw me.

"Seya's out!" I replied, too happy to be afraid of the bubbling rage in his voice.

"I don't ca- wait. You're sure?"

"I'm sure."

Releasing a breath, he muttered something, glanced back towards the bed and then held up one finger to me. Gently pressing the door to a close he moved back inside and pulled on some clothes before slipping back out.

"Come on," he said gruffly. "Let's get to my office and we can decide what to do about this."

What's there to decide? I wondered, but followed along in his wake, quickly finding myself in his office wielding a steaming cup of black coffee.

"Right," Kane said after inhaling his own scorching cup. "Seya's out you say. How? Where? Can you talk to her?"

"Yes, she's out. No, I don't know how she did it and I'm not sure where she currently is – north of us for sure and getting closer - but I know she's on the run and badly hurt. As for talking to her, not yet."

"If you can't talk to her, how do you know this?"

"We're connected," I said simply. "Sometimes that connection bleeds into my dreams, even when we are far away. I saw her fleeing multiple foes. Trolls, I think. She got hit by a club but got back up. She's... hurt Kane. Hurt bad."

Kane's expression softened and he poured himself another coffee, this time taking a sip rather than a gulp. "I know the answer to this, but I have to make sure. Are you positive that what you saw was real?"

"There's no doubt in my mind."

"Then come with me." Grabbing his coffee, he swept out of his office and soon I found myself outside a residence that I had never expected to knock on the door of.

The High Imperator opened the door with much more grace than Kane had. If I hadn't detected her getting out of bed, I would have suspected that she hadn't been sleeping at all. Regarding us both for a moment, she pursed her lips and then stepped aside, nodding us in.

I didn't know what I had been expecting but the High Imperator's chambers were tastefully decorated and quite open, providing a nice sense of space. Several tiny trees were in pots around the house, each looking like they were carefully looked after to the most minute detail, and bookcases positively overflowing with volumes lined the back wall.

"Finished your inspection?" the High Imperator asked with a hint of amusement.

Blushing, I hurriedly sat down at the kitchen table. "Sorry."

Waving a hand, she looked at Kane. "I can hazard a guess, but mind telling me what this is about?"

"Seya's free and on the run."

"Ah, good to know my instincts haven't faded just yet." Turning towards me, she asked the same questions that Kane had and I replied quickly and succinctly, leaving her with a frown on her face. Standing up, she retreated into a nearby room and came back with a scroll that she unrolled to reveal a map.

"When we spoke to the Emperor, he suggested that Seya was... here." She placed a pin in the far north. "Deep in Enemy-controlled territory. If Seya has made it out then she is likely attempting to follow her bond back to Calidan. Presuming a somewhat straight line back to here..." she got a ruler and placed it across the map, "then she's somewhere roughly along this line."

Kane let out a low whistle. "That's a long way and, with the loss of the Last Redoubt, most of it is in Enemy-held territory. How fast is she moving?"

"She's injured and she's exhausted," I replied. "She's keeping ahead of her pursuers but slowing down. Until I can talk with her it is going to be hard to judge where she is exactly."

The High Imperator stared intently at the map and I knew that she was deep in thought. Eventually she stirred. "If the Enemy truly wants her then He is going to go all out to prevent her from reaching the defensive lines in the north," she said softly. "We know that thyrkan and worse are already assaulting our forces up there in enough numbers to give concern. If they turn around then Seya will be surrounded." She tapped a finger against her lip. "We need to reach her before then."

"Will the Emperor help?" I asked eagerly. "He could portal us straight to her, right?"

"He could," she allowed. "However, the Emperor has been... distracted as of late. Unwilling to leave the citadel. And with our losses earlier this month, he might not be amenable to a high-risk rescue mission." Holding up a hand to forestall my outburst, she continued. "That doesn't mean that I won't ask him, however. With luck, we can go and get her as soon as a team is put together. If he declines then we will have to do this the old-fashioned way."

"And what's that?"

She winced. "Until you can talk to her, or see some visible landmarks, it's going to be scrying the entire way along her predicted path and hopefully we can stumble onto her. Then we can portal in."

"I thought you said that the Emperor might not approve?"

"That's true. However, whilst the Emperor is the patron of this Academy, *I* am still its leader. If he gives me a direct order against it, my hands will be tied. Until then, I will proceed as I see fit." She smiled at me. "Seya is a valuable part of our team and more than deserving of our help. I will gladly step into danger on her behalf, as will practically everyone else here."

"Thank you," I replied, choking up. "That... means a lot."

"Don't thank me just yet." The High Imperator cracked her neck from side to side and stood up. "Right. I'll catch the Emperor first thing in the morning. I know that Seya is running for her life right this instant, but I do not want to risk the Emperor's ire by disturbing his rest. In the meantime, I'll go and wake Korthan and the scryers and get them started. Calidan, I suggest you go to the canteen and brew a very large pot of coffee – some people are bound to be pretty grumpy, especially you-know-who."

I winced, already envisioning Korthan's tongue lashing of whoever dared wake him up. "I'll get on it right away."

"Excellent." She nodded firmly and stood. "Let's get to work people. We've got a friend to save."

***

The High Imperator didn't hang about. After ushering me towards the canteen, she was away, knocking on doors with impossible-to-ignore staccato bursts until the occupant opened up and then directing them to the canteen for much-needed coffee from yours truly.

Scrying, particularly scrying for something specific within a large area, is a mentally intensive task. I've never had the knack for it myself but those who can have impressive mental fortitude and are able to achieve levels of focus rarely seen in others. Riven, rest her soul, had been one of those people, which had been our primary reason for bringing her onto our team for that ill-fated rescue mission of Sarrenai.

Ella was another such individual. Though she didn't prioritise scrying, she had enough of a talent for it that she was drafted into the search group. Her eyes found mine as she walked into the canteen and a flurry of emotions flickered through them. In the end, her impassive mask dropped back into place and she accepted a coffee from me with a nod before settling down with the others.

Frankly, it didn't surprise me that she was here. Ella loved Seya, as did all of my dorm. I like to think that even if Ella and I were set on slitting each other's throats we would set our differences aside to help our favourite panther.

Once the High Imperator had woken everyone required, she returned to the canteen with the map and set about giving orders regarding search locations whilst I spent the rest of the early hours trying and failing to contact Seya.

As dawn rolled in, the High Imperator disappeared, riding to the citadel to make her case to the Emperor whilst we continued with our work. She returned past noon, her face marred by a deep frown. Meeting my gaze, she nodded towards her office and I followed, already knowing the answer from her body language.

Once her office door was shut, she let out a long, frustrated sigh.

"He's not going to do it, is he?"

A shake of the head. "The Emperor is...indisposed. Apparently, he is in a critical stage on his project and can't be disturbed. His Master of the House had been left with standing orders to refute any and all claims on the Emperor's time, including mine."

"So..."

"So we have to do this the hard way. Any luck with the scryers or contacting Seya?"

I shook my head. "Nothing yet."

"Understood. Keep at it. I'll talk with Adronicus and Kane about getting a response team assembled for when we determine her position."

Dismissed, I returned to the room we were using as an operation base. Korthan was leading the scrying team with his usual acerbic wit, providing scathing commentary regarding people's ineptitudes when they reported nothing of interest. When I walked in, his rheumy eyes locked onto me like a hawk.

"News, boy?"

"Emperor can't help."

"Pah!" Korthan scowled. "He doesn't like to make things easy for us. Like combing across an entire countryside with seraph is simple!"

Unable to resist a dig, I cocked my head quizzically. "An entire countryside? Fairly certain we have a much smaller area of focus than that, or did your old eyes miss the highlighted search area?"

The old man growled and a few of the scryers chuckled nervously before ducking their heads back to their work as his glare flashed around the room before landing back on me.

"Considering that you lost your cat in the first place, you best find a better way of keeping tabs on her. A bell, for instance."

"Tell you what, when we get Seya back, I'll let you try and put one on her. I can only imagine that going well..." I smiled wistfully and some of the pain I was trying to hide must have shone through because Korthan's voice became softer.

"We'll get her back, lad. Just you see."

"...Thanks."

"Don't mention it." Clearing his throat noisily, he turned back to his desk and waved a dismissive hand towards me. "Now kindly piss off and distract someone else."

"You got it."

Finding myself at a loose end, I wandered to the practice yard and began practicing kaschan. The movements that I had ingrained into my body acted like a meditative trance, providing relief from my thoughts and concerns as I flowed through circle after circle. People came and went but I didn't stop, moving through every circle that I knew and then starting again at the beginning. By the time darkness fell, I was drenched in sweat with my muscles burning, and a group of first and second years had gathered to watch. They scattered as I walked off the yard, no doubt terrified of meeting an actual Imperator, and I could only smile in fond remembrance of my own time during those years. It seemed a lifetime ago and felt like it had happened to a different person.

I looked down at my calloused hands. Hands that had fought and killed so many times over the years that I had lost count of my kills. Remembered Wolf's Hollow and the 'lessons' that I had learnt there.

...Maybe my subconscious was correct. Perhaps I was a completely different person now to that young idealistic child haunted by nightmares of glowing red eyes.

Whether that was a good thing or bad, remained to be seen.

Of course, instead of happening during my long hours of meditative exercise it was when I was soaking in the hot pools that the first flicker of awareness touched my mind. At first I wasn't sure if I had imagined it, so faint was our connection. Focusing, I reached out as far as I could, pushing down our bond with everything I had.

Seya?

Calidan! There was a burst of emotion that hit me like a tonne of bricks. Among the feelings were flickers of memory and flashes of the present, above it all an overwhelming sense of exhaustion.

Seya! I bolted upright in excitement, sending water sloshing everywhere. *Where are you? How are you?*

I could feel the strain as she replied. *Somewhere in Hrudan, I think. I'm hurt badly and they're closing in.*

Who is chasing you?

Thyrkan, a warlock, and some monsters – trolls mostly.

Mostly?! I waved away my incredulity at that – most people or creatures wouldn't survive a run-in with one troll, let alone multiple. *Listen, we're putting together a rescue party but I need to know, are you heading straight for me or have you detoured?*

Had to move around a lot. Too many enemies.

Shit. I frowned. *Okay, I need you to find landmarks. Something that our scryers can use to pinpoint your location.*

She didn't reply and I felt the sensation of burning pain along the bond. *Seya? What's happening?*

It's okay. I'm okay, came the weary reply alongside a fresh wave of agony. *Landmarks. Will do.*

"Oi!" someone called through the steam, distracting me from the conversation. "Stop waving that around already! Could put someone's eye out."

Rolling my eyes, I slipped out of the tub and – barely pausing to dry – pulled on fresh clothes before sprinting out the door.

Seya was much more tired and hurt than she was letting on. We needed to move fast.

CHAPTER 40
Rescue Mission

The High Imperator took one look at my face as I burst in and swivelled. "Rescue squad! Gear up for combat. You have five minutes." As her bark of command died away, she turned back. "How is she?"

"Hurt. Exhausted."

"Got a location?"

I shook my head. "Nothing concrete. Likely in Hrudan but hasn't been able to maintain a straight line so could be out of our search zone. Unless you have a better idea, I'm going to ride along and call out what I can see."

"Good plan," she agreed before clapping her hands sharply. "Scryers!" she called. "Listen to what Calidan is describing and hunt for it. We do not have long so be fast and thorough."

Taking a chair, I closed my eyes and sank deep into the bond until I could feel the power in her body, the pain of open wounds and broken bones and see the world through her eyes.

"She's running through a forest," I called out. "Pine trees mostly. Terrain appears to be predominantly flat."

Noticed any landmarks? I asked privately.

Nothing. Just forest. Though she spoke mentally, I could almost hear the wheeze in her voice from her broken ribs. *Forest and thyrkan.* Even the usual scorn as she said the name of the lizard-man race was gone. That more than anything was an indicator of just how tired she was and my concern for her grew. Now that I was in her body I had a much better understanding of how severe some of her wounds were and was honestly shocked that she was still on her feet.

Great Hearts – they practically defined the term 'durable'.

For the next hour or so I maintained my link to Seya, calling out anything useful that I could see that the scryers might be able to use to narrow down the search window as she dodged trolls and weaved around thyrkan. Unfortunately the forest she was in appeared to be extensive – a common trait of the Hrudan region – meaning that I largely wasn't much help to the scrying team.

That was, until her ears picked up a sound different to that of the thudding footsteps of trolls or lithe steps of the thyrkan. It was the rhythmic *thwack* of axes into wood. Seya moved to traverse around it when I was seized by an idea. *Wait! Go closer.*

Without arguing, she turned again and loped in the direction of the axes blows. *What are we looking for?*

If it's a big lumber camp or not. If it is, I would be surprised if you weren't close to a settlement.

The trees began to thin out and soon Seya paused at the edge of a large clearing with a sizeable lumber yard in the middle. Several burly men were wielding large hatchets with the skill of born woodsmen, each blow slicing deep into the flesh of the tree.

Looks pretty large. See if you can get behind the lumber yard and hunt for tracks.

It didn't take long for Seya to cross the open terrain, her body staying low to the ground and flowing from stump to stump. Deep rutted tracks met her eyes and she quickly followed, leaving the lumberjacks behind. I sincerely hoped that the trolls missed the men, otherwise things were about to end badly for them, but the muted roars and screams that reached her ears a few minutes later suggested that luck hadn't been on their side.

There! A small fortified town with walls of heavy timber met Seya's eyes as she crested over a low rise. Calling out the surrounding landscape and the features of the town, I heard the map-readers pouring over the parchment and barking orders at various scryers.

Come on, come on! I thought, wishing that they could work faster. *Seya, can you get any closer? See any signs that might let us know where this is?*

I'll try. My partner put on a brave face as she left the relative cover of the forest. I knew that she didn't like to be so exposed – particularly when she was already being hunted – but if she could just get a glimpse at something, *anything*, that might give us a clue then we could help her out.

Shouts from the fort walls.

They've seen me.

A little closer. Just a little closer, I pushed. *There's some kind of sign. What is that? Brun'faral?* Reading the word aloud, I heard the map-readers feverishly pour over the map once more.

Brun'farak, Seya said as she got a little closer. I repeated the word out loud just as I heard the first *thwack*. A length of wood spiralled through the air and slammed into the ground a couple of feet away. *Ballista! Run Seya!*

The massive panther was already turning away, mission done. As long as we could find the town on the map, the scryers would be able to find her and-

The world spun sideways and flipped with vertigo-inducing force, accompanied by a gut-wrenching yowl. Slowly we skidded to a halt and didn't move.

Seya?! SEYA!

The bond was faint. Weak. I could feel the heaviness in her hind-quarters, the huge bolt having struck through her abdomen – a blow that would have been instantly fatal for practically anything other than a Great Heart.

Seya, hang on!

Tears were pouring down my face as I desperately tried to cling onto her tenuous spirit. I could feel the frenzy of activity around me, the shouted questions, but focused solely on her.

C-c-cali...

Seya!

Her voice faded away and I reacted instinctively, knowing full well that what I was about to do went against everything she or Anatha had ever taught me. "Get a healer," I croaked out loud.

"For Seya?" came the questioning response.

I shook my head. "For me."

And threw myself into the bond.

Healing a Great Heart. The biggest sin in Seya's eyes that I could ever attempt. She knew that her body was too big for me to make much of a dent. That I would burn myself out long before I could make a difference.

In that moment, I didn't care. Seya was my bonded partner and she was dying. I could not, *would not,* let that happen. Throwing open my seraph pool, I drained it completely, *willing* Seya to heal.

Nothing happened.

Seya's spirit continued to diminish, her vitality plummeting.

Seya. I'm here. Just hold on. I'm going to fix it. I'm going to fix everything. Don't you dare die on me. You hear?!

I remembered how it felt when Seya healed me. She didn't – couldn't – use seraph like I did. She was an immense reservoir of the stuff, but she couldn't actively choose to use it. Her body was some kind of amalgamation of seraph and genetic modification and so it instinctively drew on her reserves for healing, but the process was slow compared to the wounds she had taken. Which meant that I had to kick it into high gear. She did something similar to me, forcibly activating something in our bond that caused me to draw everything I could from my partner. Lips curling back in a grimace, I searched my connection to Seya and there I found it. Something that was partially hidden, as though it was not meant to be used.

I didn't have time to mess around.

If I likened it to a door, some people might have tried to circle round it, or pick the lock. Not me. I bulldozed my way through.

And promptly died.

Well. The medicae say I had what looked like a massive heart attack. A series of them in fact. I'm fairly certain that if they hadn't been there I would have toppled over and never have awoken. I'm told that there was plenty of screaming and confusion. Lots of tears and swearing. Honestly? I wasn't aware of any of that. Instead, I was screaming in my soul as my very being was ripped asunder and sent flooding towards Seya.

It wasn't pleasant.

I could feel it beginning to work. Seya's body was being forced into overdrive, her healing accelerated, but it needed sustenance. It needed seraph. And as I was fresh out, my life-force was the next best thing. The bond latched on like a lamprey and refused to let go, greedily devouring my core in a series of moments that felt entirely too fleeting and yet so very eternal.

Thankfully, I managed to skip the whole 'life flashing before my eyes' malarky. I had seen that one too many times already and it had begun to get a little boring. Instead, with a realisation that could only come about when one's soul was on fire and at very real risk of being consumed, I recognised that there was one more trick I could play.

Seya couldn't actively use her seraph pool and desperately needed energy. I was fresh out of energy, but could access her pool.

With my last ounce of cognition, I ripped power out of her seraph pool and flooded mine. The energy was taken out as soon as it arrived, but that was okay. I kept pulling and so did she. Locked in an endless cycle of give and take, I burned.

The High Imperator

"Brun'farak. You heard the man. Someone find that location and find it now!" The High Imperator's voice cracked through the air and the scrying team flinched before bursting into motion. Sparing a glance at the fallen Imperator, Acana winced. Calidan didn't look too good. The number of medicae surrounding him was a dead giveaway that something was wrong, but even without them it wouldn't have been hard to see. The man's flesh was growing paler by the second, his breaths coming so rapidly that she wouldn't be surprised if his heartbeat could outpace that of a hummingbird.

He was dying – that was obvious to all – but she wasn't quite sure why. The Academy hadn't had many bonded come through its walls during her time but she was fairly certain that the death of their bonded didn't result in the death of the other.

Which meant, knowing Calidan the way she did, that he was doing something idiotic.

Her face twitched. Unless she missed her guess, Seya had to be back on her feet as soon as possible or Calidan was going to die.

A frustrated sigh escaped her lips. *Bloody typical.*

"Status update?" she snapped, receiving a chorus of negatives in return. "Korthan you old bastard, put that brain of yours to use. Where is this place?"

"Hrudan isn't a country that we have deeply detailed maps of," the old librarian replied, pain at what was happening to Calidan written across his face. "I don't recognise the name."

"I know someone who might." Rikol stepped up, face grave. "The Tracker."

"Who? Ah, wait." Acana held up a hand. "The man now in charge of the scout division."

"We never spoke much about his past, but I do know that he spent time in Hrudan," Rikol explained.

Acana eyed him. "How's your pool?"

"Full enough."

"Get over there and find me an answer."

"Yes ma'am!" Turning smartly on his feet, Rikol paused to grab his long-coat before ripping a hole in the fabric of reality. For the few seconds it was open, a blisteringly cold wind roared through the aperture, sending papers flying and causing all the scryers to lose their concentration.

"Next time," Acana roared into the portal, "do it outside!"

If Rikol heard, he chose not to answer, letting the portal close behind him and leaving a small pile of rapidly melting snowflakes on the ground.

The first medicae to attend Calidan began to shake and held up a hand to her mouth like she was about to be violently sick. A second member of the Academy medical staff moved smoothly into place, her hands placed on Calidan's sweat-covered form as she began to channel healing energy.

"I've never felt anything like it," the first gasped out between the shivers and nausea of acute seraph-withdrawal. "It's like his body is being destroyed and renewed over and over again instantly. The sheer amount of seraph he is channelling..." She shuddered and wretched, wiping her mouth before speaking again. "It shouldn't be possible."

"Whatever is happening to him," the second confirmed, her face already looking haggard in the torchlight, "our healing isn't going to help for long. Like Estasha says, his body is collapsing at a cellular level whilst at the same time those cells are being rejuvenated by seraph. Anything we do is like putting a band aid on someone missing a head."

"And then having that head regrow before vanishing again," Estasha added.

"If we don't tackle this problem at the source, he's going to be stuck like this until wherever he is pulling that seraph from stops its flow."

I can imagine where. The High Imperator pursed her lips. "And will he be alive when she- *it* does?"

The second healer grimaced. "That depends on what state he is in when the flow stops."

"Understood." Acana looked at the remaining two healers waiting for their turn and nodded to herself before snapping her fingers. "You two, you are to make sure that you don't use more than half of your seraph pools, understood? If the flow cuts off, Calidan is going to need all the help he can get, more than what you're able to provide now."

The two nodded as the door opened and Rikol stepped inside, followed by a man with a slightly twisted figure and unusual gait.

"High Imperator," Rikol began, "this is-"

"Elkona Melkhuk," the Tracker gasped, seeing Calidan on the ground and beginning to rush to his side before remembering where he was. "Apologies ma'am."

Acana waved it away. "I appreciate you coming here so swiftly."

"Rikol said it was urgent. It appears he was not wrong." The Tracker's eyes roamed the room before settling on the map on the main table. "How can I help?"

"Brun'farak? Do you know it?"

A frown creased its way down his weathered forehead. "Aye. It is known to me. Small fort."

"Can you place it on this map?"

Stomping over, the Tracker looked over the map before placing a pin in the north-eastern section of the country. "Roughly here."

"Scryers!" barked Acana. "You have your location. Find me that cat!"

"Yes ma'am!"

"Seya?" the Tracker murmured in confusion. "Is she okay?"

"She is badly hurt," the High Imperator replied, moving away from the map and going to clad on her leather long-coat. "I believe Calidan is trying to save her, but it's killing him."

"The boy has spirit. Grit. He does not die here."

"I tend to agree, but I'm going to ensure that he does not."

The grizzled man smiled at the look in her eyes. "I would help."

It was Acana's turn to inspect him properly. "She is under attack from trolls, thyrkan and possibly defenders from the fort. Can you handle that?"

A slight bend to his lip. She would have almost thought it a sneer if his body language wasn't radiating amusement. "Where I am from, trolls are the local wildlife. As for thyrkan and Sworn, they are well known to me. After all, who do you think is keeping these lands of yours safe?"

Acana couldn't help the smile. There was something about the man, something ineffable. She could see why Calidan liked him. Her eyes flickered to his leg. "Can you keep up?"

"You worry about the others. I'll worry about myself."

"Fine, you can join. Do you have a weapon?"

For the first time, the Tracker looked a little abashed. "I'm afraid that Rikol was most…insistent that I come quickly. My axe was left behind." He shook his head in feigned sorrow. "My mother would be shocked."

Acana's nose crinkled in amusement. "In that case, Rikol – take your friend to Adronicus and get him properly equipped. You have two minutes."

"Yessir!"

As the Tracker stomped out with a final worried look at the still prone and suffering Calidan, the High Imperator spoke to the room. "Reactionary team, you have two minutes. Scryers, that's how long you have to find Seya. No excuses. Get it done people."

Swivelling, she strode outside and swept straight to her office, opening her cabinet and strapping on her longsword, the gleaming silver blade looking as new as the day she had acquired it. "Time to go to work, Cinder."

Stepping back outside, she found the reactionary team assembled. The red-haired Rinoa, expression intense – doubtless she had seen Calidan on the floor. Acana's eyes narrowed slightly. She would have to remember to have a talk with her about the potential difficulties that an emotional connection could bring. Kane, her ever-trusty companion stood to her side, gauntlets prepped and ready. Scythe, Sophia, Arin and Ulessa rounded out the group, with Rikol and the Tracker walking around the corner to join as she arrived – the Tracker casually holding a massive battle-axe on one shoulder.

"Let's see… we're all here except for…"

"Sorry I'm late." Bastion strode into the square.

Acana acknowledged her with a smile. "You're right on time. Good. Right everyone, listen up. We're going into a hostile environment with one objective only. *Rescue Seya.* I want this quick and clean. We're going to portal in as close as we can, grab the cat and retreat. Bastion, get your shield up as soon as we're through."

"Understood."

"Don't engage unless you have to, but be warned, Seya was being hunted by practically everything within the Enemy's control. Expect the unexpected. And if you do have to fight," her expression hardened, "do so with extreme prejudice."

"Yessir!"

The door to the scrying chamber flung open and Korthan strode out followed by two others. "Got her!" he exclaimed. "Are you ready?" Seeing her nod, the old librarian moved to the centre of the square. "I'll keep this portal open for sixty seconds. That's about as much as I can handle. If you're not back by then you're making your own way back."

"I can do it," Rikol affirmed.

"Then save your seraph boy," Korthan replied seriously, face already starting to narrow in concentration. "Let the others do the fighting, just in case."

"Nothing new there," mumbled Scythe, causing Sophia to snigger.

Humour in the face of danger, Acana mused. *They've been trained well.*

Drawing her sword, she stepped behind Bastion and began channelling seraph to enhance her reactions and shield. "On Bastion!" The portal ripped open, Korthan swaying with the strain. Instantly the sound of a battlefield ripped through the air, the howls of monsters and the screams of men. "For the Emperor!"

They charged.

Rikol

The portal was opened directly next to Seya, surprising the squad of thyrkan who stood over her, wrapping her limbs with heavy rope. Before Rikol had even truly stepped through the portal, the heads of the six beasts were falling to the floor, Bastion's shield attack showing its value once more.

If they're not fighting here, then where is the- oh.

The Hrudan in the fort were under assault by what looked to be multiple trolls, a small horde of thyrkan and at least five other beasts that were doubtless monsters that Calidan would recognise instantly. The wooden structure was already burning in places and the stench of blood hung heavy in the frigid air. At least one troll was down, pinned to the ground in multiple places by heavy ballista bolts, but the others were too close to the fort now for the heavy weapons to be effective and Rikol knew from experience that a troll could withstand practically anything lesser in size and power. Soon enough the fort walls would succumb and the men and women within would fight a desperate last stand.

"Do you think they are Sworn?" he asked as the High Imperator went about removing the chains off Seya whilst Sophia and Rinoa began trying to remove the ballista bolt that had pierced right through her chest.

"In the fort?" replied Scythe. "Probably not, if they're fighting that hard. I figure Sworn would be opening the doors and welcoming them in."

"Keep pressure on that wound!" barked the High Imperator as the ballista pulled free. "Right, back through the-"

The world went white.

When Rikol could see again, fire raged. White flame – of a type that he had only seen apothecaries make – danced for a hundred feet in every direction, sticking to everything it touched.

"Where did that come from?!" bellowed the High Imperator. "Bastion, do you-"

"It's seraph-infused!" Bastion interrupted. "Whatever it was, it hits hard!"

Boom.

The sound was so faint that he barely heard it over the surrounding uproar but still his heart sank. *Please don't let that be...*

Boom. This time he saw Seya's ear twitch and knew that despite being near death her body was still reacting to the horrific, inexorable sound.

"It's the titan!" he roared, pointing high into the air as a canister arced towards them. Making a split-second decision, he detonated the object, causing an eruption of white flame that drifted onto the ground below, setting the grass ablaze.

"Into the portal, now!"

Wiser words had never been spoken. The High Imperator, Rinoa and Kane levitated the immobile body of Seya and carefully moved her through the portal.

"What about the fort?" Rikol asked as everyone prepared to retreat.

"Nothing we can do for them," Bastion said grimly. "That titan will finish off anything nearby. Come on, let's go."

Rikol didn't go immediately, eyes narrowing at the distant beleaguered fort.

"Rikol, come on!" Sophia's voice through the portal.

"Korthan, how long can you hold?"

"Fifteen seconds!"

Fifteen seconds. Let's do this. Knowing that he didn't have to reserve any of his pool, Rikol scanned the sky and saw the next canister spinning lazily towards his position. "Thank you kindly, titan." Wrapping seraph around the canister he adjusted its direction and smiled wolfishly before putting everything he had into throwing a shield up just in front of the fort. Creatures that had been happily smashing through heavy logs suddenly found themselves hitting a wall of light and rebounding, astonished.

It wouldn't have held them for long – he was nothing like Bastion – but it didn't need to be for long. Just long enough.

Stepping back into the portal, Rikol raised his middle finger to the sky. "This is for Seya!" he roared.

The canister hit.

The world roared back.

Flame that burned a dazzling white spewed out from the epicentre of the impact, sticking to flesh and organic material and not letting go. Just before the portal closed, Rikol could hear the bestial roars turn into high-pitched screams, the fire happily chewing its way through the Enemy's minions, the intense temperature causing skin to slough off, muscle to bubble and bone to crack.

The portal winked out and Rikol found himself face to face with the High Imperator, her expression unreadable.

"When I give an order, I expect it to be carried out immediately," she said and Rikol flinched. "What you did was dangerous and foolhardy. However," she cracked a smile, "that being said...nice job."

"Least I could do for those poor buggers."

"Quite." The High Imperator looked perturbed. "So, that was the titan, I assume?"

"Different weaponry, but no doubt in my mind," answered Rikol. "They must have really wanted Seya to warrant bringing it into the fight."

Acana frowned. "We need to step up the concept training. That *machine* is on a whole other level..." Pursing her lips, she looked up and seemed to realise that she was talking aloud. "Excellent work. We achieved our task and Seya is in the care of the healers. Get a drink and check on your friends."

"Yes sir, thank you sir."

Looking around, Rikol saw that he was the only one left. The others were either drifting away or entering the building that had been utilised for scrying, doubtless eager to check on Calidan. Watching as Bastion walked across the square, he made up his mind and jogged to catch up.

"So, er, Bastion," he began lamely. "What more can you teach me about concepts?"

As Bastion eyed him, he felt a niggle of self-doubt worm its way inside. *He should be checking on his friend*, it said. Ruthlessly he crushed it. He wouldn't become the best without working hard for it. Besides...

Calidan would be *fine*.

I was not okay.

I mean, I was alive...ish, so that was something, but I was locked into an endless cycle of give and take. Time had lost all meaning, just ceaseless agony and relief.

Have I died and gone to the Pits?

How long has it been?

I had no answer to either question. It was hard to maintain focus in this place. To understand the reason behind this eternal torment. Just as I felt like giving up, I felt the tiny tenuous flicker that was Seya solidify. Not by much, but enough.

She wasn't dying. Whatever I was doing was working. Focusing on the tiny flame in my mind, I pushed my thoughts at her.

Seya, can you hear me?

No response.

Seya, listen to me. You're staying alive no matter what.

The subtlest of changes.

Don't you dare die, you hear me? I will never forgive you.

Another quiver. I focused harder and harder.

Seya, don't give up.

I nudged her flame with my mind and instead of feeling a pressure the world became a jumble of images. Fragments of colour spiralling around me in the darkness.

Don't give up. Don't give up. Give up. Up. My words echoed around me and I could feel some unconscious tightening in the unseen walls of the area I now drifted through. Focusing on the nearest one, I willed myself towards it and suddenly-

Steam billowed out from the door as I pushed my way inside. The boy within looked suddenly terrified, unable to make out my glorious visage thanks to the clouds that swirled around him.

"Now-now Seya, let's talk about this..." he stammered.

I grinned, tongue hanging loosely. *Time for your bath.*

With a gasp, I pulled myself out of the fragment. *Memories,* I realised with awe, seeing the massive spiral that whirled around me. *They're all memories.*

Reaching out, I touched another and found myself basking in the warmth of the sun, content in the ray of light, keeping a careful eye on the stag that dutifully ignored me. The Old Man of the Forest was a wily cad. He full well knew I was there, just like he knew I was aware of his presence, but that was the game we played. Perhaps soon I would rise to his challenge and leap to the chase, but... I let out a yawn and rolled over.

Not just yet.

The feeling of agony in my soul diminished somewhat in the calming balm of such a moment. Desperate for more release, more ways to hide from the pain...and no little desire to know more of Seya, I flung myself into the memories, jumping from one to the next. One moment, I witnessed myself trying my hardest to stalk Seya in the forest and failing miserably, the next, I was leaping through the forest canopy, revelling in the majesty of being the Queen of cats. With each memory, the burden on my soul felt lesser and the flicker of Seya's flame seemed stronger. I didn't know if it was helping her somehow – more likely it was the medical attention that I was unaware at the time she was receiving in the outside world – or perhaps she was aware enough to be well and truly pissed that I was delving through her memories – but she seemed stronger for it with each one I went through.

I witnessed the first time she intervened to save my life. The rage bubbling in her chest at the temerity of the scrawny wolves that dared to try and take one of her line away. She had been lonely for so long and the hope that she thought had long been extinguished had rekindled into a blazing fire. She wouldn't, *couldn't* let this chance slip away and roared her fury to the world, shaking the trees around her, before leaping down and forcing fate to follow her paw.

The first time she came across my scent, she knew that I was a potential match. I saw myself through her eyes as she stalked me through the forest. Felt her emotions as she saw the fear and horror written across my childlike features, the devastation and despair oozing through my scent. Witnessing my pain had caused her to offer what comfort she could, slinking down to my puny fire and greeting me with her orange eyes, wishing me to sleep a dreamless sleep knowing that she would protect me.

The flicker that was Seya steadied even more and I took heart. *I'm here,* I thought in-between the bouts of screaming. *I see you and I love you.*

Pushing further, I delved into her past. I witnessed Seya on her own for years, rarely meeting anyone who could understand her or would be willing to take the chance to befriend a panther of her size and grace. I witnessed friends die. Torn from the world by old age or violence.

I witnessed her rebirth. Her old body too worn by time or damage and shutting down, her mind slowly drifting away only to wake up once more – this time as kitten. A kitten who needed to cut her way out of what had once been her body, who needed to find somewhere to hide, rest and grow in safety.

Those moments were the worst. I could feel the vulnerability of the otherwise awe-inspiring Great Heart at that time. Despite her kitten form being already as large as a wolf, she didn't have sufficient mass to be able to gestate another version of herself, so if she died during this phase it would be permanent.

That wasn't to say that she wasn't tempted to end it. Her life had been long and full of hardships. Of loss. Perhaps a final death would give her some peace?

But no. That would be giving up. Letting life rule her rather than the other way round. Seylantha did not give up. She never would.

She probably didn't know how.

Further and further I went. Years turned into decades turned into centuries, all seen through Seya's eyes. I witnessed the fall of towns and civilisations I had never heard of, saw their golden years and noticed their early beginnings. Rarely did she step foot into the places themselves – only when she detected someone of her line – but skirted the edges. Keeping close to humanity but only as a bystander to their actions. The sadness within her heart felt heavier with each memory the further back I went. I had barely felt it in her most recent memories, perhaps she had finally reconciled with whatever hurt she was carrying back then, or maybe bonding with me had helped. Either way, I didn't know, and wasn't vain enough to think that I had managed to get her to be so happy as to forget a pain as intense as the one I now knew she experienced.

There was something else too. The further I went back, the more Seya herself seemed to change. The Seya I knew was a graceful, refined queen, but the Seya back then was more...*wild*. There was an intensity to her that only grew the deeper I went. At times I almost mistook her for a wild creature, her body quivering with the need to run and hunt. Overwhelmed with the desire to kill.

Soon it barely felt like there was any cognition at all. A completely primal creature, lost in her own urges. Worryingly, considering her size and power, if I came across her like that now I would have to declare her 'monster'.

What happened to her to make her like this?

Seya was thousands of years old and her spiral of memories was likely beyond anything that anyone outside of the Powers could generate. By my best estimate, she had spent decades – perhaps a great deal more – as a wild animal. And creatures as powerful as Seya were the very top of the food chain.

With a sinking heart, I pressed on and eventually found what I knew I would.

Seya hunting humans as food.

Seya. Why? What happened to you?

Get out. The voice was a little more than a feather on the wind.

Seya?

Her life force coalesced and suddenly the flickering candle that was her steadied and flared brightly. *GET OUT!*

It felt like a door had been slammed shut in my face and I reeled, suddenly back in the burning embrace of the bond and with nothing to distract me from the agony. Reaching out, I tapped lightly on the edge of the bond. The mental equivalent of knocking on her door. There was no answer.

I'm sorry Seya. I didn't mean to pry.

Still no answer, but her life force was there and growing stronger by the second.

I needed something to numb the pain. I didn't...didn't think. Please forgive me.

For a long interminable moment there was nothing, then she replied, her mental touch lighter than I had ever experienced. Filled with pain, hurt and regret. *You're a complete and utter imbecile. You know that right?*

So I've been told.

The one thing I told you never to do and you went ahead and did it anyway!

You would have died-

I don't care! You are MY responsibility, Calidan Darkheart. MINE. It is a responsibility that I do not take lightly. Throwing your life away in a foolish attempt to save mine is ridiculous.

I gave her a mental poke. *You ARE alive though. Just saying.*

A growl that thrummed through the bond and sent shivers down my spine. *What you've done wasn't meant to be possible. They said that it couldn't be done.*

They?

She clammed up instantly.

Come on Seya, talk to me!

There is nothing to speak of.

You're a legendary creature that has been alive for millennia, so I don't think that is true.

It is...painful to remember such times Calidan. For many reasons. I felt her focus on me for a long second. *What did you see?*

To be honest, I was tempted to lie. To tell her that all I saw were sweet nothings, and not her as a raving drooling creature that reminded me of the Hound. But lies didn't build a strong relationship, and Seya's and mine had to be forged from the strongest steel. *I saw you. You as you are now but the further back I went the more you began to...change.*

Her silence was so long I thought she might have passed out. Eventually her voice came back, a little stronger than before but still little more than the faintest breath of wind. *Everyone changes. For good or for bad. It is my belief that nothing is meant to live for as long as I or the Powers have. Over that expanse of time, change is inevitable and much more pronounced. You know how when you're a child, you feel like every day is so incredibly long? Then, when you're older, the time flies by?*

I do.

It's because of time dilation. For a child of say five years, that is all they have ever known. A year to them is a fifth of their life – a vast amount of time. To an adult of fifty years, one more is just a fiftieth of their life span. Something small and easily forgettable.

When you live as long as I, days begin to feel like they pass as minutes and months as hours. If you don't focus on the present, you can become slave to the past. Wishing for it. Yearning for it. Regretting it. And when you spend days, months, years yearning for something that was long gone and drawing ever further away, you begin to lose sight of who you are. Of reality itself.

The time you saw. I...I was lost. Little more than one of the monsters you hunt. Nothing mattered to me anymore and that only compounded over time. My world became one of survival and instinct, of hunger and rage. And it stayed like that for far, far too long.

...Seya...I-

Save it. I'm not telling you this for your pity. You've seen a side of me that should never have happened. A side of me that I would rather forget.

...But it is the one thing that I cannot bring myself to. I did terrible things lost in that uncaring rage, Calidan. I became little more than animal. A beast of fury and violence. When I think of it now, I realise how fractured my mind was. My sanity. I was lost, utterly and completely. Broken beyond anything I had ever experienced. My mental faculties shut down and I survived purely on primal instinct. The flicker that was Seya wavered and then solidified. *It was a survival mechanism. I see that now. I was too ineffective at that time in dealing with everything that had happened. Unable to process. So, I simply...stopped. Tucked away the past and the problems and focused on one thing and one thing only.*

Survival.

Do you know the worst of it Calidan? The real, horrible truth that I found through the fragments of memory that I have from that time?

Her next words were almost a sob. *A Great Heart doesn't need to eat. It's purely a primal instinct. Everything and everyone I killed during that time didn't have to die. I had no need to consume them, but that's what I did.* Her voice broke. *...That's what I did.*

It's not your fault, Seya.

Of course it is. I let it happen.

Seya, the mental strain of being alive for so long in the first place must be overwhelming. I can't even begin to imagine how you have managed it! Mental health isn't something to ignore. I mean, why do you think there are the Decompression Chambers at the Academy? It's so we can process. Without that, I think I would have lost myself long ago. Hells, I'm fairly certain I was in the process of breaking when I met you.

A flash of warmth. *You were so small then. Scared.*

In my defence, you are a gigantic panther. Some find that intimidating. I reached out for her in the bond, my pain gone in the face of her revelation, and embraced the spark of her tenderly. *Nothing you've done will ever stop me from loving you.*

It's funny. These days, after all the things I've done and knowing the things I will do, I sincerely hope that the same is true for her, because I have long since stopped loving myself and I am not sure I could stand witnessing Seya turn from me.

Still. If she did turn her back on me, as long as she did it free, I would be happy.

Seya's soul had strengthened into a small blaze that no longer flickered by the time I drew back. *Do you think...?*

Yes, she answered. *I'm strong enough that my body will take over naturally. It will take a long time to heal these wounds, but it is better than this forced torment that you are putting yourself through.*

Are you positive? I will stay here as long as-

A vision of Seya booping my head with her paw reached my mind. *I'm sure. I will be safe. Sever the bond. Cease this madness.*

Sever the bond. Got it. Pulling back, I studied the bond, saw how I was drawing in the power from Seya's now dramatically reduced pool a split-second before it got pulled away again. This was going to have to be done with absolute precision. *You made it sound so easy.*

You're the one doing something that shouldn't be possible, she retorted. *Figure it out.*

Sighing through my screams, I immersed myself in the bond. Felt the flow of power in and out. Felt my own pain build and subside like a heartbeat. When the moment felt right, I reached out and cut the cord.

Darkness descended.

When I woke, it was within the Academy medical centre. An exhausted looking Sophia sat by my side, head in her arms as she napped. Almost as though she sensed my movement, she stirred, blearily looked at me through red-rimmed eyes and then shot to her feet.

"Calidan!" she exclaimed, joy lighting up her face. "You're awake!"

"H-hey," I croaked back.

Sophia turned around and pulled open the door, yelling out into the corridor. Moments later I was surrounded by my friends and no small number of rapidly growing irritated medical professionals. Before they were chased out, Sophia turned to me and told me exactly what I needed to hear.

"Seya's fine. She's growing stronger by the day. You saved her Cal."

I smiled. *I saved her.*

And in doing so, unknowingly committed her to something far worse than death.

CHAPTER 41
A BALL TO DIE FOR

"Are you ready?"

I glanced about nervously as I finished pulling on my finery. The richly woven garments still felt wrong to me, even after several years of having had to wear them, but I had to admit that when looking in the mirror, I looked *good*.

Compared to Rinoa however? I was mud on her boot.

"I think so," I replied, turning to once again stare at the red-haired beauty in front of me. A long dress of a blue so deep as to almost be black clad her figure, the lower half splaying out slightly to allow a slight swish as she walked whilst the top section hugged in all the right places. A simple necklace adorned her bosom and a pair of matching earrings sparkled in the light.

She was breathtaking.

"My, my," she murmured, stepping closer to tweak my collar, "I think you might actually be handsome. Who knew?" Winking, she drew me in for a kiss. "But for future reference, the man is meant to be ready *before* the lady."

"Sorry." I winced. "Time got away from me."

"Mhmm." Extending an arm, she cocked an eyebrow expectantly. "Come on, let's get going. The ball isn't going to wait forever."

The ball. The annual citadel ball. Something of my own creation, it had matured over the years, becoming an event that everyone looked forward to. A time to relax and to reflect. We all knew that everyone entering the citadel was being scanned by the seraph detectors to check for black seraph corruption, but thankfully we hadn't had any repeat incidents like the first event.

And hopefully we won't today.

I swallowed a nervous gulp. Rinoa smiled and gave me a comforting pat with her hand. Perhaps she thought me nervous to have such a beautiful partner on my arm, and maybe part of me was, but that wasn't the real reason.

I was nervous because today was the day. The day when whatever Ella had planned might come into fruition. Since our last blow-out argument we had been distant. She refused to speak to me about Cassius, only keeping our conversations related to either Seya or unimportant things. The others had noticed our strained relationship and some innocent questions had been asked, but no one had probed further. Being an Imperator was a stressful job and sometimes that carried over to relationships. Everyone had been through it. They just thought we needed time.

In reality, I needed answers. What had Ella planned? Was she still going to go through with it?

Most importantly, there was one question that was purely for me: what was I going to do?

Ella was my friend. My companion for the last decade. Cassius's partner. She loved him fiercely and I knew she cared for me almost as much, and it was quite possible that this plan of hers would work and Cassius would be free before the evening was over.

But what if the cost was too much? I wanted Cassius free more than anyone, save Ella. But I balked at the idea of hurting friends to do it. That was a line that I was not yet willing to cross. But if Ella was willing to take that step, did I stop her or join her?

Decisions, decisions. Mother-fucking decisions.

"Everything okay?" Rinoa asked as we settled into the carriage.

"Fine," I replied quickly before forcing myself to relax. "More than fine." I smiled warmly. "Sorry. This ball always brings back bad memories, despite how much fun it can be." It wasn't far from the truth. I still had nightmares about what had happened here.

Her face immediately became that of an understanding pity. "I know exactly how you feel. Strange how you can have such mixed emotions about the same thing."

"Tell me about it..." I murmured, eyes drifting to look out the window at the passing scenery.

Squeezing my hand, Rinoa gave me a kiss on the cheek before sitting back. "I do understand. Just note that later tonight I am going to expect some kind of *reward* for my magnanimousness." Her eyes twinkled as I coughed, taken by surprise.

"O-of course, m'lady. You'll be *rewarded* most generously."

"Generously?" she pursed her lips. "I wouldn't go making promises you might not be able to keep..."

"Oh, I'll keep them alright..."

I knew what she was doing – engaging in banter to take my mind off what she thought was the issue – but even knowing didn't make it any less effective.

What a woman.

Thoroughly distracted, the rest of the trip flew by and by the time we emerged from the carriage both of us were breathing hard and wanting nothing more than to hop back in and head straight back to the bedroom.

Unfortunately, this was the one date on the calendar that an Imperator could not miss.

"Calidan Darkheart, Rinoa Falbright," muttered the Master of the House as he checked us off the list. "Welcome, please make your way to the Great Hall."

Nodding at the man, we followed the servant-lined hallway, receiving canapés and drinks until we entered the magnificent hall. Two massive oak tables lined either side, each arrayed with a dizzying array of silver cutlery, leaving the centre for dancing and the rear of the room for the band. The Great Hall was no misnomer; it easily seated the entire population of the Academy with room to spare and served as a reminder of just how truly vast the citadel itself was. It had become almost commonplace to my eye - having spent the last decade under its shadow - and it was hard to remember when my reaction to the sheer immensity of the building had changed from jaw-dropped awe to something within the everyday scope of things.

"Calidan! Rinoa!" Sophia waved us over with a dazzling smile that complemented the stunning silver dress she was wearing. Scythe stood next to her; his powerful chest hugged tight by the uniform robes, beard neatly trimmed and oiled, deep in conversation with Oso, the slight man sparing me a nod as I approached.

"Don't you two look splendid!" gushed Sophia. "I mean, I expected it of you Rinoa but honestly, I didn't think Calidan had it in him."

"I think he sometimes prefers being covered in monster-guts," agreed Rinoa, eyes sparkling. "Lazy, if you ask me."

"Yes, yes," I groaned, "let it all out now. I'm a bumbling forest person who hates style and comfort. That about sum it up?"

"I didn't say 'bumbling' but everything else sounds about right," grinned Sophia. "How did you know?"

"It's the same jokes at every event!"

"Ah. Then obviously you never learn." She rolled her eyes and grinned with dark amusement, obviously pleased with herself.

Seeking to change the narrative, I looked around the room. "Seen the others?"

"Rikol is off talking to Bastion I believe. He's been spending a fair amount of time with her lately. Ella I haven't seen yet. Probably trying to be fashionably late."

Or already skulking around the citadel.

Forcing a smile, I nodded and starting making the rounds, laughing at jokes and telling tidbits of my own, all the time keeping an eye out for Ella. Not that I knew what I would do if she turned up or if she didn't. If she didn't turn up at all, she would need a very convincing reason for her absence and be required to go through the citadel's seraph detector at a later date, and if she did show up to the citadel but ducked away from the ball itself? Would I go after her, inform someone, or just let it lie? I honestly didn't know and I knew that my nerves were beginning to show in my posture and mannerisms when Rinoa took me aside.

"You're still not okay, are you?"

Grimacing, I shook my head. "No, not really."

"Want to get some fresh air?"

I hesitated, eyes locking onto the distant door before nodding, "Actually, yes. That sounds wonderful. Where are you thinking?"

"There's only one place to go for air when you're in the citadel," she replied, a sly smile spreading across her face before pointing her finger in the air. "Up."

Ella

Ella stepped back into the shadow of the doorway as Calidan and Rinoa glanced in her direction. When she next stepped out, she found that they were leaving the hall and heading towards the centre of the tower – if she had to guess, they were about to take the platform up to the top of the citadel, a move popular with most couples.

Couples. Ella's knuckles tightened and her heart rate spiked before she managed to wash all emotion away with an icy wave of calm. There would be no room for error today. No time for second-guessing or letting feelings get in the way of her mission. She had to be *perfect.* Nothing wrong, nothing out of place right up until the last moment when...

Well. When all hell broke loose.

She didn't exactly know what her contact had in mind, but to ensure the attention of the Emperor, his closest and strongest allies and all of the Imperators, it was going to have to be something big. She just hoped that whatever her contact had planned wasn't all talk.

And, if she listened to that little voice inside her mind, she truly did hope that it didn't involve anyone getting hurt. Unfortunately, that outcome seemed doubtful – this was the Academy, someone always got hurt.

Guards were on show throughout the citadel, with ten arrayed throughout the Great Hall alone – a consequence of that first disastrous ball. Though she surveyed them intently, she didn't recognise the person she hoped to see, though perhaps that was by design – a guard at attention couldn't move to instigate much of anything at all. No, her contact was somewhere else – close by, that was for sure – but staying out of the way.

Just like she needed to.

Make yourself known, she thought determinedly. *Get out onto the floor.* With a deep breath, she stepped through the door to the Great Hall, striding out confidently in a black and red dress. No figure-hugging wisp of a thing this, but a dress that made a statement. Heads turned as she waltzed in, eyes assessing her in all manner of ways. Smiling at several individuals as she passed, Ella sidled up next to Sophia and the others.

"Good evening," she said politely, with a warm smile. "Sorry I'm late."

"Late? No, you've timed that perfectly Ella!" replied Sophia, her eyes roving over Ella's dress appraisingly. "That dress is *phenomenal*. Where did you get it?"

"Oh, I don't know. One of the shops in the tailor's quarter. Saw it in the window and couldn't resist!"

That much, at least, was true. The dress was certainly beautiful, but it also had the extra room that she desired for a few additional *alterations*. Most people couldn't say that their clothes were functional *and* stunning. Today, Ella had that distinction.

"It's gorgeous. I wish-" Sophia broke off and shook her head regretfully. "I wish Cassius was here to see you in it."

Ella gave her a tight smile. "You and me both. Any sign of the Emperor yet?"

"None so far. I expect he will be joining for dinner at the very least, but everyone has said that he has been distracted as of late." She grinned. "Maybe he isn't aware that the ball is even on!"

"That would be...funny," Ella replied, her insides twisting at the thought. *He has to know. This can't all be for nothing. I can't wait any longer!*

A glass of champagne floated into her hand. Looking around, she saw Rikol studying her closely. Whilst she could hide her moods from most, a fellow street-rat knew when there was a performance going on. Gifting him a small smile, she raised the glass in a salute before taking a sip. When she lowered it, Rikol was back in conversation.

Good man. Rikol was astute to the emotions and mental states of those around him, but he preferred to let others sort out their own issues. In that, he and she were alike. Ella's grip tightened on the stem of the champagne flute. *And today, mine get resolved.*

The Emperor

"Sir, it's time."

"...Sir?"

"Sir, we have to go."

"Blast it Amanul, I heard you the first time!"

The short-haired woman standing outside the door didn't so much as flinch. "The ball is in progress and food is ready to be served on your arrival. It's time to take a break."

The Emperor sighed and briefly considered removing her from existence before putting his implements down with a muttered curse. "He's so nearly ready, Amanul. Motor function is looking good. Nerve responses too."

"I'm glad to hear it sir," returned the completely uninterested voice. "May I suggest that you clean up before we head upstairs? Your projects tend to be...messy."

"You know, Amanul, that whilst my mother has been dead for millennia you act just like her."

"An honour, I'm sure."

"Not really. She and I didn't see eye-to-eye." He smirked as he stood up and with a brief burst of will exchanged his medical robes for a sharply tailored, black and gold trim suit. "Probably why you remind me of her."

"Indeed."

The Emperor stepped out of the door and looked down at the woman. "Oh come now, Amanul, lighten up." He smiled broadly. "It's a party after all."

Muttered noises behind him caused a frown to cross his face. "One second." Disappearing back inside, he approached the occupant of the table who was staring at him with dilated pupils. Placing a hand against the man's head, he focused his intent. "Sleep." Problem solved, he walked back into the main room, finding both Amanul and Balthazar waiting for him, each dressed in their own finery.

"Ready!" he rumbled. "Let's go."

The two bonded spared a longing look at the tanks on opposite sides of the room before falling in behind him, doubtless staring daggers into his back. Not that he cared; despite their hostility they were the most loyal defenders of his body that he could ever ask for. They hurried to keep up with his rapid strides, the clipped heels of their boots a stark sound against the echoing *thuds* of his footfalls. Two minutes later and the silver door was closing behind them, the locking mechanism clunking shut with satisfying aplomb.

The Emperor scanned the silver door and nodded. "A good day's work!" he said, knowing that the two didn't care but stating it anyway. "Come along, you two. Try and conjure up some positive spirits for once in your lives. After all, it's a party!" With a wide smile, he began the long walk to the ground floor of the citadel, the corridors echoing with the wake of their passage.

A project nearly finished and a party to celebrate. Delightful.

"It's stunning," Rinoa breathed, awe on her face as she watched the sparkling lights of the city below.

"It certainly is."

She leaned into me. "Do you find it feels odd?"

"What, the view?"

"No, silly! The clothes, the whole thing. Pretending to be like one of those nobles out there," she waved a hand in the direction of the city. "As much as I enjoy it, I always feel like I am putting on a mask. That the real me is the one wearing the blood-stained clothes."

I snorted. "I can't believe you asked me that question."

"What? Why?"

"Because of *course* I find this odd. I've had to dress up before, sure, but my place even more than yours is out there in the wilderness, doing what I need to do to keep this place safe. I know some of the Imperators in there are much more acquainted with fancy meals and big halls, and I know how to navigate those scenarios but it definitely doesn't feel like me. It doesn't come naturally. It's...like you said, putting on a mask. But then again, isn't everything?"

"How do you mean?"

I shrugged. "Fake it until you make it. It's a fairly common expression. I'm sure if you went to one of these events regularly and pretended that you belonged there, soon enough it would become normalized and you would feel better about it all."

"Fine," she allowed. "Perhaps what I mean to say is, do you think it odd that we feel more at home in blood and guts than in the city?"

"Ah." I paused to think about that one. "I mean, honestly I don't feel it is odd, but that is perhaps the point of your entire question, isn't it?" Her bemused grin gave me all the answer I needed. "I guess it all comes down to what you are more used to. We've spent years in the Academy. Hells, more than half my life has been overshadowed by bloodshed and violence, whereas I've only spent a fraction of that time in the towns and cities that make up the empire. So, from that perspective, no I don't find it odd. It makes logical sense to me that I should feel this way: violence is something I know well, city life isn't."

"Don't you feel...I don't know, wronged somehow? Robbed of something?"

"You mean a 'normal' life?" I replied with a bark of amusement. "Perhaps? But if I had not been lucky on that day, my 'normal' life would have ended in a skyren's mouth. And if that attack had never taken place, well...I wouldn't have met you."

"Calidan Darkheart, sweet-talker, who would have thought?"

I leaned in and gave her a kiss, one that she broke off with a throaty moan. "You'll get us kicked out of here for public indecency if you keep that up."

Pretending to consider it, I winked. "Worth it."

"And miss the citadel's famous cooking? You think highly of me, good sir!"

Wrapping my arm around her, I spoke low into her ear. "I would skip citadel food forever if it meant more days like this."

Wrapping her arms around me she buried her face in my chest. "Calidan, I-"

Before she could finish her sentence, a bell chimed, low and sonorous. As one, the numerous couples up on the rooftop shiftily broke their embraces and made for the central platform.

"Another time," she whispered, kissing me on the cheek. "Dinner awaits!"

"Dinner awaits indeed," I murmured. *I just hope it is dinner and nothing more.*

Dinner, as always, was exceptional.

The Emperor sat in the centre of the long table, with the High Imperator and Bastion on either side, talking away with evident good humour whilst the others dug into the scintillating treats. Whilst I knew the Emperor could eat vast quantities, having seen him do it before, he seemingly didn't feel the same need to gorge himself as everyone else. Unsurprising really - after all, he ate this quality of food on a daily basis. Instead, he encouraged everyone else to try certain delicacies whilst picking somewhat daintily at the food himself.

I didn't mind. It meant more food for me! And what food it was: whole roasted pig stuffed with almonds and sage and topped with an orange glaze. Braised peacock with a cognac sauce. A nut roast almost a foot deep that melted on the tongue. All provided alongside array after array of side dishes that were almost as good as the centrepieces.

Heavenly.

It was so good that I almost forgot why I had been tense in the first place, finding my happy place with Rinoa by my side and engaging Rikol and the others in pleasant conversation. The wine flowed freely and the level of chatter steadily increased throughout the feast as even the sternest Imperators relaxed. After all, the citadel was a place of safety;

if they couldn't take a moment to unwind with the Emperor and his bodyguards by their side, when could they?

You would think that most remembered the attack during the first ball, but memory is a fickle thing. The last few years, the ball had taken place smoothly with no issues whatsoever and the horror of that night had begun to fade, overtaken by the numerous other horrors that we all witnessed on a frequent basis. The ball began to feel like a safe event where everyone could unwind and get away from the pressures of Academy missions.

That was our mistake.

The first I knew of something being amiss was a second of discomfort in my lower intestine. Passing it off as indigestion, I paused eating and took a sip of water to settle the stomach. For a minute I thought it had passed and then a bout of severe cramping clamped down upon my stomach, causing me to gasp in pain and clasp a hand to my gut.

And I wasn't the only one.

One by one, Imperators began to cry out, clutching their bellies and writhing in pain.

"What is the meaning of this?!" cried the Emperor, rising to his feet. If he was feeling anything adverse, he didn't show it.

"Looks like poison sir," said one of his bodyguards.

"Poison! At my feast?!" The Emperor's eyes flashed with fury. "Unforgivable. Bring me Ricard. He prepared the food; he knows who had access to it. Also, get the medicae up here and inform Andros and Geryna that there might be a situation."

"At once sir." The guard left swiftly, pulling open the door to the hall and shutting it behind him.

The Emperor reached out and touched the High Imperator's hand, brow furrowing in concentration before relaxing. "A strange prank," he muttered before standing. "Everyone, I apologise for the inconvenience. It appears that you have been exposed to a type of poison." Holding up his hands, he calmed the immediate exclamations. "Now, don't worry, it doesn't appear to be lethal but more of an inconvenience, which makes me think this is more of a prank rather than a targeted attack. After all, what would be the point in exposing all of the Imperators in the Academy to the equivalent of a mild stomach upset?" He chuckled and shook his head. "Like I said, strange, but we will get to the bottom of this. The medicae are on the way up, so we'll have you right as rain in no time."

There was a thump at the door.

"Ah, that must be the medicae now," said the Emperor. "Fast as usual." Raising his voice, he rumbled like a volcano. "Enter."

The door didn't move. Rolling his eyes, he gestured at a guard stationed near the vast door. "Let them in, will you?"

Nodding, the guard moved to the door and pulled it open. Even lost in stomach-related hell, I sensed the blood drain from his face and looked up just in time to see the poor guard disappear into the corridor beyond with a muffled yelp, yanked by something or someone with inexorable force.

"Enemies in the citadel!" the Emperor boomed. "To arms!"

As one, we tried to stand. Some made it. Most managed a half-crouched position that wouldn't have intimidated a child, let alone the owner of that hand.

"Calidan," winced Rinoa, "do you have any weapons on you?"

"None," I replied. "Anyone?"

Shakes of the heads all round. Unsurprising; the guards had made us leave all weapons behind on entry. Holding out a trembling hand, I tried to concentrate enough to will one into being but a fresh wave of cramp rendered my attempt useless.

"Damnit!" I cursed. "Can't concentrate!"

"Me neither," Rinoa groaned, her shaking legs threatening to send her to the floor.

All around us, Imperators were trying and failing to gather themselves to face whatever foe lay beyond the door, hands grasping ineffectively towards the air only for their faces to contort with fresh waves of cramps.

Whoever did this knew exactly how to interrupt seraph casting, I realised through bouts of tear-inducing pain.

The nine guards left in the room had moved to the grand door, their ceremonial armour and weapons more functional than decorative and more than capable of piercing through the toughest of armour. Standing in formation they looked resplendent and ready to take on the world. They were only missing one thing.

Knowledge of how to fight monsters.

The scent hit me and I paled.

Oh no.

"Trolls!" I screamed.

The doors slammed open and three trolls charged into the hall, barrelling through the suddenly puny looking guardsmen and sending them flying. Credit where it was due, the guards quickly rallied and blades began to sing, eliciting roars of pain from the creatures, but the wounds they inflicted quickly began to close.

Seya, can you hear me? I had refrained from contacting her as she was still recovering from her ordeal. The terrible wounds that had been inflicted on her and the stress of the bond healing had left her in a weakened state.

Calidan, what's happening?

Are you able to spare any healing? I've been poisoned and need it out of my system.

A thrum of displeasure rippled down the bond. *Poisoned?! Are you okay? Who did this? Where are they?*

Easy. I'll get some answers, I just need that healing.

Power rushed down the bond, more of a trickle than the usual torrent but still enough to immediately begin easing the cramping in my abdomen. *Thank you!*

You can thank me by staying alive. Now get to work.

"Imperators! **Focus.**" The command rippled through the air and suddenly I felt a clarity of mind that I had never before managed to obtain. The pain still coruscating through my body meant nothing in the grand scheme of things. I had to get a weapon and get to work. Reaching out a hand, I concentrated and this time a blade manifested into reality. All around me the others did the same, weapons falling into ready hands and seraph spells flaring into life.

Four guardsmen were down, their armour crumpled into bloody sheets. Grimacing, I shouted above the din. "Cauterise their wounds to stop regeneration or get something in their hearts and keep it there!"

Almost before the words were out of my mouth a dizzying array of attacks erupted out of the Imperator line and hammered into the ungainly beasts, alternating between setting them on fire, melting with acid and freezing them to the bone. The troll in front was engulfed in multi-coloured light, its screams turning impressively high-pitched for such a big creature before it collapsed into ash. A series of seraph lances bore through the second troll, leaving holes straight through its torso, most of which healed more slowly than normal which meant that my words had been listened to by at least a few. It was finally brought down when a seraph lance transformed mid-attack from piercing its heart into solid stone. With no way to heal, the troll slowly slumped to the ground with a low-gurgling groan.

The third troll was cleverer than its brethren, picking up the nearest table and using it like a discus, sending it carving through the air and causing Imperators to throw themselves to the ground. Taking advantage of the confusion, it hurdled its dying brother and crushed an unfortunate Imperator beneath its feet, stamping repeatedly on the wavering shield that the poor bloke had hurriedly erected whilst picking up nearby implements and using them as makeshift weapons. After another table, several chairs and the Imperator had gone sailing overhead, a mage of impressive power went to work, staring confidently at the troll like he could read its mind.

Maybe he could.

The beast made another grab for an Imperator and then a look of puzzlement flashed over its face. Slowly – painfully slowly – it teetered sideways before toppling over and laying still.

Rikol made a show of washing his hands in the air. "I wish I had known how to do that back in the fourth-year exam."

"What did you do?" asked a nearby Imperator.

He shrugged. "Turned its brain to stone. Wasn't hard, troll's nearly as dumb as a rock anyway."

"Guards, get to the entrances," rumbled the Emperor, his face thunderous. "Find out how they got in. Imperators, well done, the medicae will be with you shortly."

Aside from rising and helping us focus on the task at hand, I wasn't sure if the Emperor had made a move during the fight. Part of me wasn't sure why that was; surely he could have just waved a hand and made the trolls disappear? The larger – indoctrinated - part happily reasoned that he shouldn't have had to, not with that many Imperators to do the job for him.

These days, I know the truth: he likely just couldn't be bothered.

Screams erupted from the corridor down which the guards had disappeared. A second later one burst back in, blood pouring through his broken breastplate. "Sir, there's more!"

"More?!" If I had thought the Emperor annoyed before, now his face was a tempest. "This is the most defendable building in the empire – how have the outside guards fallen so easily?!"

"They're not coming from the outside sir!" the guard explained. "They're portalling in!"

"That's impossible. The citadel is warded against portal use..."

He trailed off as a ball of infinite darkness manifested in the centre of the hall. Spiralling outwards it grew at a tremendous rate until it was large enough for even the Emperor to stride through without issue. A bellowing roar cut through the air and a massive form blasted through the portal to crash into a group of shocked Imperators.

"Reaver!" I heard someone shout amidst the panic and on second glance they were correct – the bulging muscles of the thyrkan shock trooper were in full display as it crashed through hastily raised shields and sent figures flying with each blow from its massive hands. As I began to dash forwards to bring it down, I frowned.

There's something different about this. What is it?

Ducking an unconscious Imperator, I rolled and flung a seraph lance at the ridiculously over-proportioned beast, hard-earned instincts allowing me to target the weakest part of its twisted physique.

And that was when it hit me – this reaver *was* different from the others. Whatever it was that the Enemy did to create reavers, it wasn't a perfect process. I had never fought one that didn't look like some twisted, overgrown abomination with mismatched muscles. Not so this one. Its scaled body was in proportion – if still massively oversized – its scales gleamed with vibrancy and it moved with skill and alacrity. If the others had been reavers then this had to be the apex of that strange branch of the family. A beast perfected.

Its apotheotic form.

"Sir," I heard a guard yell, trying to make his way to the Emperor's side, "we need to get you out of here, it's not safe."

"This is...not possible."

For the first time since I had known him, the Emperor appeared to be at a genuine loss. The god-like figure who was always so many steps ahead that you would have to have been born *millennia* before to keep up, didn't have an answer to what was happening.

"Sir!" The guard had reached his side and tugged on his arm. "We need to leave. Now!"

That seemed to trigger something and the Emperor's gaze focused with razor intensity on the suddenly trembling guard. "Leave? No. No. Nonononnono. *No.* I am the Emperor and this is my citadel. *Mine.* If the wards are down then our role is simple." A predatory smile spread across his face and the bloodlust that I knew was often simmering just under the surface came to the fore, flooding the room with killing intent that struck like a physical blow. The reaver visibly shuddered and then roused itself, rising up to deliver a crushing blow against a nearby Imperator.

"Stop."

The word flooded the room. In that instant, I realised that the level of 'concept' that Bastion was trying to get us to was just a stepping stone to greater power. Bastion's understanding of shields would pale and crumble in the face of a Power's interpretation. What the Emperor wielded was as far above a mere *concept* as a concept was to a person without a mote of seraph.

Time stood still.

When it resumed, the Emperor was standing in front of the desperate defender and a shower of gore painted half the Great Hall. A gleaming flash and he was encased in a suit of gold and silver armour. Focusing on the rift in front of him, he frowned.

"**Break.**"

It broke. Shattering into motes of ethereal nothingness and dissipating into the air.

"Good." The Emperor spoke to the speechless room. "This is not over. I must repair the wards and for that I must have full concentration. Imperators, prepare yourselves and gather your healers." He gave us just enough time to look at him in confusion before practically everyone in the room doubled over, clutching their stomachs. The Emperor noted me still standing and gave a small nod of acknowledgement.

"There might be more already in the citadel, I need you to…"

His eyes latched onto another ripple in space. "You challenge me again in the seat of my power, Charles? Foolish. **Break.**" But before the portal had even begun to drift away, another rippled into being, then a second and a third.

"This isn't just Charles," the Emperor muttered, aghast. "He has other portal users." His frown was like a canyon through granite. "I will not be able to shut them all. I must focus on reestablishing the wards. Imperators!" He snarled the word. "Defend yourselves or die! Let there be no quarter." Raising his voice so it thundered and echoed through the citadel, he roared one final time.

"Fight!"

PRESENT DAY 11

Home. Officially it was the Academy, but I had long since stopped thinking of it as such. The wilds were more of a home to me these days but there was one place that I had started to truly think of as 'home' above all else.

The Wanderer's abode.

So...yeah. Not my home, but it was a bloody good one all the same. A home should be somewhere that makes you feel safe, secure and allows you to relax. Whilst it might seem strange that relaxation whilst in the domain of a Power was remotely possible, the Wanderer's home was sheer...simplicity.

Nowhere else had I slept such a refreshing sleep, nor drunk water so fresh and pure as to fill me with vitality.

Don't even get me started on the sunsets.

Moreover, it was a place of friendship. Don't get me wrong – I'm still not sure that anyone can truly be friends with a Power. Whenever there is a relationship where one wields power over another, things tend to get tricky and despite the Wanderer having been nothing but pleasant to me there was always the knowledge that she could squash me like an ant without a second thought. Having been on the receiving end of a Power's killing blow multiple times, it's not the most fun experience and I had no desire to repeat it, but also couldn't prevent it if she so desired.

Which meant I was helpless.

And so, in this situation I chose to do something that went against every fibre of my hard-trained being.

I chose to believe in her.

I know. My Academy Instructors would have a field-day with this one. All the training I had been put through, everything I had ever been taught, told me to find an angle. To use her. To pretend trust and then abandon when the situation called for it.

Perhaps the Academy rules didn't quite account for Powers, however. I mean, how do you 'use' a Power? Everything we do is on such a small scale compared to their plots and plans that nothing really matters. Humanity is a fleeting indulgence for these immortal beings. Something to be played with, perhaps destroyed, possibly enlightened.

So yes, a big power-gulf. But I was okay with that. I would believe that we were aligned in our goals and maybe even *friends* until the day that she revealed to me otherwise.

I truly hope that day doesn't come.

Fleeing the Dusk Court had been surprisingly simple; a series of merchant convoys got us through the depths of the desert without mishap and from there we headed deep into the wilds, losing ourselves in the vast wilderness of the world. If Rizaen had yet discovered the theft, I did not know, but I suspected that when she did the world would tremble.

She was not one to be wronged.

That, I knew all too well.

The two of us strode into the Wanderer's domain, road-weary and travel-stained yet triumphant. Eleothean met us at the edge of her true territory – the web of illusions that ensured that anyone not allowed to pass were gently diverted elsewhere without knowing that anything had happened. The humongous bear nodded at me and chuffed happily at Cassius, bumping his chest with his nose and eliciting a gurgle of delight in return, Cassius wrapping his arms around the bear and burying his head in Eleothean's soft fur.

If I didn't know Eleothean was bonded to the Wanderer I would have said that Cassius had found his spirit animal. The big bear seemed to genuinely enjoy the time he spent with Cassius regardless of fingers mistakenly in eyes and fur being teased and Cassius could rarely contain himself around the creature, laughter near-constantly bubbling up when they played.

And, of course, they both relished a good wrestle.

Climbing the carved stairs to the Wanderer's abode, Cassius giggling as he swayed behind me on Eleothean's back, I removed my pack with a sigh of relief and sunk to the mossy floor, drinking in the view whilst resting my weary muscles.

It was like a balm for my soul.

The forest was spectacular here. Curated by the Wanderer but no less special for it, it took my breath away every time I visited. Soft rays of light broke through the willowy bows to touch upon the rich, soft loam that coated the forest floor. A gentle stream meandering its way through the vista caused water droplets to glisten in the air, light refracting into all colours of the rainbow.

Seya would love it here. The thought came with that familiar tinge of sadness, but I welcomed it. One day I would bring her here and we could live the rest of our lives in peace.

Safety. Comfort. Satisfaction.

This was home.

It was two days before the Wanderer returned and I did not care in the slightest. I used that time wisely, sleeping away the aches and pains and filling my belly with the fruits of the forest, Eleothean's impressive nose tracking down the choicest of foods.

When the Power entered her domain it wasn't with the thunderous footfall of the Emperor or the trumpeted fanfare of Rizaen, instead it went largely unnoticed and she could have been just another person come to bask in the glory of the surrounding nature. That is if all of the surrounding plants and trees didn't slightly lean towards her as she entered, as though trying to bask in her rays. Perhaps it could have been the wind, but I knew better.

Strange things happen around seraph users.

Around Powers? Expect the unexpected and still manage to get your mind blown.

"Calidan, Cassius," the Wanderer said, gifting us with a warm smile, "welcome back. I trust you've been enjoying your stay?"

Considering all three of us were covered in berry juice, caught like children with their hands in the honey jar, I grinned and nodded.

"Excellent. Considering that you're here and not dead means that you have something for me?"

"I do indeed," I said around a mouthful of delicious blackberry. "It's in the bag."

Bending down, the Wanderer picked up the bag and pulled out the dully-glistening lump of metal. "Ahh, excellent. You've done very well indeed. Better than I expected, in fact."

Raising an eyebrow, I cocked my head. "And what were you expecting?"

The Wanderer at least had the decency to colour slightly. "Well, to be entirely honest, complete and abject failure ending in your imprisonment, torture or death. Likely all three. Sorry."

I waved a hand. "If we're being truthful, so did I. Yet even with the risk, I can't say it hasn't been fun stealing from under the noses of the Powers."

A wolfish smile spread across her face. "Yes, it is rather delicious isn't it? And what's life without risk?"

"Longer."

"I was going to say 'boring' but yours works too." Her nose crinkled with another smile. "Seriously, well done. With all the star-metal you've brought, I think we can move onto the next stage of the plan. But first, I have some news that you might find interesting."

"Oh? Do tell."

"I went for a stroll and just so happened to come across an old medical facility."

"That's some stroll…"

"Well, I haven't earned my nickname for nothing," she replied with a sly grin. "And, it looks like I have everything I need to perform more advanced surgery on Cassius." Raising a hand before I could explode with delight, she continued, "In terms of equipment, that is. I still don't have the knowledge, but it occurs to me that you know someone who does."

"I do?"

"A certain 'blue witch' you've mentioned a number of times."

"…You want me to ask Ash?!" I looked at her aghast. "You can't trust anything she says!"

The Wanderer frowned. "I'm not so sure about that. From what you've told me she has repeatedly told you the truth, just with the added overlay of trying to kill you at the same time."

"Like that's much of a difference."

Her eyes flashed. "That's *all* of the difference, Calidan. Think of all the lies that you've been told by those around you, by people pretending to be your friends. Your teachers at the Academy knew what the Emperor wanted from you. The Emperor groomed you to be another cog in his machine. There's likely only been one intelligence in this world who has told you the complete, whole truth about a subject. Ash."

"I don't believe this!" I snarled, picking up a rock and crushing it between my fingers. The Wanderer silently watched me fume as I tried and failed to understand her reasoning. "Even if I think you're right, how do you expect me to go and ask that bitch anything? Just wander out into the north and waltz into the Enemy's stronghold?"

The Wanderer pursed her lips, her eyes held a mischievous gleam. "Oh, dear sweet Calidan...I mean to do exactly that."

CHAPTER 42
Questions

Ella

Ella held her breath as the giant thyrkan tasted the air, its forked tongue flickering. Only when the heavy footsteps shuddered into the distance did she gasp a deep lungful, gratefully dropping her cloaking.

That had been too close.

Her contact had warned her that there might be danger in getting to the silver door, but she hadn't been specific as to what.

Well. Now she knew. Her confidence wavered and for a long second she remained crouched against the wall, taking deep, shuddering breaths.

By the Pits, what have I done?

She had known that there was going to be risk involved. That there was the potential for injury to her friends, but still... she hadn't expected trolls and worse portalling into the citadel. Her heart ached for the Imperators above and a voice in her head told her to turn back, to forget about her mission and go and assist.

But to forget about her mission was to forget about Cassius. And that she could never do.

Swallowing her guilt, she pushed away from the wall and strode forwards, each step increasing her determination. She had set the ball rolling and there was no turning back now. The least she could do was achieve her objective. Her friends – no, her *family* – would likely never forgive her, but at least she would be with him.

Cassius.

Before long she was at the door that had occupied her dreams for the last year. Gleaming silver in the light, arrayed with intricately carved sigils and looming large with intimidating solidarity, it was the last thing between her and Cassius.

Please be open. Please be open. Please be open.

Ella reached out a trembling hand and pushed. Despair clutched her heart as nothing happened and her panic spiralled out of control.

All this? For nothing?

A desperate sob broke free as she struck the door with everything she had. *Why? Why?!* And froze.

The door had moved. Another sob – this time of relief – as she leant against the metal and pushed with all her might. *Idiot, Ella. It's not locked, it's just stupidly heavy!*

On silent hinges the silver door swung open, and Ella stared.

And stared.

...And stared.

Cassius

Cassius slept.

He had grown used to sleeping. Welcomed it, in fact. It was the one place where his world made sense.

Out in the real world there was pain and there was confusion. For the most part he felt like he swam in an ocean of fog, his mind fuzzy with sparse moments of clarity. He knew things had changed. That *he* had changed. He felt it in his body but more in his mind. He barely remembered the person he was before but had flashes of happier times when his thoughts had flowed thick and fast, unburdened by aeons of torment. He wished he could be that version of himself again, not...whatever he was now.

The closest he came to that was when he slept. In his dreams – or possibly memories – he was quicker. His thoughts ran like the old him. Granted, they tended to be nightmares;

hauntings of that beautiful woman with the smile of ice and the bloody knife. He ran, he fought, he died. Over and over.

Still, it was preferable to the waking day.

"Cassius, I'm coming for you." The words sent shivers down his spine as they echoed around the dark hallway. "Traitor…"

He prepared himself as best he could. He knew that her eyes would be the last thing he would see. There was something strangely pleasing about that. He loved her eyes.

Heartless though they were.

More and more portals opened into the room as poisoned Imperators threw aside the pain ravaging their insides and desperately threw themselves into the fight. The Emperor had his eyes open but unfocused, his mouth moving as though reading an unfamiliar text, his interest in the ongoing fight apparently over. Guards and Imperators had formed a cordon around him, their faces grim but determined. Imps were ushered to the back of the room where they were most out of danger and our best fighters moved to the front, most clutching their bellies as they pushed through the pain to duck and weave amidst taloned claws.

But it wasn't just talons. Three reavers emerged from the portal, the trio wielding oversized weapons. One held a greatsword that dwarfed anything that even Adronicus would wield, the second a double-bladed great-axe, and the third had a hammer with a head bigger than me. Worse still?

They were armoured.

"By the Pits," someone breathed behind me and I couldn't help but agree. One reaver was bad enough, but armed and armoured? That couldn't be good.

Seraph surged, but a wave of obsidian washed it away as a smaller but far more terrifying figure stepped into view.

"Warlock!" someone screamed, and all hell broke loose.

Before I had even had the time to comprehend the ridiculousness of our situation, a hammer was barrelling towards my torso with the inexorable nature of a charging rhino. Darting forwards, I sought to close the gap, rolling under the swing and bringing my hastily-constructed blade up into the arm of the creature only to find it clanging off the vambrace. The reaver continued its swing, sending Imperators flying, and showed its skill for battle by sending a thunderous kick directly into my chest at the same time.

If it wasn't for my shield, I would have been dead many times over. Instead, I bounced through several ranks of Imperators before impacting a shield that stopped me dead in my tracks and made my head ring like a bell. Dazedly looking over, I saw Bastion give me an apologetic grimace before reengaging with the warlock.

Everything was chaos. Blood spattered. Imperator and beast screamed and howled. A tidal wave of frenetic motion filled the chamber, blurs of individual combat and desperate magic. I saw the familiar red blur of Scythe, the arrows of Sophia and the magic of Rikol at work...and that was when I realised something.

Ella had vanished.

What had been forgotten in the madness of the moment came crashing back. Ella wasn't here because she had done this. She had somehow brought this calamity down upon the citadel and the Imperators. People were *dying* because of her.

Before I knew it, I was up and moving. It wasn't back to the fight but around the worst of the melee, cutting and slicing where I could until I was out of the door.

The Imperators would hold without me. Filled with a burning desire to both see my best friend free and yet punish the person responsible for this madness, I hurried down the corridor.

Ella was my objective, but whether I was following to hug or to kill her, I still didn't know.

Rikol

"Where the fuck is he going?"

"Who cares?! Get killing that wanker!" screamed Sophia, pointing at the evilly grinning warlock before attempting to follow her own order and sending an arrow plunging through the air to erupt against its shield in an explosion of electrical fire.

"Make it sound so simple," muttered Rikol, shaking off the distraction of Calidan's disappearance and sinking deep into the flow of battle, his mind working overtime to calculate everything going on around him and react appropriately. To his right, the reaver with the greatsword roared with delight as it finished cleaving through two Imperators then screamed as the hilt of the weapon grew red-hot, dropping it instinctively. Threat dealt with for the moment, Rikol reacted to a blur of motion and unleashed a blast of force to counter the hammer that was threatening to crush him into paste. The reaver strained against the attack just long enough for Sophia and two other archers to put arrows into its eyes.

He watched, amazed, as the beast didn't fall to the ground like most other things did when pierced through the eye-socket. Instead it howled in agony whilst clawing at its own head, trying to manipulate its oversized claws to get past the metal helm it wore. The next instant, its screaming cut off entirely. Yet it wasn't thanks to an attack or the sheer amount of blood-loss that it must have been experiencing, but the presence of several armoured figures appearing through another portal.

Commanders.

The effect they had over the thyrkan in the room was immediate. What had been a wild melee became a more organised push as the thyrkan reavers made room for more creatures to pour out of the portals, choosing to defend the area rather than headlong charge into the fray. Each moment a portal stayed open another killer charged through, fresh and ready to fight.

Rikol knew that if they didn't find a way to shut those portals down, the Enemy would flood the citadel from the inside. He had experienced the immense numbers of the strange lizard-like creatures that the Enemy could throw at them before – this barely scratched the surface. And Pits forbid that anything worse than the thyrkan came through – he wasn't sure that the citadel could withstand the power of a titan carving up its insides.

He growled as the warlock intercepted another half-hearted attempt at an attack, wicked glee carved across its face at the paltry power he could summon.

That damn poison!

The black shield flared to life over and over, intercepting the attacks by the weakened Imperators with no apparent sign of effort on the bastard thyrkan's face. Even Bastion was struggling, her face drawn with pain. Without the Emperor's support to keep them focused, their concentration was all too easily broken and the Enemy was using that fact to pile on the pressure.

They had been well and truly played.

But by who? Did Calidan see – is that why he left? And where is Ella?

Rikol shook his head and focused on what he could do for the fight immediately in front of him. *Emperor, I really hope you can fix those wards fast. Because we don't have much time.*

CHAPTER 43

Revelations

Ella

Ella had never seen anything like it. A hall almost as vast as the one on the main floor lay before her. However, instead of something akin to the Great Hall, this one was cluttered with all manner of technology that she couldn't even begin to fathom. It had more in keeping with the facility they had found within the desert so long ago than anything she understood as 'modern' technology.

If this is all Pre-Cataclysm technology...and if it works...this place is beyond priceless.

All the more sense for it to be locked away behind such a door.

Lost in stunned awe, she walked into the room, overwhelmed by the sheer magnitude of what she was witnessing, mission temporarily forgotten. *If the Emperor had such technology all this time, why hasn't he used it to improve life outside?*

A small voice in the back of her mind scoffed at that. *Maybe it can't be used that way. Maybe it's all for something incredibly specific.*

Or maybe he just didn't want to share.

With each step, Ella found herself getting more and more outraged. To use such devices, surely the Emperor had to have an understanding of them. Even a basic understanding would be centuries ahead of anything that the outside world had. He could have worked with people to reverse engineer this technology and raise the world up. How could he not!? How...how selfish!

In less than two minutes the image of the god-like Emperor that she had cultivated over her lifetime shattered. Now she saw only the false idol, the selfish figure who kept it all for himself and who didn't have their best interests at heart. It was all so *obvious* now. Her anger snapped her out of her dazed walk and she pushed on at speed, doing her best to ignore the outrage that kept bubbling up inside.

Reaching the end of the hall, she found three unmarked doors. Pushing straight on, she walked through the door, shaking her head darkly as it moved aside at her approach, and then staggered to a halt with a horrified gasp.

Tubes, just like the ones in the desert rift, rose from floor to ceiling, each bubbling with murky liquid.

Unlike the ones in the desert, these were occupied.

Steeling herself, she pushed away from the door and walked into the room, eyes scanning the tubes. She had no idea what went on here, but it didn't feel like anything good. Something bumped against the one nearest to her and she jumped, turning to see a furred, wolf-like creature riddled with black tubes staring at her through one large golden eye. She frowned; it seemed strangely familiar.

The eye of the beast slowly shut and Ella took a trembling step backwards. Suddenly she had no desire to be in here. The walls felt like they were closing in, the tubes containing hidden monstrosities. Pivoting, she turned to flee and saw something worse than she could have expected.

Calidan strode towards her, sword in hand, covered in blood and with a face set like iron.

"Ella!" he roared. "What have you done?!"

Unable to face the betrayal in his eyes, she sprint into the next room, choking back a sob.

"Ella! What have you done?!"

My shout echoed through the air, fuelled by a rage that was soaring ever hotter. A rage at the technology surrounding me, a rage at Ella's betrayal, rage at myself for not joining her to save my best friend and a complete and all-consuming rage at the horrors being perpetrated against my friends upstairs whilst I ran around down here.

It was safe to say I wasn't in a good place.

Ella blanched and bolted into another door. Grimacing, I made to follow but then curiosity got the better of me. She had come out of that door looking like she had seen a ghost. What could possibly have been in there that had shocked her so?

I couldn't help myself. Reassuring myself that the longer I left Ella the less likely I was to put a sword through her spleen, I walked into the central room.

It was a forbidding place. The tubes that stacked up the long walls had an ominous air that made my skin crawl.

An eye opened. Brilliantly coloured, it fixed me with a predatory intensity.

I knew that eye.

"Ramuntek?" I whispered, shocked. "Is that you? What are you doing down here?"

The eye that had been slowly closing shot back open. A furred body twisted in the tube, thumping ineffectually against the walls. It was then I saw the black tubes stretching from its body and disappearing into the base of its container.

"What is this place?"

Ramuntek thrashed again, teeth exposed in a feral expression, but it couldn't give me the answers I needed.

"I-I'm sorry," I said, backpedalling. "I don't know what's going on here. I shouldn't be here. I- I need to go."

Stumbling backwards, I slammed into another tube. Something raked along the glass and I turned to see a massive hawk, talons big enough to wrap around my head, its stare both proud and immeasurably sad.

I felt something as I stared at it. A kinship with this beast.

"You're a Great Heart..." I gasped. "What is going on here?!"

The bird didn't respond, just continued tracing its claws along the glass as though lost in its own world, wings that couldn't stretch out wrapped around it tight.

Thoughts of leaving vanished at the Great Heart's appearance. I had figured this to be some kind of punishment facility for the Emperor's enemies – not that I knew that was what Ramuntek was, I was fairly certain it had helped us out in the past – but to have a Great Heart in here, with its bonded presumably upstairs?

It didn't make any sense.

Taking a deep breath, I walked further into the room. There were a dozen or so tubes. Some empty, others containing creatures that I had never seen before. A majestic ibex was the next Great Heart I came across, its eyes closed in sleep. The horns of the creature were incredible but its body looked like it had an unhealthy sheen to it, the bones showing against its skin.

Why wouldn't the two bonded be helping their Great Hearts?
Why does the Emperor need them here?
What in the world is going on?!

A soft knock on the glass caught my attention and I choked back a cry as I saw the perpetrator. Large, dexterous hands gave way to thick orange fur and a face that gleamed with intelligence. I knew this creature. Knew it well. Had known its bonded too, before she died saving us all.

Anatha's bonded. Borza.

"Borza!" I cried, rushing to the glass and pressing a hand against it. The huge ape slowly did the same and gave me the saddest smile I had ever seen. Borza's usually sparkling eyes were dull, filled with an unfathomable sadness, and his muscle hung off his frame.

"What's going on, Borza? Why are you here? The Emperor said you were helping him with something important."

Borza growled at that, momentarily reducing my visibility of him to zero as bubbles filled the chamber.

"Borza, please, tell me what's going on!"

Bad place, he signed in the language that he and Anatha had taught me over the years. *Very bad. Don't want to be here. Promise me help.*

"You've got it," I insisted. "Let's get you out."

The great ape shook his head. *No run. Always found. Only one way out.* He locked those big, curious eyes on mine. *End.*

"End?" I repeated slowly. "Wait, what? Kill you? You want me to kill you?!"

A nod. *End me. Please. End us all. This is not existence.*

I drew back from the tube, struggling to control my emotions. "Wha- what does he do to you?"

"He takes their power." The voice cut through the air, brisk and sombre. Swivelling, I found the Great Heart-bonded that had met me outside the citadel, his finery coated in blood and an axe in hand.

"What do you mean?"

His face twitched. "I mean exactly what I said. He takes their power. Their life force." His face twisted. "You're in the Emperor's emergency room. If he is ever wounded their life force is exchanged for his. He becomes strong instantaneously and the poor creature in the tube is diminished." He locked eyes with me. "This is their existence. Over and over until they eventually die."

"You're a Great Heart-bonded!" I exploded. "How can you let this happen?!"

"Let this happen?" The man scowled, eyes darkening with memory. "I railed and fought time and again, but you know the one thing you can't beat? Someone with enough power to wipe you from existence in the tip of their finger."

"The Emperor wouldn't-"

"*Boy*, you know nothing of the true nature of the Emperor!" he spat. "He takes and he takes. He is a parasite that feasts upon those around him whilst all the time getting you to believe that it is his right to do so. Regardless of what you might believe he doesn't care about you, the Academy or even his own fucking empire. All he cares about is – all he has *ever* cared about – is winning."

"Winning what?"

"Everything," he said with a shrug. "He sees himself as the best and will brook no other to be his equal. Everything he does is to undermine the other Powers and raise himself up. Eventually he will make his move and either win or lose. In either instance, it doesn't bode well for the likes of us." Walking over to the tube with the ibix inside, he gently caressed the surface, gazing longingly at the creature within. It opened a weary eye and the look of love it gave him was heartbreaking to witness.

"Delatra has been in this room for nearly six years now. She has withered before my very eyes. Any time the Emperor is hurt, something in the room is directly affected. If his wound is serious, their life force is consumed at a vastly increased rate."

"Why can't you get her out of here?"

"The same reason why you won't be able to take Seya out of here when she finally comes," he said sadly. "Delatra is branded. The Emperor can track her at all times. Furthermore, she is not the only one that is...branded." He pulled aside the collar of his jacket, revealing tattooed script. "You saw some of how this works when we last spoke. I am bound to this place. To his service. Doubly bound, you might say, for I cannot refuse to do his commands and nor can I fail in my duty to protect him lest Delatra pay the price. And that," he eyed me gravely, "is something I will never allow." He advanced slowly, sword in hand.

"Before, you couldn't say anything to me about this, why can you now?"

"I cannot talk about the specifics when outside this room. In here," he raised his arms, "I can speak freely."

"So you let Delatra stay here, trapped?" I asked, raising my own blade but taking a step backwards.

"If it means she lives, yes."

"Even if that isn't what she wants?"

The man stiffened, as though he had been punched in the gut. "In the end, her life is more important."

"Why don't you ask her?"

Gritted teeth. "I cannot."

My eyes roved over the creatures in their vats. "Communication along the bond is cut off?"

"The bond itself is largely cut off." He stopped advancing as he explained. "The reason why the Emperor likes Great Hearts specifically is because of the bond, this intangible connection regardless of distance. His machines forcibly alter the bond, giving himself overall control. As far as I know, he doesn't have remotely the same connection with them as you or I, but that isn't what he is after. Their innate need to heal their partner ensures that as soon as he is injured, power floods through the bond. Not to me. Not to anyone else. All to him. Vast quantities of it; more than any mere mortal could handle, but for him? It makes him functionally unkillable." He smiled sorrowfully. "So you see, Calidan, I cannot talk to Delatra." His eyes roamed towards her vat. "Nor she to me. Our bond is splintered and a fraction of its former self. But I will not let her die. I cannot."

I lowered the tip of my blade and nodded towards Borza. "Do you know who that is?"

"Of course."

"How long has he been here?"

"A couple of years. Why?"

"Borza has been here much less time than your Delatra, but he has asked me to end his life." I shook my head. "If he wants that to happen, how can you think that Delatra wants otherwise?"

A bitter smile. "It is easy to think like this when it is not your companion on the chopping block. You might think different were Seya here."

"Perhaps. But I refuse to believe that I would let her rot in one of these vats until she is finally consumed. I know Seya and I know that she would rather die than be caged."

For a moment I thought I had him. He lowered his blade and turned towards the ibix, shoulders slumped and head bowed. "No." He spoke the word softly but it carried the weight of certainty behind it. "No, I will not let it happen. I cannot."

He turned and raised his sword. "Prepare yourself Calidan. Though I do not desire your death, I am charged to remove all intruders."

Ignoring my cry, he swept forwards, blade humming through the air. A slash, then a second and third; fast blows that required all of my skill to avoid. "I don't want to fight you!" I barked, parrying two fluid strikes. "There has to be another way!"

"There isn't," he said sombrely, shifting quickly between attacks, his blade never letting up. "The Emperor wins." His voice cracked, becoming little more than a hoarse whisper. "...He always wins."

"Then end it!" I cried, switching between circles eight and nine to unleash my own barrage of strikes. "This is no life. Not for you and not for your bonded. Destroy his machines. Fight him if he is so terrible as you say."

Flicking my strike away, he sent me tumbling with a blast of seraph. "Destroy his machines? Do you think that he hadn't anticipated that?" He snorted. "Seraph sigils on both the creature and the machine. If one leaves the other without having been disarmed..." he grimaced and angled his blade along mine into a thrust that caused me to dance sideways. "Well. It's not pretty. No, I appreciate the anguish and horror coursing through your heart at this moment, the indignation that your life is going to end like this, but it will not change a thing. You must die. As must your little friend."

Another swing, this time enhanced by seraph, shattered the blade in my hand.

"You leave Ella out of this!" I roared, flipping backwards and conjuring seraph lances from every angle as I did so.

"She has entered the silver door. I understand her reasonings and empathise, truly, but my orders are absolute." He didn't show the slightest bit of concern regarding my attacks, lazily batting them away with his own shield whilst inexorably advancing towards me. He feinted left and then drove his sword into my shoulder as I mistakenly spun into his real attack, the tip of his blade against my shield and a spark of electricity flaring into life.

"I'm sorry Calidan."

"Not sorry enough," I grunted, forcing everything I had into my shield, looking around wildly for something, *anything*, to use as a weapon.

Something I hadn't expected made itself known. A slitted eye of amber locked onto mine, filled with profound sadness that struck me like a blow. In that moment, I knew exactly what I had to do.

"I forgive you," I said softly and the Great Heart-bonded jerked like he had been struck. The tip of his sword wavered ever so slightly and I took that as my cue, swivelling and delivering a seraph-enhanced roundhouse, the flat of my shin impacting his shield and sending him tumbling across the floor, crashing into a table with a curse.

I didn't follow. Instead I leapt forwards, sprinting back towards my chosen tube, fist clenched tight as I focused my strength into it. Behind me I heard a shout. A scream. But it didn't matter. All that mattered was the terribly tired and worn-looking goat that gently pressed the tip of its magnificent horn against the reinforced glass.

"Calidan, don't-"

Crunch.

My fist, flaming green with pure seraph, slammed into the glass, driving it into the tip of Delatra's horn with earth-shattering force.

The glass flexed. Bent.

Shattered.

The ibex fell to its side, legs weak from disuse. It blinked slowly at me and then turned its eyes onto its human.

"Delatra, wait. We can sort this out." The man was sobbing now. "Please don't do anything foolish. I can't bear it if you- wait!"

The magnificent beast blinked slowly again.

A goodbye.

She stepped out of the vat.

"Delatra! No!"

Light swirled. Golden and magnificent. Fragments of power far beyond my reckoning. Moving swiftly, it wove around Delatra, wrapping her in coil after coil of golden power. For a second she shone brighter than the sun, glorious in her freedom.

The coils snapped taught, collapsing inwards with unstoppable might.

"NO!"

Blood and gore squirted out of the seraph weave in an horrendous torrent as Delatra exploded.

"DELATRA!"

The man was on his knees, covered in the remains of his bonded, his tear tracks the only part of him that weren't red. Bowing my head to the brave creature, I rose to my feet and staggered towards Borza's vat, the orangutan blinking at me with impassive eyes.

"Do you want this, Borza? Truly?"

The great ape nodded. *I am beyond ready. It has been a long time in coming,* he signed.

"I will miss you, my friend."

Willing seraph to condense, I focused it into a drill bit and forced it to spin. Faster and faster it spun until finally the glass began to crack. Removing the drill, I let Borza's powerful hands do the rest of the work, tearing the walls of the vat apart until there was nothing keeping him from his freedom aside from the sigils embedded into his flesh.

Go now, he signed. *Thank you.*

Leaning in, I wrapped my arms around the somewhat diminished but still hulking ape. "I am so sorry," I whispered. "Rest in peace, my friend."

His fingers ran through my hair, effortlessly strong but intimately gentle. Slowly they reached under my chin and raised my gaze to his. Those intelligent orbs gazed into mine with love.

"Ook."

Smiling, I patted his hand. "You too, buddy. You too." With a final shared smile, I wiped my eyes and turned away. My gaze lingered on the broken man in the pool of his friend's blood for a moment and then I turned away, forcing myself onwards. Forcing myself to try and understand what was about to happen. To understand and to accept.

It was time to find Cassius.

A hollow voice reached me as I neared the entrance. "He will know now. Prepare yourself. He will be coming."

I paused at his words, then nodded without turning and strode out of the door, leaving the poor man to whatever fate he chose.

A blinding flash of light lit up the great hall as I walked away.

Goodbye, my friend.

Cassius

"Come out to *play*, Cassius."
"Why do you run?"
Schnick.

Cassius slunk through his dreams, always keeping a low profile, caught in the juxtaposition of thrill and fear at seeing her again.

For see her he would. She always found him. Always had that knife. The one that went *schnick* as it carved his body.

But why did she hunt him? Why did he feel a wave of love at seeing her face before they clashed? He felt like they had once been something more. Something important together. He just couldn't remember. Hated not remembering!

Fog. Colour. Light.

Laughing with people he knew. Friends? She was there. Coming at him with those eyes but less ice, more warmth.

Fog. Darkness. Pain.

Her voice echoing in the halls. Holding his guts in with his bare hands as he ran, refusing to fight.

Why did he not fight? He must fight.

"Cassius. I'm going to find you."

Fog. Nothingness. Momentary bliss.

Schnick.

"Cassius. I'm close."

Sunlight through the fog. No. He knew what that meant. He didn't want to go back to the real world. Don't make him go!

"Cassius, I'm here."

Schnick.

He floated towards the light, unable to stop. Resigned himself to the pain. At least he had managed to see her again, despite the knife.

"I've found you."

Schnick.

Burning light. Blinking eyes. Fog. Slow.

"Cassius, what have they done?"

Oval eyes. Smiling face. She found him. How did she find him? This world was safe from her!

"Cassius, can you hear me?"

She loomed closer.

"Cassius?"

Instinct honed from threat of that blade blazed into life.

Her face trembled with a sudden emotion. Just like when she turned into that ice queen.

"C-C-Cassius...w-w-ait."

His arms were longer now. Good. It meant she couldn't reach him with that knife. Why had he been scared? She was so small, dangling. But that meant nothing. If she could reach him here, she could reach him anywhere. He knew that soon enough that knife would be back to haunt him. Might as well end this whilst he could.

He squeezed.

CHAPTER 44

Rage

The Emperor

Blood sprayed across the Emperor's face but he paid it no mind, lost in his own world as he delicately repaired the final sigil deep within the bowels of the citadel. There was no doubt about it – whoever had disarmed them had thorough knowledge of his building and its security. Inwardly he sighed. *It might be past due for a purge of the staff. Trust only gets you so far.*

Fusing the last section of seraph into place he concentrated and released a pulse of will that thrummed through the building like a wave of force, igniting the sigils as it passed until they burned bright with power.

"It is done," he rumbled, finally opening his eyes to the chaos in the once-great hall. The floor was slick with blood and ichor. Thyrkan, trolls and several more unique monsters were facing off against the struggling Imperators, each ripping and tearing into the other in an impressively bloody mess. Cracking his neck from side to side, he clenched a fist and strode forwards, the hall echoing with his thundering approach. He didn't run. Didn't make haste. Just let those within the room know that his approach meant inexorable, inescapable death.

A troll flailed an impressively large warhammer in his direction. The head shattered into pieces before it could reach his body and the troll had just long enough to frown at its weapon in confusion before the Emperor reached over and tapped its chest. Blood fountained as the creature detonated and the Emperor laughed, deep and long, raising his arms into the pouring rain, glorying in the satisfaction of combat.

"Despair, fools," he thundered, lowering his gaze to encompass every hostile entity. "The time of your death fast approaches."

And he went to work.

Imperators fled from his approach like fish from a shark. He approved; they knew not to get in his way. Thyrkan advanced, their pathetic captains giving them some backbone. They advanced and he welcomed them, raising his arms out wide and letting them have the first blow. Spears jabbed, swords fell, talons slashed and yet nothing broke his skin.

Feeling the flow of battle he slipped into a pure combat role, not relying on the immensity of his seraph but his own physical form. Suddenly those claws and blades couldn't touch him as he danced between them, heightened reflexes and enhanced body allowing him to move between their attacks like they were standing still.

He snorted. *Still got it.*

He reached out as he skipped past one of the strange lizard-men and clasped a hand over the creature's head. With a gentle flex of his fingers, the thyrkan's skull imploded.

Tsk. Still too strong.

Trying his hardest to limit his physical attributes, he pulled his strikes, delivering a dozen strikes to a dozen assailants in the blink of an eye. To anyone watching, he would have barely moved. He imagined that the creatures would have been just as confused when they suddenly found themselves flung across the room, several splattering against the wall, their pathetic frames unable to withstand the merest touch of force.

Something shimmered in the far side of the hall and he felt the touch of seraph on his mind. Suddenly the thyrkan were no longer in front of him but behind. Rolling his eyes, the Emperor flexed his will and the illusion shattered into pieces. Driving his hand into the throat of the nearest troll, he sparked flame into the abscess he had created, leaving it to burn as he turned his gaze on the shimmering corner. Another flex of will and the corner was filled with a multi-limbed creature, its snake-like limbs writhing in pain at the loss of the will-combat.

You think to try to invade my mind? he sent into the beast's head, not even knowing if it could understand him. *Here is a piece of mine.*

The beast screamed in unholy agony whilst the Emperor calmly batted away his foes. When he looked again, the creature was on the ground, blood leaking out of every orifice.

Pathetic.

One of the so-called 'reavers' came for him, its oversized muscles rippling with power. Curious, he allowed the fist to impact his face, the blow landing with a thunderous *crunch*. Enemies and friends alike paused to witness the effect, then the reaver let out a roar and stumbled back, cradling its limp hand with wide eyes.

Shaking his head in disappointment, the Emperor reached out and grabbed the reaver by both shoulders. It looked at him in puzzlement, as though not understanding how this could be happening. Craning his head back, the Emperor delivered a ferocious headbutt, the force of it driving the reaver's elongated skull into its own body, skull turning to jelly as its bone structure failed, before following up with a knee to its chest. Its body managed to resist for all of a split-second before the knee broke through its ribcage, the organs beneath and its spine, before spraying gore over the array of beasts behind it. The Emperor raised both sides of the thoroughly deceased beast into the air, waved them like bloody trophies and barked a manic laugh before leaping back into battle, wielding the bloody stumps of the reaver's arms as clubs and flattening everything in sight.

By the Pits he loved to fight.

He was just about finished choking some kind of spike-covered monster with what he thought might have been its own spleen when black lightning engulfed both him and his prey. He watched as the spikey creature turned to ash with interested eyes before slowly turning to stare at the petite warlock that had the temerity to use seraph *against him*.

Granted, the little shit was relatively strong for mortals. He understood why the Imperators had difficulty with them – their understanding of the lesser concepts of seraph appeared to be particularly good. Charles had obviously trained them well. And that, more than the arcing electricity, stung. However he did it, Charles had managed to get fucking *lizards* to understand concepts, whilst his glorious Academy barely managed to produce one half-decent seraph user a generation.

Ri-fucking-diculous.

The warlock finally broke off its attack, doubtless hopeful that he would be a pile of smouldering ash like its monstrous friend. A smile twitched the corner of his mouth when the smoke cleared and the thyrkan's eyes widened in alarm and despair.

"Hi!" he said brightly. "I think you meant..." he trailed off, eyes going blank as though his concentration was completely elsewhere. The remaining thyrkan paused, uncertain of this unexpected turn of events. Slowly the Emperor's face turned red, veins throbbing and his jaw clenched so hard that the grinding of his teeth rumbled like tumbling boulders. Every muscle in his body tensed and the air surrounding him smelled like ozone. Red energy began coalescing like sparking wisps of light; personified fragmentations of his rage. Faster and faster the energy began to build until the Emperor stood in the centre of a raging whirlwind of blazing seraph. Opening his mouth, he let out a wordless scream of incoherent fury, his hair lifting into the air like it was underwater.

Just as suddenly, the power winked out and everything in the Great Hall was still, as though no man or monster could bear to break the broiling silence.

The Emperor stood in the centre of the room, no longer crackling with power but somehow even more foreboding for it.

"I must cut this short," he growled and every being in the room shuddered at the venom in his words. Scanning the room, he pinpointed everything that was unwelcome in his citadel and snapped one simple word.

"Break."

He was gone before the sound of snapping bones and imploding cartilage had finished, leaving flabbergasted Imperators, guards and serving staff in his wake.

I heard the gurgling before I reached the door. Shaken with the loss of Borza, I didn't quite register what it was at first. Suddenly it hit me and I broke into a sprint, crashing through the door just in time to see Ella's legs go limp as she dangled in the hand of a giant.

Crack.

"Ella! NO!"

The giant turned toward me and I did a double take. "C-Cassius?" I said in disbelief. "What the fuck! Cassius?! WHAT DID YOU DO?!"

Blank eyes the size of saucers stared back at me.

"Cassius, put her down. PUT ELLA DOWN!"

Still nothing. He was staring at me whilst holding her off the ground with one arm, seemingly effortlessly.

What did the Emperor do to you?

Snarling, I barrelled forwards. When he still didn't let her go, I willed the muscles in the underside of his wrist to spasm, forcing his hand to loosen. Ella dropped like a sack of stones, neck lolling strangely.

Oh no. Oh gods no!

"Ella, come on. Please!" I tapped her face, willing her to wake up, doing anything I could to fight against what my senses were telling me.

"Ella, you can't do this. You can't die! He's here. HE'S RIGHT HERE! You-" I choked back a sob. "You found him."

Cradling her to me, I rocked back and forth, tears flowing free.

I had lost yet another friend.

Ella.

"Uaaah."

It was a slow disquieting noise, one that built from nothing until it shook the room.

"Uaaaha!"

Slowly, I turned to look up at the giant that was my friend. My friend who had just killed his soulmate. His eyes were locked onto Ella and there looked to be something there. A *capacity* that hadn't been there a second ago, like the clouds had lifted from his eyes. A capacity that recognised what was going on, who I was holding and why.

His eyes filled with horror.

"UAAAHA!"

The scream tore from his throat and split the air asunder. The walls of the room trembled and I crouched low over the corpse of our dear friend, pressing against the power that emanated from her killer.

Thump.

The blow rocked Cassius's head back, his nose already bloody and bleeding.

Thwack.

A second blow caught him across the cheekbone with earth-shattering force.

A third and a fourth landed as he began to pummel his own face, unleashing devastating hits that would have pulverised any mortal. Pure anguish poured out of his throat, alternating between frenzied screams and broken moans. Wide, slitted pupils remained locked onto her body the entire time.

I froze. *Slitted pupils?*

Looking back, terrified of what I might be about to see, I breathed a silent sigh of relief. It must have been a trick of the light. Cassius's pupils weren't slitted but massively dilated, his face contorted with pain and terror. A shuddering snarl worthy of some giant beast broke free from his chest as he continued with his blows and for a second I thought his teeth were larger and more pointed than I had witnessed before.

Distantly, I heard the sound of booming feet and though I knew what it entailed; I couldn't bring myself to care. Ella was dead.

Dead.

It couldn't have happened. I refused to believe it. Refused to acknowledge reality and tried to will it away.

It didn't work of course. I was a long way short of a Power and even they might have had difficulty in bringing someone back from the dead. Still, I reached deep and tried, even knowing that every second I spent here was another second I wasn't getting Cassius out, another second that my death likely drew close in the form of a very angry Emperor – that all seemed secondary to what was in my arms.

Another snarl broke from Cassius, this one sounding much more full-throated and eminently hostile. The sound dragged my tear-filled view away from Ella and back to my friend.

What. The. Fuck?

Blinking away the tears just made the reality all the more confusing. To say Cassius was... *not himself* would be something of an understatement. Scales were beginning to emerge along his arms and torso; not the small scales of a normal thyrkan but the thick, heavy-plated armour of a reaver or – worse – a skyren. If it weren't for the scales I might have thought he was hitting hard enough to rearrange the facial structure of his head but veins were throbbing in his face and neck as muscles bunched and twisted, bone crunching as it broke and separated, his head growing more elongated. One eye remained a wide, Ella-focused dilated pupil, the other was the slitted orb of a predator, one that I couldn't help but feel was very much focused on me.

Thunderous footsteps nearby. A roar of such rage that the walls shook as the Emperor discovered the mess that we had made. I was too focused on what was unfolding in front of me to listen in to his interrogation of the ex-Great Heart-bonded but the Emperor's scent suddenly became filled with pure, murderous intent. The next moment I was in the air, feet scrabbling for purchase on nothing as one of his massive arms lifted me like I weighed little more than an apple.

Raising me up to meet his face, I realised two things: first, he was absolutely *drenched* with blood and gore, and second; he was *furious*.

"*You!*" he seethed. "How dare you do this to me!?" The tightening of his grip on my neck made any words I attempted come out as unintelligible garble. "You break into my sanctuary and destroy my *things!?*"

For the first time I realised how much he sounded like a petulant child. He didn't appear to care about the dead Imperator on the floor at his feet, but only the fact that I had 'broken his stuff'.

"I don't know what you thought you might achieve, but I promise you that you are going to die the most slow and...painful...death..." he trailed off, eyes flickering over my shoulder. The crunching sounds had largely stopped now, replaced by a monstrous breathing that immediately put me in the mind of eleven-year-old me listening to the red-eyed skyren.

"What...the?"

Not-Cassius roared, a full-throated bestial roar that promised imminent violence. I rolled my eyes as far as I could against the adamantine grip of the Emperor, just enough to see slitted eyes flick down to Ella's body, then rise to lock onto mine.

Oh shit, oh shit, oh sh-

Not-Cassius blurred into motion. Thundering forwards with lightning speed, he crossed the distance between us in the blink of an eye, hammering into my shield with a mouth determined to swallow me whole and sending the Emperor and myself careening through the wall into the main hall, the two of us spinning head over heels as we smashed into an array of vaunted artefacts from an age long gone.

I lay crumpled in the immensity of the Emperor's embrace for a moment as my senses came back to me. Not fast enough for the Emperor's sake however.

"Get. Off."

He twitched his wrist and I careened through the nearest important-looking machine, smashing it and several others like it apart like match-sticks before hitting the far obsidian wall with a bone-shaking *crunch*.

By the Pits. If I didn't have seraph I would be paste right now. I shook my head dazedly as I picked myself up, hearing the Emperor roar out a challenge at Cassius and looked over, expecting to see him clobber my poor reptilian friend back through time.

Instead, I found the behemoth completely ignoring the monstrous man and sprinting directly at me.

Oh...shit balls.

Not-Cassius's booming steps shook the room, his scaled flesh now a gleaming silvery-black, eyes burning.

Worse, he was *fast*. So damn fast. All that muscle was translating to pure power, propelling him across the hall quicker than I could react.

But one didn't just ignore the Emperor.

Crunch. The Power intercepted Not-Cassius mid-jump, sending him hurtling into another rack of machines that exploded in arcs of electricity.

"I would stop gawking and run if I were you," the Emperor rumbled, eyes not turning from the lizard. "I have no desire to kill or injure my project, whereas he might be contained quite happily whilst feasting on your flesh."

"What the fuck did you do to Cassius?!" I shouted.

He squared off as the bestial figure rose from the floor, orange eyes burning with hatred. "Simple. I made improvements."

"You Pits-damned mother fucker!"

Cassius roared and charged. The Emperor met him head on, hands wrapping around his talons and head dodging the gnashing jaws. Immense muscles strained in his back as he fought to push back the writhing mountain of power that was a full-grown skyren. If he was accessing all of his strength it would have been simple, but to do it whilst not unintentionally killing Cassius in the process? I hated how much I admired his control even in that moment.

Bang!

The Emperor fell to the ground, legs knocked from under him with a sweep of the monster's powerful tail.

It was at that point, when those flaming eyes once again picked me out amongst all the wreckage, that I realised I should have obeyed the Emperor and run. With a quick apology to Seya, I pulled everything that she could spare and flooded my muscles with power before launching into a sprint that would put any professional athlete to shame, racing a ten-tonne monstrosity to the exit.

I would like to say that it was the first time that such a thing had happened, but that would be a lie. Foot-races with monsters is not as uncommon as a non-hunter might think.

In this case it was a race that Not-Cassius was going to win. Even with my muscles steaming, his streamlined predatory form was built for explosive power and put my meagre collection of muscles to shame, his monstrous bulk flowing across the hall like water. Using all my senses, I put my life on the line as I pushed as hard as I could before slamming on the brakes and letting the bounding behemoth crash past me by a hair's breadth. Before he could turn, I was slamming through the silver door and rushing down the echoing empty corridor towards the emergency exit.

A roar of rage and the sound of razor-taloned feet soon followed.

I was in serious trouble.

CHAPTER 45
THE GREAT GAME

"Why. The. Fuck. Are. You. Chasing. Me?!" I ground out through panting breaths, my lungs burning as I pushed as fast as I could. I jumped as my senses flared and a taloned claw hissed through the air where my leg had been a split-second before. A quick willing of seraph and a small platform manifested under my foot, allowing me to jump a second time in the air and avoid the second set of equally devastating claws that threatened to remove my head.

A quick landing, roll, and I was back on my feet, momentum retained. That should have felt like a minor victory but at that point it was all I could do to keep one step ahead of the ferocious monster that was my friend. I didn't know why he was so intent on me and not the Emperor, but he was bordering on obsessed, to the extent that he ignored anything else in his path.

Even the God-Emperor.

If it had been anyone else but the man's pet project, I'm fairly certain he would have obliterated them for that insult alone.

I pushed off a nearby wall to dodge another blow, spinning as the black stone quivered under the attack and then woke up a second later, head spinning as I rebounded off the floor and the wall. Something had hit me hard enough to rattle my brain even within my shield and knock me briefly unconscious. Though my vision was tinged with grey, I created a slick pool of oil beneath my body and thrust with a burst of will, sending myself slipping down the corridor just as Not-Cassius's terrifyingly toothy jaws crunched down a finger-width away from my face. The power of his jaws did not make me want to test the strength of my shield against it. He leapt forwards again, taloned hand slamming onto the hard stone before whipping out from underneath him in the oil, sending bestial-Cassius crashing to the ground in a tumble of limbs.

Not that it stopped him for long.

Writhing like a cat, he was back on his feet in moments, hostility pouring off him in waves. *Nothing else mattered*, I realised. To him, I was the sole purpose of his existence. All of his drive, his immense capacity for slaughter, was focused on eradicating me. Whether that was because he had seen me holding Ella, I was the first person he saw, or a part of him remembered me, I had no clue, but unarmed and running out of seraph, I was rapidly running out of ideas of how to survive.

More thunderous steps behind me – erupting like an explosion of sound - and this time I realised that they weren't the cat-like *booms* of the skyren but the heavy tread of a very angry Emperor arriving at immense speed. The behemoth reached out for me again before being hit by a silver star, the impact cracking the obsidian wall as the Emperor crushed him against it.

Not-Cassius howled and snapped as the Emperor placed an immovable arm under his chin, forcing the biting jaws away from his face and up into the air. His other arm held the beast's arm at bay, pinning it to its side without issue. For a second I thought he was going to hurt Cassius but instead he just stared intently at him, like he could see right through his armoured hide and into his very soul.

I mean, I wouldn't put that kind of shit past him. Powers have the title for a reason.

"Should I...uh...still be running?" I asked after a torturously long minute or two. The Emperor jumped as though he had forgotten I was there and then scowled as he remembered who I was and what had just happened.

"Run or don't run – it makes no difference to me. I will find you and make you pay for what you have done."

"What *I've* done?" I snarled, momentarily matching the tone of Not-Cassius' foaming mouth. "Look at what you've done to my friend!"

"Yes...beautiful isn't he?" breathed the Emperor, his gaze turning back to the beast. "Unexpected but beautiful."

"What in the hells did you do to him? And why?!"

The Emperor rolled his eyes. "I already told you; I made improvements. Whether that is the case for this form, however, remains to be seen."

"You've turned him into a monster!"

"Hmm. It appears so. That strain of skyren DNA was quite potent. I thought it would allow purely for more rapid healing but to enable a transformation such as this? Unexpected, but not completely unwelcome."

"Can you change him back?"

He turned his head and arched an eyebrow at me. "I'm not just standing here for fun you know, there is a method to the-"

Something must have changed in his stance, a slight weakening or opening that hadn't been there before. Not-Cassius felt it, embraced it and exploited it without hesitation. One second the Emperor was holding it against the wall and the next he was flung down the corridor like he had been fired from a ballista, whipped around with such force that he was gone from sight almost instantly.

Once again, I was face to face with the terrifying visage of a skyren.

It stared. Drooled.

I gulped.

It pounced.

This time I had no moves to save me. The full weight of a titanic beast hammered into my hastily reinforced shield and its razor-sharp claws began bearing down, cutting into my flaring shield with devilish ease.

"Cassius!" I cried, voice choking with strain. "Cassius, it's me! You know me. Come back to me buddy. Please."

Burning eyes bore into mine. A tongue the thickness of my thigh licked the edge of my shield and drool pooled onto the floor.

"Remember who you are," I insisted, desperate. "Don't let this thing control you!"

Not-Cassius' eyes flickered and then he was gone, blasted down the corridor accompanied by a roar of anger and the shimmering metal plates of the Emperor. The sound of an impact thundered down the hall followed by the sound of percussive impacts and crumbling masonry.

That was all to be expected...until I heard the screams.

Underneath the citadel, far beyond the section available to most guests, the Emperor had a dungeon. Not a dungeon with dark slimy hallways and inefficient guards but a wide-open space filled with rows of small stone buildings where the prisoners lived out their lives. I had been here a number of times over the years, sometimes to interrogate a prisoner, other times to move into the citadel via the forest entryway and once to chase after a kyrgeth that broke free and slaughtered many of the denizens of the jail.

Today was much like that one.

A skyren is no small creature. They are powerful and vast, more than a match for your standard Great Heart in size. The Emperor too was a giant of a man, towering over mere mortals and able to deliver more power in a flick of his finger than I could ever dream of. Combined, they created a nightmare for stone walls and the likely terrified occupants within.

Arriving into the hall, I saw that one row of the cells was already completely dismantled, the stone thrown everywhere like an explosion had gone off and splatters of blood marking where the unfortunate denizens had met their untimely end.

Boom!

Another crumpling blast as another wall exploded in a cloud of dust, the whipping of a tail and flashes of silver plate the only things visible within.

"Got you!" reverberated the Emperor, clearly lost in the thrill of the fight. Not-Cassius made a shrieking yowl as he was gripped by the edge of his tail and slammed through another cell, a splash of red dust the only suggestion that someone had been inside. The Emperor continued the move, slamming the skyren over and over, spinning it whilst laughing with manic joy.

Eventually Not-Cassius got tired of the game. With a quick slash it carved through its own tail, rocketing into the distance with the force of the Emperor's swing, leaving the Power with a bloody stump and a bemused expression.

"Can't run, little Cassius," the Emperor boomed. "There is no escape."

The skyren took no notice of his mocking tone and ducked between the stone cells. Suddenly the beast went quiet, utilising that impressive stealth that skyren possessed in spades, moving with cat-like poise as it used the buildings as cover.

"Come out, come out wherever you are…" the Emperor sang, striding through the cells with complete certainty of his own might and battle prowess.

The newly grown tail of Not-Cassius blinked out of a row, hammering into the Emperor and sending him tumbling through another building. Raucous laughter filled the air as the silver-plated giant extracted himself from the rubble.

"Not bad," he boomed. "Good to see that you heal as fast as I expected. That bodes well." There was a flash of light and a clap of thunder as the billowing dust disintegrated. "And that means that I can afford to be a little less...considerate."

I hung back, worried that if I got in the way I would be squashed like a bug by either party. Not-Cassius seemingly had no such compunctions, a blur of shadow rocketing towards the Emperor only to go flying backwards with a keening screech as the man swivelled and delivered a monstrous and perfectly timed uppercut.

"Give it up, little Cassius," he said. "You can't win."

Credit where credit was due, Not-Cassius learnt fast. For its next attack it flowed over the top of the building before pouncing down on the Emperor with those wide, terribly pointy jaws. A screeching *crunch* reverberated through the room and for a second I feared the worst. Then the Emperor gripped both sides of the skyren's jaw and began to prise them apart. Not-Cassius panicked, clawing and raking at the lower half of the Emperor, but to no apparent effect. Wider and wider its jaws were forced apart, the creature scrabbling now to get away from the overwhelmingly powerful man but his grip was like a vice. Eventually, with a sickening *squelch*, the lower half of the jaw tore free from the beast in a spray of blood.

"Cassius, no!" I cried, rushing forwards.

"Take another step and it will be your last," declared the Emperor matter-of-factly. I skidded to an immediate halt.

"You've killed him!"

"Pfft. You and I both know that a skyren will survive wounds far greater than that." The Emperor moved over to the reeling creature and placed a knee against its neck, pinning it down. "Now shut up and let me concentrate if you want to see your friend again."

As he spoke, I could see the flow of blood pouring out of Not-Cassius' wound begin to slow and then stop completely as new flesh started to grow in its place. I shook my head numbly; the Emperor was right – skyren had obscene healing rates. Sarrenai had needed to immolate one from the inside out to get it to stay down for good.

Once again the Emperor stared deeply into the twitching form of the skyren, looking for something that I couldn't comprehend. Not-Cassius did his best to distract him, twisting and turning but the Emperor's grip was infallible.

"Ah, yes. I see," the Power murmured, gaze unwavering.

"See what?" I hesitantly asked.

The sigh that the Emperor let out was beyond any mortal means. I truly understood in that moment that I had gotten under his skin.

"I can see that your insatiable curiosity is not going to give me peace," he rumbled. "Perhaps I should kill you now for the insult and pain you have caused."

"Rich, coming from you."

The world froze in one of those eternal moments as soon as the words left my mouth. *Oh shit. Did I just say that?*

The Emperor's eye twitched and for a second the smallest smile graced his lips. "You know, the one thing that I have always liked about you, Calidan, is that you are direct. Even when facing down the most powerful beings in creation, you still have the spark and inclination to stand up to them. It's what has made you such a good foil for my old friend. You have the uncanny ability to annoy anyone."

"It's a gift."

"So it would seem. Having the balls to talk to me like that...I can admire it." His eyes narrowed as he looked over his shoulder at me. "It does help that I can vent my hostility towards you at any point."

That doesn't sound good. "What do you mean?"

An arched eyebrow. "Don't you remember?" A small smirk. "How about now?"

I screamed as my chest expanded, pressure building to an unbearable point.

Pop. The world went red.

Fire danced through my limbs as golden lightning filled every pore, every vein. The smell of my own burning flesh filled my nostrils as darkness fell.

My own arm clubbed me in the side of the head. My body, already weak from blood loss, unable to maintain its balance and I collapsed. A massive silver-plated boot rose and descended.

I gasped, shaking. "What the fuck?!"

"Personally, I most enjoyed the last one. You never truly know someone until you have beaten them to death with their own arm."

"W-was that real?!" My heart shuddered as my brain tried to comprehend the feeling of my own deaths.

"Oh, very much real. Localised time displacement is something of a passion of mine." The Emperor chuckled darkly. "It makes the most mundane things more fun when you're able to release any anger and tension at any point. For instance, I've killed a lot of things today, but you? Well, that tasted sweet."

Disgust etched itself onto my face. "You're sick!"

"Sick? No, I'm just not beholden to the normal laws of man. Ask yourself this: am I actually hurting anyone if it technically never happened? How many times have you wished that you could punch someone and get away with it? Well, I can. And I do."

"So, you're a murderous psychotic who prefers people to think of him as a benevolent ruler." I blew out my cheeks. "Sounds like most people in charge to be honest."

"There is no-one like me!" the Emperor snapped, the air shimmering around him as his aura flared. "Not one of you pathetic monkeys has the capacity to understand the magnitude of my skill. You can barely look after yourselves when left alone, barely able to put two and two together to make four! Pathetic! And worse," he growled the last, "weak." He sneered, the air around him darkening with hostility. "You are nothing compared to the seraphim of old. A pathetic race that clings on like cockroaches."

"But you're human too!" I interrupted.

"Human? That is too mundane a word. I am a Seraphim!" Blinding light burst out from the Emperor and he radiated raw power, causing me to flinch and Not-Cassius to wheeze in pain. "Not one of you has a fraction of the talent it takes to be a true seraphim. Born as useless as you die." He snorted. "Like mayflies. Tiny buzzing insects that offer nothing to no-one."

"And yet you still live in a citadel and demand these 'mayflies' to treat you like a god?"

A shrug of those massive shoulders. "And why shouldn't I? You are all playthings for us to do with as we see fit. Besides, you do have some uses."

"Oh please, *do tell.*"

"You are the chess pieces. All part of the Great Game." His lip arched into a sneer. "You are tools in the games of the Powers. Nothing else matters. All this," he waved a hand in the air, "all the cities and the people, the armies and the Academy, it all comes and goes. The Great Game is eternal. Like me."

"Maybe humanity should be free of your yoke."

"Perhaps, but that would require them to cast off our chains. And that, dear boy, is impossible."

I squared up to him, steeling my body as I swore with every ounce of my being. "I will make it possible. I swear it."

The Emperor looked at me completely flabbergasted before breaking into peals of laughter that thundered throughout the room. "You?" he exclaimed, wiping his eyes. "Hah! I told you I liked you Calidan. Threatening to end the reign of the Powers without any power of your own." He shook his head. "Hilarious."

Rage made me brave and foolish. "I'm a Great Heart-bonded. I have power and I will gather more. I will bring this all down."

Amusement still tinged his features and he smiled patronisingly at me. "Yes, you are. And no, no you really don't. You have less than you know."

"What do you mean?"

"You'll see, soon enough. But first," he turned back to the fully healed and struggling skyren, "let's deal with this."

Raising a finger, he slowly traced a patten of swirling lines just above the side of Not-Cassius' body, golden seraph hovering in place as he dexterously worked to create an intricate work of art. Knowing this was important, I focused on the lines, memorising their placement and reaching out with my senses to try and understand the *will* behind their formation.

"Yes..." the Emperor mused, leaning back to look at his work. "A slight tweak here," he twisted the air and the line of seraph warped before resting into a new position, "and we will be good to go."

"What are you doing to him?"

"You'll see." With that, the Emperor raised an open palm and slammed the sigil into Not-Cassius. Instantly the skyren howled, convulsing as golden light began to stream through its pores. Scales began to shed, leaving bloody flesh underneath and the horrific cracking of bones could be heard as the immense form began to twist and condense. Horrendous seconds turned into nightmarish minutes as the transformation continued, talons dropping away and leaving bloody stumps that then regrew into human fingers the size of sausages. Jaws that had once been wide enough to swallow me whole slowly shrank, once-immense bones splintering and reforming until a familiar – if larger – face reappeared. That was the worst part; the howls of the creature had been one thing - I had long inured myself to those types of screams - but as soon as Cassius had a mouth back, it became *his* screams, continuing long after the external transformation was complete, his eyes wide with horror.

"That's enough of that," murmured the Emperor, placing a finger against Cassius' head. Instantly the man dropped like he was dead and only the slight rise and fall of his chest convinced me otherwise.

"Well," the Emperor continued, clapping his hands together, "that was an exciting interlude! How truly fascinating."

"You never explained what you've done to him-"

"And I do not need to," he interrupted smoothly. "But as I know that you will not give me any peace, know this: Cassius is special. If he works as intended then he will no longer be a mere pawn in my arsenal. No, he will be more like a knight. Strong and merciless in the right scenario. Able to change the game board completely given the right opportunity."

I rolled my eyes. "Can you speak straight for once?!"

He sighed. "Cassius is still Cassius, but changed mostly for the better. There were a few side-effects; his transformation into a skyren being the obvious one. To better handle the magnitude of my mind and power I had to expand his neural pathways which has had a knock-on effect on his mental state. He is not as he was. Nor will he likely ever be."

"What?" I shook my head. "What are you talking about? What do you mean, handling your mind?"

The Emperor grinned wolfishly. "You'll see. One day. But as for now..." he grinned again and I couldn't help but feel that Cassius' skyren form had seemed less threatening, "now you and I are going to have a little...chat."

PRESENT DAY 12

"You what?"

"Did I stutter?"

"No," I shook my head vehemently, "I must have misheard because you couldn't seriously have been suggesting to sneak into the Enemy's stronghold, his place of absolute power, just to question his blasted witch-bitch!"

"Not just question Ash," the Wanderer replied calmly.

"Oh, good-"

"I mean to kill Charles too."

"And I wish to fly to the moon."

"Been there, done that. Pretty barren really and certainly not made of cheese."

...*What?*

The Wanderer noticed my confusion and grimaced before waving a hand. "Not important. Anyway. Where were we?"

"Discussing some madness about sneaking into the-"

"Ah, no, no, no." She shook her head as she spoke, her hair bouncing every which way, making her look like an innocent, playful spirit rather than the Power she was. "You must have misheard me."

I relaxed. "Thank the gods, you had me-"

"I never said anything about *sneaking*. I intend to walk right through the bastard's front door."

Maybe not so innocent and playful then.

My brain might have shut off for a moment to try and digest what she said. "...Come again?"

An infuriating smile played on her lips. "How did you think that the next phase of the plan would work, Cal?"

"Well, considering that you've never really told me all of it, I wouldn't know."

"You know enough to guess at the outlines at least."

Frowning, I thought about everything I had pieced together. "I don't know, I figured we would break into the citadel, rescue Seya and get the information needed to heal Cassius, then find some way to end the Powers for good."

"Not bad. A bit basic but not completely terrible," she replied with that same smile. "You're right in that we will break into the citadel but not until we are good and ready. There's only one way that we're doing that; by getting Melius out of it and completely distracted."

"But he always knows when anyone ventures anywhere near that blasted door!"

"Do you know how the Powers survive meeting one another?" she asked suddenly.

"No, I don't really get what you mean."

"We're some of the most powerful beings in the known universe but in some respects just as mortal as you. When we meet, which, granted, is rare – we suffer from the same foibles as other humans. We want to compete, to vie for the title of most powerful. Of most skilled. None of us made it to where we are today without honing a razor-sharp competitive edge. And after the first few meetings amongst us ended...shall we say, *badly*, we built one rule. If we were ever to meet in a group again, we were not to use a single drop of seraph."

"Wait, really?"

She nodded, eyes deadly serious. "Of course. It was the only way to make sure that our meetings could be productive. As you might imagine, we're all extremely sensitive to seraph and the merest iota of someone drawing upon it is like an alarm bell on a clear night. And so, if Melius decided to enter such an arrangement, what would that mean?"

I felt like a child in school. "That...he would have no connections to any of his wards," I breathed, realisation flooding in. "He wouldn't know that the silver door had been breached until he repaired the connection."

The Wanderer glowed like a smug kitten. "Precisely."

"But...how often do you meet?"

"Oh...maybe once every millennia or two."

"What?!"

"Relax, relax!" she chuckled, raising her hands reassuringly. "There's one surefire thing that will get all the Powers together."

"And that is?"

Her smile faded and her eyes adopted a faraway look. "The death of one of our own."

"The death of one of your own," I repeated. "So, not the first time this has happened then?"

She shook her head silently. "No, not by a long shot. Some were killed, some just decided to end things. Our numbers have dwindled to the paltry six that you know so well. But the time has come for a change. And that change has to start with Charles and that cursed kyrgeth of his, Koranth. They've gone too far." Her eyes glinted. "Any good gardener knows that some things need to be snipped to allow others to bloom."

"So, you're going to...what? Work with me to fight our way to the Enemy's fortified location, waltz through thousands of thyrkan, warlocks and worse to fight Him in some epic battle of good and evil?"

"Epic? Certainly. But if you still think this is a story about good and evil, Calidan, then you haven't been paying attention. Anyone is capable of heroic deeds, just as they are the most heinous acts. It's purely a matter of time, place and the right pressure. And no, I wasn't just thinking you and me."

"Who then?"

She grinned, canines gleaming in the light. "I was thinking...everyone."

"Come again?"

A coy look. "You can't have some grand battle between sometimes good and often evil without first summoning the armies, can you? A call to arms, as it were."

I was stunned. "What-wait..." I trailed off, desperately trying to organise my thoughts. "How?"

The Wanderer drew herself up. "I have spent aeons doing my own thing, trying to ignore the petty squabbles of my brothers and sisters. In that time I have developed something of a reputation as being the one person that should not be ignored if I come knocking. They will listen to what I have to say."

"This isn't just getting the Powers to work together, this is getting five *peoples* – all very different and mostly filled with a dislike for each other - to work as a cohesive whole." I shook my head in dismay. "This is an impossible ask."

"Well then," she murmured, her voice becoming deeper as she spoke, power curling around her until her words echoed like thunder, storm clouds gathering in the air above her domain. "It's a good thing that I'm used to doing the impossible. Because, Calidan, I swear to you that I'm going to gather the Five and we will march north, laying waste to everything that Charles has ever touched. And, once that great work is complete, you will save Seya, Cassius will be restored, and the age of pseudo-gods and Powers will be brought to a close. Mankind will be left to guide itself, for both good and bad, and I weep tears of joy to know that you will be beholden only to yourselves."

Thunder roiled across the stormy sky as I tasted ozone.

"What about you? You aren't like the others, you could stay on, teach us – there is so much that we don't know!" I blurted, suddenly panicked.

A soft, sad smile and the storm began to ease. "I'm not like the others? Perhaps not. Not now at any rate. But we've all been many things in our lives. Terrible and good. I am not beyond that, and with no-one to keep me in check perhaps I would tilt back towards something I no longer wish to be. No. It is best for you and the rest of mankind that the Powers cease to be." Her eyes locked onto mine and for the briefest moment I caught a glimpse of her soul: ageless, vast, and immeasurably tired.

"It is time to enact the beginning of the end."

CHAPTER 46
Comeuppance

Crunch. My skull splintered inwards.

Bouncing like a ragdoll, I hit the obsidian wall and left nothing but paste.

Shaking, I touched my head and frowned. *Had that happened or was I imaging things?*

"Sorry," rumbled the Emperor standing next to me, his face stoic. "Standing here and taking in everything that has happened made me lose my temper."

Happened then. I'm in such deep shit.

"Oh yes, very much so," he continued, eyes continuing to scan the broken room behind the silver door where he had dragged me. "And yes, of course I can read your thoughts. You aren't very intelligent so it isn't remotely difficult."

Prick.

A ghost of a smile traced its way across his lips. The next second I found his fist buried in my gut. Literally 'in'. It hurt. I screamed. I probably died.

And here I was, remembering things that hadn't happened. Or had happened. Or something in between – I had no fucking clue.

"Of course you don't have a clue. You're pathetic. Little more than a good blood-hound and a barely passable hand with a sword." The Emperor shook his head in dismay. "To be considered a true seraphim in my time, one had to have mastered the ability to bend time, to alter reality, and to have touched the moon without the use of a spacecraft. Some prodigies managed this before they were six years old. In comparison you're nothing but a waste of space and resources." He breathed a sigh and grimaced. "Very disappointing."

"Then why am I here and not dead?"

"Because you have something I need."

I scoffed. "Why would someone as *impressive* as you need something from someone as "pathetic" as me?"

The Emperor turned the full weight of his intense gaze upon me. "You don't know what you and that dead friend of yours have wrought do you? You don't even have the faintest clue as to how much time, effort and expense went into perfecting this system. I spent *years* getting this correct. More years than you can count." His knuckles turned white, straining with clenched fury. "And you have taken not just one, but *two* of my bonded!"

"I-"

I saw the fist coming – barely – but my shield crumpled before the sheer immensity of his blow. The backhand ripped off the lower part of my jaw, blood and bone spraying everywhere. I staggered, eyes growing dark as the man turned, his expression one of pure, unending hate. He snapped a leg out and the next moment I was on the floor on the other side of the room, a trail of blood and destruction behind me.

"Get it together Melius!" I heard him hiss as he thumped towards me. "Get it under control!"

His footsteps stopped. The world turned grey.

"Not just yet."

The foot came down.

"-have taken not just one, but *two* of my bonded!"

I jumped, twitching out of shock, feeling the apparently now phantom pain of my abrupt execution slowly recede before the knowledge that I was, once again, alive.

The Emperor watched me and then gave a mischievous grin. "Another apology is in order. I got lost in my rage."

I could do little but glare. He was right – I was nothing but a gnat to him; completely and utterly helpless.

"Yes. You should remember that." His grin turned dark. Menacing. "But I can always remind you from time to time."

Trying to change the direction of conversation before I ended up experiencing yet another unpleasant demise, I gestured at the hall filled with broken machines. "Firstly, sorry. I know this was expensive, but to clarify, most of this was done by you and Cassius. You know, the friend of mine you've experimented on and managed to mistakenly turn into a skyren."

"And still, after everything, you manage to have the audacity to speak to me like that." He shook his head in what I hoped was amazement. "If I wasn't so angry with you, I would applaud. But no, I'm not really fussed over the machines. They were beyond priceless, but I know their innermost workings. I know their designs. Which means I can repair them whenever I feel like it. No, what I am most..." anger clouded his features, slowly forced away into a fake smile, "*frustrated* by is the loss of my bonded."

"Your bonded?" I frowned – as far as I knew, the Emperor wasn't a Great Heart-bonded.

"For all intents and purposes, yes, *my* bonded. Their power flowed through me. And you killed them."

I opened my mouth to argue the technicality that he had killed them through the use of the sigils, but closed it when I saw the dangerous glint in his eye. Instead I opted for the obvious path.

"They aren't your bonded though. You forced them to be. They were trapped, helpless and imprisoned."

Ah, directly challenging his statement, much better.

"They are mine. Just as you are."

"I am my own person, not some commodity for you to use when you see fit!"

"What you are, child, is *nothing* to me. I will use everything and everyone within my empire exactly how I see fit, because they are in *my* empire. Furthermore, you act as though you haven't already agreed to this."

"I haven't agreed to-"

"You have and you did. I told you when we first met that I would have need of you, that Great Heart-bonded were too important to let go. You agreed readily enough then."

"I thought that you wanted me for my power..."

He arched an eyebrow. "I have more 'power' in my toe than you have at your beck and call. That's not to say that you haven't been useful over the years, achieving impressive results with what little life has given you. But no, I am not after you. I am and always have been after *your bond*."

I took a step back, head shaking. "N-no. Leave Seya out of this."

"That has never been an option. This was always her destiny, just when I judged the time right. Frankly, your actions have forced my hand."

"You can't!"

He stiffened. "That is a dangerous word to use in my presence, Calidan. I very much 'can' and will. If it makes you feel better, it is for the betterment of the empire, which is exactly what the Academy trains you to sacrifice for."

"You mean it is for the betterment of you!"

His eyes glinted. "And I am the empire. I have built this civilisation up with my own hands, it is mine through and through. If I were to fall, everything would crumble. Ergo, keeping me alive is your highest priority." He smiled wryly. "It's funny. The damage you've inflicted today is more debilitating to my efforts in the long run than any mortal blow I have received. Do you know how hard it is to find Great Hearts? There is a reason why they are creatures of legend. Most have died off, unable to cope with the ravages of time. The few that are left are secretive things, ones that rarely interact with humans. Their ability to bond with humans, that is the thing that makes them so useful."

"If they are that useful, why don't you have one of your own?"

"Would that I could. However Great Hearts were created not long before the end. Few were designed and my bloodline had not been processed before everything was gone. All the technology, all the research about the procedure, destroyed. What I have created here is but a shadow of that former glory; a hybrid solution that cannot create, only change."

I shook my head, confusion outweighing my fear. "But you don't just have Great Hearts in there!"

"No. The process works on anything, but it is much more effective with a creature that is designed to provide power so freely. The liathea, kyrgeth," he wrinkled his nose, "they are more of a last resort. It takes far less for them to reach their limits than a Great Heart."

"What do you mean by limits?"

He shrugged, callous in his indifference. "Everything has a limit. My process is more intensive and destructive on the body than the normal healing provided by a Great Heart. They can't really regenerate from it. Eventually – if I'm hurt enough – they will become little more than desiccated husks." He must have thought the horror on my face was directed at something else because he nodded sadly. "Yes, it's quite a mess to clean up. Pretty unpleasant really."

"And you want to put Seya in there?!" I exploded. "Not going to happen. Never."

Eyes that had seen countless years locked onto mine and bore down. "Seylantha *is* going in there. In fact, she is on her way already. I would prefer that you see reason and let it happen rather than I be forced to...*remove* you. Permanently."

My mind whirled. *On her way? How?* Reaching out, I focused on the bond between us. *Seya? Can you hear me?*

Calidan, I'm being dragged. Can't stop it. What's happening?!

The sheer fright and confusion in her voice made tears rise to my eyes. *It's the Emperor...he- he is going to take something from you. He's a monster. I should have known. Should have always known!*

The Emperor? But he-

The bond fell silent.

"And that is enough of that."

I looked around wildly, never before had I been so completely and utterly cut off from Seya. Not even in Wolf's Hollow had I not felt even the tiniest hint of her presence. "What did you do?!"

He shrugged. "I know how the bond works. It isn't too hard to suppress. Wouldn't want you unduly worrying the poor thing now, would we?"

"You son-of-a-"

He sighed and rolled his eyes. "Yes, yes. Let it out. Get your infantile rage over with so you can more quickly come to the realisation that this is going to happen whether you like it or not."

"Fuck you, you tyrannical bastard!"

I raged for what felt like hours. The Emperor merely yawned.

"Are you done?" he asked when I ran out of curses and stood there seething, barely able to hold myself back from attacking him – I knew that would be a death that I wasn't coming back from.

My head shake didn't dissuade him from continuing. "It's funny that you compare me to a tyrant. If you truly believe that now, you should have seen my previous efforts."

Even in the depths of my rage, I couldn't help but question that. "What?"

"Oh come now, you must realise that this empire is but the latest of many. All the Powers have tried their hand at running things. Some do it better than others. Some rule with an iron fist, others with love. Most, like me, have done a mixture. Keeps things fresh."

"What are you talking about?" I spat.

"This role of mine is more of a lenient, loved god-like figure. I think it works quite well. I haven't gone for the full adoration that I have done in the past, or like Rizaen has now. Nor have I gone anywhere near full tyrant with the slaves and bloodsports. That was a fun time but not the best in terms of civilisation growth."

"I...don't-"

"A bit over your head, eh? I can understand that. Hard to wrap your head around at times. Would it help or hinder to know that you aren't even the most technologically advanced civilisation that I've created? Heh," he smiled at the confused scowl on my face, "that must be a bit of a mind-fuck. Where do you think the term 'tyrant blade' came from? They were first designed to provide a wielder some semblance of power to make them more akin to me."

"...Fucking mad," I breathed.

"Mad, not mad. Tyrant, beloved." He shrugged. "I've been and done it all. Which is why I know that you're going to let Seya into one of my vats. You're going to watch and you're not going to interfere. Why? Because you know that you can't beat me. I can see it in your eyes. You're a calculating sort, Calidan. Even when pushed right up against the brink, you won't commit to a losing battle. You'll bide your time, gain your strength and strike when the time is right."

"You know nothing about me!"

"I know everything about you!" he thundered. "Every. Single. Thing." As suddenly as it had arrived his rage vanished. "And that's why you're going to agree to a deal."

I spat on the ground. "You expect me to make a deal with the likes of you?"

"Of course."

"Why?"

"Because you know that I'm good for it. I haven't lied to you yet, and you know it."

I stopped trying to will a comet into existence long enough to eye him suspiciously. "What deal?"

"I will let you go. Let you play Imperator without staying here in the citadel. Let you gain whatever power you think you can scrape together to inevitably attempt to free Seya and strike me down. There are only two requirements: firstly, you still complete the missions asked of you and secondly, you take Cassius with you as your partner."

"I-what?"

"He might be...different to how you remember him, but he is a master with a blade. Combined with his newfound size, strength and speed he will be a force to be reckoned with. Though...considering what just occurred I would refrain from making him angry."

"You think this is funny?" I hissed. "That it is some kind of game? Why would you ever think that I would agree to this instead of fighting you with every waking breath?!"

"Because you're smarter than that. You know how it ends. I've already killed you at least a dozen times in the last hour. Probably more. That means you know one universal truth. You. Can't. Stop. Me."

"To think I looked up to you."

"Mmm. Yes. It is funny how little I care."

"I'm going to kill you." I focused all my will into the five words, solidifying my intent to make them come true.

"My dear boy," the Emperor chuckled. "I sincerely hope you try. Afterall, with our guest rapidly approaching, if you did manage it you would only, in fact, be killing her. What a tragic conundrum."

The sound of claw on stone reached my ears; a long loud squealing as razor-sharp claws tried and failed to find purchase on the slick obsidian.

"And here she is now, our guest of honour."

Perfect black fur drifted into my view, Seya's magnificent length being pulled inexorably inside the silver room, her eyes wild and heart rapid. A snarling yowl of panic broke from her mouth as she recognised where she was being taken.

"Come." The Emperor said, striding forwards with those ground eating strides. "Let's get this show on the road."

Ignoring him, I ran to Seya's side. "Seya!" I shouted, running a hand down her shivering flank. Her beautiful orange eyes were filled with desperation as she swivelled towards me. I knew that she was trying to talk, but I couldn't hear her. "Seya, I'm so sorry! It's him. The Emperor!"

Confusion was evident on her face, quickly replaced by that prideful wrath that I knew so well before she settled down, not quite relaxing but forcibly stilling herself. Seeing who held her captive changed things for her. Whilst her fur still stood on end, she no longer clawed at the floor trying to be held back. She must have known that she couldn't hope to match the strength of one of the Powers, that whatever the Emperor wanted to do was going to happen, instead choosing to meet whatever was coming headfirst with as much grace and dignity as she could muster. Shifting her attention to me, she touched my hand with her nose. Even living through my own worst nightmare, I couldn't help but feel the rush of love envelop me at her touch. Feel her strength and support.

This could not, *would not*, be the end.

We were survivors. Partners.

Bonded.

I remembered the Emperor's words and rested my head against hers. "Whatever happens, I will come for you," I whispered. "However long it takes, I will bring him down and free you. I swear it."

Those glorious orange orbs blinked at me once, slowly. Another gentle touch of her nose and then a quick rasp of her tongue across my cheek.

Acceptance.

Tears trickled down my face in an unending flood as I walked with her towards that horrific place. As The Emperor stepped over the still and lifeless body of the forlorn Balthazar without so much as giving him a glance. As he reforged the vats with a wave of his hand and calmly, uncaringly, placed her inside. As sigils hummed to life and machines whirred with noise. As searing tattoos branded themselves along my flesh.

Tears of sadness. Of guilt.

Of resolve.

Of sheer-fucking-willpower.

I was going to make it all change. To free the world from this unending cycle of control. The Emperor might consider me beneath his notice but I would use that to my advantage. I would grow strong, grow hard, and find some way to destroy everything that he loved.

Seya, my cat, my bonded, my Greatest of Hearts...

...For you I will shake the very heavens themselves.

EPILOGUE

Ella's funeral was a quiet affair. The others didn't know what had happened, or why, but they suspected.

How could they not?

Her death heralded an irrevocable change to the dynamic of the group. A shift in its temperament. In its very nature. Though the words weren't uttered aloud, suddenly Ella was a potential traitor to the Academy and that was no small thing. The distrust and doubt that had been building and thought broken since Wolf's Hollow came slowly creeping back, sprouting its tendrils throughout the branches of our friendship.

They didn't know the truth about Seya. I couldn't tell them. Not when it was so fresh. The joy, confusion and horror that they expressed when they saw the hulking behemoth of Cassius was uncomfortable enough for a year let alone a few days.

They didn't understand. Hells, I was there and still didn't understand. There were questions that I couldn't or wouldn't answer. There was anger at my seeming recalcitrance. The void between us grew bigger, a chasm that I wasn't sure I would ever be able to bridge again.

Everything had changed. And yet nothing.

We were still Imperators. We still had jobs to do.

The Emperor lost himself in attempting to find the traitor in his midst, the person responsible for deactivating the wards within the citadel. He had his most ferocious bodyguards – the twins – round up all of his staff and every member of the Academy for thorough interrogation. And I do mean thorough; my brain still hurt from the scouring the Emperor gave me.

But to no avail.

Rikol was dragged away by Bastion to try and determine more effective defences against both the warlocks and the titans. Sophia and Scythe were on counter-intelligence; working missions on a need-to-know basis, likely filled with peril, intrigue and no small amount of death.

But the gap wasn't just with them. Rinoa knew I was holding something back, something life changing, and to her credit she didn't press. Didn't demand I tell her. I loved her all the more for that, but I knew that my silence hurt her, even if she didn't admit it. Soon enough her next mission came up and we said our goodbyes, leaving with fake smiles and aching hearts.

And then it was my turn. Monsters waited for no man.

Slowly, methodically, I strapped on my gear and saddled up my horse before leading her to the gate of the Academy. Scanning the outside forest, I turned to find my silent companion waiting patiently.

"You ready?"

No response. Dark blank eyes sent shivers down my spine.

Forcing a smile, I nodded. "I'll take that as a yes." Turning away from my best friend in the world, a giant of a man broken, reforged and broken again, I hopped onto the back of my horse and together we ambled into a bleak future.

A future that I had every intent of changing.

Pausing at the crest of the hill, I turned to stare at the towering citadel, centre of the empire and home to my immortal enemy.

I'll save you Seya.

I waited for a response but nothing was forthcoming. Sighing, I turned back towards my mission.

Or, perhaps 'missions' was more accurate. This might have been mission forty-three of Calidan the Imperator, but it was day one of my own.

Save Cassius.

Save Seya.

Kill a god.

Simple.

Charles

"We have confirmation from our contact that two of the Emperor's Great Hearts were destroyed."

"Hmm. Let me guess, poor Calidan is now lacking a companion?"

"That appears to be the case."

"A pity. For the brief time that I had her in my care, that panther was most impressive." Charles sighed theatrically and sat back in his chair. "Now she will rot and wither in one of those vats."

"It seems that the Emperor has been working on a project of his own," continued Ash. "Something to do with Cassius; a young man that I'm sure you remember."

"The shadow seraph boy?"

"Indeed. Apparently he has become almost as big as the Emperor. A little addled in the mind however."

"Interesting. Though…" Charles pushed himself to his feet and stretched, "if Melius has only just finished his one project, he is far behind the curve. Where do we stand on proceedings?"

"One hundred and twelve-thousand, two hundred and twenty original batch thyrkan are armed and ready. Forty-three thousand six hundred and twelve evolved thyrkan are also available. Of that number we have a thousand reavers and one hundred warlocks."

Charles's eyes gleamed. "And the titans?"

"As you know, the wreckage within Site One only allowed for two titans to be retrieved, as well as the Artemis. However we have made good progress with uncovering the second and third sites, which records show hold a substantial number of similar category devices."

"Excellent. I think, my dear, that it is long past time that we re-announced ourselves to the world."

"You believe we are ready?"

Charles snorted. "My calculations had us achieve victory with half the forces we have under our control. We are more than ready."

"In that case, I'll make the necessary arrangements."

"You do that." Charles' eyes swirled with black. "And tell Koranth that his much-desired war is about to commence, for tomorrow the legions march, and we...

...will have ourselves an ending."

The End

Afterword

Ever since I first introduced the robotic scorpion in the first novel, I have really wanted to merge sci-fi and fantasy in a big way. If you, like me, had that same desire...hopefully this scratched that itch.

Thanks for reading, you resplendent reader.

Please remember to rate / review!

Printed in Great Britain
by Amazon